OXFORD WORLD'S CLASSICS

THE DUKE'S CHILDREN

THE DUKE'S CHILDREN is the last in Trollope's six-volume sequence of novels known as the Palliser series. They chart the career of Plantagenet Palliser, and his troubled marriage to Lady Glencora. The novels depict the social milieu of the aristocracy and upper middle class of mid-Victorian England, with occasional forays into low life and the criminal underworld. They combine the machinations of politics with an intimate exploration of personal relationships to paint an unparalleled portrait of an age. The novels can be read independently and as part of a linked whole. They are:

> *Can You Forgive Her?* (1864–65)
>
> *Phineas Finn* (1869)
>
> *The Eustace Diamonds* (1872)
>
> *Phineas Redux* (1873)
>
> *The Prime Minister* (1876)
>
> *The Duke's Children* (1880)

STEVEN AMARNICK is Professor of English at the City University of New York (Kingsborough Community College). His first article about cuts to *The Duke's Children* appeared in *The Politics of Gender in Anthony Trollope's Novels: New Readings for the Twenty-First Century* (2009). A new extensive article about the cuts served as the Introduction to the Folio Society edition of the novel in 2015.

OXFORD WORLD'S CLASSICS

*For over 100 years Oxford World's Classics have brought
readers closer to the world's great literature. Now with over
700 titles—from the 4,000-year-old myths of Mesopotamia to the
twentieth century's greatest novels—the series makes available
lesser-known as well as celebrated writing.*

*The pocket-sized hardbacks of the early years contained
introductions by Virginia Woolf, T. S. Eliot, Graham Greene,
and other literary figures which enriched the experience of reading.
Today the series is recognized for its fine scholarship and
reliability in texts that span world literature, drama and poetry,
religion, philosophy, and politics. Each edition includes perceptive
commentary and essential background information to meet the
changing needs of readers.*

OXFORD WORLD'S CLASSICS

ANTHONY TROLLOPE

The Duke's Children
The Complete Text

Reconstructed and Edited by
STEVEN AMARNICK

Assisted by
ROBERT F. WISEMAN

with
SUSAN LOWELL HUMPHREYS

OXFORD
UNIVERSITY PRESS

OXFORD
UNIVERSITY PRESS

Great Clarendon Street, Oxford, OX2 6DP,
United Kingdom

Oxford University Press is a department of the University of Oxford.
It furthers the University's objective of excellence in research, scholarship,
and education by publishing worldwide. Oxford is a registered trade mark of
Oxford University Press in the UK and in certain other countries

First published as an Oxford World's Classics paperback 2020

Impression: 3

Published in the United States of America by Oxford University Press
198 Madison Avenue, New York, NY 10016, United States of America

British Library Cataloguing in Publication Data
Data available

Library of Congress Control Number: 2020938844

ISBN 978-0-19-883587-5

Printed and bound in Great Britain by
Clays Ltd, Elcograf S.p.A.

ACKNOWLEDGEMENTS

I OWE hearty thanks to the City University of New York for several research grants and two fellowship leaves. The Beinecke Rare Book and Manuscript Library, at Yale University, is an exceptional place to work—in large measure due to its peerless staff (and lovely windows and lighting too). Many colleagues, editors, Trollope scholars, and friends and relatives have offered advice and support along the way. I thank in particular Bonne August, Pamela Barrell, Marcia Babbitt, Linda Bakst, Lonny Behar, Fred Bernstein, Nicholas Birns, Joe Whitlock Blundell, Kathie Coblentz, Dominic Edwardes, Eileen Ferretti, Regenia Gagnier, Matthew Gartner, Douglas Gerlach, Iris Goodwin, Mark Green, Howard Gregg, N. John Hall, Steven Honig, Merle Keitel, John Loughery, Margaret Markwick, Deborah Denenholz Morse, Laura Saurina, Mark Schoofs, David Skilton, Stuart Suss, Kendall Thomas, Andrew Wallace, Bill Wallace, Claire Wallace, Fred Wasserman, Jo West, Randy Williams, and Karin Wiseman, as well as my late parents, Morris and Judith Amarnick, who lived long enough to see the first version of the book published by the Folio Society. Going back to my earliest days with Trollope, George Levine, Barry Qualls, and Carolyn Williams made an exemplary, and amicable, dissertation committee; I cherish the many conversations we had.

Anthony Trollope's direct descendants in Australia were gracious and encouraging when I first approached them many years ago about doing this project. Susan Lowell Humphreys, effervescent and knowledgeable, made vast contributions to the book; it was a happy day indeed when we first met at the 2006 Trollope conference in Exeter. Michael G. Williamson, cheerful and wise and level-headed, was invaluable in the final months of the Folio edition and equally invaluable in the years since. He is a founding member and immediate past chairman of the Trollope Society, and he is a keen Trollope scholar. I am fortunate not only for his guidance, but now for his close friendship too. And my sister, Phyllis Wallace, was my confidante and advisor every step of the way. It is because of her example that, as an adolescent, I developed an interest in Victorian literature in the first place, and though for many years I stubbornly (and mysteriously) resisted her entreaties to read Trollope, I am glad to say that she finally wore me down.

Finally, I owe my greatest thanks to Robert F. Wiseman. Without him, I might possibly have embarked on this endeavour, but I never would have persisted. The task would have been too lonely and too difficult—not the great labour of love, and joy, that it turned out to be.

CONTENTS

Introduction	ix
Note on the Text	xxxi
Select Bibliography	xxxii
A Chronology of Anthony Trollope	xxxvi
THE DUKE'S CHILDREN	1
Appendix: Sample of Cuts to the Manuscript	623
Explanatory Notes	641
Index of Names and Places	669

INTRODUCTION

Readers who are unfamiliar with the plot may prefer to treat the Introduction as an Afterword.

AT the very end of his autobiography, Anthony Trollope sends greetings from the dead: 'Now I stretch out my hand, and from the further shore I bid adieu to all who have cared to read any among the many words that I have written.'[1] Since he intended the book to be published posthumously, he could adopt the stance, for this one sentence, of a man whose life's work was done. Yet when he finished, on 11 April 1876, Trollope had no intention of stopping—or even of slowing down too much if his health would cooperate. Three weeks later, on 2 May, he began *The Duke's Children*, the sixth and final narrative in his Palliser series.

Trollope had already written nearly forty novels (and much more, including short stories, essays, biographies, and travel books), and ordinarily might have had no reason to think that another one or two or ten would make a huge difference to the legacy he had just been considering all through the composition of *An Autobiography*. What counted most for him was the 'gallery' of characters he had created, and how he had been able to 'live with them in the full reality of established intimacy'.[2] But in speaking from beyond the grave—his son Henry supervised the publication of the manuscript in 1883, less than a year after his father's death—Trollope makes a plea to readers to pay special attention to his depiction of Plantagenet Palliser and his wife, Lady Glencora Palliser, later known as the Duke and Duchess of Omnium. They had appeared briefly in *The Small House at Allington* (first edition published by Smith, Elder in 1864), the penultimate tale of his six-novel Barsetshire series, and then played various roles—sometimes major, sometimes minor—in *Can You Forgive Her?* (1864–65), *Phineas Finn* (1869), *The Eustace Diamonds* (1872), *Phineas Redux* (1873), and *The Prime Minister* (1876).[3] With his typical self-effacement, prevalent throughout *An Autobiography*, Trollope says, 'I do not think it probable that my name

---

[1] Anthony Trollope, *An Autobiography* (Oxford: Oxford University Press, 1999), 367.
[2] Ibid. 233.
[3] Their role is so small in *The Eustace Diamonds* that Trollope doesn't even mention this novel when he talks about the benefits of reading the series 'consecutively' (ibid. 184).

will remain among those who in the next century will be known as the writers of English prose fiction'—but then with his (also) typical self-assertion[4] he immediately notes that 'permanence of success' is quite conceivable, citing Glencora and Plantagenet (along with Mr. Crawley from the Barsetshire series) as his very greatest creations.[5] He talks in depth about the Pallisers twice in the book, both times calling attention to his feats of representation, his ability to make the tiniest of details cohere with other details hundreds—or sometimes thousands—of pages later. 'To carry out my scheme,' he says, 'I have had to spread my picture over so wide a canvas that I cannot expect that any lover of such art should trouble himself to look at it as a whole,' thereby inviting that lover to go ahead and take the plunge. He continues: 'I look upon this string of characters . . . as the best work of my life.'[6] When he indicates near the end of *An Autobiography* that he is planning another Palliser story, it would seem obvious that he was aiming to produce another detailed account of their complicated marriage, one that would help him make fresh claims for literary immortality. It turns out, however, that he had something even more ambitious in mind.

Trollope took nearly six months to complete *The Duke's Children*, finishing it in late October of 1876. It is not clear how much of an effort he made to get it published afterwards, or whether, after the calamitous response *The Prime Minister* had just received, he thought it best to wait. When he did sell the book in 1878 to Charles Dickens Jr. for serialization in *All the Year Round*, he agreed to make severe cuts—roughly 65,000 words, close to a quarter of the whole. The novel finally began to reach the public with the 4 October 1879 issue, and appeared in weekly instalments until July 1880. Chapman & Hall published the shortened version in three volumes in May 1880. Trollope still had many readers, though fewer than at the height of his popularity in the 1860s, and they were greeted with a stunning first sentence: Glencora, thoroughly vibrant at the end of *The Prime Minister*, has taken ill and died. Trollope writes in *An Autobiography* about the hazards of killing off a beloved character—in that case, Mrs Proudie, an indomitable presence through much of the Barsetshire series. Her demise, however, occurs midway

---

[4] As David Skilton notes, Trollope's 'carefully rhetorical' opening sentence in *An Autobiography*, in which Trollope calls himself an 'insignificant person', sets the stage for the entire book, as it combines 'possibly . . . mock modesty' with a strong indication that, in fact, he has 'something significant to express'. 'Reading *An Autobiography* as Advice Literature', in Frederik Van Dam, David Skilton, and Ortwin de Graef, eds, *The Edinburgh Companion to Anthony Trollope* (Edinburgh: Edinburgh University Press, 2019), 79.

[5] Trollope, *An Autobiography*, 361.   [6] Ibid. 184.

through *The Last Chronicle of Barset*, when the author had decided in effect to do away with all his important Barsetshire characters—whereas an older and wiser, but not too wise, Glencora would have offered him many possibilities. He could have kept her alive and devised a plot similar to the one he ended up using, in which the Duke and Duchess's children, Lord Silverbridge, Lord Gerald, and Lady Mary, aged 22, 20, and 19, all thwart the father's wishes as they enter adulthood, while the mother, either overtly or covertly, cheers the youngsters on. Such a novel might have been first-rate, of course, but would have unfolded in more familiar Palliser territory, with the not ideally matched couple both battling and accommodating one another. All throughout his career, Trollope had been keen to accept, or to concoct, bold challenges, so as to avoid the fate of authors who grow stale, whose work becomes 'one piece of stiff mechanism'.[7] If he saw fit to make his Duchess disappear, it was in service to a well-honed strategy that had nurtured his artistic health.

With his own advice about novel writing fresh in his mind—*An Autobiography* contains much about plot, dialogue, character, proper work habits and attitudes, and 'the opening which a literary career offers to men and women for the earning of their bread'[8]—and with keen motivation to continue writing at the highest level possible, any novel that Trollope chose to write immediately afterwards would have had a special place in his canon. That he decided to make it part of the Palliser series only raised the stakes further. As it turns out, too, he used *The Duke's Children* to explore themes that were central to *An Autobiography*. In particular, the novel is a meditation on change: how the young may turn out drastically different than anyone might expect, and how people of any age must be willing to listen and to learn if they are to avoid stultification or irrelevancy or precipitous decline. It is a novel imbued with a recognition of life's tragedies and missed opportunities, but filled with hope for the future, at least for those who are young enough in spirit to embrace the world with passion and curiosity.

In *An Autobiography*, Trollope tells the would-be novelist what he must do to render characters over time: for just as we know in the real world 'that men and women change,—become worse or better as temptation or conscience may guide them,—so should these creations of his change, and every change should be noted by him. On the last day of each month recorded, every person in his novel should be a month older than on the first.'[9] To depict such growth, or deterioration, was

---

[7] Ibid. 232.   [8] Ibid. 1.   [9] Ibid. 233.

common practice for Trollope, something he claims—a bit flippantly—that anyone with talent can do 'without much struggling'.[10] What he hadn't quite attempted until *The Duke's Children* was a particular type of *bildungsroman*: the detailed portrayal of a person who not only matures after being resolutely feckless, but who reveals a potential that had barely seemed to exist—and who may even be bound for greatness on the national stage. Trollope had gestured toward such a characterization in *An Autobiography*, in sketching his own self. The early chapters are filled with woe. He lacks 'juvenile manhood',[11] has 'a stupid boy's slowness',[12] and is devoid of 'moral courage'.[13] By the time he is done with school, he is an 'idle, desolate hanger-on, that most hopeless of human beings, a hobbledehoy of nineteen, without any idea of a career, a profession, or a trade'.[14] With parental help he gets a job at the Post Office, but for his first seven years he is, justly, often on the verge of being fired. His journals, which he kept for most of those years, expose his 'folly, ignorance, indiscretion, idleness, extravagance, and conceit'.[15] Others continue to see him as 'an evil, an encumbrance, a useless thing'.[16] When he indicates that he would like to write, his famous novelist mother scoffs: 'she did not give me credit for the sort of cleverness necessary for such work.'[17]

It all gets better, Trollope tells us, swiftly and permanently, when he takes a new Post Office job in Ireland. There are still conflicts and struggles, but as soon as he sets foot across the Channel, he is transformed, and ready for ultimate triumph. He eventually trains himself to follow 'certain self-imposed laws'[18] where he would go to his desk every morning, beginning at 5:30 a.m., read the previous day's work, and then write 250 words every fifteen minutes until 8:30 a.m.[19]—all before heading off to his full-time job. What is missing is any of that month-by-month delineation of how he grew into a man who was so work-crazed, and so adept at that work, that he became a literary giant (and in fact he quotes Nathaniel Hawthorne calling him an actual giant, whose characters were so real it is as if he had 'hewn a great lump out of the earth and put it under a glass case, with all its inhabitants going about their daily business, and not suspecting that they were being made a show of').[20] Trollope clearly had no interest in revealing how his transformation had occurred; indeed, he tells us that he destroyed his journals after consulting them a few years before starting his autobiography.

---

[10] Ibid. 233.   [11] Ibid. 2.   [12] Ibid. 6.   [13] Ibid. 12.   [14] Ibid. 28.
[15] Ibid. 42.   [16] Ibid. 60.   [17] Ibid. 74.   [18] Ibid. 118.
[19] Ibid. 272.   [20] Ibid. 144.

Besides, it was with a fiction writer's toolbox that he was most equipped to proceed. He did so by inventing a character, Lord Silverbridge, steeped in privilege and charm and innocent sweetness, unlike himself in every way—except for being such a callow, unpromising youth.

Trollope uses the word 'hobbledehoy' to describe not only himself as a young man but characters like Charlie Tudor in *The Three Clerks* (1858) and Johnny Eames in *The Small House at Allington*. As Laurie Langbauer explains, Trollope's hobbledehoys are 'graceless youths' who are 'terrible at their jobs' and 'gauche in company—they cannot fit themselves onto any kind of straightforward path. They are sidetracked or arrested or just plain fail, even when it comes to the kind of basic development—such as growing up—that we think ought to unfold naturally.'[21] Silverbridge is not quite a hobbledehoy: he doesn't need to hold on to a job, and is in no way uncouth. Yet he is strikingly hapless in the early chapters, as his failings are on full display. His tomfoolery, we learn, has resulted in his being kicked out of university; he gambles too much; he spends too much time with the horses he owns; he shows no aptitude for work. The woman he thinks he loves, Lady Mabel Grex, refuses to swoon, or even barely to flirt. She assumes she will marry him, eventually, but she won't stop looking down on him. And though his father gives both him and his brother credit for 'a dash of cleverness' (p. 46), he mostly seems none too bright. Yet Silverbridge quietly grows. When he attends a grand garden party, the hostess, Mrs. Montacute Jones, thanks him for coming 'to eat [her] strawberries', but he says it's the other guests, not the fruit, that drew him. 'You ought to have said you came to see me,' she replies with gentle humour, 'but you young men of the present day never will condescend to pay a compliment to an old woman' (p. 211)—whereupon she immediately sees to it that he makes the acquaintance of '[t]he American beauty' (p. 211), Isabel Boncassen. When later in the novel he visits again, and she calls attention to how smitten he now is with Isabel, we learn that he 'blushe[s] and stammer[s], and [i]s just able to say that his only object in life [i]s to pour out his adoration at the feet of Mrs. Montacute Jones herself' (p. 330). It is a tiny moment, but indicative of how aware and educable he is—and how Trollope builds his fiction on subtle touches. It is a subtlety that is often missed by readers, given how quickly we can race through his lucid prose if we so choose.

---

[21] Laurie Langbauer, 'The Hobbledehoy in Trollope', in Carolyn Dever and Lisa Niles, eds., *The Cambridge Companion to Anthony Trollope* (Cambridge: Cambridge University Press, 2011), 113.

Sometimes we need only observe what Silverbridge says and does to grasp how much he absorbs, such as when he recognizes why it was foolhardy for him to expect the Master of Trinity to interfere and prevent his brother's expulsion (p. 139), or when he figures out, based on what the Duke has said and not said, that he and his brother are to be 'two eldest sons', with Gerald inheriting 'the Scotch property' (p. 194). Sometimes we are privy to key information, such as when he says yes to an invitation that Mary hopes he will decline. His acceptance seems dashed off, as if he doesn't grasp how messy the situation is (because of his father's obtuseness, both Isabel and Mabel will be house guests at the same time), but in fact we discover that he has given much deliberation to the matter; it takes two well-developed paragraphs for the narrator to explain all that is hidden by the 'usual careless style' (p. 397) of Silverbridge's response. And with his most momentous choice—to marry Isabel not Mabel—we see that he is not just succumbing to novelty and to sexual attraction; rather, he has made a constant effort to understand why he feels so different in the presence of one compared to the other. Early on, he puzzles over Mabel's 'coolness and self-command and badinage' and is able to comprehend 'everything as it was only too truly' (p. 150)—though not enough, at first, to deter him from wanting to marry her. Even after meeting Isabel, he still halfheartedly plans to keep the promise he has made to his father and to marry the blue-blooded Mabel. Yet if his eventual proposal to Isabel comes somewhat impulsively, he is in full command of his reasoning several months later when he repeats his offer. Others may think that he is 'weak as water' (p. 473) and that his affections may switch once again, but Silverbridge's decisiveness is built on the bedrock of deep thought.

Trollope waxes metaphorical about 'the two fruits' in *The Small House at Allington*, and how it is the one that ripens late that is given 'the fullest flavour of the sun'—rather than the young man who in his early twenties is already a 'finished Apollo'.[22] By introducing Johnny Eames with these comments, Trollope basically assures us that he will turn out well. In *The Duke's Children*, Trollope lets the narrative proceed without such overt commentary, as Silverbridge's 'flavour' emerges in juxtaposition with Frank Tregear, his best friend and mentor when the novel begins. Frank is fully formed when we meet him, with an arrogance that is startling given that he has no money and refuses to choose a profession. The Duke abhors the arrogance and

---

[22] Anthony Trollope, *The Small House at Allington* (Oxford: Oxford University Press, 1980), 34.

convinces himself of something worse: that the supremely handsome Frank is as dissolute as Burgo Fitzgerald, the Duchess's early love in *Can You Forgive Her?* It is well understood by the Duke, and by readers of the Palliser series, that though Glencora is devoted to Burgo, her marriage to him would have been a disaster. Frank, it turns out, is no Burgo, and the Duke need not prevent Mary's marriage in order to save her. Still, a large black mark remains. Rather than become, say, a doctor, a diplomat, or an attorney (p. 25)—or even aim to rise in the Post Office and in a literary profession as Trollope had—Frank's 'one chance' (p. 436) for a future that will suit him is to wed a wealthy woman. That he openly talks about this matter with Mabel only shows how callous he is: their romance had ended because of money (they had none), and he cannot see that she is still in love with him.

Frank may be young, but he is already stuck in his ways, and embodies a more rigid form of masculinity that Trollope interrogates. To be sure, that Frank is manly is meant to be to his credit—and, ultimately, it is the 'manliness in his appeal' (p. 392) that does much to soften the Duke's opposition. In the final lines of the book, the Duke refers to him, approvingly, as 'a manly young man'. Yet we are also told that 'Silverbridge since his marriage seemed even to his father to be much more of a man than he had been before' (p. 620). The comparison is noteworthy. We have witnessed Silverbridge's growth well before the marriage; as Mabel has realized after he speaks so forcefully about his love for Isabel, 'Now at any rate he was a man. She was sure of that now. This was more, very much more, not only than she had expected from him, but more than she had thought it possible that his character should have produced' (p. 462). Silverbridge will inevitably continue to develop beyond the pages of the novel. Frank's future beyond the novel might also be bright, but as an early bloomer he remains largely what he always has been.

It might seem unfair to judge Frank more severely because he has exited boyhood without still being a boy. Yet his manliness, ultimately, is pinched and harsh compared to Silverbridge's. 'A man should never submit to blame,' Frank tells Mabel in his final meeting with her—something it is impossible to imagine Silverbridge saying. Frank is consumed with defending himself and his quick pivot to Mary, arguing that it is 'a sign of strength' to move on from heartbreak, and that 'the sooner a man can do that the more manly he is' (p. 603). By contrast, Silverbridge in his last meeting with Mabel is more compassionate and more self-critical, even though he has done little wrong; he too had pivoted quickly from Mabel, but only after he had sensed what her true feelings were. In his final meeting with Major Tifto, who in a fit of pique had purposely maimed a race horse they owned together, causing Silverbridge to lose a staggering amount of money, the young Lord offers forgiveness, and also accepts some blame, acknowledging to himself how he had raised his former racing partner's hopes, then been 'uncourteous' (p. 582) towards him. Silverbridge has come to understand that class differences are such that he and Tifto cannot really be friends, but unlike Frank, who will barely acknowledge Tifto's existence, Silverbridge knows that Tifto is a human being with actual human emotions. It is left to Mary's brother, not her fiancé, to offer patient counsel when she remains aggrieved about the Duke's grudging capitulation. 'You expect too much from him,' Silverbridge tells her. 'Of course he has not had his own way with either of us, and of course he feels it. They say that a conqueror always ought to be good-humoured. You are the conqueror here. If you are gentle with him now, he will very soon be gentle with you,—and with Tregear' (p. 574).

Both Silverbridge and Frank are manly in their own fashion, but it is only the erstwhile prankster who approaches the ideal that Trollope sets forth in a long passage from *Phineas Redux*: someone who is 'faithful to his friends, unsuspicious before the world, gentle with women, loving with children, considerate to his inferiors, kindly with servants, tender-hearted with all—and at the same time . . . frank, of open speech, with springing eager energies.'[23] Phineas Finn once had the capacity to become this sort of man, but we sense that he will always remain scarred, that despite his happy marriage at the end of *Phineas Redux*, he will never fully recover from the trauma of being accused of murder and then not being believed after he proclaims his innocence. In *The Duke's Children*, Frank falls short of the ideal from the start; and though he cannot exactly be called affected—which in Trollope's taxonomy would preclude him from manliness altogether—his character is, at least to some extent, made up of 'mere tinsel' (p. 25). Silverbridge, on the other hand, even at his shallow worst, is merely unformed. Given his immaturity at the start, it is astonishing that Silverbridge comes so far—though upon rereading the novel, one may more readily notice the early moments of promise that are obscured by all his failures. As he grows, he travels a long distance politically too, from someone who is utterly sure of his 'Conservative Convictions' (the title of Chapter 7) to someone primed for a leadership role as a stalwart Liberal.

[23] Anthony Trollope, *Phineas Redux* (Oxford: Oxford University Press, 1983), vol. II, 252.

In *An Autobiography*, Trollope devotes a number of pages to his
political views, calling himself 'an advanced, but still a conservative
Liberal',[24] and in *The Prime Minister*, written months before, the
Duke espouses similar views while taking a walk with Phineas Finn.
Silverbridge does not appear in *The Prime Minister* and so cannot join
their stroll; but the father must accept his son's 'reproach' (p. 57) for
never speaking to him about politics at all. When the Duke finally
obliges, it is understandable if Trollope does not have him pontificate
again, though the narrator's quick summary about 'the greatest benefit
of the greatest number' (p. 58) is oddly misleading with its Benthamite
implications. The Duke does care in the long term about the many
rather than the few, but utilitarianism is not at the heart of his philosophy. Rather, as he had explained to Phineas, the Liberal believes
devoutly in 'lessening distances,—of bringing the coachman and the
duke nearer together,—nearer and nearer', whereas the Conservative
strives for 'the maintenance of those distances', considering them God-
ordained.[25] The Liberal may be wary of moving too far too fast, while
the Conservative may reluctantly support far-reaching measures to
help forestall more radical jolts to the system—and thus it may sometimes be difficult to tell them apart. Nevertheless, Trollope wants us to
see a genuine difference between the two.[26]

Silverbridge at first presents his apostasy as a matter of integrity, his
own Conservative principles outweighing any rote devotion to family
heritage. Yet the Duke can 'give his reasons for being a Liberal'
(p. 28) that are also based on principles, and once he hears his father
speak, Silverbridge makes no further attempts to justify his choices.
Instead, it is relatively soon that he tells Gerald to 'stick to the Liberals.
I've made an ass of myself. I can see that already' (p. 188). He later
says how 'It does seem so hard to me . . . to find any difference between
the two sets' (p. 426), but when he finally switches parties, he asserts
that 'I like the other set'—the Liberals—'the best' (p. 589). Silverbridge
admits that he still cannot fully explain his reasoning, but he already

[24] Trollope, *An Autobiography*, 291.

[25] Anthony Trollope, *The Prime Minister* (Oxford: Oxford University Press, 1983), vol.
II, 264–65.

[26] For a thorough discussion of the 'advanced conservative Liberal'—and how we can
infer that Trollope saw himself as closer to a radical like John Stuart Mill than more
conservative thinkers like Matthew Arnold and Walter Bagehot, see Lauren M. E. Goodlad
and Frederik Van Dam, 'Trollope and Politics', in Deborah Denenholz Morse, Margaret
Markwick, and Mark W. Turner (eds.), *The Routledge Research Companion to Anthony
Trollope* (Abingdon: Routledge, 2017), 15–34.

makes it clear that his new preference for the Liberals goes beyond his long-held distaste for Sir Timothy Beeswax, the Conservative party chief. We have already seen the process by which Silverbridge reaches clarity about Isabel and Mabel, and we can assume he will become similarly clear-minded, and eloquent, about his political beliefs too. Meanwhile, he has come to think so much like his father that he even sounds like him. After reading the letter from Silverbridge in which he rejects an offer to make a major speech in Parliament on behalf of the Conservatives, Sir Timothy says, 'I can trace the Duke's hand in every word of it' (p. 523)—even though the Duke had not helped at all.

In the absence of his father's guidance, Silverbridge had been swayed by others, most importantly Frank, whose Conservative talking points he had echoed. Yet once the Duke takes an interest in him and stops treating him like a fool, Silverbridge pays careful attention. His election to Parliament is a pivotal moment. In a congratulatory letter, the Duke expresses regret that Silverbridge has chosen the Conservatives but also says, 'there is nothing disgraceful in such a change'; then he delivers stirring advice, extolling the glory of public service and urging him to work hard, 'to sit and listen so that the forms and methods of the House may as it were soak into you gradually' (p. 122). The Duke at this point may privately doubt whether his son is capable of following such advice, but he offers it without cynicism. Silverbridge doubts himself as well, saying, 'I don't suppose I shall ever go in for hard work' (p. 125). But in fact, he ruminates on everything his father says, and he does slowly pay more and more attention to politics. He playfully claims that he might 'rat' on Sir Timothy if the Liberals 'give [him] something good' (p. 397), thus suggesting that he thinks not only about switching parties but about his role once he does switch—for, as Trollope makes clear, '[t]here is a manner of joking which carries with it a great deal of serious intention' (p. 216). Near the end, after the Duke gives him permission to marry Isabel, Silverbridge feels 'forced' to attend to his 'parliamentary duties' (p. 552) first, but gets so caught up in what's going on that he finds it hard to pull away, as he reasons that Isabel is more likely to be at home an hour later anyhow—though, ironically, the delay means he just misses her (p. 553). There is no suggestion that Silverbridge is fooling himself, and that his passion for her has cooled. As Isabel says of her soon-to-be husband to the Duke, 'I do not think he likes to be kept waiting for anything' (p. 559). The sexual implications are obvious—Silverbridge has been aching to embrace her for a long time. For him to wait even an hour to deliver the ecstatic good news about their engagement indicates how much his father's advice about Parliament has taken hold. He can be head over heels in love—and still give his mind to the affairs of the nation, too.

'I shall never make a real politician' (p. 222), Silverbridge had once said, but that assessment becomes outdated, as he shows every sign of striking a healthy balance between work and play and domesticity. We have seen how, at the end, the Duke praises Frank's manliness while inwardly thinking about his son's; and he could well be thinking as much or more about his heir when in the following words too he muses about Frank's future: 'Who knows, he may live yet to be a much greater man than his father-in-law. I am certainly very glad that he has a seat in Parliament' (p. 621). The Duke has come to see that his own life had been narrowly 'jejune' (p. 477); he might recognize—though he would never say it out loud to him—Silverbridge's potential to outdo him, especially now that the young man is married and sober-minded. With a pleasantly gregarious personality and a wife who will help not hinder him—along with a newfound work ethic and the best set of connections a man could ever have—Silverbridge as a Liberal party luminary may succeed in a way that the Duke never could. Shocking as the notion may have once been to his father—and to those readers whose first impressions of Silverbridge may tarnish him forever—it is possible to imagine him, in another few decades, as a worthy and even exceptional Prime Minister.

Trollope insisted in *An Autobiography* that his 'political feelings and convictions' had never altered. 'Nor,' he says, 'do I find in myself any tendency to modify them as I have found generally in men as they grow old.'[27] It is a declaration of unchanging adherence to a world-view that embraces gradual change. And while he emphasizes class issues when he talks about what the advanced conservative Liberal stands for, it is clear from many of Trollope's novels—and in *The Duke's Children*, the relationship between Lord Silverbridge and Isabel Boncassen most particularly—that he believes in the lessening of distances between men and women as well. Indeed, while the Duke may be 'laughing' when he credits the 'republican' Isabel for his son's switch to the Liberals (p. 611), this is yet another time where humour reveals the truth, for if Silverbridge becomes an advanced conservative Liberal who embraces more modern notions about gender, it is Isabel who plays a large role in helping him to get there. It is possible, even likely,

[27] Trollope, *An Autobiography*, 291.

that Silverbridge would have changed parties anyhow as a means of supplicating his father, but he does so with conviction that he truly belongs with the Liberals. His conviction grows the more confident he becomes in his own skin—and with his exposure to the kind of woman he has never quite encountered before.

As Deborah Denenholz Morse wrote in *Women in Trollope's Palliser Novels*, Trollope had a 'limited' view of women's roles that can still be thought of as 'subversive' in Victorian England, with his 'vision of a relation between two intelligent, sexual beings who were equals within their private union.'[28] Isabel is as smart and witty and sensible and charismatic and beautiful as any woman in Trollope's oeuvre, but it is safe to assume that she will not strive for an independent career, and will assist her husband in every way possible with his. One way she will do so is by becoming an exemplary Duchess of Omnium. Isabel herself at first wonders whether, as an American, she will learn how to behave suitably. It is all to her credit that she is not over-confident, but as readers we know there is no cause for doubt. After all, she has already rid herself of 'that national nasal twang, to be free from which had been one of the great labours of her life' (p. 255). Becoming a proper Duchess of Omnium will be another great, and successful, endeavour.

Isabel will assimilate quite as much as she needs to, but she will also be a revitalizing force. After knowing Silverbridge for a long time only as 'Lord', Isabel finds out that his real name is Plantagenet, which at first she deems 'grand' (p. 374). Later, however, she says that while she will use the 'horribly historical' name, she prefers 'Thomas or Abraham' (p. 527). Later still she insists that only Abraham will do, for '[w]ho can call a man Plantagenet? I should as soon think of calling my father-in-law Coeur de Lion' (p. 616). Isabel is joking, but with a purpose: she will not be unduly awed by tradition. '[W]hat is the good of a Christian name if nobody is to use it?', she says in explaining why she has requested that Frank address her as

[28] Deborah Denenholz Morse, *Women in Trollope's Palliser Novels* (Ann Arbor: UMI Research Press, 1987), 6. In her recent article 'Trollope the Feminist' (*The Routledge Research Companion to Anthony Trollope*), she discusses a number of other articles and books about Trollope and gender in the past half century, arguing that 'most scholars have come to think that Trollope was not only intensely interested in Victorian women but also increasingly aware of the gendered strictures of his society, and often critical of these limitations. Critics writing today tend to believe that Trollope was responsive to the agitation for women's rights, although they differ in their conclusions as to the degree of that response' (60). See also her book *Reforming Trollope: Race, Gender, and Englishness in the Novels of Anthony Trollope* (Farnham: Ashgate, 2013).

Isabel—and though Silverbridge might prefer that her name be 'for his own exclusive use and benefit', he knows better than to say so (p. 591). Eventually the narrator himself follows her lead, declaring that he will stick with her first name even though he is not supposed to after she is married (p. 618). It is a gentle nod of approval on Trollope's part. Isabel will hold her own—and get others to pay attention.

The marriage between the future Duchess and Duke of Omnium will not be egalitarian in twenty-first-century terms, but it will point the way in that direction. Not long before the wedding, Silverbridge says that he is baffled about American politics, to which Isabel replies, 'If you behave yourself well you shall be taught before long' (p. 592). This is a continuation of the teasing, sexually flirtatious banter that has marked their relationship from the moment they met—early in their acquaintance she says, 'if I had a stick I'd whip you' (p. 260)—and an indication, too, that the husband will be an eager and grateful student. Isabel also decides that it would be healthy for Silverbridge to be briefly on his own after they are engaged, and so goes off to Paris for several weeks with various unnamed Americans. Though he begs to come along, she prevails, insisting 'that his time, his unlimited time for having his way, was fast coming' (p. 580). We can assume that she delivers these words with her typical lighthearted tone; nothing in her behaviour or Silverbridge's indicates that they anticipate such a moment ever arriving. Instead, they will gingerly poke fun at the conventions of a traditional marriage.

Strong, assertive, and flexible, eager to learn and grow, with a shared sense of humour, both Isabel and Silverbridge will thrive together. The fate of Mary and Frank is less certain. Having met only under idyllic conditions while on holiday in Italy, with Glencora cheering them on, and then only once in England for a few minutes by accident, they barely know one another. Even more to the point, because the circumstances of the plot make us unable to observe them together, we have little basis to determine whether they are actually a suitable match. Their wilfulness serves them well in thwarting the Duke's opposition, but what will happen when they settle into a more mundane existence? We know from early in the novel that Frank 'was one who prided himself on being the master of others in the great affairs of life and on submitting himself to no masterdom' (p. 35), and we know that he doesn't change. It is not hard to imagine the headstrong Mary struggling under the reign of such a husband. On the other hand, when we see them for the last time we are told that 'the wife thoroughly respected her husband, as did the husband his wife' (p. 620). Perhaps, then, the couple will do well together. As is so often the case in his novels, Trollope leaves plenty of room for readers to decide for themselves.

Trollope repeatedly depicts women who chafe at the restrictions placed upon them. Mary says that if she were a man, she would not be 'shut up' (p. 221), and Mabel, comparing herself to Frank, thinks that 'if she also could have been born a man, then too she might have fought her own battle' (p. 436). A bad marriage may be bad for both parties, but it is the woman who suffers far more. If, as Isabel explains to Silverbridge, their relationship were to sour, 'You would still be what you are,—with a clog round your leg, indeed, while at home,—but still, in Parliament, among your friends, at your clubs, you would be just what you are. You would be that Lord Silverbridge who had all good things at his disposal,—except that he had been unfortunate in his marriage! But what should I be?' (pp. 528–29). Dangers abound even when a marriage doesn't necessarily turn disastrous. Alice Vavasor, one of the two women who may need forgiveness in *Can You Forgive Her?* (the other is Glencora), dawdles incessantly before she agrees to wed John Grey; and though we are never given access to her private thoughts again, a passage early in *The Duke's Children* (p. 10) suggests that she was right to worry, as Grey limits her contacts with the Palliser family. Indeed, her transformation from the complex Alice Vavasor to the mostly mute Mrs. Grey is itself a statement on how women can lose their identity once they marry.

Yet while he is deeply sympathetic towards them, Trollope balks at exploring a universe in which women can thrive outside of a loving marriage. As Bill Overton writes in *The Unofficial Trollope*, 'He could vividly imagine, and realise in his writing, what the position of a woman entailed, yet he had no ear for the conclusion crying out to be drawn: that women might have abilities which only a career could fulfil.'[29] Hence, we are presented with an author who consciously held conventional, 'official' views that his fiction might still challenge in more progressive, 'unofficial' ways. It may be, as Overton says, that Trollope was unwilling to think through the implications of what he had observed and intuited. It is also possible, however, that Trollope knew where he was headed even if he had not arrived there yet. Certainly, he was able to show, with exquisite detail, how someone like the Duke can be acutely introspective and not realize that his mind is in fact changing—until suddenly it does change. Shortly before he accepts Frank Tregear as his future son-in-law, the Duke is still unaware that he is about to give in,

---

[29] Bill Overton, *The Unofficial Trollope* (Brighton: The Harvester Press, 1982), 8.

even though it has been clear for much of the book that he will do so. This is not clumsiness on Trollope's part; he wanted to depict how arduous and messy and slow the process of changing one's mind can be. An author who could create such a character might well have known something about his own movement of mind—and the direction it was ultimately going—as he contemplated the plight of women in a patriarchal society.

Of Trollope's three heroines in *The Duke's Children*, one is given a splendid happy ending; another is given a more murky ending—ostensibly happy, but possibly not; and the third is given . . . cataclysm. Mabel Grex is practically a pauper, her self-centred father and brother having squandered whatever fortune they had, including a part that she could have chosen to keep for her own. She gets to see someone else becoming the future Duchess of Omnium, and she sees the love of her life, Frank Tregear, not only marry into enormous wealth and privilege but transfer his affections, rapidly, away from her too. Two of her aunts invite her to live with them, but as she 'greatly dislike[s]' them, one being 'very high church, and the other very low', she will go somewhere with Miss Casseway, her elder companion for many years who is as close to a mother figure—but not very close—as she has ever known. They will be, as she puts it, '[t]wo old maids together!' (p. 598). Mabel is still in her early twenties and still very beautiful; if she chooses to search for a husband, she will not have difficulty finding somebody. Yet her fate appears to be dire regardless, because such a marriage would be purely mercenary on her part. 'I can never, never, never love another' (p. 605), she tells Frank soon before his marriage—thereby following in the footsteps of other heroines in Trollope's work who fall in love only once and never again. One can envision Trollope loosening up were he to write another Palliser novel, portraying an embittered Mabel who marries the least awful rich man around, then discovers that she could respect him, and like him, and someday truly love him. Needless to say, Trollope never lived to write this book—and we can only speculate about whether he ever would have wanted to.

Meanwhile, if Mabel does seem doomed whether she marries or not, it is only partially because she is a woman who has already been in love. Silverbridge is finally able to figure out what her deep affliction is: even '[w]hen he was most fond of Mabel, most anxious to make her his wife, there had always been present to him a feeling that she was—old. Though he knew her age to a day,—and knew her to be younger than himself,—yet she was old' (p. 531). Isabel, on the other hand, is 'young as Hebe' (p. 531). It is evident why Silverbridge, and the reader, should compare Mabel to Isabel. Less obvious is how Mabel measures up against another character, one who at the beginning of the novel is also much older than his years but who becomes considerably more youthful by the end. The Duke in mourning his wife looks as if 'he had at once become an old man', but it is not only her death that is to blame; we are told that for a number of years he 'had acquired a habit of stooping which, when he was not excited, gave him an appearance of age more advanced than his own' (p. 11)—a habit that surely was exacerbated by his troubled reign as Prime Minister. At the end of the novel, during Mary and Frank's wedding, his appearance is markedly different, as he seems to be 'a man with very few cares'. While there is something more complicated going on underneath, his 'good humour' is also not a pose (p. 620).

Trollope would not readily make simplistic connections between personality and political beliefs, but it seems evident in *The Duke's Children* that Mabel's deep-seated attachment to the Conservatives suits her temperament. The Duke, on the other hand, has an aversion to change that conflicts somewhat with his politics. And his inability or unwillingness to change has hurt him deeply in the past. As the eponymous Prime Minister, he does not have the right personality to succeed. Among other problems, he is too sensitive, too incapable of manipulating others—and he doesn't learn from his mistakes on the job. Yet as Trollope tells us in *An Autobiography*, 'the greed of power' builds once the Duke has 'allowed himself to taste and to enjoy it'.[30] When *The Duke's Children* begins, he has been out of office for two years but still holds a seat in the House of Lords and is eager to return to work. Nonetheless, his pride and stubbornness are such that when his lifelong colleague the Duke of St. Bungay writes a long letter urging him to become involved in 'the formation of another Liberal Ministry' (p. 166) but not as Prime Minister, he resists for a long while. It takes nearly the rest of the novel before he jumps back into the fray. The letter clearly influences him—just as his own letter about public duty has influenced Silverbridge—but not immediately, as Trollope delineates many steps along the way before the ex-Prime Minister (and ex-Chancellor of the Exchequer) accepts a lesser but still central role in a Liberal Government. Trollope had made it clear in *An Autobiography* how life would be meaningless to him if he could not continue working.

---

[30] Trollope, *An Autobiography*, 360.

For the author to give his 'political hero'[31] a chance to do work that he cares about is a loving gift from creator to creation.

The Duke's new position as President of the Council, while immensely superior to retirement, is still a comedown. In one crucial way, however, his life will be better than ever, as he will have the kinds of relationships that have previously eluded him. Earlier, he wrongly vilifies Mrs. Finn, the Duchess's closest friend, for her role in Lady Mary's engagement to Frank Tregear. When he does come around, nearly a third of the way through the novel, it is with a terse letter that temporarily satisfies Mrs. Finn, who feels that it is exactly what she would expect. But after a number of weeks go by and he doesn't visit, she again grows sore. A chance meeting in the city of Ischl allows him to apologize at greater length, and he soon solicits her advice about his ailing daughter. Yet, though he calls Mrs. Finn both 'good' and 'reasonable', he will only go so far as to say that 'you did what you thought best.' When she replies bluntly, 'I did what was best,' he is taken aback but doesn't argue (p. 324). He will need more time before he can acknowledge how loyal she has been both to him and to Mary. By the end, the Duke is effusive in his praise and respect; indeed, he reveres her, and there is no doubt that his friendship with her will be closer than any he has had with a woman or a man. Even more important is the love and respect that he feels for the future Duke of Omnium. It is a far cry from the beginning of the novel, when two days after the Duchess's funeral we learn that father and son 'had not parted altogether on pleasant terms with each other' (p. 13). They are strangers at first, but Trollope convincingly shows, through numerous details spread over numerous pages, how they forge a genuine intimacy.

The Duke's ability to change his mind, ultimately, about work, and Mrs. Finn, and Silverbridge—and about Isabel as his heir's wife, and Frank as his daughter's husband—lightens his burden and makes him capable of actual happiness. Yet there is deep melancholy too. To some extent he is 'by nature too gloomy, too little addicted to the softness and tenderness of life', too prone to 'morbid self-debasement' (pp. 13–14) to change entirely. Despite the way he seems 'thoroughly contented' at Mary's wedding, he can't help 'reminding himself of all he had suffered, and reflecting how seldom it had happened that he to whom so many good things had been given had been allowed to have his own way in the affairs of life' (p. 620). Trollope chooses not to mention the Duchess here, but he doesn't need to. The Duke misses her, but he is

---

[31] Ibid. 361.

also aware of all that went wrong. Though she was a loyal wife, he knows that she couldn't love him the way he had wished, as her heart was given first to Burgo Fitzgerald. He also knows that to a large extent he took her for granted and ignored her. A passage from early in the novel captures his feelings about that neglect:

In former days, when his wife was alive, he had been accustomed to spend many hours after dinner alone,—but then he had always had the power of seeking her, or her friends, though it were but for a moment. Now there was no one to whom he could betake himself. If you have a book with you on a journey it is very possible that you may not look at it;—but how terrible a thing it is to come on a journey unprovided with any book! So it was with him. In those former days many a long evening he had passed all alone in his library, satisfied with blue-books, newspapers, and speculations on political economy, and had never crossed the threshold of his wife's drawing-room; but now, when there was no longer a threshold that he could cross, he felt himself to be deserted. (p. 199)

By the end of the series Palliser is no longer alone, no longer clueless about where he can go for comfort. But he cannot escape the memory of his past failures.

Trollope had written about his own past failures in *An Autobiography*—but they were long past, from his woebegone youth. The harrowing tales in that book about his father's decline, and his widowed mother's desperate attempts to keep the family afloat while several of her children were dying, also came from the distant past. If Trollope kept those painful early memories fresh in his mind, he did so in part for strategic reasons: to avoid complacency, to remain as hungry and motivated as he was when he first started out as a writer. As for his more recent life—covering over three decades since everything changed for him in Ireland—Trollope writes with conviction about his happiness: 'To enjoy the excitement of pleasure, but to be free from its vices and ill effects,—to have the sweet, and leave the bitter untasted,—that has been my study. The preachers tell us that this is impossible. It seems to me that hitherto I have succeeded fairly well. I will not say that I have never scorched a finger,—but I carry no ugly wounds.'[32] His Duke has led a less balanced life than his own, with no pleasures other than work, and though Trollope is circumspect about his marriage to Rose, who ended up outliving him by over three decades, there is little to suggest that theirs was a particularly troubled union. (Some have speculated about his relationship with the American writer and lecturer Kate Field,

---

[32] Ibid. 366.

about whom he writes rapturously in one paragraph, but it is difficult to believe that Trollope was describing anything more serious than an infatuation.[33]) *An Autobiography* is an endlessly fascinating text; little in it can be taken at face value, though it would be unfair to accuse Trollope of outright fabrication. But the sense of well-being he exudes comes across as authentic. He could not have the sense of exhilaration that a young person starting out in the world might feel, but he could look back at a lifetime full of achievement with legitimate hope for more to come. It may well be that, as John Sutherland puts it, '[h]is sixties were hard for Trollope. Since 1873 he had been totally deaf in one ear. His eyesight, always poor, was increasingly poorer. He was grossly over-weight—sixteen stone on a medium frame. After a bad fall he gave up his beloved hunting.'[34] Yet if Trollope felt like an old man physically, he retained enough of his youthful spirit to feel that he was capable of writing as well as he ever had in his career. That spirit mattered more to him than a broken-down body.

Trollope wrote briefly in *An Autobiography* about his two sons, now grown. Given his deep concerns about their future, he perhaps was eager to use fiction to fulfil a wish that was out of reach in reality, as he gives both Silverbridge and Gerald an especially joyful ending. It is Gerald who has the last words of the novel, and of the entire Palliser series. 'It will be my turn next,' he says to Silverbridge. 'After what you and Mary have done, I think he must let me have my own way whatever it is' (p. 621). While some readers might believe that this opens the door to a later novel in which Gerald is a trouble-making protagonist, Trollope almost surely had no such thoughts. For him to give Gerald his own star 'turn' frustrating the Duke would be to repeat what he had already done with the plot of *The Duke's Children*. After the sacrifice of Gerald's mother to create that plot, Trollope would not have been intent on recycling it for another novel. It is also significant that, late in the narrative, after Gerald blunders yet again, he has the courage to speak to the Duke about it himself. As he writes in a letter to his brother, 'But now what do you think I've done? Directly I got home I told the governor all about it! As I was in the train I made up my mind that I would. I went slap at it' (p. 506). His language is still that of a very young man, but one who is now willing to take responsibility and

[33] See Gary Scharnhorst, *Kate Field: The Many Lives of a Nineteenth-Century American Journalist* (Syracuse: Syracuse University Press, 2008), 36–8.

[34] John Sutherland, *The Secret Trollope: Anthony Trollope Uncovered* (Brighton: Edward Everett Root Publishers, 2019), 181.

listen to his father's 'really tip-top sound good sense' (p. 507). Finally, Gerald is too kindhearted to purposely hurt his father. He will indeed largely get to have his 'own way' in the future, but not to cause needless heartbreak. Rather, he speaks with unbounded enthusiasm of a new world full of tremendous possibilities.

After reflecting on his life and work for his autobiography, and liking what he discovered, Trollope approached *The Duke's Children* with utmost confidence. While he was in the midst of composing it, *The Prime Minister* completed its serialization in June 1876 and was published by Chapman & Hall as a four-volume novel that same month. Reviews were savage and sales were poor—and this for a novel which Trollope thought contained some of his very best writing. Though in most circumstances Trollope would have been glad to sell *The Duke's Children* right away, he either could not find a suitable offer or decided not to try yet, hoping for a more welcoming publishing environment later on. In 1878, when he was making minor changes to *An Autobiography*, he included a sad single-sentence footnote referring to the 'diminution in price'[35] he had encountered from publishers just in the previous few years. He also in 1878 took up Charles Dickens Jr.'s offer to publish *The Duke's Children* serially in *All the Year Round*. It is likely that Dickens demanded he cut it, though it is also possible that Dickens merely suggested cutting, and that Trollope, feeling vulnerable, went along without putting up much of a fight. Given how he had never attempted anything similar, he may even have seen the benefit of rising to this new challenge. What is indisputable is that Trollope concluded rather quickly that he had made a colossal error in cutting so much. (See 'Sample of Cuts to the Manuscript' in the Appendix, pp. 623–24.) Yet he was not about to undertake the daunting task of trying to reconstruct the manuscript for book publication. Indeed, if the numerous and sometimes egregious errors (many corrected here for the first time) are any indication, he could barely be bothered to proofread *The Duke's Children* at all before it came out, first in *All the Year Round* and then in book form—which is to say, he was more than ready to move on. Trollope thought of himself as a man in a hurry, someone with much new work to do even though his body was failing him. What he was able to accomplish after the spring of 1878, four and a half years before his death, is often extraordinary. *Ayala's Angel* and *Mr. Scarborough's Family* may credibly be counted among his greatest longer non-series novels, while *Cousin Henry* and *Dr. Wortle's School* are two of his strongest shorter novels. *Thackeray*, *The Life of Cicero*, and *Lord Palmerston* are engaging biographical works that are also fascinatingly autobiographical. There is much more, too, that shows him continuing to try new things. His final novel, *The Landleaguers*—unfinished when he died—includes a heroine, the American opera singer Rachel O'Mahony, who at least starts out with a thriving professional career.

Trollope's pruned version of *The Duke's Children* is still a solid accomplishment, and has been well received critically since it first came out, but as J. W. Bailey wrote in a 1982 article for *The Yale University Library Gazette*, 'One has the sense that the manuscript is like a balloon from which some air has been released: the overall shape remains, but the size and density are diminished'.[36] Dinah Birch, in her introduction to the most recent Penguin edition, says that the younger people in the novel 'emerge as fixed and relatively thin creations besides their elders'[37]—which is true enough, but only for the shorter version. In particular, the arc of Silverbridge's growth—and how he ultimately outshines Frank Tregear—is impossible to appreciate without Trollope's original details. Nearly all the characters, of whatever age, including those who appear only briefly, are rendered with greater richness and complexity in the complete novel, and in fact many of the examples quoted above do not appear in the shortened work. And while characterization matters most in looking at Trollope's work, there are numerous other ways that the pared-down *Duke's Children* suffers.[38] Trollope's late flowering is no different from his early flowering or mid-career flowering; what is remarkable is that he was able to maintain his vitality for so many years. We can only be grateful that he left us with so much to relish—and that his final Palliser novel turns out to be as stellar an achievement as readers have always wanted it to be.

Steven Amarnick, 2020

---

[36] J. W. Bailey, '*The Duke's Children*: Rediscovering a Trollope Manuscript', *The Yale University Library Gazette* 57.1–2 (October 1982), 36.

[37] Anthony Trollope, *The Duke's Children* (London: Penguin Books, 1995), x.

[38] I have written about these cuts in depth in my Introduction to the Folio Society edition (*Commentary to the First Complete Edition of* The Duke's Children *by Anthony Trollope* (London: The Folio Society, 2015), 1–32, as well as in my article 'Trollope at Fuller Length: Lord Silverbridge and the Manuscript of *The Duke's Children*', in Margaret Markwick, Deborah Denenholz Morse, and Regenia Gagnier (eds.), *The Politics of Gender in Anthony Trollope's Novels: New Readings for the Twenty-First Century* (Aldershot: Ashgate, 2009), 193–206. My most detailed comments on the cuts appear both on the Trollope Society's website ('Notes on Selected Restored Passages', https://www.trollopesociety.org/works/dukes-children/notes-restored-passages/) and on https://www.dukeschildrencomplete.com.

NOTE ON THE TEXT

TROLLOPE first wrote *The Duke's Children* between May and October of 1876. His working papers at the Bodleian Library reveal that he originally titled the novel *The Ex-Prime Minister* and planned to publish it in four volumes. In April and May of 1878 he returned to the manuscript, cutting roughly 65,000 words, over twenty-two percent of the whole. A Memorandum of Agreement signed by Trollope and Charles Dickens Jr., owner and editor of the literary magazine *All the Year Round*, indicates that Trollope would supply a novel in three volumes called *Lord Silverbridge* or 'any other name'. That novel, by then titled *The Duke's Children*, appeared in *All the Year Round* in weekly instalments from 4 October 1879 to 24 July 1880. In May 1880, Chapman & Hall published the book in three volumes. Trollope received £1400 total for the serial and book rights—down from the £2500 he was paid for each of the three previous Palliser novels, *The Eustace Diamonds*, *Phineas Redux*, and *The Prime Minister*. According to a note attached to the autograph manuscript, Trollope's elder son, Henry, offered to sell it to raise money for the British Red Cross in February 1918. The manuscript was eventually acquired by Professor Chauncey Brewster Tinker of Yale University, who later donated it to the school's Beinecke Library. (For more about the circumstances regarding the book's original publication, see the Introduction, p. x and xxviii, and Appendix, pp. 623–5.)

SELECT BIBLIOGRAPHY

Biographical

Anyone wishing to learn more about Trollope's life should start with his highly entertaining *An Autobiography*, published soon after his death. Not everything is factually accurate, but it is more than possible to believe that he did not purposely lie—even if his memory was faulty, or if he was willing to playfully mislead those readers who did not parse his words carefully. The most authoritative biography is by N. John Hall (*Trollope: A Biography*, 1991); at around the same time, three other biographies also appeared, all of them worthwhile: R. H. Super, *The Chronicler of Barsetshire: A Life of Anthony Trollope* (1988); Richard Mullen, *Anthony Trollope: A Victorian in His World* (1990); and Victoria Glendinning, *Anthony Trollope* (1993). Earlier in the twentieth century, the most significant Trollope scholar was Michael Sadleir, and his *Trollope: A Commentary* (1927) contains valuable biographical details and insights into his novels.

Trollope is one of the greatest letter writers in English fiction—that is, within the novels themselves. His own letters are more businesslike and less illuminating, though there is still much to be learned about him from what has survived. They are collected in N. John Hall's two-volume *The Letters of Anthony Trollope* (1983).

General

apRoberts, Ruth, *Trollope: Artist and Moralist* (London: Chatto and Windus, 1971; later titled *The Moral Trollope* for the U.S. publication).

Clark, John W., *The Language and Style of Anthony Trollope* (London: André Deutsch, 1975).

Cockshut, A. O. J., *Anthony Trollope: A Critical Study* (London: Collins, 1955).

Edwards, P. D., *Anthony Trollope: His Art and Scope* (Brisbane: University of Queensland Press, 1977).

Epperly, Elizabeth R., *Patterns of Repetition in Trollope* (Washington, DC: Catholic University of America Press, 1989).

Halperin, John, *Trollope and Politics: A Study of the Pallisers and Others* (London: Macmillan, 1977).

Hamer, Mary, *Writing by Numbers: Trollope's Serial Fiction* (Cambridge, UK: Cambridge University Press, 1987).

Herbert, Christopher, *Trollope and Comic Pleasure* (Chicago: University of Chicago Press, 1987).

Kincaid, James R., *The Novels of Anthony Trollope* (Oxford: Clarendon Press, 1977).

Letwin, Shirley Robin, *The Gentleman in Trollope: Individuality and Moral Conduct* (Cambridge, MA: Harvard University Press, 1982).

McMaster, Juliet, *Trollope's Palliser Novels: Theme and Pattern* (London: Macmillan, 1978).

Moody, Ellen, *Trollope on the Net* (London: Trollope Society, 1999).

Morse, Deborah Denenholz, *Women in Trollope's Palliser Novels* (Ann Arbor: UMI Research Press, 1987).

Nardin, Jane, *He Knew She Was Right: The Independent Woman in the Novels of Anthony Trollope* (Carbondale, IL: Southern Illinois University Press, 1989).

Overton, Bill, *The Unofficial Trollope* (Brighton: The Harvester Press, 1982).

Polhemus, Robert M., *The Changing World of Anthony Trollope* (Berkeley: University of California Press, 1968).

Skilton, David, *Anthony Trollope and His Contemporaries: A Study in the Theory and Conventions of Mid-Victorian Fiction* (New York: St. Martin's Press, 1972).

Tracy, Robert, *Trollope's Later Novels* (Berkeley: University of California Press, 1978).

Wright, Andrew, *Anthony Trollope: Dream and Art* (London: Macmillan, 1983).

TWENTY-FIRST-CENTURY STUDIES

Markwick, Margaret, *New Men in Trollope's Novels: Rewriting the Victorian Male* (Aldershot: Ashgate, 2007).

McCourt, John, *Writing the Frontier: Anthony Trollope between Britain and Ireland* (Oxford: Oxford University Press, 2015).

Morse, Deborah Denenholz, *Reforming Trollope: Race, Gender, and Englishness in the Novels of Anthony Trollope* (Farnham: Ashgate, 2013).

Sutherland, John, *The Secret Trollope: Anthony Trollope Uncovered* (Brighton: Edward Everett Root Publishers, 2019).

Turner, Mark W., *Trollope and the Magazines: Gendered Issues in Mid-Victorian Britain* (London: Macmillan, 2000).

Van Dam, Frederik, *Trollope's Late Style: Victorian Liberalism and Literary Form* (Edinburgh: Edinburgh University Press, 2016).

CONFERENCES AND ESSAYS

In recent years there have been two large international conferences devoted to Trollope, out of which these volumes of collected essays have appeared: Margaret Markwick, Deborah Denenholz Morse, and Regenia Gagnier (eds.), *The Politics of Gender in Anthony Trollope's Novels: New Readings for the Twenty-First Century* (Ashgate, 2009; from the 2006 conference in Exeter); Frederik Van Dam, David Skilton, and Ortwin de Graef, *The Edinburgh Companion to Anthony Trollope* (Edinburgh University Press, 2019; from the 2015 bicentenary conference in Leuven). Two other fine collections are Carolyn Dever and Lisa Niles (eds.), *The Cambridge Companion to Anthony Trollope* (Cambridge University Press, 2011), and Deborah Denenholz Morse, Margaret Markwick, and Mark W. Turner (eds.), *The Routledge Research Companion to Anthony Trollope* (Routledge, 2017).

There are of course innumerable essays on Trollope that are worth reading, none more important, or enjoyable, than Henry James's long obituary piece in 1883; it can be found in Library of America's *Henry James: Literary Criticism*, Vol. 1: *Essays on Literature, American Writers, English Writers* (1984). James arguably gets a lot wrong in his condescending assessment, but he also calls Trollope a genius, and seems to mean it; his essay is fascinating both for what it says about Trollope and what it says about James's own aesthetic.

On The Duke's Children *in particular*

Birch, Dinah, Introduction to *The Duke's Children* (London: Penguin Books, 1995), vii–xxi.

Butte, George, 'Ambivalence and Affirmation in *The Duke's Children*', *Studies in English Literature, 1500–1900*, 17(4) (1977), 709–27.

Egremont, Max, Introduction to *The Duke's Children: The Complete Text* (London: Everyman's Library, 2017), ix–xxv.

Franklin, J. Jeffrey, 'The Victorian Discourse of Gambling: Speculations on *Middlemarch* and *The Duke's Children*', *ELH*, 61(4) (1994), 899–921.

Hagan, John H., '*The Duke's Children*: Trollope's Psychological Masterpiece', *Nineteenth-Century Fiction*, 13(1) (1958), 1–21.

Herbert, Christopher, 'Trollope and the Fixity of the Self', *PMLA*, 93(2) (1978), 228–39.

Mullin, Katherine, and Francis O'Gorman, Introduction to *The Duke's Children* (Oxford: Oxford World's Classics, 2011), xi–xxxii.

Lee, Hermione, Introduction to *The Duke's Children* (Oxford: Oxford World's Classics, 1983), xi–xxv.

Pei, Lowry, '*The Duke's Children*: Reflection and Reconciliation', *Modern Language Quarterly*, 39 (1978), 284–302. '

On Trollope's cuts to the manuscript of The Duke's Children

Amarnick, Steven, Introduction, *Commentary to the First Complete Edition of* The Duke's Children *by Anthony Trollope* (London: The Folio Society, 2015), 1–32.

Amarnick, Steven, 'Trollope at Fuller Length: Lord Silverbridge and the Manuscript of *The Duke's Children*', in Margaret Markwick, Deborah Denenholz Morse, and Regenia Gagnier (eds.), *The Politics of Gender in Anthony Trollope's Novels: New Readings for the Twenty-First Century* (Aldershot: Ashgate, 2009), 193–206.

Bailey, J. W., '*The Duke's Children*: Rediscovering a Trollope Manuscript', *The Yale University Library Gazette* 57.1–2 (October 1982), 34–8.

Birch, Dinah, 'A Note on the Manuscript', in Anthony Trollope, *The Duke's Children* (London: Penguin Books, 1995), 507–10.

McMaster, Juliet, *Trollope's Palliser Novels: Theme and Pattern*, Chapter 7 (London: Macmillan 1978).

Wright, Andrew, 'Trollope Revises Trollope', in John Halperin, ed., *Trollope Centenary Essays* (New York: St. Martin's Press, 1982), 109–33.

Useful websites (containing extensive notes about reconstructing and editing *The Duke's Children*)

https://www.trollopesociety.org/works/dukes-children
https://www.dukeschildrencomplete.com

A CHRONOLOGY OF ANTHONY TROLLOPE

Michael G. Williamson

Life History	Literary Output

1815 24 April: Born at 16, Keppel St., Bloomsbury, London, as the youngest son of Thomas Anthony Trollope and Frances (Fanny) Trollope, née Milton. Family moves to Harrow-on-the-Hill later in the year.

1823 Summer: Enrolled at Harrow School as a day-boy.

1824 Summer: Death of brother Arthur William (aged 12).

1825 Transferred to Arthur Drury's School at Sunbury early in the year.

1827 April: Admitted to Winchester College.

1830 Summer: Leaves Winchester College.

1831 January: Sent again to Harrow School.

1834 April: Leaves Harrow School. Family move to Bruges to avoid creditors.
Summer: Becomes a classical usher at William Drury's School in Brussels for six weeks.
November: Appointed Junior Clerk in the General Post Office, London, and moves to lodgings in Little Marlborough St. with his brother Thomas Adolphus.
December: Death of brother Henry (aged 23).

1835 Moves to lodgings in Northumberland St.
October: Death of father, Thomas Anthony, at Bruges.

Life History	*Literary Output*
1836 February: Death of sister Emily (aged 18) at Hadley.	
1838 Moves with Fanny, Thomas Adolphus, and sister Cecilia to 20, York St., Portman Square.	
1839 Marriage of Cecilia to John Tilley, Trollope's friend and colleague. Travels to Paris with Fanny, where they meet up with Thomas Adolphus.	
1840 Moves to lodgings at 3, Wyndham St. Summer: Becomes seriously ill.	Plans and begins to write *A History of World Literature* but abandons it in 1841.
1841 July: Appointed Surveyor's Clerk in the Central Postal District of Ireland. Moves to Banagher, King's County, Headquarters of the Central District.	
1843	Begins *The Macdermotts of Ballycloran* in September (completed in March 1845; published by Thomas C. Newby in March 1847).
1844 11 June: Marries Rose Heseltine, at Rotherham, Yorkshire. August: Transferred to the Southern Postal District of Ireland as Assistant Surveyor. Moves to Cork, County Cork.	
1845 March: Moves to Clonmel, County Tipperary.	
1846 13 March: Birth of elder son Henry Merivale.	Begins *The Kellys and the O'Kellys* (completed in 1847; published by Henry Colburn & Co. in June 1848).
1847 27 September: Birth of younger son Frederic James Anthony.	
1848 April: Thomas Adolphus marries Theodosia Garrow. Autumn: Moves to Mallow, County Cork.	Begins *La Vendée* (completed in 1849; published by Henry Colburn & Co. in June 1850).
1849 April: Death of Cecilia (aged 32).	

	Life History	*Literary Output*
1850		Writes *The Noble Jilt* (play). On advice, it is not submitted for publication or production.
1851	August: Sent on postal work to the West of England and Channel Islands. Recommends the use of free-standing pillar boxes. December: Returns to Ireland.	
1852	Returns again on postal work to the West of England and Wales.	
1853	Travels abroad on leave with Rose and brother-in-law, John. May: Spends in Florence with Thomas Adolphus. Appointed Acting Surveyor of the Northern Postal District of Ireland. 29 August: Moves to Belfast. Birth of Beatrice (Bice) to Thomas Adolphus and Theodosia Trollope.	July: Begins *The Warden* (completed in autumn 1854; published by William Longman in January 1855).
1854	9 October: Officially appointed as Surveyor of the Northern Postal District of Ireland.	
1855	May/June: Travels abroad on leave with Rose and meets Fanny, and Thomas Adolphus, in Venice. June: Moves to Donnybrook, near Dublin.	January: Begins *Barchester Towers* (completed in November 1856; published by William Longman in May 1857). March–May: Writes and revises *The New Zealander* but it remains unpublished.
1856	August/September: Travels abroad on leave with Rose and John.	
1857	September: Travels abroad on leave with Rose, Fanny, and Thomas Adolphus.	February: Begins *The Three Clerks* (completed in August; published by Richard Bentley in November 1858). August: Begins *The Struggles of Brown, Jones, and Robinson* (abandoned for several years, then completed in August 1861; serialized in the *Cornhill Magazine* from August 1861 until March 1862 and published in book form by Smith, Elder & Co. in November 1870). October: Begins *Dr. Thorne* (completed in March 1858; published by Chapman & Hall in May 1858).

Life History	*Literary Output*
1858 February: Sets off from London on postal work to Egypt. Arrives in Alexandria. March: Visits the Holy Land. April/May: Returns home via Malta, Gibraltar, and Spain. May–September: Resumes postal duties in Scotland and the North of England. November: Sails from Southampton on postal duties to the West Indies. December–May 1859: Arrives at St. Thomas and travels to Jamaica, Cuba, other islands of the West Indies, and Central America.	April: Begins *The Bertrams* (completed in January 1859; published by Chapman & Hall in March 1859).
1859 May: Starts for home from West Indies via the Niagara Falls and New York City. 3 July: Arrives back in Liverpool. September/October: Travels abroad on leave to the South of France with Rose, Fanny, Thomas Adolphus, and John. 21 November: Transferred to the Eastern Postal District of England as Surveyor.	June: Writes *The West Indies and the Spanish Main* (published by Chapman & Hall in October). August: Begins *Castle Richmond* (completed in March 1860; published by Chapman & Hall in May 1860). November: Begins *Framley Parsonage* (completed in June 1860; serialized in the *The Cornhill Magazine* from January 1860 until April 1861; published in book form by Smith, Elder & Co. in April 1861).
1860 10 January: Moves to Waltham House, Waltham Cross, Hertfordshire. September–November: Travels abroad on leave with Rose, visiting his mother and brother in Florence, and begins a lifelong friendship with American journalist Kate Field.	July: Begins *Orley Farm* (completed in June 1861; serialized in twenty monthly parts by Chapman & Hall from March until October 1862; published in book form by Chapman & Hall: Vol. 1 in December 1861, Vol. 2 in September 1862).
1861 April: Elected to the Cosmopolitan Club. August/September: Leaves with Rose from Liverpool on his visit to the United States and Canada and arrives in Boston. November: Rose returns home.	January: Lecture on 'The Civil Service as a Profession' delivered for the first time. September: Begins *North America* (completed in April 1862; published by Chapman & Hall in May 1862). November: *Tales of All Countries: First Series* published by Chapman & Hall; contains short stories mainly first published in magazines between July 1859 and November 1860.

Life History	Literary Output
1862 March: Leaves New York and arrives in Liverpool. April: Elected to the Garrick Club. Autumn: Extensions built on to Waltham House. September: Travels to Holland on leave.	May: Begins *The Small House at Allington* (completed in February 1863; serialized in *The Cornhill Magazine* from September 1863 until April 1864; published in book form by Smith, Elder & Co. in March 1864). Lecture on 'The Present Condition of the Northern States of the American Union' delivered for the first time (either late in 1862 or early in 1863).
1863 March: Trollope's niece, Florence Bland, the orphaned daughter of Rose's sister Isabella, joins his household. July/August: Travels on leave to Switzerland, the Rhine, and Cologne with Rose, their niece Edith Tilley, and their two sons, Henry and Frederic. October: Death of Fanny.	February: *Tales of All Countries: Second Series* published by Chapman & Hall; contains short stories mainly first published in magazines between January and December. March: Begins *Rachel Ray* (completed in June; published by Chapman & Hall in October). August: Using plot elements from *The Noble Jilt*, begins the first Palliser novel, *Can You Forgive Her?* (completed in April 1864; appears in monthly numbers from January until August 1865; published in book form by Chapman & Hall: Vol. 1 in September 1864 and Vol. 2 in July 1865).
1864 March: Elected to the General Committee of the Royal Literary Club. April: Selected for membership of the Athenaeum Club. October: Travels on leave with Henry to Paris and, in the same month, travels with Rose to the Isle of Wight. Leads discussions on founding *The Fortnightly Review.*	May: Begins *Miss Mackenzie* (completed in August; published by Chapman & Hall in February 1865). August: Begins *The Claverings* (completed in December; serialized in *The Cornhill* from February 1866 until May 1867; published in book form by Smith, Elder & Co. in April 1867).
1865 Travels on leave to Florence following the death of Theodosia, and returns home to England with his niece Beatrice (Bice) Trollope aged 10. May/June: On postal duties in Scotland and Ireland.	January: Begins *The Belton Estate* (completed in September; serialized in *The Fortnightly Review* from May 1865 until January 1866; published in book form by Chapman & Hall in December). February: First issue of the *Pall Mall Gazette* appears, with two articles by Trollope, including the first of the series *Hunting Sketches* (full series completed in March; published in book form by Chapman & Hall in May).

Life History	*Literary Output*
1865 Travels on leave with Rose and Frederic to Koblenz where they are joined by Henry. September/October: Frederic travels to Vienna and Australia with the intention of eventually settling in Australia.	August: Provides the first of *Travelling Sketches* for the *Pall Mall Gazette* (completed in September; published by Chapman & Hall in February 1866). November: Provides the first of *Clerical Sketches* for the *Pall Mall Gazette* (published in book form by Chapman & Hall in March 1866, as *Clergymen of the Church of England*). November: Begins *Nina Balatka* (completed in December; serialized anonymously by *Blackwood's Magazine* from July 1866 until January 1867; published anonymously in book form by Blackwood in January 1867).
1866 September: On leave with Rose at Bantry Bay in Ireland. 29 October: Travels on leave to Paris, where he is joined by Rose and Henry for Thomas Adolphus's second wedding, to Frances Ternan. Invited by James Virtue to edit a new monthly magazine called *The Saint Pauls Magazine*.	Begins to write *History of English Prose Fiction* but later abandons it. January: Begins *The Last Chronicle of Barset* (completed in September; issued in weekly parts by Smith, Elder & Co., from December until July 1867; published in book form by Smith, Elder & Co.: Vol. 1 in March 1867, Vol. 2 in May 1867). November: Begins *Phineas Finn*, the second novel in the Palliser series (completed in April 1867; serialized in *Saint Pauls* from October 1867 until May 1869; published in book form by Virtue & Co. in March 1869).
1867 July/August: On leave in Europe. Rose joins him in Paris, and they visit Switzerland together. 1 September: Resigns from the Civil Service. 31 October: Attends Farewell Dinner, at the end of nearly thirty-three years of working for the Post Office.	June: Begins *Linda Tressel* (completed in July; serialized in *Blackwood's Magazine* from October until May 1868; published anonymously in book form by Blackwood in May 1868). August: *Lottie Schmidt*, a collection of short stories, published by Alexander Strahan. September: Begins *The Golden Lion of Granpère* (completed in October; serialized in *Good Words* from January 1872 until August 1872; published in book form by Tinsley Brothers in May 1872). November: Begins *He Knew He Was Right* (completed in June 1868; published in weekly numbers by Virtue & Co. from October 1868 until May 1869; published in book form by Alexander Strahan in May 1869).

Life History

Literary Output

1868 17 March: Presented at Court, before travelling to negotiate a postal convention between Great Britain and the United States of America.
11 April: Sails from Liverpool, arriving in New York on 22 April and continuing on to Washington.
15 July: Sails for home, arriving on 26 July.
30 October: Stands for election as the Liberal candidate for Beverley, Yorkshire, and gives his first speech to electors.
17 November: On election day, finishes last out of four candidates. The result is eventually overturned on appeal and the seat is disenfranchised.
December: Frederic returns from Australia and remains until 26 April 1869, after which he returns to Australia to settle permanently.

Begins to deliver his lecture on 'The Higher Education of Women' at several locations.
British Sports and Pastimes published in book form by Virtue & Co., reprinted from *Saint Pauls* and edited by Trollope, including Trollope's two-part article 'On Hunting'.
January: The first issue of *Saint Pauls* to be edited by Trollope appears.
June: Begins *The Vicar of Bullhampton* (completed in November; issued in monthly numbers by Bradbury & Evans from July until May 1870; published in book form in April 1870).
December: Begins *Sir Harry Hotspur of Humblethwaite* (completed in January 1869; serialized in *McMillan's Magazine* from May to December 1870; published in book form by Hurst & Blackett in November 1870).

1869 September: Travels with Rose to Normandy and Brittany.

March: Produces a dramatized version of *The Last Chronicle of Barset* as *Did He Steal It?* It is rejected for production.
April: Begins *Ralph the Heir* (completed in August; issued in monthly parts by Alexander Strahan from January 1870 until July 1871 and, at the same time, as supplements to *Saint Pauls*; published in book form by Hurst & Blackett in April 1871).
December: Begins *The Eustace Diamonds*, the third novel of the Palliser series (completed in August 1870; serialized in *The Fortnightly Review* from July 1871 until February 1873; published in book form by Chapman & Hall in October 1872).

1870 Gives up editorship of *Saint Pauls* after July issue.

January: Begins *The Commentaries of Caesar* (completed in April; published by Blackwood in June).
Delivers lecture 'On English Prose Fiction as a Rational Amusement' for the first time.

Life History	Literary Output
1870	June: *An Editor's Tales*, a collection of short stories, appears in *Saint Pauls*. September: Begins *An Eye for an Eye* (completed in October; serialized in the *Whitehall Review* from August 1878 until February 1879; published in book form by Chapman & Hall in October 1879). October: Begins *Phineas Redux*, the fourth novel of the Palliser series (completed in April 1871; serialized in *The Graphic* from July 1873 to January 1874; published in book form by Chapman & Hall in December 1873).
1871 April: Gives up Waltham House, and sails with Rose from Liverpool to Australia on 24 May to visit Frederic in New South Wales. July: Arrives in Melbourne to begin a tour to Sydney, New South Wales, and Brisbane, Queensland. Stays with Frederic in late October at his sheep station.	May: Begins *Lady Anna* (completed in July; serialized in *The Fortnightly Review* from April 1873 until April 1874; published in book form by Chapman & Hall in March 1874). October: Begins *Australia and New Zealand* (completed in January 1873; published by Chapman & Hall in February 1873).
1872 April: Tours South Australia. 29 July: Sails from Melbourne to New Zealand. October: Begins the journey home, changing ships at Honolulu. 6 November: Arrives in San Francisco, and crosses America by train, calling at Salt Lake City. December: Arrives home, and lodges at 3, Holles St.	April: *Shilly Shally*, a pirated version of *Ralph the Heir*, is dramatized by Charles Reade and staged at the Gaiety Theatre, London.
1873 April: Moves into his new house at 39, Montagu Square. August: On holiday with Rose to Killarney.	May: Begins *The Way We Live Now* (completed in December; issued in monthly numbers from February 1874 until September 1875; published in book form by Chapman & Hall in June 1875). June: Begins and completes *Harry Heathcote of Gangoil* (appears in the Christmas issue of *The Graphic*; published in book form by Sampson Low in October 1874).

Life History	Literary Output

1874 July/August: On holiday with Rose in Switzerland.

April: Begins *The Prime Minister*, the fifth novel in the Palliser series (completed in September; published in monthly parts by Chapman & Hall from November 1875 until June 1876; published in book form by Chapman & Hall in June 1876). October: Begins *Is He Popenjoy?* (completed in May 1875; serialized in *All the Year Round* from October 1877 until July 1878; published in book form by Chapman & Hall in April 1878).

1875 1 March: Leaves London for Australia, calling at Rome and Naples.
March/April: Visits Ceylon.
May: Arrives at Melbourne and travels to Frederic's sheep station in New South Wales.
28 August: Sails from Sydney, calling at Auckland, Honolulu, San Francisco, Boston, and New York.
20 October: Sails from New York and reaches Liverpool on 30 October.

June: Begins *The American Senator* (completed in September; serialized in *Temple Bar* from May 1876 until July 1877; published in book form by Chapman & Hall in June 1877). July: The first of twenty letters (mainly about Australia) is published in the *Liverpool Mercury*; these continue each week until November. October: Begins *An Autobiography* (completed in April 1876; published, posthumously, in October 1883). 6–11 December: 'Never, Never—Never, Never', a parody written for *Sheets for the Cradle*, is produced for charitable purposes. The short story appears in issues 1, 3, and 5.

1876 March: Finally gives up hunting.
July–October: On holiday with Rose and Florence in Switzerland.

May: Begins *The Duke's Children* as the sixth novel in the Palliser series (completed in October; severely cut by Trollope in 1878; serialized in *All the Year Round* from October 1879 until July 1880; published in book form by Chapman & Hall in May 1880).

1877 29 June: Sails from Dartmouth for South Africa.
22 July: Arrives in Cape Town and travels throughout South Africa until December.
11 December: Leaves Cape Town and reaches home in January 1878.

February: Begins *John Caldigate* (completed in July; serialized in *Blackwood's Magazine* from April 1878 until June 1879; published in book form by Chapman & Hall in May 1879). Writes a two-part article, 'Cicero', which appears in *The Fortnightly Review* in April and September. Continues intermittently to write *The Life of Cicero* until 1880 when it is published by Chapman & Hall, in two volumes, in December 1880. July: Begins *South Africa* (completed in January 1878; published by Chapman & Hall in February 1878).

Life History	*Literary Output*
1878 April: Visits Bolton Abbey, Yorkshire. June/July: Travels to Iceland in the yacht *Mastiff*. Late July–September: On holiday with Rose and Florence in Switzerland and Germany.	March: Completes arrangements with Chapman & Hall for the publication, in eight volumes, of *The Chronicles of Barsetshire*, which appear from November 1878 until July 1879. April: Begins *Ayala's Angel* (completed in September; published by Chapman & Hall in May 1881). June/July: Writes *How the 'Mastiffs' Went to Iceland*; it is privately printed by Virtue & Co. and presented to the participants of the trip. October: Begins *Cousin Henry* (completed in December; serialized simultaneously in the *Manchester Weekly Times* and the *North British Weekly Mail* from March 1878 until April 1879; published in book form by Chapman & Hall in October 1879). December: Begins *Marion Fay* (completed in November 1879; serialized in *The Graphic* from December 1881 until June 1882; published in book form by Chapman & Hall in May 1882).
1879 August/September: On holiday with Rose and Florence to Germany, France, and Switzerland.	February: Begins *Thackeray* (completed in March; published by Macmillan in May). April: Begins *Dr. Wortle's School* (completed in December 1880; serialized in *Blackwood's Magazine* from May until December 1880; published in book form by Chapman & Hall in January 1881). The article 'A Walk in a Wood' appears in *Good Words*.
1880 July: Moves from Montagu Square to North End, South Harting, near Petersfield.	July–September: 'London Tradesmen', a series of eleven sketches, appears at intervals in *The Pall Mall Gazette*. July: Begins *Kept in the Dark* (completed in August; serialized in *Good Words* from May to December 1882; published in book form by Chatto & Windus in October 1882). December: Begins *The Fixed Period* (completed in February 1881; serialized in *Blackwood's Magazine* from October to March 1882; published in book form by Blackwood in March 1882).

Life History | *Literary Output*

1881 March: Travels to Rome with Rose and Florence to visit Thomas Adolphus and Frances.
July: Death of Beatrice (Bice).

March: Begins *Mr. Scarborough's Family* (completed in October; serialized in *All the Year Round* from May 1882 until June 1883; published in book form by Chatto & Windus in April 1883).
Autumn: Begins *Lord Palmerston* (completed in 1882; published by William Isbister in June 1882).
December: *Why Frau Frohmann Raised Her Prices*, a collection of short stories, published by William Isbister.

1882 May/June: Travels to Dublin with Florence to undertake research for *The Landleaguers*.
August/September: Visits Dublin again with Florence.
2 October: Takes rooms at Garlant's Hotel, Suffolk Street.
3 November: Suffers a stroke while dining with John.
6 December: Dies in a nursing home at 34, Welbeck St.
9 December: Buried at Kensal Green Cemetery.

February: Begins and completes *An Old Man's Love* (published by Blackwood in March 1884).
June: Begins *The Landleaguers* (remains uncompleted; serialized in *Life* from November until October 1883; published in book form by Chatto & Windus in October 1883).
'The Two Heroines of Plumplington' is written for *Good Cheer*, the Christmas issue of *Good Words*, but remains officially unpublished in book form until 1953.
'Not If I Know It', a short story, appears in the Christmas Annual of *Life*.

1923 *The Noble Jilt* (play) is published by Constable and Co.

1927 *London Tradesmen* is published privately by Elkin Mathews & Marrot Ltd.

1938 *Four Lectures* is published by Constable and Co. Ltd in a limited edition.

1941 *The Tireless Traveller*, bringing together the twenty letters to the *Liverpool Mercury* written by Trollope in 1875, is published by the University of California Press.

1952 *Did He Steal It?* (play) is published by Princeton University Library.

1953 November: *The Two Heroines of Plumplington* is published (limited edition) by André Deutsch Ltd.

1971 *Never, Never—Never, Never* is privately printed by the Valley Press.

Life History	*Literary Output*
1972	*The New Zealander* is published by Clarendon Press, Oxford.
1987 The Trollope Society is founded by John Letts.	The Trollope Society begins publishing the first uniform edition of Trollope's work (largely completed in 2003).
1993 25 March: Following a special appeal by the Trollope Society, a Memorial to Anthony Trollope is installed in Poet's Corner, in Westminster Abbey.	
2015	Coinciding with the 200th anniversary of Trollope's birth, *The Duke's Children* is published in its original, extended form by the Folio Society, as a fine edition. It contains approximately 65,000 additional words.
2017	*The Duke's Children*, in its extended form, is published by Everyman's Library in hardback format.

THE DUKE'S CHILDREN

THE DUKE'S CHILDREN

CONTENTS

VOLUME 1

1. When the Duchess Was Dead   7
2. Lady Mary Palliser   14
3. Francis Oliphant Tregear   23
4. Park Lane   30
5. 'It is impossible'   37
6. Major Tifto   46
7. Conservative Convictions   54
8. 'He is a gentleman'   61
9. *In medias res*   68
10. 'Why not like a Romeo, if I feel like a Romeo?'   76
11. 'Cruel'   83
12. At Richmond   91
13. The Duke's Injustice   98
14. The New Member for Silverbridge   103
15. The Duke Receives a Letter,—and Writes One   114
16. 'Poor boy!'   122
17. The Derby   128
18. One of the Results of the Derby   137
19. 'No, my Lord, I do not'   144
20. 'Then he will come again'   151
21. Sir Timothy Beeswax   158
22. The Duke in His Study   164
23. Frank Tregear Wants a Friend   174
24. 'She must be made to obey'   181
25. A Family Breakfast-Table   187
26. Dinner at the Beargarden   194

VOLUME 2

27. Major Tifto and the Duke   205
28. Mrs. Montacute Jones's Garden-Party   210
29. The Lovers Meet   219
30. What Came of the Meeting   226
31. Miss Boncassen's River-Party, No. 1   233
32. Miss Boncassen's River-Party, No. 2   242

33. The Langham Hotel   251
34. Lord Popplecourt   261
35. 'Don't you think ——?'   268
36. Tally-ho Lodge   278
37. Grex   283
38. Crummie-Toddie   291
39. Killancodlem   298
40. 'And then?'   307
41. Ischl   315
42. Again at Killancodlem   326
43. What Happened at Doncaster   333
44. How It Was Done   340
45. 'There shall not be another word said about it'   346
46. Lady Mary's Dream   355
47. Miss Boncassen's Idea of Heaven   364
48. The Party at Custins Is Broken Up   371
49. The Major's Fate   378
50. The Duke's Arguments   384
51. The Duke's Guests   392
52. Miss Boncassen Tells the Truth   398
53. 'Then I am as proud as a queen'   407

VOLUME 3

54. 'He must be made to please something else'   417
55. Polpenno   423
56. The News Is Sent to Matching   432
57. The Meeting at The Bobtailed Fox   438
58. The Major Is Deposed   444
59. 'No one can tell what may come to pass'   451
60. Lord Gerald in Further Trouble   464
61. 'Bone of my bone'   469
62. The Brake Country   479
63. 'I've seen 'em like that before'   488
64. 'I believe him to be a worthy young man'   495
65. 'Do you ever think what money is?'   500
66. The Three Attacks   507
67. 'He is such a beast'   517
68. Brook Street   523
69. 'Pert poppet!'   531
70. 'Love may be a great misfortune'   538

71. 'What am I to say, sir?'   545
72. Carlton Terrace   554
73. 'I have never loved you'   561
74. 'Let us drink a glass of wine together'   569
75. The Major's Story   580
76. On Deportment   586
77. 'Mabel, good-bye'   592
78. The Duke Returns to Office   605
79. The First Wedding   612
80. The Second Wedding   618

VOLUME 1

CHAPTER 1

WHEN THE DUCHESS WAS DEAD

No one, probably, ever felt himself to be more alone in the world than our old friend,* the Duke of Omnium,* when the Duchess died. When this sad event happened he had ceased to be Prime Minister just two years. Those who are conversant with the political changes which have taken place of late in the Government of the country will remember that when the coalition Ministry of which he had been the head was broken up, the old Liberal party came back to power under the leading of Mr. Gresham. That arrangement did not remain in force very long;—but at the present moment we need not allude to ministerial changes, except to say that the Duke of Omnium had not as yet returned to office. During the first nine months he and the Duchess remained in England. Then they had gone abroad, taking with them their three children. The eldest, Lord Silverbridge, had been at Oxford, but had had his career there cut short by some more than ordinary youthful folly, which had induced his father to agree with the college authorities that his name had better be taken off the college books,—all which had been cause of very great sorrow to the Duke. The other boy was to go to Cambridge;* but his father had thought it well to give him a twelvemonth's run on the Continent, under his own inspection. Lady Mary, the only daughter,* was the youngest of the family, and she also had been with them on the Continent. They remained the full year abroad, travelling with a large accompaniment of tutors, lady's-maids, couriers, and sometimes friends. I do not know that the Duchess or the Duke had enjoyed it much; but the young people had seen something of foreign courts and much of foreign scenery, and had perhaps perfected their French and added something to their German. The Duke had gone to work at his travels with a full determination to create for himself occupation out of a new kind of life. He had studied Dante, and had striven to arouse himself to ecstatic joy amidst the loveliness of the Italian lakes. But through it all he had been aware that he had failed. The Duchess had made no such resolution,—had hardly, perhaps, made any attempt; and her impatience had militated against his efforts. But, in truth, they

had both sighed to be back among the war-trumpets. They had both
suffered much among the trumpets, and yet they longed to return. He
told himself from day to day, that though he had been banished from
the House of Commons, still, as a peer, he had a seat in Parliament; and
that, though he was no longer a British minister, still he might be useful
as a British legislator. She, in her career as a leader of fashion, had no
doubt met with some trouble,—with some trouble but with no disgrace; and as she had been carried about among the lakes and mountains, among the pictures and statues, among the counts and countesses,
she had once more felt that there was no happiness except in that
dominion which circumstances had enabled her to achieve once, and
might enable her to achieve again, in the realms of London society. And
so they had both sighed to be again among the trumpets, without any
free communication of their thoughts one to the other.

Then, in the early spring of 187—,* they came back to England, having
persistently carried out their project, at any rate in regard to time. Lord
Gerald, the younger son, was at once sent up to Trinity. For the eldest son
a seat was to be found in the House of Commons, and the fact that a dissol-
ution of Parliament was expected served to prevent any prolonged sojourn
abroad. Lady Mary Palliser was at that time nineteen, and her entrance into
the world was to be her mother's great care and great delight. In March
they spent a few days in London, and then went down to Matching Priory.*
When she left town the Duchess was complaining of cold, sore throat, and
debility. A week after their arrival at Matching she was dead.

Had the heavens fallen and mixed themselves with the earth, had the
people of London risen in rebellion with French ideas of equality, had
the Queen persistently declined to comply with the constitutional
advice of her ministers, had a majority in the House of Commons lost
its influence in the country,—the utter prostration of the bereft husband could not have been more complete. It was not only that his heart
was torn to pieces, but that he did not know how to look out into the
world. It was as though a man should be suddenly called upon to live
without hands or even arms. He was helpless, and knew himself to be
helpless. Hitherto he had never specially acknowledged to himself that
his wife was necessary to him as a component part of his life. Though
he had loved her dearly, and had in all things consulted her welfare and
happiness, he had at times been inclined to think that in the exuberance
of her spirits she had been a trouble rather than a support to him. But
now it was as though all outside appliances and comforts were taken
away from him. He was alone in the world, and there was no one of
whom he could ask a question.

For it may be said of this man that, though throughout his life he had had many Honourable and Right Honourable friends, and that, though he had entertained guests by the score, and though he had achieved for himself the respect of all good men and the thorough admiration of some few who knew him, he had hardly made for himself a single intimate friend in the world,—except that one friend who had now passed away from him. To her he had been able to say what he thought, even though she would occasionally ridicule him while he was declaring his feelings. But there had been no other human soul to whom he could thus open himself. There were one or two whom he loved, and perhaps liked; but his loving and his liking had been almost exclusively political. He had so habituated himself to devote his mind and his heart to the service of his country, that he had almost risen above or sunk below humanity. But she, who had been essentially human, had been a link between him and the world. Now there was no longer a link, and he felt himself to be dissevered from the world.

There were his three children, the youngest of whom was now nine-teen,* and they surely were links! At the first moment of his bereave-ment they were felt to be hardly more than burdens. The loss was so great that nothing remaining seemed to him to be of value. A more loving father there was not in England, but nature had made him so undemonstrative that as yet they had hardly known his love. In all their joys and in all their troubles, in all their desires and all their disappoint-ments, they had ever gone to their mother. She had been conversant with everything about them, from the boys' bills and the girl's gloves to the innermost turn in the heart and the disposition of each. She had known with the utmost accuracy the nature of the scrapes into which Lord Silverbridge had precipitated himself, and had known also how probable it was that Lord Gerald would do the same. The results of such scrapes she, of course, deplored; and therefore she would give good counsel, pointing out how imperative it was that such evil-doings should be avoided; but with the spirit that produced the scrapes she fully sympathised. The father disliked the spirit almost worse than the results; and was therefore often irritated and unhappy. How should he now control them, when she was gone?

And the difficulties about the girl were almost worse to bear than those about the boys. She had done nothing wrong. She had given no signs of extravagance or other juvenile misconduct. But she was beau-tiful, young, and as full of life and energy as her mother had been. How was he to bring her out into the world? How was he to decide whom she should or whom she should not marry? How was he to guide her through the shoals and rocks which lay in the path of such a girl before she can achieve matrimony?

It was the singularity of the position of the family that, with a world of acquaintance, they had not many friends. From all close connection with relatives on the side of the Duchess they had been dissevered, by old feelings on her part at first, and afterwards by want of any similitude in the habits of life. She had, when young, been repressed by male and female guardians with an iron hand. Such repression had been needed, and had been perhaps salutary, but it had not left behind it much affection. And then her nearest relatives were not sympathetic with the Duke. There was an old Lady Midlothian and a young Lord Nidderdale with whom he and she had maintained but a very cold acquaintance. He could obtain no assistance in the care of his girl from that source. Nor could he even do it from his own cousins' wives, who were his nearest connections on the side of the Pallisers. They were women to whom he had ever been kind, but to whom he had never opened his heart. When, in the midst of the stunning sorrow of the first week, he tried to think of all this, it seemed to him that there was nobody.

The friend whom he most trusted was a certain Mrs. Grey.* She had been a distant cousin of his wife, and with her he had always maintained something like real friendship. He and his wife, who on such matters were often at variance, had agreed in valuing the society of this lady, and in the early days of the Duke's married life she had been much with them; but any close social intercourse with persons so far above him in rank had hardly suited Mr. Grey's views, and he had somewhat discouraged the near intimacy which the Duchess certainly would have liked. But the poor widower, when he looked about thinking where he might find assistance, turned his mind more frequently to Mrs. Grey than to any other female friend.

There had been one lady, a very dear ally, staying in the house with them when the Duchess had died. This was Mrs. Finn, the wife of Phineas Finn, who had been one of the Duke's colleagues when in office. How it had come to pass that Mrs. Finn and the Duchess had become singularly bound together has been told elsewhere.* But there had been very close bonds,—so close that when the Duchess on their return from the Continent had passed through London on her way to Matching, ill at the time and very comfortless, it had been almost a thing of course that Mrs. Finn should go with her. And as she had sunk, and then despaired, and then died, it was this woman who had always been at her side, who had ministered to her, and had listened to the fears and the wishes and hopes she had expressed respecting the children in almost the last words she had spoken. Then death had come, and Mrs. Finn was still there with the bereaved family.

At Matching, amidst the ruins of the old Priory, there is a parish burying-ground, and there, in accordance with her own wish, almost within sight of her own bedroom-window, she was buried. On the day of the funeral a dozen relatives came, Pallisers and M'Cluskies,* who on such an occasion were bound to show themselves, as members of the family. With them and his two sons the Duke walked across to the grave-yard, and then walked back; but even to those who stayed the night at the house he hardly spoke a word. By noon on the following day they had all left him, and the only stranger in the house was Mrs. Finn.

On the afternoon of the day after the funeral the Duke and his guest met, almost for the first time since the sad event. There had been just a pressure of the hand, just a glance of compassion, just some murmur of deep sorrow,—but there had been no real speech between them. Now he had sent for her, and she went down to him in the room in which he commonly sat at work. He was seated at his table when she entered, but there was no book open before him, and no pen ready to his hand. He was dressed of course in black. That, indeed, was usual with him, but now the tailor by his funereal art had added some deeper dye of blackness to his appearance, some other outer sign of utter deso-lation which struck her eye at once. When he rose and turned to her she thought that he had at once become an old man. His hair had already become grey in parts, and he had never accustomed himself to use that skill in managing his outside person by which many men are able to preserve for themselves a look, if not of youth, at any rate of youthful freshness. He was thin, of an adust complexion, and in latter years had acquired a habit of stooping which, when he was not excited, gave him an appearance of age more advanced than his own. All that was com-mon to him; but now it was so much exaggerated that he who was not yet fifty might have been taken to be over sixty.

He put out his hand to greet her as she came up to him. 'Silverbridge,' he said, 'tells me that you go back to London to-morrow.'

'I thought it would be best, Duke. My presence here can be of no comfort to you.'

'I will not say that anything can be of comfort. But of course it is right that you should go. I can have no excuse for asking you to remain. While there was yet a hope for her——' Then he stopped, unable to say a word further in that direction, and yet there was no sign of a tear and no sound of a sob.

'Of course I would stay, Duke, if I could be of any service.'

'Mr. Finn will expect you to return to him.'

'Perhaps it would be better that I should say that I would stay were it not that I know that I can be of no real service.'

'What do you mean by that, Mrs. Finn?'

'Lady Mary should have with her at such a time some other friend.'

'There was none other whom her mother loved as she loved you;—none, none.' This he said almost with energy.

'There was no one lately, Duke, with whom circumstances caused her mother to be so closely intimate. But even that perhaps was unfortunate.'

'I never thought so.'

'That is a great compliment. But, as to Lady Mary,—will it not be as well that she should have with her as soon as possible someone,—perhaps someone of her own kindred if it be possible, or, if not that, at least one of her own kind?'

'Who is there? Whom do you mean?'

'I mean no one. It is hard, Duke, to say what I do mean, but perhaps I had better try. There will be, probably there have been, some among your friends who have regretted the great intimacy which chance produced between me and my lost friend. While she was with us no such feeling would have sufficed to drive me from her. She had chosen for herself, and if others disapproved her choice that was nothing to me. But as regards Lady Mary,—it will be better I think that from the beginning she should be taught to look for friendship and guidance to those,—to those who are more naturally connected with her.'

'I was not thinking of any guidance,' said the Duke.

'Of course not. But with one so young, where there is intimacy there will be guidance. What I mean is that there should be somebody with her. It was I think almost the last thought that occupied her mother's mind. I could not tell her, Duke, but I can tell you that I cannot, with advantage to your girl, be that somebody.'

'Cora wished it.'

'Her wishes probably were sudden and hardly fixed.'

'Who should it be then?' asked the father, after a pause.

'Who am I, Duke, that I should answer such a question?'

After that there was another pause, and then the conference was ended by a request from the Duke that Mrs. Finn would stay at Matching for yet two days longer. When she left the room he was almost harsh to her in his manner, saying little or nothing to thank her for her compliance, but showing plainly that he wished to be alone again. At dinner they all met,—the father, the three children, and Mrs. Finn.

How far the young people among themselves had been able to throw off something of the gloom of death need not here be asked; but in the presence of their father they were sad and sombre, almost as he was. On the next day, early in the morning, the younger lad returned to his college, and Lord Silverbridge went up to London, where he was supposed to have his home. From a word or two that was said by Lady Mary, Mrs. Finn learned that the father and his eldest son had not parted altogether on pleasant terms with each other.

'Perhaps you would not mind reading these letters,' the Duke said to her, when she again went to him, in compliance with a message from him asking for her presence. Then she sat down and read two letters, one from Lady Cantrip, and the other from a Mrs. Jeffrey Palliser, each of which contained an invitation for his daughter, and expressed a hope that Lady Mary would not be unwilling to spend some time with the writer. Lady Cantrip's letter was long, and went minutely into circumstances. If Lady Mary would come to her, she would abstain from having other company in the house till her young friend's spirits should have somewhat recovered themselves. Nothing could be more kind, or proposed in a sweeter fashion. There had, however, been present to the Duke's mind as he read it a feeling that a proposition to a bereaved husband to relieve him of the society of an only daughter, was not one which would usually be made to a father. In such a position a child's company would probably be his best solace. But he knew,—at this moment he painfully remembered,—that he was not as are other men. Lady Cantrip when she wrote the letter had no doubt felt that he was by nature too gloomy, too little addicted to the softness and tenderness of life, to be left as the only companion of a young girl. He acknowledged the truth of this, but he was not the less grieved and irritated by the reminder. The letter from Mrs. Jeffrey Palliser was to the same effect, but was much shorter. If it would suit Mary to come to them for a month or six weeks at their place in Gloucestershire, they would both be delighted.

'I should not choose her to go there,' said the Duke, as Mrs. Finn refolded the latter letter. 'My cousin's wife is a very good woman, but Mary would not be happy there with her.'

'Lady Cantrip is an excellent friend for her.'

'Excellent. I know no one whom I esteem more than Lady Cantrip.'

'Would you wish her to go there, Duke?'

There came a wistful piteous look over the father's face. Why should he be treated as no other father would be treated? Why should it be supposed that he would desire to send his girl away from him? But yet he felt that it would be better that she should go. It was his present purpose to remain at Matching through a portion of the summer. What could he do to make a girl happy? What comfort would there be in his companionship? 'I suppose she ought to go somewhere,' he said.

'I had not thought of it,' said Mrs. Finn.

'I understood you to say,' replied the Duke, almost angrily, 'that she ought to go to someone who would take care of her.'

'I was thinking of some friend coming to her.'

'Who would come? Who is there that I could possibly ask? You will not stay.'

'I certainly would stay,—if it were for her good. I was thinking, Duke, that perhaps you might ask the Greys to come to you.'

'They would not come,' he said, after a pause.

'When she was told that it was for her sake, she would come,—I think.'

Then there was another pause. 'I could not ask them,' he said. 'For his sake I could not have it put to her in that way. Perhaps Mary had better go to Lady Cantrip. Perhaps I had better be alone here for a time. I do not think that I am fit to have any human being here with me in my sorrow. I would not be very loquacious, you know.' This he said with a faint attempt at a most sorry smile.

At last it was decided that Mrs. Finn should discuss the matter with Lady Mary herself, and that she should go to this discussion prepared to recommend a short visit to Lady Cantrip. She was very eager in counselling the Duke to talk the matter over himself with his daughter; but in his morbid self-debasement he declared that were he to do so he would simply seem to dictate to his child. He thought it much better that she should hear what there was to be said from Mrs. Finn, and that she should make known her decision to that lady.

CHAPTER 2

LADY MARY PALLISER

I⊤ may as well be said at once that Mrs. Finn knew something of Lady Mary which was not known to the father, and which she was not pre-pared,—at any rate not as yet prepared,—to make known to him. The last winter abroad had been passed at Rome, and there Lady Mary Palliser had become acquainted with a certain Mr. Tregear,—Francis Oliphant Tregear. The Duchess, who had been in constant correspond-ence with her friend, had asked questions by letter as to Mr. Tregear, of whom she had only known that he was the younger son of a Cornish gentleman, who had become Lord Silverbridge's friend at Oxford. In this there had certainly been but little to recommend him to the intimacy of such a girl as Lady Mary Palliser. Nor had the Duchess, when writing, ever spoken of him as a probable suitor for her daughter's hand. She had not in any of her letters connected the two names together. But Mrs. Finn had been clever enough to perceive that the Duchess had become fond of Mr. Tregear, and would willingly have heard something to his advantage. And she did hear something to his advantage,—something also to his disadvantage. At his mother's death this young man would inherit a property amounting to about fifteen hundred a year.* 'And I am told,' said Mrs. Finn, 'that he is quite likely to spend his money before it comes to him.' In answer to this the Duchess had said something of enormous wealth being no more than an enormous burden. There had been nothing more written specially about Mr. Tregear; but Mrs. Finn had feared not only that the young man loved the girl, but that the young man's love had in some imprudent way been fostered by the mother.

Then there had been some fitful confidence during those few days of acute illness. Why should not the girl love the man if he were lovable? And the Duchess referred to her own early days when she had loved, and to the great ruin which had come upon her heart when she had been severed from the man she had loved. 'Not but that it has been all for the best,' she had said;—'not but that Plantagenet has been to me the best husband which Providence could have given me. Only if she can be spared what I suffered, let her be spared.' Even when these things had been said to her, Mrs. Finn had found herself unable to ask questions. She could not bring herself to inquire whether the girl had in truth given her heart to this young Tregear. The one was nineteen, and the other as yet but two-and-twenty! But though she asked no questions she almost knew that it must be so. And she knew also that the father, as yet, was quite in the dark on the matter. How was it possible that in such circumstances she should assume the part of the girl's confidential friend and monitress? Were she to do so she must immediately tell the father everything. In such a position no one could be a better friend than Lady Cantrip, and Mrs. Finn had already almost made up her mind that, should Lady Cantrip occupy the place, she would tell her ladyship all that had passed between herself and the Duchess on the subject.

Of what hopes she might have, or what fears, about her girl, the Duchess had said no word to her husband. But when she had believed that the things of the world were fading away from her, and when he was sitting by her bedside,—dumb, because at such a moment he knew not how to express the tenderness of his heart,—holding her hand, and trying so to listen to her words, that he might collect and remember every wish, she had murmured something about the ultimate division of the great wealth with which she herself had been endowed. 'She had never,' she said, 'even tried to remember what arrangements had been made by lawyers, but she hoped that Mary might be so circumstanced, that if her happiness depended on marrying a poor man, want of money need not prevent it.' The Duke suspecting nothing, believing this to be a not unnatural expression of maternal interest, had assured her that Mary's fortune would be ample.

On the afternoon of the day on which the young men had left Matching, Mrs. Finn made the proposition to Lady Mary in respect to Lady Cantrip's invitation. Lady Mary was very like her mother, especially in having exactly her mother's tone of voice, her quick manner of speech, and her sharp intelligence. She had also her mother's eyes, large and round, and almost blue, full of life and full of courage, eyes which never seemed to quail, and her mother's dark brown hair, never long but very copious in its thickness. She was, however, taller than her mother, and very much more graceful in her movement. And she could already assume a personal dignity of manner which had never been within her mother's reach. She had become aware of a certain brusqueness of speech in her mother, a certain aptitude to say sharp things without thinking whether the sharpness was becoming to the position which she held, and, taking advantage of the example, the girl had already learned that she might gain more than she would lose by controlling her words. Those who knew the Duchess well and who would declare that the daughter was the image of the mother would generally add something to signify that both in manner and appearance the copy excelled the original.

'Papa wants me to go to Lady Cantrip?' she said.

'I think he would like it,—just for the present, Lady Mary.'

Though there had been the closest possible intimacy between the Duchess and Mrs. Finn, this had hardly been extended to the intercourse between Mrs. Finn and the children. The latter had now been more than twelve months abroad, and previously to that had been subject to governesses and teachers. And, of Mrs. Finn, it must be acknowledged that she was, perhaps fastidiously, afraid of appearing to take advantage of her friendship with the Duke's family. She would tell herself that though circumstances had compelled her to be the closest and nearest friend of a duchess, still her natural place was not among dukes and their children, and therefore in her intercourse with this girl she did not at first assume the manner and bearing which her position in the house would have seemed to warrant. Hence the 'Lady Mary.'

'Why does he want to send me away, Mrs. Finn?'

'It is not that he wants to send you away, but that he thinks it will be better for you to be with some friend. Here you must be so much alone! He thinks that at present that will not be good for you.'

'Why don't you stay? But I suppose Mr. Finn wants you to be back in London.'

'It is not that only;—or to speak the truth not that at all. Mr. Finn could come here,—if it were suitable. Or for a week or two he might do very well without me. But there are other reasons. There is no one whom your mother respected more highly than Lady Cantrip.'

'I never heard her speak a word of Lady Cantrip that I can remember.'

'And both he and she are your father's intimate friends.'

'Does papa want to be—alone here?'

'It is you, not himself, of whom he is thinking.'

'Therefore I must think of him, Mrs. Finn. I do not wish him to be alone. I am sure it would be better that I should stay with him.'

'He feels that it would not be well that you should be here without the companionship of some lady.'

'Then let him find some lady. You would be the best because he knows you so well. I, however, am not afraid of being alone. I am sure he ought not to be here quite by himself. If he bids me go I must go, and then of course I shall go where he sends me. But I won't say that I think it best that I should go, and certainly I do not want to go to Lady Cantrip.' This she said with great decision, as though the matter was one on which she had altogether made up her mind. Then she added in a lower voice, 'Why doesn't papa speak to me about it? If he wants me to go away, why does he not tell me so himself? I don't think he ought to want me to go away because the boys have gone.'

'He is thinking only of what may be best for you.'

'It would be best for me to stay near him. Whom else has he got?'

All this Mrs. Finn repeated to the Duke as closely as she could, and then of course the father was obliged to speak to his daughter. 'Don't send me away, papa,' she said at once.

'Your life here, Mary, will be inexpressibly sad.'

'It must be sad anywhere. I cannot go to college like Gerald, or live anywhere, just as I please, like Silverbridge.'

'Do you envy them that?'

'Sometimes, papa. Only I shall think more of poor mamma by being alone, and I should like to be thinking of her always.' He shook his head mournfully. 'I do not mean that I shall always be unhappy as I am now.'

'No, dear;—you are too young for that. It is only the old who suffer in that way.'

'You will suffer less if I am with you,—won't you, papa? I do not want to go to Lady Cantrip. I hardly remember her at all.'

'She is very good.'

'Oh yes. That is what they used to say to mamma about Lady Midlothian. Papa, pray do not send me to Lady Cantrip.'

Of course it was decided that she should not go to Lady Cantrip at once, or to Mrs. Jeffrey Palliser, and, after a short interval of doubt, it was decided also that Mrs. Finn should remain at Matching for at least a fortnight. The Duke declared that he would be glad to see Mr. Finn, and spoke of our old friend Phineas as one of his established friends; but she knew that in his present mood the society of any one man to whom he would feel himself called upon to devote his time would be a burden to him, and she plainly said that Mr. Finn had better not come to Matching at present. 'There are old associations,' she said, 'which will enable you to bear with me as you will with your butler or your groom; but you are not as yet quite able to make yourself happy with company.' This he bore with perfect equanimity, and then, as it were, handed over his daughter to Mrs. Finn's care.

Very quickly there came to be close intimacy between Mrs. Finn and Lady Mary. For a day or two the elder woman, though the place she filled was one of absolute confidence, rather resisted than encouraged the intimacy. She always remembered that the girl was the only daughter of a great duke, of one who had been Prime Minister, and who was perhaps the richest nobleman in England; and that her position in the house had sprung from circumstances which would not, perhaps, in the eyes of the world at large, have recommended her for such friendship. No one was more fully aware than Mrs. Finn herself that there were rumours still afloat as to the manner in which she had made good her footing in the house of the Pallisers. She knew,—the reader may possibly know,—that nothing had ever been purer, nothing more disinterested than her friendship. But she knew also,—no one knew better,—that the judgment of men and women does not always run parallel with facts. She entertained, too, a conviction in regard to herself, that hard words and hard judgments were to be expected from the world,—were to be accepted by her without any strong feeling of injustice,—because she had been elevated by chance to the possession

of more good things than she had merited. She weighed all this with
a very fine balance, and even after the encouragement she had received
from the Duke, was intent on confining herself to some position about
the girl inferior to that which such a friend as Lady Cantrip might have
occupied. But the girl's manner, and the girl's speech about her own
mother, overcame her. It was the unintentional revelation of the
Duchess's constant reference to her,—the way in which Lady Mary
would assert that 'mamma used always to say this of you; mamma
always knew that you would think so and so; mamma used to say that
you had told her.' It was the feeling thus conveyed, that the mother who
was now dead had in her daily dealings with her own child spoken of
her as her nearest friend, which mainly served to conquer the deference
of manner which she had assumed.

Then gradually there came confidences,—and at last absolute confidence. The whole story about Mr. Tregear was told. Yes; she loved Mr.
Tregear. She had given him her heart, and had told him so.

'Then, my dear, your father ought to know it,' said Mrs. Finn.

'No;—not yet. Mamma knew it.'

'Did she know all that you have told me?'

'Yes; all,—and Mr. Tregear spoke to her. And she said that papa
ought not to be told quite yet.' Mrs. Finn could not but remember that
the friend she had lost was not, among women, the one best able to give
a girl good counsel in such a crisis, but of that she could of course say
nothing to the daughter.

'Why not yet, dear?'

'Well;—because——; it is very hard to explain. In the first place
because Mr. Tregear himself does not wish it.'

'That is a very bad reason;—the worst in the world.'

'Of course you will say so. Of course everybody would say so. But
when there is one person whom one loves better than all the rest, for
whom one would be ready to die, to whom one is determined that
everything shall be devoted, surely the wishes of a person so dear as
that ought to have weight.'

'Not in persuading you to do that which is acknowledged to be
wrong.'

'What wrong? I am going to do nothing wrong.'

'The very concealment of your love is wrong, after that love has been
not only given but declared. A girl's position in such matters is so delicate,—especially that of such a girl as you!'

'I know all about that,' said Lady Mary, with something almost
approaching to scorn in her tone. 'Of course I have to be—delicate.

I don't quite know what the word means, but I intend at any rate to do nothing to be ashamed of. I am not a bit ashamed of being in love with Mr. Tregear. He is a gentleman, highly educated, very clever, of a very old family,—older I believe a great deal than papa's. And he is manly, and handsome;—just what a young man ought to be. Only he is not rich.'

'If he be all that you say, ought you not to trust your papa? If he approve of it, he could give you money.'

'Of course he must be told,—at last. But not now. He is nearly broken-hearted about dear mamma. He could not bring himself to care about anything of that kind quite at present. And then it is Mr. Tregear that should speak to him first.'

'Not now, Mary.'

'How do you mean, not now?'

'If you had a mother,—you would talk to her about it.'

'Mamma knew.'

'If she were still living, she would tell your father.'

'But she didn't tell him though she did know. She didn't mean to tell him quite yet. She wanted to see Mr. Tregear here in England first. Of course I shall do nothing till papa does know.'

'You will not see him?'

'How can I see him here? He will not come here if you mean that.'

'You do not correspond with him?' Here for the first time the girl blushed. 'Oh, Mary, if you are writing to him your father ought to know it.'

'I have not written to him, but when he heard how ill poor mamma was, then he wrote to me,—twice.'

'Has he written since?'

'Yes, once again. You may see his letters. It is all about her. No one worshipped mamma as he did.'

Gradually the whole story was told. These two young persons considered themselves to be engaged, but had agreed that their engagement should not be made known to the Duke till something had occurred, or some time had arrived, as to which Mr. Tregear was to be the judge. In Mrs. Finn's opinion nothing could be more unwise than this, and she said much to induce the girl to confess everything to her father at once. But in all her arguments she was opposed by the girl's reference to her mother. 'Mamma knew it.' And it did certainly seem to Mrs. Finn as though the mother had assented to this imprudent concealment. When she endeavoured, in her own mind, to make excuse for her friend, she felt almost sure that the Duchess, with all her courage, had been afraid to propose to her husband that their daughter should marry a commoner without any immediate income of his own, and almost without prospects.

But in thinking of all that, there could now be nothing gained. What ought she to do—at once? The girl, in telling her, had exacted no promises of secrecy, nor would she have given any such promise; but yet she did not like the idea of telling the tale behind the girl's back. It was evident that Lady Mary had considered herself to be quite safe in confiding her story to her mother's old friend. Lady Mary no doubt had had her confidences with her mother,—confidences from which it had been intended by both that the father should be excluded; and now she seemed naturally to expect that this new ally, between whom and her mother there had been so much sympathy, should look at this great question as her mother had looked at it. The father had been regarded as a great outside power, which could hardly be overcome, but which might be evaded, or made inoperative by stratagem. It was not that the daughter did not love him. She loved him, and venerated him highly,—the veneration perhaps being stronger than the love. The Duchess, too, had loved him dearly,—more dearly in late years than in her early life. But her husband to her had always been an outside power which had in many cases to be evaded. Lady Mary, though she did not express all this, evidently thought that in this new friend she had found a woman whose wishes and aspirations for her would be those which her mother had entertained. It did not seem to have occurred to her that Mrs. Finn would commit the unwomanly crime of telling her secret to her father.

But Mrs. Finn was much troubled in her mind, thinking that it was her duty to tell the story to the Duke. It was not only the daughter who had trusted her, but the father also; and the father's confidence had been not only the first but by far the holier of the two. And then the question was one of such vital importance to the girl's future happiness! There could be no doubt that the peril of her present position was very great. Who was Mr. Tregear that so great a trust should be put in him? Mrs. Finn only knew of him that he was a young man of fashion without means, and Lord Silverbridge's particular friend. In this there was nothing certainly to justify Lady Mary's engagement and subsequent silence. It must be presumed that the Duke would object to the marriage, and if such objection were to be made and sustained it would certainly be better for the young lady that her father's purpose should be known at once. If, on the other hand, the Duke should show himself disposed to indulge his daughter's wishes and to give the young pair a start in life together, then certainly the sooner the engagement were made known to him, the greater would be his good-will. At any rate as father he was entitled to know. Mrs. Finn, as she thought of all this, already repented her prolonged sojourn at Matching.

'Mary,' she said one morning when the fortnight was nearly at an end, 'your father ought to know all this. I should feel that I had betrayed him were I to go away leaving him in ignorance.'

'You do not mean to say that you will tell?' said the girl, horrified at the idea of such treachery.

'I wish that I could induce you to do so. Every day that he is kept in the dark is an injury to you.'

'I am doing nothing. What harm can come? It is not as though I were seeing him every day.'

'This harm will come. Your father of course will know that you became engaged to Mr. Tregear in Italy and that a fact so important to him has been kept back from him.'

'If there is anything in that, the evil has been done already. Of course poor mamma did mean to tell him.'

'She cannot tell him now, and therefore you ought to do what she would have done.'

'I cannot break my promise to him.' 'Him' always meant Mr. Tregear. 'I have told him that I would not do so till I had his consent;—and I will not.'

This was very dreadful to Mrs. Finn, and yet she was most unwilling to take upon herself the part of a stern elder, and declare that under the circumstances she must tell the tale. The story had been told to her under the supposition that she was not a stern elder, that she was regarded as the special friend of the dear mother who was gone, that she might be trusted to assist against the terrible weight of parental authority. She could not endure to be regarded at once as a traitor by this young friend who had sweetly inherited the affection with which the Duchess had regarded her. And yet if she were to be silent how could she forgive herself? 'The Duke certainly ought to know,—at once!' said she, repeating her words merely that she might gain some time for thinking, and pluck up courage to declare her purpose, should she resolve on betraying the secret.

'If you tell him now, I will never forgive you,' said Lady Mary.

'I do not know what I ought to do. I wish you had never spoken to me about it. I am bound in honour to see that your father knows a thing which is of such vital importance to him and to you. Having heard all this I have no right to keep it from him. If Mr. Tregear really loves you,'—Lady Mary smiled at the doubt implied by this suggestion,—'he ought to feel that for your sake there should be no secret from your father.' Then she paused a moment to think. 'Will you let me see Mr. Tregear myself and talk to him about it?'

To this Lady Mary at first demurred, but when she found that in no other way could she prevent Mrs. Finn from going at once to the Duke and telling him everything, she consented. Under Mrs. Finn's directions she wrote a note to her lover, which Mrs. Finn saw and then undertook to send together with a letter from herself, to Mr. Tregear's address at London. The note was very short, and was indeed dictated by the elder lady, with some little dispute, however, as to certain terms, in which the younger lady had her way. It was as follows:

'DEAREST FRANK,

'I wish you to see Mrs. Finn who, as you know, was dear mamma's most particular friend. Please go to her, as she will ask you to do. When you hear what she says, I think you ought to do what she advises.

'Yours for ever and always,

'M.P.'

This Mrs. Finn sent enclosed in an envelope, with a few words from herself, asking the gentleman to call upon her in Park Lane, on a day and at an hour fixed. And this letter was directed to the Beargarden Club,* that being the only address for her lover which the young lady knew. 'Of course he has a residence,' she said, with some touch of disdain in her voice. 'When he is at home he lives at Polwenning where the Tregears have lived from before the Conquest. But a young man isn't always under his mother's apron string. No;—I don't know where he sleeps when he is in London. The Tregears have no town house. They don't come to town. I suppose they are not rich enough. I don't think they are a bit inferior because of that.'

'Certainly not; only I did not know whether you might not have a better address than the gentleman's club.'

'I have no address, and had no intention of writing to him. But the name of the club is on the note which I got from him immediately after poor mamma's death.'

CHAPTER 3

FRANCIS OLIPHANT TREGEAR

MR. FRANCIS OLIPHANT TREGEAR was a young man who might not improbably make a figure in the world, should circumstances be kind to him, but as to whom it might be doubted whether circumstances would be sufficiently kind to enable him to use serviceably his unquestionable talents and great personal gifts. He had taught himself to regard himself as a young English gentleman of the first water, qualified by his birth and position to live with all that was most noble and most elegant; and he could have lived in that sphere naturally and gracefully were it not that the part of the 'sphere' which he specially affected requires wealth as well as birth and intellect. Wealth he had not, and yet he did not abandon the sphere. As a consequence of all this, it was possible that the predictions of his friends as to that figure which he was to make in the world might be disappointed.

He had been educated at Eton, from whence he had been sent to Christ Church; and both at school and at college had been the most intimate friend of the son and heir of a great and wealthy duke. He and Lord Silverbridge had been always together, and they who were interested in the career of the young nobleman had generally thought he had chosen his friend well. Tregear had been at the top of the school, and had achieved a character for scholarship. And at Oxford, though he had done nothing very great, still as a young man of fashion he was supposed to have done well. He had gone out in honours and had been a second-class man, whereas his tutor and his college had expected a lower rank for him. His friend Silverbridge, we know, had been allowed to take no degree at all; but the terrible practical joke by which the whole front of the Dean's house had been coloured scarlet in the middle of the night, had been carried on without any assistance from Tregear. The two young men had then been separated for a year; but immediately after taking his degree, Tregear, at the invitation of Lord Silverbridge, had gone to Italy and had there completely made good his footing with the Duchess,—with what effect on another member of the Palliser family the reader already knows.

The young man was certainly abnormally clever. When the Duchess found that he could talk without any shyness, that he could speak French fluently, and that after a month in Italy he could chatter Italian, at any rate without reticence or shame; when she perceived that all the women liked the lad's society and impudence, and that all the young men were anxious to know him, she was glad to find that Silverbridge had chosen so valuable a friend. And then he was beautiful to look at,—putting her almost in mind of another man on whom her eyes had once loved to dwell. He was dark, with hair that was almost black, but yet was not black; with clear brown eyes, a nose as regular as Apollo's, and a mouth in which was ever to be found that expression of manliness, which of all characteristics is the one which women love the best. He was five feet ten in height. He was always well dressed, and yet always so dressed as to seem to show that his outside garniture had not been a matter of trouble to him. Before the Duchess had dreamed what might take place between this young man and her daughter she had been urgent in her congratulations to her son as to the possession of such a friend.

For though she now and then would catch a glimpse of the outer man, which would remind her of that other beautiful one whom she had known in her youth, and though, as these glimpses came, she would remember how poor in spirit and how unmanly that other one had been, though she would confess to herself how terrible had been the heart-shipwreck which that other one had brought upon herself; still she was able completely to assure herself that this man, though not superior in external grace, was altogether different in mind and character. She was old enough now to see all this and to appreciate it. Young Tregear had his own ideas about the politics of the day, and they were ideas with which she sympathised, though they were antagonistic to the politics of her life.* He had his ideas about books too, as to manners of life, as to art, and even ethics. Whether or no in all this there was not much that was superficial only, much that was mere tinsel, she was not herself deep enough to discover. Nor would she have been deterred from admiring him had she been told that it was tinsel. Such were the acquirements, such the charms, that she loved. Here was a young man who dared to speak, and had always something ready to be spoken; who was not afraid of beauty, nor daunted by superiority of rank; who, if he had not money, could carry himself on equal terms among those who had. In this way he won the Duchess's heart, and having done that, was it odd that he should win the heart of the daughter also?

When he had taken his degree his friends were urgent with him to enter some profession. At that time there was but one profession open to him. Were he to submit to work at all he must work as a barrister. The church was out of the question. The whole tone of his mind and his mode of life made medicine and surgery impossible to him. It was already too late with him for diplomacy,—which he told his friends he would have liked; or at any rate for that regular entrance into the lower ranks by which alone, we are given to understand though not always made to believe, can the good things of the Civil Service be reached. For the army and the navy he was also too old, and, as he himself thought, by far too well educated. But to the bar he made many objections. He did not, he said, like the duplicity. He did not, in truth, like the labour. He liked to be a gentleman at large, having certain vague ideas as to a future career in Parliament; and he tried, very much in

vain, to satisfy himself by thinking that he could be content to live
among gentlemen as a poor man.

His father was a Cornwall squire of comfortable means, having
joined the property of his wife to his own for the period of his own life.
She had possessed land also in Cornwall, supposed to be worth fifteen
hundred a year, and his own paternal estate at Polwenning was said to
be double that value. Being a prudent man, he lived at home as a country gentleman, and thus was able in his county to hold his head as high
as richer men. But Frank Tregear was only his second son; and though
Frank would hereafter inherit his mother's fortune, he was by no means
now in a position to assume the right of living as an idle man. Yet he was
idle. The elder brother, who was considerably older than Frank, was an
odd man, much addicted to quarrelling with his family, and who spent
his time chiefly in travelling about the world. Frank's mother, who was
not the mother of the heir also, would sometimes surmise, in Frank's
hearing, that the entire property must ultimately come to him. That
other Tregear, who was now supposed to be investigating the mountains of Crim Tartary,* would surely never marry. And Frank was the
favourite also with his father, who paid his debts at Oxford with not
much grumbling; who was proud of his friendship with a future duke;
who did not urge, as he ought to have urged, that vital question of
a profession; and who, when he allowed his son four hundred pounds
a year, was almost content with that son's protestations that he knew
how to live as a poor man among rich men, without chagrin and without trouble.

Such was the young man who now, in lieu of a profession, had taken
upon himself the responsibility of an engagement with Lady Mary
Palliser. He was tolerably certain that, should he be able to overcome
the parental obstacles which he would no doubt find in his path, money
would be forthcoming sufficient for the purposes of matrimonial life.
The Duke's wealth was fabulous, and as a great part of it, if not the
greater, had come from his wife, there would probably be ample provision for the younger children. And when the Duchess had found out
how things were going, and had yielded to her daughter, after an opposition which had never had the appearance even of being earnest, she
had taken upon herself to say that she would use her influence to prevent any great weight of trouble from pecuniary matters. Frank Tregear,
young and bright, and full of hearty ambitions, was certainly not the
man to pursue a girl simply because of her fortune; nor was he weak
enough to be attracted simply by the glitter of rank; but he was wise
enough with worldly wisdom to understand thoroughly the comforts of

a good income, and he was sufficiently attached to high position to feel the advantage of marrying a daughter of the Duke of Omnium. At this moment therefore he was somewhat elated, and was certainly very much in love. But with all his audacity he dreaded the Duke.

When the Duchess was leaving Italy, it had been her declared purpose to tell her husband the story as soon as they were at home in England. And it was on this understanding that Frank Tregear had explained to the girl that he would not as yet ask her father for his permission to be received into the family as a suitor. Everyone concerned had felt that the Duke would not easily be reconciled to such a son-in-law, and that the Duchess should be the one to bell the cat. Then the Duchess had been ill, and then, alas, the Duchess had died. Tregear had during this period twice written to the lady of his love,—as she had confessed to Mrs. Finn. No doubt the subject matter of these letters had been,—of the first, hope as to the mother's health, and of the second, grief; but in each there had been a word indicating that in the present circumstances this new affair should not be mentioned to the Duke.

There was one member of the family who had hitherto been half-hearted in the matter. Lord Silverbridge had vacillated between loyalty to his friend and a certain feeling as to the impropriety of such a match for his sister. He was aware that something very much better should be expected for her, and still was unable to explain his objections to Tregear. He had not at first been admitted into confidence, either by his sister or by Tregear, but had questioned his friend when he saw what was going on. 'Certainly I love your sister,' Tregear had said. 'Do you object?' Lord Silverbridge, though he was the weaker of the two and very much subject to the influence of his friend, could on occasion be firm, and he did at first object. But he did not object strongly, and allowed himself at last to be content with declaring that the Duke would never give his consent to such a marriage.

While Tregear was with his love, or near her, his hopes and his fears were sufficient to occupy his mind; and immediately on his return, all the world was nothing to him, except as far as all the world was concerned with Lady Mary Palliser. He and Silverbridge had come back to England somewhat before the ducal party, and as was not unnatural the pleasures and occupations of London life had not abated his love, but enabled him to feel that there was something in life over and beyond his love; whereas to Lady Mary, down at Matching, there had been nothing over and beyond her love,—except the infinite grief and desolation produced by her mother's death.

She had not known what address to give to Mrs. Finn for her lover except that of the club from whence he had written to her, and had said that she did not know where he slept in town. He was in truth staying at her own father's house in Carlton Terrace.* Silverbridge was there, and, on leaving Matching, had asked the Duke's permission to have his friend with him. The Duke at that time was not well pleased with his son as to a matter of politics, and gave his son's friend credit for the evil counsel which had produced this displeasure. But still he had not refused his assent to this proposition. Had he done so, Silverbridge would probably have gone elsewhere; and though there was a matter in respect to Tregear of which the Duke disapproved, it was not a matter, as he thought, which would have justified him in expelling the young man from his house. The young man was a strong Conservative; and now Silverbridge had declared his purpose of entering the House of Commons, if he did enter it, as one of the Conservative party!

This had been a terrible blow to the Duke. The Pallisers had always been Whigs. He himself was doubly a Whig,—or rather doubly a Liberal. It was his family party, and therefore he was bound by that bond which generally constrains our aristocrats to follow this or that side in politics. But he also had opinions of his own, very strong opinions, and had thought the matter out. He could give his reasons for being a Liberal, believing that by fighting on that side he could do something, though it might be ever so little, to help his country and his countrymen. It was very grievous to him that a Palliser, that the future head of the Pallisers, should desert the political creed of the family; but it was a matter to him of most profound sorrow that his own eldest son should be so misguided. And he believed that it all came from this young Tregear. Still he must do his duty, and not more than his duty. He knew nothing against Tregear. That a Tregear should be a Conservative was perhaps natural enough,—at any rate, was not disgraceful; that he should have his political creed sufficiently at heart to be able to persuade another man, was to his credit. He was a gentleman, well educated, superior in many things to Silverbridge himself. There were those who said that Silverbridge had redeemed himself from contempt,—from that sort of contempt which might be supposed to await a young nobleman who had painted scarlet the residence of the head of his college,—by the very fact of his having chosen such a friend. The Duke was essentially a just man; and though, at the very moment in which the request was made, his heart was half crushed by his son's apostasy, he gave the permission asked. At this moment therefore Frank Tregear was occupying a room in the Duke's London house.

'You know Mrs. Finn,' Tregear said to his friend one morning at breakfast.

'I remember her all my life. She used to be a great deal with my grandfather.* I believe he left her a lot of diamonds and money and that she wouldn't have them. I don't know whether the diamonds are not locked up somewhere now, so that she can take them when she pleases.'

'What a singular woman!'

'It was odd; but she had some fad* about it. What makes you ask about Mrs. Finn?'

'She wants me to go and see her.'

'What about?'

'I think I have heard your mother speak of her as though she loved her dearly,' said Tregear, not as yet answering the last question.

'I don't know about loving her dearly. They were intimate, and Mrs. Finn used to be with her very much when she was in the country. She was at Matching just now, when my poor mother died. Why does she want to see you?'

'She has written to me from Matching. She wants to see me——'

'Well?'

'To tell you the truth I do not know what she has to say to me;—though I can guess.'

'What do you guess?'

'It is something about your sister.'

'You will have to give that up, Tregear.'

'I think not.'

'Yes, you will. My father will never stand it.'

'I don't know what there is to stand. I am not noble, nor am I rich, but I am as good a gentleman as he is.'

'My dear fellow,' said the young Lord, 'you know very well what I think about all that. A fellow is not any better to me because he has got a title, nor yet because he owns half a county. But men have their ideas and feelings about it. My father is a rich man and of course he'll want his daughter to marry a rich man. My father is noble and he'll want his daughter to marry a nobleman. You can't very well marry Mary without his permission, and therefore you had better let it alone.'

'I haven't even asked his permission as yet.'

'*Ça va sans dire.** Even my mother was afraid to speak to him about it, and I never knew her to be afraid to say anything else to him.'

'I shall not be afraid,' said Tregear, looking grimly.

'I should. That's the difference between us.'

'He can't very well eat me.'

'Nor even bite you;—nor will he abuse you. But he can look at you, and he can say a word or two which you will find it very hard to bear. My governor is the quietest man I know, but he has a way of making himself disagreeable when he wishes that I never saw equalled. When that row came up at Oxford all that he said to me did not take two minutes, but it took the very life out of me for the time.'

'I don't propose to do anything quite so absurd as that.'

'But something quite as much opposed to his wishes.'

'At any rate I had better go and see your Mrs. Finn.' Then Tregear wrote a line to Mrs. Finn, and made his appointment.

CHAPTER 4

PARK LANE

FROM the beginning of the affair Tregear had found the necessity of bolstering himself up inwardly in his great attempt by mottoes, proverbs, and instigations to courage addressed to himself. 'None but the brave deserve the fair.'* '*De l'audace, et encore de l'audace, et toujours de l'audace.*'* He was a man naturally of good heart in such matters, who was not afraid of his brother-men, nor yet of women, his sisters. But in this affair he knew that very much persistence would be required of him, and that even with such persistence he might probably fail, unless he should find a more than ordinary strength of constancy in the girl. That the Duke could not eat him, indeed that nobody could eat him as long as he carried himself as an honest man and a gentleman, was to him an inward assurance on which he leaned much. And yet he was conscious, almost with a feeling of shame, that in Italy he had not spoken to the Duke about his daughter because he was afraid lest the Duke might eat him. He had no doubt been counselled by the Duchess to hold his peace at present,—but he had been so counselled because she also had been afraid of the Duke. In such an affair he should have been careful from the first to keep his own hands thoroughly clean. Had it not been his duty as a gentleman to communicate with the father, if not before he had gained the girl's heart, at any rate as soon as he knew he had done so? And now it would be impossible even to feign that he did so. He had left Italy thinking that he would certainly meet the Duchess and her daughter in London, and that then he might go to the Duke as though this love of his had arisen from, or at any rate had been confirmed by, the sweetness of those meetings in London. But all these

ideas had been dissipated by the great misfortune of the death of Lady
Mary's mother. There could be no meetings now in London or in the
country for some months, no probability of familiar meetings anywhere,—unless he could induce the Duke to accept him as a son-in-
law. From all this he was driven to acknowledge to himself that his
silence in Italy had been wrong, that he had been weak in allowing himself to be guided by the counsel of the Duchess, and that he had already
armed the Duke with one strong argument against him.

He did not doubt but that Mrs. Finn would be opposed to him. Of
course he could not doubt but that all the world would now be opposed
to him,—except the girl herself. He would find no other friend so generous, so romantic, so unworldly as the Duchess had been. It was of
course clear to him that Lady Mary had told the story of her engagement to Mrs. Finn, and that Mrs. Finn had not, as yet, told it to the
Duke. From this he was to a certain extent justified in regarding Mrs.
Finn as the girl's friend. The request made was that he should at once
do something which Mrs. Finn was to ask him to do. He would hardly
have been so requested, and that in terms of such warm affection, had
it been Mrs. Finn's intention to ask him to desist altogether from his
courtship. This woman was regarded by Lady Mary as her mother's
dearest friend, and very much might depend on her assistance as on her
opposition. It was therefore incumbent on him now to do his best to
win her good graces, and to induce her to believe in him,—as the
Duchess had believed.

He knocked at the door of Mrs. Finn's little house in Park Lane
a few minutes before the time appointed, and found himself alone when
he was shown into the drawing-room. He had heard much of this lady
though he had never seen her, and had heard much also of her husband.
There had been,—so at least he thought he had understood,—a kind
of mystery about her. People did not quite understand how it was that
she had been so intimate with the Duchess, nor why the late Duke had
left to her an enormous legacy, which as yet had never been claimed.
There was supposed, too, to have been something especially romantic
in her marriage with her present husband. It was believed also that she
was very rich. The rumours of all these things together had made her
a person of note, and Tregear, when he found himself alone in the
drawing-room, looked round about him as though a special interest was
to be attached to the belongings of such a woman. It was a pretty room,
somewhat dark, because the curtains were almost closed across the windows, but furnished with a pretty taste, and now, in these early April
days, filled with flowers.

'I have to apologise, Mr. Tregear, for keeping you waiting,' she said as she entered the room.

'I fear I was before my time.'

'I know that I am after mine,—a few minutes,' said the lady. He told himself that though she certainly was not a young woman, yet she was very pretty. She was dark, and still wore her black hair in curls, such as are now seldom seen with ladies. Perhaps the reduced light of the chamber had been regulated with some regard to her complexion and to her age. The effect, however, was good, and Frank Tregear felt at once that she was a power in whom he was bound to be interested.

'You have just come up from Matching?' he said.

'Yes,—only the day before yesterday. It is very good of you to come to me so soon.'

'Of course I came when you sent for me. I am afraid the Duke felt his loss very heavily.'

'How should he not;—such a loss as it was? Few people knew how much he trusted her, and how dearly he loved her.'

'Silverbridge has told me that he is awfully cut up.'

'You have seen Lord Silverbridge then?'

'Just at present I am living with him, at Carlton Terrace.'

'In the Duke's house?' she asked with some surprise.

'Yes;—in the Duke's house. Silverbridge and I have been very intimate. I can't afford lodgings for myself and so he puts me up. Of course the Duke knows that I am there. Is there any chance of his coming to town?'

'Not yet I fear. He is determined to be alone. I wish it were otherwise, as I am sure he would better bear his sorrow if he would go about among other men, and at least attend to public business in the House of Lords.'

'No doubt he would suffer less,' said Tregear. Then there was a pause. Each wished that the other should introduce the matter which both knew was to be the subject of their conversation. The man had reason on his side in waiting, as the meeting had not originated with him. But the lady, who found that the task before her was difficult, hoped that her companion might feel himself bound to begin it if she abstained awhile from doing so. But Tregear would not begin. 'When I left them all at Florence,' he said, 'I little thought that I should never see her again.'

'You had been intimate with them, Mr. Tregear?'

'Yes;—I think I may say that I have been intimate with them. I had been at Eton and at Christ Church with Silverbridge, and we have always been much together.'

'I have understood that. Have you and the Duke been good friends?'

'We have never been enemies,' said the young man laughing.

'I suppose not that.'

'The Duke, I think, does not much care about young people. I hardly know what he used to do with himself. When I dined with them, I saw him, but I did not often do that. I think he used to read a good deal, and walk about alone. We were always riding.'

'Lady Mary used to ride?'

'Oh yes,—and Silverbridge, and Lord Gerald. And the Duchess used to drive. One of us would always be with her.'

'And so you became intimate with the whole family.'

'So I became intimate with the whole family.'

'And especially so with Lady Mary?' This she said in her sweetest possible tone, and with a most gracious smile.

'Especially so with Lady Mary,' he replied.

'It will be very good of you, Mr. Tregear, if you endure and forgive all this cross-questioning from me who am a perfect stranger to you.'

'But you are not a perfect stranger to her.'

'That is it,—of course. Now, if you will allow me, I will explain to you exactly what my footing with her is. When the Duchess returned, and when I found her to be so ill as she passed through London, I went down with her into the country,—quite as a matter of course. There had been that between us which made it a matter of course.'

'So I understand.'

'And there she died,—in my arms. I will not try to harass you by telling you what those few days were;—how absolutely he was struck to the ground, how terrible was the grief of the daughter, how the boys were astounded by the feeling of their loss! After a few days they went away. It was, I think, their father's wish that they should go. And I too was going away,—and had felt indeed, directly her spirit had parted from her, that I was only in the way in his house. But I stayed at his request, because he did not wish his daughter to be alone.'

'I can easily understand that, Mrs. Finn.'

'I wanted her to go to Lady Cantrip, who had invited her;—but she would not. In that way we were thrown together in the closest intercourse for two or three weeks. Then she told me the story of your engagement.'

'That was natural, I suppose.'

'Surely so. Think of her position, left as she is without a mother! It was incumbent on her to tell someone. There was, however, one other person in whom it would have been much better that she should have confided.'

'What person?'

'Her father.'

'I rather fancy that it is I who ought to tell him.'

'As far as I understand these things, Mr. Tregear,—which indeed is very imperfectly,—I think it is natural that a girl should at once tell her mother when a gentleman has made her understand that he loves her.'

'She did so, Mrs. Finn.'

'And I suppose that generally the mother would tell the father.'

'She did not.'

'No. And therefore the position of the young lady is now one of great embarrassment. No one, of course, at that time foresaw the death of my poor friend. The Duchess has gone from us; and we must now make up our minds as to what had better be done. It is out of the question that Lady Mary should be allowed to consider herself to be engaged, and that the father should be kept in ignorance of her position.' She paused for his reply,—but as he said nothing she continued. 'Either you must tell the Duke, or she must do so,—or I must do so.'

'I suppose she told you in confidence.'

'No doubt. She told it me, presuming that I would not betray her. But I shall,—if that be a betrayal. The Duke must know it. It will be infinitely better that he should know it through you or through her, than through me. But he must be told.'

'I don't quite see why,' said Tregear, who had now assumed a tone almost of anger.

'For her sake—whom I suppose you love.'

'Certainly I love her.'

'In order that she may not suffer, he must be told. I wonder you do not see it, Mr. Tregear. Perhaps you have a sister.'

'I have no sister, as it happens.'*

'But you can imagine what your feelings would be. Should you like to think of a sister as being engaged to a man without the knowledge of any of her family?'

'It was not so. The Duchess knew it. The present condition of things is altogether an accident arising from her unfortunate death.'

'It is an accident that must be brought to an end.'

'Of course it must be brought to an end! I am not such a fool as to suppose that I can make her my wife without telling her father.'

'I mean at once, Mr. Tregear.'

'It seems to me that you are rather dictating to me, Mrs. Finn.'

'I owe you an apology of course for meddling in your affairs at all. But as it will be, I think, more conducive to your success that the Duke should hear this from you than from me, and as I feel that I am bound by my duty to him and to Lady Mary to see that he be not left in ignorance, I think that I am doing you a service by speaking as I have done.'

'I do not like to have a constraint put upon me.'

'That, Mr. Tregear, is what gentlemen, I fancy, very often feel in regard to ladies. But the constraint of which you speak is necessary for their protection. Are you unwilling to see the Duke?'

He was very unwilling, but he would not confess so much. He gave various reasons for delay, urging repeatedly that the question of his marriage was one which he could not press upon the Duke so soon after the death of the Duchess. And when she assured him that this was a matter of importance so great, that even the death of the man's wife should not be held by him to justify delay, he became angry, and for a while insisted that he must be allowed to follow his own judgment. But the conference was at last ended by an assertion on his part that he was not afraid of the Duke, and by an assurance that he would take steps to see the Duke before a week was over. Nevertheless he left the house in dudgeon, having told Mrs. Finn more than once that she was taking advantage of Lady Mary's confidence. They hardly parted as friends, and her feeling was, on the whole, hostile to him and to his love. It could not, she thought, be for the happiness of such a one as Lady Mary Palliser that she should give herself in marriage to one who seemed to have so little beyond his personal appearance to recommend him.

He, when he had left her, was angry with his own weakness. He had not only promised that he would make his application to the Duke, but that he would do so within the period of a week. Who was she that she should exact terms from him after this fashion, and prescribe days and hours? He was one who prided himself on being the master of others in the great affairs of life and on submitting himself to no masterdom. With the Duchess he had found that he could generally have his own way. Over Lady Mary his dominion had of course been supreme. And in his intercourse with Lord Silverbridge his influence had always been the more powerful of the two. And now, because this strange woman had spoken to him, he was compelled to make a journey down to the Duke's country-house, and to seek an interview in which he would surely be snubbed! And yet he told himself over and over again that he was not afraid of the Duke,—that the Duke could not 'eat him.'

This occurred on a Wednesday, and he resolved that he would go down to Matching on the next Monday. He would not allow himself to postpone his journey till the last day which his compact with Mrs. Finn would have allowed, because by doing so he would seem to himself to be in truth afraid. He said nothing of his plan to anyone, and not a word passed between him and Lord Silverbridge about Lady Mary during the first two or three days. But on the Saturday Silverbridge appeared at breakfast with a letter in his hand. 'The governor is coming up to town,' he said.

'Immediately?'

'In the course of next week. He says that he thinks he shall be here on Wednesday.'

It immediately struck Tregear that this sudden journey must have some reference to Lady Mary and her engagement. 'Do you know why he is coming?'

'Because of these vacancies in Parliament.'

'Why should that bring him up?'

'I suppose he hopes to be able to talk me into obedience. He wants me to stand for the county,—as a Liberal of course. I intend to stand for the borough as a Conservative,* and I have told them so down there at Silverbridge. I am very sorry to annoy him, and all that kind of thing. But what the deuce is a fellow to do? If a man has got political convictions of his own of course he must stick to them.' This the young Lord said with a good deal of self-assurance, as though he, by the light of his own reason, had ascertained on which side the truth lay in the political contests of the day.

'There is a good deal to be said on both sides of the question, my boy.' At this particular moment Tregear felt that the Duke ought to be propitiated, and thought that if it could be done by Silverbridge obeying his behests in this matter of politics the sacrifice made would not be very great.

'You wouldn't have me give up my convictions!'

'A seat in Parliament is a great thing.'

'I can probably secure that whichever side I take. I thought you were so devilish hot against the Radicals.'*

'So I am. But then you are as it were bound by family allegiance.'

'I'll be shot if I am. One never knows how to understand you nowadays. It used to be a great doctrine with you that nothing should induce a man to vote against his political opinions.'

'So it is,—if he has really got any. However—as your father is coming to London I need not go down to Matching.'

'You don't mean to say that you were going to Matching?'

'I had intended to beard the lion in his country den; but now the lion will find me in his own town den, and I must beard him here. I suppose I shall have to look out for other lodgings.'

'If you are going to speak to him about my sister, I think you must,' said Lord Silverbridge.

Then Tregear wrote a most chilly note* to Mrs. Finn, informing her with great precision, that, as the Duke of Omnium intended to be in town one day next week, he would postpone the performance of his promise for a day or two beyond the allotted time. He began the note by presenting his compliments, and did his best to make it stiff and almost uncivil. 'Silly boy!' she said to herself as she read the effusion. 'Even if he had money he would not be fit to marry her.'

CHAPTER 5

'IT IS IMPOSSIBLE'

DOWN at Matching Lady Mary's life was very dull after Mrs. Finn had left her. She had a horse to ride, but had no one to ride with her; she had a carriage in which to be driven, but no one to be driven with her, and no special places whither to go. Her father would walk daily for two hours, and she would accompany him when he encouraged her to do so; but she had an idea that he preferred taking his walks alone, and when they were together there was no feeling of mutual confidence between them. There could be none on her part, as she knew that she was keeping back information which he was entitled to possess. On this matter she received two letters from Mrs. Finn, in the first of which she was told that Mr. Tregear intended to present himself at Matching within a few days, and was advised in the same letter not to endeavour to see her lover on that occasion,—at any rate until after his interview with her father; and then in the second letter she was informed that this interview was to be sought not at Matching but in London. From this latter letter there was of course some disappointment, though also some feeling of relief. Had he come there she might possibly have seen him whether before or after the interview. But then she would have been subjected to the immediate sternness of her father's anger. That she would now escape. She would not be called on to meet him after the first blow had fallen upon him,—not at once, nor till time and consideration should have restored to him the habitual tenderness of his manner.

She was quite sure that he would disapprove of the thing. She was quite sure that he would be very angry. She knew that he was a peculiarly just man, and yet she thought that in this he would be most unjust. Had she been called upon to sing the praises of her father she would have insisted above all things on the absolute integrity of his mind, which would not allow him to swerve a tittle either to the left or right, even where by doing so he could serve his own dearest interests. She already possessed sufficient power of insight to see all this. And yet, knowing as she did that he would be opposed to her marriage with Mr. Tregear, she assured herself every day and every hour that he had no right to make any such objection. The man she loved was a gentleman, and an honest man, by no means a fool, and subject to no vices. Her father had no right to demand that she should give her heart to a rich man, or to one of high rank. Rank! As for rank, she told herself that she had the most supreme contempt for it. She thought that she had seen it near enough already to be sure that it ought to have no special allurements. What was it doing for her? Simply restraining her choice among comparatively a few who seemed to her by no means the best endowed of God's creatures. She was sick of lords and countesses;—so at least she told herself, instigated no doubt by her love for one who was no lord and the son of no countess.

Of one thing she was very sure, that under no pressure whatsoever would she abandon her engagement with Mr. Tregear. That to her had become a bond almost as holy as matrimony itself could be. She had told the man that she loved him, and after that there could be no retreat. He had kissed her, and she had returned his caress. He had told her that she was his, as his arm was round her; and she had acknowledged that it was so, that she belonged to him, and could not be taken away from him. All this was to her a compact so sacred that nothing could break it but a desire on his part to have it annulled. No other man had ever whispered a word of love to her, of no other man had an idea entered her mind that it could be pleasant to join her lot in life with his. With her it had been all new and all sacred. Love with her had that religion which nothing but freshness can give it. That freshness, that bloom, may last through a long life. But every change impairs it, and after many changes it has perished for ever. There was no question with her but that she must bear her father's anger, should he be angry; put up with his continued opposition, should he resolutely oppose her; bear all that the countesses of the world might say to her;—for it was thus that she thought of Lady Cantrip now. Any retrogression was beyond her power. She loved the man,—and as he also loved her, there was an end of all consideration on the matter.

She felt herself, moreover, bound to obey him. She knew, as well as Mrs. Finn did, that her father ought to be told of her purpose without delay. She could make excuse for the delay, feeling that it had been caused by her mother's illness and sudden death. She wished, indeed, that there might be an end to this state of suspense. But it never occurred to her that she ought to disobey her lover's injunctions, or even to feel angry with him because he insisted on them. There was nothing in which she would not obey him,—nothing that would not touch her own honour. But she was glad when she heard that he intended at once to see her father, and again relieved when she heard that the interview would not take place at Matching.

She was walking with her father when she first heard of his intended visit to London. At that time she had received Mrs. Finn's first letter, but not the second. 'I suppose you'll see Silverbridge,' she said. She knew then that Frank Tregear was living with her brother, but of him of course she said nothing.

'I am going up on purpose to see him. He is causing me much annoyance.'

'Is he extravagant?'

'It is not that,—at present.' He winced even as he said this, for he had in truth suffered somewhat from demands made upon him for money, which had hurt him not so much by their amount as by their nature. Lord Silverbridge had taken upon himself to 'own a horse or two,' very much to his father's chagrin, and was at this moment part proprietor of an animal supposed to stand well for the Derby. The fact was not announced in the papers with his lordship's name, but his father was aware of it, and did not like it the better because his son held the horse in partnership with a certain Major Tifto, who was well known in the sporting world. But, as he had said to his daughter, it was not that special extravagance which was irritating him now and forcing upon him a journey up to London.

'What is it, papa?'

'Of course he ought to go into Parliament.'*

'I think he wishes it himself.'

'Yes,—but how? By a piece of extreme good fortune West Barsetshire is open to him. The two seats are vacant together.* There is hardly another agricultural county in England that will return a Liberal, and I fear I am not asserting too much in saying that no other Liberal could carry the seat but one of our family.'

'You used to sit for Silverbridge, papa.'*

'Yes;—I did. In those days the county returned four Conservatives. I cannot explain it all to you, but it is his duty to contest the county on the Liberal side.'

'But if he is a Conservative himself, papa?' asked Lady Mary, who had had some political ideas suggested to her own mind by her lover.

'It is all rubbish. It has come from that young man Tregear with whom he has been associating.'

'But, papa,'—said Lady Mary, who felt that even in this matter she was bound to be firm on what was now her side of the question,—'I suppose it is as,—as,—as respectable to be a Conservative as a Liberal.'

'I don't know that at all,' said the Duke angrily.

'I thought that—the two sides were——'

She was going to express an opinion that the two parties might be supposed to stand as equal in the respect of the country, when he interrupted her. 'The Pallisers have always been Liberal. It will be a blow to me indeed if Silverbridge deserts his colours. Of course if it came from conviction I could put up with it,—though I should be sorry to see him convinced by error. But when I know that as yet he himself has had no deep thoughts on the subject, that unfortunately he does not give himself much to thinking, and that in this matter he is being talked over by a young man whose position in life has hardly justified the great intimacy which has existed, I own that I am most annoyed.'

This was very far from being comfortable to her, but of course she said nothing in defence of Tregear's politics. Nor at present was she disposed to say anything as to his position in life, though at some future time she might not be so silent. The Duke went on, discussing the subject with its political bearings, and declaring how grievous it would be to him if he should find himself once and for ever dissevered from his son in public life. A few days later they were again walking together, when he spoke to her about herself. 'I cannot bear that you should be left here alone while I am away,' he said.

'You will not be long gone, I suppose.'

'Only for three or four days now.'

'I shall not mind that, papa.'

'But very probably I may have to go into Barsetshire. Would you not be happier if you would let me write to Lady Cantrip and tell her that you will go to her?'

'No, papa, I think not. There are times when one feels that one ought to be almost alone. Don't you feel that?'

'I do not wish you to feel it, nor would you do so when you had had other people around you for a short time. With me it is different. I am an old man, and cannot look for new pleasures in society. It has been the fault of my life to be too much alone. I do not want to see my children follow me in that.'

'It is so very short a time as yet,' said she, thinking of her mother's death.

'I do not wish to drive you into society.'

'Do not drive me away at all, papa.'

'But I think that you should be with somebody,—with some woman who would be kind to you. I like to see you with books, but books alone should not be sufficient at your age.' How little, she thought, did he know of the state either of her heart or mind! 'I wish you would be persuaded to go to Lady Cantrip.'

'Oh, papa!'

'Do you dislike Lady Cantrip?'

'I do not know her. I can't say that I dislike a person whom I don't think I ever spoke to and never saw above once or twice. But how can I say that I like her? And how could I learn to like anyone just now?' She did, however, know that Lady Cantrip was a countess all over, and would be shocked at the idea of the daughter of a Duke of Omnium marrying the younger son of a country squire. Just then nothing further was said on the matter, and when the Duke went to town Lady Mary was left there quite alone; with a sort of understanding that if he were compelled to go into Barsetshire he should come back and take her with him.

He arrived at his own house in Carlton Terrace about five o'clock in the afternoon, and immediately went to his study, intending to dine and spend the evening there alone. His son had already pleaded an engagement for that afternoon, but had consented to devote the following morning to his father's wishes. Of the other sojourner in his house the Duke had thought nothing; but the other sojourner had thought very much of the Duke. As the thing was to be done would it not be better that it should be done at once? Frank Tregear was fully possessed of that courage which induces a man who knows that he must be thrown over a precipice to choose the first possible moment for his fall. He had sounded Silverbridge about this change in his politics, and had found his friend quite determined not to go back to the family doctrine. Such being the case, the Duke's ill-will and hardness and general severity would probably be enhanced by his interview with his son. Tregear, therefore, thinking that nothing could be got by delay, sent his name in to the Duke before he had been an hour in the house, and asked for an interview. The servant brought back word that his Grace was fatigued, but would certainly see Mr. Tregear if the matter in question was one of any importance. Frank's heart quailed for a moment, but only for a moment. He took up a pen, and wrote a note.

'MY DEAR DUKE OF OMNIUM,

'If your Grace can spare me a moment, I think you will feel that what I have to say will justify the intrusion.

'Your very faithful servant,

'F.O. TREGEAR.'

Of course the Duke admitted him. Equally of course during the five minutes of interval before the meeting he was driven to consider what was the subject on which the young man wished to speak to him. There was but one idea in his head. His son had taken this way of making some communication to him respecting his political creed. Some overture or some demand was to be preferred through Tregear. If so, it was proof of a certain anxiety as to the matter on his son's part which was not displeasing to him. But he was not left long in this mistake after Tregear had entered the room. 'Sir,' he said, speaking quite at once, as soon as the door was closed behind him, but still speaking very slowly, looking beautiful as Apollo as he stood upright before his wished-for father-in-law,—'Sir, I have come to you to ask you to give me the hand of your daughter.' The few words had been all arranged beforehand, and were now spoken without any appearance of fear or shame. No one hearing them would have imagined that an almost penniless young gentleman was asking in marriage the daughter of the richest and greatest nobleman in England.

'The hand of my daughter!' said the Duke, rising from his chair. Surely the young man was mad!

'I know how very great is the prize,' said Frank, 'and how unworthy I am of it. But,—as she thinks me worthy——'

'She! What she?'

'Lady Mary.'

'She think you worthy!'

'Yes,—your Grace.'

'I do not believe it.' On hearing this, Frank simply bowed his head. 'I beg your pardon, Mr. Tregear. I do not mean to say that I do not believe you. I never yet gave the lie to a gentleman, and I hope I never may be driven to do so. But there must be some mistake in this. What is it that you do mean?'

'I mean that I am complying with Lady Mary's wishes in asking your permission to enter your house as her suitor.'

The Duke stood for a moment biting his lips in silence. 'I cannot believe it,' he said at last. 'I cannot bring myself to believe it. There must be some mistake. My daughter! Lady Mary Palliser!' Again the young man bowed his head. 'What are your pretensions?'

'Simply her regard.'

'Of course it is impossible. Of course it is out of the question. You are not so ignorant but that you must have known as much when you came to me. Perhaps I had better hear from her what is really the truth of this.'

There was so much scorn in his words, and in the tone in which they were uttered, that Tregear in his turn was becoming angry. He had prepared himself to bow humbly before the great man, before the Duke, before the Croesus,* before the late Prime Minister, before the man who was to be regarded as certainly being one of the most exalted of the earth; but he had not prepared himself to be looked at as the Duke looked at him. 'The truth, my Lord Duke, is this,' he said, 'that your daughter loves me and that we are engaged to each other,—as far as that engagement can be made without your sanction as her father.'

'It cannot have been made at all,' said the Duke.

'I can only hope,—we can both of us only hope, that a little time may soften——'

'It is out of the question. There must be an end of this altogether. You must neither see her, nor hear from her, nor in any way communicate with her. It is altogether impossible. I believe, sir, that you have no means.'

'Very little, at present, Duke.'

'How did you think you were to live? But it is altogether unnecessary to speak of any such matter as that. There are so many reasons to make this impossible, that it would be useless to discuss one as being more important than others. Has any other one of my family known of this?' This he asked wishing to ascertain whether Lord Silverbridge had disgraced himself by lending his hand to such a disposition of his sister.

'Oh, yes,' said Tregear.

'Who has known it?'

'The Duchess, sir. We had all her sympathy and approval.'

'I do not believe a word of it,' said the Duke, becoming extremely red in the face. He was forced to do now that which he had just declared that he had never done in his life,—driven by the desire of his heart to acquit the wife he had just lost of the terrible imprudence,—worse than imprudence,—of which she was now accused.

'That is the second time, my Lord, that you have found it necessary to tell me that you have not believed direct assertions which I made you. But, luckily for me, the two assertions are capable of the easiest and most direct proof. You will believe Lady Mary, and she will confirm me in the one and in the other.'

The Duke was almost beside himself with emotion and grief. He did know,—though now at this moment he was most loath to own to himself that it was so,—that his dear wife had been the most imprudent of

women. And he recognised in her encouragement of this most pernicious courtship,—if she had encouraged it,—a repetition of that
romantic folly by which she had so nearly brought herself to shipwreck
in her own early life. If it had been so,—even whether it had been so or
not,—he had been wrong to tell the man that he did not believe him.
And the man had rebuked him with firmness and dignity. 'At any rate it
is impossible,' he repeated. 'When I have said that, I do not think there
is any more to be said.'

'I cannot allow that it is impossible.'

'That is for me to judge, sir.'

'I trust that you will excuse me when I say that I also must hold
myself to be in some degree a judge in the matter. If you were in my
place, you would feel——'

'I could not possibly be in your place.'

'If your Grace were in my place you would feel that as long as you
were assured by the young lady that your affection was valued by her
you would not be deterred by the opposition of her father. That you
should yield to me of course I do not expect;—that Lady Mary should
be persistent in her present feelings when she knows your mind, perhaps, I have no right to hope;—but should she be so persistent as to
make you feel that her happiness depends, as mine does, on our marriage, then I shall believe that you will yield at last.'

'Never,' said the Duke. 'Never. I shall never believe that my daughter's happiness can be assured by a step which I should regard as disgraceful to her.'

'Disgraceful is a violent word, my Lord.'

'It is the only word that will express my meaning.'

'And one which I must be bold enough to say you are not justified in
using. Should she become my wife to-morrow no one in England would
think that she had disgraced herself. The Queen would receive her
on her marriage. All your friends would hold out their hands to us,—
presuming that we had your good-will.'

'But you would not have it.'

'Her disgrace would not depend upon that, my Lord. Should your
daughter so dispose of herself, as to disgrace herself,—which I think to
be impossible,—your countenance could not set her right. Nor can the
withdrawal of your countenance condemn her before the world, if she
does that with herself which any other lady might do and remain a lady.'

The Duke, when he heard this, even in the midst of his wrath, which
was very violent, and in the midst of his anger, which was very acute,
felt that he had to deal with a man,—with one whom he could not put

off from him into the gutter, and there leave as buried in the mud. And there came, too, a feeling upon him, which he had no time to analyse, but of which he was part aware, that this terrible indiscretion on the part of his daughter and of his late wife was less wonderful than it had at first appeared to be. But not on that account was he the less determined to make the young man feel that his paternal opposition would be invincible. 'It is quite impossible, sir. I do not think that I need say anything more.' Then, while Tregear was meditating whether he would make any reply, whether on the whole he had not better submit now, before he might be tempted to speak a word which might have been better left unspoken, the Duke asked a question which certainly had better have been left unasked. The asking of it diminished somewhat from that ducal, grand-ducal, quasi-archducal, almost godlike superiority which he had assumed, and showed the curiosity of a mere man. 'Has anybody else been aware of this?' he said, still wishing to know whether he had cause for anger against Silverbridge in the matter.

'Mrs. Finn is aware of it,' answered Tregear.

'Mrs. Finn!' exclaimed the Duke as though he had been stung by an adder.

Tregear saw the emotion but did not understand the cause of it. He had known how intimate the Duchess had been with that lady, and was now led to imagine that that intimacy had been disagreeable to the Duke. But the feeling now at work in the Duke's mind was very different from that. This was the woman whom he had prayed to remain awhile with his daughter after his wife had been laid in her grave, in order that there might be someone near whom he could trust! And this very woman whom he had so trusted,—whom, in his early associations with her, he had disliked and distrusted, but had taught himself both to like and to trust because his wife had loved her,—this woman was the she-Pandarus* who had managed matters between Tregear and his daughter! His wife had been too much subject to her influence. That he had always known. And now, in this last act of her life, she had allowed herself to be persuaded to give up her daughter by the baneful wiles of this most pernicious woman. Such were the workings of the Duke's mind when the young man told him that Mrs. Finn was acquainted with the whole affair. As the reader is aware, nothing could have been more unjust.

'I mentioned her name,' said Tregear, 'because I thought she had been a friend of the family.'

'That will do, sir. I do not think there can be any necessity that you should remain here longer. I do not deny that I have been greatly pained as well as surprised by what I have heard. Of the real state of the case

I can form no opinion till I see my daughter. You of course will hold no further intercourse with her.' He paused as though for a promise, but Tregear did not feel himself called upon to say a word in one direction or in the other. 'It will at any rate be my care that you shall not do so. That the whole thing is impossible I imagine that you yourself must be aware. Good-morning, sir.'*

Tregear, who during the whole interview had been standing, then bowed, turned upon his heel, and left the room.

The Duke seated himself when he was alone, and, crossing his arms upon his chest, sat for nearly an hour looking up at the ceiling. Why was it that, for him, such a world of misery had been prepared? What wrong had he done, of what imprudence had he been guilty, that, at every turn of life, something should occur so grievous to him as to make him think himself the most wretched of men? No man had ever loved his wife more dearly than he had done; and yet now, in that very access of tenderness* which her death would be sure to occasion, he was driven to accuse her, not only of gross imprudence, but also of a great sin against himself, in that she had kept back from him her knowledge of this affair;—for, when he came to turn the matter over in his mind, he did believe the statement made to him as to her cognisance of the matter and encouragement. Then, too, he had been proud of his daughter. He was a man so reticent and undemonstrative in his manner that he had never known how to make confidential friends of his children. In his sons hitherto he had not taken much pride. They were gallant, well-grown, handsome boys, with a certain dash of cleverness,—more like their mother than their father; but they had not as yet done anything quite as he would have had them do it. But the girl, in the perfection of her beauty, in the quiescence of her manner, in the nature of her studies, and in the general dignity of her bearing, was,—or had appeared to be,—all that he had desired. And now she had engaged herself, behind his back, to the younger son of a little country squire!

But his anger against Mrs. Finn was hotter than his anger against anyone in his own family.

CHAPTER 6

MAJOR TIFTO

THE engagement which prevented Lord Silverbridge from waiting upon his father immediately upon the Duke's arrival, and which thus enabled Tregear to undertake his task at once, was one which perhaps might have been postponed had the son been very anxious for the meeting. He was to dine with his friend Major Tifto at the Beargarden, of which club the Major, under his noble young friend's auspices, had lately become a member.

It was believed, by those who had made some inquiry into the matter, that the Major had really served a campaign as a volunteer in the Carlist army in the north of Spain, and that he had there held some command equal in rank to that of a major in the British army. When, therefore, it was declared by some who were his enemies that he was not a major at all, his friends were able to contradict the assertion, and to impute it to slander. Instances were brought up,—declared by these friends to be innumerable, but which did, in truth, amount to three or four,—of English gentlemen who had come home from a former Carlist war,* bearing the title of colonel, without any contradiction or invidious remark. Had this gallant officer appeared as Colonel Tifto, perhaps less might have been said about it. There was perhaps a little lack of courage in the title which he did choose. But it was accepted at last, and, as Major Tifto, he was proposed, seconded, and elected at the Beargarden.

But he had other points in his favour over and beyond the friendship of Lord Silverbridge,—points which had probably led to that friendship. He was, without doubt, one of the best horsemen in England. There were some who said that, across country, he was the very best, and that, as a judge of a hunter, few excelled him. Of late years he had crept into credit as a betting man. No one supposed that he had much capital to work with; but still, when he lost a bet he paid it. He was well known upon race-courses, and it would be unjust to him to say that he was better known than trusted.

Soon after his return from Spain, he was chosen as Master of the Runnymede Foxhounds, and was thus enabled to write the letters M.F.H.* after his name. The gentlemen who rode with the Runnymede were not very liberal in their terms, and had lately been compelled to change their Master rather more frequently than was good for that quasi-suburban hunt; but now they had fitted themselves well. How he was to hunt the country five days a fortnight, finding servants and horses, and feeding the hounds, for eight hundred pounds a year, no one could understand. But Major Tifto not only undertook to do it, but did it. And he actually succeeded in obtaining for the Runnymede a degree of popularity which for many years previous it had not possessed. Such a man,—even though no one did know anything of his father or mother, though no one had ever heard him speak of a brother or a sister or a family friend, though it was believed that he had no real income,—was felt by many to be the very man for the Beargarden; and when his name was brought up at the committee, Lord Silverbridge was able to say so much in his favour that only two blackballs* were given against him. Under the mild rules of the club, three would have been necessary to exclude him; and therefore Major Tifto was now as good a member as anyone else.

He was a well-made little man, and good-looking too for those who like such good looks. He was light-haired and blue-eyed, with regular and yet not inexpressive features. But his eyes were small and never tranquil, and rarely capable of looking at the person who was speaking to him. He had small, well-trimmed, glossy whiskers, with the best-kept moustache and the best-kept tuft on his chin which were to be seen anywhere. His face still bore all the freshness of youth, which was a marvel to many, who declared that, from facts within their knowledge, Tifto must be far on the wrong side of forty. At a first glance you would hardly have called him thirty. No doubt, when, on close inspection, you came to look close into his eyes, you could see something of the hand of time. But even then it was impossible not to admire his state of preservation. Even if you believed the common assertion that he painted,—which it was very hard to believe of a man who passed the most of his time in the hunting field or on a race-course,—yet the paint on his cheeks would not enable him to move with the marvellous elasticity which seemed to belong to all his limbs. He rode flat races and steeple chases,—if jump races may still be so called; and with his own hounds and with the Queen's* did almost incredible things on horseback. He could jump over chairs too,—the backs of four chairs in a dining-room after dinner,—a feat which surely no gentleman of forty-five could perform, even though he painted himself ever so.

So much in praise of Major Tifto honesty has compelled the present chronicler to say. And it must be added also to the above good things that he had a way of making himself decidedly pleasant with young men. He could be authoritative about horses, as is required from a man who is a Master of Foxhounds and a pundit on race-courses, and at the same time could be short of speech, flattering in manner, and not dictatorial. He could yield when he knew himself to be right. At the same time, even when wrong, he could be very positive if he had the flower of his company* with him. But whether yielding or insisting, he could do it with an easy air and with a certain amount of pleasant drollery.

But there were traits of character in which he fell off a little, even in the estimation of those whose pursuits endeared him to them. He could not refrain from boasting,—and especially from boasting about women.

It was the special pride of his life to be held to be a favourite with the sex. With a certain portion of the sex it was believed that he did prevail. But his desire for glory in that direction knew no bounds, and he would sometimes mention names, and bring himself into trouble. It was told of him that at one period of his life, when misfortune had almost overcome him, when sorrow had produced prostration, and prostration some expression of truth, he had owned to someone whom at that moment he could regard as a friend, his own conviction that could he have kept his tongue from talking of women, he might have risen to prosperity and comfort in his profession. From those misfortunes he had emerged, and, no doubt, being in many things a thoughtful man as must be he who has to live entirely on his wits, had often reflected on what he himself had then said. But we know that the drunkard, though he hates drunkenness, cannot but drink,—that the gambler cannot keep from the dice, or the opium-taker from his laudanum. Major Tifto still lied about women, and could not keep his tongue from the subject. He would boast, too, about other matters,—much to his own disadvantage. He was, too, very 'deep,' and some men, who could put up with his other failings, could not endure that. Whatever he wanted to do he would attempt round three corners. Though he could ride straight, he could do nothing else straight. He was full of mysteries. If he wanted to draw Charter Wood he would take his hounds out of the street at Egham directly in the other direction. If he had made up his mind to ride Lord Pottlepot's horse for the Great Leamington handicap,* he would be sure to tell even his intimate friends that he was almost determined to take 'the baronet's' offer of a mount. This he would do even when there was no possible turn in the betting to be effected by such falsehood. So that his companions were apt to complain that there was no knowing where to have Tifto. And then, they who were old enough in the world to have had some experience in men, had perceived that peculiar quality of his eyes, which never allowed him to look anyone in the face,—and they feared him accordingly.

That Major Tifto should make money by selling horses was, perhaps, a necessity of his position. No one at any rate grumbled at him because he did so, or thought that such a pursuit was incompatible with his character as a sporting gentleman or his position as Master of the Runnymede hunt. But there were some who considered that they had suffered unduly under his hands, and in their bargains with him had been made to pay more than a proper amount of tax for the advantages of his general assistance and guidance. When a man has perhaps made fifty pounds by using a 'straight tip'* as to a horse at Newmarket, in doing which he had of course encountered some risk, he feels that he ought not to be made to pay the amount back into the pockets of the 'tipper,' and at the same time to find himself saddled with the possession of a perfectly useless animal. In this way there were many rocks in the course through which the Major was called on to steer his bark.* Of course he was anxious, when preying upon his acquaintances, to spare those who were really useful friends to him. Now and again he would sell a serviceable animal at a fair price, and would endeavour to make such sale in favour of someone whose countenance would be a rock to him. He knew his business very well, but sometimes there would be mistakes.

Now, at this very moment, was the culmination of the Major's life. He was Master of the Runnymede Hounds; he was partner with the eldest son of a duke in the possession of a colt and of a filly,* Prime Minister and Coalition, both of which stood high in the betting, one for the Derby and the other for the Oaks; and he was a member of the Beargarden. He was a man who had often been despondent about himself, but was now disposed to be a little triumphant. He had finished his season well with the Runnymede, and were it not that, let him work as he would, his expenses always exceeded his means, he would have been fairly comfortable.

At eight o'clock Lord Silverbridge and his friend met in the dining-room of the Beargarden. 'Have you been here before?' asked the Lord.

'Not in here, my Lord. I just looked in at the smoking-room last night. Glasslough and Nidderdale were there. I thought we should have got up a rubber, but they didn't seem to see it.'

'There is whist here generally. You'll find out all about it before long. Perhaps they are a little afraid of you, you know.'

'I'm the worst hand at cards, I suppose, in England. A dash at loo for about an hour, and half-a-dozen cuts at blind hookey,*—that's about my form. I know I drop a good deal more than I pick up at the card-table. If I knew what I was about I should never touch a card.'

'Horses; eh, Tifto?'

'Horses, yes. They've pretty good claret here, eh, Silverbridge?' He could never hit off his familiarity quite right. He had my-Lorded his young friend at first, and now brought out the name with a hesitating twang, which even the young nobleman, though not as yet much experienced in such matters, appreciated. But then the young nobleman was quite aware that the Major was a friend for club purposes, and sporting purposes, and not for home use.

'Everything of that kind is pretty good here, I take it,' said the Lord.

'You were saying, horses!'

'I dare say you do better with them than with cards.'

'If I didn't I don't know where I should be, seeing what a lot pass through my hands in the year. Any one of our fellows who has a horse to sell thinks that I am bound to buy him. And I do buy 'em. Last May I had forty-two hunters on my hands.'

'How many of them have you got now?'

'Three. Three of that lot, though a goodish many have come up since. But what does it amount to? When I have anything that is very good some fellow that I like gets him from me.'

'After paying for him.'

'After paying for him! Yes. I don't mean that I make a fellow a present. But the man who buys has a deal the best of it. Did you ever get anything better than that spotted chestnut in your life?'

'What,—old Sarcinet?'

'You had her for one hundred and sixty pounds. Now if you were on your oath what is she worth?'

'She suits me, Major, and of course I shouldn't sell her.'

'I rather think not. I knew what that mare was well enough. A dealer would have had three hundred and fifty pounds for her. I could have got the money easily if I had taken her down into the shires and ridden her a day or two myself.'

'I gave you what you asked.'

'Yes, you did. It isn't often that I take less than I ask. But the fact is, about horses, I don't know whether I shouldn't do better if I never owned an animal at all, but those I want for my own use. Of course I don't give 'em away; but when I'm dealing with a man I call a friend I can't bear to make money of him. I don't think fellows give me all the credit they should do for sticking to them.' The Major, as he said this, leaned back in his chair, put his hand up to his moustache, and looked sadly away into the vacancy of the room, as though he were meditating sorrowfully on the ingratitude of the world.

'I suppose it's all right about Cream Cheese?' asked the Lord.

'Well;—it ought to be.' And now the Major spoke like an oracle, leaning forward on the table, uttering his words in a low voice, but very plainly, so that not a syllable might be lost. 'When you remember how he ran at the Craven with nine stone twelve pound on him,—that it took Archbishop all he knew to beat him with only nine stone two pound,—and what the lot at Chester are likely to be, I don't think that there can be seven to one against him. I should be very glad to take it off your hands, only the figures are a little too heavy for me.'

'I suppose Sunflower'll be the best animal there?'

'Not a doubt of it if he's all right, and if his temper will stand. Think what a course Chester is for an ill-conditioned brute like that! And then he's the most uncertain horse in training. There are times he won't feed. From what I hear I shouldn't wonder if he don't turn up at all.'

'Solomon says he's all right.'

'You won't get Solomon to take four to one against him, nor yet four and a half. I suppose you'll go down, my Lord.'

'Well;—yes; if there's nothing else doing just then. I don't know how it may be about this electioneering business. I shall go and smoke upstairs.'

At the Beargarden there were,—I was going to say, two smoking-rooms. The rules of the house, however, did in fact allow gentlemen to smoke everywhere except in the dining-room. But it was the custom of those who habitually played cards at the club to take their cigars and coffee upstairs. Into this sanctum Major Tifto had not yet been introduced, but now he was taken there under Lord Silverbridge's wing. There were already four or five assembled, among whom was Mr. Adolphus Longstaffe, a young man of about thirty-five years of age, who spent very much of his time at the Beargarden. 'Do you know my friend Tifto?' said the Lord. 'Tifto, this is Mr. Longstaffe,—whom men within the walls of this asylum sometimes call Dolly.' Whereupon the Major bowed and smiled graciously.

'I have heard of Major Tifto,' said Dolly.

'Who has not?' said Lord Nidderdale, another middle-aged young man who made one of the company. Again the Major bowed.

'Last season I was always intending to get down to your country and have a day with the Tiftoes,' said Dolly. 'Don't they call your hounds the Tiftoes?'

'They shall be called so, if you like,' said the Major. 'And why didn't you come?'

'It always was such a grind.'

'Train down from Paddington every day at 10:30.'

'That's all very well if you happen to be up at that hour. Well, Silverbridge, how's the Prime Minister?'

'How is he, Tifto?' asked the noble partner.

'I don't think there's a man in England just at present enjoying a very much better state of health,' said the Major pleasantly.

'Safe to run?' asked Dolly.

'Safe to run! Why shouldn't he be safe to run?'

'I mean sure to start?'

'I think we mean him to start;—don't we, Silverbridge?' said the Major.

There was something perhaps in the tone in which the last remark was made which jarred a little against the young Lord's dignity. At any rate he got up and declared his purpose of going to the opera. He should look in, he said, and hear a song from Mdlle. Stuffa. Mdlle. Stuffa was the nightingale of the season,* and Lord Silverbridge, when he had nothing else to do, would sometimes think that he was fond of music. Soon after he was gone Major Tifto had some whisky-and-water, lit his third cigar, and began to feel the glory of belonging to the Beargarden. With Lord Silverbridge, to whom it was essentially necessary that he should make himself agreeable at all times, he was somewhat overweighted as it were. Though he attempted an easy familiarity, he was a little afraid of Lord Silverbridge. With Dolly Longstaffe he felt that he might be quite comfortable,—not, perhaps, quite understanding that gentleman's character. With Lord Nidderdale he had previously had some acquaintance, and had always found him to be good-natured. There were two other men there who were very young, and did not seem to be frightful. So as he sipped his whisky he became confidential—and comfortable.

'I never thought so much about her good looks,' he said. They were talking of the singer, the charms of whose voice had carried Lord Silverbridge away.

'Did you ever see her off the stage?' asked Nidderdale.

'Oh, dear yes.'

'She does not go about very much, I fancy,' said one of the young men.

'I dare say not,' said Tifto. 'But she and I have had a day or two together for all that.'

'You must have been very much favoured,' said Dolly.

'We've been pals ever since she has been over here,' said Tifto with an enormous lie.

'How do you get on with her husband?' asked Dolly,—in the simplest voice, as though not in the least surprised at his companion's statement.

'Husband!' exclaimed the Major, who was not possessed of sufficient presence of mind to suppress all signs of his ignorance.

'Ah,' said Dolly; 'you are not probably aware that your pal has been married to Mr. Thomas Jones for the last year and a half.' Soon after that Major Tifto left the club,—with considerably enhanced respect for Mr. Longstaffe.

CHAPTER 7

CONSERVATIVE CONVICTIONS

LORD SILVERBRIDGE had engaged himself to be with his father the next morning at half-past nine, and he entered the breakfast-room a very few minutes after that hour. He had been made aware of the subject on which his father wished to speak to him, and had determined what he would say in reply. He meant to call himself a Conservative, and to enter Parliament, if he did go into the House of Commons, under that denomination. All the men among whom he lived were Conservatives, or so called themselves. It was a matter on which, as he thought, his father could have no right to control him. Down in Barsetshire, as well as up in London, there was some little difference of opinion in this matter. The people of Silverbridge declared that they would prefer to have a Conservative member, as indeed they had had one for the last session. They had loyally returned the Duke himself while he was a commoner, but they had returned him as being part and parcel of the Omnium appanages. That was all over now, and they were allowed to elect whom they themselves might choose. As a constituency they were endowed with no peculiarly advanced views, and thought that a Conservative would suit them best. That being so, and as they had been allowed to understand that the Duke's son was a Conservative, they fancied that by electing him they would be pleasing everybody. But, in truth, by so doing they would by no means please their landlord, the Duke. He had told them on previous occasions that they might elect whom they pleased, and felt no anger because they had elected a Conservative. They might send up to Parliament the most antediluvian old Tory they could find in England if they wished, only not his son, not a Palliser as a Tory or Conservative!* And then, though the little town had gone back in the ways of the world, the county, or the Duke's division of the county, had made so much progress, according to his views, that a Liberal candidate recommended by him would almost certainly be returned. It was just the occasion on which a Palliser should show himself ready to serve his country. There would be an expense, but he would think nothing of expense in such a matter. Ten thousand pounds spent on such an object would not in the least vex him. The very contest would have given him new and pleasant life. All this Lord Silverbridge in a good measure understood, but yet had said to himself and to all his friends that it was a matter in which he did not intend to be controlled.

He was not afraid of his father,—who had in truth always been indulgent to him; but he had taught himself to think that fixed conversations with his father were disagreeable and should if possible be avoided. He had never been intimate with the Duke,—as are some sons and some fathers,—and would usually set himself to work to get through the business of a parental interview as quickly as possible. It was with some such determination that he entered the room this morning. There would be their breakfast to eat, but the Duke would probably not begin his political lecture,—for Silverbridge was sure that that would be the shape which the conversation would take,—till after breakfast. Of course he had no idea of the revelation that had been made to the Duke on the previous evening. He had declared to himself whenever that matter of his sister's love had been brought to his mind, and had declared also to Tregear whenever the question had been discussed between them, that the Duke would be found to be utterly impregnable on that question. But it was no affair of his. He had not encouraged Tregear. He had not been in confidence with his sister. In the one or two words which he had spoken to his mother on the subject he had opposed the idea of such a marriage. But at the present moment of meeting his father there was no special weight on his mind in reference to his sister's engagement.

The Duke had passed a very unhappy night. He had told himself over and over again that any such marriage was of course out of the question. He believed that the matter might be so represented to his girl as to make her feel that it was out of the question. He hardly doubted but that he could stamp it out. Though he should have to take her away into some furthest corner of the world, he would stamp it out. But she, when this foolish passion of hers should have been thus stamped out, could never be the pure, the bright, the unsullied, unsoiled thing, of the possession of which he had thought so much. He had never spoken of his hopes about her even to his wife, but in the silence of his very silent life he had thought much of the day when he would give her to some noble youth,—noble with all gifts of nobility, including rank and wealth,—who might be fit to receive her. Now, even though no one else should know it,—and all would know it,—she would be the girl who had condescended to love young Tregear.

His own Duchess, she whose loss to him now was as though he had lost half his limbs,—had not she in the same way loved a Tregear, or worse than a Tregear, in her early days? Ah yes! And though his Cora had been so much to him, had he not often felt, had he not been feeling all his days, that Fate had robbed him of the sweetest joy that is given to man, in that she had not come to him loving him with her early spring of love, as she had loved that poor ne'er-do-well? How infinite had been his regrets. How often had he told himself that, with all that Fortune had given him, still Fortune had been unjust to him because he had been robbed of that. Not to save his life could he have whispered a word of this to anyone, but he had felt it. He had felt it for years. Dear as she had been, she had not been quite what she should have been but for that. And now this girl of his, who was so much dearer to him than anything else left to him in the world, was doing exactly as her mother had done. The young man might be stamped out. He might be made to vanish as that other young man had vanished,—probably with less of absolute danger. But the fact that he had been there, cherished in the girl's heart,—that could not be stamped out.

He struggled gallantly to acquit the memory of his wife,—or at any rate to make excuse for her. And he found that he could best do so by leaning with the full weight of his mind on the presumed iniquity of Mrs. Finn. Had he not from the first known that the woman was an adventuress? And had he not declared to himself over and over again that between such a one and himself there should be no intercourse, no common feeling? He had allowed himself to be talked into an intimacy, to be talked almost into an affection. And this was the result!

And how should he treat this matter in his coming interview with his son;—or should he make no allusion to it? At first it seemed as though it would be impossible for him to give his mind to that other subject. How could he enforce the merits of political liberalism, and the duty of adhering to the old family party, while his mind was entirely preoccupied with his daughter? It had suddenly become almost indifferent to him whether Silverbridge should be a Conservative or a Liberal,—so infinitely greater to him was that other misfortune. But as he dressed he told himself that, as a man, he ought to be able to do a plain duty, marked out for him as this had been by his own judgment, without regard to any suffering that he might be enduring. The hedger and ditcher must make his hedge and clean his ditch even though he be tormented by rheumatism. His son was his son and heir, and would be the future Duke of Omnium. His duty by his son he must do, even though his heart were torn to pieces.

During breakfast he tried even to be gracious, and condescended to ask his son a question about Prime Minister. Racing was an amusement to which English noblemen had been addicted for many ages, and had been held to be serviceable rather than disgraceful, if conducted in a noble fashion. He did not credit Tifto with much nobility. He knew but little about the Major. He would much have preferred that his son should have owned a horse alone, if he must have anything to do with ownership;—but partnerships he had been told were not uncommon. 'Would it not be better to buy the other share?' asked the Duke.

'It would take a deal of money, sir. The Major would ask a couple of thousand, I should think.'

'That is a great deal.'

'And then the Major is a very useful man. He thoroughly understands the turf.'

'I hope he doesn't live by it.'

'Oh no; he doesn't live by it. That is he has a great many irons in the fire.'

'I do not mind a young man owning a horse,—if he can afford the expense, as you perhaps can do; but I hope you don't bet.'

'Nothing to speak of.'

'Nothing to speak of is so apt to grow into that which has to be much spoken of.' So much the father said at breakfast, hardly giving his mind to the matter discussed,—his mind being on other things. But when their breakfast was eaten, then it was necessary that he should begin. 'Silverbridge,' he said, 'I hope you have thought better of what we were talking about as to these coming elections.'

'Well, sir;—of course I have thought about it.'

'And you can do as I would have you?'

'You see, sir, a man's political opinion is a kind of thing he can't get rid of and take up another just as he may wish it.'

'You can hardly as yet have had any very confirmed political opinion. You have never spoken to me on the subject in your life before.'

'Nor you to me, sir.'

This was true, or very nearly so, and the Duke felt that the reproach was just. 'You are still very young, and I do not suppose that you have thought much about politics.'

'Well, sir; I think I have. I've got my own ideas. We've got to protect our position as well as we can against the Radicals and Communists, who no doubt would take away our property if they could get it.'

'I cannot admit that at all, Silverbridge. There is no great political party in this country anxious either for communism or for revolution. But, putting all that aside for the present, do you think that a man's political opinions should be held in regard to his own individual interests, or to the much wider interests of others,—whom we call the public?'

'To his own interests,' said the young man with decision.

'It is simply self-protection then?'

'His own, and his class. The people will look after themselves and we must look after ourselves. We are so few and they are so many that we shall have quite enough to do. Besides if all your property was taken away, where would be the people who depend on you?'

Then the Duke gave his son a somewhat lengthy political lecture, which need not be repeated here, but which was intended to teach him that the greatest benefit of the greatest number* was the object to which all political studies should tend. The son listened to it with praiseworthy attention, and when it was over, expressed his opinion that there was a great deal in what his father had said. 'I trust, if you will consider all that,' said the Duke, 'that you will not find yourself obliged to desert the school of politics in which your father has not been an inactive supporter, and to which your family has belonged for many generations.'

'I could not call myself a Liberal,' said the young politician.

'Why not?'

'Because I am a Conservative.'

'And you won't stand for the county on the Liberal interest?'

'I should be obliged to tell them that I should always give a Conservative vote.'

'Then you refuse to do what I ask?'

'I do not know how I can help refusing. If you wanted me to grow a couple of inches taller I couldn't do it even though I should be ever so anxious to oblige you. If a man is of one way of thinking, he can't make himself of another.'

'But a very young man, as you are, may have so much deference for his elders as to be induced to believe that he has been in error.'

'Oh yes;—of course.'

'You cannot but be aware that the political condition of the country is the one subject to which I have devoted all the labour of my life.'

'I know that very well;—and of course I know how much they all think of you.'

'Then my opinion, my convictions, might go for something with you.'

'So they do, sir. I shouldn't have doubted at all only for that. Still, you see, as the thing is;—how am I to help myself?'

'You believe that you must be right;—you, who have never given an hour's study to the subject. You surely think yourself a very clever fellow!'

'No, sir;—that certainly isn't so. In comparison with a great many men, I know that I am a fool. Perhaps it is because I know that, that I am a Conservative. The Radicals are always saying that a Conservative must be a fool. Therefore a fool ought to be a Conservative. Therefore I'm a Conservative.'

Hereupon the father got up from his chair and turned round, facing the fire, with his back to his son. He was becoming very angry, but endeavoured to restrain his anger, which he himself knew to be in a certain degree unreasonable. In what way, however, should he proceed? The matter in dispute between them was of so great importance, that he could hardly be justified in abandoning it in consequence of arguments so trifling in themselves as these which his son adduced. As he stood there for some minutes thinking of it all, he was tempted again and again to burst out in wrath and threaten the lad,—to threaten him as to money, as to his amusements, as to the general tenor of his life. The pity was so great that the lad should be so stubborn and so foolish! If only he would go properly and quietly into political harness, everything would be granted to him. And the political harness need not entail heavy political work,—as it had done on himself. He would never ask his son to be a slave to the Liberal party, as he had been. But that a Palliser should not be a Liberal,—and his son, as the first recreant Palliser,—was wormwood to him! As he stood there he more than once clenched his fist in eager desire to turn upon the young man; but he restrained himself, telling himself that in justice he should not be angry for such offence as this. To be a Conservative,—to become a Conservative when the path to liberalism was so fairly open,—might be the part of a fool, but could not fairly be imputed as a crime. To endeavour to be just was the study of his life, and in no condition of life can justice be more imperatively due than from a father to his son. But yet he was sorely tried! 'You mean to stand for Silverbridge?' he said at last.

'Not if you object, sir.'

This made it worse. It became now still more difficult for him to scold the young man. 'Of course you are aware that I should not meddle in any way.'

'That was what I supposed. They will return a Conservative at any rate.'

'What is to become of Mr. Fletcher?' said the Duke, asking after the sitting, or rather, as it now was, the late member.

'There's to be some arrangement about him. If I stand he won't. I think, you know, the people there would rather like me to be the member.' No doubt they would, many of them! No doubt the Conservative party would like it, and in order to seduce from his allegiance the heir of the house of Omnium would take care that arrangements should be made so that this family borough of Silverbridge should help him in his apostasy. The Duke could understand all that very well and could remember with increased bitterness of spirit that but for his own patriotic self-abnegation he might now send whatever Liberal he pleased to name to Parliament for the borough. 'Of course if you say that you do not want me to stand for Silverbridge, I will look elsewhere,' said the young man.

'It is not the place that I care about,' said the Duke sadly.

'Upon my word, sir, I am very sorry to vex you;—but what would you have me do? I will give up Parliament altogether if you say that you wish it.'

'No. I do not wish that.'

'You wouldn't have me tell a lie about my opinions.'

'No!'

'What can I do then?'

'Learn what there is to learn from some master fit to teach you.'

'There are so many masters.'

'I believe it to be that most arrogant, ill-behaved young man who was with me yesterday who has done this evil.' Now his mind was reverting to that other and greater trouble.

'You mean Frank Tregear?'

'I do mean Mr. Tregear.'

'He's a Conservative of course. And of course he and I have been much together. But I think it would have been the same if I had never known him. Was he with you yesterday, sir?'

'Yes,—he was.'

'What was that about?' asked Lord Silverbridge in a voice that almost betrayed fear, for he knew very well what cause had produced the interview.

If Silverbridge had been a sinner in this matter, then justice would not require the father to refrain from anger. But it was necessary that the fact should be ascertained before the anger was shown. 'He has been speaking to me——' When the Duke had got so far as this he paused, finding himself to be hardly able to declare the disgrace which had fallen upon himself and his family. As he did tell the story, both his face and his voice were altered, so that the son, in truth, was scared. 'He has been speaking to me—about your sister.'

'Oh, indeed;—yes.'

'Did you know of this?'

'I knew there was something up between them.'

'And you have encouraged it?'

'No, sir. Just the contrary. I have told him that I was quite sure it would never do.'

'And why did you not tell me? In a matter of such moment to the family why did you not come to me?'

'Well, sir;—that was hardly my business; was it?'

'Not to guard the honour of your sister?'

'You see, sir, how many things have happened all at once.'

'What things?'

'My dear mother, sir, thought well of him.' The Duke uttered a deep sigh and turned again round to the fire. 'I did not like to interfere much. I always told him that you would never consent.'

'I should think not.'

'It has come all so suddenly. I should have spoken to you about it as soon as,—as soon as——' He had meant to say as soon as the husband's grief for the loss of his wife had been in some degree appeased, but he could not speak the words. The Duke, however, perfectly understood him. 'In the meantime they were not seeing each other.'

'Nor writing.'

'I think not.'

'Mrs. Finn has known it all.'

'Mrs. Finn!'

'Certainly she has known it all through.'

'I do not see how it can have been so. Of course it is possible.'

'He told me so himself,' said the Duke, unwittingly putting words into Tregear's mouth which Tregear had never uttered. Then there was another pause after which he spoke again, very solemnly. 'There must be an end of this. I will speak to your sister. In the meantime the less, I think, you see of Mr. Tregear, the better. Of course it is out of the question he should be allowed to remain in this house. You will make him understand that at once, if you please.'

'Oh, certainly,' said Silverbridge,—who after that was allowed to take his departure.

CHAPTER 8

'HE IS A GENTLEMAN'

THE DUKE on that very day returned to Matching an almost broken-hearted man. He had intended to go down into Barsetshire, in reference to the coming elections;—not with the view of interfering in any unlordly, or rather unpeerlike fashion, but thinking that if his eldest son were to stand for the county in a proper constitutional spirit, as the eldest son of so great a county magnate ought to do, his own presence at Gatherum Castle,* among his own people, might probably be serviceable, and would certainly be gracious. Of course there would be no question of entertainment. His late bereavement would make that impossible. But there would come from his presence a certain savour of proprietorship, and a sense of power, which would be beneficial to his son, and would not, as the Duke thought, be contrary to the spirit of the constitution. But all this was now at an end. He told himself that he did not care how the elections might go;—that he did not care much how anything might go. Silverbridge might stand for Silverbridge if he so pleased. He would give neither assistance nor obstruction, either in the county or in the borough. He wrote to this effect to his agent, Mr. Moreton;—but at the same time desired that gentleman to pay Lord Silverbridge's electioneering expenses, feeling it to be his duty as a father to do so much for his son.

But though he endeavoured to engage his thoughts in these parliamentary matters, though he wrote to Mr. Moreton,—and indeed also to his son telling him that his expenses would be paid,—though he tried to make himself believe that this political apostasy was the trouble which now vexed him, in truth that other misery was so crushing a burden to him, as to make the affairs of his son of comparatively little effect. How should he express himself to her? That was the reflection most constantly present to his mind as he went down to Matching. Should he content himself with simply telling her that such a wish on her part was disgraceful, and that it could never be fulfilled; or should he argue the matter with her, endeavouring as he did so to persuade her gently that she was wrong to place her affections so low, that her rank and position demanded from her a constraint to which another girl need not, perhaps, subject herself, and so to obtain from her an assurance that the idea should be abandoned?

The latter course would be infinitely the better,—if only he could accomplish it. But he was conscious of his own hardness of manner, and was aware that he had never quite succeeded in establishing confidence between himself and his daughter. It was a thing for which he had longed,—as a plain girl might long to possess the charms of an acknowledged beauty, as a poor little fellow five feet in height might long to have a cubit added to his stature,—but which seemed to be almost as impossible to him as the faintest of those other wishes would seem to them. Though he was angry with her, how willingly would he take her into his arms and assure her of his forgiveness! How anxious he would be to make her understand that nothing should be spared by him to add beauty and glory and grace to her life! Only, as a matter of course, Mr. Tregear must be abandoned. But he felt of himself that he would not know how to begin to be tender and caressing and forgiving. He knew that he would not know how not to be stern and hard to her.

But he must find out the history of it all;—how it had come to pass. No doubt the man had been his son's friend, and had joined his party in Italy at his son's invitation. There could surely be no mystery to him on that subject. But yet he had come to entertain an idea that Mrs. Finn had been the great promoter of the sin, and he really did think that Tregear had told him that that lady had been concerned with the matter from the beginning. In all this there was a craving in his heart to lessen the amount of culpable responsibility which might seem to attach itself to the wife he had lost.

He reached Matching about eight on that evening, and directed that he might have dinner brought to him in his own study. Another man would have sent word home and would have dined with his daughter. He was so much in the habit of living alone that this did not occur to him. When Lady Mary came to welcome him, he kissed her forehead and bade her come to him after his dinner. 'Shall I not sit with you, papa, whilst you are eating it?' she asked; but he merely told her that he would not trouble her to do that. Even in saying this he was almost more tender to her than usual;—so that she assured herself for the moment that her lover had not as yet done as he had promised.

The Duke's meals were not generally feasts for a Lucullus.* No man living, perhaps, cared less what he ate, or knew less what he drank. In such matters he took what was provided for him, making his dinner off the first bit of meat that was brought to him, and simply ignoring anything offered to him afterwards. And he would drink what wine the servant would pour out for him, mixing it, whatever it might be, with seltzer water. He had never been much given to the pleasures of the table; but this habit of simplicity had grown on him of late, till the Duchess used to tell him that his wants were so few that it was a pity he was not a hermit, vowed to poverty.

Very shortly after he had sat down a message was brought to Lady Mary, saying that her father wished to see her. She went at once, and found him seated on a sofa, which stood close along the bookshelves on one side of the room. The table had already been cleared, and he was alone. He not only was alone, but had not even a pamphlet or news-paper in his hand, or a book lying open near him;—from all which she was sure that there was some special matter for conversation on his mind. If it were so, then Tregear must have told the story. As this occurred to her, her legs almost gave way under her. 'Come and sit down, Mary,' he said, pointing to the seat on the sofa beside himself.

She sat down and took one of his hands within her own. Then, as he did not begin at once, she asked a question. 'Will Silverbridge stand for the county, papa?'

'No, my dear.'

'But for the town?'

'Yes, my dear. At least I suppose so.'

'And he won't be a Liberal?'

'I am afraid not. It is a cause of great unhappiness to me; but I do not know that I should be justified in any absolute opposition. A man is entitled to his own opinion, even though he be a very young man, and a son.' He was almost inclined to add,—'and though he be as ignorant as your brother,'—but he stopped himself.

'I am so sorry that it should be so, papa,—because it vexes you.'

'I have many things to vex me;—things to break my heart.'

'Poor mamma!' she exclaimed.

'Yes;—that above all others;—that first. But life and death are in God's hands and even though we may complain, we can alter nothing. But whatever our sorrows are while we are here, we must do our duty.'

'I suppose he may be a good member of Parliament, though he has turned Conservative.'

'I am not thinking about your brother just at present. I am thinking about you.' The poor girl gave a little start on the sofa. 'Do you know—Mr. Tregear?' he added.

'Yes, papa; of course I know him. You used to see him in Italy.'

'I believe I did. I understood that he was there as a sort of friend of Silverbridge.'

'His most intimate friend, papa.'

'I dare say. He came to me in London yesterday, and told me;—oh, Mary, can it be true?'

'Yes, papa,' she said, covered up to her forehead with blushes, and with her eyes turned down onto her lap. In the ordinary affairs of life she was a girl of great courage, who was not given to be shaken from her constancy by the pressure of any present difficulty; but now, at this trying moment, the terror inspired by her father's voice almost overpowered her.

'Do you mean to tell me that you have engaged yourself to that young man without my approval and without my knowledge?'

'Of course you were to have been asked, papa.'

'Is that in accordance with your idea of what should be the conduct of a young lady in your position?'

'Nobody meant to conceal anything from you, papa.'

'It has been so far concealed. And yet this young man has the self-confidence to come to me and to demand your hand as though it were a matter of course that I should accede to so trivial a request. It is, as a matter of course, quite impossible. You understand that; do you not?' When she did not answer him at once, he repeated the question. 'I ask you whether you do not feel that it is altogether impossible?'

'No, papa,' she said, in the lowest possible whisper, but still in such a whisper that he could hear the word, and with so much clearness that he could judge from her voice of the obstinacy of her mind.

'Then, Mary, it becomes my duty to tell you that it is quite impossible. I will not have it thought of. There must be an end of it.'

'Why, papa?'

'Why! I am astonished that you should ask me why.'

'I should not have allowed him, papa, to go to you unless I had—unless I had loved him—very much.'

'Then you must conquer your love. It is disgraceful and must be conquered.'

'Disgraceful!'

'Yes. I am sorry to use such a word to my own child, but it is so. If you will promise to be guided by me in this matter, if you will undertake not to see him any more, I will,—if not forget it,—at any rate pardon it, and be silent. I will excuse it because you were young and were thrown imprudently in his way. There has, I believe, been someone at work in the matter with whom I ought to be more angry than with you. Say that you will obey me, and there is nothing within a father's power that I will not do for you, to make your life happy.' It was in this way that he endeavoured to practise the lessons which he had been teaching himself. It was thus that he strove not to be stern. His heart, indeed, was tender enough, but there was nothing tender in the tone of his voice or in the glance of his eye. Though he was very positive in what he said, yet he was shy and shamefaced even with his own daughter. He, too, had blushed when he told her that she must conquer her love.

She could not see his blushes, nor could she learn from his voice and manner so much of the workings of his heart and mind as an older woman might have done. That she should be told that she had disgraced herself was terrible to her. That her father should speak of her marriage with this man as an event that was quite impossible made her very unhappy. That he should talk of pardoning her, as for some great fault, was in itself a misery. But she had not on that account the least idea of giving up her lover. Young as she was, she had her own peculiar theory on that matter, her own code of conduct and honour, from which she did not mean to be driven. Of course she had not expected that her father would yield at the first word. He, no doubt, would wish that she should make a more exalted marriage;—one in which there would be more of wealth and rank. She had known that she would have to encounter opposition, though she had not expected to be told that she had disgraced herself. As she sat there she resolved that under no pressure would she give up her lover;—but she was so far abashed and beaten down that she could not at first find words in which to express herself. He, too, had been silent for a few moments before he again asked her for her promise.

'Will you tell me, Mary, that you will not see him again?'

'I don't think that I can say that, papa.'

'Why not?'

'Oh, papa, how can I, when of all the people in the world I love him the best?'

It is not without a pang that anyone can be told that she who is of all the dearest has some other one who to her is the dearest. Such pain fathers and mothers have to bear; and though, I think, the arrow is never so blunted but that it leaves something of a wound behind, there is in most cases, if not a perfect salve, still an ample consolation. The mother knows that it is good that her child should love some man better than all the world beside, and that she should be taken away to become a wife and a mother herself. And the father, when that delight of his eyes ceases to assure him that he is her nearest, dearest, closest friend, though he abandon the treasure of that nearestness and dearestness with a soft melancholy, still knows that it is as it should be. Of course that other 'him' is the person she loves the best in the world. Were it not so how evil a thing it would be that she should marry him! Were it not so with reference to some 'him,' how void would her life be! But now, to the poor Duke the wound had no salve, no consolation. When he was told that this young Tregear was the owner of his girl's sweet love, was the treasure of her heart,—though he must have known that it was so from the moment in which Tregear had spoken to him,—he shrank as though arrows with sharp points were pricking him all over. 'I will not hear of such love,' he said.

'What am I to say, papa?'

'Say that you will obey me. Say that you will never see him again.' Then she sat silent. 'Do you not know that he is not fit to be your husband?'

'No, papa.'

'Then you cannot have thought much either of your position or of mine.'

'He is a gentleman, papa.'

'So is my private secretary. So I suppose is the young man who acts as his assistant——'

'I do not know whom you mean.'

'Well; not now, because he has gone.* There is not a clerk in one of our public offices who does not consider himself to be a gentleman. The curate of the parish is a gentleman, and the medical man who comes here from Bridstock. The word is too vague to carry with it any meaning that ought to be serviceable to you in thinking of such a matter.'

'I do not know any other way of dividing people,' said she, showing thereby that she had altogether made up her mind as to what ought to be serviceable to her.

'You are not called upon to divide people. That division is so difficult and requires so much experience that you are bound in this matter to rely upon those to whom your obedience is due. I cannot but think you must have known that you were not entitled to give your love to any man without being assured that the man would be approved of by—by—by me.' He was going to say, 'your parents,' but was stopped by the remembrance of his poor wife's imprudence.

She saw it all, and was too noble to plead her mother's authority. But she was not too dutiful to cast a reproach upon him, when he was so stern to her. 'You have been so little with me, papa.'

'That is true,' he said after a pause. 'That is true. It has been a fault and I will mend it. It is a reason for forgiveness, Mary, and I will forgive you. But you must tell me that there shall be an end to all this.'

'No, papa.'

'What do you mean?'

'That as I love Mr. Tregear, and as I have told him so, and as I have promised him that I will be true to him, I cannot let there be an end to it.'

'You do not suppose that you will be allowed to see him again?'

'I hope so.'

'Most assuredly not. Do you write to him?'

'No, papa.'

'Never?'

'Never since we have been back in England.'

'Promise me in the first place that you will not write to him.'

She paused a moment before she answered him, and now she was looking him full in the face. 'I shall not write to him. I do not think I shall write to him. But I will not promise.'

'Not promise me,—your father!'

'No, papa. It might be that,—that I should do it.'

'You would not wish me so to guard you that you should have no power of sending a letter but by permission?'

'I should not like that.'

'But it will have to be so.'

'If I do write, I will tell you.'

'And show me what you write.'

'No, papa;—not that; but I will tell you what I have written.'

Then it occurred to him that this bargaining was altogether derogatory to his parental authority, and by no means likely to impress upon her mind the conviction that Tregear must be completely banished from her thoughts. He began already to find how difficult it would be for him to have the charge of such a daughter,—how impossible that he should conduct such a charge with sufficient firmness, and yet with sufficient tenderness! At present he had done no good. He had only been made more wretched than ever by her obstinacy. Surely he must pass her over to the charge of some lady,—but of some lady who would be as determined as was he himself that she should not throw herself away by marrying Mr. Tregear. 'There shall be no writing,' he said, 'no visiting, no communication of any kind. As you refuse to obey me now, you had better go to your room.' Then she went to her room, and left him alone in his unhappiness.

CHAPTER 9

IN MEDIAS RES

PERHAPS the method of rushing at once *in medias res** is, of all the ways of beginning a story, or a separate branch of a story, the least objectionable. The reader is made to think that the gold lies so near the surface that he will be required to take very little trouble in digging for it. And the writer is enabled,—at any rate for a time, and till his neck has become, as it were, warm to the collar,—to throw off from him the difficulties and dangers, the tedium and prolixity, of description. For this rushing *in medias res* has doubtless the charm of ease. 'Certainly when I threw her from the garret window onto the stony pavement below, I did not anticipate that she would fall so far without injury to life or limb.' When a story has been begun after this fashion, without any prelude, without description of the garret or of the pavement, or of the lady thrown, or of the speaker, a great amount of trouble seems to have been saved. The mind of the reader fills up the blanks,—if erroneously, still satisfactorily. He knows, at least, that the heroine has encountered a terrible danger, and has escaped from it with almost incredible good fortune; that the demon of the piece is a bold demon, not ashamed to speak of his own iniquity, and that the heroine and the demon are so far united that they have been in a garret together. Unless indeed the demon's story be a lie altogether, and the lady has never been in the garret and never thrown out of the window! In which case the lie and the reader's belief in the lie will add much to the mystery and consequently to the interest of the story. But there is this drawback in the *in medias res* system,—that it is almost impossible to avoid the necessity of doing, sooner or later, that which would most naturally be done at first. It answers, perhaps, for a half-a-dozen chapters;—and to carry the reader pleasantly for half-a-dozen chapters is a great matter!—but after that a certain nebulous darkness gradually seems to envelop the characters and the incidents. 'Is all this going on in the country, or is it in town,—or perhaps in the Colonies? How old was she? Was she tall? Is she fair? Is she heroine-like in her form and gait? And, after all, how high was the garret window?' I have always found that the details would insist on being told at last, and that by rushing *in medias res* I was simply presenting the cart before the horse. But as readers like the cart the best, I will do it once again,—trying it only for a branch of my story,—and will endeavour to let as little as possible of the horse be seen afterwards.

'And so poor Frank has been turned out of heaven,' said Lady Mabel Grex* to young Lord Silverbridge.

'Who told you that? I have said nothing about his going to anybody.'

'Of course he told me himself,' said the young beauty. I am aware that, in the word 'beauty,' and perhaps, also, in the word 'young,' a little bit of the horse is appearing; and I am already sure that I shall have to show his head and neck, even if not his very tail. 'Poor Frank. Did you hear it all?'

'I heard nothing, Lady Mab, and know nothing.'

'You know that your awful governor,—for of all men he is the most awful,—won't let him stay any longer in Carlton Terrace.'

'Yes; I know that.'

'And why not?'

'Would Lord Grex allow Percival to have his friends living here?' Earl Grex was Lady Mabel's father. Lord Percival was the Earl's son;—and the Earl lived in Belgrave Square.* All these are little bits of the horse.

'Certainly not. In the first place I am here.'

'That makes a difference certainly.'

'Of course it makes a difference. They would be wanting to make love to me.'

'No doubt. I should, I know.'

'And therefore it wouldn't do for you to live here. And then papa is living here himself. And then the permission never has been given. I suppose Frank did not go there at first without the Duke knowing it.'

'I dare say that I had mentioned it.'

'You might as well tell me all about it. We are cousins, you know.' Frank Tregear, through his mother's family, was second cousin to Lady Mabel; as was also Lord Silverbridge, one of the Grexes having, at some remote period, married a Palliser. This is another bit of the horse.

'The governor merely seemed to think that he would like to have his own house to himself,—like other people. What an ass Tregear was to say anything to you about it!'

'I don't think he was an ass at all. Of course he had to tell us that he was changing his residence. He says that he is going to take a back bedroom somewhere near the Seven Dials.'*

'He has got very nice rooms in Duke Street.'

'Have you seen him there?'

'Of course I have.'

'Poor fellow! I wish he had a little money; he is so nice. And now, Lord Silverbridge, do you mean to say that there is not something in the wind about Lady Mary?'

'If there were I should not talk about it,' said Lord Silverbridge, who was as yet too young, being of the male sex, to lie decently. 'Nor, indeed, should I probably know about it.'

'You are a very innocent young gentleman.'

'And you are a very interesting young lady.'

'You ought to think me so, for I interest myself very much about you. Was the Duke very angry about your not standing for the county?'

'He was vexed, I think.'

'I do think it is so odd that a man should be expected to be this or that in politics because his father happened to be so before him! I don't understand how he should expect that you should remain with a party so utterly snobbish and down in the world as the Radicals. Everybody that is worth anything is leaving them.'

'He has not left them.'

'No; I don't suppose he could. But you have.'

'I never belonged to them, Lady Mab.'

'And never will, I hope. I always told papa that you would certainly be one of us.' All this took place in the drawing-room of Lord Grex's house, in which the two young persons were sitting alone at about five o'clock on Sunday afternoon. They were cousins, though only second cousins, and therefore perhaps did not require to be looked after specially.* There was no Lady Grex alive, but there lived with the Earl a certain elderly lady, reputed also to be in some distant way a cousin of the family, named Miss Casseway, who, in the matter of looking after Lady Mab, did what was supposed to be absolutely necessary. She now entered the room with her bonnet on, having just returned from church. 'What was the text?' asked Lady Mab at once.

'If you had gone to church as you ought to have done, my dear, you would have heard it.'

'But as I didn't——'

'I don't think the text alone will do you any good.'

'And probably you forget it.'

'No, I don't, my dear. How do you do, Lord Silverbridge? I hope I see you very well.'

'He is a Conservative, Miss Cass.'

'Of course he is. I am quite sure that a young nobleman of so much taste and intellect would take the better side.'

'You forget that all you are saying is against my father and my family, Miss Cassewary.'

'I dare say it was different when your father was a young man. And your father, too, was, not very long since, at the head of a Government which contained many Conservatives. I don't look upon your father as being in the least given to radicalism, though perhaps I should not be justified in calling him a Conservative.'

'Well; certainly not, I think.'

'But now it is necessary that all noblemen in England should rally to the defence of their order.' Miss Cassewary was a great politician, and was one of those who are always foreseeing the ruin of their country. 'My dear, I will go and take my bonnet off. Perhaps you will have tea, when I come down.'

'Don't you go,' said Lady Mabel when Silverbridge got up to take his departure.

'I always do when tea comes.'

'But you are going to dine here?'

'Not that I know of. In the first place nobody has asked me. In the next place I am engaged. Thirdly I don't care about having to talk politics to Miss Cass. And fourthly I hate family dinners on Sunday.'

'In the first place I ask you. Secondly I know you were going to dine with Frank Tregear at the club. Thirdly I want you to talk to me and not to Miss Cass. And fourthly you are an uncivil young—young,—young,—I should say cub if I dared, to tell me that you don't like dining with me any day of the week!'

'Of course you know what I mean is that I don't like troubling your father.'

'Leave that to me. I shall tell him you are coming. And Frank too. Of course you can bring him. Then he can talk to me when papa goes down to his club, and you can arrange the politics of the nation with Miss Cass.' So it was settled, and at eight o'clock Lord Silverbridge reappeared in Belgrave Square with his friend Frank Tregear.

Earl Grex was a nobleman of very ancient family, the Grexes having held the parish of Grex, in Yorkshire, from some time long prior to the Conquest. In saying all this, I am, I know, allowing the horse to appear wholesale;—but I find that he cannot be kept out. I may as well therefore go on to say at once that the present Earl was better known at Newmarket and the Beaufort,*—where he spent a large part of his life in playing whist,—than in the House of Lords. He was a grey-haired, handsome, worn-out old man, who through a long life of pleasure had greatly impaired a fortune which, for an earl, had never been magnificent, and who now strove hard, but not always successfully, to remedy that evil by gambling. As he could no longer eat and drink as he had used to do, and as he cared no longer for the light that lies in a lady's eye, there was not much left to him in the world but cards and the race-course. Nevertheless he was a handsome old man, of polished manners, when he chose to use them; a staunch Conservative and much regarded by his party, for whom in his early life he had done some work in the House of Commons. He had been honoured too by his Sovereign, having the Garter.* 'Silverbridge is all very well,' he had said to his daughter;—'but I don't see why that young Tregear is to dine here every night of his life.'

'This is the second time since he has been up in town, papa.'

'He was here last week, I know.'

'Silverbridge wouldn't come without him.'

'That's d —— nonsense,' said the Earl. Miss Cassewary gave a start,—not, we may presume, because she was shocked, for she could not be much shocked, having heard the same word from the same lips very often; but she thought it right always to enter a protest. Then the two young men were announced.

Frank Tregear, having been known by the family as a boy, was Frank to all of them,—as was Lady Mabel, Mabel to him, somewhat to the disgust of the father and not altogether with the approbation of Miss Cass. But Lady Mabel had declared that she would not be guilty of the folly of changing old habits. Silverbridge, being Silverbridge to all his own people, hardly seemed to have a Christian name;—his godfathers and godmothers had indeed called him Plantagenet;—but having only become acquainted with the family since his Oxford days he was Lord Silverbridge to Lady Mabel. Lady Mabel had not as yet become Mabel to him, but, as by her very intimate friends she was called Mab, had allowed herself to be addressed by him as Lady Mab. There was thus between them all considerable intimacy,—though with regard to Lord Silverbridge it had at present been but short-lived.

'I'm deuced glad to hear it,' said the Earl when dinner was announced. For, though he could not eat much, Lord Grex was always impatient when the time of eating was at hand. Then he walked down alone. Lord Silverbridge followed with his daughter, and Frank Tregear gave his arm to Miss Cassewary. 'If that woman can't clear her soup better than that, she might as well go to the d——,' said the Earl;—upon which remark no one in the company made any observation. As there were two men-servants in the room when it was made, the cook probably had the advantage of it. It may be almost unnecessary to add that though the Earl had polished manners for certain occasions he would sometimes throw them off in the bosom of his own family.

'My Lord,' said Miss Cassewary,—she always called him my Lord,—'Lord Silverbridge is going to stand for the Duke's borough in the Conservative interest.'

'I didn't know the Duke had a borough,' said the Earl.

'He had one till he thought it proper to give it up,' said the son, taking his father's part.

'And you are going to pay him off for what he has done by standing against him. It's just the sort of thing for a son to do in these days. If I had a borough Percival would go down and make Radical speeches there.'

'There isn't a better Conservative in England than Percival,' said Lady Mabel, bridling up.

'Nor a worse son,' said the father. 'I believe he would do anything he could lay his hand on to oppose me.' During the past week there had been some little difference of opinion between the father and the son as to the signing of a deed.

'My father doesn't take it in bad part at all,' said Silverbridge.

'Your father is a man in a hundred,' said Frank, who in spite of his own little difficulties felt disposed to take the Duke's part.

'Perhaps he's ratting* himself,' said the Earl. 'When a man lends himself to a coalition he is as good as half gone already.'

'No indeed,' said the son. 'I do not think that in all England there is so thorough a Liberal as my father, and when I say that he doesn't take this badly of me, I don't mean that it doesn't vex him. I know it vexes him. But he doesn't quarrel with me. He even wrote down to his man of business in Barsetshire to say that all my expenses at Silverbridge were to be paid,—just as though I were standing in obedience to him.'

'I call that very bad politics,' said the Earl.

'It seems to me to be very grand,' said Frank.

'Perhaps, sir, you don't know what is good or what is bad in politics,' said the Earl, trying to snub his guest.

But it was difficult to snub Frank. 'I know a gentleman when I see him, I think,' he said. 'Of course Silverbridge is right to be a Conservative. Nobody has a stronger opinion about that than I have. But the Duke is behaving so well that if I were he I should almost regret it.'

'And so I do,' said Silverbridge.

'No; no; not that,' said Lady Mabel.

When the ladies were gone the old Earl turned himself toward the fire, having filled his glass and pushed the bottles away from him, as though he meant to leave the two young men to themselves. He sat leaning with his head on his hand, looking the picture of woe. It was now only nine o'clock, and there would be no whist at the Beaufort till nearly eleven. There was still more than an hour to be endured before the brougham would come to fetch him. 'I suppose we shall have a majority?' said Frank, trying to rouse him.

'Who does "we" mean?' asked the Earl.

'The Conservatives,—of whom I take the liberty to call myself one.'

'It sounded as though you were a very influential member of the party.'

'I consider myself to be at any rate one of the party; and so I say "we." ' To this the Earl condescended to make no reply.

On this evening, the Earl having declined to go upstairs before he went to his club, the two young men joined the ladies without his company. On such occasions Miss Cassewary did her duty loyally. It was quite right that young ladies and young gentlemen should be allowed to talk together, and very right indeed that such a young gentleman as Lord Silverbridge should be allowed to talk to such a young lady as Lady Mabel. What could be so nice as a marriage between the heir of the house of Omnium and Lady Mabel Grex? Lady Mabel looked indeed to be the elder,—but they were in truth the same age. All the world acknowledged that Lady Mabel was very clever and very beautiful and in all respects fit to be a duchess. Even the Earl, when Miss Cassewary hinted at the matter to him, grunted an assent. Lady Mabel had already refused one or two not ineligible offers, and it was necessary that something should be done. There had been at one time a fear in Miss Cassewary's bosom lest her charge should fall too deeply in love with Frank Tregear;—but now, though the two young persons were very intimate, Miss Cassewary knew that whatever danger there might have been in that respect had passed away. Frank was quite willing to talk to her, while Mabel and Lord Silverbridge were in a corner together.

'I shall be on tenterhooks now till I know how it is to be at Silverbridge,' said the young lady.

'It is very good of you to feel so much interest.'

'Of course I feel an interest. Are not you one of us? If you were standing as a Liberal I should not care so much about it. When is it to be?'

'They say that the elections will be over before the Derby.'

'And which do you care for the most?'

'I should like to pull off the Derby, I own.'

'From what papa says I should think the other event is the more probable.'

'Doesn't the Earl stand to win on Prime Minister?'

'I never know anything about his betting. But,—you know his way,—he said you were going to drop a lot of money like a ——. I can't quite tell you what he likened you to.'

'The Earl may be mistaken, you know.'

'You are not betting much, I hope.'

'Not plunging. I never do that kind of thing. But I have a little money on.'

'Don't get into a way of betting.'

'Why;—what difference does it make,—to you?'

'Is that kind, Lord Silverbridge?'

'I meant to say that if I did make a mess of it you wouldn't care about it.'

'Yes, I should. I should care very much if you made a mess, as you call it. I dare say you could lose a great deal of money and care nothing about it.'

'Indeed I could not.'

'What would be a great deal of money to me. But, of course, you would want to get it back again. And in that way you would be regularly on the turf.'

'And why not?'

'I want to see better things from you.'

'You ought not to preach against the turf, Lady Mab.'

'Because of papa? But I am not preaching against the turf. If I were such as you are, I would have a horse or two myself. A man in your position should do a little of everything. You should hunt, and have a yacht, and stalk deer, and keep your own trainer at Newmarket.'

'I wish you'd say all that to my father.'

'Of course I mean if you can afford it. I like a man to like pleasure. But I despise a man who makes a business of his pleasures. When I hear that this man is the best whist-player in London, and that man the best billiard-player, and that another plays cricket like a professional, I always know that they can do nothing else. That is the one thing they live for,—and then I despise them.'

'You needn't despise me, because I do nothing well,' said the young Lord as he got up to take his leave.

'I do so hope you'll get the seat;—and win the Derby.' These were her last words to him as she wished him good-night.

'What an old brute he is!' said Frank as they were walking home together along Piccadilly.

'Yes;—he doesn't make himself pleasant when he's cross. I was afraid you were going to cut up rough.'

'I'm too fond of Mabel for that. We have known each other so long that she is almost like a sister to me. I sometimes fancy the Earl wants to quarrel with me, so that I should not go there any more;—but I don't mean to let him. I can, perhaps, be of some service to her. Don't you call her very handsome?'

'Certainly I do.'

'I look at her just as I would at a picture, and in that way I think she is the most beautiful thing to be seen in London. And then how clever she is!'

'I wonder she is not married.'

'She never seems to think that she has found anybody good enough. Good-night, old fellow. No, I won't go down to the club now. I am a little out of sorts about my own affairs;—as you may understand.'

CHAPTER 10

'WHY NOT LIKE A ROMEO, IF I FEEL
LIKE A ROMEO?'

'THAT'S nonsense, Miss Cass, and I shall,' said Lady Mabel. They were together, on the morning after the little dinner-party described in the last chapter, in a small back sitting-room which was supposed to be

Lady Mabel's own, and the servant had just announced the fact that Mr. Tregear was below.

'Then I shall go down too,' said Miss Cassewary.

'You'll do nothing of the kind. Will you please to tell me what it is you are afraid of? Do you think that Frank is going to make love to me again?'

'No.'

'Or that if I chose that he should I would let you stop me? He is in love with somebody else,—and perhaps I am too. At any rate we are two paupers, and though we are the best friends in the world, we can't afford to be anything else.'

'My Lord would not approve of it.'

'If you know what my Lord approves of and what he disapproves you understand him a great deal better than I do. And if you mind what he approves or disapproves, you care for his opinion a great deal more than I do. My cousin is here now to talk to me,—about his own affairs, and I mean to see him,—alone. I shan't ask him to stay to lunch because papa might get up and come in.'

'That is because you are afraid of my Lord.'

'No, I'm not;—not in the least. But I don't want to have Frank snubbed.' Then she left the little room and went down into that in which Frank was waiting for her, without the company of Miss Cassewary.

'Do you really mean,' she said, after they had been together for some ten or fifteen minutes, 'that you had the courage to ask the Duke for his daughter's hand?'

'Why not?'

'I believe you would dare do anything.'

'I couldn't very well take it without asking him.'

'As I am not acquainted with the young lady myself, I don't know how that might be.'

'And if I took her so, I should have to take her empty-handed.'

'Which wouldn't suit;—would it?'

'It wouldn't suit for her,—whose comforts and happiness are now much more to me than my own.'

'No doubt! Of course you are terribly in love.'

'Very thoroughly in love, I think, I am.'

'For the tenth time, I should say.'

'For the second only. I don't regard myself as a monument of constancy, but I think I am less fickle than some other people.'

'Meaning me!'

'Not especially,—unless you like to take it so.'

'Frank, that is ill-natured, and almost unmanly,—and false also. When have I been fickle? You say that there was one before with you. I say that there has never really been one with me at all. No one knows that better than yourself. I cannot afford to be in love till I am quite sure that the man is fit to be, and will be, my husband.'

'I doubt sometimes whether you are capable of being in love with anyone.'

'I think I am,' she said very gently. 'But I am at any rate capable of not being in love till I wish it. Come, Frank; do not quarrel with me. You know,—you ought to know,—that I should have loved you had it not been that such love would have been bad for both of us?'

'It is a kind of self-restraint I do not understand.'

'Because you are not a woman.'

'Why did you twit me with changing my love?'

'Because I am a woman. Can't you forgive as much as that to me?'

'Certainly. Only you must not think that I have been false because I now love her so dearly.'

'I do not think you are false. I would do anything to help you if there were anything I could do. But when you spoke so like a Romeo of your love——'

'Why not like a Romeo, if I feel like a Romeo?'

'But I doubt whether Romeo talked much to Rosaline* of his love for Juliet. But you shall talk to me of yours for Lady Mary, and I will listen to you patiently and encourage you, and will not even think of those former sweet speeches.'

'The former sweet speeches were foolish.'

'Oh,—of course.'

'You at least used to say so.'

'I say so now, and they shall be as though they had been never spoken. So you bearded the Duke in his den, and asked him for Lady Mary's hand,—just as though you had been a young duke yourself and owned half a county?'

'Just the same.'

'And what did he say?'

'He swore that it was impossible. Of course I knew all that before. It was a form which it was necessary to go through.'

'How will it be now? You will not give it up?'

'Certainly not.'

'And Lady Mary?'

'One human being can perhaps never answer for another with perfect security.'

'But you feel sure of her.'

'I do.'

'He, I should think, can be very imperious.'

'And so can she. The Pallisers are all obstinate.'

'Is Silverbridge obstinate?' she asked.

'Stiff-necked as a bull if he takes it into his head to be so.'

'I shouldn't have thought it.'

'No;—because he is so soft in his manner, and often finds it easier to be led by others than to direct himself. He stuck to his own opinion fast enough when his father wanted him to stand for the county.'

Then she remained silent for a few seconds, during which he stood with his back to the fire while she was seated in a low chair. They were both thinking of the same thing, and both wishing to speak of it. But the words came to her first, though the subject must have been more difficult for her even than for him. 'I wonder what he thinks of me,' she said. Whereupon Tregear only smiled. 'I suppose he has spoken to you about me?'

'Why do you ask?'

'Why!'

'And why should I tell you? Supposing he should have said to me in the confidence of friendship that he thinks you ugly and stupid——'

'I am sure he has not said that. He has eyes to see and ears to hear. But, though I am neither ugly nor stupid he needn't like me.'

'Do you want him to like you?'

'Yes, I do. You know that I do. It would suit me to be Duchess of Omnium and I believe that I should be to him a good and a loving wife. Oh, yes; you may laugh; but if I did not think so I would not take his hand even to become Duchess of Omnium.'

'Do you mean that you love him, Mabel?'

'No; I do not mean that. But I would learn to love him. You do not believe that?' Here he smiled again and shook his head. 'It is as I said before, because you are not a woman and do not understand how women are trammelled. Do you think ill of me because I say this?'

'No, indeed.'

'Do not think ill of me if you can help it, because you are almost the only friend that I trust. I almost trust dear old Cass, but not quite. She is old-fashioned and I shock her. As for other women, there isn't one anywhere to whom I would say a word. Only think how a girl such as I am is placed;—or indeed any girl. You, if you see a woman that you fancy, can pursue her, can win her and triumph, or lose her and gnaw your heart;—at any rate you can do something. You can tell her that you love her;—can tell her so again and again even though she should scorn you. You can set yourself about the business you have taken in hand and, if it be important to you, can work hard at it. What can a girl do?'

'Girls work hard too sometimes.'

'Of course they do;—but everybody feels that they are sinning against their sex. Of love, such as a man's is, a woman ought to know nothing. How can she love with passion when she should never give her love till it has been asked, and not then unless her friends tell her that the thing is suitable? Love such as that to me is out of the question. But, as it is fit that I should be married, I wish to be married as well as possible. And, having a conscience in the matter, I mean to do my duty by my husband whoever he be.'

'And to love him after a fashion?'

'Yes;—to love him—after a very sterling fashion. I will make his wishes my wishes, his ways my ways, his ideas my ideas, his party my party, his home my home, his ambition my ambition,—his heaven my heaven.' As she said this she stood up with her hands clenched and head erect, and her eyes flashing. 'Do you not know me well enough to be sure that I should be loyal to him?'

'Yes;—I think that you would be loyal.'

'Whether I loved him or not, he should love me.'

'And you think that Silverbridge would do?'

'Yes, I think that Silverbridge would do. And I think that I should do for Silverbridge. You, no doubt, will say that I am flying high.'

'Not too high. Why should you not fly high? If I can justify myself, surely I cannot accuse you.'

'It is hardly the same thing, Frank. Of course there is not a girl in London to whom Lord Silverbridge would not be the best match that she could make. He has the choice of us all, does he not?'

'Most girls would think twice about it before refusing him.'

'Very few would have to think twice before accepting him. Perhaps he wishes to add to his wealth by marrying richly,—as his father did.'

'No thought on that subject will ever trouble him. That will be all as it happens. As soon as he takes a sufficient fancy to a girl he will ask her straight off. I do not say that he might not change afterwards, but he would mean it at the time.'

'If he had once said the word to me, he should not change. But then what right have I to expect it? What has he ever said about me?'

'Very little. But had he said much I should not tell you.'

'You are my friend?'

'Certainly I am.'

'But you are his also?'

'And his too.'

'And he, perhaps, is more to you than I am. As his friend it may be your duty to tell him all that I am saying. If so I have been wrong. Perhaps you will put him on his guard against me.'

'Do you think that I shall do that, Mabel?'

'I do not know. Men are so strong in their friendships.'

'Mine with you is the older, and the sweeter. Though we may not be more than friends I will say that it is the more tender. In my heart of hearts I do not think that Silverbridge could do better.'

'Thanks for that at any rate, Frank.'

'I shall tell him nothing of you certainly that can set him against you.'

'You would be glad to see me his wife?' she said.

'As you must be somebody's wife, and not mine——'

'I cannot be yours, Frank; can I?'

'And not mine,' he repeated, 'I will endeavour to be glad. Who can explain his feelings in such a matter? Though I most truly love the girl I hope to marry, yet my heart goes back to former things and opens itself to past regrets.'

'I know it all,' she whispered.

'But you and I must be too wise to permit ourselves to be tormented by such foolish melancholy.' As he said this he took her hand, half with the purpose of bidding her good-bye, but partly with the idea of giving some expression to the tenderness of his feelings. But as he did so, the door was opened, and the old Earl shambled into the room.

'What the deuce are you doing here?' he said.

'I have been talking to Lady Mabel.'

'For about an hour.'

'Indeed I do not know for how long.'

'Papa, he is going to be married.' When she said this Frank Tregear turned round and looked at her almost in anger.

'Going to be married, is he? Who is the fortunate woman?' Had he said unfortunate, his meaning would have been the same, and his expression not a whit more clear.

'I don't know whether he will let me tell you.'

'Not yet, I think,' said Frank gloomily. 'There is nothing settled.'

The old Earl looked puzzled, but Lady Mabel's craft had been in a great measure successful. If this objectionable young second cousin had come there to talk about his marriage with another young woman, the conversation must at any rate have been innocent. 'Where is Miss Cassewary?' asked the Earl.

'I asked her not to come down with me,' said Lady Mabel, 'because Frank wished to speak about his own affairs. You have no objection to his coming, papa?'

There had been objections raised to any intimacy with Frank Tregear; but all that was now nearly two years since. The father had then been, if not satisfied, at least pacified. He had been assured over and over again by Miss Casseway that he need not be afraid of Frank Tregear, and had in a sort of way assented to the young man's visits. But, still, he did not like his presence. 'I think he might find something better to do with his time than hanging about here all day.' Frank, shrugging his shoulders, and having shaken hands both with the daughter and father, took his hat and departed. 'Who is the girl?' asked the Earl.

'You heard him say that I was not to tell.'

'Has she got money?'

'I believe she will have a great deal.'

'Then she is a great fool for her pains,' said the Earl, shambling off again.

Lady Mabel spent the greater part of that afternoon alone, endeavouring to recall to her mind all that she had said to Frank Tregear, and questioning herself as to the wisdom and truth of her own words. She had intended to tell the truth,—but hardly, hardly perhaps the whole truth. The life which was before her,—which it was necessary that she should lead,—seemed to her to be so difficult! She could not clearly see her way to be pure and good and feminine, and at the same time wise. She had been false now;—so far false that she had told her friend that she had never been in love. But she was in love;—in love with him, Frank Tregear. She knew it as thoroughly as it was possible for her to know anything;—and had acknowledged it to herself a score of times.

But she could not marry him. And it was expedient, nay, almost necessary that she should marry someone. To that someone, how good she would be! How she would strive by duty and attention, and if possible by affection, to make up for that misfortune of her early love!

The reader may not approve of Lady Mabel. My female reader certainly will not do so. But I hope she will understand that with all her faults my heroine was a woman anxious to do her duty according to her lights.

And so I hope that I have brought my cart in to its appointed place in the front, without showing too much of the horse.

CHAPTER 11

'CRUEL'

FOR two or three days after the first scene between the Duke and his daughter,—that scene in which she was forbidden either to see or to write to her lover,—not a word was said at Matching about Mr. Tregear, nor were any steps taken towards curtailing her liberty of action. She had said at any rate that she would not write to him without telling her father, and the Duke was too proud of the honour of his family to believe it to be possible that she should deceive him. Nor was it possible. Not only would her own idea of duty prevent her from writing to her lover,—although she had stipulated for the right to do so in some possible emergency,—but, carried far beyond that in her sense of what was right and wrong, she felt it now incumbent on her to have no secret from her father at all. The secret, as long as it had been a secret, had been a legacy from her mother,—and had been kept, at her lover's instance, during that period of mourning for her mother in which it would, she thought, have been indecorous that there should be any question of love or of giving in marriage. It had been a burden to her, though a necessary burden. She had been very clear that the revelation should be made to her father, when it was made, by her lover. That had been done,—and now it was open to her to live without any secrecy,—as was her nature. She meant to cling to her lover. She was quite sure of that. Nothing could divide her from him but his death or hers,—or falseness on his part. She belonged to him and could not in any way be made to belong to another. But as to marriage, that would not be possible till her father had assented. And as to seeing the man,—ah, yes, if she could do so with her father's assent! She would not be ashamed to own her great desire to see him. She would tell her father that all her happiness depended upon seeing him. She would not be coy in speaking of her love. But she would obey her father.

It was, at any rate, after that fashion that she made up her mind in her present emergency. But she had, I think, a strong idea that she would ultimately prevail,—an idea also that that 'ultimately' should not be postponed to some undefined middle-aged period of her life. As she intended to belong to Frank Tregear, she thought it expedient that he should have the best of her days as well as what might be supposed to be the worst; and she therefore resolved that it would be her duty to make her father understand that though she would certainly obey him, she would look to be treated humanly* by him, and not to be made miserable for an indefinite term of years. She owed him much, but she was fully aware that he also owed something to her. If he were inhuman, so perhaps might she be,—but yet obedient.

The first word spoken between them on the subject,—the first word after that first discussion,—began with him and was caused by his feeling that her present life at Matching must be sad and lonely. At present there was no lady there, nor was there any lady whom at the present moment he would wish to have as her intimate. But Lord Cantrip was with him for a day or two, having come to him chiefly in reference to certain political movements with which the reader's mind shall not be burdened quite immediately; and to Lord Cantrip he had told,—not his sorrow in regard to his daughter's misplaced affection, which was a disgrace which he could not bring his tongue to utter, at any rate to another man,—but his fears lest the life at Matching should be oppressive to his girl's spirit. Then there had been some discussion between them as to how relief had best be afforded. Lady Cantrip would be delighted to take her;—but Lady Cantrip was in London and must be in London, at any rate when Parliament should again be sitting. A London life would perhaps, at present, hardly suit Lady Mary. Then a plan was proposed between them which might be convenient. The Duke had a house at Richmond, on the river, called The Horns.* That should be lent to Lady Cantrip, and Mary should there be her guest. Richmond was so nearly a part of London that the Earl, if sojourning there, might be at the same time sufficiently domestic, and sufficiently parliamentary. So it was settled between the Duke and the Earl. But as yet Lady Mary knew nothing of the arrangement.

'I think I shall go up to town with Lord Cantrip to-morrow,' said the Duke to his daughter.

'For long?'

'I shall be gone only one night. It is on your behalf that I am going.'

'On my behalf, papa?'

'I have been talking to him about you.'

'Not about Mr. Tregear?'

'No;—not about Mr. Tregear,' said the father with a mixture of anger and solemnity in his tone. 'It is my desire to regard Mr. Tregear as though he did not exist.'

'That is not possible, papa.'

'But I was speaking to Lord Cantrip of the inconvenience of your position here.'

'Why is it inconvenient?'

'You are too young to be without a companion. It is not fit that you should be so much alone.'

'I do not feel it.'

'It is very melancholy for you, and cannot be good for you in any way. They will go down to The Horns, so that you will not be absolutely in London, and you will find Lady Cantrip a very nice person.'

'I don't care for new people just now, papa,' she said. But to this he paid but little heed; nor was she prepared to say that she would not do as he directed. When therefore he left Matching with his friend, she understood that he was going to prepare a temporary home for her. Nothing further was said at the moment about Tregear. She was too proud to ask that no mention of his name should be made to Lady Cantrip. And he when he left the house did not think that he would find himself called upon to allude to the subject.

But when Lady Cantrip made some inquiry about the girl and her habits,—asking what were her ordinary occupations, how she was accustomed to pass her hours, to what she chiefly devoted herself,— then at last with much difficulty the Duke did bring himself to tell the story. 'Perhaps it is better you should know it all,' he said as he told it.

'Poor girl! Yes, Duke; upon the whole it is better that I should know it all,' said Lady Cantrip. 'Of course he will not come here.'

'Oh, dear; I hope not.'

'Nor to The Horns.'

'I hope he will never see her again anywhere,' said the Duke. 'I have told her that there is to be no intercourse;—no possibility of intercourse.'

'Poor girl!'

'Have I not been right? Is it not best to put an end to such a thing at once?'

'Certainly at once, if it has to be put an end to,—and can be put an end to.'

'It must be put an end to,' said the Duke very decisively. 'Do you not see that it must be so? Who is Mr. Tregear?'

'I suppose they were allowed to be together.'

'He was unfortunately intimate with Silverbridge, who took him over to Italy. You know how young people do get together in that way. He has nothing;—not even a profession.' Lady Cantrip could not but smile when she remembered the immense wealth of the man who was speaking to her;—and the Duke saw the smile and understood it. 'You will understand what I mean, Lady Cantrip. If this young man were in other respects suitable, of course I could find an income for them. But he is nothing;—just an idle seeker for pleasure without the means of obtaining it.'

'That is very bad.'

'As for rank,' continued the Duke energetically, 'I do not think that I am specially wedded to it. I have found myself as willing to associate with those who are without it as with those who have it. I feel no special regard for those who hold it. But for my child, I would wish her to mate with one of her own class.'

'It would be best, certainly.'

'When a young man comes to me who, though I believe him to be what is called a gentleman, has neither rank, nor means, nor profession, nor name, and asks for my daughter, surely I am right to say that such a marriage shall not be thought of?'

As this proposition was made in such a form and with such a tone as to demand an answer, Lady Cantrip had to pause till she should have resolved what answer she would give. 'Was I not right?' demanded the Duke persistently.

'I suppose you were right.'

'What else could I have said?'

'But it is a pity that it should be so. It is a pity that they should ever have come together.'

'It is indeed, indeed to be lamented,' said the Duke almost with eloquence. 'And I will own at once that the fault was not hers. Though I must be firm in this you are not to suppose that I am angry with her. I have myself been to blame.' This he said with a resolution that,—as he and his wife had been one flesh,—all faults committed by her should, now that she was dead, be accepted by him as his faults. 'It had not occurred to me that as yet she would love any man.'

'Has it gone deep with her, Duke?'

'I fear that all things go deep with her.'

'Poor girl!'

'But they shall be kept apart? As long as your great kindness is continued to her they shall be kept apart?'

'I do not think that I should be found good at watching a young lady.'

'She will require no watching.'

'Then of course they will not meet. She had better know that you have told me.'

'She shall know it.'

'And let her know also that anything I can do to make her happy shall be done. But, Duke, there is but one cure.'

'Time you mean.'

'Yes; time; but I did not mean time.' Then she smiled as she went on. 'You must not suppose that I am speaking against my own sex if I say that she will not forget Mr. Tregear till someone else has made himself agreeable to her. We must wait till she can go out a little into society. Then she will find out that there are others in the world besides Mr. Tregear. It so often is the case that a girl's love means her sympathy for him who has chanced to be nearest to her.'

The Duke as he went away thought very much of what Lady Cantrip had said to him;—particularly of those last words, 'till someone else has made himself agreeable to her.' Was he to send his girl into the world in order that she might find a lover? There was something in the idea which was thoroughly distasteful to him. He had not given his mind much to the matter, but he had felt that a woman should be sought for,—sought for and extracted, cunningly, as it were, from some hiding-place, and not sent out into a market to be exposed as for sale. In his own personal history there had been, as he was well aware, a misfortune,—a misfortune, the sense of which he could never, at any moment, have expressed to any ears, the memory of which had been always buried deep in his own bosom,—but a misfortune in that no such cunning extraction on his part had won for him the woman to whose hands had been confided the strings of his heart. His wife had undergone that process of extraction before he had seen her, and his marriage with her had been a matter of sagacious bargaining. He was now told that his daughter must be sent out among young men in order that she might become sufficiently fond of some special one to be regardless of Tregear. There was a feeling that in doing so she must lose something of the freshness of the bloom of her innocence. How was this transfer of her love to be effected? Let her go here because she will meet the heir of this wealthy house who may probably be smitten by her charms; or there because that other young lordling would make a fit husband for her. Let us contrive to throw her into the arms of this man,—or at any rate put her in the way of that man. Was his girl to be exposed to this? Surely that method of bargaining to which he had owed his own wife would be better than that. Let it be said,—only he himself most certainly could not be the person to say it,—let it be said to some man of rank and means and fairly good character, 'Here is a wife for you with so many thousand pounds, with beauty as you can see for yourself, with rank and belongings of the highest, very good in every respect;—only that as regards her heart she thinks she has given it to a young man named Tregear. No marriage there is possible; but perhaps the young lady might suit you?' It was thus he had been married. There was an absence in it of that romance which, though he had never experienced it in his own life, was always present to his imagination. His wife had often ridiculed him because he could only live among figures and official details; but to her had not been given the power of looking into a man's heart and finding all that was there. Yes;—in such bargaining for a wife, in such bargaining for a husband, there could be nothing of the tremulous delicacy of feminine romance; but it would be better than standing at a stall in the market till the sufficient purchaser should come. It never occurred to him that the delicacy, the innocence, the romance, the bloom might all be preserved if he would give his girl to the man whom she said she loved. That course did not for a moment recommend itself to him. That was, as he had said from the first, quite impossible. Could he have modelled her future course according to his own wishes, he would have had her live a gentle life for the next three years,—a life chiefly among books and music, with a pencil perhaps in her hand or a music-book before her,—and then come forth, cleansed as it were by such quarantine from the impurity to which she had been subjected by her contact with this man.

It filled his mind so completely that he had hardly heart enough to be made additionally miserable by his son's apostasy. Of course he saw Lord Silverbridge when he was in town, and asked sundry questions about the coming election. It was quite arranged that the young man should stand for the borough. Mr. Fletcher, who had sat for it, was required down in Herefordshire, his own county,—so that nothing could possibly be more convenient. There was some talk of an opposition. Mr. Du Boung, the brewer, thought of coming forward again, and had declared himself to be a supporter of the Duke. But the general opinion in the borough was that on the day of nomination there would be no second candidate, and that any second candidate, should there be one, would find himself nowhere. 'You see,' said Lord Silverbridge, apparently thinking that he would receive all his father's sympathy, 'I have your influence and my own politics to support me.'

'My influence ought to be worth nothing,' said the angry Duke, 'and your politics worth less.'

'Less than nothing!' exclaimed the son.

'As belonging to you. The facts that you are my son and that being so you call yourself a Conservative ought, together, to debar you from receiving a single vote. But of course I shall not interfere.'

'I thought it so good of you, sir, to tell Moreton to pay the bills.'

'That is another matter entirely. It is right that you should go into Parliament and not right that your income should be crippled by doing so.' After that nothing further was said between them on the matter.

When he was back at Matching he at once told his daughter what he had arranged for her, and then there took place a prolonged discussion both as to his view of her future life and as to her own. 'You did tell her, then, about Mr. Tregear?' she asked.

'As she is to have the charge of you for a time I thought it best.'

'Perhaps it is. Perhaps—you were afraid.'

'No; I was not afraid,' he said angrily.

'You need not be afraid. I shall do nothing elsewhere that I would not do here, and nothing anywhere without telling you.'

'I am sure you would not. I know I can trust you.'

'But, papa, I shall always intend to marry Mr. Tregear.'

'No!' he exclaimed.

'Yes;—always. I want you to understand exactly how it is. Nothing you can do can separate me from him.'

'Mary, that is very wicked.'

'It cannot be wicked to tell the truth, papa. I mean to try to do all that you tell me. I shall not see him, or write to him,—unless there should be some very particular reason. And if I did see him or write to him I would tell you. And of course I should not think of—of marrying, without your leave——'

'No, Mary.'

'But I shall expect you to let me marry him.'

'Never!'

'Then I shall think you are—cruel; and you will break my heart.'

'You should not call your father cruel.'

'I hope you will not be cruel.'

'I can never permit you to marry this man. It would be altogether improper. I cannot allow you to say that I am cruel because I do what I feel to be my duty. How would it be—if—if the man were even something lower?'

'He is a gentleman.'

'But if he were not, then should I be cruel? The cruelty would be the same.'

'That would be impossible, papa,' she said proudly.

'And so is this,—quite impossible. You will see other people——'

'A great many perhaps.'

'And will learn to,—to,—to forget him.'

'Never. I will not forget him. I should hate myself if I thought it possible. What would love be worth if it could be forgotten in that way?' As
he heard this he reflected whether his own wife, this girl's mother, had
ever forgotten her early love for that Burgo Fitzgerald whom in her
girlhood she had wished to marry. 'When do you want me to go, papa?'

'Lady Cantrip will write to you.'

'But about when? This is May Day. Shall I stay here a week longer?'

'She will hardly be ready at The Horns so soon as that.'

'Then I may expect to remain here ten days. I am not the least in
a hurry to go.' When he was leaving her she called him back again.
'There is one other thing I think I ought to say, papa. If Lady Cantrip
speaks to me about Mr. Tregear, I can only tell her what I have told you.
I shall never give him up.' When he heard this he turned angrily from
her, almost stamping his foot upon the ground, while she quietly left
the room.

Cruel! She had told him that he would be cruel, if he opposed her
love. He thought he knew of himself that he could not be cruel,—even
to a fly, even to a political opponent. There could be no cruelty without
dishonesty, and did he not always struggle to be honest? Cruel to his
own daughter! And on what ground was the charge based? There was
certainly some position,—a position possible at any rate to be thought
of,—in which it would be absolutely, clearly, his duty to debar his
daughter from marrying, let her pain in the matter be what it might. If
the man were a murderer, or an idiot! These were cases, possible cases,
in which he would have to do so, though she should die from the sufferings produced.* And, if a duty, then it could not be cruel. No conduct
can, at the same time, be good and bad. Yes;—though it would kill her,
he would have to do it. If so, then it was clear that he could not be justly
called cruel, simply because he debarred her from this marriage. The
cruelty, if there were cruelty, must depend on the fitness of the man. He
must make a line in his own mind, and declare that any man below that
line should be regarded unfit, and that he would reject the charge of
cruelty,—this most oppressive, wounding charge,—with reference to
any such man. But such a line could not be made palpable to any eyes
but his own. It must be a vague meandering line as to which, though he
should see it and know it thoroughly, he would be unable to lay down
any rules why it ascended here or descended here. But he was quite sure
that Mr. Tregear was below the line, infinitely below it, and that he
must be firm with his girl, allowing himself to be moved by no accusation of cruelty. If he were right he could not also be cruel,—and he
was sure that in doing this he would be right.

CHAPTER 12

AT RICHMOND

THE pity of it! The pity of it!* It was thus that Lady Cantrip looked at it. From what the girl's father had said to her she was disposed to believe that the malady had gone deep with her. 'All things go deep with her,' he had said. And she too from other sources had heard something of this girl. She was afraid that it would go deep. It was a thousand pities! Then she asked herself whether the marriage ought to be regarded as impossible. The Duke had been very positive,—had declared again and again that it was quite impossible, had so expressed himself as to make her aware that he intended her to understand that he would not yield, whatever the sufferings of the girl might be. But Lady Cantrip knew the world well and was aware that in such matters daughters are apt to be stronger than their fathers. He had declared Tregear to be a young man with very small means, and intent on such pleasures as require great means for their enjoyment. No worse character could be given to a gentleman who had proposed himself as a son-in-law. But Lady Cantrip thought it possible that the Duke might be mistaken in this. She had never seen Mr. Tregear, but she fancied that she had heard his name, and that the name had been connected with a character different from that which the Duke had given him. She therefore gave herself the task of making some inquiry on the subject.

Lady Cantrip, who at this time was a young-looking woman not much above forty, had two daughters, both of whom were married. The younger about a year since had become the wife of Lord Nidderdale,*— a middle-aged young man who had been long about town, a cousin of the late Duchess, the heir to a marquisate, and a member of Parliament. The marriage, however, had not been considered to be very brilliant, as the greater part of the income necessary for the newly married couple had for the present to be supplied by the lady's father. But the husband was himself good-natured and pleasant, and Lady Cantrip was fond of him. In the first place she went to him for information.

'Oh, yes,' he said, 'I know him. He's one of our set at the Beargarden.'

'Not your set, now, I hope,' she said laughing.

'Well,—I don't see so much of them certainly as I used to do. Tregear is not a bad fellow at all. He's always with Silverbridge. When Silverbridge does what Tregear tells him, he goes along pretty straight. But unfortunately there's another man called Tifto, and when Tifto is in the ascendant then Silverbridge is apt to get a little astray.'

'He's not in debt, then?'

'Who? Tregear? I should think he's the last man in the world to owe a penny to anyone.'

'Is he a betting man?'

'Oh dear no;—quite the other way up. He's a severe, sarcastic, bookish sort of fellow,—a chap who knows everything and turns up his nose at people who know nothing. The odd thing is that he and Silverbridge should suit each other.'

'Has he got anything of his own?'

'Not much, I should say. If he had had any money he would have married Lady Mab Grex last year. Don't you remember hearing it talked about?'

Lady Cantrip thought that she did remember hearing some gossip about it, and was inclined from what she now learned to think that the Duke must be wrong about the young man. But before Lady Mary joined her she made further inquiry. She too knew Lady Mabel, and knowing Lady Mabel, she knew Miss Casseway. She contrived to find herself alone with Miss Cassewary, and asked some further questions about Mr. Tregear. 'He is a cousin of my Lord's,' said Miss Cass.

'So I thought. I wonder what sort of a young man he is. He is a good deal with Lord Silverbridge.'

Then Miss Cassewary spoke her opinion very plainly. 'If Lord Silverbridge had nobody worse about him than Mr. Tregear he would not come to much harm. He is a very clever young man, and I know nothing evil of him.'

'I suppose he's not very well off.'

'No;—certainly not. He will have a property of some kind, I believe, when his mother dies. I think very well of Mr. Tregear;—only I wish that he had a profession.'

'What does he do then?'

'Nothing, as far as I know. But why are you asking about him, Lady Cantrip?'

'Nidderdale was talking to me about him and saying that he was so much with Lord Silverbridge. Lord Silverbridge is going into Parliament now, and, as it were, beginning the world, and it would be a thousand pities that he should get into bad hands.' It may, however, be doubted whether Miss Cassewary was hoodwinked by this little story. Miss Cassewary was a lady who generally saw things very plainly.

Early in the second week of May the Duke brought his daughter up to The Horns, and at the same time expressed his intention of remaining in London. When he did so Lady Mary at once asked whether she might not be with him, but he would not permit it. The house in London would, he said, be more gloomy even than Matching. It was his intention to resume his duties in the House of Lords. If he could be of any service to the country he ought not, he thought, to allow himself to be hindered by his personal sorrow from performing that service. On that same day he was even in his usual place on the opposition bench in the House of Lords,—in the place which had been usual to him when he himself was not in office.

'I am quite ashamed of giving you so much trouble,' Lady Mary said to her new friend.

'We are delighted to have you, my dear.'

'But I know that you have been obliged to leave London, because I am with you.'

'There is nothing I like so much as this place which your father has been kind enough to lend us. As for London there is nothing now to make me like being there. Both my girls are married, you know, and therefore I regard myself as an old woman who has done her work. Don't you think this place very much nicer than London at this time of the year?'

'I don't know London at all, hardly. I had only just been brought out when poor mamma went abroad. I seem to know much more about Florence than I do of London.'

The life they led was very quiet, and must probably have been felt to be dull by Lady Cantrip, in spite of her old age and desire for retirement. But the place itself was very lovely. May of all the months of the year is in England the most insidious, the most dangerous, and the most inclement. A greatcoat cannot be endured, and without a greatcoat who can endure a May wind and live? But of all months it is the prettiest. The grasses are then the greenest, and the young foliage of the trees, while it has all the glory and all the colour of spring vegetation, does not hide the form of the branches as do the heavy masses of the larger leaves which come in the advancing summer. And of all villas near London The Horns was the sweetest. The broad green lawn swept down to the very margin of the Thames, which absolutely washed the fringe of grass when the tide was high. And here, along the bank, was a row of flowering ashes, the drooping boughs of which in places touched the water. It was one of those spots which when they are first seen make the beholder feel that to be able to live there and look at it always would be happiness enough for life. Alas, it is a happiness which soon wears itself out. The joys of scenery will last a man his life, so that there be ever and again some novelty in it, or that some trouble be taken to reach it. But Alps and lakes, or rivers and plains, just before the window, will make no man or woman happy long. Lady Mary had that in her young heart which did suffice,—either for happiness or for sorrow. And as yet she had not so far recognised the difficulty of her position or the power of her father's opposition as to feel her love to be a cause for sorrow rather than joy. She could yet take pride to herself in the assurance of her constancy to the man she loved, and in her full conviction of his truth. To have a lover was all the world to her! To have one and never to have had another is all the world! To have had a dozen, even though one or two may still be left, is nothing. In this way Lady Mary's life was full enough; but before a week was over Lady Cantrip began to find that hers would be dull.

At the end of the first week there came a visitor to see Lady Mary. A very pretty carriage was driven up to the door of The Horns, and the servant asked for Lady Mary Palliser. The owner of that carriage was Mrs. Finn. Now it must be explained to the reader that there had never been any friendship between Mrs. Finn and Lady Cantrip, though the ladies had met each other. The great political intimacy which had existed between the Duke and Lord Cantrip had created some intimacy also between their wives. The Duchess and Lady Cantrip had been friends,—after a fashion. But Mrs. Finn had never been cordially accepted by those among whom Lady Cantrip chiefly lived. There was a certain amount of mystery attached to the very close alliance between Mrs. Finn and the late Duchess, and also between Mrs. Finn and the old Duke. Lady Cantrip did not like mystery, and she had never opened her arms to Mrs. Finn. When therefore the name was announced, the servant expressly stating that the visitor had asked for Lady Mary, Lady Cantrip, who was with her guest, had to bethink herself what she would do. The Duke, who as the reader will perhaps remember was at this time very full of wrath against Mrs. Finn, had not mentioned this lady's name when delivering up the charge of his daughter to Lady Cantrip. At this moment it occurred to her that not improbably Mrs. Finn would cease to be included in the intimacies of the Palliser family from the time of the death of the Duchess,—that the Duke would not care to maintain the old relations, and that he would be as little anxious to do it for his daughter as for himself. If so, could it be right that Mrs. Finn should come down here, to a house which was now in the occupation of a lady with whom she was not on visiting terms, in order that she might thus force herself on the Duke's daughter? Mrs. Finn had not left her carriage, but had sent in to ask if Lady Mary could see her. In all this there was considerable embarrassment, which was not lessened by a consciousness on the part of the older lady that Mrs. Finn's husband had been, and still was, very highly esteemed by her own husband. She looked round at her guest, who had at once risen from her chair. 'Would you wish to see her?' asked Lady Cantrip.

'Oh yes;—certainly.'

'Have you seen her since,—since you came home from Italy?'

'Oh dear, yes! She was down at Matching when poor mamma died. And papa persuaded her to remain afterwards. Of course I will see her.' Then the servant was desired to ask Mrs. Finn to come in;—and while this was being done Lady Cantrip retired.

Mrs. Finn embraced her young friend, and asked after her welfare, and after the welfare of the house in which she was staying,—a house with which Mrs. Finn herself had been well acquainted,—and said half-a-dozen pretty little things in her own quiet pretty way, before she spoke of the matter which had really brought her to The Horns on that day.

'I have had a correspondence with your father, Mary.'

'Indeed.'

'And unfortunately one that has been far indeed from agreeable to me.'

'I am sorry for that, Mrs. Finn.'

'So am I; very sorry. I may say with perfect truth that there is no man in the world, except my own husband, for whom I feel so perfect an esteem as I do for your father. If it were not that I do not like to be carried away by strong language I would speak of more than esteem. Through your dear mother I have watched his conduct closely and have come to think that there is, perhaps, no other man at the same time so just and so patriotic. Now he is very angry with me,—and most unjustly angry.'

'Is it about me?'

'Yes;—it is about you. Had it not been altogether about you I would not have troubled you with a matter so disagreeable.'

'And about——?'

'Yes;—about Mr. Tregear also. When I tell you that there has been a correspondence I must explain that I have written one long letter to the Duke, and that in answer I have received a very short one. That has been the whole correspondence. Here is your father's letter to me.' Then she brought out of her pocket a note, which Lady Mary read,—covered with blushes as she did so. The note was as follows:

'The Duke of Omnium understands from Mrs. Finn's letter that Mrs. Finn, while she was the Duke's guest at Matching, was aware of a certain circumstance affecting the Duke's honour and happiness,—which circumstance she certainly did not communicate to the Duke. The Duke thinks that the trust which had been placed in Mrs. Finn should have made such a communication imperative. The Duke feels that no further correspondence between himself and Mrs. Finn on the matter could lead to any good result.'

'Do you understand it?' asked Mrs. Finn.

'I think so.'

'It simply means this,—that when at Matching he had thought me worthy of having for a time the charge of you and of your welfare, that he had trusted me, who was the friend of your dear mother, to take for a time in regard to you the place which had been so unhappily left vacant by her death;—and it means also that I deceived him and betrayed that trust by being privy to an engagement on your part of which he disapproves and of which he was not then aware.'

'I suppose he does mean that.'

'Yes, Lady Mary; that is what he means. And he means further to let me know that as I did so foully betray the trust which he had placed in me,—that as I had consented to play the part of assistant to you in that secret engagement,—therefore he casts me off as altogether unworthy of his esteem and acquaintance. It is as though he had told me in so many words that among women he had known none more vile or more false than I.'

'Not that, Mrs. Finn.'

'Yes; that;—all of that. He tells me that, and then says that there shall be no more words spoken or written about it. I can hardly submit to so stern a judgment. You know the truth, Lady Mary.'

'Do not call me Lady Mary. Do not quarrel with me.'

'If your father has quarrelled with me, it would not be fit that you and I should be friends. Your duty to him would forbid it. I should not have come to you now did I not feel that I am bound to justify myself. The charge against me is so heavy, the thing of which I am accused is so repugnant to me, that I am obliged to do something and to say something, even though the subject itself be one on which I would so willingly be silent.'

'What can I do, Mrs. Finn?'

'It was Mr. Tregear who first told me that your father was angry with me. It had been talked of I think between him and your brother. But he knew what I had done and why, and he, I think, was bound to do as he did in order that I might have an opportunity of setting myself right with the Duke. Then I wrote and explained everything,—how you had told me of the engagement and how I had then urged Mr. Tregear that he should not keep such a matter secret from your father. In answer to my letter I have received—that.'

'Shall I write and tell papa;—or shall I talk to him?'

'I wish that he should be made to understand that from the moment in which I heard of the engagement I was urgent with you and with Mr. Tregear that he should be informed of it. You will remember what passed.'

'I remember it all.'

'I did not conceive it to be my duty to tell the Duke myself, but I did conceive it to be my duty to see that he should be told. Now he writes as though I had known the secret from the first, and as though I had been concealing it from him at the very moment in which he was asking me to remain at Matching on your behalf. That I consider to be hard,—and unjust. I cannot deny what he says. I did know of it while I was at Matching, for it was at Matching that you told me. But he implies that I knew it before. When you told me your story I did feel that it was my duty to see that the matter was not kept longer from him;—and I did my duty. Now your father takes upon himself to rebuke me,—and takes upon himself at the same time to forbid me to write to him again!'

'I will tell him all, Mrs. Finn.'

'Let him understand this. I do not wish to write to him again. After what has passed I cannot say I wish to see him again. But I think he should write me to acknowledge that he has been mistaken. He need not then fear that I shall trouble him with any reply. But I shall know that he has acquitted me of a fault of which I cannot bear to think I should be accused.' Then she took a somewhat formal though still an affectionate farewell of the girl, kissing her, and expressing strongly her wish for Lady Mary's future happiness.

'I want to see papa as soon as possible,' said Lady Mary when she was again with Lady Cantrip. Of course the reason for her wish was soon given, and then the whole story told. 'You do not think that she should have gone to papa at once?' Lady Mary asked. It was a point of moral law on which the elder woman, who had had girls of her own, found it hard to give an immediate answer. It certainly is expedient that parents should know at once of any engagement by which their daughters may seek to contract themselves. It is expedient that they should be able to prevent any secret contracts. Lady Cantrip was quite well assured of that. And she was quite sure that Mrs. Finn, having accepted, as it were, from the father's hands the confidential charge of the daughter, could not with any honesty, could not without gross fraud and betrayal of trust, allow herself to be the depositary of such a secret. 'But she did not allow herself,' said Lady Mary, pleading for her friend.

'But she left the house without telling him, my dear.'

'But it was because of what she did that he was told.'

'That is true;—but I doubt whether she should have left him an hour in ignorance.'

'But it was I who told her. She would have betrayed me.'

'She was not a fit recipient for your confidence, Mary. But I do not wish to accuse her. She seems to be a high-minded woman and I think that your papa has been a little hard upon her.'

'And mamma knew it, always,' said Mary. To this Lady Cantrip could give no answer. Whatever cause for anger the Duke might have against Mrs. Finn, there had been cause for much more against his wife. But she had freed herself from all accusation by death. What a pity it was, Lady Cantrip thought, that the whole matter should not be settled and put an end to by a marriage. The Duke could give them ample money. Persons who are less rich always fancy that they who are more rich have super-abundant means for everything. Three or four hundred thousand pounds would be as nothing to the Duke of Omnium;—and then Tregear might go into Parliament and probably become a Speaker, and possibly a member of Government. One of her own daughters was married to a commoner,—but then he fortunately was a man of large possessions.

Lady Mary wrote to her father, declaring that she was most 'particularly anxious to see him and talk to him about Mrs. Finn.'

CHAPTER 13

THE DUKE'S INJUSTICE

No advantage whatever was obtained by Lady Mary's interview with her father. He persisted that Mrs. Finn had been untrue to him and to the charge which she had accepted from his hands when she left Matching without telling him all that she knew of his daughter's engagement with Mr. Tregear. No doubt by degrees that idea which he at first entertained was expelled from his head,—the idea that she had been cognisant of the whole thing before she came to Matching; but even this was done so slowly that there was no moment at which he became aware of any lessened feeling of indignation. The fact at any rate remained that she had been aware of this iniquity while she was holding intercourse with him about his daughter, and that she had concealed it.

No doubt there returned at this time to the Duke's mind something of the feeling towards this woman which had been strong with him when first his wife had proposed her to him as a friend. He too had thought,—he as well as Lady Cantrip and others,—that she had been in some degree mysterious and, in the same degree, objectionable. At any rate she was not one of his class. She had then been a widow, and even up to this day he had heard nothing of her first husband except that he had died leaving her a rich woman. She had no doubt behaved well in very peculiar circumstances. She might herself have been at this very moment a Duchess of Omnium, the old Duke having asked her to marry him. She had refused,—no doubt very wisely in reference to her own happiness;—but there had seemed to be something noble in her refusal. The late Duchess had so regarded it, and had consequently opened her heart to the woman. He had gradually been carried along with his wife, and had submitted himself to an intimacy which had been contrary to his taste.* Other matters also had acted much in her favour,—first and chiefly, no doubt, his own appreciation of a certain modesty on her part. Intimate as she had been in the house, she had never been familiar in her manner with himself. She had borne herself in those days as though there must always be something of a gulf between the Duke of Omnium and Madame Max Goesler, as she was then called. He was the last man in the world to tell himself that this was a recommendation; but he had felt it as such. Then it had chanced that she had married a man with whom he had close political relations. And then too there had been the matter of a legacy, a very large legacy, left her by the old Duke, as to which, though he had strenuously opposed her, still he had admired her conduct. Of what the old man had left her she would take nothing,—and even at this very day there was lying packed up in the vaults beneath the premises of the Duke's bankers near Charing Cross a collection of diamonds, said to be worth a very great sum of money, which was in truth the property of this woman but which she had hitherto positively refused to accept. These things had, after a fashion, reconciled even his stubborn nature to his wife's friend. He had become, if not absolutely intimate with her, at least so much more intimate than with any other woman, that he had asked her to remain with his daughter at Matching. Even when doing so he remembered that she had been the mysterious widow of an unheard-of old husband; but still he had asked her. And she had betrayed his trust! So he declared to himself; and he asked himself at the same time what else he had a right to expect from the mysterious widow of an unheard-of old husband.

To his thinking she had betrayed her trust, and he could not be got by his daughter to say that he would forgive her. He certainly could not be got to say that he would apologise for the accusation he had made. It was nothing less that his daughter asked; and he could hardly refrain himself from anger when she asked it. 'There should not have been a moment,' he said, 'before she came to me and told me all.' Poor Lady Mary's position was certainly uncomfortable enough. The great sin,—the sin which was so great that to have known it for a day without revealing it was in itself a damning sin on the part of Mrs. Finn,—was Lady Mary's sin. And she differed so entirely from her father as to think that this sin of her own was a virtue, and that to have spoken of it to him would have been, on the part of Mrs. Finn, a treachery so deep that no woman ought to have forgiven it! Each of them in this interview tried to avoid any special reference to Mr. Tregear;—but it was difficult. When he spoke of a matter which deeply affected his honour,—clearly implying that his honour was touched even by the thought of such an alliance,—she could hardly refrain from asserting that his honour was quite safe in his daughter's hands, and when in his heat he declared that it should have been Mrs. Finn's first care to save him from disgrace, Lady Mary did break out. 'Papa,' she said, 'there could be no disgrace.' 'That for a moment shall be laid aside,' he said, with that manner by which even his peers in council had never been able not to be awed, 'but, if you communicate with Mrs. Finn at all you must make her understand that as I regard her conduct as inexcusable, I cannot apologise for what she thinks is the severity of my letter to her.'

Nothing had been gained, and poor Lady Mary was compelled to write a few lines which were to her most painful in the writing.

'MY DEAR MRS. FINN,

'I have seen papa, and he thinks that you ought to have told him when I told you. It seems to me that that would have been a cruel thing to do, and most unfair to Mr. Tregear, who was quite willing to go to papa and had only put off doing so because of the circumstances of poor dear mamma's death. As I had told mamma, of course it was right that he should tell papa. Then I told you, because you were so kind to me! I am so sorry that I have got you into this trouble; but what can I do? I hope you will not be angry with me because papa is so severe.

'I told him I must write to you. I suppose it is better that I should, although what I have to say is so unpleasant. I hope it will all blow over in time because I love you dearly. You may be quite sure of one thing,—that I shall never change.' In this assurance the writer was alluding not to her friendship for her friend but her love for her lover,—and so the friend understood her. 'I hope things will be settled some day, and that then we may be able to meet.

'Your very affectionate Friend,
'MARY PALLISER.'

Mrs. Finn, when she received this, was alone in her house in Park Lane. Her husband, who had to look after his seat in the House of Commons,* was down in the North of England canvassing. On this sub-ject she had not spoken to him, fearing that he would feel himself bound to take some steps to support his wife under the treatment she had received. Even though she must quarrel with the Duke,—and that now did seem to be altogether necessary,—she was most anxious that her hus-band should not be compelled to do so. Their connection had been not only personal, but political also;—and, indeed, political rather than per-sonal. There were many reasons why there should be no open cause of disruption between them. But her husband was hot-headed, and, were all this to be told him and that letter shown to him which the Duke had written, there would be words between him and the Duke which would probably make impossible any further connection between them, even of a political nature. She was, therefore, obliged to bear her trouble alone.

And it troubled her very much. She was by no means not alive to the honour of the Duke's friendship. Throughout her intimacy with the Duchess she had abstained from pressing herself on him, not because she had been indifferent about him but that, having watched him closely and having thought much of his character, she had perceived that she might make her way with him better by standing aloof than by thrusting herself forward. And she had known that she had been successful. She could tell herself with pride that her conduct towards him had been always such as would become a lady of high spirit and fine feeling. She knew that she had deserved well of him, that in all her intercourse with him, with his uncle, and with his wife, she had given much and had taken little. She was the last woman in the world to let a word on such a matter pass her lips, even to her husband; but not the less was she conscious of her merit towards him. And she had been led to act as she had done by sincere admiration for the man,—and especially by admiration for his justice. In all their political troubles,—and there had been such troubles in which the Duke and his wife had been concerned,—she had under-stood him better than the Duchess had done. Looking on from a distance and seldom having an opportunity of hearing much from himself, she had understood the man's character as it had come to her both from his wife and from her own husband. The man's honesty had specially endeared itself to her,—his honesty and strong sense of justice. And now she was being treated with the greatest injustice by this most just of men!

That he was unjust to her,—cruelly unjust,—she was quite sure. He accused her of intentional privity as to a secret which it behoved him to know, and of being a party to that secrecy. Whereas from the moment in which she heard the secret, she had determined that it must be made known to him without delay and had been successful in carrying out that determination. She felt that she had deserved his good opinion in all things, but in nothing more than in the way in which she had acted in this matter. And yet he had treated her with an imperious harshness which amounted to insolence. What a letter it was that he had written to her! The very tips of her ears tingled with heat as she read it again to herself. None of the ordinary courtesies of epistle-craft had been preserved either in the beginning or in the end. It was worse even than if he had called her 'Madam' without an epithet. 'The Duke understands——!' 'The Duke thinks——!' 'The Duke feels——!' feels that he should not be troubled with either letters or conversation; the upshot of it all being that the Duke declared her to have shown herself to be unworthy of being treated like a lady! And this after all that she had done!

She would not bear it. That at present was all that she could say to herself. Lady Mary's note certainly did not improve her position. She was not at all angry with Lady Mary. She did not doubt but that the girl had done the best in her power to bring her father to reason. But because Lady Mary had failed, she, Mrs. Finn, was not going to put up with so grievous an injury. And she was forced to bear all this alone! There was none with whom she could communicate;—no one from whom she could ask advice. She would not bring her husband into a quarrel which might be prejudicial to his position as a member of his political party. There was no one else to whom she would tell the secret of Lady Mary's love. And yet she could not bear this injustice done to her.

On the day after that on which she received Lady Mary's note she wrote as follows to the Duke:

'Mrs. Finn presents her compliments to the Duke of Omnium. Mrs. Finn finds it to be essential to her that she should see the Duke in reference to his letter to her. If his Grace will let her know on what day and at what hour he will be kind enough to call on her, Mrs. Finn will be at home to receive him.

'Park Lane. Thursday, 12th May, 187—.'

CHAPTER 14

THE NEW MEMBER FOR SILVERBRIDGE

LORD SILVERBRIDGE was informed that it would be right that he should go down to Silverbridge a few days before the election, to make himself known to the electors. As the day for the election drew near it was understood that there would be no other candidate. The young Lord had no doubt had some true insights as to the matter when he told his father that he would be supported both by his own politics and by the family interest. There could be no doubt but that the Conservative side was the popular side among the tradesmen of Silverbridge. Silverbridge had been proud to be honoured by the services of the heir of the house of Omnium, even while that heir had been a Liberal,—had regarded it as so much a matter of course that the borough should be at his disposal that no question as to politics had ever arisen while he retained the seat. And had the Duke chosen to continue to send them Liberals, one after another, when he went into the House of Lords, there would have been no question as to the fitness of the man or men so sent. Silverbridge had been Liberal as a matter of course,*—because the Pallisers were Liberal. It had never occurred to the voters in the borough to look into their own minds and find out what were their own opinions. It was to them not at all a grievance that they were called on to return a Liberal. But when the matter was remitted to themselves,—when the Duke declared that he would not interfere any more, for it was thus that the borough had obtained its freedom;—then the borough had scratched its head, had bethought itself, and had begun to feel Conservative pre-dilections. 'If his Grace really does mean us to do just what we please ourselves, which is a thing we never thought of asking from his Grace, then we find, having turned the matter over among ourselves, that we are, upon the whole, Conservative.' In this spirit the borough had elected a certain Mr. Fletcher; but in doing so the borough had still a shade of fear,—in spite of reiterated assurances from the Duke to the contrary,—that it would offend the Duke. The house of Palliser, Gatherum Castle, the Duke of Omnium, and this special Duke himself, were all so great in the eyes of the borough, that the first and only strong feeling in the borough was one of duty. The borough did not altogether enjoy being enfranchised. But when the Duke had spoken once, twice, and thrice, then with a hesitating heart, and activated by causes which have been described elsewhere,* the borough returned

Mr. Fletcher. Now Mr. Fletcher was wanted elsewhere, having been persuaded to stand for the county, and it was a great comfort to the borough that it could in some sort resettle itself beneath the warmth of the wings of the Pallisers.

Mr. Du Boung,* who was a brewer, a native, rich and popular, and a Liberal, vainly endeavoured at certain meetings to make the borough understand that the Duke was honest enough in his politics to prefer a Liberal even to his own son, when he insinuated that the father was much offended by his son's apostasy, and would be offended with the borough, should the borough aid the apostate. The borough altogether refused to believe him. A landlord,—such a landlord at any rate as the Duke,—could not be offended with his tenants for sending his own son to Parliament. So they argued it among themselves, and Mr. Du Boung found that he would not have a chance. He retired therefore, putting forth a very graceful document in which he declared his opinion that no differences in politics could justify an opposition to a scion of the house of Palliser in the borough of Silverbridge. This he took care to send to the Duke,—who was fortified in his opinion by it as to the worthlessness of Mr. Du Boung as a politician.

So the matter stood when Lord Silverbridge was told that his presence in the borough for a few hours would be taken as a compliment. Hitherto no one knew him at Silverbridge. During his boyhood he had not been much at Gatherum Castle, and had done his best to eschew the place since he had ceased to be a boy. All the Pallisers took a pride in Gatherum Castle and its vicinity,—but they all disliked it. 'Oh yes, I'll go down,' he said to Mr. Moreton, who was up in town. 'I needn't go to the great barrack, I suppose.' The great barrack was the Castle. 'I'll put up at the inn.' Mr. Moreton begged the heir to come to his own house, but Silverbridge declared that he would prefer the inn, and so the matter was settled. He was to meet sundry politicians,— Mr. Sprugeon and Mr. Sprout, and Mr. Du Boung himself,—who of course would like to be thanked for what they had done. But who was to go with him? He would naturally have asked Tregear, but from Tregear he had for the last week or two been, not perhaps estranged, but separated. He had been much taken up with racing. He had gone down to Chester with Major Tifto, and under the Major's auspicious influences had won a little money there. And now he was very anxiously preparing himself for the Newmarket Second Spring Meeting, on which occasion he intended to run a horse,—also under the Major's auspices. He had therefore passed much of his time with Major Tifto. And when this visit to Silverbridge was pressed on him he thoughtlessly asked Tifto to go with him. Tifto was delighted. Lord Silverbridge was to be met at Silverbridge by various well-known politicians from the neighbourhood, and Major Tifto was greatly elated by the prospect of such an introduction into the political world.

But no sooner had the offer been made by Lord Silverbridge than he acknowledged to himself that he had been guilty of an indiscretion. Tifto was very well for Chester or Newmarket, very well perhaps for the Beargarden, but not very well for an electioneering expedition. An idea came to the young nobleman that if it should be his fate to represent Silverbridge in Parliament for the next twenty years, it would be well that Silverbridge should entertain respecting him some exalted estimation,—that Silverbridge should be taught to regard him as a fit son of his father and a worthy specimen of the young British political nobility. Struck by serious reflections of this nature he did open his mind to Tregear, whom he met by chance at the club. 'I am very fond of Tifto,' he said, 'but I don't know whether he's just the sort of fellow to take down to an election.'

'I should think not,' said Tregear very decidedly.

'He's a very good fellow, you know,' said Silverbridge, arguing as men are apt to do on such occasions against his own original proposition. 'I don't know an honester man than Tifto anywhere.'

'I dare say. Or rather, I don't dare say. I know nothing about the Major's honesty and I doubt whether you do. He rides very well.'

'What has that to do with it?'

'Nothing on earth. Therefore I advise you not to take him to Silverbridge. The matter is important, and therefore I have no hesitation in saying that it would be a very foolish thing to do.'

'You needn't preach.'

'You may call it what you like. Tifto would not hold his tongue and there is nothing he could say there which would not be to your prejudice.'

'Will you go?'

'If you wish it,' said Tregear.

'What will the governor say?'

'That must be your look-out. In a political point of view I shall not disgrace you. I shall hold my tongue and look like a gentleman,—neither of which is in Tifto's power. I don't suppose the Duke could be more offended than he is at present. He has no objection to me, I take it, except in so far as I am a suitor for your sister's hand.' And so it was settled,—that on the day but one after this conversation Lord Silverbridge and Tregear should go together to Silverbridge.

But the Major, when on that same night his noble friend's altered plans were explained to him, did not bear the disappointment with equanimity. 'Isn't that a little strange?' he said, becoming very red in the face. He had said so much about this political movement that many of his second-class friends had almost been made to believe that he was going to become a member of Parliament himself.

'What do you call strange?' said the Lord.

'Well;—I'd made all my arrangements. When a man has been asked to do a thing like that, he doesn't like to be put off. I know whose doing it is.'

'Whose doing is it?'

'Never mind. I shall mention no names.'

'The truth is, Tifto, when I came to think of it I saw that, going down to these fellows about Parliament and all that sort of thing, I ought to have a political atmosphere and not a racing, or a betting, or a hunting atmosphere.'

'There isn't a man in London who cares more about politics than I do;—and not very many perhaps who understand them better. To tell you the truth, my Lord, I think you're throwing me over.'

'I'll make it up to you,' said Silverbridge, meaning to be kind. 'I'll go down to Newmarket with you and stick to you like wax.'

'No doubt you'll do that,' said Tifto, who, like a fool, failed to see where his advantage lay. 'I can be useful at Newmarket and so you'll stick to me. I like a friend who will stick to me all round.'

'Look here, Major Tifto,' said Silverbridge, 'if you are dissatisfied you and I can easily separate ourselves. You can go one way and I can go another.'

'I am not dissatisfied,' said the little man, almost crying.

'Then don't talk as though you were. As to Silverbridge I shall not want you to go there with me. When I asked you I was only thinking what would be pleasant for both of us; but since that I have remembered that business must be business.' Even this, in which he ought to have found a compliment, did not reconcile the angry little man, who as he turned away declared within his own little bosom that he would 'take it out of Silverbridge for that.'

Lord Silverbridge and Tregear went down to the borough together, and on the journey something was said about Lady Mary,—and something also about Lady Mabel. 'From the first, you know,' said Lady Mary's brother, 'I never thought it would answer.'

'Why not answer?'

'Because I knew the governor would not have it. Money and rank and those sort of things are not particularly charming to me. I believe that I think as little about them as most men. But still things should go together. It is all very well for you and me to be pals, but of course it will be expected that Mary should marry some——'

'Some swell?'

'Some swell if you will have it.'

'You mean to call yourself a swell?'

'Yes I do,' said Silverbridge, with considerable resolution. 'You ought not to make yourself disagreeable, because you understand all about it as well as anybody. Chance has made me the eldest son of a duke and the heir to an enormous fortune. Chance has made my sister the daughter of a duke, and an heiress also. My intimacy with you ought to be proof at any rate to you that I don't on that account set myself up above other fellows. I think a deal more of a fellow being clever than of his having rank or money. But when you come to talk of marriage of course it's a different thing.'

'But you have told me more than once that you have no objection on your own score.'

'Nor have I.'

'You are only saying what the Duke will think.'

'I am telling you that it is impossible, and I told you so before. You and she will be kept apart, and so——'

'And so she'll forget me?'

'Something of that kind.'

'Of course I have to trust to her for that. If she forgets me, well and good.'

'She needn't forget you. Lord bless me! You talk as though the thing were not done every day. You'll hear some morning that she is going to marry some fellow who has a lot of money and a good position; and what difference will it make then whether she has forgotten you or not?' It might almost have been supposed that the young man had been acquainted with his mother's history.

After this there was a pause, and there arose conversation about other things, and a cigar was smoked. Then Tregear returned once more to the subject. 'There is one thing I wish to say about it all.'

'What is that?'

'I want you to understand that nothing else will turn me away from my intention but such a marriage on her part as that of which you speak. That is of course possible. I may be deceived about her. But nothing that your father can do will turn me.'

'She can't marry without his leave.'

'Perhaps not.'

'That he'll never give,—and I don't suppose you look forward to waiting till his death.'

'If he sees that her happiness really depends on it he will give his leave. It all depends on that. If I judge your father rightly, he's just as soft-hearted as other people. The man who holds out is not the man of the firmest opinion, but the man of the hardest heart.'

'Somebody will talk Mary over.'

'If so, the thing is over. It all depends on her.' Then he went on to tell his friend that he had spoken of his engagement to Lady Mabel. 'I have mentioned it to no soul but to your father and to her.'

'Why to her?'

'Because we were friends together as children. I never had a sister, but she has been more like a sister to me than anyone else. Do you object to her knowing it?'

'Not particularly. It seems to me now that everybody knows everything. There are no longer any secrets.'

'But she is a special friend.'

'Of yours,' said Silverbridge.

'And of yours,' said Tregear.

'Well, yes;—in a sort of a way. She is the jolliest girl I know;—but I should hardly think of talking to her about things of that sort.'

'That is because you don't know her well enough. Take her all round, for beauty, intellect, good sense, and fun at the same time, I don't know anyone equal to her.'

'It's a pity you didn't fall in love with her.'

'We knew each other too early for that. And then she has not a shilling. I should think myself dishonest if I did not tell you that I could not afford to love any girl who hadn't money. A man must live,—and a woman too. I don't think I'm at all mercenary. Such a girl as Mabel Grex is to me like the throne of the Sultan. Whatever place I may be able to get to, I know that at any rate I cannot get there.'

At the station they were met by Mr. Sprugeon and Mr. Sprout, who, with many apologies for the meanness of such entertainment, took them up to the George and Vulture,* which was supposed for the nonce to be the Conservative hotel in the town. Here they were met by other men of importance in the borough, and among them by Mr. Du Boung. Now Mr. Sprout and Mr. Sprugeon were Conservatives, but Mr. Du Boung was a strong Liberal.

'We are, all of us, particularly glad to see your lordship among us,' said Mr. Du Boung.

'I have told his lordship how perfectly satisfied you are to see the borough in his lordship's hands,' said Mr. Sprugeon.

'I am sure it could not be in better hands,' said Mr. Du Boung. 'For myself I am quite willing to postpone any peculiar shade of politics to the advantage of having your father's son as our representative.' This Mr. Du Boung said with much intention of imparting both grace and dignity to the occasion. He thought that he was doing a great thing for the house of Omnium, and that the house of Omnium ought to know it.

'That's very kind of you,' said Lord Silverbridge, who had not read as carefully as he should have done the letters which had been sent to him, and did not therefore quite understand the position.

'Mr. Du Boung had intended to stand himself,' said Mr. Sprout.

'But retired in your lordship's favour,' said Mr. Sprugeon.

'In doing which I considered that I studied the interests of the borough,' said Mr. Du Boung.

'I thought you gave it up because there was hardly a footing for a Liberal,' said his lordship, very imprudently.

'The borough was always Liberal till the last election,' said Mr. Du Boung, drawing himself up.

'The borough wishes on this occasion to be magnanimous,' said Mr. Sprout, probably having in his mind some confusion between magnanimity and unanimity.

'As your lordship is coming among us, the borough is anxious to sink politics altogether for the moment,' said Mr. Sprugeon. There had no doubt been a compact between the Sprugeon and Sprout party and the Du Boung party in accordance with which it had been arranged that Mr. Du Boung should be entitled to a certain amount of glorification in the presence of Lord Silverbridge.

'And it was in compliance with that wish on the part of the borough, my Lord,' said Mr. Du Boung,—'as to which my own feelings were certainly quite as strong as that of any other gentleman in the borough,—that I conceived it to be my duty to give way. There are those in the borough who, thinking that they would have secured my return on Liberal principles, do not hesitate to tell me that I have been wrong. But it has been a matter of feeling, my Lord;—and I have obeyed my feelings.'

'His lordship is quite aware how much he owes to Mr. Du Boung,' said Tregear. Whereupon Lord Silverbridge bowed, perhaps not quite understanding the position even yet, and at the same time being unwilling, in so far as he did understand it, to express any gratitude to Mr. Du

Boung for retiring from a position which would have been untenable. Whereupon Mr. Du Boung held his head a little higher than before, and put his hands into his trowser pockets. Mr. Sprugeon, very cautiously, just with a corner of his eye, winked at Mr. Sprout, and a gentleman who was in the corner of the room, a staunch Conservative and no less a person than the landlord of the George and Vulture himself, whispered to his neighbour, Mr. Cloral the chemist, that his lordship seemed to have cut his eye-teeth.*

'And now what are we to do?' said Lord Silverbridge.

Then there was a little whispering between Mr. Sprout and Mr. Sprugeon. 'Perhaps, Mr. Du Boung,' said Sprugeon, 'his lordship had better call first on Dr. Tempest.'

'Perhaps,' said the injured brewer, 'as it is to be a party affair after all, I had better retire from the scene.'

'I thought all that was to be given up,' said Tregear.

'Oh, certainly,' said Sprout. 'Suppose we go to Mr. Walker first.'

'I'm up to anything,' said Lord Silverbridge, 'and am quite ready to express my gratitude to Liberals or Conservatives who will help to return me. But of course everybody understands that I am a Conservative.'

'Oh dear, yes,' said Sprugeon.

'We are all aware of that,' said Sprout.

'And very glad we've, all of us, been to hear it,' said the landlord.

'Though there are some in the borough who could have wished, my Lord, that you had stuck to the old Palliser politics,' said Mr. Du Boung, who found himself able to say an honest word as to his own opinion now that so poor a response had been made to his just claim for gratitude.

'But I haven't stuck to the Palliser politics. I couldn't for worlds let there be any misunderstanding. Just at present I think that order and all that sort of thing should be maintained.'

'Hear, hear!' said the landlord.

'And now, as I have expressed my views generally, I am willing to go anywhere.'

'Then we'll go to Mr. Walker first,' said Sprugeon. Now it was understood that in the borough, among those who really had opinions of their own, Mr. Walker the old attorney stood first as a Liberal, and Dr. Tempest the old rector first as a Conservative. There had been a great deal of conversation in the borough as to priority between the parties,—both of which were to be represented by this new member; and now, when Mr. Sprout suggested and Mr.

Sprugeon afterwards agreed that the first visit should be made to Mr. Walker, those around, with the exception of the two strangers from London, were aware that a sop was being offered to Mr. Du Boung. After what had passed he would not have accompanied them to Dr. Tempest's house, had Dr. Tempest been taken before Mr. Walker. But, as it was, with an ill grace, walking not behind but a little on one side so as to be very visible almost in the centre of the street, he did go with them.

'I am glad to see your lordship in the town which gives you its name,' said Mr. Walker, who was a hale old gentleman with silvery-white hair, over seventy years of age. 'I proposed your father for this borough on, I think, six or seven different occasions. They used to go in and out then whenever they changed their offices.'

'We hope you'll propose Lord Silverbridge now,' said Mr. Sprugeon. This, too, was intended to propitiate Mr. Du Boung.

'Oh; well;—yes. He's his father's son, and I never knew anything but good of the family. I wish you were going to sit on the same side, my Lord. I don't like these new lights.'

'Times are changed a little, perhaps,' said his lordship.

'The matter is not to be discussed now,' said the old attorney. 'I understand that. Only I hope you'll excuse me if I say that a man ought to get up very early in the morning if he means to see further into politics than your father.'

'Very early indeed,' said Mr. Du Boung, shaking his head.

'That's all right,' said Lord Silverbridge.

'I'll propose you, my Lord. I need not wish you success, because there is no one to stand against you. Good-morning.'

Then they went to Dr. Tempest, who was also an old man. 'Yes, my Lord, I shall be proud to second you,' said the rector. 'I didn't think that I should ever do that to one of your name in Silverbridge.'

'I hope you think I've made a change for the better,' said the candidate.

'You've come over to my school of course, and I suppose I am bound to think that a change for the better. Nevertheless I have a kind of idea that certain people ought to be Tories and that other certain people ought to be Whigs.* What does your father say about it?'

'My father wishes me to be in the House, and that he has not quarrelled with me you may know by the fact that had there been a contest he would have paid my expenses.'

'A father generally has to do that whether he approves of what his son is about or not,' said the caustic old gentleman.

Then Mr. Du Boung took one further opportunity,—the last which probably would be allowed him,—of setting himself right with the borough. 'I am sure Dr. Tempest,' said he, 'will agree with me in thinking that our chief duty at present is to maintain the kindly relations which have ever existed between his Grace and the borough.' He paused for the rector's assent, but the rector only smiled. 'That, at least, has been my feeling in the matter. That is the sentiment by which my conduct has been governed. I am a Liberal. I don't care who knows it. I am proud of my political creed. But the circumstances of this borough are very peculiar, and I think it to be for the advantage of the borough generally that it should be represented in Parliament by the son of the Duke of Omnium.'

'I'm sure I'm very much obliged to you,' said Lord Silverbridge. Then there was another pause, but as Dr. Tempest would not say a word in answer to Mr. Du Boung,—as he only smiled,—Mr. Du Boung led the way out of the room; and with a great shaking of hands that little conference was brought to an end.

There was nothing else to be done. They all went back to the hotel, and Mr. Sprugeon with Mr. Sprout and the landlord drank a glass of sherry at the candidate's expense, wishing him political long life and prosperity. Mr. Du Boung was of course invited to join them, but excused himself. For the advantage of the borough he had come forward, but of gala doings in such company he would know nothing. There was no one else whom it was thought necessary that the candidate should visit, and on the next day he returned to town with the understanding that on the day appointed in the next week he should come back again to be elected. He was not even asked to make a speech, which was a relief to him,—though in a certain way a disappointment also, as he had spent an hour or two in the composition of a few words in which he had intended to explain his politics. He thought he had done this rather well;—but at the same time he doubted his memory, and told himself that upon the whole it was as well that he should have been spared.

'I can't conceive why you should have been so uncivil to that fellow Du Boung,' Tregear said to him in the train.

'Because he told lies. Only I didn't think I was uncivil to him.'

'Oh yes, you were. What lies did he tell?'

'He wanted to make out that if he had stood against me he would have been elected. Everybody knows that he did give up because he hadn't a chance.'

'But when a man does give up, of course he expects to be thanked. He probably saved you six or seven hundred pounds.'

'And himself too. I'm not going to thank a fellow when I'm not a bit obliged to him. I hate a fellow who talks trash to me about feeling. If he's a Liberal he ought to stick to his party and keep me out if he can. The only person I'm obliged to in the whole matter is my governor,— and to you, old chap, for coming down with me.'

On the day appointed the two young men again went to Silverbridge, and on this occasion, after he had been declared duly elected, the new member of Parliament was allowed to make his speech. There was a meeting in the town-hall, and many were assembled anxious to hear,—not the lad's opinions, for which probably nobody cared much,—but the tone of his voice, and to see his manner. Of what sort was the eldest son of the man of whom the neighbourhood had been so proud? For the county was in truth proud of their Duke. Of this son whom they had now made a member of Parliament they at present only knew that he had been sent away from Oxford,—not so very long ago,—for painting the Dean's house scarlet. At no time of his life could the father have done such a thing as that. The speech was not very brilliant. He told them that he was very much obliged to them for the honour they had done him. Though he could not follow exactly his father's political opinions,—for in these matters, as they knew, there would be differences,—he would always have before his eyes his father's political honesty and independence. He broke down two or three times and blushed, and repeated himself, and knocked his words a great deal too quickly one on the top of another. But it was taken very well, and was better than was expected by those who remembered that affair of the house-painting.

When it was over, and he had returned to London, he wrote a line to the Duke.

'MY DEAR FATHER,

'I am member of Parliament for Silverbridge,—as you used to be in the days which I can first remember. I hope you won't think that it does not make me unhappy to have differed from you. Indeed it does. I don't think that anybody has ever done so well in politics as you have. But when a man does take up an opinion I don't see how he can help himself. Of course I could have kept myself quiet;—but then you wished me to be in the House. They were all civil to me at Silverbridge, but there was very little said.

'I do not care very much for that Mr. Du Boung.

'Your affectionate Son,

'SILVERBRIDGE.'

CHAPTER 15

THE DUKE RECEIVES A LETTER,

—AND WRITES ONE

THE Duke, when he received Mrs. Finn's note demanding an interview, thought much upon the matter before he replied. She had simply desired him to go to her, declaring that it was essential to herself that she should see him; and he liked this simplicity. She had made her demand as though the Duke had been no more than any other gentleman, almost as though she had a right to call upon him to wait upon her. He understood and admired the courage of this;—but nevertheless he would not go to her. He had trusted her with that which of all things was the most sacred to him, and she had deceived him! That secret should not have been in her keeping for a moment before she brought it to him! He wrote to her as follows:

'The Duke of Omnium presents his compliments to Mrs. Finn. As the Duke thinks that no good could result either to Mrs. Finn or to himself from an interview he is obliged to say that he would rather not do as Mrs. Finn has requested.

'But for the strength of this conviction the Duke would have waited upon Mrs. Finn most willingly.'

Mrs. Finn when she received this was certainly not surprised. She had felt almost sure that such would be the nature of the Duke's answer; but she was quite sure also that if such an answer did come she would not let the matter rest. The more she thought about it the more certain she was that he was treating her badly. Mr. Finn was still away in the North of England, and she hardly went into society at all. She remained at home during these days, quite alone, thinking of all this. The matter was so present to her mind, with all its different hues and shades, that she had come to know exactly what words she would use to him if she should succeed in getting him into her presence. The accusation was so bitter to her that she would spare nothing in defending herself,—nothing in labour, nothing in time, and nothing in effort. She would make him know at any rate that she was in earnest. As she could not succeed in getting into his presence she must do this by letter,— and she wrote her letter, as follows, after taking two days to think of her words.

'May 18, 187—.

'MY DEAR DUKE OF OMNIUM,

'As you will not come to me, I must trouble your Grace to read what I fear will be a long letter. For it is absolutely necessary that I should explain my conduct to you. That you have condemned me I am sure you will not deny;—nor that you have punished me as far as the power of punishment was in your hands. If I can succeed in making you see that you have judged me wrongly, I think you will admit your error and beg my pardon. You are not one who from your nature can be brought easily to do this; but you are one who will certainly do it if you can be made to feel that by not doing so you would be unjust. I am myself so clear as to my own rectitude both of purpose and conduct, and am so well aware of your perspicuity, that I venture to believe that if you will read this letter I shall convince you.

'Before I go any further I will confess that the matter is one,—I was going to say almost of life and death to me. Circumstances, certainly not in the first instance of my own seeking, have for some years past thrown me so closely into intercourse with your family that now to be cast off, and to be put on one side as a disgraced person,—and that so quickly after the death of her who loved me so dearly and who was so dear to me,—is such an affront as I cannot bear and hold up my head afterwards. I have come to be known as her whom your uncle trusted and loved, as her whom your wife trusted and loved,—obscure as I was before;—and as her whom, may I not say, you yourself trusted? As there was much of honour and very much of pleasure in this, so also was there something of misfortune. Friendships are safest when the friends are of the same standing in life. I have always felt that there was danger;—and now the thing I feared has come home to me. From all this you will know how important to me is a matter which no doubt is trivial to you; and will understand why it is that I find it so necessary to defend myself and to demand from you a reversal of the verdict you have given against me.

'Now I will plead my case. I fancy, that when first you heard that I had been cognisant of your daughter's engagement, you imagined that I was aware of it before I went to Matching. Had I been so, I think I should have been guilty of that treachery of which you now accuse me. I fancy also that you have changed your opinion on that point. At any rate I did know nothing of it till Lady Mary told me on the day, as I think, before I left Matching. That she should tell me was natural enough. Her mother had known it, and for the moment,—if I am not assuming too much in saying so,—I was filling her mother's place. But, in reference to you, I could not exercise the discretion which a mother might have used, and

I told her at once, most decidedly, that you must be made acquainted with the fact. Up to that point at any rate I did my duty by you.

'Then Lady Mary expressed to me her wish,—not that the matter should be kept any longer from you, for that it should be told to you she was as anxious as I was myself,—but that it should be told to you by Mr. Tregear. That I think is generally the desire of a girl in such a position. She tells her own secret to her mother and expects that the man who has won her heart should ask her father's leave to take her hand. It was not for me to raise any question as to Mr. Tregear's fitness or unfitness,—as to which, indeed, I could know nothing. All I could do was to say that if Mr. Tregear would make the communication at once, I should feel that I had done my duty. The upshot was that Mr. Tregear came to me, immediately on my return to London, and agreeing with me that it was imperative that you should be informed, went to you at once and did inform you. In all of that, if I have told the story truly, where has been my offence? I suppose you will believe me, but your daughter can give evidence as to every word that I have written.

'I think that you have got it into your mind that I have befriended Mr. Tregear's suit, and that, having received this impression, you hold it with the tenacity which is usual to you. There never was a greater mistake. I went to Matching as the friend of my dear friend;—but I stayed there at your request, as your friend. Had I been, at the moment when you asked me to do so, a participator in that secret,—as might have been possible,—I could not have honestly remained in the position you assigned to me. Had I done so, I should have deserved your ill opinion. As it is I have not deserved it and your condemnation of me has been altogether unjust. Should I not now receive from you a full withdrawal of all charge against me, I shall be driven to think that after all the insight which circumstances have given me into your character, I have nevertheless been mistaken in the reading of it.

'I remain,

'Dear Duke of Omnium,

'Yours truly,

'M. FINN.

'I find on looking over my letter that I must add one word further. It might seem that I am asking for a return of your friendship,—or I might perhaps better say for a return of friendly relations with your family. Such is not my purpose. Neither can you forget that you have accused me,—nor can I. The very letter which I am now writing is itself sufficient to make friendly relations impossible. What I expect is that you should tell me that you in your conduct to me have been wrong, and that I in mine to you have been right. I must be able at any rate to feel that the separation between us has come from injury done to me, and not by me.'

He did read the letter more than once, and read it with tingling ears, and hot cheeks, and a knitted brow. As the letter went on, and as the woman's sense of wrong grew hot from her own telling of her own story, her words became stronger and still stronger, till at last they were almost insolent in their strength. Were it not that they came from one who did think herself to have been wronged, or rather if, when writing them, she did not think that she had been most cruelly wronged, then certainly they would be insolent. A sense of injury, a burning conviction of wrong sustained, will justify language which otherwise would be unbearable. The Duke felt that, and though his ears were tingling and his brow knitted, he could have forgiven the language, if only he could have admitted the argument. The letter was a good letter, though the cause which it supported might be bad. He understood every word of it. When she spoke of tenacity she intended to charge him with obstinacy. Though she had dwelt but lightly on her own services she had made her thoughts on the matter clear enough. 'I, Mrs. Finn, who am nobody, have done much to succour and assist you, the Duke of Omnium; and this is the return which I have received!' Words such as these he found interwritten between the lines. And then she told him to his face that unless he did something which it would be impossible that he should do,—unless he begged her pardon and confessed that he had done wrong,—she would revoke that opinion of his honesty which she had already formed. He tried to persuade himself that her opinion about his honesty was nothing to him;—but he failed. Her opinion was very much to him. Though in his anger he had determined to throw her off from him, he knew her to be one whose good opinion was worth having. Had it not been so she could not have written that letter.

There were various other matters which disturbed his mind and for a time warded off from him the necessity of going into the very argument itself. Not a word of overt accusation had been made against his late wife. Every phrase alluding to her was full of love. But yet how heavy a charge was really made! That such a secret should be kept from him, the father, was acknowledged to be a heinous fault;—but the wife had known the secret and had kept it from him the father! And then how wretched a thing it was for him that anyone should dare to write to him about the wife that had been taken away from him! In spite of all her faults her name was so holy to him that it had never once passed his lips since her death, except in low whispers to himself,—low whispers made in the perfect, double-guarded seclusion of his own chamber.

'Cora, Cora,' he had murmured, so that the sense of the sound and not the sound itself had come to him from his own lips. And now this woman wrote to him about her freely, as though there were nothing sacred, no religion in the memory of her!

'It was not for me to raise any question as to Mr. Tregear's fitness.' Was it not palpable to all the world that he was altogether unfit? Heavens and earth, to what was the world coming! Unfit! How could a man be more unfit? He was asking for the hand of one who was second only to royalty,—who was possessed of everything, who was beautiful, well born, rich, who was the daughter of the Duke of Omnium, and he had absolutely nothing of his own to offer in exchange for all this. Fit indeed! Within his own heart he almost thought that Mrs. Finn should have been so shocked by the proposition as to have sunk beneath the weight of it. And now she seemed to say that there might be a question on the subject!

But it was necessary that he should at last come to the consideration of the actual point as to which she had written to him so forcibly. He tried to set himself to the task in perfect honesty. He certainly had condemned her. In all that she had said on that matter she had spoken truly enough. He had condemned her and had no doubt punished her to the extent of his power. And if he could be brought to see that he had done this unjustly, then certainly must he beg her pardon. And when he considered it all, he had to own that her intimacy with his uncle and his wife had not been so much of her seeking as of theirs. And the services rendered had been from her to him and his, and not from him and his to her. It grieved him now that it should have been so, but so it was. And after all this,—after the affectionate surrender of herself to his wife's caprices which had been spread over some years before his wife's death,—he had turned upon her and driven her away with ignominy. That all was true. As he thought of it he became hot, and was conscious of a quivering feeling round his heart. These were bonds indeed; but they were bonds of such a nature as to be capable of being rescinded and cut away altogether by absolute bad conduct. If he could make it good to himself that in a matter of such magnitude as the charge of his daughter she had been untrue to him and had leagued herself against him, despite the trust placed in her, with an unworthy lover, then, then—all bonds would be rescinded! Then would his wrath be altogether justified! Then would it have been impossible that he should have done aught else than cast her out! As he thought of this he felt sure that she had betrayed him. How great would be the ignominy to him should he be driven to own to himself that she had not betrayed him! 'There should not have been a moment,' he said to himself over and over again,—'not a moment!' Yes;—she certainly had betrayed him.

But had she leagued herself against him with that man? He did find himself compelled at last to ask himself that question. There might still be safety for him in that confident assertion of 'not a moment'; but had there been anything of that conspiracy of which he had certainly at first judged her to be guilty? She had told her story, and had then appealed to Lady Mary for evidence here in her favour. After five minutes of perfect stillness,—but five minutes of great misery, five minutes during which great beads of perspiration broke out from him and stood upon his brow, he had to confess to himself that he did not want any evidence. He did believe her story. When he allowed himself to think that she had been in league with Tregear he had wronged her. She certainly was not lying to him in that. He wiped away the beads from his brow, and again repeated to himself those words which were now his only comfort, 'There should not have been a moment;—not a moment!'

Then he turned over that plea of hers as to the conventional position of a lover. The girl tells her mother, and then the lover applies to the father. He did not know much about such things, but he thought that he had heard that such was generally the fashion of their management. No doubt had this young man sought a bride for himself among his equals, all that would have been fit and proper,—though any prudent father, even of those who were his equals, would have rejected him. But was it possible that Mrs. Finn should have thought that this case should have been governed after that fashion? By parity of reasoning,—though no doubt with greater absurdity,—it might be argued that a beggar aspiring to the daughter of royalty should simply make known his wishes to the royal father. It was not for her, she had said, to raise a question of fitness! Her great fault had consisted in this,—that she had not seen that no such question was possible. 'There should not have been a moment;—not a moment!'

In this way he was enabled, at any rate for a time, to assure himself that there need be no acknowledgment of wrong done on his part. Having settled this in his own mind he now forced himself to attend a meeting at which his assistance had been asked and to listen to a complex debate on law reform. Two or three ex-Lord Chancellors there present were very sure, each that the others were wrong, but were all unified in thinking that the Lord Chancellor who was not ex and who was not present was the most in error of them all. The Duke endeavoured to give himself up entirely to the matter; but through it all there was the picture before him of Mrs. Finn waiting for an answer to her letter. If he should confirm himself in his opinion that he had been right,—as of course he had done and would continue to do, for should she not have told it to him without the delay of a moment?,—then would any answer be necessary? He might just acknowledge the letter, after the fashion which has come up in official life, than which silence is an insult much more bearable. But he did not wish to insult, nor to punish her further. He would willingly have withdrawn the punishment under which she was groaning could he have done so without self-abasement. Or he might write as she had done,—advocating his own cause with all his strength, using that last one strong argument,—'there should not have been a moment.' But there would be something repulsive to his personal dignity in the continued correspondence which this would produce. 'The Duke of Omnium regrets to say in answer to Mrs. Finn's letter, that he thinks no good can be attained by a prolonged correspondence.' Such, or of such kind, he thought, must be his answer. But had she not deserved better from him than this? Was this a fair return for the solicitude shown by her to his uncle, for the love which had made her so patient a friend to his wife, for the nobility of her own conduct in many things? Then, as he sat there listening to a very strong argument in which Lord Weazeling was destroying Lord Ramsden and all the other law-lords,* his mind reverted to certain jewels,—supposed to be of enormous value,—which were still in his possession though they were the property of this woman. They had been left to her by his uncle, and she had obstinately refused to take them. Now they were lying packed in the cellars of certain bankers near Charing Cross,—but still they were in his custody. He had always wished that she would take them, but still had admired her for refusing them. What should he now do in this matter? Hitherto, perhaps once in every six months, he had notified to her that he was keeping them as her curator, and she had always responded that it was a charge from which she could never relieve him. It had become almost a joke between them. But how could he joke with a woman with whom he had quarrelled after this internecine fashion?

What if he were to consult Lady Cantrip on the subject? He could not do so without a pang that would be very bitter to him,—but any pang, any agony would be better than that arising from a fear that he had been unjust to one who had deserved well of him. No doubt Lady Cantrip would see it in the same light as he had done. She no doubt would feel and would exclaim that there should not have been a minute lost. And then he would be able to support himself by the assurance that that which he had judged to be right was felt to be right also by one whom all the world would acknowledge to be a good judge on such a matter.

When he got home that evening he found his son's letter telling him of the election at Silverbridge. There was something in it which softened his heart to the young man,—or perhaps it was that in the midst of his many discomforts he wished to find something which at least was not painful to him. That his son and heir should insist on entering political life in opposition to him was of course a source of pain; but, putting that aside, the thing had been done pleasantly enough, and the young member's letter had been written with some good feeling. So he answered the letter as pleasantly as he knew how.

'MY DEAR SILVERBRIDGE,

'I am glad that you are in Parliament and am glad also that you should have been returned by the old borough; though I would that you could have reconciled yourself to adhering to the politics of your family. But though there is something painful there is nothing disgraceful in such a change, and I am able to congratulate you as a father should a son, and to wish you long life and success as a legislator.

'There are one or two things I would ask you to remember;—and firstly this,—that as you have voluntarily undertaken certain duties you are bound as an honest man and a gentleman to perform them as scrupulously as though you were paid for doing them. There was no obligation on you to seek the post;—but having sought it and acquired it you cannot neglect the work attached to it without being untrue to the covenant you have made. It is especially necessary that a young member of Parliament should bear this in his mind, and especially a member who has not worked his way up to notoriety outside the House, because to him there will be great facility for idleness and neglect.

'And then I would have you always remember the purport for which there is a Parliament elected in this happy and free country of ours. It is not that some men may shine there, that some may acquire power, or that all may plume themselves on being the elect of the nation. It often appears to me that some members of Parliament so regard their success in life,—as the fellows of our colleges do too often, very improperly, thinking that their fellowships were awarded for their comfort and not for the furtherance of any object such as education or religion. I have known gentlemen who have clearly felt that in becoming members of Parliament they had achieved an object for themselves instead of thinking that they had put themselves in the way of achieving something for others. A member of Parliament should feel himself to be the servant of his country,—and like every other servant, he should serve. If this be distasteful to a man he need not go into Parliament. If the harness gall him he need not wear it. But if he takes the trappings, then he should draw the coach. You are there as the guardian of your fellow-countrymen,—that they may be safe, that they may be prosperous, that they may be well governed and lightly burdened,—above all that they may be free. If you cannot feel this to be your duty, you should not be there at all.

'And I would have you remember also that the work of a member of Parliament can seldom be of that brilliant nature which is of itself charming; and that the young member should think of such brilliancy as being possible to him only at a distance. It should be your care to sit and listen so that the forms and methods of the House may as it were soak into you gradually. Even this is a study which many members have not diligence enough to pursue, thereby neglecting, as I think, their very first duty. And then you must bear in mind that speaking in the House is but a very small part of a member's work,—perhaps that part which he may lay aside altogether with the least strain on his conscience. A good member of Parliament will be good upstairs in the Committee Rooms, good downstairs to make and to keep a House, good to vote, for his party if it may be nothing better, but for the measures also which he believes to be for the good of his country when he has sufficiently educated himself to have an opinion respecting them.

'Gradually, if you will give your thoughts to it, and above all your time, the theory of legislation will sink into your mind, and you will find that there will come upon you the ineffable delight of having served your country to the best of your ability.

'It is the only pleasure in life which has been enjoyed without alloy by your affectionate father,

'OMNIUM.'

The Duke in writing this letter was able for a few moments to forget Mrs. Finn, and to enjoy the work which he had on hand.

CHAPTER 16

'POOR BOY!'

THE new member for Silverbridge, when he entered the House to take the oath, was supported on the right and left by Sir Timothy Beeswax and Sir Orlando Drought,—the two men against whom his father would have been most prone to warn him, had any such warning in existing circumstances been possible. The Duke was too noble to say a word against men to whom his son must now be an ally, but who, as he thought, had been treacherously false to him;* and they were too ignoble to be aware that they should have abstained from the triumph which they displayed in thus attaching themselves openly to the apostate child of the Pallisers. It did not much matter, as nothing of it could be known to the Duke. It was, after all, only the way in which the atoms of a crowd had formed themselves. But still there were those who saw it and who knew that it was not accidental.

Mr. Monk had seen him a few minutes previously,—Mr. Monk who of all Liberals was the firmest* and than whom no one had been more staunch to the Duke,—and had congratulated him on his election, expressing at the same time some gentle regrets. 'I only wish you could have come among us on the other side,' he said.

'But I couldn't,' said the young Lord.

'I am sure nothing but a conscientious feeling would have separated you from your father's friends,' said the old Liberal. And then they were parted, and the member for Silverbridge was hustled up to the table between the baronet and the law-knight* who had been members of the Duke's Government, but had been the Duke's most bitter opponents.

Of what else was done on that occasion, or on the next day when two middle-aged young politicians in gorgeous apparel moved and seconded the address, nothing shall be said here. For the present we will follow our young member, from whom no political work was required except that of helping for an hour or two to crowd the Government benches. There were, however, one or two others quite as anxious as to his political career as Sir Orlando and Sir Timothy,—at any rate one other. He had promised that as soon as he could get away from the House he would go to Belgrave Square and tell Lady Mabel Grex all about it.

When he reached the Square it was past seven, but Lady Mabel and Miss Cassewary were still sitting in the drawing-room. 'There seemed to be a great deal of bustle and I didn't understand much about it,' said the member.

'But you heard the speeches?' These were the speeches made on the proposing and seconding of the address.

'Oh yes;—Lupton did it very well. Lord George didn't seem to be quite so good. Then Sir Timothy Beeswax made a speech, and then Mr. Monk. After that, I saw other fellows going away, so I bolted too.'

'If I were a member of Parliament I would never leave it while the House was sitting,' said Miss Cassewary.

'If all were like that, there wouldn't be seats for them to sit upon,' said Silverbridge.

'A persistent member will always find a seat,' continued the patriotic old lady, whose sentiments as to the duty of a legislator were almost as high as those conveyed in the letter which our young member at this moment had in his pocket.

'I am sure Lord Silverbridge means to do his duty,' said Lady Mabel.

'Oh, yes;—I've thought a good deal about it, and I mean to try. As long as a man isn't called upon to speak I don't see why it shouldn't be easy enough. I mean to make a business of it.'

'I'm so glad to hear you say so! Of course after a little time you will speak. I wonder whether I shall ever hear you. I should so like to hear you make your first speech.'

'If I thought you were there, I'm sure I should not make it at all.' Just at this period Miss Cassewary, saying something as to the necessity of dressing, and cautioning her young friend that there was not much time to be lost, as there were people coming to dinner, left the room.

'Dressing does not take me more than ten minutes,' said Lady Mabel. Miss Cassewary declared this to be nonsense, but she nevertheless left the room. Whether she would have done so if Lord Silverbridge had not been Lord Silverbridge, but had been some young man with whom it would not have been expedient that Lady Mabel should fall in love, may perhaps be doubted. But then it may be taken as certain that under such circumstances Lady Mabel herself would not have remained. She had quite realised the duties of life, had had her little romance,—and had acknowledged that it was foolish.

'I do so hope that you will do well,' she said, going back to the parliamentary duties. 'I shall watch to see,—you may be sure of that.'

'I don't think I shall ever do much. I shall never be like my father.'

'I don't see why not.'

'There never was anybody like him. I am always amusing myself, but he never cared about amusement. I am an idle fellow, and I don't suppose he was ever idle for a moment in his life.'

'You are very young.'

'As far as I can learn he was just as he is now at my age. My mother has told me that long before she married him he used to spend all his time in the House, and now he is always at work. I wonder whether you would mind reading the letter he wrote me when he heard of my election.' Then he took the epistle out of his pocket and handed it to Lady Mabel.

'He means all that he says.'

'He always does that.'

'And he really hopes that you will put your shoulder to the wheel,— even though you must do so in opposition to him.'

'That makes no difference. I think my father is a very fine fellow, though he is so hard and severe.'

'Shall you do all that he tells you?'

'Well;—I suppose not;—except that he advises me to hold my tongue. I think that I shall do that. I mean to go down there, you know, and I dare say I shall be much the same as others. I don't suppose I shall ever go in for hard work.'

'Has he talked to you much about it?'

'No;—he never talks much,—at least with me. Every now and then he will give me a downright lecture, or he will write me a letter like that; but he never talks to any of us much, I think.'

'How very odd.'

'Yes; he is odd. He seems to be fretful when we are with him. A good many things make him unhappy.'

'Your poor mother's death?'

'That first;—and then there are other things. I suppose he didn't like the way I came to an end at Oxford.'

'You were a boy then.'

'Of course I was very sorry for it,—though I hated Oxford. It was neither one thing nor another. You were your own master and yet you were not. It was much more jolly at Eton.'

'Now you must be your own master.'

'I suppose so.'

'You must marry, and become a lord of the Treasury. When I was a child* I acted as a child. You know all about that.'

'Oh yes. And now I must throw off childish things. You mean that I mustn't paint any more houses. Eh, Lady Mab?'

'That, and the rest of it. You are a legislator now.'

'So is Popplecourt, who took his seat in the House of Lords two or three months ago. He is the biggest young fool I know out. He couldn't even paint a house.'

'He is not an elected legislator. It makes all the difference. I quite agree with what the Duke says. Lord Popplecourt can't help himself. Whether he's an idle young scamp or not, he must be a legislator. But when a man goes in for it himself, as you have done, he should make up his mind to be useful. Don't you think so?'

'I shall vote with my party of course.'

'More than that;—much more than that, I hope. If you didn't care for politics you wouldn't have taken a line of your own.' When she said this she knew well enough that he had been talked into what he had done by Tregear,—by Tregear, who had ambition, and intelligence, and capacity for forming an opinion of his own. 'If you do not do it for your own sake, you will for the sake of those who,—who;—who are your friends,' she said at last, not feeling quite able to tell him that he must do it for the sake of those who loved him.

'There are not very many I suppose who care much about it.'

'Your father.'

'Oh yes,—my father!'

'And Tregear.'

'Tregear has got his own fish to fry.'

'Are there none others? Do you think that we care nothing about it here?'

'Miss Cassewary!'

'Well;—Miss Cassewary. A man might have a worse friend than Miss Cassewary. And my father.'

'I don't suppose Lord Grex cares a straw about me.'

'Indeed he does,—a great many straws. And so do I. Do you think I don't care a straw about it?'

'I don't know why you should.'

'Because it is my nature to be earnest. A girl comes out into the world so young that she becomes serious, and steady as it were, so much sooner than a man does.'

'Are you steady?'

'Yes;—when things really affect me.'

'I always think that nobody is so full of chaff as you are, Lady Mab.'

'I am not chaffing now at any rate in recommending you to go to work in the world like a man.' As she said this they were sitting on the same sofa, but with some space between them,—with space enough for a third person, had any third person been there to occupy it. When Miss Cassewary had left the room Lord Silverbridge was standing, but after a little he had fallen into the seat, at the extreme corner, and had gradually come a little nearer to her. Now in her energy she put out her hand, meaning perhaps to touch lightly the sleeve of his coat, meaning perhaps not quite to touch him at all. But as she did so he put out his hand and took hold of hers.

She drew it away, not seeming to allow it to remain in his grasp for a moment; but she did so, not angrily, or hurriedly, or with any flurry. She did it as though it were natural that he should take her hand and as natural that she should recover it. 'Indeed I have hardly more than ten minutes left for dressing,' she said, rising from her seat.

'If you will say that you care about it, you yourself, I will do my best.' As he made this declaration blushes covered his cheeks and forehead.

'I do care about it,—very much; I myself,' said Lady Mabel, not blushing at all. Then there was a knock at the door, and Lady Mabel's maid, putting her head in, declared that 'my Lord' had come in and had already been some time in his dressing-room. 'Good-bye, Lord Silverbridge,' she said quite gaily, and rather more aloud than would have been necessary, had she not intended that the maid also should hear her. 'If you do not let me know when you are going to make your first speech I will never forgive you.'

'Poor boy!' she said to herself as she was dressing. 'Poor boy!' Then, when the evening was over she spoke to herself again about him. 'Dear, sweet boy!' And then she sat and thought. How was it that she was so old a woman, while he was so little more than a child? How fair he was, how far removed from conceit, how capable of being made into a man,—in the process of time! What might not be expected from him if he could be kept in good hands for the next ten years! But in whose hands? What would she be in ten years, she who already seemed to know the town and all its belongings so well? And yet,—as she did not forget to tell herself,—she was as young in years as he. He, as she knew, had passed his twenty-second birthday,—and so had she. That was all. It might be good for her that she should marry him. She was ambitious. And such a marriage would satisfy her ambition. Through her father's faults, and her brother's, she was likely to be poor. This man would certainly be very rich. Many of those who were buzzing around her from day to day were distasteful to her. From among them she knew that she could not take a husband, let their rank and wealth be what it might. She was too fastidious, too proud, too prone to think that things should be with her as she liked them! This lad was in all things pleasant to her. Though he was but a boy there was a certain boyish manliness about him. The very way in which he had grasped at her hand, and had then blushed ruby-red at his own daring, had gone far with her. How gracious he was to look at! Dear, sweet boy! Love him? No;—she did not know that she loved him. That dream was over. She was sure however that she liked him.

But how would it be with him? It might be well for her to become his wife, but could it be well for him that he should become her husband? In sober earnest and with anxious thought she turned all this in her mind. Did she not feel that it would be better for him that he should become a man before he married at all? Perhaps so;—but then if she desisted would others desist? If she did not put out her bait, would there not be other hooks,—other and worse? Would not such a one, so soft, so easy, so prone to be caught and so desirable for the catching, be sure to be made prey of by some snare?

But could she love him? That a woman should not marry a man without loving him, she partly knew. But she thought she knew also that there must be exceptions. Should she succeed in bringing him to her feet she would certainly love him. She would do her very best to love him. That other man should be banished from her very thoughts. She would be such a wife to him that he should never know that he lacked anything. It would, she acknowledged, be better for him that he should remain unmarried for a while; but as he was destined to be caught at once she thought that for his sake as well as for her own it would be best that he should be caught by her. Poor boy! Sweet, dear boy!

He, as he went away to his dinner, had his thoughts also about her. Of all the girls he knew she was the jolliest,—and of all his friends she was the pleasantest. As she was anxious that he should go to work in the House of Commons he would go to work there. As for loving her! Well;—of course he must marry someone, and why not Lady Mab as well as anyone else?

CHAPTER 17

THE DERBY

An attendance at the Newmarket Second Spring Meeting had unfortunately not been compatible with the Silverbridge election. Major Tifto had therefore been obliged to look after the affair alone. 'A very useful mare,' as Tifto had been in the habit of calling a leggy, thoroughbred, meagre-looking brute named Coalition who, as she was unfitted by her proportions to be a mother of horses, and could never by any chance do anything useful, was on this occasion confided to the Major's sole care and judgment. But Coalition failed, as coalitions always will do, and Tifto had to report to his noble patron that they had not pulled off the event. It had been a match for four hundred pounds, made indeed by Lord Silverbridge, but made at the suggestion of Tifto;—and now Tifto wrote in a very bad humour about it. It had been altogether his lordship's fault in submitting to carry two pounds more* than Tifto had thought to be fair and equitable. Tifto, so he declared, had he been allowed to use his own judgment would never have dreamed of allowing the mare to run with such a crushing weight upon her back! Was Lord Silverbridge aware that two pounds extra would make all the difference in the world in such a match as this? But the match had been lost. Would Lord Silverbridge be so good as to pay the money to Mr. Green Griffin, the happy owner of the victorious horse, and debit him, Tifto, with his share of the loss?

In giving Major Tifto his due, we must acknowledge that the very unpleasant tone of his letter was due quite as much to the ill-usage he had received in reference to that journey to Silverbridge, as to the loss of the race. Within that little body there was a high-mounting heart, and that heart had been greatly wounded by his lordship's treatment. Tifto had felt himself to be shoved aside almost as though he had been a servant. Hardly an excuse had even been made. He had been simply told that he was not wanted;—or worse even than that, that he was not quite fit for the occasion. He was apt sometimes to tell himself that he knew on which side his bread was buttered,—and seeing that he had begun the world with nothing, and that he had hitherto eaten very well-buttered bread, perhaps he had reason for such self-confidence. But yet perhaps he hardly did know how best to keep the butter going. There was a little pride about him which was antagonistic to the best interests of such a trade as his. Perhaps it was well that he should inwardly suffer,—perhaps well that he should determine inwardly to resent such injury as he had received. But it could not be well that he should declare to such men as Nidderdale, and Dolly Longstaffe, and Popplecourt, and others that he didn't mean to put up with that sort of thing. And had he really known on which side his bread was buttered he certainly would not have spoken in this strain before Tregear. Of all men living he hated Tregear the worst, and in truth feared him the most. And he knew that of all men living,—that is, of all young men,—no one loved Silverbridge as did Tregear. Had he been thinking of his bread and butter, instead of giving way most uncautiously to the mighty anger of his little bosom, he would have hardly declared before Tregear at the club that he would let Lord Silverbridge know that he did not mean to stand any man's airs;—nor would he have said even in the presence of Dolly Longstaffe that the young Lord's comb would want cutting before long.* But these extravagances were due perhaps to whisky-and-water, and that kind of intoxication which comes to certain men from momentary triumphs. Tifto could always be got to make a fool of himself when surrounded by three or four men of rank who, for the occasion, would flatter him and talk to him as an equal. There was a moment in which he almost declared that Coalition had lost her match because he had not been taken down to Silverbridge.

'Tifto is in a deuce of a way with you,' said Dolly Longstaffe to the young member.

'I know all about it,' said Silverbridge, who had received Tifto's letter and had also had an interview with his partner since the race.

'He says that you have about ruined him. If you don't take care he'll dismiss you.'

Silverbridge did not care much about this, knowing that words of wisdom did not ordinarily fall from the mouth of Dolly Longstaffe. But he was more moved when his friend Tregear spoke to him. 'I wish you knew the kind of things which that fellow Tifto says behind your back.'

'As if I cared.'

'But you ought to care.'

'I don't see that at all. Do you care what every fellow says about you?'

'I care very much what those say whom I choose to live with me. Whatever Tifto might say about me would be quite indifferent to me because we have nothing in common. But you and he are so bound together that people will naturally suppose that he knows what he is talking about.'

'We have a horse or two in common;—that's all.'

'But that is a great deal. The truth is he's a nasty, brawling, boasting, ill-conditioned little reptile, and the sooner you can get quit of him the better for you.'

Silverbridge of course did not acknowledge that this was true. When does anyone acknowledge the truth of advice from a friend? But he felt it, and almost repented him of his trust in Tifto. But still Prime Minister stood very well for the Derby.* He was second favourite, the odds against him being only four to one; and at this very hour was supposed to be rising a little. The glory of being part owner of a probable winner of the Derby was so much to him that he could not bring himself to be altogether angry with Tifto. There was no doubt that the horse's present condition was due entirely to Tifto's care. Tifto spent, in these few days just before the race, the greatest part of his time in the close vicinity of the horse, down at Newmarket, only running up to London now and then, as a fish comes to the surface, for a breath of air. Some men said that he slept in the stable. He certainly saw Prime Minister take all his gallops. It was impossible that Lord Silverbridge should separate himself from the Major,—at any rate till after the Epsom meeting.

He had paid the money for the match and certain other sums for stable expenses without a word of reproach to his partner, but still with a feeling that things were not quite as they ought to be. In money matters his father had been very liberal to him, but not very definite. He had been told that he ought not to spend at the most above two thousand pounds a year, and had been reminded that there was a house for him always to use both in town and in the country. But he had been given to understand also that any application made to Mr. Moreton, if not very unreasonable, would be attended with success. A solemn promise had been exacted from him that he would have no dealings with money-lenders;—and then he had been set afloat. This had been on his withdrawal from Oxford, and from that day to the present time there had not been a word between him and his father about money. There had been a rather frequent correspondence with Mr. Moreton, who had on one or two occasions ventured to submit a total of the money paid on behalf of his correspondent. Lord Silverbridge, who imagined himself to be anything but an extravagant young man, had sometimes wondered how the figures could mount up so rapidly. But the money needed was always forthcoming, and the raising of objections never seemed to be carried back beyond Mr. Moreton. His promise to his father about the money-lenders had been scrupulously kept. As long as ready money can be made to be forthcoming without any charge for interest, a young man must be very foolish indeed who will prefer to borrow it at twenty-five or fifty per cent.

Now had come the night before the Derby, and it must be acknowledged that not only the young Lord, but Tifto also, was much fluttered by the greatness of the coming struggle. Tifto, having seen his horse conveyed to Epsom, had come up to London in order that he might dine with his partner and hear what was being said about the race at the Beargarden. The party dining there consisted of Silverbridge, Dolly Longstaffe, Popplecourt, and Tifto. Lord Nidderdale was to have joined them, but he told them on the day before, with a sigh, that domestic duties were too strong for him. Lady Nidderdale,—or if not Lady Nidderdale herself, then Lady Nidderdale's mother,—was so far potent over the young nobleman as to induce him to confine his Derby practices to the Derby day. Tregear had been asked to join the party, but he had flatly told Silverbridge that he would not willingly sit down in company with Major Tifto.

Another guest had also been expected, the reason for whose non-appearance must be explained somewhat at length. Lord Gerald Palliser, the Duke's second son, was at this time at Cambridge,—being almost as popular at Trinity as his brother had been at Christ Church. It was to him quite a matter of course that he should see his brother's horse run for the Derby. What chance was there that Silverbridge should ever again possess a favourite for the great race of the year? That he should see the race seemed to him to be so natural that he almost felt that his going would be a thing of course to the college authorities. But, unfortunately, in this very year a stand was being made by the University pundits against a practice which they thought had become too general. For the last year or two it had been considered almost as much a matter of course that a Cambridge undergraduate should go to the Derby as that a member of Parliament should do so. Indeed it had seemed to become a question whether the whole Derby week should not be regarded as a period devoted to Saturnalia. Against this three or four rigid disciplinarians had raised their voices,—and as a result, no young man up at Trinity could get leave to be away on the Derby pretext.

Lord Gerald, when he found that he must consider himself to be bound by this law, raged against the restriction very loudly. He at first proclaimed his intention of ignoring the college authorities altogether, and of dealing with his time as a man may do who is subject to no control. Of course he would be expelled. But the order itself was to his thinking so absurd,—the idea that he should not see his brother's horse run was so extravagant,—that he argued that his father could not be angry with him for incurring dismissal in so excellent a cause. But his brother saw things in a different light. He knew how his father had looked at him when he had been sent away from Oxford, and he counselled moderation. Gerald should see the Derby, but should not encounter that heaviest wrath of all which comes from a man's not sleeping beneath his college roof. There was a train which left Cambridge at an early hour, and would bring him into London quite in time to accompany his friends to the race-course;—and another train, a special, was arranged which would take him down after dinner, so that he and others should reach Cambridge before the college gates were shut. The day would be no doubt stolen from the University as far as any purposes of hall, chapel, or lecture-room were concerned;—but if a man even has a headache he cannot go to hall, chapel, or lecture-room. In fact it was considered that if he only slept each night within his college no great harm would come, although he would have done exactly what it was intended that he should not do in going to the Derby.

The dinner at the Beargarden was very joyous, and after dinner the young men joined themselves to others. Of course the state of the betting in regard to Prime Minister was the subject generally popular for the night. Mr. Lupton came in, a gentleman well known in all fashionable circles, parliamentary, social, and racing,* who was rather older than his company on this occasion, but still not so much so as to be found to be an encumbrance. Lord Glasslough, too, and others joined them, and a good deal was said about the horse. 'I never keep these things dark,' said Tifto. 'Of course he's an uncertain horse.'

'Most horses are,' said Lupton.

'Just so, Mr. Lupton. What I mean is the Minister has got a bit of temper. But if he likes to do his best I don't think there is anything in England at this moment can get his nose past him;—that is, of course, anything three years old.'

'For half a mile he'd be nowhere with the Provence filly,' said Glasslough.

'I'm speaking of a Derby distance, my Lord.'

'That's a kind of thing nobody really knows,' said Lupton.

'I've seen him 'ave his gallops,' said the little man, who in his moments of excitement would sometimes fall away from that exact pronunciation which had been one of the studies of his life, 'and 'ave measured his stride. I think I know what pace means as well as any man out at present. Of course I'm not going to answer for the 'orse. He's a temper, and, like most other animals I've seen in training, his legs are not made of steel. But if things go favourably no animal that ever showed on the Downs was more likely to do the trick. Is there any gentleman here who would like to bet me fifteen to one in hundreds against the two events,—the Derby and the Leger?' The desired odds were at once offered by Mr. Lupton, and the bet was booked.

This gave rise to other betting, and before the evening was over Lord Silverbridge had taken three and a half to one against his horse to such an extent that he stood to lose twelve hundred pounds by the bets made then and there in that room; but then he also stood to win over four thousand on an event which at the present moment he conceived to be almost probable. The champagne which he had drunk, and the news that Quousque,* the first favourite, had so gone to pieces that now there was a question which was the first favourite, had so inflated him that, had he been left alone, he would almost have wagered even money on his horse. He had told his father that he didn't bet much. He had assured her whom he regarded as the dearest of his friends, Lady Mab, that he did not and would not 'plunge.' Not a week since, he had informed Mr. Moreton in his good-humoured way that that gentleman need not be a bit afraid of his losing money on the turf. Now, in the midst of his excitement, there came to him a feeling that he was allowing himself to do just that which he had intended to avoid. But then the occasion was so peculiar! How often can it happen to a man in his life that he shall own a favourite for the Derby? And when before had it ever happened to one so young as he? The affair was one in which it was almost necessary that he should risk a little money. In this way he consoled himself,—though as he got into bed he knew that he had been doing that of which he ought to be ashamed.

Tifto, when he got into his bed, was altogether happy. He had added whisky-and-water to his champagne, and was moreover so circumstanced in the world that an even chance of obtaining great pecuniary success was to him itself ground for triumph. If Prime Minister could be made to win the Derby he would be able to pay all that he owed and to make a start with money in his pocket. And then there would be at once attached to him all the infinite glory of being the owner of a winner of the Derby. The horse was being run in his name. Thoughts as to great successes crowded themselves upon his heated brain. What might not be open to him? Parliament! The Jockey Club! The Mastership of one of the crack shire packs! Might it not come to pass that he should some day become the great authority in England upon races, race-horses, and hunters? If he could be the winner of a Derby and Leger he thought that Popplecourt and Glasslough and Lupton would snub him no longer, that even Tregear would speak to him, and that his pal, the Duke's son, would not throw him aside again when once he had invited him to go down into the country. Thinking of all this, Major Tifto was quite happy with himself when he went to bed.

Lord Silverbridge had bought a drag with all its appendages. There was the coach, the four bay horses, the harness, and the two regulation grooms. They had belonged to a certain sporting baronet named Sir Damask Monogram who had come to some grief in his money matters, and had been transferred wholesale to the young Lord. When making this purchase he had condescended to say a word to his father on the subject. 'Everybody belongs to the four-in-hand club, now,' said the son.

'I never did,' said the Duke.

'Ah,—if I could be like you! We can't all be Statesmen when we are young.' The Duke had said that he would think about it, and then had told Mr. Moreton that he was to pay the bill for this new toy. He had thought about it, and had assured himself that driving a coach and four was at present regarded as a fitting amusement for young men of rank and wealth. He did not understand it himself. It seemed to him to be as unnatural as though a gentleman should turn blacksmith and make horseshoes for his amusement. Driving four horses was hard work,—and the power of doing so a desirable accomplishment for a professional coachman. But the same might be said of rowing. There were men, he knew, who would spend their days standing at a lathe, making little boxes for their recreation. He did not sympathise with it. But the fact was so, and this driving of coaches was regarded with favour;—the only recognised objection to it being that of expense. On that score there was no reason why Silverbridge should not do anything that was not on other grounds objectionable. He had been a little touched by that word his son had spoken. 'We cannot all be Statesmen when we are young.' So he had given the permission; the drag, horses, harness, and grooms had come into the possession of Lord Silverbridge; and now they were put into requisition to take their triumphant owner and his party down to Epsom to see Prime Minister win the great race of the year. Dolly Longstaffe's team was sent down to meet them half-way. Gerald Palliser, who had come up from Cambridge that morning, was allowed to drive the first stage out of town to compensate him for the cruelty done to him by the University pundits. Tifto, with a cigar in his mouth, with a white hat and a blue veil, and a new light-coloured coat, new bright pantaloons, and a ruby-coloured silk handkerchief round his neck, was by no means the least happy or least confident of the party.

How that race was run, and how both Prime Minister and Quousque were beaten by an outsider named Fishknife, Prime Minister, however, coming in a good second, the present writer, having no aptitude in that way, cannot describe. Such, however, were the facts, and then Dolly Longstaffe and Lord Silverbridge drove the coach back to London. The coming back was not so triumphant, though the young fellows bore their failure well. Dolly Longstaffe had lost a 'pot of money.' Silverbridge would have to draw upon that inexhaustible Mr. Moreton for something over two thousand pounds,—in regard to which he had no doubt as to the certainty with which the money would be forthcoming, but he feared that it would give rise to special notice from his father. Even the poor younger brother had lost a couple of hundred pounds, for which he would have to make his own special application to Mr. Moreton. Prime Minister certainly had not done any good as yet.

But Tifto probably felt it more than anyone. The horse ought to have won. Nobody doubted that. Fishknife, of whom nobody had known anything, had been favoured by such a series of accidents that the whole affair had been a miracle performed in his favour. Tifto had all these circumstances at his fingers' ends, and in the course of the afternoon and evening explained them accurately to all who would listen to him. I do not know that, if explained here, they would be interesting to the general reader. He had, however, this to say on his own behalf,—that before the party had left the course their horse stood first favourite for the Leger. As it happened Fishknife had not even been entered for the Yorkshire race. But Tifto was very unhappy as he came back to town, and in spite of the lunch, which had been very glorious, sat moody and sometimes even silent within his gay apparel.

'It was the unfairest start I ever saw,' said Tifto, almost getting up from his seat on the coach so as to address Dolly and Silverbridge on the box, and speaking after an interval of ten minutes.

'What the —— is the good of that?' said Dolly from the coach-box. 'Take your licking and don't squeal.'

'That's all very well. I can take my licking as well as another man. But one has to look to the causes of these things. I never saw Peppermint ride so badly. Before he got round the corner I wished I'd been on the horse myself. He has the name of a jockey, but I never saw anything so awkward.'

'I don't believe it was Peppermint's fault a bit,' said Silverbridge.

'Well;—perhaps not. Only I did think that I was a pretty good judge of riding. Perhaps you are better.' Then Tifto again settled down into silence.

But though a great deal of money had been lost, and a great deal of disappointment had to be endured by our party in reference to the Derby, the most injurious and most deplorable event in the day's history had not occurred yet. Dinner had been ordered at the Beargarden at seven,—an hour earlier than would have been named had it not been that Lord Gerald must be at the Eastern Counties Railway station* at 9 p.m. An hour and a half for dinner and a cigar afterwards, and half an hour to get to the railway station would not be more than time enough. And so the hour had been arranged for the young man.

But of all men alive Dolly Longstaffe was the most unpunctual. He did not arrive till nearly eight. The others were not there till half-past seven, and it was very nearly eight before any of them sat down. At half-past eight Silverbridge began to be very anxious about his brother, and told him more than once that he ought to start without further delay. A hansom cab* was waiting at the door, but Lord Gerald still delayed. He knew, he said, that in fact the special would not start till half-past nine. There were a lot of fellows who were dining about everywhere, and they would never get to the station punctually by the hour fixed. It soon became apparent to the elder brother that Gerald would stay altogether unless he were forced to go, and at last he did absolutely get up and almost push the young fellow out. 'Drive like the very devil,' he said to the cabman, explaining to him something of the circumstances. The cabman did do his best, but a cab cannot be made to travel from the Beargarden, which as all the world knows is close to St. James's Street, to Liverpool Street* in the City in ten minutes. When Lord Gerald reached the station the train had started, and he was impeded in the frantic effort he made to jump onto the guard's brake* as the carriages were passing away.

At twenty minutes to ten the young man reappeared at the club. 'Why on earth didn't you take a special for yourself?' exclaimed Silverbridge.

'They wouldn't give me one.'* After that it was apparent to all of them that what had just happened had done more to ruffle our hero's temper than his failure and loss at the races. He had taken a good deal of wine, but, nevertheless, he was silenced. There was nothing to be done. It was impossible to waft the young lad down to Trinity during the night watches.

'I wouldn't have had it to happen for any money you could name,' said the elder brother to the younger, as he took him home to Carlton Terrace.

'If they do send me down, what's the odds?' said the younger brother, who was not quite as sober as he might have been.

'After what happened to me it will almost break the governor's heart,' said the heir.

CHAPTER 18

ONE OF THE RESULTS OF THE DERBY

ON the following morning at about eleven Silverbridge and his brother were at breakfast at an hotel in Jermyn Street. They had slept in Carlton Terrace, but Lord Gerald had done so without the knowledge of the Duke. Lord Silverbridge had at one time, just as he was putting himself to bed, made up his mind to tell the whole story to the Duke, but when the morning came his courage failed him. The two young men therefore slunk out of the house, and as there was no breakfasting at the Beargarden they went to this hotel. They were both rather gloomy, but the elder brother was certainly the more sad of the two. 'I'd give anything I have in the world,' he said, 'that you hadn't come up at all.'

'Things have been so unfortunate!'

'Why the deuce wouldn't you go when I told you?'

'Who on earth would have thought that they'd have been so punctual? They never are punctual on the Great Eastern. It was an infernal shame.' But what was to be done? 'I think I shall go at once to Harnage and tell him all about it,' said Lord Gerald. Now Mr. Harnage was Lord Gerald's tutor.

'But you've been in ever so many scrapes before.'

'Well,—I've been gated, and once when they'd gated me I came right upon Harnage on the bridge at King's.'

'What an ass you must have been. What sort of a fellow is he?'

'He used to be good-natured. At least they all say so. Now he has taken ever so many crotchets into his head. It was he who began all this about none of the men going to the Derby.'

'Did you ask him yourself for leave?'

'Yes;—and he wouldn't give it me. And when I told him about your owning Prime Minister and all that, he got savage and declared that was the very reason why I shouldn't go.'

'You didn't tell me all that.'

'I was determined I would go. I wasn't going to be made a child of.'

At last it was decided that the two brothers should go down to Cambridge together. Silverbridge would be able to come back to London the same evening, so as to take his drag down to the Oaks on the Friday,—a duty from which even his present misery would not deter him. They reached Cambridge at about three, and Lord Silverbridge, according to the plan which had been made, at once called at the Master's lodge and sent in his card. The Master of Trinity is a man so great that he cannot be supposed to see all comers, but on this occasion Lord Silverbridge was fortunate. With much trepidation he told his story. Such being the circumstances, could anything be done to moderate the vials of wrath which must doubtless be poured out over the head of his unfortunate brother?

'Why come to me?' said the Master. 'From what you say yourself it is evident that you know that this must rest with the college tutor.'

'I thought, sir, if you would say a word.'

'Do you think it would be right that I should interfere for one special man, and that a man of special rank?'

'Nobody thinks that would count for anything. But——'

'But what?' asked the Master.

'If you knew my father, sir!'

'Everybody knows your father;—every Englishman I mean. Of course I know your father,—as a public man, and I know how much the country owes to him.'

'Yes, it does. But it is not that I mean. If you knew how this would,—would,—would break his heart.' Then there came a tear into the young man's eye,—and there was something almost like a tear in the eye of the old man too. 'Of course it was my fault. I got him to come because I had a horse of my own running. He hadn't the slightest intention of staying. I think you will believe what I say about that, sir.'

'I believe every word you say, my Lord.'

'I got into a row at Oxford. I dare say you heard. There never was anything so stupid. That was a great grief to my father,—a very great grief. It is so hard upon him because he never did anything foolish in all his life.'

'You should try to imitate him.' Silverbridge shook his head. 'Or at least not to grieve him.'

'That is it. He has got over the affair about me. As I'm the eldest son I've got into Parliament, and he thinks, perhaps, that all has been forgotten. An eldest son may, I fancy, be a greater ass than his younger brother.' The Master could not but smile as he thought of the selection which had been made of a legislator. 'But if Gerald is sent down, I don't know how he'll get over it. If you could do anything for my father's sake I should think so much of it.' And now the tears absolutely rolled down the young man's face, so that he was forced to wipe them from his eyes.

The Master was much moved. That a young man should pray for himself would be nothing to him. The discipline of the college was not in his hands, and such prayers ought not to avail and would not avail anything. Nor would a brother praying simply for a brother avail much. A father asking for his son might be resisted. But the brother asking pardon for the brother on behalf of the father was almost irresistible. But this man had long been in a position in which he knew that no such prayers should ever prevail at all. In the first place it was not his business. If he did anything, it would only be by asking a favour when he knew that no favour should be granted;—and a favour which he of all men should not ask, because to him of all men it could hardly be refused. And then the very altitude of the great Statesman whom he was invited to befriend,—the position of this Duke who had made bishops and who might so probably be called on to make them again,—was against any such interference. He himself might know of himself that he had nothing to wish for,—that as Master of Trinity he would accept no bishopric;—but others could not know it of him. Of himself he might be sure that he would certainly have done this as readily for any Mr. Jones as for the Duke of Omnium; but were he to do it, it would be said of him that it had been done because the man was Duke of Omnium and might so probably be again Prime Minister of England. There are positions exalted beyond the reach of benevolence, because benevolence would seem to be self-seeking. 'Your father if he were here,' said he, 'would know that I could not interfere in this matter without doing wrong.'

'And will he be sent down?'

'I do not know all the circumstances. From your own showing the case seems to be one of great insubordination. To tell the truth, Lord Silverbridge, I ought not to have spoken to you on the subject at all.'

'You mean that I should not have spoken to you.'

'Well;—I did not say so. And if you have been indiscreet I certainly can pardon that. I wish I could have served you; but I fear that it is not in my power.' Then Lord Silverbridge took his leave, and going to his brother's rooms waited there till Lord Gerald had returned from his interview with the tutor.

'It's all up,' said he, chucking down his cap and striving to be cheerful as he entered the room. 'I may pack up and go—just where I please. He says that on no account will he have anything more to do with me. And that means that I am to go down. I asked him what I was to do, and he said that the governor had better take my name off the books of the college. I did ask whether I couldn't go over to Maclean.'

'Who is Maclean?'

'One of the other tutors. But the brute only smiled.'

'He thought you meant it for chaff.'

'Well;—I suppose I did mean to show him that I was not going to be exterminated by him. He will write to the governor to-day, and he was kind enough to say that I might do what I liked about keeping my rooms for a day or two. You will have to talk to the governor.'

Yes! As Lord Silverbridge went back that afternoon to London he thought very much of that talking to the governor! Never yet had he been able to say anything very pleasant to 'the governor.' He had himself been always in disgrace at Eton, and had been sent away from Oxford. He had introduced Tregear to the family, which of all the troubles perhaps was the worst. He had changed his politics. He had spent more money than he ought to have done, and now at this very moment must ask for a large sum. And he had brought Gerald up to see the Derby, thereby causing him to be sent away from Cambridge! Had ever a father more reason to be displeased with a son? And through it all there was present to him a feeling that by no words which he could use would he be able to make his father understand how deeply he felt all this. His father, who seemed to expect that he should all at once become a first-class member of Parliament,—which he knew to be impossible,—seemed to him to give him no credit whatever for the good qualities which he did possess.

He could not bring himself to see the Duke that evening, and the next morning he was sent for before he was out of bed. He found his father at breakfast with the tutor's letter before him. 'Do you know anything about this?' asked the Duke very calmly.

'I suppose I know all about it.'

'What is it?'

'Gerald ran up to see the Derby and in the evening missed his train.'

'Mr. Harnage tells me that he had been expressly ordered not to go to these races.'

'I suppose he was, sir.'

Then there was silence between them for some minutes. 'You might as well sit down and eat your breakfast,' said the father. Then Lord Silverbridge did sit down and poured himself out a cup of tea. There was no servant in the room, and he dreaded to ring the bell. 'Is there anything you want?' asked the Duke. There was a small dish of fried bacon on the table, and some cold mutton on the sideboard. Silverbridge, declaring that he had everything that was necessary, got up and helped himself to the cold mutton. Then again there was silence, during which the Duke crunched his toast and made an attempt at reading the newspaper. But, soon pushing that aside, he again took up Mr. Harnage's letter. Silverbridge watched every motion of his father as he slowly made his way through the slice of cold mutton. 'It seems that Gerald is to be sent away, altogether?'

'I fear so, sir.'

'He has profited by your example at Oxford?' This he put as a question, but his son did not feel himself bound to answer it. Then another question was asked, the answering of which could not be avoided. 'Did you persuade him to come to these wretched races?'

'I am afraid I did.'

'Though you knew the orders which had been given?'

'I thought it was meant that he should not be away the night. That was altogether an accident.'

'He had asked permission to go to the Derby and had been positively refused. Did you know that?'

Silverbridge sat for some moments considering. He could not at first quite remember what he had known and what he had not known. Perhaps he entertained some faint hope that the question would be allowed to pass unanswered. He saw, however, from his father's eye that that was impossible. And then he did remember it all. 'I suppose I did know it.'

'And you were willing to imperil your brother's position in life, and my happiness, in order that he might see a horse, of which I believe you call yourself part owner, run a race?'

'I thought there would be no risk if he got back the same night. I don't suppose there is any good in my saying it, but I never was so sorry for anything in all my life. I didn't think very much about it. Of course Gerald wanted to be there, and I was anxious to please him. Now, as it has gone in this way, I feel as if I could go and hang myself.'

'That is absurd,—and unmanly,' said the Duke. The expression of sorrow, as it had been made, might be absurd and unmanly, but nevertheless it had touched him. He was severe because he did not know how far his severity wounded, but no father could be less willing to add to any sorrow that his son might feel. 'It is a great blow;—another great blow! What he had better do I cannot say. Races! A congregation of all the worst blackguards in the country mixed with the greatest fools.'

'Lord Cantrip was there,' said Silverbridge;—'and I'm sure I saw Sir Timothy Beeswax.'

The stroke would have been a good stroke if Silverbridge had contented himself with quoting Lord Cantrip, who, as the reader knows, was a man much respected by the Duke. But the second venture was not so good. There was perhaps no man in England at the present moment whom the Duke both disliked and despised more thoroughly than he did Sir Timothy Beeswax. 'If the presence of Sir Timothy Beeswax be an allurement to you, I pity you indeed. I have nothing further to say about it. You have ruined your brother.'

'Don't say that, sir.'

'What am I to do about him?'

'Let him be—an attaché, or something of that kind.'

'Do you believe it possible that he should pass any examination? I do not know what to do. I think that my children between them will bring me to the grave. You had better go now. I suppose you will want to be—at the races again.' Then the young man crept out of the room, and going to his own part of the house shut himself up alone for nearly an hour. What had he better do to give his father some comfort? Should he abandon racing altogether, sell his share of Prime Minister and Coalition, and go in hard and strong for committees, debates, and divisions? Should he get rid of his drag, and resolve to read up parliamentary literature? He might determine to do all this, but he found that he was not strong enough to keep to any such determination. He was resolved upon one thing at any rate. He would not go to the Oaks that day. And then he was resolved on another thing. He would call on Lady Mab Grex and ask her advice. No one could give him advice so good as Lady Mab Grex. He felt so disconsolate and insufficient for himself that he wanted advice from someone whom he could trust.

He found Tifto, Dolly Longstaffe, and one or two others at the stables, from whence it was intended that the drag should start. They were waiting, and rather angry because they had been kept waiting for a quarter of an hour. But the news, when it came, was very sad indeed. 'You wouldn't mind taking the team down and back yourself; would you, Dolly?' he said to Longstaffe.

'You ain't going!' said Dolly, assuming a look of mock-heroic horror.

'No;—I am not going to-day.'

'What's up?' asked Popplecourt.

'Not going!' said Tifto.

'Not to-day, Major.'

'That's rather sudden;—isn't it?' asked the Major.

'Well; yes; I suppose it is sudden.'

'It's throwing us over a little, isn't it?'

'Not that I see. You've got the trap and the horses.'

'Yes;—we've got the trap and the horses,' said Dolly, 'and I vote we make a start. Silverbridge is wanted to make a House,* no doubt.'

'As you are not going yourself, perhaps I'd better drive your horses,' said Tifto.

'Dolly will take the team,' said his lordship.

'Yes;—decidedly. I will take the team,' said Dolly. 'There isn't a deal of driving wanted on the road to Epsom, but a man should know how to hold his reins.' This of course gave rise to some angry words, but Silverbridge did not stop to hear them.

The poor Duke had no one to whom he could go for advice and consolation. When his son left him he turned to his newspaper, and tried to read it—in vain. His mind was too ill at ease to admit even of political matters. He was greatly grieved by this new misfortune as to Gerald. He was disappointed at finding that his elder son gave his mind to all mean things rather than to the House of Commons and to public matters. It was not that he had expected much immediate work from the young member, but that he had thought,—at any rate had hoped,—that the possession of the privileges of Parliament would have had an immediate if not a permanent effect on the young man's mind. As far as he could see, getting into Parliament had been no more to his heir than getting into some Beargarden Club might have been.

But though these sorrows were heavy, there was a sorrow heavier than these. Lady Cantrip had expressed an opinion almost in favour of Tregear,—and had certainly expressed an opinion in favour of Mrs. Finn. The whole affair in regard to Mrs. Finn had been explained to her,—with perfect justice and truth,—and she had told the Duke that, according to her thinking, Mrs. Finn had behaved well! When the Duke, with an energy which was by no means customary with him, had asked that question on the answer to which so much depended,—'Should there have been a moment lost?'—Lady Cantrip had assured him that not a moment had been lost. Mrs. Finn had at once gone to work, and had arranged that the whole affair should be told to him, the Duke, in the proper way. 'I think she did,' said Lady Cantrip, 'what I myself should have done in similar circumstances. I could not have made myself the informer, but I should have taken care that the gentleman should tell his own tale without delay. That, I take it, is the usual and the proper course.'

This was altogether terrible to the Duke. In the first place it conveyed to him the opinion of this lady, whom he had been willing to trust in the matter, that Tregear was to be regarded as a suitor who had been entitled at any rate to make his suit. He himself had felt that the young man should have been regarded as having travelled as it were out of his own hemisphere in what he had done;—as an Ixion who had tried to fly into the heavens, as a Phaethon who had thought that he could drive the horses of the sun, as a Marsyas who had piped in emulation of the god,—and that the punishment of an Ixion, a Phaethon, or a Marsyas should befall the arrogant intruder.* He was especially desirous that his daughter should be imbued with this idea;—but how could that be if Lady Cantrip, who had the charge of his daughter, would not allow herself to be so imbued?

And then how was he to answer that letter of Mrs. Finn's? If Lady Cantrip was right, then must his apology to Mrs. Finn be ample and abject. Perhaps it was this latter feeling which at the moment was most vexatious to him.

CHAPTER 19

'NO, MY LORD, I DO NOT'

BETWEEN two and three o'clock Lord Silverbridge, in spite of his sorrow, found himself able to eat a good lunch at his club. He had not enjoyed his breakfast, and was hungry. The place was quite deserted, at any rate so far as his own friends were concerned, the Beargarden world having gone to the races. As he sat there alone eating cold lamb and drinking soda-and-brandy he did confirm himself in certain resolutions,—modified resolutions, which, as he had told himself, might be more probably kept than those sterner laws of absolute renunciation to which he had thought of pledging himself in his half-starved morning condition. His father had spoken in very strong language against racing,—saying that those who went were either fools or rascals. He was sure that this was exaggerated. Half the House of Lords and two-thirds of the House of Commons were to be seen at the Derby; but no doubt there were many rascals and fools, and he could not associate with the legislators without finding himself among the fools and rascals. He would,—as soon as he could,—separate himself from the Major. And he would not bet. It was on that side of the sport that the rascals and the fools showed themselves. Of what service could betting be to him whom Providence had provided with all things wanted to make life pleasant? He would certainly give up betting. As to the drag, his father had in a certain measure approved of that, and he would keep the drag. He must have some relaxation, and there could be no reason why that relaxation should not consist in driving four horses. But his great effort of all should be made in the House of Commons. He would endeavour to make his father perceive that he had read and appreciated that letter. He would always be in the House soon after four, and would remain

there,—for, if possible, as long as the Speaker sat in the chair. He had
already begun to feel that there was a difficulty in keeping his seat upon
those benches. The half-hours there would be longer than he had ever
known them to be elsewhere. An irresistible desire of sauntering out, at
any rate as far as the smoking-room, would come upon him. There were
men the very sound of whose voices had already become odious to him.
Already there had come upon him a feeling in regard to certain habitual
orators, that when once they had begun to speak there was no reason why
they should ever stop. Words of some sort were always forthcoming like
spiders' webs, and as for matter it could be spread out so thin that the
smallest fragment of an idea might be made to last for an hour. He did
not think that he could learn to take a pleasure in sitting in the House; but
he hoped that he might be man enough to do it, though it was not pleasant. He would at any rate begin to-day, instead of going to the Oaks.

But before he went to the House he would endeavour to see Lady
Mabel Grex. And here it may be well to state that in making his resolutions as to a better life,—a life which might be better for his father's
sake rather than his own,—he had considered much whether it would
not be well for him to take a wife. His father had once told him that
when he married, the house in Carlton Terrace should be his own.
'I will be a lodger, if you will have me,' said the Duke, 'or if your wife
should not like that, I will find a lodging elsewhere.' This had been in
the sadness and tenderness which had immediately followed the death
of the Duchess. It had been evident that the Duke had then thought
that he ought to marry. Marriage would steady him. Were he a married
man, Tifto would of course disappear. Upon the whole he thought it
would be good that he should marry. And, if so, who could be so nice as
Lady Mabel? That his father would be contented with Lady Mab, he
was inclined to believe. His father, he knew well, had no great respect
for Lord Grex, who was a gambler and a roué, and had never attended
much to his parliamentary duties in the House of Lords. But there was
no better blood in England, and Lady Mabel was known to be clever,
beautiful, and, in her peculiar circumstances, very wise. There was an
attraction about Lady Mabel which he had found in no other girl.

He was aware, however, of a certain drawback, though he had never
as yet succeeded in defining it to himself. Lady Mabel as his wife
would be his superior, and in some degree his master. Though not
older she was wiser than he,—and not only wiser but more powerful
also. She might perhaps require of him more than he would be willing
to give. And he was not quite sure but that she regarded him as a boy.
He thought that she did love him,—or would do so if he asked

her,—but that her love would be bestowed upon him as on an inferior creature. He could not bring the phrases to his mind by which he could explain all this to himself,—but he did not like to think that she should patronise him and be kind to him, and perhaps at last become his wife, partly because he was the eldest son of a duke and partly because she liked him as a boy. He was already jealous of his own dignity, and fearful lest he should miss the glory of being loved by this lovely one for his own sake,—for his own manhood, and his own gifts and his own character.

And yet his attraction to her was so great that now in the day of his sorrow he could think of no solace but what was to be found in her company. 'Not at the Oaks!' she said as soon as he was shown into the drawing-room.

'No;—not at the Oaks. Lord Grex is there, I suppose.'

'Oh, yes;—that is a matter of course. He has been down in the neighbourhood since Wednesday. He comes up to-day to dinner. Why are you a recreant?'

'The House sits to-day.'

'How virtuous! Is it coming to that,—that when the House sits you will never be absent?'

'That's the kind of life I'm going to lead. You haven't heard anything about Gerald?'

'About your brother?'

'Yes. You haven't heard?'

'Not a word. I hope there is no misfortune.'

'But indeed there is,—a most terrible misfortune.' Then he told the whole story,—how Gerald had been kept in London, and how he had gone down to Cambridge,—all in vain; how his father had taken the matter to heart, telling him that he had ruined his brother; and how he, in consequence, had determined not to go to the races. 'Then he said,' continued Silverbridge, 'that his children between them would bring him to his grave.'

'That was terrible.'

'Very terrible;—was it not?'

'But what did he mean by that?' asked Lady Mabel, anxious to hear something about Lady Mary and Tregear.

'Well;—of course what I did at Oxford made him unhappy, and now there is this affair of Gerald's.'

'He did not allude to your sister?'

'Yes, he did. You have heard of all that, I know. Tregear told you.'

'He told me something.'

'Of course my father does not like it. In fact he looks upon it as quite out of the question. I suppose Mary will not give it up.'

'Do you approve of it?'

'No,' said he,—curtly and sturdily.

'Why not? You like Tregear.'

'Certainly I like Tregear. He is the friend, among men, whom I like the best. I have only two real friends in the world,—two that I care for.'

'Who are they?' she asked, sinking her voice very low,—feeling herself to be almost sure what his answer would be, but yet anxious to hear it.

'He is one,—and you are the other. You knew that.'

'I hoped that I was one, though I didn't know that there were only two,' she said. 'But if you love Tregear so dearly,—that is if you are so fond of him,—why do you not approve of him for your sister?'

'I always knew it would not do.'

'But why not?'

'Mary ought to marry a man of higher standing.'

'Of higher rank you mean. The daughters of dukes have married commoners before.'

'It is not exactly that. I don't like to talk of it in that way. I knew it would make my father unhappy. It isn't as though he had got any money. In point of fact he can't marry her. What is the good of approving of a thing that is impossible?'

'I wish I knew your sister. Is she—firm? When she takes a thing in her head does she stick to it?'

'Indeed she does.'

'I am not so sure that you are.'

'No,' said he, after considering awhile; 'nor am I. But she is not like Gerald or me. She is much more obstinate.'

'Less fickle, perhaps.'

'Yes,—if you choose to call it fickle. I don't know that I am fickle.'

'I think you would be.'

'Then you don't know me. If I were in love with a girl I should be true to her.'

'Are you sure of that?'

'Quite sure. If I were really in love with her I certainly should not change. It is possible that I might be bullied out of it.'

'But she will not be bullied out of it?'

'Mary? No. That is just it. She will stick to it if he does. And yet what is the use?'

'I would if I were she. Where will you find any young man equal to Frank Tregear? Do you know anyone? I don't.'

'Perhaps you mean to cut poor Mary out.'

'That isn't a nice thing for you to say, Lord Silverbridge. Frank is my cousin,—as indeed you are also; but it so happens that I have seen a great deal of him all my life. And, though I don't want to cut your sister out, as you so prettily say, I love him well enough to understand that any girl whom he loves ought to be true to him.' So far what she said was very well, but she afterwards added a word which might have been wisely omitted. 'Frank and I are almost beggars, and therefore, though we may be dear cousins,—the same as brother and sister almost,—we never could have been anything else.'

'What an accursed thing money is,' he exclaimed, jumping up from his chair with energy.

'I don't agree with you at all. I think it is a very blessed thing. I am sure it is a very comfortable thing.'

'How is anybody who has got it to know if anybody cares for him?'

'You must find that out. There is such a thing I suppose as real sympathy. The rich people are loved, I take it, quite as dearly as the poor.'

'You tell me to my face that you and Tregear would have been lovers, only that you are both poor.'

'I never said anything of the kind.'

'And that he is to be passed on to my sister because it is supposed that she will have some money.'

'You are putting words into my mouth which I never spoke, and ideas into my mind which I never thought, in a most unfair manner.'

'And of course I feel the same about myself. How can a fellow help it? I wish you had a lot of money, I know.'

'It is very kind of you;—but why?'

'Well;—I can't quite explain myself,' he said, blushing as was his wont. 'I dare say it wouldn't make any difference.'

'It would make a great difference to me. As it is, having none, and knowing as I do that papa and Percival are getting things into a worse mess every day, I am obliged to hope that I may some day marry a man who has got an income.'

'I suppose so,' said he, still blushing, but frowning at the same time.

'You see I can be very frank with a real friend. But I am sure of myself in this,—that I will never marry a man I do not love. A girl needn't love a man unless she likes it, I suppose. She doesn't tumble into love as she does into the fire. It would not suit me to marry a poor man, and so I don't mean to fall in love with a poor man.'

'But you do mean to fall in love with a rich one?'

'That remains to be seen, Lord Silverbridge. The rich man will at any rate have to fall in love with me first. What may happen then must depend on circumstances. If you know of anyone you need not tell him to be too sure because he has a good income.'

'There's Popplecourt. He's his own master, and, fool as he is, he knows how to keep his money.'

'I don't want a fool. You must do better for me than Lord Popplecourt.'

'What do you say to Dolly Longstaffe?'

'He would be just the man, only he never would take the trouble to come out and be married.'

'Or Glasslough?'

'I'm afraid he is cross, and wouldn't let me have my own way.'

'I can only think of one other;—but I know you wouldn't take him.'

'Then you had better not mention him. It is no good crowding the list with impossibles.'

'I was thinking of—myself.'

'You are certainly one of the impossibles.'

'Why, Lady Mab?'

'For twenty reasons. You are too young, and you are bound to oblige your father, and you are to be wedded to Parliament,—at any rate for the next ten years. And altogether it wouldn't do—for a great many reasons.'

'I suppose you don't like me well enough?'

'What a question to ask! No, my Lord, I do not. There. That's what you may call an answer. Don't you pretend to look offended, because if you do I shall laugh at you. If you may have your joke, surely I may have mine.'

'I don't see any joke in it.'

'But I do. Suppose I were to say the other thing. "Oh, Lord Silverbridge, you do me so much honour! And now I come to think about it, there is no one in the world I am so fond of as you." Would that suit you?'

'Exactly.'

'But it wouldn't suit me. There's papa. Don't run away.'

'It's ever so much past five,' said the legislator, 'and I had intended to be in the House more than an hour ago. Besides, I don't care about seeing your father. He would chaff me about that brute of a horse that did not win the race. Good-bye. Give my love to Miss Cassewary.'

'Certainly. Miss Cassewary is your most devoted friend. Won't you bring your sister to see me some day?'

'When she is in town, I will.'

'I should so like to know her. Good-bye.' Then, as he was shaking hands with her, he stood for a moment as though he would say yet another word. But he went at last without saying it.

As he hurried down to the House in a hansom he thought over it all, and told himself that he feared it would not do. She might perhaps accept him, but if so, she would do it simply in order that she might become Duchess of Omnium. And yet he was far from accusing her of mercenary feelings. She might, he thought, have accepted him then, had she chosen. He had spoken plainly enough. But she had laughed at him,—had told him that he was too young, had reminded him that he was bound to his father, and had quizzed him about his parliamentary duties. He felt that if she loved him, there ought to have been something of that feminine tremor, of that doubting, hesitating half avowal of which he had perhaps read in novels, and which his own instincts taught him to desire. But there had been no tremor nor hesitating. 'No, my Lord, I do not,' she had said when he asked her to her face whether she liked him well enough to be his wife. 'No, my Lord, I do not.' It was not the refusal conveyed in these words which annoyed him. He did believe that if he were to press his suit with the usual forms she would accept him. All that she had said as to her want of money tended that way. But it was that there should be such a total absence of trepidation in her words and manner. Before her he trembled and blushed and hesitated and felt that he did not know how to express himself. If she would only have done the same, then there would have been an equality. Then he could have seized her in his arms and sworn that never, never, never would he care for anyone but her. But her coolness and self-command and badinage cowed him.

In truth he saw everything as it was only too truly. Though she might choose to marry him if he pressed his request, she would never subject herself to him as he would have the girl do whom he loved. She was his superior, and in every word uttered between them showed that it was so. She knew so much more of the world than he did,—was so much more confident of herself,—in fact so much older! But yet how beautiful she was;—how much more beautiful than any other thing he had ever seen! If he could seize her in his arms and kiss her, what an Elysium of happiness would it not be to him! And perhaps it might be fortunate for him that he should have a wife in some degree superior to him. He sat on one of the high seats behind Sir Timothy Beeswax and Sir Orlando Drought, listening, or pretending to listen, to the speeches of three or four gentlemen respecting sugar, thinking of all this till half-past seven;—and then he went to dine at his club with the proud consciousness of having done his duty. The forms and methods of the House were, he flattered himself, soaking into him gradually,—as his father had desired. The theory of legislation was sinking into his mind. The welfare of the nation depended chiefly on sugar. That he had thoroughly learned. But he thought that, after all, his own welfare must depend on the possession of Mab Grex.

CHAPTER 20
'THEN HE WILL COME AGAIN'

LADY MABEL, when her young lover left her, was for a time freed from the necessity of thinking about him by her father. He had returned from the Oaks very early, but in a very bad humour. Lord Grex had been very badly treated by his son, whom he perhaps hated worse than anyone else in the world. On the Derby day he had won a large sum of money, which had been to him at the time a matter of intense delight,—for he was in great want of ready money. But on this day he had discovered that Lord Percival, his son and heir, had lost rather more than he had won, and an arrangement had been suggested to him that his winnings should go to pay Percival's losings. This was a mode of settling affairs to which the Earl would not listen for a moment, had he possessed the power of putting a veto upon it. But there had been a transaction lately between him and his son with reference to the cutting off a certain entail under which money was to be paid to Lord Percival. This money had not yet been forthcoming, and therefore the Earl was constrained to assent. Lord Percival put it in this way. I owe A.B. a thousand pounds. A.B. owes the same sum to C.D. C.D. owes it again to the Earl. The Earl owes that, and ever so much more, to me. To the extent of the thousand pounds, let us cry quits. There was some rounding off needed, but such was the nature of the suggestion generally. It was very distasteful to the Earl, and he came home therefore in a bad humour, and said a great many disagreeable things to his daughter. 'You know, papa, if I could do anything I would.' This she said in answer to a threat, which he had made often before and now repeated, of getting rid altogether of the house in Belgrave Square. Whenever he made this threat he did not scruple to tell her that the house had to be kept up solely for her welfare, and then he would say very nasty words about Miss Cassewary. 'I don't see why the deuce you don't get married to somebody. You'll have to do it sooner or later.' That was not a pleasant speech for a daughter to hear from her father. 'As to that,' she said, 'it must come or not as chance will have it. If you want me to sign anything, I will sign it.' For she had been asked to sign papers, or in other words to surrender rights. 'But for that other matter, it must be left to myself.' Then he had been very disagreeable indeed.

They dined out together,—of course with all the luxury that wealth can give. There was a well-appointed carriage to take them backwards and forwards to the next square, such as an earl should have. She was splendidly dressed, as became an earl's daughter, and he was brilliant with some star which had been accorded to him* by his grateful Sovereign, or by his Sovereign's grateful minister, in return for staunch parliamentary support. No one looking at them could have imagined that such a father could have told such a daughter that she must marry herself out of the way, because as an unmarried girl she was a burden too heavy to be borne! And yet something very like that had occurred.

During the dinner she was very gay. To be gay was the habit,—we may almost say the work,—of her life. It so chanced that she sat between Sir Timothy Beeswax, who in these days was a very great man indeed, and that very Mr. Longstaffe, Dolly Longstaffe, whom Silverbridge in his irony had proposed to her as a fitting suitor for her hand.

'Isn't Lord Silverbridge a cousin of yours?' asked Sir Timothy.

'A very distant one.'

'He has come over to us, you know. It is such a triumph.'

'I was so sorry to hear it.' This, however, as the reader knows, was a fib.

'Sorry!' said Sir Timothy. 'Surely Lord Grex's daughter must be a Conservative.'

'Oh yes;—I am a Conservative because I was born one. I think that people in politics should remain as they are born,—unless they are very wise indeed. When men come to be Statesmen and all that kind of thing of course they can change backwards and forwards.'

'I hope that is not intended for me, Lady Mabel.'

'Certainly not. I don't know enough about it to be personal.' That, however, was again not quite true. 'But I have the greatest possible respect for the Duke, and I think it such a pity that he should be made unhappy by his son. Don't you like the Duke?'

'Well;—yes;—in a way. He is a most respectable man; and has been a good public servant.'

'Is that all?'

'What more am I to say? He certainly is not a friendly man. He never could keep a Cabinet together. He is as cold as ice, you know;—and then he thinks so much of his own dignity.'

'All our lot are ruined, you know,' said Dolly, talking of the races.

'Who are your lot, Mr. Longstaffe?'

'I'm one myself.'

'I suppose so.'

'I'm utterly smashed. I don't know what I shall have to do to raise the money. Then there's Percival.'

'I hope he has not lost much. Of course you know he's my brother.'

'Oh laws;—so he is. I always put my foot in it, if it's possible. Well;—he has lost a lot. And so have Silverbridge and Tifto. Perhaps you don't know Tifto.'

'I have not the pleasure of knowing Mr. Tifto.'

'He is a major. I think you'd like Major Tifto. He's a sort of racing coach to Silverbridge. You ought to know Tifto. And Tregear is pretty nearly cleared out.'

'Mr. Tregear! Frank Tregear!'

'I'm told he has been hit very heavy. I hope he's not a friend of yours, Lady Mabel.'

'Indeed he is;—a very dear friend, and a cousin. I did not think that he ever betted.'

'That's what I hear. He's very much with Silverbridge, you know. All of them who went in for the Prime Minister have had a bad time of it.'

'I cannot think that Mr. Tregear has lost money.'

'I hope he hasn't. I know I have. I wish someone would stick up for me, and say that it was impossible.'

'But that is not Mr. Tregear's way of living at all. I can understand that Lord Silverbridge or Percival should lose money.'

'Or me?'

'Or you, if you like to say so.'

'Or Tifto?'

'I don't know anything about Mr. Tifto.'

'Major Tifto.'

'Or Major Tifto;—what does it signify?'

'No;—of course. We inferior people may lose our money just as we please. But a man who can look as clever as Mr. Tregear ought to win always.'

'I told you just now that he was a friend of mine.'

'But don't you think that he does look clever?' There could be no question but that Tregear, when he disliked his company, could show his dislike by his countenance; and it was not improbable that he had done so in the presence of Mr. Adolphus Longstaffe, who was a gentleman quite able to appreciate such signs of disfavour. 'Now, tell the truth, Lady Mabel;—does he not look conceited sometimes?'

'He generally looks as if he knew what he was talking about;—which is more than some other people do sometimes.'

'Of course he is a great deal more clever than I am. I know that. But I don't think even he can be so clever as he looks. "Or you so stupid";—that's what you ought to say now.'

'Sometimes, Mr. Longstaffe, I deny myself the pleasure of saying what I think.'

When all this was over she was very angry with herself for the anxiety she had expressed about Tregear and his affairs. This Mr. Longstaffe was, she thought, exactly the man to report all she had said in the public room at the club. But she had been annoyed by what she had heard as to her friend,—that he should have been betting and losing money. She knew that he of all men should keep himself free from such follies. Those others had, as it were, a right to make fools of themselves. She would not have said that they were born to do so,—but she almost felt it. It had seemed so natural that the young men of her own class should dissipate their fortunes and their reputations by every kind of indulgence and extravagance! Her father had done so, and she had never even ventured to hope that her brother would not follow her father's example. That Lord Silverbridge should be one of the same set was natural too; but then it was almost impossible that he should injure himself very much. Losses that would ruin others' properties would hardly be felt by the wealth which supported the house of Omnium. But Tregear, if he gave way to such follies as these, would soon fall headlong into a pit from which there would be no extrication. And if he did fall, she knew herself well enough to be aware that she could not stifle, nor even conceal, the misery which this would occasion her. As long as he stood well before the world she would be well able to assume indifference, almost to feel it. But were he to be precipitated into some bottomless misfortune, then she thought that she could only throw herself after him. She could see him marry, and smile,—and perhaps even like his wife. And while he was doing so, she could also marry, and resolve that the husband whom she took should be made to think that he had the most loving wife in England. But were Frank to die,—then must she fall upon his body as though he had been known by all the world to be her lover. Something of this feeling came upon her now, when she heard that he had been betting and had been unfortunate.

She had been unable so to subdue herself as to seem to be perfectly careless about it. She had begun by saying that she had not believed it;—but she had believed it. It was so natural that Tregear should have done as the others did with whom he lived! But then the misfortune would be to him so terrible,—so irremediable! The reader, however, may as well know at once that there was not a word of truth in the assertion;—that when Silverbridge had suggested to his poorer friend that he could 'put a very good thing in his way,' the poorer friend had absolutely refused to have anything to do with good things of that sort. Somebody had said at the club that Tregear had been carried away by the energy of the owner of the unfortunate horse, and hence had come Dolly Longstaffe's report. But at the present moment Lady Mabel did believe it, and the belief added much to her unhappiness.

After the dinner she went home alone. There were other festivities to be attended, had she pleased to attend them; and poor Miss Cassewary was dressed ready to go with her as chaperone;—but Miss Cassewary, in spite of the trouble she had thus taken, was quite satisfied to be allowed to go to bed in lieu of Mrs. Montacute Jones's great ball.* And she had gone to her bedroom and had begun to strip herself of her finery when Lady Mabel went to her. 'I am glad you are alone,' she said, 'because I must speak to you.'

'Is anything wrong?'

'Everything is wrong,—everything. Papa says he must give up this house.'

'He says that almost always when he comes back from the races, and very often when he comes back from the club. No doubt he wins sometimes, and then he says nothing about it.'

'Percival has lost ever so much.'

'I don't think my Lord will hamper himself for your brother.'

'I can't explain it, but there is some horrible money complication. It is hard upon you and me.'

'Who am I?' said Miss Cassewary.

'About the dearest friend that ever a poor girl had. It is hard upon you,—and upon me. I have given up everything;—as far as I can understand, everything. And what good have I done?'

'It is hard, my dear.'

'But after all I do not care much for all that. I suppose papa and Percival will not become beggars altogether. The thing has been going on so long that one is used to it.'

'What is it then?'

'Ah;—yes; what is it? How am I to tell you?'

'Surely you can tell me,' said the old woman, putting out her hand so as to caress the arm of the younger one.

'I could tell no one else; I am sure of that. Frank Tregear has taken to gambling,—like the rest of them.'

'Who says so?'

'He has lost a lot of money at these races. A man who sat next to me at dinner,—one of those stupid gaping do-nothing fools that one meets everywhere,—told me so. He is one of the Beargarden set, and of course he knows all about it. How is Frank to pay a large sum of money?'

'Did he say how much?'

'How is he to pay anything? Of all the things that men do this is I think the worst. A man who would think himself disgraced for ever if he accepted a present of money will not scruple to use all his wits to rob his friend of everything that he has by studying the run of cards or by watching the paces of some brutes of horses! And they consider themselves to be fine gentlemen! A real gentleman should never want the money out of another man's pocket;—should never think of it. He should never think of money at all.'

'I don't know how that is to be helped, my dear. I have got to think of it, and you have got to think of it.'

'Yes;—I have to think of it, and do think of it. And because I do so, I am not what I call a gentleman.'

'No;—my dear; you're a lady.'

'Psha! You know what I mean. I might have had the feelings of a gentleman as well as the best man that ever was born. I haven't; things have gone against me. But I have never done anything so mean as gambling. Now I have got something else to tell you.'

'What is it? You do frighten me so when you look like that!'

'You may well be frightened,—for if this all comes round I shall very soon be able to dispense with you altogether. His Royal Highness, Lord Silverbridge——'

'What do you mean, Mabel?'

'He's next door to a Royal Highness at any rate, and a much more topping man than most of them. Well then;—His Serene Highness the heir of the Duke of Omnium has done me the inexpressible honour of asking me—to marry him.'

'No!'

'You may well say, No. And to tell the truth exactly, he didn't.'

'Then why do you say he did?'

'I don't think he did quite ask me, but he gave me to understand that he would like to do so if I would give him any encouragement.'

'Did he mean it?'

'Yes;—poor boy! He meant it. With a word;—with a look, he would have been down there, kneeling. He asked me whether I liked him well enough. What do you think I did?'

'What did you do?'

'I spared him;—out of sheer, downright, Christian charity! I said to myself, "Love your neighbour." "Don't be selfish." "Do unto him as you would he should do unto you";—that is think of his welfare. Though I had him in my net, I let him go. Shall I go to heaven for doing that?'

'I don't know,' said Miss Cassewary, who was so much perturbed by the news she had heard as to be unable to come to any opinion on the point just raised.

'Or mayn't I rather go to the other place? From how much embarrassment should I have relieved my father! What a friend I should have made for Percival! How much might I have been able to do for Frank! And then what a wife I should have made him!'

'I think you would.'

'He'll never get another half so good; and he'll be sure to get one before long. It is a sort of tenderness that is quite inefficacious,—and indeed injurious. He will become a prey, as I should have made him a prey. But where is there another who will treat him so well?'

'I cannot bear to hear you speak of yourself in that way.'

'But it is true. I know the sort of girl he should marry. In the first place she should be two years younger, and four years fresher. She should be able not only to like him and love him but to worship him. How well I can see her! She should have fair hair, and bright green-grey eyes, with the sweetest complexion, and the prettiest little dimples,—two inches shorter than me,—and the delight of her life should be to hang with two hands on his arm. She should have a feeling that her Silverbridge is an Apollo upon earth. To me he is a rather foolish, but very, very sweet-tempered young man;—anything rather than a god. If I thought that he would get the fresh young girl with the dimples, then I ought to abstain.'

'If he was in earnest,' said Miss Cassewary, throwing aside all this badinage and thinking of the main point,—than which nothing could be more important,—'if he was in earnest, he will come again.'

'He was quite in earnest.'

'Then he will come again.'

'I don't think he will,' said Lady Mabel. 'I told him that I was too old for him; and I tried to laugh him out of it. He does not like being laughed at. He has been saved, and he will know it.'

'But if he should come again?'

'I shall not spare him again; no,—not twice. I felt it to be hard to do so once, because I so nearly love him. There are so many of them who are odious to me,—with whom I could not bear to think that I should be linked for a life,—as to whom the idea of marriage seems to be mixed somehow with an idea of suicide.'

'Oh, Mabel!'

'But he is as sweet as a rose. If I were his sister, or his servant, or his dog I could be devoted to him. I can fancy that his comfort and his success and his name should be everything to me.'

'That is what a wife ought to feel.'

'But I could never feel him to be my superior. That is what a wife ought in truth to feel. Think of those two young men and the difference between them! Well;—don't look like that at me. I don't often give way, and I dare say after all I shall live to be the Duchess of Omnium.' Then she kissed her friend and went away to her own room.

CHAPTER 21

SIR TIMOTHY BEESWAX

AT the time with which we are at present concerned the country was not, I think, very proud of its Ministry. Lord Drummond, the Prime Minister, sat in the House of Lords,—a man who in inferior offices had been much respected, but was now known to be a fainéant Premier,* placed in that position because the man who had succeeded in making himself the most powerful politician of the day had not as yet quite succeeded so far as to grasp the name and dignity of the first place.

There had lately been a great Conservative reaction* in the country, brought about in part, no doubt, by the industry and good management of gentlemen who were strong on that side;—but due also in part to the blunders and quarrels of their opponents. That these opponents should have blundered and quarrelled, being men active and in earnest, was to have been expected. Such blunderings and quarrellings have been a matter of course since politics have been politics, and since religion has been religion. When men combine to do nothing, how should there be disagreement? When men combine to do much, how should there not be disagreement? Thirty men can sit still, each as like the other as peas. But put your thirty men up to run a race, and they will go at different paces and soon assume different forms. And in doing nothing, you can hardly do amiss. To rest and be thankful is easy, so that a man's disposition be that way inclined. But who ever did a great work,—or even a little one,—without finding that there were blunders for him to fall into on the right side and on the left? The Roman Catholics are apt to point with pride to their own unanimity, and with scorn to the dissevered sects of Protestantism. But the Roman Catholic who has to think of nothing in his religion may well be of the same mind with others who also have no need of thinking. Whereas the Protestant has no such rampart of security. He must think. And men who think will differ. The wonder is that there should ever be in a reforming party enough of consentaneous action to carry any reform. The reforming or Liberal party in British politics had thus stumbled,—and stumbled,—and stumbled till it fell. And now there had been a great Conservative reaction! Many of the most Liberal constituencies in the country had been untrue to their old political convictions, desiring some change. And, as the result, Lord Drummond was Prime Minister in the House of Lords,—with Sir Timothy Beeswax acting as first man* in the House of Commons.

It cannot be denied that Sir Timothy had his good points as a politician. He was industrious, patient, clear-sighted, intelligent, courageous, and determined. Long before the time when he first sat in the House, when he was simply working his way up to the probability of a seat by making a reputation as an advocate, he had resolved that he would be more than an Attorney- or Solicitor-General, more than a judge,—more, as he thought it, than a Chief Justice; but at any rate something different. When by means of the law he had brought himself sufficiently forward for his purpose, he would take to politics as apart from law, and would bid high for the highest place in politics. This place he had all but gained,—and it must be acknowledged that he had been moved by a grand and manly ambition. When there is no such ambition in the heart of any citizen, the State must be at a low ebb indeed! But there were drawbacks to the utility and beauty of Sir Timothy's character as a Statesman. He had no idea as to the necessity or non-necessity of any measure whatsoever in reference to the well-being of the country. It may, indeed, be said that all such ideas were to him absurd, and the fact that they should be held by his friends and supporters was an inconvenience. That there must be a certain amount of legislation was of course a necessity; but, to his thinking, the less the better. He was not at all in accord with those who declare that a Parliament is a collection of windbags which puff, and blow, and crack only to the annoyance of honest men. He fully believed in Parliaments, and talked quite as frequently as anybody in the British House of Commons of the glory of the four walls which contained him and his fellow members. But to him Parliament was a debating place, by having a majority in which, and by no other means, he,—or another,—might become the great man of the day. By no other than parliamentary means could such a one as he come to be the chief governor. And this use of Parliament, either on his own behalf or on behalf of others, had been for so many years present to his mind, that there seemed to him to be nothing absurd in an institution supported for such a purpose. Parliament was a club so aristocratic and eligible in its nature that all Englishmen wished to belong to it. They who succeeded were acknowledged to be the cream of the land. They who dominated in it were the cream of the cream. Those two who were elected to be the chiefs of the two parties had more of cream in their composition than any others. But he who could be the chief of the strongest party, and who therefore, in accordance with the prevailing arrangements of the country, should have the power of making dukes and bestowing garters and appointing bishops, he who by attaining the first seat should achieve the right of snubbing all below him, whether friends or foes, he, according to the feelings of Sir Timothy, would have gained an Elysium of creaminess* not to be found in any other position on the earth's surface. No man was more warmly attached to parliamentary government than Sir Timothy Beeswax; but I do not think that he ever cared much for legislation.

Parliamentary management was his forte. There have been various rocks on which great men have shattered their barks in their attempts to sail successfully into the harbours of parliamentary management. There is the great Senator who declares to himself that personally he will have neither friend nor foe. There is his country before him and its welfare. Within his bosom is the fire of patriotism, and within his mind the examples of all past time. He knows that he can be just, he teaches himself to be eloquent, and he strives to be wise. But he will not bend;—and at last, in some great solitude, though closely surrounded by those whose love he had neglected to acquire,—he breaks his heart.

Then there is he who, seeing the misfortune of that great one, tells himself that patriotism, judgment, industry, and eloquence will not suffice for him unless he himself can be loved. To do great things a man must have a great following, and to achieve that he must be popular. So he smiles and learns the necessary wiles. He is all for his country and his friends,—but for his friends first. He too must be eloquent and well instructed in the ways of Parliament, must be wise and diligent. It is not by love only that he can sit on that high seat. But in all that he does and all that he says, and in every measure by which he strives to serve his country, he must first study his party. It is well with him for a time;—but he has closed the door of his Elysium too rigidly, and those who are without gradually become stronger than his friends within, and so he falls and—becomes almost nobody.

But may not the door be occasionally opened and an outsider admitted, so that the exterior force be diminished and brought down to a bearable quantity? We all know how great is the pressure of water; how the peril of an overwhelming weight of it may be removed by opening the way for a small current. There comes therefore the Statesman who acknowledges to himself that he will be pregnable. That, as a Statesman, he should have enemies is a matter of course. Against moderate enemies he will hold his own. But when there comes one immoderately, forcibly, violently inimical, then to that man he will open his bosom. In fact he will tempt into his camp, with an offer of high command, any foe that may be worth his purchase. This too has answered well; but there is a flabbiness about the proceeding which will not bear the wear and tear of much time. The loyalty of officers so procured must ever be open to suspicion. The man who has once said bitter things against you will never sit at your feet in contented submission, nor will your friend, who has been your friend all through, long endure to be superseded in favour of such converts.

All these dangers Sir Timothy had seen and studied, and for each of them he had hoped to be able to provide an antidote. Love could not do all,—if anything. Fear may do more. Fear acknowledges a superior. Love desires an equal. Love is to be created by benefits done, and means gratitude, which we all know to be weak. But hope, which refers itself to benefits to come, is of all our feelings the strongest. And Sir Timothy had parliamentary doctrines, concealed in the depth of his own bosom, beyond these and almost more important. The Statesman who falls is he who tries to do much, and thus injures many. The Statesman who stands the longest is he who does nothing and injures no one. He soon began to find that the work to which he had attached himself required all the art of a great conjurer. He must be possessed of tricks so marvellous that not even those friends who sat nearest to him might know how they were performed;—but these tricks should have nothing to do with either the executive or legislative business of the country. The one should be left in the hands of men who liked to work;—of the other there should be little, or, if possible, none. But Parliament must be managed,—and his party. It was in this that the conjuring was so necessary. Of patriotism he did not know the meaning;—perhaps few men do, beyond a feeling that they would like to lick the French or perhaps the Russians, or to get the better of the Americans in a matter of fisheries or frontiers.* But there would, he felt, be much need of a pseudo-patriotic conjuring by phraseology which no one should understand but which many might admire. It would have to be said,—if success were to be achieved,—that he was far-and-away the cleverest of his party. He knew himself to be clever. But he could only be far-and-away the cleverest by saying and doing that which no one else could understand. If he could become master of some great hocus-pocus system which could be made to be graceful to the ears and eyes of many, which might for a while seem to have within it some semi-divine attribute, which should have all but divine power of mastering the loaves and fishes, then would they who followed him believe in him more firmly than other followers who had believed in their leaders. When you see a young woman read a closed book placed on her dorsal vertebrae,—if you do believe that she so reads it,—you think that she is endowed with a very wonderful faculty! And should you also be made to believe that this same young woman had direct communication with Abraham, by means of some invisible wire, you would be apt to do a great many things as that young woman might tell you. Conjuring, when not known to be conjuring, must be very effective indeed.

There can be no doubt that much of Sir Timothy's power, much rather of his opportunity, had come from his most praiseworthy industry. Though he cared nothing for the making of laws, though he knew nothing of finance, which should now have been his own peculiar business, though he had abandoned his legal studies, still he worked very hard. And because he had worked harder in a special direction than others around him, therefore he was enabled to lead them. The management of a party is a very great work in itself; and when to that is added the management of the House of Commons, a man has enough upon his hands even though he neglects altogether the more ordinary pursuits of a Statesman. Those around Sir Timothy were fond of their party; but they were for the most part men who had not condescended to put their shoulders to the wheel as he had done. Had there been any very great light among them, had there been a Pitt or a Peel,* Sir Timothy would have probably become Attorney-General and in due course have made his way to the bench;*—but there had been no Pitt and no Peel, and he had seen his opening. He had studied the ways of members. Parliamentary practice had become familiar to him. He had shown himself to be ready at all hours to fight the battle of the party he had joined. And no man knew so well as did Sir Timothy how to elevate a simple legislative attempt into a good faction fight. And so he had been successful.

His parliamentary career had been versatile. For, though it might be true, as he had once boasted, that he had never changed his political principles, he had more than once changed his political friends. Not having had political principles, he could not but be consistent. He had been Solicitor-General to a Conservative minister,* and had thence, with many other Conservatives, joined the coalition which had been made under the auspices of the Duke of Omnium. When that was broken up he remained for a while with the Liberals. But the Liberal Government which was then formed by Mr. Monk had in it from the first so much of weakness that Sir Timothy did not see his way to remain. It would weary the reader were he to be called on here to read the remarkably clever explanation which he then gave of his conduct. It was, however, so clever that it enabled him without a blush to commence his attack upon his late colleagues from the very day on which he left them, and this he had done in a manner that had greatly assisted in producing their defeat. Now he was reaping his reward,—not so great a reward as he hoped might come in time, for he looked forward to the glory of making a duke or two out of his own bosom, and this could be done only when he should have succeeded in getting rid of the Lord who still was the Prime Minister of England,—but still a great reward. He had so mastered his tricks of conjuring that no one could get to the bottom of them, and had assumed a look of preternatural gravity which made many young members think that Sir Timothy was born to be a king of men.

There were no doubt some among his older supporters who felt their thraldom grievously. There were some lords in the Upper House and some sons of the lords in the Lower,—with pedigrees going back far enough for pride,—who found it irksome to recognise Sir Timothy as a master. No doubt he had worked very hard, and had worked for them. No doubt he knew how to do the work, and they did not. There was no other man among them to whom the lead could be conveniently transferred. But yet they were uncomfortable,—and perhaps a little ashamed.

It had arisen partly from this cause that there had been something of a counter reaction at the last general election. When the Houses met, the ministers had indeed a majority, but a very much lessened majority. The great old Liberal constituencies had returned to an expression of their real feeling. This reassertion of the progress of the tide, this recovery from the partial ebb which checks the violence of every flow, is common enough in politics; but at the present moment there were many who said that all this had been accelerated by a feeling in the country that Sir Timothy was hardly all that the country required as the Leader of the country party.

In some of the counties the reaction had been as palpable as in the large towns. In West Barset, where, as the reader may perhaps remember, the Duke of Omnium had been anxious that his son should stand in the Liberal interest, a Liberal had been returned for the first time since the first Reform Bill. The fight had been very severe, and the Conservative party declared that the Duke's money had flown like water. In fact the Duke had spent nothing. Mr. Moreton, the Duke's agent, was a hot politician* and had doubtless done all that he could; but he had scrupulously abstained from mentioning the Duke's name. At Silverbridge, as we know, a Conservative had been returned without a contest, and as this Conservative had been the Duke's son a great deal was made of it;—but that could go but a very little way towards consoling Sir Timothy and his friends for the great blow which they had received.

Then it was alleged that there was some little disagreement in the Cabinet. Lord Drummond had been heard to express himself strongly, and his very words had been repeated. 'I certainly shall not attempt to carry on Her Majesty's Government without a good working majority,'—and it had been added that peculiar emphasis was given to the word 'I,'—that emphasis which men are apt to use when they attempt to give strength to weakness by the tone of the voice. But the dictum of Sir Timothy in answer to this had also been repeated. 'Drummond doesn't know what he's talking about. He seldom does.' It was not at all probable that Sir Timothy had in truth committed himself by language so foolish as this. 'The men who as ministers have the strongest party at their back must carry on the Government. As far as I can see that is our position. If we are beaten on some particular point it may be necessary that we should go out. But everybody would know that we must come back again.' That was said to be Sir Timothy's view of the present state of affairs; but we all know how easy it is to put words into the mouths of great men.

CHAPTER 22

THE DUKE IN HIS STUDY

It was not unnatural that at such a time, when success greater than had been expected had attended the efforts of the Liberals, when some dozen votes more than anyone had ventured to hope had been acquired, the leading politicians of that party should have found themselves compelled to look about them and see how these good things might be utilised. In February they certainly had not expected to be called to power in the course of the existing session. Perhaps they did not expect it even yet. There was still a Conservative majority in the House of Commons,—though but a small majority. But the strength of the minority consisted, not in the fact that the majority against them was small, but that it was decreasing. How quickly does the snowball grow into hugeness as it is rolled on,—but when the change comes in the weather how quickly does it melt, and before it is gone become a thing ugly, weak, and formless! As increase does in itself produce increase, so does decrease decrease. Where is the individual who does not assert to himself that he would be more loyal to a falling than to a rising friend? Such is perhaps the nature of each one of us. But when any large number of men act together, the falling friend is apt to be deserted. There was a general feeling among politicians that Lord Drummond's Ministry,—or Sir Timothy's,—was failing, and the Liberals, though they certainly could not yet count the votes by which they might hope to be supported in power, nevertheless felt that they ought to be looking to their arms.*

There had been a coalition. They who are well read in the political literature of their country will remember all about that. It had perhaps succeeded in doing that for which it had been intended. The Queen's Government had been carried on for two or three years without difficulty, and without inconvenience to anyone,—except, perhaps, to the poor ministers themselves. The Duke of Omnium had been the head of that Ministry; and he certainly had suffered so much as to have become utterly ashamed of the coalition,—so much as to have said often to himself that under no circumstances would he again join any Ministry. All this, I think, must be remembered by readers of our political literature. At this time there was no idea of another coalition. That is a state of things which cannot come about frequently,—which can only be reproduced by men who have never hitherto felt the mean insipidity of such a condition. But they who had served on the Liberal side in that coalition must again put their shoulders to the wheel, and now they must be true to themselves and to their party. Of course it was in every man's mouth that the Duke must be induced to forget his miseries and once more to take upon himself the duties of an active servant of the State.

But they who were most anxious on the subject, such men as Lord Cantrip, Mr. Monk, our old friend Phineas Finn, and a few others, were almost afraid to approach him. At the moment when the coalition was broken up he had been very bitter in spirit, apparently almost arrogant, holding himself aloof from his late colleagues, and wrapping himself up either in silence or in solitude. And since that, great troubles had come to him which, as these men understood, had aggravated the soreness of his heart. His wife had died. All the world knew that, and seemed to know also how hard to bear the loss had been. And he had suffered much through his children. What Lord Silverbridge had done at Oxford was of course matter of general conversation, and also what he had not done. That the heir of the family should have become a renegade in politics was supposed greatly to have afflicted the father. Now Lord Gerald had been expelled from Cambridge, and Silverbridge was on the turf in conjunction with Major Tifto! Something too had oozed out into general ears about Lady Mary and her lover,—something which should have been kept secret as the grave. It is the misfortune of greatness that even its littlenesses should be made public. It had therefore come to pass that so much had been said of the Duke's sorrows past and present, political and private, that it was difficult even to address him.

There was one man, and but one, who could do this with ease to himself;—and that man was at last put into motion. It is not here necessary to explain with accuracy how that idea went from Phineas Finn to Mr. Monk, and from Mr. Monk to Lord Cantrip, and so on to the man himself. But the result was that the old Duke of St. Bungay* wrote the following letter to the Duke of Omnium. The letter purported to be rather an excuse for the writer's own defalcation than an incentive to the man addressed. But the chief object of the writer was to induce the younger Duke once more to submit to harness.

'Longroyston, 3rd June, 187—
'Dear Duke Of Omnium,

'How quickly the things come round! I had thought that very probably I should never again have been called upon even to think of the formation of another Liberal Ministry; and now, though it was but yesterday that we were all telling ourselves that we were thoroughly manumitted from the labours of governing by the altered opinions of the country, sundry of our old friends are again putting their heads together, and not unnaturally have addressed themselves to me.

'That they should put their heads together is a matter of course. Did they not do so they would neglect a manifest duty. Nothing is more essential to the political well-being of the country than that the leaders on both sides in politics should be prepared for their duties. But for myself, I am bound at last to put in the old plea with a determination that it shall be respected,—at any rate by myself. "*Solve senescentem*——*."

It is now, if I calculate rightly, exactly fifty years since I first entered public life in obedience to the advice of Lord Grey and under the immediate tuition of Mr. Huskisson.* I had then already sat five years in the House of Commons. I assisted humbly in the emancipation of the Roman Catholics,* and have learned by the legislative troubles of just half a century that those whom we then invited to sit with us in Parliament have been in all things our worst enemies. But what then? Had we benefited only those who love us, would not the sinners also,—or even the Tories,—have done as much as that?

'But such memories are of no avail now. I write to say that after so much of active political life, and so much of passive endeavours, I will at last retire altogether. My friends when they see me anxiously inspecting a pigsty or assiduously picking a peach are apt to remind me that I can still stand on my legs, and with more of compliment than of kindness will argue therefore that I ought still to undertake active duties in Parliament. I can select my own hours for pigs and peaches, and should I, through the dotage of age, make mistakes as to the breeding of the one or the flavour of the other, the harm done will not go far. In politics I have done my work. What you and others in the arena do will interest me more than all other things of this world, I think and hope, to my dying day. But I will not trouble the workers with the garrulousness of old age.

'So much for myself. And now, my dear friend, let me, as I go, say a parting word to him with whom in politics I have been for many years more in accord than with any other living man. As nothing but age or infirmity would to my own mind have justified me in retiring,—me whose services have never risen above the second class, whose intellect has never been clear enough for the carrying out of any special work,—so do I think that you, who can plead neither age nor infirmity, will find yourself at last to want self-justification, if you permit yourself to be driven from the task which seems to have been appointed for you either by pride or by diffidence.*

'I might perhaps express my real feeling better were I to say by pride *and* diffidence. I look to our old friendship, to the authority given to me by my age, and to the thorough goodness of your heart for pardon in thus accusing you. That little men should have ventured to ill-use you, has hurt your pride. That these little men should have been able to do so, has created your diffidence. Put you to a piece of work that a man may do, you have less false pride as to the way in which you may do it than any man I have known; and, let the way be open to you, as little diffidence as any. But in this political mill of ours in England, a man cannot always find the way open to do things. It does not often happen that an English Statesman can go in and make a great score off his own bat. But not the less is he bound to play the game and to go to the wicket when he finds that his time has come.

'There are, I think, two things for you to consider in this matter, and two only. The first is your capacity, and the other is your duty. A man may have found by experience that he is unfitted for public life. You and I have known men in regard to whom we have thoroughly wished that such experience had been reached. But this is a subject in which a man who doubts himself is bound to take the evidence of those around him. The whole party is most anxious for your cooperation. There is not a leading man in it who if he were asked to construct a Liberal Cabinet would not put your name down among the three first. If this be so,—and I make you the assurance from most conclusive evidence,—you are bound to accept the common consent of your political friends on that matter. You perhaps think that at a certain period of your life you failed. They all agree with me that you did not fail, but served your country well, faithfully, and most usefully. It is a matter on which you should be bound by our opinion rather than by your own. Where is the man that can ever see his own merits clearly?

'As to that matter of duty I shall have less difficulty in carrying you with me because I know well that in all your public life duty has been the mainspring of your actions. Though this renewed task may be personally disagreeable to you, though by undertaking it you can obtain nothing personally desirable by yourself, even though your tastes should lead you to some other life,—which I think is not the case,—still if your country wants you, you should serve your country. It is a work as to which such a one as you has no option. A demand equally strong cannot be made on many. Of most of those who choose public life,—as of myself,—it may be said that were they not there, there would be others as serviceable. But when a man such as you has shown himself to be necessary, as long as health and age permits he cannot recede without breach of manifest duty. The work to be done is so important, the numbers to be benefited are so great, that he cannot be justified in even remembering that he has a self.

'As I have said before, I trust that my own age and your goodness will induce you to pardon this great interference. But whether pardoned or not I shall always be

'Your most affectionate Friend,

'ST. BUNGAY.'

The Duke,—our Duke,—on reading this letter was by no means pleased by its contents. He could ill bear to be reminded either of his pride or of his diffidence. And yet the accusations which others made against him were as nothing to those with which he daily charged himself. He would do this till at last he was forced to defend himself against himself, by asking himself whether he could be other than as God had made him. It is the last and the poorest makeshift of a defence to which a man can be brought in his own court! And then though he would accuse himself of pride, he would plead that in very truth the vice of which he was anxious was not pride. Was it his fault that he was so thin-skinned that all things hurt him, and that he shrank from being hurt? When some coarse man said to him that which ought not to have been said,—as coarse men had done from day to day during that wretched time in which he had been Prime Minister,—was it his fault that at every word a penknife had stabbed him? Other men had borne these buffets without shrinking, and had shown themselves thereby to be much more useful, much more efficacious; but he could no more imitate them than he could procure for himself the skin of a rhinoceros or the tusk of an elephant. And this shrinking was what men called pride,—was the pride of which his old friend wrote! 'Have I ever been haughty, unless in my own defence?' he asked himself, remembering certain passages of humility in his life,—and certain passages of haughtiness also. And yet, though he thus argued his own cause, he would not give himself a verdict of not guilty.

And the Duke told him also that he was diffident. Of course he was diffident. Was it not one and the same thing? The very pride of which he was accused was no more than that shrinking which comes from the want of trust in oneself. He knew that nothing could be more easy than his own manner when he was quite sure of himself;—but then it so often happened that he was not sure. He was a shy man. All his friends, and all his enemies, knew that;—it was thus that he still discoursed with himself;—a shy, self-conscious, timid, shrinking, thin-skinned man! Of course he was diffident. Then why urge him on to tasks for which he was by nature unfitted? Was it consistent that he should be told in one and the same letter that he was proud and diffident, and be told also that it was his duty to devote himself to a work for the performance of which pride and diffidence were peculiar disqualifications?

And yet there was much in his old friend's letter which moved him. There were certain words which he kept on repeating to himself. 'He cannot be justified in even remembering that he has a self.' It was a hard thing to say of any man, but yet a true thing of such a man as his correspondent had described. His correspondent had spoken of a man who should know himself to be capable of serving the State. If a man were capable, and was sure within his own bosom of his own capacity, it would be his duty. Such a man would not be justified in remembering that he had a self. But what if he were not so satisfied? What if he felt that any labours of his would be vain, and all self-abnegation useless? His friend had told him that on that matter he was bound to take the opinion of others. Perhaps so. But if so, had not that opinion been given to him very plainly when he was told that he was both proud and diffident? That he was called upon,—imperatively called upon,—to serve his country by good service, if such were within his power, he did acknowledge freely; but not that he should allow himself to be stuck up as a ninepin only to be knocked down! There are politicians, so-called Statesmen, for whom such occupation seems to be proper;—and who like it too. A little office, a little power, a little rank, a little pay, a little niche in the ephemeral history of the year will reward many men adequately for being knocked down. There had been a time when he himself had not much cared about such knocks. But that time had gone.

And yet he loved power, and even when thinking of all this allowed his mind from time to time to run away into a dreamland of prosperous political labours. He thought what it would be to be an all-beneficent Prime Minister, with a loyal majority, with a well-conditioned unanimous Cabinet, with a grateful people, and an appreciative Sovereign. How well might a man spend himself night and day, and how glorious would be his enthusiasm, if in the midst of labours such as these human nature should give way.

He received the Duke's letter as he was sitting in his library in Carlton Terrace; and then, when he had been turning it over in his mind for half an hour, he suddenly jumped up and sat himself down at his writing-desk. He felt it to be necessary that he should at once write to his old friend;—and the more necessary that he should do so at once, because he had from the first resolved that he would do so before he had quite made up his mind on the chief subject of that letter. It did not suit him to say either that he would or that he would not do as his friend advised him. And yet the letter must be answered. The sooner such an answer was written the easier it would be. The reply was made in a very few words. 'As to myself,' he said, after expressing his regret that the Duke should find it necessary to retire from public life,—'as to myself, pray understand that whatever I may do I shall never cease to be grateful for your affectionate and high-spirited counsels.' After that he put the subject away from him. There was no necessity for a decision to-day or probably to-morrow.

Then his mind recurred to a more immediate and, for the moment, a heavier trouble. It was now over a fortnight since he had received from Mrs. Finn that letter which the reader will perhaps remember, and as yet he had given no answer to it. It might indeed be passed over without an answer. By this time she would probably have learned to think that that was his intention. But he knew that that was impossible to him. She had accused him in the very strongest language of injustice, and had made him understand that if he were unjust to her, then would he be most ungrateful. He, looking at the matter with his own lights, had thought that he had been right,—had at any rate hoped that he had been right, but had, in downright honesty, resolved to entrust the question to another person. As judge in the matter he had chosen Lady Cantrip, and Lady Cantrip had given judgment altogether against him.

He had pressed Lady Cantrip for a decided opinion, and she had told him that she, in the same position, would have done just as Mrs. Finn had done. After this there was no possibility that he should get a verdict in his favour from that judge, and he had resolved that the judgment of that judge should be final. He still thought that Mrs. Finn's conduct had been,—he would not say wrong, but the opposite of that which ought to have been esteemed right. There are in all such matters unwritten laws, and if she had obeyed those laws he could not justly demand more from her. The laws ought to have been different, but that was not her fault. What,—that anyone concerned with his interest should know that such a man as Francis Tregear was thinking of marrying his daughter, that any simply honest person, whether immediately concerned with his interest or not, should know this and not tell him at once! If a man's house be on fire, do you think of certain rules of etiquette before you bid him send for the engines? If a wild beast be loose, do you go through some ceremony before you caution the wanderers abroad? There should not have been a moment! But, nevertheless, it was now necessary that he should conform himself to the opinion of Lady Cantrip, and in doing so he must apologise for the bitter scorn with which he had allowed himself to treat his wife's most loyal and loving friend.

That letter also must be written. The few words to the Duke had not been difficult, but this letter seemed to be an Herculean task. It was made infinitely more difficult by the fact that Lady Cantrip had not seemed to think that the marriage was impossible. 'Young people when they have set their minds upon it do so generally prevail at last!' These had been her very words, and they discomforted him greatly. She would not have spoken them unless she had thought the marriage to be at any rate possible. Did it not almost indicate an opinion on her part that they ought to be allowed to marry? And if so, would it not be his duty to take his girl away from Lady Cantrip? As to that idea that young people, because they have declared themselves to be in love, were to have just what they wanted,—with that he did not agree at all. Lady Cantrip had told him that young people generally did prevail at last. He knew the story of one young person, whose position in her youth had been very much the same as that of his daughter now, and she had not prevailed. And in her case had not the opposition which had been made to her wishes been most fortunate for everybody? That young person had become his wife, his Glencora, his Duchess. Had that argument been used in regard to her, had she been allowed to have her own way when she was a child, what would have been her fate? Ah what! Then he had to think of it all. Might she not have been alive now, and perhaps happier than she had ever been with him? And had he remained always unmarried, devoted simply to politics, would not the troubles of the world have been lighter on him? But what had that to do with it? In these matters it was not the happiness of this or that individual which should be considered. Even he or she who might have to make the decision should not think overmuch of his or her own happiness. There is a propriety in things;—and only by an adherence to that propriety on the part of individuals can the general welfare be maintained. A king in this country, or the heir or the possible heir to the throne, is debarred from a humble and what might possibly be a happy marriage by regard for the good of his subjects. To the Duke's thinking the maintenance of the aristocracy of the country was second only in importance to the maintenance of the Crown. And then how should the aristocracy be maintained if its wealth were allowed to fall into the hands of an adventurer! That the wealth of the aristocracy should be recruited from time to time by the wealth of trade was well enough,—nay, was in the utmost degree desirable, as without such provision the grandeur of the aristocracy could hardly be preserved; but they among them who were alive to their duty would take care that nothing should be robbed from them by those who were without.

Such were the opinions with regard to his own order of one who was as truly liberal in his ideas as any man in England, and who had argued out these ideas to their consequences,—and had acknowledged that those consequences were desirable. As by the spread of education and increase of general well-being every proletaire was brought nearer to a duke, so by such action would the duke be brought nearer to a prole- taire. Such drawing-nearer of the classes was the object to which all this man's political action tended. It was to him the one desirable object of a liberal policy. And yet it was a dreadful thing to him that his own daughter should desire to marry a man so much beneath her own rank and fortune as Frank Tregear.

He would not allow himself to believe that the young people could ever prevail; but nevertheless, as the idea of the thing had not alarmed Lady Cantrip as it had him, it was necessary that he should make some apology to Mrs. Finn. And it must be done at once. He had already put it off for some days, simply from unwillingness to do a thing that was disagreeable. But he was not a man who could do this with any internal comfort. Each moment of procrastination was a prick to his conscience. He now therefore dragged out from the secrecy of some close drawer Mrs. Finn's long letter and read it through to himself once again. Yes—it was true that he had condemned her, and true that he had punished her. Though he had done nothing to her, and said nothing, and written but very little, still he had punished her with the whole weight of his severe displeasure. Feeling this, he could not protect himself by pleading to himself that he had neither done or said anything. She had written as though the matter was almost one of life and death to her. He could understand that too. His uncle's conduct to this woman, and his wife's, had created the intimacy which had existed. It had not come from any seeking on her part. Through their efforts she had become almost as one of the family. And now to be dismissed, like a servant who had misbehaved herself, must be grievous indeed to her! That she had been dismissed would become known to so many, who might only too probably have envied her her intimacy with a duchess! And then her arguments in her own defence were all so good,—if only that which Lady Cantrip had laid down as law was to be held as law. He was quite aware now that she had had no knowledge of the matter till his daughter had told her of the engagement at Matching. Then it was evident also that she had taken steps to send this Tregear to him immediately on her return to London. And at the end of the letter she accused him of what she had been pleased to call his usual tenacity in believing ill of her! He had been obstinate,—too obstinate in this respect; but he did not love her the better for having told him of it. And now, how was he to put his apology to her into words?

At last he did put it into words.

'MY DEAR MRS. FINN,

'I believe I had better acknowledge to you at once that I have been wrong in my judgment as to your conduct in a certain matter. You tell me that I owe it you to make this acknowledgment to you,—and I make it. The subject itself is, as you may imagine, so painful that I will spare myself, if possible, any further allusion to it. I believe I did you a wrong, and therefore I write to ask your pardon.

'I should perhaps apologise also for delay in my reply. I have had much to think of in this matter, and have had many others also on my mind.

'Believe me to be,

'My dear Mrs. Finn,

'Yours very faithfully,

'OMNIUM.'

It was very short, and as being short was infinitely less troublesome at the moment than a fuller epistle; but he was angry with himself, knowing that it was too short, feeling that it was ungenerous. He should have expressed a hope that he might soon see her again,—only he had no such wish. Her presence could not be pleasant to him, because he had been proved to have done her a wrong! There had been times at which he had liked her, but he knew that he did not like her now. And yet he was bound to be her friend! If he could only do some great thing for her, and thus satisfy his feeling of indebtedness towards her! But all the favours had been from her to him and his. Now, at this moment, those gems, certainly worth a prince's ransom and which certainly belonged to her, were lying at his bankers'. He must at any rate take steps to free himself from the feeling that he had her property in his hands.

CHAPTER 23

FRANK TREGEAR WANTS A FRIEND

SIX or seven weeks had passed since Tregear had made his communication to the Duke, and during that time he had heard not a word about the girl he loved. He knew, indeed, that she was at The Horns under the custody of Lady Cantrip, and probably had reason to suppose that she was being guarded there, and shut up, as it were, out of his reach. This did not surprise him; nor did he regard it as a hardship. It was of course to be expected that she should be kept out of his sight. But this was a state of things to which, as he thought, there should not be more than a moderate amount of submission. Six weeks was not a very long period, but it was, perhaps, long enough for evincing that respect and awe which he owed to the young lady's father. Something must be done some day, or else nothing would come of his love. How could he expect her to be true to him unless he took some means of showing himself to be true to her? But then what means?

In these days he did not live very much with her brother, in regard to whom he entertained something like anger on account of the Major. He not only disliked, but distrusted Major Tifto, and had so expressed himself as to give rise to angry words. Silverbridge had said that he knew how to take care of himself. Tregear had replied that he had his doubts on that matter. Then the member of Parliament had declared that at any rate he did not intend to be taken care of by Frank Tregear,—all of which had led to some little coolness between the men. In such a state of things it was not possible that there should be any close confidence as to Lady Mary. Nor does it often come to pass that the brother is the confidant of the sister's lover. Brothers hardly like their sisters to have lovers, though they are often well satisfied that their sisters should find husbands. There still exists some half relic of the barbarous idea that a lover is improper. The father and mother are aware that the girl will not become a wife,—at any rate can hardly become a wife happily,—unless she be in love first. But the brother is apt to look upon the thing as being an impertinence on both sides. Tregear's want of rank and wealth added something to this feeling in the mind of this brother; so that Silverbridge, though he felt himself to be deterred by friendship from any open opposition, and though he had under his mother's influence, when the affair began, given a cold assent to it, still was almost inimical. 'It won't do, you know,' he had said to his brother Gerald, shaking his head.

Tregear, however, was determined to be active in the matter, to make some effort, to speak to somebody. But how to make an effort,—and to whom should he speak? Thinking of all this he remembered that Mrs. Finn had sent for him and had told him to go with his love story to the Duke. Since the death of his friend the Duchess there had been no moment so hopeful to him as that in which she had assured him that the affair should not be kept as a secret from the lady's father. She had been almost severe with him, but she had not made him understand that she thought the marriage to be impossible. He had during his interview been angry with her, thinking that she was interfering with him;—but after the interview was over, and from that time to the present, he had continued to assure himself that she had acted well and wisely. He therefore determined that he would go to Mrs. Finn.

When he was shown up into her presence she had as yet received no answer from the Duke, though nearly a fortnight had elapsed since she had written her letter. During that time she had become very angry with the man. She felt that he was not treating her as a gentleman should treat a lady, and certainly not as the husband of her late friend should have treated the friend of his late wife. She had a proud consciousness of having behaved well in all things to the Pallisers, and now this head of the Pallisers was rewarding her by very evil treatment. She had been generous; he was most ungenerous. She had been honest; he was deficient now even in that honesty for which she had specially given him credit. And she had been unable to obtain any of that consolation which could have come to her from talking of the wrongs she endured. She could not complain to her husband, because there were reasons which made it essential that her husband should not quarrel with the Duke. She was hot with indignation at the very moment in which Tregear was announced.

He began by apologising for his intrusion, and she of course assured him that he was welcome. 'After the liberty which I took with you, Mr. Tregear, I am only too well pleased that you should come and see me.'

'I am afraid,' he said, 'that I was a little rough.'

'A little warm;—but that was to be expected. A gentleman never likes to be interfered with on such a matter. Upon the whole I thought that you bore it very well.'

'The position was and is difficult, Mrs. Finn.'

'And I am bound, now that I see you, to acknowledge the very ready way in which you did what I asked you to do.'

'And now, Mrs. Finn, what is to come next?'

'Ah!'

'Something must be done! You know, of course, that the Duke did not receive me with any great favour.'

'I did not suppose he would.'

'Nor did I. It was not to be supposed. Of course he would object to such a marriage. I can understand that very well. But a man in these days cannot dictate to his daughter what husband she should marry.'

'Perhaps he can dictate to her what husband she shall not marry.'

'Hardly that. He may put impediments in the way; and the Duke, no doubt, will do so. But if I am happy enough to have won the affections of his daughter in such a way as to keep them,—so as to make it essential to her happiness that she should become my wife,—he will give way. Do not you think so?'

'What am I to say, Mr. Tregear?'

'Just what you think.'

'Why should I be made to say what I think on so delicate a matter? Or of what use would be my thoughts? Remember how far I am removed from her!'

'You are his friend.'

'Not at all! No one less so!' As she said this she could not hinder the colour from coming into her face. She did not intend to express her indignation to this young man, but the glow of it was then betraying, as she feared, her feelings. 'I was her friend,—Lady Glencora's; but with the death of my friend there was an end of all that.'

'You were staying with him,—at his request. You told me so yourself.'

'I shall never stay with him again. But all that, Mr. Tregear, is of no matter. I do not mean to say a word against him,—not a word. But if you wish to interest anyone as being the Duke's friend, then I can assure you I am the last person in London to whom you should come. I know no one to whom the Duke is likely to entertain feelings so little kind as towards me.' This she said in a peculiarly solemn way which startled Tregear. But before he could answer her, almost as she was speaking, a servant entered the room with a letter. As she took it into her hand, she recognised the Duke's writing. Here was the answer for which she had been so long waiting in silent expectation! Again came the colour, and again she was sure that he saw it. She could not keep it unread till he was gone. 'Will you allow me a moment?' she whispered, and then she opened the envelope. As she read the few words her eyes became laden with tears. They quite sufficed to relieve the injured pride which had sat so heavy at her heart. 'I believe I did you a wrong, and therefore I ask your pardon!' That was all she had wanted,—that he should feel that her conduct to him had been at least honest, and that he should be honest enough to acknowledge his mistake in misjudging her. This he had done now completely. 'I believe I did you a wrong, and I write to ask your pardon.' It was so like what she had believed the man to be! She could not be longer angry with him. And yet the very last words she had spoken were words complaining of his conduct. She felt that she must in some way withdraw those words. 'This is from the Duke,' she said, putting the letter back into its envelope.

'Oh, indeed.'

'It is odd that it should have come while you are here.'

'Is it,—is it,—about Lady Mary?'

'No;—at least, not directly. I perhaps spoke more harshly about him than I should have done,—as to his feelings I mean to myself. The truth is I had expected a line from him, and it had not come. Now it is here; but I do not suppose that I shall ever see much of him. My intimacy was with her. But I would not wish you to remember what I said just now, if,—if——'

'If what, Mrs. Finn? You mean, perhaps, if I should ever be allowed to call myself his son-in-law. It may seem to you to be arrogant, but it is an honour which I expect to win.'

'Faint heart,*—you know, Mr. Tregear.'

'Exactly. One has to tell oneself that very often. You will help me?'

'Certainly not,' she said, as though she were much startled. 'How can I help you?'

'By telling me what I should do. I suppose if I were to go down to Richmond I should not be admitted.'

'If you ask me, I think not;—not to see Lady Mary. Lady Cantrip would perhaps see you.'

'I do not know Lady Cantrip.'

'Nor do I. She probably thinks as the Duke thinks.'

'She is acting the part of—duenna.'

'As I should do also, if Lady Mary were staying with me. You don't suppose that if she were here I would let her see you in my house without her father's leave?'

'I suppose not.'

'Certainly not;—and therefore I conceive that Lady Cantrip will not do so either.'

'I wish she were here.'

'It would be of no use. I should be a dragon in guarding her.' Of course as she said this she smiled, and this woman when she smiled was always charming.

'I wish you would let me feel that you were like a sister to me in this matter.'

'But I am not your sister, nor yet your aunt, nor yet your grandmother. What I mean is that I cannot be on your side.'

'Can you not?'

'No, Mr. Tregear. Think how long I have known these other people.'

'But just now you said that he was your enemy.'

'I did say so, but, as I have unsaid it since, you as a gentleman will not remember my words. But whether he be my enemy or whether he be my friend, it must be the same. I cannot help you in this.'

'I shall write to her.'

'It can be nothing to me. If you write she will show your letter either to her father or to Lady Cantrip, and they will forbid her to answer it.'

'But she will read it first?'

'I cannot tell how that may be. In fact I am the very last person in the world to whom you should come for assistance in this matter. If I gave any assistance to anybody I should be bound to give it to the Duke.'

'I cannot understand that, Mrs. Finn.'

'Nor can I explain it, but it would be so. As it is I should have no power of meddling if I wished to do so,—but I certainly do not. I shall always be very glad to see you. And I do feel that we ought to be friends,—because I took such a liberty with you, and because you bore it so well. But in this matter I cannot help you.'

When she said this he had to take his leave. It was impossible that he should further press his case upon her, though he would have been very glad to extract from her some acknowledgment that the marriage was in her opinion at any rate possible. It is such a help in a difficulty to have somebody who will express even a hope that the difficulty is perhaps not invincible! If you have a book to publish and know that the chances against your success are a thousand to one, still there will be comfort if one dear one will tell you that the book ought to be successful! He had no one to comfort him in this matter. There was one dear friend,—as a friend dearer than any other,—to whom he might go, and who would after some fashion bid him prosper. Mabel would encourage him. She had said that she would do so. But in making that promise she had said also that she would not think of his former sweet speeches,—from which he understood only too well that those former sweet speeches would always be in her thoughts. She had told him that Romeo would not have spoken of his love for Juliet to Rosaline, whom he had loved before he saw Juliet. No doubt she had gone on to tell him that he might come to her and talk freely of his love for Lady Mary,—but after what had been said before he felt that he could not do so without leaving a sting behind. There was no one to whom he could have recourse in his difficulty. When a man's love goes well with him,—so well as to be in some degree oppressive to him even by its prosperity,—when the young lady has jumped into his arms, and the father and the mother have been quite willing, then he wants no confidant. He does not care to speak very much of the matter which among his friends is apt to become a subject for raillery. When you call a man Benedick he does not come to you with ecstatic descriptions of the beauty and the wit of his Beatrice. But no one was likely to call him Benedick in reference to Lady Mary.

Among his friends, who were not very numerous, this young man was considered to be more than ordinarily self-confident and self-sufficient. And there was ground for this opinion as to his character, both in his manners and in his ways of life. But such manners and such ways of life come as frequently from outward effort as from inward disposition. He had taught himself to assert himself, thinking that men would rate him at his own value. And he was right. He who can assume dignity will be treated with respect whether he deserve it or not. But in spite of his manner, in spite of his apparent self-sufficiency, this man was very soft within.* Less than two years back he had been willing to sacrifice all the world for his cousin Mabel, and his cousin Mabel had told him that he was wrong. 'It does not pay to sacrifice the world for love.' So cousin Mabel had then said, and had added something as to its being necessary that she should marry a rich man, and expedient that he should marry a rich woman. He had thought much about it, and had declared to himself that on no account would he marry a woman for her money, and in so resolving had almost concluded that he had better not marry at all. But whilst he was coming to this conclusion he had encountered Lady Mary Palliser. There had been no conclusions, no resolutions after that, no thinking about it;—but downright love. There was nothing left of real regret for his cousin in his bosom. She had been right. That love had been impossible. But this would be possible,—ah, so deliciously possible,—if only her father and mother would assent! The mother, imprudent in this as in all things,—in real truth, absolutely delighted with the imprudence,—had assented. The reader knows the rest.

It was in every way possible. 'She will have money enough,' the Duchess had said, 'if only her father can be brought to give it you.' So Tregear had set his heart upon it, and had said to himself that the thing was to be done. A man, he thought, should always have before him something difficult to be achieved, and this should be his destined achievement. Then his friend the Duchess had died, and the real difficulties had commenced. From that day he had not seen his love, or heard from her. How was he to know whether she would be true to him? And where was he to seek for that sympathy which he felt to be so necessary to him? A wild idea had come into his head that Mrs. Finn would be his friend;—but she had repudiated him, and he could now see that such repudiation was a matter of course.

He went straight home and at once wrote to the girl. The letter was a simple love-letter, and as such need not be given here. In what sweetest language he could find he assured her that even though he should never be allowed to see her or to hear from her, that still he should cling to her. And then he added this passage: 'If your love for me be what I think it to be, no one can have a right to keep us apart,—and no one can have the power to do so permanently. Pray be sure that I shall not change. If you change let me know it;—but I shall as soon expect the heavens to fall.' This letter he addressed to her without any attempted secrecy, and entrusted to the post.

CHAPTER 24

'SHE MUST BE MADE TO OBEY'

LADY MARY PALLISER down at The Horns had as much liberty allowed to her as is usually given to young ladies in these very free days. There was indeed no restriction placed upon her at all. Had Tregear gone down to Richmond and asked for the young lady, and had Lady Cantrip at the time been out and the young lady at home, it would have depended altogether upon the young lady's wishes whether she would have seen her lover or not. Nevertheless Lady Cantrip kept her eyes open, and when the letter came from Tregear she was aware that a letter had come. But the letter found its way into Lady Mary's hands without any delay, and was read in the seclusion of her own bedroom. 'I wonder whether you would mind reading that,' she said very shortly afterwards to Lady Cantrip, handing to her Tregear's letter. Of course Lady Cantrip read it. 'What answer ought I to make?' the girl asked before the elder lady had had time to speak.

'Do you think any answer ought to be made, my dear?'

'Oh yes; I must answer him.'

'Would your papa wish it?'

'I told papa that I would not promise not to write to him. I think I told him that he should see any letters that there were. But if I show them to you, I suppose that will do as well.'

'You had better at any rate keep your word to him absolutely.'

'I am not afraid of doing so, if you mean that, Lady Cantrip. I cannot bear to give him pain, but this is a matter in which I mean to have my own way.'

'Mean to have your own way!' said Lady Cantrip, much surprised by the determined tone of the young lady.

'Certainly I do. I want you to understand so much! I suppose papa could keep us from marrying for ever and ever if he pleases, but he never will make me say that I will give up Mr. Tregear. I should despise myself if I should think it possible. And if he does not yield I shall think him very cruel. Why should he wish to make me unhappy all my life?'

'He certainly does not wish that, my dear.'

'But he will do it. Mr. Tregear is a gentleman and that ought to be enough.'

'I cannot go against your father, Mary.'

'No, I suppose not. I shall write to Mr. Tregear, and then I will show you what I have written. Papa shall see it too, if he pleases. I will do nothing secret, but I will never give up Mr. Tregear.'

Lord Cantrip came down to Richmond that evening, and his wife told him that in her opinion it would be best that the Duke should allow the young people to marry, and should give them money enough to live upon. 'Is not that a strong order,' asked the Earl, 'considering the great aversion he has to the whole affair?' The Countess acknowledged that it was a 'strong order,' but suggested that for the happiness of them all it might quite as well be done at first as at last.

The next morning Lady Mary showed her a copy of the reply which she had already sent to her lover. It was as follows.

'DEAR FRANK,

'You may be *quite sure* that I shall *never* give you up. I will not write more at present because papa does not wish me to do so. I shall show papa your letter and my answer.

'Your own most affectionate

'Mary.'

'Has it gone?' asked the Countess.

'I put it myself into the pillar letter-box yesterday.' Then Lady Cantrip felt that she had to deal with a very self-willed young lady indeed.

That afternoon Lady Cantrip was going up to town and asked Mary whether she might be allowed to take the two letters with the express purpose of showing them to the Duke. 'Oh yes,' said Mary. 'I think it would be so much the best. Give papa my kindest love, and tell him from me that if he wants to make his poor little girl happy he will forgive her and be kind to her in all this.' Then the Countess made some attempt to argue the matter with her young friend. There were proprieties! High rank might be a blessing or might be the reverse,—as people thought of it;—but all men acknowledged that very much was due to it. *Noblesse oblige.* It was so often the case in life that women were called upon by circumstances to sacrifice their early inclinations! What right had a gentleman to talk of marriage who had no means? All these things she said and very many more. She talked for an hour, but it was to no purpose. The young lady asserted that as the gentleman was a gentleman there need be no question as to rank, and that in regard to money there need be no difficulty if one of them had sufficient. 'But you have none but what your father may give you,' said Lady Cantrip,—as though that argument must at least be conclusive. 'Papa can give it to us without any trouble,' said Lady Mary. Lady Cantrip found that the conversation was quite useless. This child had a clear idea of what she thought to be her own rights in the world. Being the child of rich parents she had a right to money. Being a woman she had a right to a husband. Having been born free she had a right to choose a husband for herself. Having had a man's love given to her she had a right to keep it. 'One doesn't know which she is most like, her father or her mother,' Lady Cantrip said afterwards to her husband. 'She has his cool determination, and her hot-headed obstinacy.'

She did show the letters to the Duke, and in answer to a word or two from him explained that she could not take upon herself to debar her guest from the use of the post. 'But you need not be afraid of that,' she said. 'She will write nothing without letting you know it.'

'She ought to write nothing at all.'

'What she feels is much worse than what she writes.'

'If there were no intercourse she would forget him.'

'Ah; I don't know,' said the Countess sorrowfully. 'I thought so once. But the more I see her the more I feel how determined she is.'

'All children are determined as long as they are allowed to have their own way.'

'I mean to say that it is the nature of her character to be obstinate. Most girls, as far as I have seen them, are only too prone to yield. They have not character enough of their own to stand against any opposition. I am not speaking now only of affairs like this. It would be the same with her in anything, I should say. Have you not always found it so?'

Then he endeavoured to remember what he had found out in reference to his daughter's character, and had to acknowledge to himself that he had never found out anything. She had been properly educated;—at least he hoped so. He had seen her grow up, pretty, sweet, affectionate, always obedient to him on the few occasions in which he had exercised authority over her;—the most charming plaything in the world on the quite fewer occasions in which he had allowed himself to play. But as to her actual disposition, he had never taken any trouble to inform himself. She had been left to her mother,—as other girls are left. And his sons had been left to their tutors. And now he had no control over any of them. That question from his friend made him very unhappy. 'She must be made to obey like others,' he said at last, speaking through his teeth.

There was something in this which almost frightened Lady Cantrip. She did not wish to give way, nor did she think it reasonable to ask him to do so. But she could not bear to hear him say that the girl must be made to yield with that spirit of despotic power under which we are told that women were restrained in years now passed. If she could have spoken her own mind quite freely it would have been to this effect: 'Let us do what we can to lead her away from this desire of hers; and in order that we may do so, let us tell her just at present that her marriage with Mr. Tregear is quite out of the question. But if we do not succeed,—say in the course of the next twelve months,—let us give way. As far as my own opinion goes, I feel sure that we shall have to give way. And therefore let us make it a matter of joy that the young man himself is so acceptable and well-behaved.' That was her idea, and with that she would have indoctrinated the Duke had she been able. But his seemed to be altogether different. 'She must be made to obey,' he said. And, as he said it, he seemed to be indifferent as to the sorrow which such enforced obedience might bring upon his child. In answer to this she could only shake her head. 'What do you mean?' he asked. 'Do you think we ought to give way to her?'

'Not at once certainly.'

'But at last?'

'What can you do, Duke? If she be as firm as you, can you bear to see her suffer? Can you see her become thin, and ill, and miserable,— absolutely pining away in her misery!'

'Girls do not do like that,' he said.

'Girls, like men, are very different. They generally will yield to external influences. English girls, though they become the most loving wives in the world, do not, I think, generally become so riven by an attachment, before that attachment has been sanctioned, as to become deep sufferers when it is disallowed. But here, I fear, we have to deal with one who will suffer after this fashion.'

'Why should she not be like others?'

'It may be so. We will try. But you see what she says in her letter to him. She at any rate believes of herself that she can be obstinate. She writes as though your authority were to be nothing in that matter of giving up, though she adds that she does not wish to write to him lest she should displease you. In all that she says to me there is the same spirit. If she is firm, Duke, you must yield.'

'Never. She shall never marry him with my sanction.'

There was nothing more to be said on that occasion, and Lady Cantrip went her way. But the Duke, though he could say nothing more, continued to think of it hour after hour. He went down to the House of Lords to listen to a debate on some subject connected with the law reform of the day on which it was considered expedient to oppose Sir Timothy Beeswax, under whose direction some mistake had been made as to legal proceedings. Parliament during the year last past had carried some provision which would not work, and now it was thought that the Government must be beaten or own itself to have been wrong. As

a Government can never be brought to do the latter, a victory was antici-
pated; and the Duke, though his politics generally were almost as
troublesome as his domestic affairs, was eager in the matter. When
things have so come round that the vanquished may hope again to be the
victors, the struggle always becomes interesting, let the subject matter
be what it may. But now, though Lord Weazeling really was very funny
as he recapitulated the legal absurdities and forensic deadlock which
recent legislation had produced, the Duke could not listen to him. He
could listen to nothing as he thought of the condition of his children.

He had been asked whether he could bear to see his girl suffer, and had
been so asked as though it was thought that he was indifferent to the sufferings of his child. Did he not know of himself that there was no father
who would do more than he for the welfare of his daughter? Was he not
sure of the tenderness of his own heart towards her? In all this that he was
doing was he governed by anything but a sense of duty? Was it personal
pride or love of personal aggrandisement? He thought that he could
assure himself safely that he was open to no such charge. Would he not
willingly die for her,—or rather for them,—if he could so serve them?
Surely then this woman had accused him most wrongfully when she had
intimated that he could look on and see his girl suffer without caring for
it. In his indignation he determined,—for a while,—that he would
remove her from the custody of Lady Cantrip. But then, where should he
place her? He was aware that his own house, whether in town or country,
would be like a grave to a girl just fit to come out into the world. Now, in
a month or two, when the mourning for her mother should have been
mitigated, of course some gaiety must be provided for her. In this coming
autumn she must go somewhere,—with someone. He himself, in his
present frame of mind, would be but a sorry travelling companion.

An idea had been hinted to him by Lady Cantrip,—not at their last
interview but when they had previously conferred on the same subject,—
that the chief hope of escape would lie in the prospect of another lover.
When he came to pick this idea to pieces, and to look at it in and out and all
around, he did not altogether like it;—but it was an idea which had led to
safety in a previous case. He knew enough of the history of his own wife to
be aware of that. Before he had ever seen her as Lady Glencora M'Cluskie
she had been desirous of giving herself and all her wealth to one Burgo
Fitzgerald, who had been altogether unworthy of her. The Duke could
remember well how a certain old Lady Midlothian had first hinted to him
that Lady Glencora's property was very large, and had then added that the
young lady herself was very beautiful. And he could remember how his
uncle, the late Duke, who had seldom taken much trouble in merely human

affairs, had actually taken upon himself to say a word or two—'I have heard a whisper about you and Lady Glencora M'Cluskie. Nothing could be better.' That was all the Duke had said, but it had been efficacious. The result had been undoubtedly good. His Cora and all her money had been saved from a worthless spendthrift. He had found a wife who he now thought had made him happy. And she had found at any rate a respectable husband. The idea when picked to pieces is not a nice idea. 'Let us look out for a husband for this girl, so that we may get her married,—out of the way of her lover.' It is not nice. But it had succeeded in one case, and why should it not succeed in another?

But how was it to be done? Who should do it? Whom should he select to play the part which he had undertaken in that other arrangement? He did conceive of himself that no worse person could be found for managing such an affair. When the idea had first been raised he had thought that Lady Cantrip would do it all; but now he was angry with Lady Cantrip. And, at any rate, he must have some voice as to the man to be chosen.

How was it to be done? How should it be commenced? Then his mind was carried away to the consideration of what might have been the commencement of his own affair. He did not in the least know how he had been chosen, or who first thought of him as the lady's future husband. Was it possible that his uncle, who was the proudest man in England, should have condescended to make a bargain with an old dowager whom almost everybody had despised? And in what way had he been selected? No doubt he had been known to be the heir-apparent to a dukedom and to ducal revenues. But it seemed odd to him that anybody should in such a matter be able to come to an absolute decision. Yet in his case old Lady Midlothian had begun the matter with him. It occurred to him that in royal marriages such beginnings are quite common.

But who should be the happy man? Then, though he thoroughly despised himself for what he was doing, he began to count up the requisite attributes. The man must be of high rank, and an eldest son, and the possessor of, or the heir to, a good estate. He did despise himself when he found that he put these things first,—as a matter of course. Nevertheless he did put them first. He was rejecting this other man because he possessed none of these attributes. He hurried himself on to add that the man must be of good character, and temper, and such as a young girl might learn to love. But yet he was aware that he added these things for his conscience's sake. Tregear's character was good,— and temper also, very probably,—and certainly the girl loved him. But was it not clear to all who knew anything of such matters that

Mr. Francis Tregear should not have dared even to think of marrying the daughter of the Duke of Omnium?

Who should be the happy man? Though some woman probably must take the management of the matter, though it would be left to him simply to signify his approval, still he might form an opinion on that matter. There were so many who evidently were unfit. Young Lord Percival was heir only to a ruined estate and a beggared peerage. Lord Glasslough was odious to all men. There were three or four others of whom he knew or thought that he knew something that was fatal. But when he remembered Lord Popplecourt there seemed to him to be no objection which need be fatal.

Lord Popplecourt was a young peer whose father had died some two years since and whose estates were large and quite unembarrassed. The late Lord, who had been a Whig of the old fashion, had in early days been the Duke's friend. They had been at Oxford and in the House of Commons together, and though Lord Popplecourt had never been an active politician he had always been true to his party. As to the son, the Duke remembered to have heard lately that he was by no means given to waste his money. He drove a coach about London a good deal, but had as yet not done anything very foolish. He had taken his degree at Oxford, thereby showing himself to be better than Silverbridge. He had also taken his seat in the House of Lords and had once opened his mouth. He had not indeed appeared often again; but at Lord Popplecourt's age much legislation is not to be expected from a young peer. Then he thought of the man's appearance. Popplecourt was not specially attractive,—was not an Adonis, whereas Tregear was a very handsome man. But so also had been Burgo Fitzgerald,—almost abnormally beautiful, while he, Plantagenet Palliser, as he was then, had been quite as insignificant in appearance as Lord Popplecourt. So at least the Duke told himself as he thought of it all.

Lord Popplecourt might possibly do. But then how should the matter be broken to the young man? After all, would it not be best that he should trust Lady Cantrip?

CHAPTER 25

A FAMILY BREAKFAST-TABLE

LORD SILVERBRIDGE had paid all his Derby losses, and indeed most of those incurred also by Major Tifto, without any difficulty. They had not been very heavy for a man in his position, and the money had come without remonstrance from Mr. Moreton. When asking for it he was half ashamed of himself, but could still find consolation by remembering how very much worse had befallen many young men whom he knew. He had never 'plunged.' In fact he had made the most prudent book in the world; and had so managed affairs that even now the horse which he and Tifto owned between them was worth more than all he had lost and paid. 'This is getting serious,' he had said to his partner when, on making out a rough account, he had brought the Major in a debtor to him of more than a thousand pounds. The Major had owned that it was serious, but had hinted that as he was half owner of the horse, his partner had good security for the money. Then something of an arrangement in words was made,— which, however, even in words was not very accurately arranged. Prime Minister was now one of the favourites for the Leger. If the horse won that race there would be money enough for everything. If that race were lost, then there should be a settlement,—the settlement to be made by a transfer of the steed to the younger partner. 'He's safe to pull it off,' said the Major, to whose comfort it was essentially necessary that Lord Silverbridge should be of the opinion he had so expressed.

At this time both his sons were living with the Duke in London. It had been found impracticable to send Lord Gerald back to Cambridge with any good prospect. The doors of Trinity were certainly closed against him. But some interest had been made in his favour, and he was to be transferred to Oxford. All the truth had been told, and there had been a feeling that the lad should be allowed another chance. He could not however go to his new Alma Mater till after the long vacation, and it had been decided that in the meantime he should be taken by a tutor down to a cottage on Dartmoor and there be made to read,—with such amusement in the meantime as might be got from fishing, and playing cricket with the West Devon county club. 'It isn't a very bright look-out for the summer,' his brother had said to him, 'but it's better than breaking out on the loose altogether. If I were you I'd read like bricks, and be a credit to the family, and all that sort of thing. Then I'll give up the borough to you. But mind you stick to the Liberals. I've made an ass of myself. I can see that already.' However in these early days of June Lord Gerald had not yet got his tutor. A gentleman had been found, after much inquiry,—the Rev. Somerset Lennox, an Oxford man of course, who was to have a hundred pounds and all his expenses paid for four months' attendance.

Though the father and the two young men were at this time living together they did not see very much of each other. The Duke always breakfasted at nine and the repast was a very simple one. When they failed to appear, he did not scold,—but would simply be disappointed. At dinner they never met. It was supposed that Lord Gerald passed his mornings in reading, and some little attempts were made in that direction, chiefly under his brother's direction. It is to be feared they did not come to much. Silverbridge was very kind to Gerald, feeling an increased tenderness for him on account of that Cambridge mishap, which had been primarily due to the fact that he had been tempted to the races to see Prime Minister run. Now they were very much together, and occasionally, by a strong effort, would grace their father's breakfast-table with their company.

It was not often that he either reproached them or preached to them. Though he could not live with them on almost equal terms, as some fathers can live with their sons, though he could not laugh at their fun or make them laugh at his wit, he knew very well that it would have been better both for him and them if he had possessed this capacity. Though the life which they lived as young men was distasteful to him,—though race-horses were an abomination to him, and the driving of coaches a folly, and club-life a manifest waste of time, still he recognised these things as being, if not necessary to them, at any rate unavoidable costs. To Gerald he would talk about Oxford, avoiding all allusions to past Cambridge misfortunes; but in the presence of Silverbridge, whose Oxford career had been so peculiarly unfortunate, he would make no allusion to either of the Universities. To his eldest son he would talk of Parliament, which of all subjects would have been the most congenial to him had they agreed in politics. As it was he could speak more freely to him on that than any other matter, and was light and almost jocose when he spoke of the blunderings of Sir Timothy Beeswax.

One Thursday night as the two brothers went to bed on returning from the Beargarden, at a not very late hour, they agreed that they would 'give the governor a turn' the next morning,—by which they meant that they would drag themselves out of bed in time to breakfast with him at nine o'clock. 'The worst of it is that he will never let them get anything to eat,' said Gerald. But Silverbridge explained that he had taken that matter into his own hands, and had specially ordered broiled salmon and stewed kidneys. 'He won't like it, you know,' said Gerald. 'I'm sure he thinks it wicked to eat anything but toasted bacon before lunch.'

At a very little after nine Silverbridge was in the breakfast-room, and there he found his father. 'I suppose Gerald is not up yet,' said the Duke almost crossly.

'Oh yes he is, sir. He'll be here directly.'

'Have you seen him this morning?'

'No; I haven't seen him. But I know he'll be here. He said he would, last night.'

'You speak of it as if it were an undertaking.'

'No; not that, sir. But we are not always quite up to time.'

'No;—indeed you are not. Perhaps you sit late at the House.'

'Sometimes I do,' said the young member, with a feeling almost akin to shame as he remembered that on the last night or two he had spent more of his hours at the Beargarden than in the House of Commons. 'I have had Gerald there in the gallery sometimes. It is just as well that he should know what is being done. Don't you think so, sir?'

'Quite as well.'

'I shouldn't wonder if he gets a seat some day.'

'I don't know how that may be.'

'He won't change as I have done. He'll stick to your side. Indeed I think he'd do better in the House than I ever shall. He has more gift of the gab.'

'That is not the first thing requisite.'

'I know all that, sir. I've read your letter more than once, and I showed it to him.'

There was something sweet and pleasant in the young man's manner by which the father could hardly not be captivated. They had now sat down, and the servant had brought in the unusual accessories for a morning feast. 'What is all that?' asked the Duke.

'Gerald and I are so awfully hungry of a morning,' said the son apologising.

'Well;—it's a very good thing to be hungry;—that is if you can get plenty to eat. Salmon is it? I don't think I'll have any myself. Kidneys! Not for me. I think I'll take a bit of fried bacon. I also am hungry, but not awfully hungry.'

'You never seem to me to eat anything, sir.'

'Eating is an occupation from which I think a man takes the more pleasure the less he considers it. A rural labourer who sits on the ditch-side with his bread and cheese and an onion has more enjoyment out of it I fancy than any Lucullus.'

'But he likes a good deal of it, I suppose.'

'I do not think he ever over-eats himself,—which Lucullus does. All that wealth and luxury can add to the pleasure of eating seems to me to be very little, whereas appetite when it is genuine can add so much! I have envied a ploughman his power,—his *dura ilia*,*—but never an epicure the appreciative skill of his palate. If Gerald does not make haste he will be able to exercise neither the one nor the other upon that fish.'

'I will leave a bit for him, sir,—and here he is. You are twenty minutes late, Gerald. My father says that bread and cheese and onions would be better for you than salmon and stewed kidneys.'

'No, Silverbridge;—I said no such thing; but that if he were a hedger and ditcher the bread and cheese and onions would be as good.'

'I should not mind trying them at all,' said Gerald. 'Only one never does have such things for breakfast. Last winter a lot of us skated to Ely and we ate two or three loaves of bread and a whole cheese at a pot-house! Nothing ever was so good! And as for beer, we pretty nearly drank the public dry.'

'It was because for the time you had been a hedger and ditcher.'

'Proby was a ditcher, I know, when he went right through into one of the dikes. Just push on that dish, Silverbridge. It's no good you having the trouble of helping me half-a-dozen times. I don't think things are a bit the nicer because they cost a lot of money. I suppose that is what you mean, sir.'

'Something of that kind, Gerald. Not to have money,—not to have enough for your wants;—that must be troublesome.'

'Very bad indeed,' said Silverbridge, shaking his head wisely, as a member of Parliament might do who felt that something should be done to put down such a lamentable state of things.

'I don't complain,' said Gerald. 'No fellow ever had less right to complain. But I never felt that I had quite enough. Of course it was my own fault.'

'I should say so, my boy. But then there are a great many like you. Let their means be what they may they never have quite enough. To be in any difficulty in regard to money,—to owe what you cannot pay, or even to have to abstain from things which you have told yourself are necessary either to yourself or to those who depend on you,—creates a feeling of meanness.'

'That is what I have always felt,' said Silverbridge. 'I cannot bear to think that I should like to have a thing and that I cannot afford it.'

'You do not quite understand me, I fear. The only case in which you can be justified in desiring that which you cannot afford is when the thing is absolutely necessary;—as bread may be, or clothes.'

'As when a fellow wants a lot of new breeches before he has paid his tailor's last bill.'

'As when a poor man,' said the Duke impressively, 'may long to give his wife a new gown, or his children boots to keep their feet from the mud and snow.' Then he paused a moment, but the serious tone of his voice and the energy of his words had sent Gerald headlong among his kidneys, while Silverbridge sat back in his chair prepared to listen with filial patience. 'I say that in such cases money must be regarded as a blessing.'

'A ten-pound note will do so much,' said Silverbridge.

'But beyond that it ought to have no power of conferring happiness, and certainly cannot drive away sorrow. Not though you build palaces out into the deep, can that help you. You read your Horace I hope. "*Scandunt eodem quo dominus minae.*" '

'I recollect that,' said Gerald. 'Black care sits behind the horseman.'

'Even though he have a groom riding after him beautiful with exquisite boots.* As far as I have been able to look out into the world——'

'I suppose you know it as well as anybody,' said Silverbridge,—who was simply desirous of making himself pleasant to the 'dear old governor.'

'As far as my experience goes the happiest man is he who being above the troubles which money brings, or the want of money, has his hands the fullest of work. If I were to name the class of men whose lives are spent with the most thorough enjoyment I think I should name that of barristers who are in large practice and also in Parliament.'

'Isn't it a great grind, sir?' asked Silverbridge.

'A very great grind, as you call it. And there may be the grind and not the success. But——' He had now got up from his seat at the table and was standing with his back against the chimney-piece, and as he went on with his lecture,—just as the word 'but' came from his lips,—he struck the fingers of one hand lightly on the palm of the other as he had been known to do at some happy flight of oratory in the House of Commons. 'But it is the grind that makes the happiness. To feel that your hours are filled to overflowing, that you can barely steal minutes enough for sleep, that the welfare of many is entrusted to you, that the world looks on and approves, that some good is always being done to others,—above all things some good to your country;—that is happiness. For myself I can conceive none other.'

'Books!' suggested Gerald, as he put the last morsel of the last kidney into his mouth.

'Yes, books! Cicero and Ovid have told us that to literature only could they look for consolation in their banishment. But then they speak of a remedy for sorrow, not of a source of joy. No young man should dare to neglect literature. At some period of his life he will surely need consolation. And he may be certain that should he live to be an old man, there will be none other,—except religion, except religion. But, for that feeling of self-contentment,—and a man cannot be happy unless he be contented with himself,—you may be sure that hard work, and hard work alone, can give it to you.'

'Books are hard work themselves sometimes,' said Gerald.

'As for money,' continued the father, not caring to notice this interruption, 'if it be regarded in any other light than as a shield against want, as a rampart under the protection of which you may carry on your battle, it will certainly fail you. I was born a rich man.'

'Few people have cared about it so little as you,' said the elder son.

'And you, both of you, have been born to be rich.' This assertion did not take the elder brother by surprise. It was a matter of course. But Lord Gerald, who had never as yet heard anything as to his future destiny from his father, was interested by the statement. 'When I think of all this,—of what constitutes happiness,—I am almost tempted to grieve that it should be so.'

'If a large fortune were really a bad thing,' said Gerald, 'a man could I suppose get rid of it. But nobody does. I mean nobody tries to.'

'No;—it is a thing of which a man cannot get rid,—unless by shameful means. It is a burden which he must carry to the end.'

'Does anybody wish to get rid of it,—as Sinbad did of the Old Man?'* asked Gerald pertinaciously.

'No one,' replied the father almost angrily. 'I did not say that anyone wished it. It all began about that breakfast which your brother had ordered. Though you add luxury to luxury you will not really gratify your taste.'

'I did enjoy the kidneys, sir.'

'You assured us just now that the bread and cheese at Ely were just as good.' The Duke as he said this looked as though he knew that he had taken all the wind out of his adversary's sails. 'Though you add carriage to carriage, you will not be carried more comfortably.'

'A second horse out hunting is a comfort,' said Silverbridge.

'Then at any rate don't desire a third for show. But those comforts will cease to be joys when they become to you matters of course. That a boy who does not see a pudding once a year should enjoy a pudding when it comes in his way I can understand; but the daily pudding, or the pudding twice a day, is soon no more than simple daily bread,—which will or will not be sweet as it shall or shall not have been earned.' Then he went slowly to the door, but, as he stood with the handle of it in his hand, he turned round and spoke another word. 'When hereafter, Gerald, you may chance to think of that bread and cheese at Ely always remember that you had skated from Cambridge.'

'I will, sir,' said Gerald as the door was closed.

Immediately after this the two brothers took themselves to some remote part of the house where arrangements had been made for smoking, and there they finished the conversation. 'I was very glad to hear what he said about you, old boy.' This of course came from Silverbridge.

'I didn't quite understand him.'

'He meant you to understand that you wouldn't be like other younger brothers.'

'Then what I have will be taken from you.'

'There is lots for three or four of us. I do agree that if a fellow has as much as he can spend he ought not to want anything more. Moreton was telling me the other day something about the settled estates. I sat in that office with him all one morning when I was down at Silverbridge. I could not understand it all but I observed that he said nothing about the Scotch property. You'll be a laird and I wish you joy with all my heart. The governor will tell you all about it before long. I'm sure of that from his manner. He's going to have two eldest sons.'*

'What an unnatural piece of cruelty to me,—and so unnecessary!'

'Why?'

'According to his way of thinking! He says that a property is no better than a burden. But I'll try and bear it.'

CHAPTER 26

DINNER AT THE BEARGARDEN

IT was some three or four days after the breakfast scene described in the last chapter that a little communication on family political matters took place between the Duke and his eldest son in the galleries of the House of Commons. The Duke was in the gallery which is devoted to the use of peers, and Silverbridge, having heard that his father was there, had come up to shake hands with him from his own part of the enclosures. It was then about half-past five, and the House had settled down to business. Prayers had been read, petitions had been presented, and ministers had gone through their course of baiting with that equanimity and affectation of superiority which always belongs to a well-trained occupant of the Treasury bench. At the present moment, Sir Timothy Beeswax was advocating the second reading* of a bill which had come down from the House of Lords and was intended to remedy certain defects in legal reform, to which allusion has been already made. Sir Timothy, being a distinguished lawyer as well as Leader of the House of Commons, of course had the matter in his own hands,—not altogether to the grief of his Attorney-General, who was well aware that a mess had been made of this matter in the previous session.

In these days the Duke was very anxious that his son should attend to his parliamentary duties, but he was too proud a man and too generous to come to the House as a spy. It was his present habit always to be in his own place when the Lords were sitting, and to remain there while the Lords sat. It was not, for many reasons, an altogether satisfactory occupation, but it was the best which his life afforded him. He would never, however, come across into the other House without letting his son know of his coming, and Lord Silverbridge had on this occasion been on the look-out, and had come up to his father at once. 'Don't let me take you away,' said the Duke, 'if you are particularly interested in your chief's defence.'

'I can hear it up here, you know, sir,' said Silverbridge.

'Hardly if you are talking to me.'

'To tell the truth it's a matter I don't care very much about. They've got into some mess as to the number of judges and what they ought to do. There was something about it the night before, and Finn was saying that they had so arranged that there was one judge who never could possibly do anything.'

'If Mr. Finn said so it would probably be so, with some little allowance for Irish exaggeration. He is a clever man, with much less of his country's hyperbole than others;—but still, not without his share.'

'You know him well, I suppose.'

'Yes;—as one man does know another in the political world.'

'But he is a friend of yours? I don't mean an "Honourable friend," which is great bosh, I think; but you know him at home as we used to say at Eton?'

'Oh yes;—certainly. He has been staying with me at Matching. In public life such intimacies come from politics.'

'You don't care very much about him then?'

The Duke paused a moment before he answered. 'Yes I do. And in what I said just now perhaps I wronged him,—or rather gave you a wrong impression of my feelings towards him. I have been under obligations to Mr. Finn,—in a matter as to which he behaved to me very well.* I have found him to be a gentleman. If you happen to come across him in the House I would wish you to be courteous to him. I have not seen him since we came from abroad. Indeed I have seen nobody. I have been able to see nobody. But if ever again I should entertain my friends at my table, Mr. Finn would be one who would always be welcome there.' This he said with a sadly serious air as though wishing that his words should be noted. It was quite true that Mr. Finn had once done him a kindness, and true also that he had esteemed the man as a gentleman. But at the present moment he was remembering that he owed recompense to Mrs. Finn, and was making an effort to pay the debt. 'But your Leader is striking out into unwonted eloquence, is he not? Surely we ought to listen to him.'

Sir Timothy was a very fluent speaker, and when there was nothing to be said was possessed of great plenty of words. And he was gifted with that peculiar power which enables a man to have the last word in every little encounter,—a power which we are apt to call repartee, which is in truth the readiness which comes from continual practice. You shall meet two men of whom you shall know the one to be endowed with the brilliancy of true genius, and the other to be possessed of but moderate parts, and shall find the former never able to hold his own against the latter, even in the ordinary conversation of everyday society. And as the ordinary conversation of everyday society is the arena in which men are most generally seen, then the man of moderate parts will seem to be greater than the man of genius. But this skill of tongue, this glibness of speech is hardly an affair of intellect at all. It is,—as is style to the writer,—not the wares which he has to take to market, but the vehicle in which those wares may be carried. Of what avail to you is it to have filled granaries with corn produced from your own land if you cannot get your corn to the consumer? The vehicle and the road are so much! Now Sir Timothy was very great on roads and vehicles, but he had not in truth much corn to send. He could turn a laugh against an adversary;—no man better. He could seize, at the moment, every advantage which the opportunity of the moment might give him. The Treasury bench on which he sat and the big box on the table before him were to him fortifications of which he knew how to use every stone. The cheers and the jeers of the House had been so measured by him that he knew the value and force of every sound that was uttered. Politics had never been to him a study; but to parliamentary strategy he had devoted all his faculties. No one knew so well as Sir Timothy how to make arrangements for business, so that every detail arranged should be troublesome to his opponents. He could foresee a month beforehand that on a certain day a royal concert would make the House empty,* and would generously give that day to a less observant adversary. He knew how to blind the eyes of members to the truth without making any assurance with words of which they could afterwards complain. Those on the opposite side of the House would again and again find themselves checkmated by his astuteness,—when, with all their pieces on the board, there should be none which they could move. And this to him was Government! It was to purposes such as this that he conceived that a great Statesman should devote himself! Parliamentary management! That, in his mind, was under this constitution of ours the art most essential for the well-being of the country!

In all this he was very great; but when it might fall to his duty either to suggest or to defend any real piece of proposed legislation he was less happy. On this occasion he had been driven to take the matter in hand because he had previously been concerned in it as a lawyer. He had allowed himself to wax angry as he endeavoured to answer certain personal criticisms which had been made on his measure by Phineas Finn. Now Sir Timothy was never stronger than when he simulated anger. His mock indignation, which was of course altogether under control, was perhaps his most powerful weapon. But real anger is a passion which few men can use with judgment. And now Sir Timothy was really angry, and condescended to speak of our old friend Phineas as a bellicose Irishman. There was an over-true story as to our friend having once been seduced into fighting a duel* since he had been a member of Parliament, and those who wished to decry him sometimes made a good deal of this adventure. Sir Timothy had been called to order by some restive Irish members, but the Speaker had ruled that 'bellicose Irishman' was not beyond the latitude of parliamentary animadversion. Then Sir Timothy had repeated the phrase with a good deal of emphasis, and the Duke hearing it in the gallery had made his little caustic remark as to the unwonted eloquence of his son's parliamentary chief.

'Surely we ought to listen to him,' said the Duke. And for a short time they did listen. 'Sir Timothy is not a man I like, you know,' said the son, feeling himself obliged to apologise in some sort for his subjection to such a chief.

'I never particularly loved him myself.'

'They say that he is a sort of necessity.'

'A Conservative Fate,' said the Duke.

'Well, yes; he is so,—so awfully clever. We all feel that we could not get on without him, you know. When you were in, he was one of your party.'

'Oh yes;—he was one of us. I have no right to complain of you for using him. But when you say you could not get on without him, does it not occur to you that should he,—let us say be taken at once up to heaven,—you would have to get on without him?'

'Yes, we should.'

'And what then?'

'Then, why, he would be,—out of the way, you see, sir.'

'What you mean perhaps is that you do not know how to get rid of him.'

'Of course I am a very young hand at it and I don't pretend to understand much about it; but they all seem to think that he does know how to keep the party together. I don't think we are very proud of him.'

'Hardly that.'

'But he is awfully useful. A man has to look out so sharp to be always ready for those other fellows! I beg your pardon, sir, but I mean your side.'

'I understand who the other fellows are.'

'And it isn't everybody who will go through such a grind. You see he never must forget anything. He always must be ready. He has so many little things to think of. As far as I can see we all feel that we could not get along very well without him.'

Upon the whole the Duke was pleased with what he heard from his son. The young man's ideas about politics were boyish, but they were, he thought, the ideas of an attentive boy. Silverbridge had picked up some of the ways of the place, though he had not as yet formed any sound political opinions. He seemed to know something of the nature of the fight which was always going on, and to take an interest in it.

Then Sir Timothy finished a somewhat long speech with a flowery peroration, in which he declared that if Parliament were desirous of keeping the realms of Her Majesty free from the invasions of foreigners it must be done by maintaining the dignity of the judicial bench. There were some clamours at this; and although it was now nearly dinner-time Phineas Finn, who had been called a bellicose Irishman, was able to say a word or two. 'The Right Honourable gentleman no doubt means,' said Phineas, 'that we must carry ourselves with some increased external dignity. The world is bewigging itself, and we must buy a bigger wig than any we have got, in order to confront the world with proper self-respect. Turveydrop* and deportment will suffice for us against any odds.' No one quite understood why the security of the Queen's realms, as against foreign aggression, was dragged into such a debate as this; but there came, as the result, great anger on the part of one side of the House against Sir Timothy, and on the other great anger against Phineas Finn.

Then the House about half-past seven suddenly became very empty. 'Where are you going to dine, sir?' asked Silverbridge, who was still close to his father. The Duke, with something like a sigh, said he supposed he should dine at home, hinting with a muttered word or two that his dinner was not to him a matter of very much consequence. His dinner was of no consequence to him, but his evenings after dinner were at this period of his life very sad. In former days, when his wife was alive, he had been accustomed to spend many hours after dinner alone,—but then he had always had the power of seeking her, or her friends, though it were but for a moment. Now there was no one to whom he could betake himself. If you have a book with you on a journey it is very possible that you may not look at it;—but how terrible a thing it is to come on a journey unprovided with any book! So it was with him. In those former days many a long evening he had passed all alone in his library, satisfied with blue-books,* newspapers, and speculations on political economy, and had never crossed the threshold of his wife's drawing-room; but now, when there was no longer a threshold that he could cross, he felt himself to be deserted. 'You never were at the Beargarden;—were you, sir?' asked Silverbridge suddenly.

'Never,' said the Duke.

'Come and dine with me.'

'I am not a member of the club.'

'We don't care at all about that. Anybody can take in anybody.'

'Does not that make it promiscuous?'

'Well;—no; I don't know that it does. It seems to go on very well. I dare say there are some cads there sometimes.' Then Silverbridge bethought himself of Tifto. 'But I don't know where one doesn't meet cads. There are plenty in the House of Commons.'

'There is something in that, Silverbridge, which makes me think that you have not quite realised the difference between private and public life. In the former you choose your own associates and are responsible for your choice. In the latter you are concerned with others for the good of the State; and though, even for the State's sake, you would not willingly be closely allied with those whom you think dishonest, the outward manners and fashions of life need create no barriers. I certainly should not turn up my nose at the House of Commons because some constituency might send there an illiterate shoemaker; but I might probably find the illiterate shoemaker an unprofitable companion for my private hours.'

'I don't think there will be any shoemakers at the Beargarden.'

'Even if there were I would go and dine with you. I shall be very glad to see the place where you, I suppose, pass many of your hours.'

'I find it a very good shop to dine at. The place at the House is so stuffy and nasty,—and they do cook so badly! Besides one likes to get away for a little time.'

'Certainly. I never was an advocate for living in the House. One should always change the atmosphere.' Then they got into a cab and went away to the club. Silverbridge was, perhaps, a little afraid of what he was doing. The invitation had come from him on the spur of the moment, and he hardly ventured to think that his father would accept it. And now he did not quite know how the Duke would go through the ceremony. 'The other fellows' would all come and stare so at a man whom he and they had all been taught to regard as the most un-Beargardenish of men. But, nevertheless, he was a little proud of himself, and was especially anxious to make things pleasant for his father.

'What shall I order?' said the son as he took the Duke into a dressing-room to wash his hands. The Duke suggested that anything sufficient for his son would certainly be sufficient for him.

Nothing especial occurred during the dinner, which the Duke appeared to enjoy very much. 'Yes; I think it is very good soup,' he said. 'I don't think they ever give me any soup at home.' Then the son expressed his opinion very energetically that unless his father looked about rather more sharply, 'they' very soon would provide no dinner at all, and went on to remark that his experience had taught him that the less people demanded the more they were 'sat upon.' The Duke did like his dinner,—or, rather, it might perhaps be better said, he liked the feeling that he was dining with his son. A report that the Duke of Omnium was dining with Lord Silverbridge soon went round the room, and they who were justified by some previous acquaintance came up to greet him. To all who did so he was very gracious, and was specially so to Lord Popplecourt, who happened to pass close by the table at which he was sitting.

'I think he is a fool,' whispered Silverbridge as soon as the young Lord had passed.

'What makes you think so?'

'We always thought him an ass at Eton.'

'He has done pretty well I am told.'

'Oh yes,—in a way.'

'Somebody has told me that he is a careful man about his property.'

'I believe he is all that,' said Silverbridge.

'Then I don't see why you should think him a fool.'

To this Silverbridge made no reply; partly perhaps because he had nothing to say,—but hindered also in thinking of anything by the coming in of Tregear. This was an accident the possibility of which had escaped him. Unfortunately too the Duke's back was turned, so that Tregear, as he walked up the room, could not see who was sitting at his friend's table. Tregear coming up stood close at the Duke's elbow before

he recognised the man, and spoke some word or two to Silverbridge.
'How do you do, Mr. Tregear,' said the Duke, turning round.

'Oh, my Lord, I did not know that it was you.'

'You hardly would. I am quite a stranger here. Silverbridge and
I came up from the House together and he has been hospitable enough
to give me a dinner. I will tell you a very odd thing for a London man,
Mr. Tregear. I don't think that I have dined at a London club for fifteen
years before this.'

'I hope you like it, sir,' said Silverbridge.

'Very much indeed. Good-evening, Mr. Tregear. I suppose you have
to go to your dinner now.'

Then they went into one of the rooms upstairs to have coffee, the son
declining to go into the smoking-room, and assuring his father that he
did not in the least care about having a cigar after dinner. 'You would
be smothered, sir.' The Duke did as he was bidden and went upstairs.
Silverbridge was in truth much more anxious to please his father than
to gratify himself by smoking; but there was, in truth, a further reason
for avoiding the publicity of the smoking-room. When bringing his
father to the club he had thought nothing about Tregear but he had
thought much about Tifto. There was nothing in the club which he
feared to present to his father except Tifto. As he entered the room he
had seen Tifto at a table dining alone, and had bobbed his head at him.
Then he had taken the Duke to the further end of the room, and had
trusted that fear would keep the Major in his place. Fear had kept the
Major in his place. When the Major learned who the stranger was, he
had become silent, reserved, and stationary. Before the father and son
had finished their dinner, Tifto had gone to his cigar; and so that danger was over.

'By George, there's Silverbridge has got his governor to dinner,' said
Tifto, standing in the middle of the room, and looking round as though
he were announcing some confusion of the heavens and earth.

'Why shouldn't Lord Silverbridge have his father to dine with him?'
asked Mr. Lupton.

'I believe I know Silverbridge as well as any man, and by George, it
is the very last thing of the kind that I should have expected. There
have been no end of quarrels.'

'There has been no quarrel at all,' said Tregear, who had then just
entered the room. 'Nothing on earth would make Silverbridge quarrel
with his father, and I think it would break the Duke's heart to quarrel
with his son. They happen to have taken different sides in politics;—
that is all.' Tifto was rather oppressed by this and endeavoured to argue

the matter out; but Tregear, having made the assertion on behalf of his friend and his friend's father, would not allow himself to be enticed into further speech. Nevertheless there was a good deal said by others, during which the Major drank two glasses of whisky-and-water. In the dining-room he had been struck with absolute awe by the Duke's presence, and had certainly no idea of presenting himself personally to the great man. But Bacchus lent him foreign aid, and when the discussion was over and the whisky had been swallowed, it occurred to him that he owed it to his friend to go upstairs and ask to be introduced.

In the meantime the Duke and his son were seated in close conversation on one of the upstairs sofas. It was a rule at the Beargarden that men might smoke all over the house except in the dining-room;—but there was one small chamber, absurdly enough called the library, in which the practice was not often followed. But the room was generally deserted, and at this moment the father and son were the only occupants. 'A club,' said the Duke, as he sipped his coffee, 'is a comfortable and an economical residence. A man gets what he wants well served, and gets it cheap. But it has its drawbacks.'

'You always see the same fellows,' said Silverbridge.

'A man who lives much at a club is too apt to fall into a selfish mode of life. He is taught to think that his own comfort should always be the first object. A man can never, I think, be happy unless his first objects are outside himself. Personal self-indulgence begets a sense of meanness which still sticks to a man even when he has got beyond all hope of rescue. It is for that reason,—among others,—that marriage is so desirable.'

'A man should marry, I suppose.'

'Unless a man has on his shoulders the burden of a wife and children he should, I think, feel that he has shirked out of school as it were. He is not doing his share of the work of the Commonwealth.'

'Pitt was not married, sir.'

'No;—and a great many other good men have remained unmarried. Do you mean to be another Pitt?'

'I don't intend to be a Prime Minister.'

'I would not recommend you to entertain any such ambition. Pitt perhaps hardly had time for marriage. You may be more lucky.'

'I suppose I shall marry some day.'

'I hope so.'

'At any rate the pleasures of the Beargarden won't keep me single.'

'I should be glad to see you marry early,' said the Duke, speaking in a low voice, almost solemnly, but in his quietest, sweetest tone of voice. 'You are peculiarly situated. Though you are as yet only the heir to the property and honours of our family, still, were you married, almost everything would be at your disposal. There is so much which I should only be too ready to give up to you!'

'I can't bear to hear you talking of giving up anything,' said Silverbridge energetically.

Then the father looked round the room furtively, and seeing that the door was shut, and that they were assuredly alone, he put out his hand and gently stroked the young man's hair. It was almost a caress,—as though he would have said to himself, 'Were he my daughter, I would kiss him.' 'There is much I would fain give up,' he said. 'If you were a married man the house in Carlton Terrace would be fitter for you than for me. I have disqualified myself for taking that part in society which should be filled by the head of our family. You who have inherited so much from your mother would, if you married pleasantly, do all that right well.' He paused for a moment and then asked a straightforward question, very quickly—'You have never thought of anyone yet, I suppose?'

But Silverbridge had thought very much of somebody. He was quite aware that he had almost made an offer to Lady Mabel, and was, he fancied, ready to do so completely. She certainly had not given him any encouragement; but the very fact that she had not done so allured him the more. He did believe that he was thoroughly in love with Lady Mabel. She had told him that he was too young,—but he was older than Lady Mab herself by a week. She was beautiful;—that was certain. It was acknowledged by all that she was clever. As for blood, of which he believed his father thought much, there was perhaps none better in England,—the Grex barony dating from the time of Richard II. He had heard it said of her,—as he now well remembered, in his father's presence,—that she had behaved remarkably well in trying circumstances.* She had no fortune;—everybody knew that; but then he did not want fortune. Would not this be a good opportunity for breaking the matter to his father? 'You have never thought of anyone?' said the Duke,—again very sweetly, very softly.

'But I have.' Lord Silverbridge as he made the announcement blushed up to the eyes. Then there came over the father something almost of fear. If he was to be told, how would it be if he could not approve? 'Yes, I have,' said Silverbridge, recovering himself. 'If you wish it, I will tell you who it is.'

'Nay, my boy;—as to that, consult your own feelings. Are you sure of yourself?'

'Oh, yes.'

'Have you spoken to her?'

'Well;—yes; in part. She has not accepted me if you mean that. Rather the contrary.' Now the Duke would have been very unwilling to say that his son would certainly be accepted by any girl in England to whom he might choose to offer his hand, his coronet, and his fortune,— nor probably did he so think. But when the idea of a doubt was suggested to him, it did seem to be odd that his son should ask in vain. What other young man was there who could offer so much, and who was at the same time so likely to be loved for his own sake? He smiled however and was silent. 'I suppose I may as well out with it,' continued Silverbridge. 'You know Lady Mabel Grex.'

'Lady Mabel Grex. Yes;—I know her.'

'Is there any objection?'

'Is she not your senior?'

'No, sir; no; she is younger than I am.'

'Her father is not a man I esteem.'

'But she has always been so good!' Then the Duke was again silent. 'Have you not heard that, sir?'

'I think I have.'

'Is not that a great deal?'

'A very great deal. To be good must of all qualities be the best. She is very beautiful.'

'I think so, sir. Of course she has no money.'

'It is not needed. It is not needed. I have no objection to make. If you are sure of your own mind——'

'I am quite sure of that, sir.'

'Then I will raise no objection. Lady Mabel Grex! Her father I fear is not altogether a worthy man. I hear that he is a gambler.'

'He is so poor!'

'That makes it worse, Silverbridge. A man who gambles because he has money that he can afford to lose is, to my thinking, a fool. But he who gambles because he has none, is,——Well, let us hope the best of him. I remember to have heard your dear mother say that Lady Mabel had in certain circumstances behaved very well. We are related to them, you know.'

'Oh, yes. We are always joking about being cousins.'

'You may give her my love.'

'She has not accepted me.'

'But should she do so, you may.'

'She almost rejected me. But I am not sure that she was in earnest, and I mean to try again.' Just at that moment the door was opened and Major Tifto walked into the room.

VOLUME 2

CHAPTER 27

MAJOR TIFTO AND THE DUKE

'I BEG your pardon, Silverbridge,' said the Major, entering the room, 'but I was looking for Longstaffe. He hasn't been here I suppose.'

'No; he has not,' said Silverbridge, who did not at this moment at all wish to be interrupted by his racing friend.

'Your father, I believe?' said Tifto. He was rather red in the face but was in other respects perhaps improved in appearance by the liquor which he had taken. In his more sober moments he was not always able to assume that appearance of equality with his companions which it was the ambition of his soul to achieve. There would be fits and starts,—starts of impudence and fits of putting his tail between his legs. But a second glass of whisky-and-water would always enable him to cock his tail and bark before the company with all the courage of my lady's pug. 'Would you do me the great honour to introduce me to his Grace?'

Silverbridge was a young man who would not willingly turn his back upon a friend, however low in the world that friend might be. He had begun to understand that he had made a mistake by connecting himself with the Major, but at the club he always defended his partner, and, whenever he met the man there, would always devote a few moments to him. Though he not unfrequently found himself obliged to snub the Major himself, he nonetheless always countenanced the objectionable little Master of Hounds, and was true to his own idea of 'standing by a fellow.' Nevertheless he did not wish to introduce his friend to his father. The Duke saw it all at a glance, and felt that the introduction should be made. 'Perhaps,' said he, getting up from his chair, 'this is Major Tifto, of whom I have heard.'

'Yes;—my Lord Duke. That is my name. I am Major Tifto.'

The Duke bowed graciously. 'My father and I were engaged about private matters,' said Silverbridge.

'I beg ten thousand pardons,' exclaimed the Major. 'I certainly did not intend to intrude.'

'I think that we had done,' said the Duke. 'Pray sit down, Major Tifto.' The Major sat down. 'Though, now I bethink myself, I have to beg your pardon;—that I a stranger should ask you to sit down in your own club.'

'Don't mention it, my Lord Duke.'

'I had become so immersed in what I was saying to my son, and am so unused to clubs, that I forgot where I was.'

'Quite so, my Lord Duke. I hope you think that Silverbridge is looking well.' This he said as though he were in a manner responsible for his friend's state of health as well as for his stables.

'Yes;—yes. I think so.' Silverbridge bit his lips and turned his face away to the door.

'We didn't make a very good thing of our Derby nag the other day. Perhaps your Grace has heard all that.'

'I did hear that the horse in which you are both interested had failed to win the race.'

'Yes, he did. The Prime Minister, we call him, your Grace,—out of compliment to a certain Ministry which I wish it was going on to-day instead of the seedy lot we've got in. I think, my Lord Duke, that anyone you may ask will tell you that I know what running is. Well;—I can assure you,—your Grace, that is,—that since I've seen 'orses I've never seen a 'orse fitter than him. When he got his canter that morning after saddling, it was nearly even betting. Not that I or Silverbridge were fools enough to put on anything at that rate. But I never saw a 'orse so bad ridden in all my life. I don't mean to say anything, my Lord Duke, against the man. I never like to take away a man's character. But if that fellow hadn't been squared, or else wasn't drunk, or else wasn't off his head, that 'orse must have won,—my Lord Duke.'

'I do not know anything about racing, Major Tifto.'

'I suppose not, your Grace. I think I've heard Silverbridge say as much before. But as I and Silverbridge are together in this matter I thought I'd just let your Grace know that we ought to have had a very good thing. Though I say it as shouldn't, it is not as though he'd been joined with a man who didn't know what he was doing. I thought that perhaps your Grace might like to know that.'

'Tifto, you are making an ass of yourself,' said Silverbridge, unable any longer to restrain himself.

'Making an ass of myself!' exclaimed the Major.

'Yes;—considerably.'

'I think you are a little hard upon your friend,' said the Duke, with an attempt at a laugh. 'It is not to be supposed that he should know how utterly indifferent I am to everything connected with the turf.'

'I thought, my Lord Duke, you might care about hearing how Silverbridge was going on.' This the poor little man said almost with a whine. His partner's roughness had knocked out of him nearly all the courage which Bacchus had given him.

'So I do. Anything that interests him, interests me. But perhaps of all his pursuits racing is the one to which I am least able to lend an attentive ear. That every horse has a head, and that all did have tails till they were ill-used, is the extent of my stable knowledge.'

'Very good indeed, my Lord Duke; very good, indeed! Ha, ha, ha. All horses have heads, and all have tails! Heads and tails. Upon my word that is the best thing I have heard for a long time. I will do myself the honour of wishing your Grace good-night. By-bye, Silverbridge.' Then he left the room, having been made supremely happy by what he considered to have been the Duke's joke. To have had a joke made for his express behoof by the Duke of Omnium,—a fact of which he could talk in all societies without lying for the next two years,—was more than consolation to him for his friend's ill nature. Nevertheless he would remember the snubbing and would be even with Silverbridge some day. Did Lord Silverbridge think that he was going to look after his lordship's 'orses, and do this always on the square, and then be snubbed for doing it! Squareness in such matters is a virtue for which Major Tifto thought that his partner should be willing to pay highly,—even to the amount of being gracious to him in the father's presence. Silverbridge had not regarded the matter in this light;—and it was possible that Silverbridge might be made to pay for his mistake! Such were the feelings with which Major Tifto left the room.

'I am very sorry that he should have come in to trouble you,' said the son.

'He has not troubled me much. I do not know whether he has troubled you. If you are going down to the House again I will walk with you.' Under these circumstances Silverbridge of course had to go down to the House again, and they started together. 'That man did not trouble me, Silverbridge; but the question is whether such an acquaintance must not be troublesome to you.'

'I'm not very proud of him, sir.'

'But I think one ought to be proud of one's friends. Otherwise there can be no true delight in friendship.'

'He isn't my friend in that way at all.'

'In what way then?'

'He understands racing, and therefore I have got myself, as it were, joined with him.'

'He is the partner of your pleasures then;—the man in whose society it pleases you to enjoy the recreation of the race-course.'

'It is, sir, because he understands it.'

'I thought that a gentleman on the turf would have a trainer for that purpose,—not a companion whom he would be supposed to treat in terms of equality. What you mean to imply is that you can save money by leaguing yourself with Major Tifto.'

'No, sir,—indeed.'

'If you associate with him, not for pleasure, then it surely must be for profit. That you should do the former would be to me so surprising that I must regard it as impossible. That you should do the latter is—is, I think, a reproach.' This he said with no slightest tone of anger in his voice,—so gently that Silverbridge at first hardly understood the force of the words. But gradually all that was meant came in upon him, and he felt himself to be ashamed of himself.

'He is bad,' he said at last.

'Whether he be bad or not, I will not say; but I have seen enough of him to be sure that you can gain nothing by his companionship.'

'I will get rid of him,' said Silverbridge, after a considerable pause. 'I cannot do so all at once, but I will do it.'

'It will be better, I think.'

'Tregear has been telling me the same thing.'

'Is he objectionable to Mr. Tregear?' asked the Duke.

'Oh yes. Tregear cannot bear him. You treated him a great deal better than Tregear ever does.'

'I do not deny that he is entitled to be treated well;—but so also is your groom. Let us say no more about him at present. And so it is to be Mabel Grex?'

'I did not say so, sir. How can I answer for her? Only it was so pleasant for me to know that you would approve if it should come off.'

'Yes,—I will approve. When she has accepted you——'

'But I don't think she will.'

'If she should, tell her that I will go to her at once. It will be very much to me to have a new daughter;—very much that you should have a wife. Where would she like to live?'

'Oh, sir, we haven't got as far as that yet.'

'I dare say not; I dare say not,' said the Duke, almost chuckling. 'Gatherum is always thought to be dull.'

'She wouldn't like Gatherum at all, I'm sure.'

'Have you asked her?'

'No, sir. But nobody ever did like Gatherum.'

'I suppose not. And yet, Silverbridge, what a sum of money it cost!'
'I believe it did.'

'All vanity; and vexation of spirit!'* The money was there and the spending of it did not signify; but why should one have the vexation of spirit? The Duke no doubt was thinking of certain scenes passed at the great house in question, which scenes had not been delightful to him. 'No, I don't suppose she would wish to live at Gatherum. The Horns was given expressly by my uncle to your dear mother, and I should like Mary to have the place.'

'Certainly.'

'You should live among your tenantry. I don't care so very much for Matching.'

'It is the one place you do like, sir.'

'However we can manage all that. She shall not want for a house. Carlton Terrace I do not particularly like; but it is a very good house, and there you should hang up your hat when in London. She would find room there for her bonnets also. When it is settled let me know at once.'

'But if it should never be settled!'

'I will ask no questions;—but if it be settled tell me.' Then in Palace Yard he was turning to go, but before he did so, he said another word leaning on his son's shoulder. 'I do not think that Mabel Grex and Major Tifto would do well together at all.'

'There shall be an end to that, sir.'

'God bless you, my boy,' said the Duke.

Lord Silverbridge sat in the House,—or to speak more accurately, in the smoking-room of the House,—for about an hour thinking over all that had passed between himself and his father. He certainly had not intended to say anything about Lady Mab, but on the spur of the moment it had all come out. Now at any rate it was decided for him that he must, in set terms, ask her to be his wife. He had told the Duke that he had quite made up his mind, and the thing must be done. He was glad that it was so because he was sure that he loved her. Nothing ever was so pretty, so nice, so sweet, as Mabel Grex,—or nobody ever so clever! And then he himself felt that he was a young man who ought to marry. The scene which had just occurred had made him thoroughly sick of Major Tifto. He must get rid of the Major, and there could be no way of doing this at once so easy and so little open to observation as marriage. And he felt that without some such strongly operating cause very likely he might not really get rid of Tifto. He was conscious of his own weakness. If he were but once engaged to Mabel Grex the dismissal of Tifto would be quite a matter of course;—but, under any other circumstances, there might be a difficulty. He would see Lady Mabel again on the morrow and ask her in direct language to be his wife. It would be a great thing for him to be able to plead his father's good-will.

CHAPTER 28

MRS. MONTACUTE JONES'S GARDEN-PARTY

IT was known to all the world that Mrs. Montacute Jones's first great garden-party was to come off on Wednesday, 16th June, at Roehampton. Mrs. Montacute Jones, who lived in Grosvenor Place and who also had a country-house in Gloucestershire, and a place for young men to shoot at in Scotland, also kept a suburban Elysium at Roehampton, in order that she might give two garden-parties every year. When it is said that all these costly luxuries appertained to Mrs. Montacute Jones, it is to be understood that they did in truth belong to Mr. Jones, of whom nobody ever heard much. But of Mrs. Jones,—that is, Mrs. Montacute Jones,—everybody heard a great deal. She was an old lady who devoted her life to the amusement of—not only her friends, but very many who were not her friends. No doubt she was fond of lords and countesses, and did work very hard to get around her all the rank and fashion of the day. It must be acknowledged that she was a worldly old woman. But no more good-natured old woman lived in London, and everybody liked to be asked to her garden-parties. On this occasion there was to be a considerable infusion of royal blood,—German, Belgian, French, Spanish, and of native growth. Everybody who was asked would be sure to go, and everybody had been asked,—who was anybody. Of course Lord Silverbridge had been asked, and of course Lord Silverbridge intended to be there. Lady Mary, his sister, could not even be asked, because her mother was hardly more than three months dead; but it is quite understood in the world that women mourn longer than men.

Silverbridge in these days had mounted a private hansom cab in which he could be taken about rapidly,—and, as he said himself, without being shut up in a coffin. In this vehicle he had himself taken to Roehampton, purporting to kill two birds with one stone. He had not as yet seen his sister since she had been with Lady Cantrip. He would on this day come back by The Horns and call on his way.

He was well aware that Lady Mab would be at the garden-party with Miss Cassewary. What place could be better for putting the question he had to ask her? No place would be better if only she would allow herself to be separated from others and taken apart among some of the walks, as may be so easily done on such occasions. But if she did not intend to accept him, if that half-jocose rejection of a half-jocose offer had been made with a serious purpose, then of course she would not allow herself to be so separated and carried off. He was by no means so confident as the heir to so many good things might perhaps have been without undue self-confidence,—or as he probably would become after living a year or two longer in London.

Entering through the house onto the lawn he encountered Mrs. Montacute Jones, who, with a seat behind her on the terrace, surrounded by flowers, was prepared to go through the immense labour of receiving her guests, with all the vigour and courage of a British fashionable matron. 'How very good of you to come all this way, Lord Silverbridge, to eat my strawberries.'

'How very good of you to ask me! I did not come to eat your strawberries, but to see your friends.'

'You ought to have said you came to see me, but you young men of the present day never will condescend to pay a compliment to an old woman. Have you met Miss Boncassen yet?'

'The American beauty? No; but I have heard ever so much about her. Is she here?'

'Yes, and she particularly wants to be introduced to you. You won't betray me;—will you?'

'Certainly not. I am as true as steel.'

'She wanted, she said, to see whether the eldest son of the Duke of Omnium really did look like any other man.'

'Then I don't want to see her,' said Silverbridge, with a look of vexation.

'There you are wrong, for there was real downright fun in the way she said it. Of course you have to remember that she is a republican and an American,—and to remember also that she has heard ever so much about you. There they are, and I shall introduce you.' Then Mrs. Montacute Jones absolutely left her post for a minute or two, and taking the young Lord down the steps of the terrace did introduce him to Mr. Boncassen, who was standing there amidst a crowd of new acquaintances, and to Miss Boncassen the daughter.

Mr. Boncassen was an American from New York who had lately arrived in England with the object of carrying out certain literary pursuits in which he was engaged within the British Museum.* Much had been said about his coming, and all in his praise. He was an American who had nothing to do with politics and nothing to do with trade, both of which circumstances were in his favour. He was also a man of wealth and a man of letters, which two other circumstances added so much to his credit, that he was regarded quite as an American phoenix. And then he had a daughter who was said to be the prettiest young woman either in Europe or in America at the present time. So much had been said about her beauty that Silverbridge had already heard it mentioned with enthusiasm.

Isabel Boncassen, who was standing close by her father's elbow when the introduction took place, was certainly a very pretty girl. I wish that my reader would believe my simple assurance that imagination could conceive no greater perfection of feminine loveliness. But no such simple assurance was ever believed, and I doubt even whether any description will procure for me from the reader that amount of faith which I desire to achieve. But I must make some attempt, even though I may know that I shall fail. General opinion generally considered Miss Boncassen to be small, but she was in truth something above the average height of English women. She was slight, without that look of slimness which is so common to girls, and especially to American girls. That her figure was perfect the reader must believe on my word, as any detailed description of her arms, legs, bust, and waist, would be wearisome and ineffective. Her hair was dark brown in hue and sufficiently plentiful; but it added but little to her charms, which depended altogether on other matters. Perhaps what struck the beholder first was the excessive brilliancy of her complexion. No pink was ever pinker, no alabaster whiteness was ever more like alabaster; but under and around and through it all there was a continually changing hue which gave a vitality to her countenance which no fixed colours can ever produce. Her eyes, too, were full of life and brilliancy, and even when she was silent her mouth would be speaking. Nor was there a fault within the oval of her face upon which the hypercriticism of mature age could set a finger. Her teeth were excellent both in form and colour, but were seen but seldom. Who does not know that look of ubiquitous ivory produced by teeth which are too perfect in a face which is otherwise poor? Her nose at the base spread a little,—so that it was not purely Grecian. But who has ever seen a nose to be eloquent and expressive, which did not so spread? And who that has watched noses will deny that a nose may be most eloquent and expressive? It was, I think, the vitality of her countenance,—the way in which she could speak with every feature, the command which she had of pathos, of humour, of sympathy, of satire, the assurance which she gave by every glance of her eye, every elevation of her brow, every curl of her lip, every expansion of her nostrils, that she was alive to all that was going on,—it was all this rather than those feminine charms which can be catalogued and ticketed and labelled that made all who saw her acknowledge that she was most beautiful.

'Lord Silverbridge,' said Mr. Boncassen, speaking a little through his nose, 'I am proud to make your acquaintance, sir. Your father is a man for whom we in our country have a great respect. I think, sir, you must be proud of such a father.'

'Oh yes,—no doubt,' said Silverbridge awkwardly. Then Mr. Boncassen continued his discourse with the other gentlemen around him. Upon this our young friend turned of course to the young lady. 'Have you been long in England, Miss Boncassen?'

'Long enough to have heard about you and your father,' she said, speaking with no slightest twang,*—which delighted him.

'I hope you have not heard any evil of me?'

'Well!'

'I'm sure you can't have heard much good.'

'I know you didn't win the Derby.'

'You've been long enough to hear that then?'

'Do you suppose we don't interest ourselves about the Derby in New York? Why, when we arrived at Queenstown I was leaning over the taffrail so that I might ask the first man on board the tender* whether the Prime Minister had won.'

'And he said he hadn't.'

'I can't conceive why you of all men should call your horse by such a name. If my father had been President of the United States I don't think I'd call a horse President.'

'I didn't name the horse.'

'I'd have changed it. But is it not very impudent in me to be finding fault with you in this way the first time I have ever seen you? Shall you have a horse at Ascot?'

'There will be something going, I suppose. Nothing that I care about.' Lord Silverbridge had made up his mind that he would go to no races with Tifto before the Leger. And as Tifto would assuredly go to almost all that were run, he could only keep his resolve by staying away. The Leger would be an affair of such moment as to demand his presence. After that should come the complete rupture between him and Tifto.

Then there was a movement among the elders, and after a little while Lord Silverbridge found himself walking alone with Miss Boncassen. It seemed to her to be quite natural to do so, and there certainly was no reason why he should decline so pleasant a way of passing his morning.

It was thus that he had intended to walk with Mabel Grex. It was thus that he still intended to walk with Mabel Grex;—only as yet he had not found her. 'Oh, yes,' said Miss Boncassen, when they had been together about twenty minutes; 'we shall be here all the summer, and all the fall, and all the winter. Indeed father means to read every book in the British Museum before he goes back.'

'He'll have something to do then.'

'He reads by steam, and he has two or three young men with him to take it all down and make other books out of it;—just as you'll see a lady take a lace shawl and turn it all about till she has trimmed a petti-coat with it. It is the same lace all through,—and so I tell father it's the same knowledge.'

'But he puts it where more people will find it.'

'The lady endeavours to do the same with the lace. That depends on whether people look up or down. Father, however, is a very learned man. You mustn't suppose that I am laughing at him. And he is going to write a very learned book. Only everybody will be dead before it can be half finished.' They still went on together, and then he gave her his arm and took her into the place where the strawberries and cream were prepared,—or in other words one of those magnificent morning banquets which people never can eat because of their breakfasts, but which serve altogether to destroy their subsequent dinners. As he was going in he saw Mabel Grex walking with Tregear, and she bowed to him pleasantly and playfully. 'Is that lady a great friend of yours?' asked Miss Boncassen.

'A very great friend indeed.'

'She is very beautiful.'

'And clever as well,—and as good as gold.'

'Dear me! Do tell me who it is that owns all these qualities.'

'Lady Mabel Grex. She is daughter of Lord Grex. That man with her is my particular friend. His name is Frank Tregear, and they are cousins. Now I've told you all about them.'

'I am so glad they are cousins.'

'Why glad?'

'Because his being with her won't make you unhappy.'

'Supposing I was in love with her,—which of course I am not';—he need hardly have said this;—'do you suppose it would make me jealous to see her with another man?'

'In our country it would not. We do not think of such things at all. A young lady may walk about with a young gentleman just as she might with another young lady; but I thought it was different here. Do you know, judging by English ways, I believe I am behaving very improperly now in allowing you to go about with me so long. Ought I not to tell you to go away?'

'Pray do not.'

'As I am going to stay here so long I wish to behave well to English eyes. There isn't any fault so great as people thinking that it is enough for them to attend to the morals of their own people when they are away from their own country.'

'People know who you are, and discount all that.'

'If the difference be very marked they do. For instance I needn't wear a hideous long bit of cloth over my face in Constantinople because I am a woman. Everyone understands the difference between a Mohammedan and a Christian female. But when the discrepancies are small then they have to be attended to. So I shan't walk about with you any more.'

'Oh yes, you will,' said Silverbridge, who began to think that he liked walking about with Miss Boncassen.

'Certainly not. There is Mr. Sprottle. He is father's secretary. He will take me back.'

'Cannot I take you back as well as Mr. Sprottle,—if you have to be taken back? We will go round by the haycocks once again and then when we find your father we will talk about it.'

'Indeed no;—I am not going to monopolise such a man as you. Do you think that I don't understand that everybody will be making remarks upon the American girl who won't leave the son of the Duke of Omnium alone? There is your particular friend Lady Mabel, and here is my particular friend Mr. Sprottle.'

'May I come and call?'

'Certainly. Father will only be too proud,—and I shall be prouder. Mother will be the proudest of all. Mother very seldom goes out. Till we get a house we are at the Langham. You know that great American caravansary.* Thank you, Mr. Sprottle. I think we'll go and find father.'

Lord Silverbridge when he was thus dismissed found himself close to Lady Mabel and Tregear, and also to Miss Cassewary, who had now joined Lady Mabel. He had been very much struck with the American beauty, but was not on that account the less anxious to carry out his great plan. It was essentially necessary that he should do so at once, not only,—though of course chiefly,—for his own happiness, but also because the matter had been settled between him and his father. He was anxious to assure her that if she would consent, then the Duke would be ready to pour out all kinds of paternal blessings on their heads. 'Come and take a turn among the haycocks,' he said, not quite in a whisper, but yet so as to make her understand that the invitation was given specially to her.

'Frank declares,' said Lady Mabel, 'that the hay is hired for the occasion. I wonder whether that is true.'

'Anybody can see,' said Tregear, 'that it has not been cut off the grass it stands upon.'

'If I could find Mrs. Montacute Jones I'd ask her where she got it,' said Lady Mabel.

'And how much she pays for it,' suggested Tregear.

'Are you coming?' asked Silverbridge impatiently.

'I don't think I am. I have been walking round the haycocks till I am tired of them.'

'Anywhere else then?'

'There isn't anywhere else. What have you done with your American beauty? The truth is, Lord Silverbridge, you ask me for my company when she won't give you hers any longer.' He looked up at her as though he were really annoyed by her speech. 'Doesn't it look like it, Miss Cassewary?'

'I don't think Lord Silverbridge is the man to forget an old friend for a new one,' said the old lady.

'Not though the new friend be as lovely as Miss Boncassen?' asked Lady Mabel.

'Upon my word I don't know that I ever saw a prettier girl,' said Tregear.

'I quite admit it,' said Lady Mabel. 'But that is no salve for my injured feelings. I have heard so much about Miss Boncassen's beauty for the last week, that I mean to get up a company of British females, limited, for the express purpose of putting her down. Who is Miss Boncassen that we are all to be cast on one side for her? I am not going to stand it, Lord Silverbridge. Good-morning!'

Of course he knew that she was joking, but he hardly knew how to take her joke. There is a manner of joking which carries with it a great deal of serious intention. Who has not been persecuted by a joke, which can defend itself if attacked by its jocosity, but which nevertheless has carried with it the gravest censure? He did feel that Lady Mabel was not gracious to him because he had spent half an hour with this new beauty, and he was half inclined to be angry with her. Was it fitting that she should be cross with him, seeing that he was resolved to throw at her feet all the good things that he had in the world? 'Bother Miss Boncassen,' he said; 'you might as well come and take a turn with a fellow.'

'Come along, Miss Cassewary,' said she. 'We will go round the hay-cocks yet once again.' So they turned. Tregear went off another way, and the two ladies accompanied Lord Silverbridge.

But this was by no means what he wanted. Miss Cassewary was, no doubt, his very good friend, but he could not say what he had to say in the presence of Miss Cassewary,—nor could he ask her to take herself off in another direction. But even that was not the extent of his misfortune. He could not take himself off. Now that he had joined himself to these two ladies he could not escape till he had made with them the tour of the grounds. All this made him cross. 'These kind of things are a great bore,' he said.

'I dare say you would rather be in the House of Commons;—or, better still, at the Beargarden.'

'You mean to be ill-natured when you say that, Lady Mab.'

'You ask us to come and walk with you, and then you tell us that we are bores!'

'I did nothing of the kind.'

'I hope you two are not going to quarrel,' said Miss Cassewary.

'I should have thought that you would be particularly pleased with yourself for coming here to-day,' said Lady Mabel, 'seeing that you have made Miss Boncassen's acquaintance. To be allowed to walk half an hour alone with the acknowledged beauty of the two hemispheres ought to be enough even for Lord Silverbridge.'

'That is nonsense, Lady Mab;—absolute nonsense.'

'Nothing gives so much zest to admiration as novelty. A republican charmer must be charming indeed after all the blasé well-born habituées of the London drawing-rooms.'

'How can you talk such nonsense, Mabel?' said Miss Cassewary.

'But it is so. I sometimes feel that people must be sick of seeing me. I know I am very often sick of seeing them. Here is something quite fresh,—and not only unlike, but so much more lovely. I quite acknow-ledge that. I may be jealous, but no one can say that I am spiteful. I wish that some republican Adonis or Apollo would crop up,—so that we might have our turn. But I don't think the republican gentlemen ever are equal to the republican ladies. Do you, Lord Silverbridge?'

'I haven't thought much about it.'

'Mr. Sprottle for instance?'

'I have not the pleasure of knowing Mr. Sprottle.'

'Now we've been round the haycocks, and really, Lord Silverbridge, I don't think we have gained much by it. I quite feel that I haven't made myself pleasant, and you have been as cross as ever you can be. Those

forced marches never do any good. I dare say I shall meet you somewhere to-night, and then I hope I shall be pleasanter and you better-
humoured. Ta, ta.' And so they parted.

He was thinking with a bitter spirit of the ill result of his morning's
work,—or of the absence of any result,—when he again found himself
close to Miss Boncassen in the crowd of departing people on the terrace. People were going away and were hurrying through to their carriages. Mr. Sprottle had been sent on in advance, and Miss Boncassen
was hanging on her father's arm. 'Mind you keep your word,' she said.
And then she turned to her father. 'Lord Silverbridge has promised
to call.'

'Your mother will be delighted to make his acquaintance.'

'We are dining to-day with Sir Oliver Crumblewit, the president of
the Phrenological Society.* I suppose you don't go there.'

'Well; no; I don't think I know Sir Oliver.'

'And to-morrow with General Vansinoff, the great Dutch traveller.'

'I don't think I know the General either.'

'I dare say not. We always go to learned places;—never anywhere
else. On the next evening there is a grand meeting of vivisectors. You
won't be there I dare say.'

'My Lord, you mustn't believe all the nonsense that my girl talks,'
said the father.

'Oh yes, I do,' said Lord Silverbridge cheerfully, as he made his way
through the crowd. 'At any rate I shall be sure to come and call.' Then
Miss Boncassen smiled and nodded to him familiarly. At that moment
he saw that Lady Mabel was just at his other elbow. She also smiled and
nodded, but it seemed to him that there was more of sarcasm than of
good humour in her smile.

He got into his cab and was driven off towards Richmond. As he
went he began to think of the two young women with whom he had
passed his morning. Of course he was still fully prepared to ask Lady
Mabel to be his wife. He assured himself that he was not the man to be
put off his intention by the absurd nonsense of a few minutes. But
Mabel had certainly behaved badly to him. Even if she suspected nothing of his object, did she not owe it to their friendship to be more courteous to him than she had been? And if she suspected that object,
should she not at any rate have given him his opportunity? Or could it
be possible that she intended him to take what she had before said as
a rejection in earnest, and that therefore she would not give him that
opportunity? If so,—if he could feel convinced that it were so,—then
why should he undergo the annoyance of a more positive repulse? And

yet her manner had hardly been such as in that condition of affairs he would have expected!

Or could it be that she was really jealous of the American girl? No;—that idea he rejected instantly. It was not compatible with the innate modesty of his disposition. But no doubt the American girl was very lovely. Merely as a thing to be looked at she was superior to Mabel. He did feel that as to mere personal beauty she was in truth superior to anything he had ever seen before. And she was clever too;—and good-humoured;—whereas Mabel had been both ill-natured and unpleasant. Thinking of all this he found himself suddenly at The Horns.

CHAPTER 29

THE LOVERS MEET

LORD SILVERBRIDGE found his sister alone. Lady Cantrip, though he had not seen her, had been at the garden-party and had not yet come home. 'I particularly want you,' said the brother, 'to come up and call on Mabel Grex. She wishes to know you, and I am sure you would like her. You ought to know each other because you are cousins.'

'But I haven't been out anywhere yet,' she said. 'I don't feel as though I wanted to go anywhere.'

Nevertheless she was very anxious to know Lady Mabel Grex, of whom she had heard much. A girl if she has had a former love passage says nothing of it to her new lover; but a man is not so reticent. Frank Tregear had perhaps not told her everything, but he had told her something. 'I was very fond of her;—very fond of her, very fond of her,' he had said. 'And so I am still,' he had added. 'As you are my love of loves, she is my friend of friends.' Lady Mary had been satisfied by the assurance, but had become anxious to see the friend of friends. Nevertheless she resisted at first her brother's entreaties. She felt that her father in delivering her over to Lady Cantrip and to the seclusion of The Horns had intended to preclude her from showing herself in London at all. She was conscious that she was being treated with cruelty, but, like other martyrs, had a certain pride in her martyrdom. She would obey her father to the letter, and much beyond the letter; she would give him no right to call her conduct in question; but he and any other to whom he might entrust the care of her, should be made to know that she thought him cruel. He had his power to which she must submit. But she also had hers,—to which it was possible he might be made to submit. 'I do not know that papa would wish me to go,' she said.

'But it is just what he would wish. He thinks a good deal about Mabel.'

'Why should he think about her at all?'

'I can't exactly explain,' said Silverbridge awkwardly, 'but he does.'

'If you mean to tell me, Silverbridge, that Mabel Grex is anything particular to you, and that papa approves of it, I will go all round the world to see her.' But he had not meant to tell her any such thing. The request had been made at Lady Mabel's instance. When his sister had spoken of her father's possible objection, then he had become eager in explaining the Duke's feeling, not remembering that such anxiety might betray himself. Just at that moment Lady Cantrip came in, and the question was referred to her. She did not see any objection to such a visit, and expressed her opinion that it would be a very good thing that Mary should be taken out. 'She should begin to go somewhere,' said Lady Cantrip. And so it was decided. This was Wednesday. On the next Friday he would come down early in his hansom cab and drive her up to Belgrave Square. Then he would take her to Carlton Terrace, and Lady Cantrip's carriage should pick her up there and bring her home. He would arrange it all with Lady Mabel, so that there should be no difficulty about their meeting.

'What did you think of the American beauty?' asked Lady Cantrip when all that was settled.

'I thought she was a beauty.'

'So we perceived. You had eyes for nobody else, Lord Silverbridge.'

'Somebody introduced her to me at once, and then I had to walk about the grounds with her. That's the kind of thing one always does at those places.'

'Just so. That is what "those places" are meant for, I suppose. But it was not apparently a great infliction.' Lord Silverbridge had to explain that it was not an infliction;—that it was a privilege, seeing that Miss Boncassen was both clever and lovely, but that it did not mean anything in particular, and that he, though he admired her beauty and intellect, did not care very much about her. All this he thought it necessary to explain, but as he was not very good at explanation he blundered over it a little.

When he took his leave he asked his sister to go out into the grounds with him for a moment. This she did almost unwillingly, fearing that he was about to speak to her of Tregear, and determined if he did so to stand up for her love boldly. But he had no such purpose on his mind. 'Of course you know,' he began as soon as they were alone, 'all that was nonsense you were saying about Mabel.'

'I did not know.'

'I was afraid you might blurt out something before her.'

'I should not be so imprudent as that.'

'Girls do make such fools of themselves sometimes. They are always thinking about people being in love. But it is really the truth that my father said to me the other day how very much he liked what he had heard of her, so that I am able to say that I know he would like you to know her.' Nevertheless, in spite of all this, Lady Mary thought it very probable that Lady Mabel Grex might become her sister-in-law.

On that same evening Silverbridge wrote from the Beargarden the shortest possible note to Lady Mabel, telling her what he had arranged. 'I and Mary propose to call in B. Square on Friday at two. I must be early because of the House. You will give us lunch. S.' There was no word of endearment,—none even of those ordinary words which people who hate each other use to one another. He would take his sister to see her because he had promised. In other respects he would be as cold to her as possible till she had shown a willingness to come round. But he received the next day at home a much more kindly written note from her,—in which it appeared that she was willing to 'come round.'

'DEAR LORD SILVERBRIDGE,

'You are so good! You always do just what you think people will like best. Nothing could please me so much as seeing your sister, of whom of course I have heard *very very* much. There shall be nobody here but Miss Cass.

'Yours most sincerely,

'M.G.

'I saw your American beauty last night, and got myself introduced to her. I found her charming. I hope you were not angry because I chaffed you about her.'

'How I do wish I were a man,' his sister said to him when they were in the hansom together.

'You'd have a great deal more trouble.'

'But I'd have a hansom of my own, and go about where I pleased. How would you like to be shut up at a place like The Horns?'

'You can go out if you please, I suppose.'

'Not like you. Papa thinks it's the proper place for me to live in and so I must live there. I don't think a woman ever chooses how or where she shall live herself. She has always got to do what some man tells her.'

'You are not going to take up women's rights, I hope.'

'I think I shall if I stay at The Horns much longer. What would papa say if he heard that I was going to give a lecture at an Institute?'

'The governor has had so many things to bear that a trifle such as that would make but little difference.'

'Poor papa!'

'He was dreadfully cut up about Gerald. And then he is so good! He said more to me about Gerald than he ever did about my own little misfortune at Oxford; but to Gerald himself he said almost nothing. And now he has forgiven me everything because he thinks I am constant at the House.'

'And are you?'

'Not so much as he thinks. I do go there,—for his sake. But I get so sick of it that I am always running out. I shall never make a real politician. And he has been so good about my changing sides.'

'I think you were quite right there.'

'I am beginning to think I was quite wrong. If a fellow means to stick to politics it's all very well that he should have an opinion of his own; but I shall never do that. What did it matter to me?'

'I suppose it did make papa unhappy.'

'Of course it did. And then this affair of yours.' As soon as this was said Lady Mary at once hardened her heart against her father. Whether Silverbridge was or was not entitled to his own political opinions,—seeing that the Pallisers had for ages been known as staunch Whigs and Liberals,—might be a matter for question. But that she had a right to her own lover she thought that there could be no question. There should at any rate be no question within her own bosom. On that matter she could be as hard as a rock to anything that either father or brother might say to her. As they were sitting in the cab he could hardly see her face, but he was aware that she was in some fashion arming herself against opposition,— putting her back up as a cat does when a dog invades her territory. 'I am sure that this makes him very unhappy,' continued Silverbridge.

'It cannot at any rate be altered,' she said.

'It will have to be altered.'

'Nothing can alter it. He might die, indeed;—or so might I.'

'Or he might see that it is no good,—and change his mind,' suggested Silverbridge.

'Of course that is possible,' said Lady Mary very curtly,—showing plainly by her manner that the subject was one which she did not choose to discuss any further. And there was no further discussion.

'It is very good of you to come to me,' said Lady Mabel, kissing her new acquaintance. 'I should never have thought of asking it, if your brother had not wished it too. I have heard so much about you.'

'And I also of you.'

'I, you know, am one of your brother's stern Mentors. There are three or four of us determined to make him a pattern young legislator. Miss Cassewary is another.' Miss Cass had already been introduced to the stranger. 'Only she is not quite so stern as I am.'

'He ought to be very much obliged.'

'But he is not,—not a bit. Are you, Lord Silverbridge?'

'Not so much as I ought to be perhaps.'

'Of course there is an opposing force. There are the race-horses, and the drag, and Major Tifto. No doubt you have heard of Major Tifto.' Mary said that she had heard of Major Tifto. 'The Major is the Mr. Worldly-Wiseman who won't let Christian go to the Strait Gate.* Is it not so, Lord Silverbridge?'

'I don't quite know what you are talking about.'

'I am afraid he hasn't read his *Pilgrim's Progress*. But we shall prevail, Lady Mary, and he will get to the beautiful city at last.'

'What is the beautiful city?' he asked.

'A seat in the Cabinet, I suppose,—or that general respect which a young nobleman achieves when he has shown himself able to sit on a bench for six consecutive hours without appearing to go to sleep.'

Then they went to lunch, and Lady Mary did find herself to be happy with her new acquaintances. Her life since her mother's death had been so sad, that this short escape from it was in itself a relief to her. The sadness had probably come chiefly from its solitariness, but she thought that it had arisen from her father's opposition to her lover. Now for a while she found herself almost gay. There was an easy liveliness about Lady Mabel,—a grain of humour and playfulness conjoined,—which made her feel almost at home at once. And it seemed to her as though her brother were quite at home. He called the girl Lady Mab, and Queen Mab, and once plain Mabel, and the old woman, whose name Mary had never heard before, he called Miss Cass. It surely, she thought, must be the case that Lady Mabel and her brother were engaged to each other. But if it were so, why should he not have told her?

'Come upstairs into my own room,—it is nicer than this,' said Lady Mabel, and they went from the dining-room into a pretty little sitting-room with which Silverbridge was very well acquainted. 'Have you heard of Miss Boncassen?' Lady Mabel asked. Mary said she had heard something of Miss Boncassen's very great beauty. 'Everybody is talking about her. Your brother met her at Mrs. Montacute Jones's garden-party and was made a conquest of instantly.'

'I wasn't made a conquest of at all,' said Silverbridge.

'Then he ought to have been made a conquest of. I should be if I were a man. Indeed I am as a woman. I think she is the loveliest person to look at and the nicest person to listen to that I ever came across. We all feel that, as far as this season is concerned, we are going to be cut out; but we don't mind it so much because she is a foreigner.'

'Americans are not foreigners,' suggested Silverbridge. Then there arose a question on that subject which was strongly debated, Miss Cassewary expressing an opinion that Americans are by no means so foreign as Frenchmen and Italians, but, still, are to a certain extent foreign; and Lady Mary holding with her brother that nobody could be a foreigner who did not speak a foreign language. In the middle of this argument, over which the four persons pretended to excite themselves considerably, the door was opened and Frank Tregear was announced.

Everybody there present knew as well as does the reader, what was the connection between Tregear and Lady Mary Palliser. And each knew, or was nearly certain, that the other knew it. It was therefore impossible for them not to feel themselves guilty among themselves. The two lovers had not seen each other since the death of the Duchess,—since, indeed, they had been together in Italy. Now they were brought face to face in this unexpected manner! And nobody was quite sure whether somebody had not done something to arrange the meeting,—nobody at least except Tregear, who was well aware that his coming at that moment was quite accidental. Mary might naturally suspect that Lady Mabel had done this in the interest of her friend Tregear, and Silverbridge could hardly not suspect that it was so. Lady Mabel, who had never before met the other girl, could hardly refrain from thinking that there had been some underhand communication with Tregear,—and Miss Cassewary was clearly of opinion that there must have been some such understanding. Tregear however must have been a hardened hypocrite if his surprise had been assumed.

Silverbridge was the first to speak. 'Halloa, Tregear, I didn't know that we were to see you.'

'Nor I, that I should see you,' said he. Then of course there was a shaking of hands all round, in the course of which ceremony he came to Mary the last. She gave him her hand, but had not a word to say to him. 'If I had known that you were here,' he said, 'I should not have come; but I need hardly say how glad I am to see you,—even in this way.' Then the two girls were convinced that the meeting was accidental; but Miss Cass still had her doubts, and Silverbridge also as to the possibility of some treachery between Lady Mabel and Tregear.

Conversation became at once very difficult. Tregear seated himself near, but not very near, to Lady Mary, and made some attempt to talk to both the girls at once. Lady Mabel, in her flighty way, spoke about various things, but in a manner which clearly showed that she was not at her ease;—whereas Mary seemed to be stricken dumb by the presence of her lover. Silverbridge was so much annoyed by a feeling that every moment of this interview was a treason to his father, that he sat cudgelling his brain to think how he should bring it to an end. Miss Cassewary was dumbfounded by the occasion. She was the one elder in the company. She was the person who ought to see that no wrong was committed. She was not directly responsible to the Duke of Omnium, but she was thoroughly permeated by a feeling that it was her duty to take care that there should be no clandestine love meetings in Lord Grex's house. At last Silverbridge jumped up from his chair. 'Upon my word, Tregear, I think you had better go,' said he.

'So do I,' said Miss Cassewary. 'If it is an accident——'

'Of course it is an accident,' said Tregear, angrily,—looking round at Mary, who blushed up to her eyes.

'I did not mean to doubt it in the least,' said the old lady. 'But as it has occurred, Mabel, don't you think that he had better go?'

'He won't bite anybody, Miss Cass.'

'She would not have come if she had expected it,' said Silverbridge.

'Certainly not,' said Mary, speaking now for the first time. 'But now he is here——' Then she stopped herself, rose from the sofa, sat down, and then rising again, stepped up to her lover,—who rose at the same moment,—and threw herself into his arms and put up her lips to be kissed.

'This won't do at all,' said Silverbridge. Miss Cassewary clasped her hands together and looked up to heaven. She probably had never seen such a thing done before. Lady Mabel's eyes were filled with tears, and though in all this there was much to cause her anguish, still in her heart of hearts she admired the brave girl who could thus show her truth to her lover.

'Now go,' said Mary through her sobs.

'My own one!' Tregear ejaculated.

'Yes, yes, yes; always your own. Go;—go; go.' She was weeping and sobbing as she said this, and hiding her face with her handkerchief. He stood for a moment irresolute, and then left the room without a word of adieu to anyone.

'You have behaved very badly,' said the brother.

'She has behaved like an angel,' said Mabel, throwing her arms round Mary as she spoke, '—like an angel. If there had been a girl whom you loved and who loved you, would you not have wished it? And would you not have worshipped her for showing that she was not ashamed of her love?'

'I am not a bit ashamed,' said Mary.

'And I say that you have no cause. No one knows him as I do,—how good he is, and how worthy!' Immediately after that Silverbridge took his sister away, and Lady Mabel, escaping from Miss Cass, was alone. 'She loves him almost as I have loved him,' she said to herself. 'I wonder whether he can love her as he did me!'

CHAPTER 30

WHAT CAME OF THE MEETING

NOT a word was said in the cab as Lord Silverbridge took his sister to Carlton Terrace, nor for some time after their arrival there. He had indeed left her without any reference to the scene which had just taken place, intending to go at once down to the House;—but an idea struck him that this would be cruel, or at any rate harsh. So he returned. 'Mary,' he said, 'I was very sorry for all that.'

'It was not my doing.'

'I suppose it was nobody's doing. It was an accident. But I am very sorry that it occurred. I think that you should have controlled yourself.'

'No!' she almost shouted.

'I think so.'

'No;—if you mean by controlling myself holding my tongue. He is the man I love,—whom I have promised to marry. In that way I will treat him whenever I see him.'

'But Mary,—do ladies generally embrace their lovers in public?'

'No,—nor should I. I never did such a thing in my life before. But as he was there I had to show that I was not ashamed of him. You talk of—"public"! Do you think I should have done it if you all had not been there? It was because you were there to see!' Then again she burst out into tears.

He did not quite know what to make of it. Mabel Grex had declared that she had behaved like an angel, and Mabel Grex ought to know. But yet, as he thought of what he had seen, he shuddered with vexation. 'I was thinking of the governor,' he said.

'And I have thought of papa too. He shall be told everything.'

'That you met Tregear?'

'Certainly; and that I—kissed him. I will do nothing that I am ashamed to tell everybody.'

'He will be very angry.'

'I cannot help it. He should not treat me as he is doing. Mr. Tregear is a gentleman. Why did he let him come? Why did you bring him? But it is of no use. The thing is settled. Papa can break my heart if he chooses, but he cannot make me say that I am not engaged to marry Mr. Tregear.' He waited with her till Lady Cantrip's carriage came to take her back to Richmond, and then he walked away to his legislative duties.

On that night Mary told the whole of her story to Lady Cantrip;—the story, that is, of her trip to London. There was nothing that she tried to conceal. 'I got up,' she said, 'and threw my arms round him. Of course I did. Is he not all the world to me?'

'Had it been planned?' asked Lady Cantrip.

'No;—no! Nothing had been planned. It seemed like it at first because of course I did not expect it. But it was not so. They are cousins and very intimate and he goes there constantly. And so he came in. Now I want you to tell papa all about it.'

Lady Cantrip began to think that it had been an evil day for her when she had agreed to take the charge of this very determined young lady; but she consented at once to write the letter to the Duke. As the girl was in her hands she must take care not to lay herself open to reproaches such as those which had fallen to the lot of poor Mrs. Finn. She had refused to act the part of a duenna;—but, nevertheless, as this objectionable lover had either contrived a meeting, or had met the young lady without contriving, it was necessary that the Duke should be informed. 'I would rather you wrote it,' said Lady Mary. 'I should be sure to write something that he would not like. But pray tell him that all along I have meant him to know all about it.'

Then Lady Cantrip wrote her letter,—not without very great difficulty. Till she seated herself at her table and searched for her words, she did not know how very great the difficulty would be. It cannot in any circumstances be easy to write to a father as to his daughter's love for an objectionable lover; but the Duke's character added much to the severity of the task. And then that embrace! How was it to be described? She knew that the Duke would be struck with horror as he read any such description, and she found herself to be struck almost with horror herself as she attempted to write it. When she came to the point she found she could not write it. 'I fear there was a good deal of warmth shown on both sides,' she said, feeling as she wrote the words that she was calumniating the man, as to whose warmth she had in truth heard nothing. 'It is quite clear to me,' she added, 'that this is not a passing fancy on her part.' Had she dared, she would have advised the Duke to give way at once. It was becoming quite evident to her that the young people would prevail.

It was impossible that the Duke should be made to understand exactly what had occurred. That Silverbridge had taken Mary up to London he did understand, and that they had together gone to Lord Grex's house. He understood also that the meeting had taken place in the presence of Silverbridge and of Lady Mabel. It seemed to him at the first glance that everybody concerned must have behaved treacherously to him. 'No doubt it was all an accident,' Lady Cantrip wrote. How could it be an accident? Or, if so, what must he do to prevent a recurrence of such accidents?

'You had Mary up in town on Friday,' he said to his son on the following Sunday morning.

'Yes, sir.'

'What was that for?'

'I wanted her and Lady Mabel Grex to know each other.'

'And that—friend of yours came in?'

'Yes, sir.'

'Do you not know what my wishes are?'

'Certainly I do;—but I could not help his coming. You do not suppose that anybody had planned it!'

'I hope not.'

'It was simply an accident,—which could not be helped, and such an accident as must occur over and over again,—unless Mary is to be locked up.'

'Who talks of locking anybody up? What right have you to speak in that way?'

'I only meant to say that of course they will stumble across each other in London.'

'I think I will go abroad,' said the Duke. He was silent for a while, and then repeated his words. 'I think I will go abroad.'

'Not for long I hope, sir.'

'Yes;—to live there. Why should I stay here? What is there to give me any pleasure here? What good can I do here? Everything I see and everything I hear is a pain to me.' The young man of course could not but go back in his mind to the last interview which he had had with his father, when the Duke had been so gracious and apparently so well pleased,—when he had appeared to be so happily intent on his son's marriage.

'Is there anything else wrong,—except about Mary?' Silverbridge asked.

'I am told that Gerald owes about fifteen hundred pounds at Cambridge.'

'So much as that! I knew he had four or five horses there.'

'It is not the money, but the absence of principle;—that a young man should have no feeling that he ought to live within certain prescribed means! Do you know what you have had from Mr. Moreton?'

'Not exactly, sir.'

'Of course it is different with you,—now that you are in Parliament. But a man, let him be who he may, should live within certain means. As for your sister, I think she will break my heart.' Silverbridge found it to be quite impossible to say anything in answer to this. 'Are you going to church?' asked the Duke.

'I was not thinking of doing so, particularly.'

'Do you not ever go?'

'Yes;—sometimes. I will go with you now if you like it, sir.'

'I had thought of going, but my mind is too much harassed. It is better not to go, than to go and attend to nothing. I do not see why you should not go.'

But Silverbridge, though he had been willing to sacrifice his morning to his father,—for it was, I fear, in that way that he had looked at it,—did not see any reason for performing a duty which his father himself omitted. When therefore he had escaped from the Duke's presence,—which he did in a half-apologetic manner, as though he was aware that he ought to stay a little longer,—he had his morning before him. He let himself down into the park by a small iron gate which opened into the Mall from the back of the house, and, strolling into the enclosure, began to roam about slowly under the trees. There were various matters which required a good deal of thought. In the first place he was aware that on the previous evening,—after dinner, at which he had been somewhat liberal with his champagne,—he had allowed himself to back Prime Minister for the Leger to a very serious amount. He had both taken the odds against his horse in a good many thousands, and had also laid the odds against another horse to quite as great an extent. In fact he had plunged, and now stood to lose some twenty thousand pounds on the doings of the last night. And he had made these bets under the direct influence of Major Tifto. It was the remembrance of this, after the promise made to his father, after the assurance given by himself to himself, that annoyed him the most. He was imbued with a feeling that it behoved him as a man who had commenced upon life, as one who was called upon by circumstance to fill a great part, to 'pull himself together' as he would have said himself, and to live in accordance with certain rules of the wisdom of which he himself should be the judge. He could make the rules easily enough, but he had never yet succeeded in keeping any one of them. He had determined to sever himself from Tifto; and, in doing that, had intended to sever himself from the affairs of the turf generally,— certainly from betting. This resolution was not yet a week old. It was only on the last Tuesday that the Major had intruded himself upon them when he was talking with his father at the Beargarden, and had so thoroughly disgusted him. It was on that evening that he had resolved that Tifto should no longer be his companion; and now he had to confess to himself that because he had drunk three or four glasses of champagne he had been induced by Tifto to wager a great deal more money than he could possibly have of his own to pay!

And he had told his father that he intended to ask Mabel Grex to be his wife. He felt that in that matter he had absolutely committed himself. He had so committed himself that the offer must now be made. He did not specially regret that, though he wished that he had been more reticent. 'What a fool a man is to blurt out everything!' he said to himself. But he did not reject his purpose. A wife would be a good thing for him. He was quite conscious of that himself, and where could he possibly find a better wife than Mabel Grex? How thoroughly handsome she had looked when she stood up to take his sister's part! In beauty she was no doubt inferior to Miss Boncassen. There was something about Miss Boncassen which made it impossible to forget her. But Miss Boncassen was an American, a stranger, and on many accounts out of the question. It did not occur to him that he would fall in love with Miss Boncassen; but still it seemed hard to him that this immediate intention of marriage should stand in the way of his having a good time with Miss Boncassen for a few weeks. As he thought of this he almost felt that it was a pity he should be in a hurry. No doubt there were objections to marriage. It clipped a fellow's wings, and all that kind of thing. But then, if he were married, he might be sure that Tifto would be laid aside. It was such a great thing to have got his father's assured consent to a marriage. It meant complete independence in money matters,—independence so complete that he would never again be driven to write in half-apologetic strains to Mr. Moreton!

Then his mind ran away to a review of his father's affairs. It was a genuine trouble to him that his father should be so unhappy. Of all the griefs which weighed upon the Duke's mind, that in reference to his sister was, he thought, the heaviest. The money which Gerald owed at

Cambridge would be nothing if that other sorrow could be conquered. Nor had Tifto and his own extravagance caused the Duke any incurable wounds. If Tregear could be got out of the way, his father, he thought, might be reconciled to other things. In turning all this over in his mind it did not occur to him that this getting Tregear out of the way might be altogether prejudicial to his sister's happiness. Brothers but seldom feel respect for the love affairs in which their sisters are interested. He did feel very tender-hearted about his father; but he had no remorse in regard to his sister as he made up his mind that he would speak very seriously to Tregear.

He was now sitting within the park, on a bench beneath the trees, and had lighted by this time half-a-dozen cigarettes one after another. He was a very handsome youth, about six feet high, with light hair, with his mother's round blue eyes, and with all that aristocratic look which had belonged so peculiarly to the late Duke but which was less conspicuous in the present head of the family than in any of the Pallisers. He was a young man whom you would hardly pass in a crowd without observing,—but of whom you would say, after due observation, that he had not as yet put off all his childish ways. He now sat with his legs stretched out, with his cane in his hands, looking down upon the water. He was trying to think. He worked hard at thinking. But the bench was hard and, upon the whole, he was not satisfied with his position. He had just made up his mind that he would look up Tregear in order that he might express his opinion as to that necessity of 'putting an end to all that stuff between him and Mary,' when Tregear himself appeared on the path before him.

'Tregear!' exclaimed Silverbridge.

'Silverbridge!' exclaimed Tregear.

'What on earth makes you walk about here on a Sunday morning?'

'But what makes you sit there? That I should walk here, which I often do, does not seem to me odd. But that I should find you is marvellous. Do you often come?'

'Never was here in my life before. I strolled in because I had things to think of.'

'Questions to be asked in Parliament? Notices of motions? Amendments in Committee, and that kind of thing? A member of Parliament must have an uneasy time of it.'

'Go on, old fellow.'

'Or perhaps Major Tifto has made important revelations as to the stables at Newmarket.'

'D—— Major Tifto.'

'With all my heart,' said Tregear.

'Sit down here,' said Silverbridge. 'As it happened, at the very moment when you came up I was thinking of you.'

'That was kind of you.'

'And I was determined to go to you. All this about my sister must be given up.'

'Must be given up!'

'It can never lead to any good. I mean that there never can be a marriage.' Then he paused, but Tregear was determined to hear him out. 'It is making my father so miserable that you would pity him if you could hear him talk about it.'

'I dare say I should. When I see people unhappy I always pity them. What I would ask you to think of is this. If I were to commission you to tell your sister that everything between us should be "given up,"—as of course I might do,—would not she also be so unhappy that you would have to pity her? What is your honest opinion about that?'

'She would get over it.'

'And so will your father. Whatever the unhappiness may be, people generally do get over it after some fashion. But would his unhappiness be worse than hers?'

'He has a right to have his own opinion on such a matter.'

'And so have I. And so has she. His rights in this matter are very clear and very potential. I am quite ready to admit that we cannot marry for many years to come unless he will provide the money. You are quite at liberty to tell him that I say so, and to tell her. Not but what he knows it, and knows that I know it. I have no right to ask your father for a penny, and I will never do so. The power is all in his hands. I shall not attempt to run away with her. As far as I know my own purposes, I shall not make any immediate attempt even to see her. Though,—mind,—on that matter I make no promise. We did meet, as you saw, the other day, by the merest chance. After that do you think that your sister wishes me to give her up?'

'As for supposing that girls are to have what they wish, that is nonsense.'

'For young men I suppose equally so. This life ought to be a life of self-denial no doubt. Perhaps it might be my duty to retire from this affair, if by doing so I should sacrifice only myself. The one person of whom I am bound to think in this matter is the girl I love.'

'That is just what she would say about you.'

'I hope so.'

'In that way you support each other, though it must be manifest to anybody that the whole thing is as wrong as it can be. If it were any other man circumstanced just like you are, and any other girl placed like

Mary, you would be the first to say that the man was behaving badly. I don't like to use hard language to you, whom I always liked better than any other fellow I've known; but in such a case you would be the first to say of another man—that he was looking after the girl's money.'

Silverbridge as he said this looked forward steadfastly onto the water, regretting much that cause for quarrel should have arisen, but thinking that Tregear would find himself obliged to quarrel. But Tregear, after a few moments' silence, having thought it out, determined that he would not quarrel. 'I think I probably might,' he said, laying his hand on Silverbridge's arm. 'I think I perhaps might express such an opinion.'

'Well, then!'

'I have to examine myself, and find out whether I am guilty of the meanness which I might perhaps be too ready to impute to another. I have done so, and I am quite sure that I am not drawn to your sister by any desire for her money. I am certain of myself that no man was ever more firmly devoted to a girl, or with a surer singleness of heart and purpose. I did not seek her because she was a rich man's daughter, nor,—because she is a rich man's daughter,—will I give her up. She shall be mistress of the occasion. Nothing but a word from her shall induce me to leave her;—but a word from her, if it comes from her own lips,—shall do so.' Then he took his friend's hand in his, and, having grasped it, walked away without saying another word. Silverbridge remained on the bench yet for another half-hour, hard though it was,—thinking of it all.

CHAPTER 31

MISS BONCASSEN'S RIVER-PARTY, NO. 1

TWICE before the expiration of that June month, and once early in July, did Lord Silverbridge sally forth from his own house, or from the club, or from the House of Commons with the full intention of asking Mabel Grex to be his wife; but on none of the occasions were either Venus or Hymen kind to him. On the first attempt he did not find the lady; on the second he could not at first secure her solitary ear for a moment, and, when he did so, had got into so strong an argument about his sister that it had become impossible to adapt himself to the other matter. 'Of course I was very sorry at first that he should have come in,' Lady Mabel had said. 'But I was glad of it afterwards, because I could see what sort of a girl she was. Of course she will marry him.

Cart-ropes won't keep them apart.' Then Silverbridge had become angry and had expressed an opinion that they would have to be kept apart, whether by cart-ropes or other means. He had altogether taken his father's part and had become rather violent. 'It was monstrous,' he had said, 'that a girl like that should think that she was going to have her own way!' When there had been this difference between them he had found himself compelled to leave the house without pleading his own cause.

Then he tried again, but on the third attempt Miss Cassewary was with her, and did not leave the room,—as she had done on the former occasion, discreetly though to no purpose. And the conversation turned in a very disagreeable way on Miss Boncassen, as to whom he could not but think that Lady Mabel said some very ill-natured things. It was no doubt true that he, during the last three weeks, had often been in Miss Boncassen's company, that he had danced with her, ridden with her, taken her to the House of Lords and to the House of Commons, had even gone to church with her at Westminster Abbey, and was now engaged to attend upon her at a river-party up above Maidenhead. But Mabel had certainly no right to complain. Had he not thrice during the same period come there to lay his coronet at her feet;—and now, at this very moment, was it not her fault that he was not going through the ceremony?

'I suppose,' she said, laughing, 'that it is all settled.'

'What is all settled?'

'About you and the American beauty?' Of course Miss Cass heard every word of all this.

'I am not aware that anything particular has been settled.'

'Then it ought to be,—oughtn't it? For her sake I mean.'

'That is so like an English woman,' said Lord Silverbridge. 'Because you cannot understand a manner of life a little different from your own you will impute evil.'

'I have imputed no evil, Lord Silverbridge, and you have no right to say so.'

'If you mean to assert,' said Miss Cass, 'that the manners of American young ladies are freer than those of English young ladies, it is you, I think, that are taking away their characters.'

'Because you can't understand that they should differ from ourselves without being bad.'

'I don't say it would be at all bad,' continued Lady Mabel. 'She is a beautiful girl, and very clever, and would make a charming duchess. And then it would be such a delicious change to have an American duchess.'

'She wouldn't be a duchess.'

'Well, countess, with duchessship before her in the remote future. Wouldn't it be a change, Miss Cass?'

'Oh, decidedly!' said Miss Cass, who thought that all such changes were objectionable.

'And very much for the better. Quite a case of new blood, you know. Pray don't suppose that I mean to object. Everybody who talks about it approves,—and that is everybody. I haven't heard a dissentient voice. Only as it has gone so far, and as English people are too stupid, you know, to understand all these new ways,—don't you think perhaps——?'

'No, I don't think. I don't think anything except that you are very ill-natured.' Then he got up and, after making formal adieux to both the ladies, left the house. He certainly had not in this way got any nearer to his object in reference to Mabel Grex.

As soon as he was gone Lady Mabel began to laugh, but the least apprehensive ears would have perceived that the laughter was forced and affected. Miss Cassewary did not laugh at all, but sat bolt upright and looked very serious. 'Upon my honour,' said the younger lady, 'he is the most beautifully simple-minded human being I ever knew in my life.'

'Then I wouldn't laugh at him.'

'How can one help it? But of course I do it with a purpose.'

'What purpose?'

'I think he is making a fool of himself. If somebody does not interfere he will go so far that he will not be able to draw back without misbehaving! Don't you think it would be very bad if he were to marry this American?'

'Very bad indeed!'

'But it must come to that unless somebody stops him.'

'I thought,' said Miss Casseway, in a very low voice, almost whispering, 'I thought that he was looking for a wife elsewhere.'

'You need not think of that ever again,' said Lady Mab, jumping up from her seat. 'I had thought of it too. But as I told you before, I spared him. He did not really mean it with me;—nor does he mean it with this American girl. Such young men seldom mean. They drift into matrimony. But she will not spare him. How would it be possible that she should do so? It would be a national triumph. All the States would sing a paean of glory. Fancy a New York belle having compassed a duke!'

'I don't think it possible. It would be too horrid.'

'I think it quite possible. As for me I could teach myself to think it best as it is, were I not so sure that I should be better for him than so many others. But still I should not be very good. I shouldn't love him for instance.'

'Why not love him?'

'He is such a boy. I should always be treating him like a boy,—spoiling him and petting him, but never respecting him. Don't run away with any idea that I should really refuse him from conscientious motives, if he were really to ask me. I too should like to be a duchess. I should like to bring all this misery at home to an end. There can be no girl in all England more in want of a magnificent husband than I am.'

'But you did refuse him.'

'Not exactly;—because he never asked me. Had I chosen to set my wits to work I could have made him ask me. He almost did it;—but for the moment I was weak and so I let him have another chance. I shall not have been a good friend to him if it ends in his marrying this Yankee.'

Lord Silverbridge went out of the house in a very ill humour,—which however left him when in the course of the afternoon he found himself up at Maidenhead with Miss Boncassen. Miss Boncassen at any rate did not laugh at him. And then she was so pleasant, so full of common sense, and so completely intelligent! 'I like you,' she had said, 'because I feel that you will not think that you ought to make love to me. There is nothing I hate so much as the idea that a young man and a young woman can't be acquainted with each other, without some such tomfoolery as that.' This had exactly expressed his own feeling. Nothing could be so pleasant as his intimacy with Isabel Boncassen;—but he was quite sure that he had never made love to her, and almost equally sure that he never would.

Mrs. Boncassen seemed to be a most homely person, with very little desire either to speak to anyone else, or to be spoken to. She went out but seldom, and on those rare occasions did not in any way interfere with her daughter. It seemed that she completely understood that it was her duty in life to be a sort of upper servant to Isabel. Mr. Boncassen filled a much prouder situation. Everybody knew that Miss Boncassen was in England because it suited Mr. Boncassen to spend many hours in the British Museum. But still the daughter hardly seemed to be under control from the father. She went where she liked; talked to those she liked; and did what she liked. She had a hired carriage at her own disposal and had more than once altogether shocked the Miss Cassewarys of the world by going home from parties alone. Some of the young ladies, however, had expressed an opinion that there was a good deal to be said in favour of this practice.

There is however a good deal to be said against it. All young ladies cannot be Miss Boncassens, with such an assurance of admirers as to be free from all fear of being left alone. There is a comfort for a young lady in having a pied-à-terre to which she may retreat in case of need. In American circles, where girls congregate without their mothers, there is a danger felt by young men that if a lady be once taken in hand, there will be no possibility of getting rid of her,—no mamma to whom she may be taken and under whose wings she may be dropped. And in consequence of this danger some young gentlemen are becoming cautious. And that caution on the side of the gentlemen begets the necessity for a correspondingly strong action on the side of the ladies. 'My dear,' said an old gentleman the other day walking through an American ballroom, and addressing himself to a girl whom he knew well,—'My dear——' But the girl bowed and passed on, still clinging to the arm of the young man who accompanied her. But the old gentleman was cruel, tyrannical, and possessed of a determined purpose. 'My dear,' said he again, catching the young man tight by the collar and holding him fast. 'Don't be afraid; I've got him; he shan't desert you; I'll hold him here till you have told me how your father does.' The young lady looked as if she didn't like it, and the sight of her misery gave rise to a feeling that, after all, mammas perhaps may be a comfort to their daughters in a ball-room.

But in her present phase of life Miss Boncassen suffered no misfortune of this kind. There was no need to catch and hold a young man for her. It had become a privilege to be allowed to attend upon Miss Boncassen, and the feeling of this privilege had certainly been enhanced by the manner in which Lord Silverbridge had devoted himself to her. Fashion of course makes fashion. Had not Lord Silverbridge been so very much struck by the charm of the young lady, Lords Glasslough and Popplecourt would not perhaps have found it necessary to run after her. As it was, even that most unenergetic of young men, Dolly Longstaffe, was moved to profound admiration and had been heard to say that the American beauty was better than all the English pullets that had come out of British eggs.

On this occasion they were all up the river at Maidenhead. The party was given by Mr. Boncassen himself, and therefore Mrs. Boncassen also was present. He had looked about for some means of returning the civilities offered to him, and had been instigated by Mrs. Montacute Jones to do it after this fashion. There was a magnificent banquet spread in a summer-house on the river bank,—so spread that ladies and gentlemen might sit in chairs, if such was their will, or be waited upon with lobster-salad and champagne-cup* under the trees. There were boats, and there was a band, and there was a sward* for dancing. There was lawn-tennis, and fishing-rods,—which nobody used,—and better still, long shady secluded walks in which gentlemen might stroll,—and ladies too, if they were kind enough. The whole thing had been arranged by Mrs. Montacute Jones, who had explained to Miss Boncassen the theory on which her invitations should be sent out. As the day was fine, as many of the old people had kindly abstained from coming, as there were plenty of young men of the best sort, and as nothing had been spared in reference to external comforts, the party promised to be a success. Every most lovely girl in London of course was there,—except Lady Mabel Grex. Lady Mabel was in the habit of going everywhere, but on this occasion she had refused Mrs. Boncassen's invitation. 'I don't want to see her triumphs,' she had said to Miss Cass.

Everybody went down by railway of course, and innumerable flies and carriages had been prepared to take them to the scene of action. Some immediately got into boats and rowed themselves up from the bridge,—which, as the thermometer was standing at eighty in the shade, was an inconsiderate proceeding. 'I don't think I am quite up to that,' said Dolly Longstaffe, when it was proposed to him to take an oar. 'Miss Amazon will do it. She rows so well, and is so strong!' Whereupon Miss Amazon, not at all abashed, did take the oar; and as Lord Silverbridge was on the seat behind her with the other oar she probably enjoyed her task. Miss Boncassen was not in the boat, and therefore neither did Dolly Longstaffe nor Lord Silverbridge remain there long.

'What a very nice sort of person Lady Cantrip is.' This was said to Silverbridge by that generally silent young nobleman Lord Popplecourt, to whom Silverbridge was by no means peculiarly well inclined. The two young men were on the bank together looking at the struggles of other watermen and waterwomen in another boat, and had come together apparently by accident. Silverbridge a moment before had been talking to Mrs. Montacute Jones, who had been singing the praises of Isabel Boncassen, but being cautious as well as old, had declined to come down quite so close to the water's edge. 'What a very nice person Lady Cantrip is.' The remark was the more singular because Lady Cantrip was not at the party,—and the more so again because, as Silverbridge thought, there could be but little in common between the very steady Countess who had his sister in charge and the young Lord beside him, who was not fast only because he did not like to risk his money.

'Well,—yes; I dare say she is.'

'I thought so, peculiarly. I was at that place at Richmond yesterday.'

'The devil you were. I didn't know that anybody ever was let in there. What were you doing at The Horns?'

'Lady Cantrip's grandmother was—I don't quite know what she was, but something to us. I know I've got a picture of her at Popplecourt. Lady Cantrip wanted to ask me something about it, and so I went down. I was so glad to make acquaintance with your sister.'

'You saw Mary, did you?'

'Oh yes. I lunched there. I'm to go down and meet the Duke some day.'

'Meet the Duke!'

'Why not?'

'No reason on earth,—only I can't imagine the governor going to Richmond for his dinner, or, indeed, dining anywhere.'

'I saw him eating his dinner with you at the club the other day.'

'Yes; he did that. Well! I am very glad to hear it. I hope you'll get on well with him. You may take your oath of this. He'll talk as much good sense to you as any man in the kingdom.'

'I was so much struck with your sister.'

'Yes; I dare say,' said Silverbridge, turning away into the path where he saw Miss Boncassen standing with some other ladies. What Popplecourt had said to him did induce him to think a little, but it certainly did not occur to him that Popplecourt was to be brought forward as a suitor for his sister's hand.

'I believe this is the most lovely place in the world,' Miss Boncassen said to him.

'We are so much the more obliged to you for bringing us here.'

'We don't bring you. You allow us to come with you and see all that is pretty and lovely.'

'Is it not your party?'

'Father will pay the bill, I suppose,—as far as that goes. And mother's name was put on the cards. But of course we know what that means. It is because you and a few others like you have been so kind to us, that we are able to be here at all.'

'Everybody, I should think, must be kind to you,—everywhere.'

'I do have a good time pretty much;—but nowhere so good as here. I fear that when I get back I shall not like New York and Newport.'*

'I have heard you say, Miss Boncassen, that Americans were more likeable than the English.'

'Have you? Well; yes; I think I have said so. And I think it is so. I'd sooner have to dance with a bank clerk in New York, than with a bank clerk here.'

'Do you ever dance with bank clerks?'

'Oh dear, yes. At least I suppose so. I dance with whoever comes up. We haven't got lords in America, you know.'

'You have got gentlemen?'

'Plenty of them;—but they are not so easily defined as lords. I do like lords.'

'Do you?'

'Oh yes—and ladies;—countesses I mean and women of that sort. Your Lady Mabel Grex is not here. Why wouldn't she come?'

'Perhaps you didn't ask her.'

'Oh yes, I did;—especially for your sake.'

'She is not my Lady Mabel Grex,' said Lord Silverbridge with unnecessary energy.

'But she will be.'

'What makes you think that?'

'You are devoted to her.'

'Much more to you, Miss Boncassen.'

'That is nonsense, Lord Silverbridge.'

'Not at all.'

'It is also—untrue.'

'Surely I must be the best judge of that myself.'

'Not a doubt; a judge not only whether it be true, but if true whether expedient,—or even possible. What did I say to you when we first began to know each other well?'

'What did you say?'

'That I liked knowing you;—that was frank enough;—that I liked knowing you because I knew that there would be no tomfoolery of love-making.' Then she paused; but he did not quite know how to go on with the conversation at once, and she continued her speech. 'When you condescend to tell me that you are devoted to me, as though that were the kind of thing that I expect to have said when I take a walk with a young man in a wood, is not that the tomfoolery of love-making?' Then she stopped and looked at him, so that he was obliged to answer.

'Then why do you ask me if I am devoted to Lady Mabel? Would not that be tomfoolery too?'

'No. If I thought so, I would not have asked the question. I did specially invite her to come here because I thought you would like it. You have got to marry somebody.'

'Some day, perhaps.'

'And why not her?'

'If you come to that, why not you?' He felt himself to be getting into deep waters as he said this,—but he had a meaning to express if only he could find the words to express it. 'I don't say whether it is tomfoolery, as you call it, or not; but whatever it is, you began it.'

'Yes;—yes. I see. You punish me for my unpremeditated impertinence in suggesting that you are devoted to Lady Mabel, by the premedi-
tated impertinence of pretending to be devoted to me,—having all
along the intention of letting me know that it is pretence.'

'Stop a moment. I cannot follow that.' Then she stood and laughed.
'I will swear that I did not intend to be impertinent.'

'I hope not.'

'I am devoted to you.'

'Lord Silverbridge!'

'I think you are——'

'Stop, stop. Do not say it.'

'Well I won't;—not now. But there has been no tomfoolery.'

'May I ask a question, Lord Silverbridge?'

'What question, Miss Boncassen?'

'It is altogether about yourself.'

'I think you may.'

'You will not be angry? I would not have you angry with me.'

'I will not be angry,' he said.

'Are you not engaged to marry Lady Mabel Grex?'

'No.'

'Then I beg your pardon. I was told that you were engaged to her.'

'Who told you?' he asked.

'That would only be to make mischief. I was so told. And I thought
your choice was so fortunate, so happy! I have seen no girl here that
I admire half so much. She almost completely comes up to my idea of
what a young woman should be.'

'Almost!'

'Now I am sure that if not engaged to her you must be in love with her,
or my praise would have sufficed. One can imagine angels, you know.'

'Though one knows a Lady Mabel Grex, one may yet become
acquainted with a Miss Boncassen.'

There are moments in which stupid people say clever things, obtuse
people say sharp things, and good-natured people say ill-natured
things. This young Lord of ours was not stupid or obtuse, and he
certainly had not intended to be clever or sharp. He was thoroughly
good-natured, and manifestly did not wish to wound his present
companion. But the rebuke seemed to her sharp. 'Lord Silverbridge,'
she said, 'I did not expect that from you.'

'Expect what? I meant it simply.'

'I have no doubt you meant it simply. We Americans think ourselves
sharp, but I have long since found out that we may meet more than our

matches over here. I think we will go back. Mother means to try to get up a quadrille.'

'You will dance with me?'

'I think not. I have been walking with you, and I think I had better dance with someone else.'

'You can let me have one dance.'

'I think not. There will not be many.'

'Are you angry with me?'

'Yes, I am; there.' But as she said this she smiled. 'The truth is I thought I was getting the better of you, and you turned round and gave me a pat on the head to show me that you could be master when it pleased you. You have defended your intelligence at the expense of your good nature.'

'I'll be shot if I know what it all means,' he said, just as he was parting with her. 'But I will go back to my first assertion and declare again that I am devoted to you.' Then he took off his hat, made a bow, and went away in another direction.

CHAPTER 32

MISS BONCASSEN'S RIVER-PARTY, NO. 2

LORD SILVERBRIDGE soon made up his mind that as he could not dance with Miss Boncassen he would not dance at all. He was by no means angry at being rejected, and when, soon after, he saw her stand up with Dolly Longstaffe he felt no jealousy whatever. She had refused to dance with him not because she did not like him, but because she did not wish to show that she liked him too well. He could understand that from her manner, though he had not quite followed all the ins and outs of her little accusations against him. She had flattered him,—without perhaps any intention of flattery on her part. She had spoken of his intelligence and had complained that he had been too sharp to her. Mabel Grex when most sweet to him, when most loving, always made him feel that he was her inferior. He dearly loved Mabel Grex, but with her he felt himself to be hardly more than a boy. She took no trouble to hide her conviction of his youthfulness. This was anything but flattering. Miss Boncassen, on the other hand, professed herself to be almost afraid of him. There had been in some sort a tacit understanding between them, that she refused to dance with him because she thought too much of him.

'There shall be no tomfoolery of love-making,' she had said. But what if it were not tomfoolery at all? What if it were good, genuine, earnest love-making? He certainly was not pledged to Lady Mabel. Indeed as far as the matter had yet gone, she had rejected him. As regarded his father there certainly would be a difficulty,—a double difficulty. In the first place he had been foolish enough to tell his father that he was going to make an offer to Mabel Grex,—foolish because it was possible that the girl might reject him, and foolish again because he might have cause to change his mind. And then his father would surely refuse his consent to a marriage with an American stranger. In such case there would be no unlimited income, no immediate pleasantness of magnificent life such as he knew would be poured out upon him if he were to marry Mabel Grex. As he thought of this, however, he told himself that it would be base indeed to sell himself for money and magnificence,—especially when the money and magnificence must come at last. He at any rate could afford to be independent, and gratify his own taste. Just at this moment he was of opinion, after balancing the matter well in his mind, that Isabel Boncassen would be the sweeter companion of the two.

He had sauntered down to the place where they were dancing and stood by, saying a few words to Mrs. Boncassen, who was seated on a bench, looking at her daughter. 'Why are you not dancing, my Lord?' she asked.

'There are enough without me.'

'I guess you young aristocrats are never over-fond of doing much with your own arms and legs.'

'I don't know about that;—polo, you know, for the legs, and lawn-tennis for the arms. It is hard work enough.'

'But it must always be something new-fangled; and after all it ain't of much account. Our young men like to have quite a time at dancing.'

It all came through her nose. Every syllable of it! And she looked so common! What a woman to have for a mother-in-law! What would the Duke say to her, or Mary, or even Gerald? But then she would probably have been sent back to America before that;—or it might perhaps be better that he should go to New York and be married there. The father was by no means so objectionable. He was a tall, straight, ungainly man, who always wore black clothes and seemed to keep himself ready to dine out by simply changing his black tie for a white one. He had dark, stiff, short hair, a long nose, and a forehead that was both high and broad. Ezekiel Boncassen was the very man,—from his appearance,— for a President of the United States;* and there were men who talked of him for that high office. That he had never attended to politics was supposed to be in his favour. He had the reputation of being the most learned man in the States, and reputation itself often suffices to give a man dignity of manner. He, too, spoke through his nose, but the peculiar twang coming from a man would be supposed to be virile and incisive. From a woman, Lord Silverbridge thought it to be unbearable. But as to Isabel, had she been born in Belgravia* or within the confines of some lordly park in Hertfordshire, she could not have been more completely free from the abomination.

'I am sorry that you should not be enjoying yourself,' said Mr. Boncassen, coming up to his wife's relief.

'Nothing could have been nicer. To tell the truth I am standing idle by way of showing my anger against your daughter, who would not dance with me.'

'I am sure she would have felt herself honoured,' said Mr. Boncassen, bowing.

'Who is the gentleman with her?' asked the mother.

'A particular friend of mine,—Dolly Longstaffe!'

'Dolly!' ejaculated Mrs. Boncassen, with peculiar intonation of the strongest kind.

'Everybody calls him so. His real name I believe to be Adolphus.'

'Is he,—is he,—just anybody?' asked the anxious mother.

'He is a very great deal,—as people go here. Everybody knows him. He is asked everywhere, but he goes nowhere. The greatest compliment paid to you here is his presence.'

'Why, my Lord, there are the Countess Montague, and the Marchioness of Capulet, and Lord Tybalt,* and——'

'They go everywhere. They are nobodies. It is a charity to even invite them. But to have had Dolly Longstaffe once is a triumph for life.'

'Laws!'* said Mrs. Boncassen, looking hard at the young man who was dancing. 'What has he done?'

'He never did anything in his life.'

'I suppose he's very rich.'

'I don't know. I should think not. A man of that sort generally owes a lot of money. I don't know anything about his riches, but I can assure you that having had him down here will quite give a character to the day.'

In the meantime Dolly Longstaffe was in a state of great excitement. Some part of the character assigned to him by Lord Silverbridge was true. He very rarely did go anywhere, and yet was asked to a great many places. He was a young man,—though not a very young man,—with a fortune of his own and the expectation of a further fortune from his father. Few men

living could have done less for the world than Dolly Longstaffe,—and yet
he had a position of his own. Now he had taken it into his head to fall in
love with Miss Boncassen. This was an accident which had probably never
happened to him before, and which had disturbed him very much. He had
known Miss Boncassen a week or two before Lord Silverbridge had seen
her, having by some chance dined out and sat next to her at dinner. From
that moment he had become greatly changed, and had gone hither and
thither in pursuit of the American beauty. His passion, having become
suspected by his companions, had excited their ridicule. But though he
had more than once shown himself to be annoyed he had nevertheless
persevered;—and now he was absolutely dancing with the lady out in the
open air. 'If this goes on, your friends will have to look after you, and put
you somewhere where you will be safe.' Mr. Lupton had said this to him
in one of the intervals of the dance. Dolly had turned round and scowled,
and then suggested that if Mr. Lupton would mind his own affairs it
would be just as well for the world at large.

At the present crisis Dolly was very much excited. When the dance
was over, as a matter of course, he offered the lady his arm, and as a matter of course she accepted it. 'You'll take a turn; won't you?' he said.

'It must be a very short turn, Mr. Longstaffe,' she said,—'as I am of
course expected to make myself busy.'

'Oh, bother that.'

'It bothers me;—but it has to be done.'

'You have set everything going now, and it will all go on like clock-
work. They'll begin dancing again without your telling them.'

'I hope so.'

'And I've got something I want to say.'

'Dear me;—what is it?'

They were now on a path close to the riverside, in which there were
many loungers. Every now and again Dolly looked behind him to see if
there were others close upon their heels;—and there always was another
couple close upon their heels. 'Would you mind coming up to the temple?' he said.

'What temple?'

'Oh, such a beautiful place. The Temple of the Winds, I think they
call it, or Venus;—or—or—Mrs. Arthur de Bever.'

'Was she a goddess?'

'I remember now. It is something built to her memory. Such a view
of the river! I was here once before and they took me up there.
Everybody who comes here goes and sees Mrs. Arthur de Bever. They
ought to have told you.'

'Let us go then,' said Miss Boncassen. 'Only it must not be long.'

'Five minutes will do it all.' Then he walked rather quickly up a flight of rural steps which it was necessary that they should ascend alone. 'Lovely spot; isn't it?'

'Yes, indeed.'

'That's Maidenhead Bridge. That's—somebody's place; I don't know who. And now I've got something to say to you.'

'You're not going to murder me now you've got me up here alone?' said Miss Boncassen laughing.

'Murder you!' said Dolly, throwing himself into an attitude that was intended to express the most devoted affection. 'Oh, no!'

'I am glad of that.'

'Miss Boncassen!'

'Mr. Longstaffe! If you sigh like that you'll burst yourself.'

'I'll—what?'

'Burst yourself!' And she nodded her head at him.

Then he clapped his hands together, and turned his head away from her towards the little temple. 'I wonder whether she knows what love is,' he said, as though he were addressing himself to Mrs. Arthur de Bever.

'No; she don't,' said Miss Boncassen.

'But I do,' he shouted, turning back towards her. 'I do. If any man was ever absolutely, actually, really in love I am the man.'

'Are you indeed, Mr. Longstaffe?'

'I am.'

'But is it not pleasant?'

'Pleasant;—pleasant? Oh, it could be so pleasant!'

'But who is the lady? Perhaps you don't mean to tell me that.'

'You mean to say you don't know?'

'Haven't the least idea in life,' said Miss Boncassen, looking as though she were, in truth, very much in the dark on the subject.

'Let me tell you then that it could only be one person. It never was but one person. It never could have been but one person. It is you, of course!' Then he put his hand well on his heart.

'Me!' said Miss Boncassen, choosing to be ungrammatical in order that he might be made the more absurd.

'Of course it is you. Do you think that I should have brought you all the way up here to tell you that I was in love with anybody else?'

'I thought I was brought to see Mrs. de Somebody,—and the view.'

'Not at all,' said Dolly emphatically.

'Then you have deceived me.'

'I will never deceive you. Only say that you will love me, and I will be as true to you as the North Pole.'

'Is that true to me?'

'You know what I mean.'

'But if I don't love you?'

'Yes, you do!'

'Do I?'

'I beg your pardon,' said Dolly. 'I didn't mean to say that. Of course a man shouldn't make sure of a thing.'

'Not in this case, Mr. Longstaffe; because, really, in honest sober truth, I entertain no such feeling.'

'But you can if you please.'

'I rather think not.'

'Yes you can. Just let me tell you who I am.'

'That will do no good whatever, Mr. Longstaffe.'

'Let me tell you at any rate. I have a very good income of my own as it is.'

'Money can have nothing to do with it.'

'But I want you to know that I can afford it. You might perhaps have thought that I wanted your money.'

'I will attribute nothing evil to you, Mr. Longstaffe. Only it is quite out of the question that I should—respond as I suppose you wish me to; and therefore, pray, do not say anything further. Now I think I will go down to my friends.'

She went to the head of the little steps but he interrupted her. 'You ought to hear me,' he said.

'I have heard you.'

'I can give you as good a position as any man without a title in England.'

'Mr. Longstaffe, I rather fancy that wherever I may be I can make a position for myself. At any rate I shall not marry a husband with the view of getting one. If my husband were an English duke I should think myself nothing, unless I was something as Isabel Boncassen. My name I should have to change; but unless I could be something as having been Isabel Boncassen, I should be quite discontented with myself.'

When she said this she certainly did not bethink herself that Lord Silverbridge would in the course of nature become an English duke. She possibly did not know the fact, or if she had heard it, she probably was too little acquainted with the intricacies of English rank to bear it in her mind. But the allusion to an English duke told instantly on Dolly, who had become quite aware that he had a noble rival. 'English dukes ain't so easily got,' he said.

'Very likely not. I might have expressed my meaning better had I said an English prince.'

'That's quite out of the question,' said Dolly. 'They can't do it,—by Act of Parliament,—except in a hugger-mugger left-handed way that wouldn't suit you at all.'

'Mr. Longstaffe,—you must forgive me—if I say—that of all the gentlemen—I have ever met in this country or in any other—you are the—most obtuse.' This she brought out in little disjointed sentences, not with any hesitation, but in a way to make every word she uttered more clear to an intelligence which she did not believe to be bright. But in this belief she did some injustice to Dolly, who was generally sharp enough, though he had failed to understand exactly what she had meant when she told him that it would be nothing to her to marry a duke or a prince. He was at any rate quite alive to the disgrace of being called obtuse, and quick enough to avenge himself at the moment.

'Am I?' said he. 'How humble-minded you must be when you think me a fool because I have fallen in love with such a one as yourself.'

'I like you for that,' she replied laughing, 'and withdraw the word "obtuse" as not being applicable. Now we are quits and can forget and forgive, and be the very best friends in the world;—only let there be the forgetting.'

'Never,' said Dolly, with his hand again on his heart.

'Then let it be a little dream of your youth,—that you once met a pretty American girl who when you offered her your love was too foolish to accept all that you would have given her.'

'So pretty! So awfully pretty!' Thereupon she curtsied. 'I have seen all the handsome women in England going for the last ten years, and there has not been one who has made me think that it would be worth my while to get off my perch for her.'

'And now you would desert your perch for me!'

'I have already.'

'But you can get up again?'

'I should not know how to set about it.'

'Oh, yes. Let it be all a dream. I know men like to have had such dreams. And in order that the dream may be pleasant the last word between us shall be kind. Such admiration from such a one as you is an honour,—and I will reckon it among my honours. But there is no accounting for taste, and it can be no more than a dream.' Then she gave him her hand. 'It shall be so;—shall it not?' In his dilemma he put his hand up under his hat and scratched his head. 'It must be so, Mr. Longstaffe.'

'Must it?'

'That and no more. Now I wish to go down. Will you come with me? Yes; I know you will. It will be better.' Then she put her hand upon his arm, knowing that she would have to leave it at the steps, but feeling that in this way she would best recreate a feeling of companionship. 'Don't you think it is going to rain?'

Dolly looked up at the clouds. 'I wish it would with all my heart,' he said.

'I know you are not so ill-natured. Think what a trouble it would be to us. It would spoil all.'

'You have spoiled all.'

'No, no. I have spoiled nothing. It will only be a little dream about "that strange American girl, who really did make me feel queer for half an hour!" That's the way you'll talk about it next evening. Look at that. A great big drop. And the cloud has come over us as black as Erebus.* Do hurry down.' He was leading the way. 'What shall we do for carriages to get us to the inn?'

'There's the summer-house.'

'It will hold about half of us. And think what it will be to be in there waiting till the day's rain shall be over! Everybody has been so good-humoured and now they will be so cross!' They did hurry down and when they got onto the walk below everyone was now scurrying along towards the summer-house. The rain was now falling in big heavy drops, slow and far between, but almost black with their size. And the heaviness of the cloud which had gathered over them now made everything dark.

'Will you have my arm?' said Silverbridge, who saw Miss Boncassen scudding along, with Dolly Longstaffe following as fast as he could.

'Oh dear no. I have got to mind my dress. There;—I have gone right into a puddle. Oh, dear!' So she ran on, and Silverbridge followed close behind her, leaving Dolly Longstaffe in the distance.

It was not only Miss Boncassen who got her feet into a puddle and splashed her stockings. Many did so who were not obliged by their position to maintain good humour under their misfortunes. The storm had come on with such unexpected force and quickness that there had been a general stampede to the summer-house. As Isabel had said, there was comfortable room for not more than half of them, and seats for nothing like that number. In a very few minutes people were crushed who never ought to be crushed. A Countess for whom treble-piled sofas* were hardly good enough was putting up with the corner of a table till some younger and less gorgeous lady could be made to give way for her. And the Marchioness was declaring she was as wet through as though she had been dragged in a river. Mrs. Boncassen was so absolutely quelled as to have retired into the kitchen or back office attached to the summer-house, having felt herself unable to encounter the unhappiness of her guests. Mr. Boncassen, with all his country's pluck and pride, was proving to a knot of gentlemen round him on the verandah, that such treachery in the weather was a thing unknown in his happier country. Miss Boncassen had to do her best to console the splashed ladies. 'Oh Mrs. Jones. Is it not a pity! What can I do for you?'

'We must bear it, my dear. It often does rain, but why on this special day should it come down out of buckets?'

'I never was so wet in all my life,' said Dolly Longstaffe, poking in his head.

'There's somebody smoking,' said the Countess angrily. There was a crowd of men smoking out on the verandah,—of men who could not get into the room. 'I never knew anything so nasty in my life,' the Countess continued, leaving it in doubt whether the rain, or the smoke, or the party generally were the nastiest thing she had ever known. Nothing special, however, was done to lessen the nastiness, for the men went on smoking.

Damp gauzes, splashed stockings, trampled muslins, and features which have perhaps known something of rouge and certainly encountered something of rain may be made—but can only, by supreme high breeding, be made—compatible with good humour. To be moist, muddy, rumpled, and smeared, when by the very nature of your position it is your duty to be clear-starched up to the pellucidity of crystal, to be spotless as the lily, to be crisp as the ivy-leaf, and as clear in complexion as a rose,—is it not, O gentle readers, felt to be a disgrace? It is a disgrace when many see it, even though those many be fellow-sufferers. It came to pass, therefore, that many were now surly, and some very cross. Carriages were ordered under the idea that some improvement might be made at the inn which was nearly a mile distant. Very few, however, had their own carriages; and there was jockeying for the vehicles, and all the inevitable consequences,—insolence on the part of servants, almost quarrels among the men, and a want of civility among the ladies. In the midst of all this Silverbridge remained as near to Miss Boncassen as circumstances would admit. 'You are not waiting for me,' she said.

'Yes, I am. Why not? We might as well go up to town together.'

'Leave me with father and mother. We are at any rate bound to bear this misfortune patiently. Like the captain of a ship I must be the last to leave the wreck.'

'But I'll be the gallant sailor of the day who always at the risk of his life sticks to the skipper to the last moment.'

'Not at all;—just because there will be no gallantry. The wretched should always be left in their misery. They like that best. But come and see us to-morrow and find out whether we have got through it alive.'

CHAPTER 33

THE LANGHAM HOTEL

THE Boncassens were still living at the Langham Hotel, and had now resolved to remain there till they should return to town after some short autumn excursion to be made either to Devonshire, or to the Lakes, or to Scotland. His search after knowledge would then keep him in London all through the next winter and probably to the end of the next season. They had large and expensive rooms, and, living after their fashion, were probably more comfortable than they would have been in a hired house. When all their guests had left them after their garden-party, they themselves returned to town by a later train,—thus being the last to leave the ship, as Miss Boncassen had told Lord Silverbridge would be the case. 'What an abominable climate,' Mrs. Boncassen had said when they were quite alone at Maidenhead.

'My dear, you didn't think you were to bring New York along with you when you came here,' replied her husband.

'I wish I was going back to-morrow.'

'That's a foolish thing to say. People here are very kind, and you are seeing a great deal more of the world than you would ever see at home. I am having a very good time. What do you say, Bell?'

'I wish I could have kept my stockings clean.'

'But what about the young men?'

'Young men are pretty much the same everywhere, I guess. They never have their wits about them. They never mean what they say because they don't understand the use of words. They are generally half impudent and half timid. When in love they are as though in a fit, not at all understanding what has befallen them. What they want, they try to compass as a cow does when it stands stretching out its head towards a stack of hay which it cannot reach. Indeed there is no such thing as a young man, for a man is not really a man till he is middle-aged. But take them at their worst they are a deal too good for us, for they will probably be men some day, whereas we must only be women to the end.'

'My word, Bella,' exclaimed the mother.

'You have managed to be tolerably heavy upon God's creatures taking them in a lump,' said the father. 'Boys, girls, and cows! Something has gone wrong with you besides the rain.'

'Nothing on earth, sir,—except the boredom, which was to be expected.'

'Some young man has been talking to you, Bella.'

'One or two, mother; and I got to be thinking if any one of them should ask me to marry him, and if, moved by some evil Destiny, I were to take him, whether I should murder him, or myself, or run away with one of the others.'

'Couldn't you bear with him till according to your own theory he would grow out of his folly?' said the father.

'Being a woman,—no. The present moment is always everything to me. When that horrid old harridan halloed out that somebody was smoking, I thought I should have died. It was very bad just then.'

'Awful!' said Mrs. Boncassen, shaking her head.

'I didn't seem to feel it much,' said the father. 'Of course one doesn't look to have everything just what one wants always. If I did I should go out nowhere;—but my total of life would be less enjoyable. If ever you do get married, Bell, you should remember that.'

'I mean to get married some day, so that I shouldn't be made love to any longer.'

'I hope it will have that effect,' said the father.

'Mr. Boncassen!' ejaculated the mother.

'What I say is true. I hope it will have that effect. It had with you, my dear; and I hope your daughter will follow your footsteps.'

'I don't know that people didn't think of me as much as of anybody else, even though I was married.'

'Then, my dear, I never knew it. But I think we may go down to the station now.'

Miss Boncassen, though she had behaved serenely and with much good temper during the process of Dolly's proposal, had not at all liked it. She had a very high opinion of herself, and was certainly entitled to have it by the undisguised admiration of all that came near her. Of course at her age, let her say what she might, the admiration of which she thought the most was the admiration of young men. How can it be otherwise with a girl when she knows that it is to be her lot to marry some young man? How can it be otherwise when it is by the eyes of young men that she is most admired? How can it be otherwise when all nature has so ordained it? Miss Boncassen was not more indifferent to the admiration of young men than are other young ladies. But she was not proud of the admiration of Dolly Longstaffe. She was here among strangers whose ways were unknown to her, whose position and rank and general standing in the world were all vague to her, and wonderful in their dimness. She knew that she was associating with men very different from those at home where almost all men of her acquaintance were supposed to be under the necessity of earning their bread. At New York she would dance, as she had said, with bank clerks. She was not at all prepared to admit that a young London lord was better than a New York bank clerk. Judging the men on their own individual merits she might probably find the bank clerk to be the better of the two. But a certain sweetness of the aroma of rank was beginning to permeate her republican senses. The rich softness of a life in which no occupation was compulsory had its charms for her. Though she had told her father that young men do not understand the use of words,—thinking at the moment of some flaws of intelligence displayed by poor Dolly,—she was alive to the delight of having nothings said to her pleasantly. All this had affected her so strongly that she had—not reflected, but almost felt that a life among these English luxuries would be a pleasant life. Like most Americans who do not as yet know this country, she had come here with an inward feeling that as an American and a republican she might probably be despised.

There is not uncommonly a savageness of self-assertion about Americans which arises in fact from a too great anxiety to be admitted to fellowship with Britons. She had felt this, and knowing how great had been the reputation already made by herself in the social life of New York, she had half trusted that she would be well received in London, and had half convinced herself that she would be rejected. She certainly had not been rejected. She must now have become quite aware of that. By degrees, by very quick degrees, she had dropped the idea that she would be scorned. Ignorant as she had been of English life, she perceived that she had, almost at once, become a personage. And this had been so in spite of her mother's homeliness and her father's awkwardness. By herself and by her own gifts she had done it. She had found out concerning herself that she had that which would commend her to other society than that of the Fifth Avenue. Those lords of whom she had heard were as plenty with her as blackberries.* And the young Lord Silverbridge, of whom she was told that of all the young lords of the day he stood first in rank and wealth and general desirability, was peculiarly her friend. Her brain was firmer than that of most girls of her age, but even her brain was a little turned. She never told herself that it would be well for her to become the wife of such a one. In her more thoughtful moments she almost told herself that it would not be well. But still the allurement was strong upon her. Park Lane was sweeter than the Fifth Avenue. Lord Silverbridge was nicer than the bank clerk.

But Dolly Longstaffe was not. She would certainly prefer the bank clerk to Dolly Longstaffe. And yet Dolly Longstaffe was the one among her English admirers who had come forward and spoken out. I should be misleading the reader altogether were I to leave an impression that the girl expected or desired that anyone should come forward and speak out. But it was an annoyance to her that this special man should have done so. It was a trifle not at all worth talking about. She certainly would not mention it either to her father or mother. But it annoyed her.

She had asked Lord Silverbridge to see her on the following morning, and perhaps it was this which induced her to decline going with her mother to Westminster Abbey in the afternoon. She pleaded that the heat and general mugginess of the weather kept her in. The weather was generally muggy, but perhaps no injury will be done to her by the suggestion that when she thought of the weather she thought also of Lord Silverbridge. But it must not be supposed that she intended to deceive her mother in regard to the visit of a young man. She would have had no hesitation in saying that he was coming to see her, had she been sure of the fact. Her mind and conscience in the matter were just as they might have been had she been a young man instead of a young woman. Upon the whole she did not want to go to the Abbey, and she made the first excuse which came to her hand.

The waiter at the Langham understood American ways perfectly, and when a young man called between three and four o'clock, asking for Mrs. Boncassen, said that Miss Boncassen was at home. The young man took off his hat, brushed up his hair, and followed the waiter up to the sitting-room. The door was opened and the young man was announced. 'Mr. Longstaffe.'

Miss Boncassen certainly was disgusted. She had had enough at any rate of this English lover. Why should he have come after what had occurred yesterday? He ought to have felt that he was absolved from the necessity of making personal inquiries. It would have been well that they should have met as friends when they met by chance, but a forced meeting was assuredly a mistake. 'I am glad to see that you got home safe,' she said as she gave him her hand.

'And you too, I hope?'

'Well;—so, so; with my clothes a good deal damaged and my temper rather worse.'

'I am so sorry!'

'It should not rain on such days. Mother is out. She has gone to church.'

'Oh;—indeed. I like going to church myself sometimes.'

'Do you now?'

'I know what would make me like to go to church.'

'And father is at the Athenaeum. He goes there to do a little light reading in the library on Sunday afternoon.'

'I shall never forget yesterday, Miss Boncassen.'

'You wouldn't, if your clothes had been spoilt as mine were.'

'Money will repair that.'

'Well; yes; but when I've had a petticoat flounced particularly to order I don't like to see it ill-treated. There are emotions of the heart which money can't touch.'

'Just so;—emotions of the heart! That's the very phrase. I begin to recognise the fact that emotions of the heart may be stronger than—than anything else.'

She was determined if possible to prevent a repetition of the scene which had taken place up at Mrs. de Bever's temple, but almost doubted her power. There was a force of obstinacy about the man which seemed to her to be hardly compatible with the weakness of his absurdity. 'All my emotions are about my dress,' she said as she thought the matter over.

'All!'

'Well; yes; all. I guess I don't care much for eating and drinking.' In saying this she actually contrived to produce something of that national nasal twang, to be free from which had been one of the great labours of her life.

'Eating and drinking!' said Dolly. 'Of course they are necessities;— and so are clothes.'

'But new things are such ducks! Don't you think so?'

'Trowsers may be,'* said Dolly.

Then she took a prolonged gaze at him, wondering whether he looked a greater fool than he was or was a greater fool than he looked. She was almost minded to ask him the celebrated question, but did not quite dare to do it. 'How funny you are,' she said.

'A man does not, I suppose, generally feel funny after going through what I suffered yesterday. Miss Boncassen,——'

'Would you mind ringing the bell?'

'Must it be done quite at once?'

'Quite,—quite,' she said. 'I can do it myself for the matter of that.' And she rang the bell somewhat violently. Dolly sank back again into his seat, simply remarking in his usual apathetic way that he had intended to obey her behest but had not understood that she was in so great a hurry. 'I am always in a hurry,' she said. 'I like things to be done—sharp,' and she hit the table a crack. 'Please bring me some iced water.' This of course was addressed to the waiter. 'And a glass for Mr. Longstaffe.'

'None for me, thank you.'

'Perhaps you'd like soda-and-brandy?'

'Oh dear no;—nothing of the kind. But I am so much obliged to you all the same.' As the water-bottle was in fact standing in the room, and as the waiter had only to hand the glass, all this created but little obstacle. Still it had its effect, and Dolly, when the man had retired, felt that there was a difficulty in proceeding. 'I have called to-day——' he began.

'That has been so kind of you. But mother has gone to church.'

'I am very glad that she has gone to church, because I wish to——'

'Oh. Laws! There's a horse has tumbled down in the street. I heard it.'

'He has got up again,' said Dolly, looking leisurely out of the window. 'They do skip about dreadfully this weather. But as I was saying——'

'I don't think that the water we Americans drink can do us any good. It makes all the women become ugly so very young.'

'You will never become ugly.'

She got up and curtsied to him, and then, still standing, made him a speech. 'Mr. Longstaffe, it would be absurd of me to pretend not to understand what you mean. But I won't have any more of it. Whether you are making fun of me, or whether you are in earnest, it is just the same.'

'Making fun of you!'

'It does not signify in the least. I don't care which it is. But I won't have it. There!'

'A gentleman should be allowed to express his feelings and to explain his position.'

'You have expressed and explained more than enough already, and I won't have any more. If you will sit down and talk about something else, or else go away, just as you please, there shall be an end of it;—but if you go on, I will ring the bell and go upstairs.'

'In that case I would only send the waiter after you.'

'Then I should desire him to get you a cab and to see you off the premises. What can a man gain by going on when a girl has spoken as I have,—unless it be his object to give annoyance?' They were both at this time standing up, and he was now quite as angry as she was.

'I've paid you the greatest compliment a man can pay a woman,' he began.

'Very well. If I remember rightly I thanked you for it yesterday. If you wish it, I will thank you again to-day. But it is a compliment which becomes very much the reverse of a compliment if it be repeated once too often. You are sharp enough to understand that I have done everything in my power to save us both from this trouble. Now let there be an end of it.'

'What makes you so fierce, Miss Boncassen?'

'What makes you so foolish?'

'I suppose it must be something peculiar to American ladies.'

'Just that;—something peculiar to American ladies. They don't like——; well, I don't want to say anything more that can be called fierce. Only don't provoke me.'

At this moment the door was again opened and Lord Silverbridge was announced. 'Halloa, Dolly;—are you here?' That was the young Lord's first salutation.

'It seems that I am.'

'And I am here too,' said Miss Boncassen, smiling her prettiest.

'None the worse for yesterday's troubles, I hope?'

'A good deal the worse. I have been explaining all that to Mr. Longstaffe, who has been quite sympathetic with me about my things. We did get so berained, and bespattered, and bedaubed.'

'A terrible pity, that shower,' said Dolly.

'For you,' said Silverbridge, 'because if I remember right Miss Boncassen was walking with you;—but I was rather glad of it.'

'Lord Silverbridge!'

'I regarded it as a direct interposition of Providence because you would not dance with me.'

'And if I had the rain would not have come?'

'I think not.'

'Then I wish I had danced with you certainly.'

'Any news to-day, Silverbridge?' asked Dolly.

'Nothing particular. They say that Coalheaver can't run for the Leger.'

'What's the matter?' asked Dolly vigorously.

'Broke down at Ascot. But I dare say it's a lie.'

'Sure to be a lie,' said Dolly. 'What do you think of Madame Schotzdam, Miss Boncassen?'

'I am not a good judge;—but I suppose she sings very well.'

'Never heard anything equal to it yet in this world,' said Dolly. 'I wonder whether that's true about Coalheaver?'

'Tifto says so.'

'Which at the present moment,' asked Miss Boncassen, 'is the greater favourite with the public, Madame Schotzdam or Coalheaver?'

'Coalheaver is a horse, Miss Boncassen.'

'Oh,—a horse!'

'Perhaps I ought to say a colt.'

'Oh,—a colt!'

'Do you suppose, Dolly, that Miss Boncassen doesn't know all that?' asked Silverbridge.

'He supposes that my American ferocity has never been sufficiently softened for the reception of such polite erudition.'

'You two have been quarrelling, I fear.'

'I never quarrel with a woman,' said Dolly.

'Nor with a man in my presence, I hope,' said Miss Boncassen.

'Not with me certainly,' said Lord Silverbridge. 'I have done nothing. But somebody does seem to have got out of bed at the wrong side.'

'I did,' said Miss Boncassen. 'I got out of bed at the wrong side. I am cross. I can't get over the spoiling of my flounces yesterday. I think you had better both go away and leave me. If I could walk about the room for half an hour and stamp my feet, I should get better.' Silverbridge thought that as he had come last, he certainly ought to be left last. Miss Boncassen felt that, at any rate, Mr. Longstaffe should go, taking the other man with him if the two were so disposed;—but that he at least should go. Dolly was of opinion that his manhood required him to remain till Silverbridge should have departed. After what had taken place he was not going to leave the field vacant for another. It might be that on reconsideration he should see the wisdom of retiring from his suit,—and the more especially as the lady certainly was ferocious. Or again it might seem to be more in accordance with his own virile persistency to continue his courtship,—mindful that he had heard that ladies will often say 'yes' after half-a-dozen 'noes.' To go and to leave the other man there was not in accordance with his principles;—and therefore he made no effort to move.

'That seems rather hard upon me,' said Silverbridge.

'It is hard upon you,' said the lady.

'You told me to come.'

'I told you to come and ask after us all. You have come and asked after us all and been informed that we are all very bad. What more can I say? You accuse me of getting out of bed the wrong side, and I own that I did.'

'I meant to say that Dolly Longstaffe had done so.'

'And I say it was Silverbridge,' said Dolly.

'We ain't very agreeable together, are we? Upon my word I think you'd better both go.' Silverbridge immediately got up from his chair;—upon which Dolly also moved.

'Good-morning,' said Silverbridge.

'Good-morning,'* said Dolly. And then they both left the room together.

'What the mischief is up?' asked Silverbridge, when they were under the porch together.

'The truth is you never can tell where you are with those American girls, or how you ought to treat them.'

'I suppose you have been making up to her.'

'Nothing in earnest. She seemed to me to like admiration;—so I told her I admired her.'

'What did she say then?'

'Upon my word you seem to be very great at cross-examining. Perhaps you had better go back and ask her.'

'I will, next time I see her.' Then he stepped into his cab that was waiting for him, and in a loud voice ordered the man to drive him to the Zoo. But when he had gone a little way up Portland Place, he stopped the driver and desired he might be taken back again to the hotel. As he left the vehicle he looked round for Dolly, but Dolly had certainly gone. Then he told the waiter to take his card up to Miss Boncassen, and explain that he had something to say which he had forgotten.

'So you have come back again,' said Miss Boncassen, laughing.

'Of course I have. You didn't suppose I was going to let that fellow get the better of me. I had come here to have half an hour of "good time" as you call it. Why should I be turned out because he had made an ass of himself!'

'Who said he made an ass of himself?'

'But he had;—hadn't he?'

'No;—by no means,' said she after a little pause.

'Tell me what he had been saying.'

'Indeed I shall do nothing of the kind. If I told you all he said, then I should have to tell the next man all that you may say. Would that be fair?'

'I should not mind,' said Silverbridge.

'I dare say not, because you have nothing particular to say. But the principle is the same. Lawyers and doctors and parsons all talk of privileged communications. I don't see why a young lady should not have her privileged communications.'

'But I have something particular to say.'

'I hope not.'

'Why should you hope not?'

'I hate having things said particularly. Nobody likes conversation so well as I do;—but it should never be about anything particular.'

'I was going to tell you that I came back to London yesterday in the same carriage with old Lady Clanfiddle, and that she swore that no consideration on earth would ever induce her to go to Maidenhead again.'

'That isn't particular.'

'She went on to say,—you won't tell of me; will you?'

'It shall all be privileged.'

'She went on to say that Americans couldn't be expected to understand English manners.'

'Perhaps they may be all the better for that.'

'Then I spoke up. I swore I was awfully in love with you.'

'You didn't.'

'I did;—that you were, out and away, the finest girl I ever saw in my life. Of course you understand that her two daughters were there, and that as for manners,—unless the rain could be attributed to American bad manners,—I did not think anything had gone wrong.'

'What about the smoking?'

'I told her they were all Englishmen, and that if she had been giving the party herself they would have smoked just as much. You must understand that she never does give any parties.'

'How could you be so ill-natured?'

'There was ever so much more of it. And it ended in her telling me that I was a schoolboy and that my father ought to look after me. I found out the cause of it all. A great spout of rain had come upon her daughter's hat, and that had produced a most melancholy catastrophe.'

'I would have given her mine willingly.'

'An American hat;—to be worn by Lady Violet Clanfiddle!'

'It came from Paris last week, sir.'

'But must have been contaminated by American contact.'

'Now, Lord Silverbridge,' said she, getting up, 'if I had a stick I'd whip you.'

'It was such fun.'

'And you come here and tell it all to me!'

'Of course I do. It was a deal too good to keep it to myself. "American manners!"' As he said this he did almost succeed in looking like Lady Clanfiddle.

At that moment Mr. Boncassen entered the room, and was immediately appealed to by his daughter. 'Father, you must turn Lord Silverbridge out of the room.'

'Dear me! If I must,—of course I must. But why?'

'He is saying everything horrid he can about Americans.'

After this they settled down for a few minutes to general conversation, and then Lord Silverbridge again took his leave. When he was gone Isabel Boncassen almost regretted that the 'something particular' which he had threatened to say had not been less comic in its nature.

CHAPTER 34

LORD POPPLECOURT

WHEN the reader was told that Lord Popplecourt had found Lady Cantrip very agreeable it is to be hoped that the reader was disgusted. Lord Popplecourt would certainly not have given a second thought to Lady Cantrip unless he had been specially flattered. And why should such a man have been flattered by a woman who was in all respects his superior? The reader will understand. It had been settled by the wisdom of the elders that it would be a good thing that Lord Popplecourt should marry Lady Mary Palliser.

There are certain circumstances and occurrences in life,—so common that but few of us escape all contact with them,—in which a certain thing seems very desirable to be done, and when done may seem to be almost equally desirable, but which, in the doing, is not altogether nice. What can seem to be more proper than that a father, anxious for the happiness and prosperity of his daughter, should look about for a fitting husband for her? Or what more friendly act can be performed than assisting a father in such a search? The first was the Duke's position, and the second that of Lady Cantrip. The Duke was strengthened in his conviction of the propriety of his conduct by his vivid remembrances of his wife's history;—and Lady Cantrip also in some degree by her knowledge of the same. Everybody who had heard anything of the tale was aware from how great an evil Lady Glencora had been saved, when she was separated from that poor wretch Burgo Fitzgerald who had at last destroyed himself with brandy-and-water. They who had interfered had interfered successfully; and unalloyed good,—good apparently unalloyed,—had been the result. Nobody knew whether on that occasion anybody had felt soiled by his or her share in the performance. But now that the matter was in the doing, the soil was felt both by Lady Cantrip and by the Duke.

The mutual assent which leads to marriage should no doubt be spontaneous. Who does not feel that? Young love should spread from its first doubtful, hesitating, unconscious spark,—a spark which any drawn breath of air may quench or cherish,—till it becomes a flame which nothing can satisfy but the union of the two lovers. No one should be told to love, or bidden to marry, this young man or that young woman. The theory of this is plain to us all, and till we have sons or daughters whom we feel imperatively obliged to control, the theory is unassailable. But the duty is so imperative! The Duke had taught himself to believe that as his wife would have been thrown away on the world had she been allowed to marry Burgo Fitzgerald, so would his daughter be thrown away were she allowed to marry Mr. Tregear. Therefore the theory of spontaneous love must in this case be set aside. Therefore the spark,—would that it had been no more,—must be quenched. Therefore there could be no union of two lovers;—but simply a prudent and perhaps splendid marriage, such as had joined him to Lady Glencora M'Cluskie.

Lord Popplecourt was a man undoubtedly in possession of a very large estate which was altogether unencumbered. His rank in the peerage was not high; but his barony was of a very old date,—and, if things went well with him, something higher in rank might be open to him. He had good looks of that sort which recommend themselves to pastors and masters, to elders and betters. He had regular features. He looked as though he were steady. He was neither impatient nor rollicking. Silverbridge was also good-looking;—but his good looks were such as would give a pang to the hearts of some anxious mothers of daughters. Tregear was good-looking too,—no doubt the handsomest man of the three;—but then he looked as though he had no betters and did not care for his elders. Lord Popplecourt, though a very young man, had once stammered through half-a-dozen words in the House of Lords, and had been known to dine with the 'Benevolent Funds,' on behalf both of literature and art. Lord Silverbridge had declared him to be a fool. A great many who knew him spoke of him as though he were not a bright young man. But in the eyes of the Duke,—and of Lady Cantrip,—he had his good qualities. Looking about them they could find no one more worthy of the great honour intended.

But the work was very disagreeable. It was the more hard upon Lady Cantrip because she did not believe in the work. If it could be done, it would be expedient. So far she did believe. But she felt very strongly that it could not be done. No doubt that Lady Glencora had been turned from her evil destiny; but at the time Lady Glencora had been younger than her daughter was now, and possessed of very much less character. Nor was Lady Cantrip blind to the difference between a poor man with a bad character, such as that Burgo had been, and a poor man with a good character, such as was Tregear. Nevertheless she undertook to aid the work, and condescended to pretend to be so interested in the portrait of some common ancestor as to persuade the young man to have it photographed, in order that the bringing down of the photograph might lead to something. This had been rather hard upon Popplecourt, as it entailed on him the necessity of sending a photographer expressly down to his country-house.

But he took the photograph, and Lady Cantrip said very much to him about his grandmother, who was the old lady in question. 'She could,' she said, 'just remember the features of the dear old woman.' She was by no means habitually a hypocrite, and she hated herself for what she was doing, and yet her object was simply good,—to bring together two young people who might advantageously marry each other. The mere talking about the old woman would be of no service. She longed to bring out the offer plainly, and say, 'There is Lady Mary Palliser. Don't you think she'd make a good wife for you?' But she could not quite as yet bring herself to be so indelicately plain. 'You haven't seen the Duke since?' she asked.

'He spoke to me only yesterday in the House, and was recommending what I ought to do. I like the Duke.'

'If I may be allowed to say so, it would be for your advantage that he should like you;—that is if you mean to take a part in politics.'

'I suppose I shall,' said Popplecourt. 'There isn't very much else to do.'

'You don't go to races.' He shook his head. 'I am very glad of that,' said Lady Cantrip. 'Nothing is so bad as the turf. I fear Lord Silverbridge is devoting himself to the turf.'

'I am afraid he is a good deal in with that fellow, Tifto.'

'That can't be good for him.'

'Well, Lady Cantrip, I don't think it can be good for any man to have much to do with Major Tifto. I suppose Silverbridge knows what he's about. He thinks he does, at any rate.'

Here was an opportunity which might have been used wisely. Lady Cantrip saw it at once and almost made up her mind that she would use it. It would have been so easy for her to glide from the imperfections of the brother to the perfections of the sister. But she could not bring herself to do it quite at once. She approached the matter however as nearly as she could without making her grand proposition. She shook her head sadly in reference to Silverbridge and Tifto, and then spoke of the Duke. 'His father is so anxious about him!'

'I dare say.'

'I don't know any man who is more painfully anxious about his children. He feels the responsibility so very much since his wife's death. There is Lady Mary.'

'She's all right, I should say.'

'All right! Oh yes; she's all right. But when a girl is possessed of so many things,—rank, beauty, intelligence, large fortune,——'

'Will Lady Mary have much?'

'A large portion of her mother's money, I should say. When all these things are joined together a father of course feels most anxious as to their disposal.'

'I suppose she is clever.'

'Very clever,' said Lady Cantrip.

'I think a girl may be too clever, you know,' said Lord Popplecourt.

'Perhaps she may. But I know a great many more who are too foolish. I am so much obliged to you for all the trouble you have taken about the photograph.'

'Don't mention it.'

'I really did not mean that you should send a man down.'

On that occasion the two young people did not see each other. Lady Mary did not come down from her room, and Lady Cantrip actually lacked the courage to send for her. As it was, might it not be possible that the young man should be induced to make himself agreeable to the young lady without any further explanation? He had certainly seemed to be alive to the catalogue which had been given of her charms, and especially to that which had been said as to her presumed wealth. But love-making between young people cannot well take place unless they be brought together. It was understood that Lady Mary should remain at The Horns while Parliament was sitting and should then be carried somewhither by her father. There was a difficulty in bringing them together at Richmond. The Duke had indeed spoken of meeting Lord Popplecourt at dinner there;—but this was to have followed the direct proposition which Lady Cantrip should make to him. She could not bring herself to make the proposition, and therefore she hardly knew how to arrange the dinner. She was obliged at last to let the wished-for lover go away without arranging anything. When the Duke should have settled his autumn plans, then an attempt must be made to induce Lord Popplecourt to travel in the same direction.

That evening Lady Cantrip said a few words to Mary respecting the proposed suitor;—but they were not very successful. 'There is nothing I have such a horror of as gambling,' she said.

'It is dreadful.'

'I am very glad to think that Nidderdale does not do anything of that sort.' It was perhaps on the cards that Nidderdale should do things of which she knew nothing. 'I hope Silverbridge does not bet.'

'I don't think he does. He told me he wouldn't.'

'There's Lord Popplecourt,—quite a young man,—with everything at his own disposal, and a very large estate indeed. Think of the evil he might do if he were given that way.'

'Does he gamble?'

'Not at all. It must be such a comfort to his mother!'

'He looks to me as though he never would do anything,' said Lady Mary. Then the subject was dropped. Lady Cantrip was woman enough to have liked to say, 'Oh yes,—you care for nobody but that odious Mr. Tregear!' That, however, in the present circumstances would have been indiscreet.

It was a week after this, towards the end of July, the period at which all legislation seems always to have got itself into such a state of inextricable confusion that outsiders feel that Parliament should not be dissolved at all that year, and when ministers are beginning to see their way through it to rest and rural delights, that the Duke wrote a line to Lady Cantrip, apologising for what he had done, but explaining that he had asked Lord Popplecourt to dine at The Horns on a certain Sunday. He had, he said, been assured by Lord Cantrip that such an arrangement would be quite convenient. But the arrangement if not convenient to Lady Cantrip could easily be altered. He was very apologetic, but it was clear from his letter that he was much in earnest. Of course there was no reason why the dinner should not be eaten. Only the specialty of the invitation to Lord Popplecourt must not be so glaring that he himself should be struck by the strangeness of it. There must be a little party made up, an explanation made to Popplecourt that it was not at all a dinner-party,—as neither the Duke nor Mary was going into society,—but that he was asked as a particular friend. Lord Nidderdale and his wife were therefore bidden to come down, and Silverbridge, who at first consented rather unwillingly,—and Lady Mabel Grex, as to whom the Duke made a special request that she might be asked. This last invitation was sent express from Lady Mary, and included Miss Cass. So the party was made up. The careful reader will perceive that there were to be ten of them,—a number which would, it was thought, prevent perturbation in the mind of Lord Popplecourt.

'Isn't it odd papa wanting to have Lady Mabel?' Mary said to Lady Cantrip.

'Does he not know her, my dear?'

'He hardly ever spoke to her. I'll tell you what I expect; Silverbridge is going to marry her.'

'Why shouldn't he?'

'I don't know why he shouldn't. She is very beautiful and very clever. But if so papa must know all about it. It does seem so odd that papa of all people should turn match-maker.'

'I don't suppose he arranged it;—if it is so.'

'Or even that he should think of it.'

'So much is thrown upon him now,' said Lady Cantrip in a sad tone.

'Poor papa!' Then she remembered herself, and spoke with a little start. 'Of course I am not thinking of myself. Arranging a marriage is very different from preventing anyone from marrying.'

'Whatever he may think to be his duty, he will be sure to do it,' said the elder lady very solemnly.

Lady Mabel was surprised by the invitation, but she was not slow to accept it, and of course she made Miss Cassewary accept it also. 'Papa will be here and will be so glad to meet you,' Lady Mary had said. Why should the Duke of Omnium wish to meet her? 'Silverbridge will be here too,' Mary had gone on to say. 'It is just a family party. Papa, you know, is not going anywhere; nor am I.' By all this Lady Mabel's thoughts were much stirred, and her bosom somewhat moved. And Silverbridge also was moved by it. Of course he could not but remember that he had pledged himself to his father to ask Lady Mabel to be his wife. He remembered also well enough how determined he himself had been on the matter. No doubt he had faltered since. She had been, he thought, unkind to him, or at any rate indifferent. He had surely said enough to her to make her know what he meant; and yet she had taken no trouble to meet him half-way,—had indeed almost ceased to be kind to him. And then Isabel Boncassen had intervened. Now he was asked to dinner in a most unusual manner, and asked apparently on purpose that he might meet Mabel Grex. Of course he was much moved.

Of all the guests invited Lord Popplecourt was perhaps the least disturbed. He was quite alive to the honour of being noticed by the Duke of Omnium, and alive also to the flattering courtesy shown to him by Lady Cantrip. But justice would not be done him unless it were acknowledged that he had as yet flattered himself with no hopes in regard to Lady Mary Palliser. He was made very proud by the Duke's notice, and began to think that it might be within the scope of his abilities to make a political figure in the country. He was induced by it to look a little down upon such fellows as Nidderdale,

Silverbridge, and others who spent their time and their money in going to races. And Lady Cantrip's friendship increased this effect. She evidently regarded him as one of the rising young men of the day. He of course had advantages which those other young men did not possess. He was his own master, was burdened with no father, and was the head of his own family. He, when he prepared himself for his journey down to Richmond, thought much more of the Duke than of the Duke's daughter. He was very keen against Sir Timothy Beeswax, and was quite prepared to give reasons why the Duke should accept office.

'Oh yes, I can drive you down if you like that kind of thing,' Silverbridge said to him on the Saturday evening.

'And bring me back?'

'If you will come when I am coming. I hate waiting for a fellow.'

'Suppose we leave at half-past ten.'

'I won't fix any time; but if we can't make it suit there'll be the governor's carriage. He'll bring you up with certain punctuality.'

'Will the Duke go down in his carriage?'

'I suppose so. It's quicker and less trouble than the railway.' Then Lord Popplecourt reflected that he would certainly come back with the Duke if he could so manage it, and there floated before his eyes visions of under-secretaryships, all of which might owe their origin to this proposed drive up from Richmond. We remember a noble Duke who boasted in the House of Lords* that he had once travelled in the same post-chaise with Sir Robert Peel. Lord Popplecourt's feelings were now of the same kind,—humble and exalted also.

At six o'clock on the Sunday evening Silverbridge called for Lord Popplecourt at his mother's house in Grosvenor Place. 'Upon my word,' said he, 'I didn't ever expect to see you in my cab.'

'Why not me especially?'

'Because you're not one of our lot at all.'

'You'd sooner have Tifto I dare say.'

'No, I wouldn't. Tifto is not at all a pleasant companion, though he understands horses. You're going in for heavy politics, I suppose.'

'Not particularly heavy.'

'If not why on earth does my governor take you up?' This was not flattering, and Lord Popplecourt held his tongue. 'You won't mind my smoking I dare say.' After this there was no conversation between them; but Silverbridge turned it all over very much in his mind. Why on earth should his father or Lady Cantrip want to have Lord Popplecourt down at Richmond?

CHAPTER 35

'DON'T YOU THINK——?'

IT was pretty to see the Duke's reception of Lady Mabel,—whom he remembered to have met before, but only just remembered it. 'I knew your mother many years ago,' he said, 'when I was young myself. Her mother and my mother were first cousins and dear friends.' He held her hand as he spoke and looked at her as though he meant to love her,—just as he might have looked at the girl whom he was making welcome to his house and his heart as a future daughter. Lady Mabel, who in such matters was very clever, could not but acknowledge this to herself. Could it be possible that the Duke had heard anything;—that he should wish so to receive her? She had told herself and had told Miss Cassewary that though she had spared Silverbridge, yet she knew that she would make him a good wife. If the Duke thought so also, then surely she need have no further doubt.

'I always knew we were cousins,' she said, 'and have been so proud of the connection! Lord Silverbridge does come and see us some-times;—does he not, Miss Cassewary?' Then the Duke shook hands with the old lady and said a few words by which he showed that he knew something also about her and her belongings.

Soon after that Silverbridge and Popplecourt came in. If the story of the old woman in the portrait may be taken as evidence of some family connection between Lady Cantrip and Lord Popplecourt, everybody there was more or less connected with everybody else. Nidderdale had been a first cousin of Lady Glencora, and he had married a daughter of Lady Cantrip. They were manifestly a family party,—thanks to the old woman in the picture. The Duke too remembered something about the old woman. It is a point of conscience that among the—perhaps not ten thousand, but say one thousand of bluest blood,—that everybody should know who everybody else is. Our Duke, though he had not given his mind much to the pursuit,—though he had spent his time dili-gently on other matters,—had nevertheless learned his lesson. It is a knowledge which the very possession of the blue blood itself pro-duces. There are countries in which the blood is bluer, less mixed, in which to be without such knowledge is a crime.

When the old lady in the portrait had been discussed, Popplecourt found himself standing opposite to Lady Mary. They two had no idea why such vicinity had been planned. The Duke knew of course, and

Lady Cantrip. Lady Cantrip had whispered to her daughter that such a marriage would be suitable, and the daughter had hinted it to her husband. Lord Cantrip of course was not in the dark. Lady Mabel had expressed a hint on the matter to Miss Cass, who had not repudiated it. Even Silverbridge had suggested to himself that something of the kind might be in the wind, remarking to himself at the same time that, if so, none of them knew much about his sister Mary. But Popplecourt himself was divinely innocent. His ideas of marriage had as yet gone no further than a conviction that girls generally were things which would be pressed on him, and against which he must arm himself with some thickest shield. Marriage would have to come, no doubt; but not the less was it his duty to live at present as though it were a pit towards which he was to be tempted by female allurements. Against this he was thoroughly on his guard. But that a net should be spread over him here he was much too humble-minded to imagine.

'Very hot,' he said to Lady Mary. The weather had been hot.

'We found it very warm in church to-day.'

'I dare say.' He would not confess that he himself had 'skipped' church, not knowing whether the Duke had any strong opinions on the matter. 'I came down here with your brother in his hansom cab. What a very odd thing to have a hansom cab.'

'I should like one.'

'Should you indeed?'

'Particularly if I could drive it myself. Silverbridge does, at night, when he thinks people won't recognise him.'

'Drive the cab in the streets! What does he do with his man?'

'Puts him inside. He was out once without the man and took up a fare;—an old woman he said,—and when she was going to pay him he touched his hat and said he never took money from ladies.'

'Do you believe that?'

'Oh yes. I call that good fun because it did no harm to anyone. He had his lark. The lady was taken where she wanted to go, and she saved her money.'

'Suppose he had upset her,' said Lord Popplecourt, looking as an old philosopher might have looked when he had found some clinching answer to another philosopher's argument. The hypothesis was one which Lady Mary had not considered and from the too speedy consideration of which she was now preserved by the announcing of dinner.

Questions of rank had to be preserved, and Popplecourt, as in duty bound, took Miss Cass out to dinner, but questions of rank enabled Lady Cantrip so to manage matters that Silverbridge should sit next to

Lady Mabel, and Popplecourt to Lady Mary. It is a convenience that at dinner-parties ladies and gentlemen should all of them have two sides.*

'The real cabman might have upset her worse,' said Lady Mary as she took her seat,—having had time to consider the matter.

'Don't you feel it odd that we should meet here?' said Lord Silverbridge at the same moment to his neighbour, Lady Mabel.

'Anything unexpected is, I suppose, odd,' said Lady Mabel, not quite knowing what answer to make to such a question. It seemed to her to be very odd,—unless certain people had made up their minds as to the expediency of a certain event.

'That is what you call logic;—isn't it? "Anything unexpected is odd!"'

'Lord Silverbridge, I won't be laughed at. You have been at Oxford and ought to know what logic is.'

'That at any rate is ill-natured,' he replied, turning very red in the face.

'You don't think I meant it. Oh, Lord Silverbridge, say that you don't think I meant it. You cannot think I would wilfully wound you. Indeed, indeed I was not thinking.' It had in truth been an accident, that allusion to Oxford where, as everyone knew, his career had been unfortunate. She could not speak aloud because they were closely surrounded by others, but she looked up in his face to see whether he were still angry with her. 'Say that you do not think I meant it.'

'I do not think you meant it.'

'I would not say a word to hurt you,—oh, for more than I can tell you.'

'It is all bosh of course,' he said laughing; 'but, somehow, I do not like to hear the old place named. I have always made a fool of myself. Some men do it and seem not to care about it. But I do it, and yet it makes me miserable.'

'If that be so you will soon give over making—what you call a fool of yourself. For myself I like the idea of wild oats.'

'Do you?'

'I look upon them like measles. It has to be gone through sooner or later. Only you should have a doctor ready when the disease shows itself,—or it may become virulent.'

'What sort of a doctor ought I to have?'

'Ah;—you must find out that yourself. That sort of feeling which makes you feel miserable after your escapades. That is a doctor itself.'

'Or a wife?'

'Or a wife,—if you can find a good one. There are wives, you know, who only aggravate the disease. If I had a fast husband I should only make him faster by wanting to be fast myself. There is nothing I envy so much as the power of doing half-mad things.'

'Women can do that too.'

'But they go utterly to the dogs,—and I don't intend to do that. But we are dreadfully restricted. If you like champagne you can have a bucketful. I am obliged to pretend that I only want a very little. You can bet thousands. I must confine myself to gloves. You can flirt with any woman you please. I must wait till somebody comes,—and put up with it if nobody does come.'

'Plenty come,—no doubt.'

'But I want to pick and choose. I suppose a man turns the girls over one after another as one does the papers when one is fitting up a room, or rolls them out as one rolls out the carpets, till one finds what pleases one's eyes. I can fancy that a very careful young man like Lord Popplecourt might reject a young woman because her hair didn't suit the colour of his furniture. Of course we know that we are dealt with after this fashion,—unless we have a lot of money.'

'I won't answer for Popplecourt, but I don't think that I shall ever choose my wife as I would papers and carpets.'

The Duke, who sat between Lady Cantrip and her daughter, did his best to make himself agreeable and by the end of dinner had worked himself into a good humour, as he had done when he dined with his son at the club. The conversation had been semi-political,—political to the usual feminine extent, and had consisted chiefly of sarcasms from Lady Cantrip against Sir Timothy Beeswax, Sir Orlando Drought, and other offending members of the present administration. 'That England should put up with such a man as Sir Timothy,' Lady Cantrip had said, 'strikes me as being so shocking! There used to be a feeling at any rate in favour of gentlemen.' To this the Duke had responded by asserting that Sir Timothy had displayed great aptitude for parliamentary life, that he knew the House of Commons better than most men, and that he was a very dangerous adversary. He said nothing against his foe, and very much in his foe's praise. But Lady Cantrip knew very well what she was about and had succeeded in pleasing him.

When the ladies were gone the politics became more serious. 'That unfortunate quarrel is to go on the same as ever, I suppose,' said the Duke, addressing himself to the two young men present who had seats in the House of Commons. They were both on the Conservative or ministerial side in politics. The three peers present were all Liberals.

'Till next session, I think, sir,' said Silverbridge.

'Sir Timothy, though he did lose his temper, has managed it very well,' said the Duke.

'To keep his position till next February with a majority of a dozen, is to manage it well,' said Lord Cantrip.

'Phineas Finn lost his temper worse than Sir Timothy,' said Lord Nidderdale.

'But yet I think he had the feeling of the House with him,' said the Duke. 'I happened to be present in the gallery at the time.'

'Yes,' said Nidderdale, 'because he "owned up," as we used to say at school. The fact is if you "own up" in a genial sort of way the House will forgive anything. If I were to murder my grandmother, and, when questioned about it in the House, were to acknowledge that I had done it——' Then Lord Nidderdale stood up and made his speech as he might have made it in the House of Commons, addressing the Duke as though he had been the Speaker. ' "I regret to say, sir, that the cantankerous old woman did get in my way when I was in a passion. Unfortunately I had a heavy stick in my hand and I did strike her over the head. Nobody can regret it so much as I do! Nobody can feel so acutely the position in which I am placed! I have sat in this House for many years, and many gentlemen know me well. I think, sir, that they will acknowledge that I am a man not deficient in filial piety or general humanity. Sir, I am sorry for what I did in a moment of heat. I shall regret it as long as I live. I have now spoken at any rate the truth, and I shall leave myself in the hands of the House." My belief is I should get such a round of applause as I certainly shall never achieve in any other way. It is not only that a popular man may do it,—like Phineas Finn, whom everybody thinks a fine fellow because he didn't murder a man* in the streets; but the most unpopular man in the House may make himself liked by owning freely that he has done something that he ought to be ashamed of.' Nidderdale's unwonted eloquence was received in good part by the assembled legislators, and then the ways and customs of the House were discussed at length by the two senior peers for the advantage of their juniors around them.

'Taking it altogether,' said the Duke, 'I know of no assembly in any country in which good humour prevails so generally, in which the members behave to each other with equal courtesy, in which rules are so universally followed, or in which the President, Chairman, or Speaker is so thoroughly sustained by the feeling of the members.'

'I hear men say that it isn't quite what it used to be,' said Silverbridge.

'Nothing will ever be quite what it used to be. There will always be changes.'

'Changes for the worse, I mean. Men are doing all kinds of things, just because the rules of the House allow them. A few men whom we all could name move the adjournment every day to enable them to do what they oughtn't to do.'

'If they be within rule,' said the Duke, 'I don't know who is to blame them. In my time if any man stretched a rule too far the House would not put up with it.'

'That's just it,' said Nidderdale. 'The House puts up with anything now. There is a great deal of good feeling, I don't doubt, but there's no earnestness about anything. Our party go and come just as Beeswax wants us. If any man has life enough in him to have a little job of his own to get done, he is let to have his own way. The comfort is so very few ever have.'

'We are better on our side than that,' said Lord Cantrip.

'I think you are more earnest than we;—but then you are such horrid bores. And each earnest man is in earnest about something that nobody else cares for. Go ask anybody whether there isn't a feeling that Home Rule* hasn't been the most important matter discussed this session.'

'Nobody believes in Home Rule,' said Silverbridge.

'Nobody does believe in it; but so many gentlemen agree to pretend to believe in it that it assumes a look of reality. Nobody will take the trouble even to pretend to believe about most things that are brought up. I am going to move that arms be put up on the benches, as the chief use of the House is to go to sleep in.' This was received with almost solemn disapprobation by the Duke, but was cheered by the younger legislators present. Lord Cantrip only shrugged his shoulders as they all went through to the drawing-room.

It soon came to pass that Lord Popplecourt was again sitting next to Lady Mary. 'Where are you going this autumn?' he asked.

'I don't know in the least. Papa has said something about going abroad somewhere.'

'You won't be at Custins?' Custins was Lord Cantrip's country seat in Dorsetshire.

'I know nothing about myself as yet. But I don't think I shall go any-where unless papa goes too.'

'Lady Cantrip has asked me to be at Custins in the middle of October. It is awfully good-natured. They say it is about the best pheasant-shooting in England.'

'Do you shoot much?'

'A great deal. I shall be in Scotland on the Twelfth.* I and Reginald Dobbes have a place together. He has booked our party to kill more grouse and shoot more deer than any other six guns this year. I shall get to my own partridges on the first of September. I always mean to manage that. Popplecourt is in Suffolk, and I don't think any man in England can beat me for partridges.'

'What a slayer of animals you must be.'

'Yes, I am rather.'

'What do you do with them all, Lord Popplecourt?'

'Leadenhall Market. I make it pay,—or very nearly. Then I shall run back to Scotland for the end of the stalking, and I can easily manage to be at Custins by the middle of October. I never touch my own pheasants till November.'

'Why are you so abstemious?'

'The birds are heavier and it answers better. But if I thought you would be at Custins it would be much nicer.' Lady Mary, who did not respond with enthusiasm to the compliment, again told him that as yet she knew nothing of her father's autumn movements.

But at the same moment in another part of the house the Duke was arranging his autumn movements, or at any rate those of his daughter. Lady Cantrip had told him that the desirable son-in-law had promised to go to Custins, and suggested that he and Lady Mary should also be there. In his daughter's name he promised, but he would not bind himself. Would it not be better that he should be absent? What personal aid could he lend to the arrangement? Lady Cantrip too would know his own mind on the subject,—did, indeed, know it already. Lady Cantrip pleaded that there might be arrangements to be made as to money. Then he frowned, but added that his lawyer would be prepared with an answer as to that. The arrangements prepared would be such that Lord Popplecourt could not possibly object to them. 'The young man, I think, is not indifferent to money,' said Lady Cantrip. The Duke asked no question as to Lord Popplecourt's present condition of mind on the subject, not venturing to inquire whether any, and what, communication had been made. Now that the doing of this thing was brought nearer to him so that he could see and feel its details, he was disgusted by it. And yet it had answered so well with his wife!

'Is Lord Popplecourt intimate here?' Lady Mabel asked her friend, Lord Silverbridge.

'I don't know. I am not.'

'Lady Cantrip seems to think a great deal about him.'

'I dare say. I don't. But then it is so natural that Lady Cantrip and I should have different ideas about a young man.'

'Your father seems to like him.'

'That's possible too. They're going back to London together in the governor's carriage. My father will talk high politics all the way, and Popplecourt will agree with everything.'

'He isn't intended to—to——? You know what I mean.'

'I can't say that I do.'

'To cut out poor Frank.'

'It's quite possible.'

'Poor Frank!'

'You had a great deal better say, "poor Popplecourt!"—or "poor governor!" or "poor Lady Cantrip!" Anyone can lead a horse to water, you know.'

'But a hundred countesses can't make your sister marry a man she doesn't like. That's what you mean.'

'Just that. They don't go the right way about it.'

'What would you do?'

'Leave her alone. Let her find out gradually that what she wants can't be done.'

'And so linger on for ten years,' said Lady Mabel reproachfully.

'I say nothing about that. It is a matter in which I will not meddle or make. The man is my friend.'

'And you ought to be proud of him.'

'I never knew anybody yet that was proud of his friends. I like him well enough, but I can quite understand that the governor should object. We all know that Tregear has got nothing.'

'Yes, we all know that,' said the girl sadly, who something over twelve months since had been at such infinite trouble to explain to the very man of whom they were talking that she could not marry him on that same ground.

'What would your father say if you wanted to marry someone who hadn't a shilling?'

'I should object myself,—without waiting for my father. But then,— neither have I a shilling. If I had money, do you think I wouldn't like to give it to the man I loved?'

'But this is a case of giving somebody else's money. I know all about it, Lady Mab. They won't make her give it up by bringing such a young ass as that down here. If my father has persistency enough to stick to his purpose and let her cry her eyes out, he'll succeed.'

'And break her heart.'

'Very likely;—as hearts are broken.'

'Could you do that?'

'Certainly not. But then I'm soft. I'm not persistent. I can't refuse when I'm asked.'

'Can't you?'

'Not if the person who asks me is in my good books. You try me.'

'I am not in your good books.'

'Nobody stands so well in them. You ask me for anything, and see.'

'What shall I ask for?'

'Anything.'

'The Prime Minister.'

'I would not introduce you to a partnership with such a man as my friend the Major, else you should have my half of the beast.'

'Give me that ring off your finger,' she said. He at once took it off his hand. 'Of course you know I am in joke. You don't imagine that I would take it from you.' He still held it towards her. 'Lord Silverbridge, I expect that with you I may say a foolish word without being brought to sorrow by it. I know that that ring belonged to your great-uncle,— and to fifty Pallisers before, probably.'

'What would it matter?'

'And it would be wholly useless to me, as I could not wear it.'

'Of course it would be too big,' said he, replacing the ring on his own finger. 'But when I talk of anyone being in my good books, I don't mean a thing like that. Don't you know there is nobody on earth I——'; then he paused and blushed, and she sat motionless, looking at him, expecting, with her colour too somewhat raised,— 'whom I like so well as I do you?' It was a very lame conclusion. She felt it to be lame. But as regarded him, the lameness at the moment had come from bashfulness on his part, from a certain timidity which forbade him to say the word 'love' even though he had meant to say it.

She recovered herself instantly. 'I do believe it,' she said. 'I do think that we are real friends.'

'Would you not take a ring from a—real friend?'

'Not that ring; nor a ring at all after I had asked for it in joke. You understand it all, I am quite sure. But to go back to what we were talking about, if you can do anything for Frank, pray do. You say yourself that your sister will break her heart. A man of course bears it all better, but he does not perhaps suffer the less. It is all his life to him. He can do nothing while this is going on. Are you not true enough to your friendship for him to exert yourself on his behalf?' Silverbridge put his hand up and rubbed his head as though he were vexed. 'Your aid would just turn everything in his favour.'

'You do not know my father.'

'Is he so inexorable?'

'It is not that, Mabel. But he is so unhappy. I cannot add to his unhappiness by taking part against him.'

In another part of the room,—or rather in another room, for there were two or three opening into each other,—Lady Cantrip was busy on the same matter with Lord Popplecourt. She had talked about pheasants, and had talked about grouse, had talked about moving the address in the House of Lords in some coming session, and the great value of forming political alliances early in life, till the young peer began to think that Lady Cantrip was the nicest of women. Then after a short pause she changed the subject. 'Don't you think Lady Mary very beautiful?'

'Uncommon,' said his lordship.

'And her manners so perfect! She has all her mother's ease without any of that—— You know what I mean.'

'Quite so,' said his lordship energetically.

'And then she has got so much in her!'

'Has she though?'

'I don't know any girl of her age so thoroughly well educated. The Duke seems to take to you.'

'Well, yes;—the Duke is very kind.'

'Don't you think——?'

'Eh!'

'You have heard of her mother's fortune.'

'Tremendous!'

'She will have I take it quite a third of it. Whatever I say I'm sure you will take in confidence;—but she is a dear, dear girl; and I am anxious for her happiness almost as though she belonged to me.' Then the Countess got up and moved away.

Lord Popplecourt went back to town in the Duke's carriage, but was unable to say a word about politics,—or to listen or even to appear to listen. His mind was altogether filled with the wonderful words that had been spoken to him. Could it be that Lady Mary had fallen violently in love with him? He would not at once give himself up to the pleasing idea. Having so thoroughly grounded himself in the belief that female nets were to be avoided, that he must be on his guard against all those matrimonial hooks which would encounter him at every turn in his stream of life, he would not give himself up, freely and at once, even to the allurements of a proposition so delightful as that which had been made to him. But when he got home to his own chamber he did think favourably of it. The daughter of a duke,—and such a duke! So lovely a girl, and with such gifts! And then a fortune which would make a material addition to his own large property! Though it were a hook, would it not be worth his while to swallow it?

CHAPTER 36

TALLY-HO LODGE

WE all know that very clever distich concerning the great fleas and the little fleas* and the lesson which it teaches us that no animal is too humble to have its parasite. Even Major Tifto had his inferior friend. This was a certain Captain Green,—for the friend also affected military honours. He was a man somewhat older than Tifto of whose antecedents no one was supposed to know anything. But he could ride a horse, understand something of farriery,* and called himself a sporting gentleman. It was presumed of him that he lived by betting, and it was always boasted by those who wished to defend his character that when he lost he paid his money like a gentleman. Tifto during the last year or two had been anxious to support Captain Green, and had always made use of this argument: 'Where the d—— he gets his money I don't know;—but when he loses, there it is. No one will say that he was ever welched by Green.' It was thus that Tifto had spoken of his friend to Lord Silverbridge.

Major Tifto had a little 'box' of his own* in the neighbourhood of Egham, at which he had a set of stables a little bigger than his house, and a set of kennels a little bigger than his stables. It was here he kept his horses and hounds, and himself too when business connected with his sporting life did not take him up to town. It was now the middle of August. Everybody had left London, and he had failed in a little attempt he had made to be taken down to a Scotch shooting. He therefore had come to Tally-ho Lodge, there to look after his establishments, to make arrangements for cub-hunting, and to prepare for the autumn racing campaign. On this occasion Captain Green was enjoying his hospitality and assisting him by sage counsels and the lessons of a lengthened experience. Behind the little box was a little garden,— a garden that was very little; but, still, thus close to the parlour window, there was room for a small table to be put on the grass-plat,* and for a couple of arm-chairs. Here the Major and the Captain were seated about eight o'clock one evening, with convivial good things within their reach. The good things were gin-and-water and pipes. The two gentlemen had not dressed strictly for dinner. They had spent a great part of the day handling the hounds and the horses, dressing wounds, curing sores, and ministering to canine ailments, and had probably been detained over their work too long to think of their toilet. As it was they had an eye to business. The stables at one corner and the kennels at the other were close to the little garden, and the doings of a man and a boy who were still at work among the animals could be inspected and directed from the arm-chairs on which the two sportsmen were sitting.

It must be explained, before the matter then under discussion between these gentlemen be touched upon by us, that ever since the Silverbridge election there had been a growing feeling in Tifto's mind that he had been ill-treated by his partner. The feeling was greatly strengthened by the admirable condition of Prime Minister and the place which the horse held in the betting for the Leger. Surely more consideration had been due to a man who had produced such a state of things! Silverbridge, he thought, could hardly know what winning a Leger meant, or he would pay more respect to the man who was preparing for him so great a triumph! Tifto had previously talked magnificently to his friend of his position at the Beargarden and of his intimacy with all the young lords, members of Parliament, and opulent 'swells' by whom that aristocratic institution was supported, and the Captain, with a partial belief in these boastings, had once, in a thoughtful moment, suggested that he also would like to be a member of the Beargarden. Tifto knew well how impossible this would be; and indeed looked upon the request as monstrous impertinence. 'He hasn't got toggery fit to go to such a place,' Tifto said to himself. Nevertheless it was necessary that he should excuse himself after some civil fashion. Though the Captain's clothes were not bright,—with the exception of his red coat, breeches, and boots, which were always decent,—still the Major owed him a little money and in many ways could hardly get on without him. 'The truth is,' he said, 'that Silverbridge and I are going to have a tiff.'

'I wouldn't quarrel with him, but I'd make him pay his way,' said the prudent Captain, who saw at a moment that his aspirations in regard to the club were vain.

'As for that of course he does pay—his share.'

'Who does all the work?'

'That's true.'

'The fact is, Tifto, you don't make enough out of it. You'll excuse me if I speak my mind.'

'Oh, yes.'

'When a small man like you has to deal with a big man like that, he may take it out of him in one of two ways. But he must be deuced clever if he can get it both ways.'

'What are you driving at?' asked Tifto, who did not like being called a small man, feeling himself to be every inch a Master of Foxhounds.

'Why this! Look at that d—— fellow, fretting that 'orse with a switch. If you can't strap a 'orse* without a stick in your hand, don't you strap him at all, you————.' Then there came a volley of abuse out of the Captain's mouth, in the middle of which the man threw down the rubber he was using and walked away, as though he were going for the night, leaving the horse fastened by a headstall* to a ring outside the stable.

'You come back,' halloed Tifto, jumping up from his seat with his pipe in his mouth. Then there was a general quarrel between the man and his two masters, in which the man at last was victorious. The Captain swore that no groom ought to stand over a horse with a stick in his hand, and the man swore that he would not go near such a brute as that without a stick. The matter was compromised at last by the horse being taken into the stable in an unfinished condition. 'It's all very well to say, "get rid of him," but where am I to get anybody better? It has come to such a pass that now if you speak to a fellow he walks out of the yard. It all comes of them school-books and suffrage* and unions. When a fellow knew that if he didn't do what he was told he'd get a month at the treadmill and a month of starvation* when he came out, things were much better attended to. I explained all that to Silverbridge when he first thought about Parliament.' These were Tifto's ideas on political economy.

This brought them back to the state of affairs as it was between Tifto and Lord Silverbridge at the present moment. 'What I was saying is this,' continued the Captain. 'If you choose to put yourself up to live with a fellow like that on equal terms——'

'One gentleman with another;—you mean that.'

'Put it so. It don't quite hit it off, but put it so. Why then you get your wages when you take his arm and call him Silverbridge.'

'I don't want wages from any man,' said the indignant Major.

'That comes from not knowing what wages is. I do want wages. If I do a thing I like to be paid for it. You are paid for it,—after one fashion. I should prefer the other fashion.'

'Do you mean he should give me—a salary?'

'I'd have it out of him some way for looking after his affairs. What's the good of young chaps of that sort if they ain't made to pay? You've got this young swell in tow. As far as I can hear he's going to be about the richest man in England;—and what the deuce better are you for it?' Then the Captain paused, emptied his glass, refilled it, and lit his pipe, which had been allowed to extinguish itself in the heat of the argument with the groom. Tifto sat meditating, thinking of the wisdom which was being spoken. The same ideas had occurred to him. The happy chance which had made him intimate with Lord Silverbridge had not yet enriched him. He owed Lord Silverbridge money, but even that money had never been in his own pocket. 'What is the good of chaps of that sort if they are not made to pay?' The words were wise words. But yet how glorious he had felt his position to be when he had been elected at the Beargarden, and had entered the club as the special friend of the heir of the Duke of Omnium.

After a short pause, Captain Green pursued his discourse. 'You said salary.'

'I did mention the word.'

'Salary and wages I take it is all one. A salary is a very nice thing if you're only sure that it'll be paid regular. I had a salary once myself for looking after a stud of 'orses at Newmarket, only the gentleman broke up and it never went farther than the first half-year.'

'Was that Marley Bullock?'

'Yes,—that was Marley Bullock. He's abroad somewhere now with nothing a year paid quarterly to live on. I think he does a little at cards with some of the young English. He'd had a good bit of money once, but most of it was gone when he came my way.'

'You didn't make by him.'

'I didn't lose nothing. I didn't have a lot of 'orses under me without getting some picking out of it. I didn't trust to the salary altogether.'

'What am I to do?' asked Tifto. 'I can sell him a horse now and again. But if I give him anything good there isn't much to come out of that.'

'Very little I should say.' Then there was a pause. 'Don't he put his money on his 'orses?'

'Not very free. He does bet a little, and I think he's coming out freer now. It seems to me his governor stumps up for everything.'

'What did he stand to win on the Derby?'

'A thousand or two perhaps.'

'There may be something made very handsome out of that,' said the Captain, not venturing to allow his voice to rise above a whisper. Major Tifto looked hard at him but said nothing. 'Of course you must see your way.'

'I don't quite understand.'

'Race 'orses are expensive animals,—and races generally is expensive. There are some who drop a deal of money at it,—and some who pick it up.'

'That's true.'

'When so much is dropped, somebody has to pick it up. That's what I've always said to myself. I'm as honest as another man.'

'That's of course,' said the Major civilly.

'But if I don't keep my mouth shut, somebody'll have my teeth out of my head. I know that. Everyone for himself and God for us all; that's my motto. I suppose there's a deal of money flying about with this young Marquis.'

'He ain't a marquis.'

'He's a duke's son anyhow. He'll put a lot of money on this 'orse of yours for the Leger if he's managed right. There's more to be got out of that than calling him Silverbridge and walking arm-in-arm. Business is business. I don't know whether I make myself understood.'

The gentleman did not quite make himself understood; and Tifto sat for a time endeavouring to read the riddle. Tifto did understand something of the lesson intended to be taught, and determined to profit by it. He must in some way make money out of his friend Lord Silverbridge. Hitherto he had contented himself with the brilliancy of the connection; but now he began to find that this was not so glorious as it had at first appeared. His brilliant friend had taken to snubbing him, and had on more than one occasion made himself thoroughly disagreeable. It seemed to him that Captain Green counselled him to put up with all that, but counselled him at the same time to—pick up some of his friend's money. He filled another pipe and another glass of gin-and-water as he thought of this in silence. He didn't think that he could ask Lord Silverbridge for a salary,—he who was a Master of Foxhounds, and a member of the Beargarden. Then his friend the Captain had suggested something about the young Lord's bets. He was endeavouring to unravel all this with a brain that was already somewhat muddled with alcohol, when Captain Green got up from his chair and, standing over the Major,—not quite in a vertical position, for the gin-and-water had had considerable effect upon his legs though none apparently as to intellect,—spoke his last words for that night as from an oracle. 'Square is all very well, as long as others are square to you;—but when they ain't then I say square be d——. Square! What comes of it? Work your heart out, and then it's no good.' After that the Captain made his way off to his bed.

The Major thought about it much that night, and was thinking about it still when he awoke on the next morning. It would quite answer his purpose to make Lord Silverbridge pay for his late insolence. It would answer his purpose to make a little money,—as he told himself,—in any honest way. At the present moment he was in want of money, and on looking into his affairs declared to himself that he had certainly impoverished himself by his devotion to Lord Silverbridge's interests during the past summer and spring. At breakfast on the following morning he endeavoured to bring his friend back to the subject. But the Captain was cross, rather than oracular. 'Everybody,' he said, 'ought to know his own business. He wasn't going to meddle or make. What he had said had been taken amiss.' This was hard upon Tifto, who had taken nothing amiss. 'But what he would like,' said the Captain, 'was to get that sixty pounds that was due to him. He had to pay other people, and he couldn't carry on unless other people paid him.' This was again hard, because there had been an understanding that this money was not to be asked for until after the Leger had been run.

'Square be d——!' There was a great deal in the lesson thus enunciated which demanded consideration. Hitherto the Major had fought his battles with a certain adherence to squareness. If his angles had not all been perfect angles, still there had always been an attempt at geometrical accuracy. He might now and again have told a lie about a horse—but who that deals in horses has not done as much as that? He had been alive to the value of underhand information from racing stables, but what racing man is there who won't use a tip if he can get it? He had lied about the expense of his hounds, in order to enhance the subscription of his members. He had enticed young men to play cards with him when they were far gone with wine. But those were things which everybody did in his line,—things which he would hardly be ashamed to acknowledge. But old Green had meant something beyond this. What was it that old Green had meant?

As far as he could see out in the world at large, nobody was square. You had to keep your mouth shut, or your teeth would be stolen out of it. He didn't look into a paper without seeing that on all sides of him men had abandoned the idea of squareness. Chairmen, directors, members of Parliament, baronets, ambassadors,—all the world, as he told himself,—were trying to get on by their wits. He didn't see why he should be more square than anybody else. Why hadn't Silverbridge taken him down to Scotland for the grouse?

CHAPTER 37

GREX

FAR away from all known places, in the northern limit of the Craven district, on the borders of Westmorland but in Yorkshire, there stands a large, rambling, most picturesque old house called Grex. The people around call it the Castle, but it is not a castle, nor is that name ever given to it by the family, who always call the place simply Grex. It is an old brick building supposed to have been erected in the days of James the First, having oriel windows, twisted chimneys, long galleries, gable ends, a quadrangle of which the house surrounds three sides, terraces, sun-dials, and fishponds. But unfortunately it is so sadly out of repair as to be altogether unfit for the residence of a gentleman and his family. It stands not in a park, for the land about it, very nearly up to the house, is divided into paddocks by low stone walls, but in the midst of lovely scenery, the ground rising all round it in low irregular hills or fells; and close to it, within a quarter of a mile from the unused outhouses which stand at the back of the house, there is a small dark lake,—not serenely lovely as are some of the lakes in Westmorland, but attractive by the darkness of its waters and the gloom of the rocks around it.

This is the country seat of Earl Grex,—which however he had not visited for some years. Gradually the place had got into such a condition that his absence should not be wondered at. Who does not know how one want begets another, till ruin follows upon ruin? An old house always requires care and is always expensive;—but if the work be done continuously the cost may be brought within bounds. But when once the evil has been allowed to grow, then the affair becomes almost hopeless. An owner of Grex with large means at his disposal and with a taste for the picturesque to gratify,—one who could afford to pay for memories and who was willing to pay dearly for such luxuries,—might no doubt restore Grex. But it would be a cheaper work to build a new house, if not as large, yet more commodious. The present owner of Grex had no idea of doing either the one or the other. As the place was entailed he could not sell it;* but the entail could not force him to keep the house in repair.

Lord Grex had latterly never gone near the place, nor was his son Lord Percival very fond of looking upon the ruin of his property. But Lady Mabel loved the place with a fond love. With all her lightness of spirit she was prone to memories, prone to melancholy, prone at times almost to seek the gratification of sorrow. Year after year when the London season was over she would come down to Grex and spend a week or two amidst its desolation before she went to enjoy the hospitable luxury of some rich friend's country mansion. She was now going on to a seat in Scotland belonging to Mrs. Montacute Jones called Killancodlem; but she was having what she thought to be the greatest luxury of the year in spending what must have been a desolate fortnight at Grex in company with Miss Cassewary. The land was let up to the back door. Even the gardens were let,—and being let of course were not kept in further order than as profit might require. The man who rented them lived in the big house with his wife, and they on such occasions as this would cook what was needed for Lady Mabel. She had her own maid, for an earl's daughter, even in poverty, must have her own maid. But in truth the ruin of the family was not as yet absolute ruin. There was a handsome house still maintained in Belgrave Square. During the season there was a carriage and horses, and there were servants with white plastered heads.* Lady Mabel dressed handsomely. Lord Percival lived luxuriously,—though of his living little was seen either by the father or sister. The old sinner himself always had money for gambling and had now taken himself off to some German baths,—so he said,—with his own valet and a courier. Lady Mabel presumed that he had gone to Monaco. Money could still be made to be forthcoming for such absolute needs as these. But still anyone who saw Grex would say that the family was ruined.

And now Lady Mabel was at the home of her ancestors, and the faithful Miss Cass was with her. But at the moment and at the spot at which the reader shall see her, Miss Cass was not with her. She was sitting, at about six o'clock in the afternoon, on a rock about twelve feet above the lake looking upon the black water; and on another rock a few feet from her was seated Frank Tregear. 'No,' she said. 'You should not have come. Nothing can justify it. Of course as you are here I could not refuse to come out with you. To make a fuss about it would be the worst of all. But you should not have come.'

'Why not?'

'Why not! For you to ask why not! For you to pretend to be thick-headed!'

'I do not know that my head is thicker than other people's; but still I say, why not? Whom does it hurt? It is a pleasure to me. If it be the reverse to you, I will go.'

'Men are so unmanly! They take such mean advantages. You know it is a pleasure to me to see you.'

'I had hoped so.'

'But it is a pleasure I ought not to have,—at least not here.'

'That is what I do not understand,' said he. 'In London where the Earl could bark at me if he happened to find me, I could see the inconvenience of it. But here, where there is nobody but my particular friend Miss Cass——'

'There are a great many others. There are the rocks and stones and walls and old women;—all of which have ears.'

'But of what is there to be ashamed?'

'Certainly nothing on my part.'

'I don't see what you mean. There is nothing in the world to me so pleasant as the companionship of my friends.'

'Then go after Silverbridge. He is your friend.'

'I mean to do so;—but I am taking you by the way.'

'It is all unmanly,' she said, rising from her stone and standing near him. 'You know that it is so. Friends! Do you mean to say that it would make no difference whether you were here with me or with Miss Cass?'

'The greatest difference in the world.'

'What difference? Why?'

'Because I like you better than Miss Cass.'

'Because she is an old woman and I am a young one, and because in intercourse between young men and young women there is something dangerous to the woman and therefore pleasant to the man.'

'I never heard anything more far-fetched or more unjust. You cannot think I desire anything which may be hurtful or injurious to you.'

'I do think so.' She was still standing and spoke now with great vehemence. 'I do think so. You force me to throw aside the reticence I ought to keep. Would it help me in my prospects if your friend Lord Silverbridge knew that you were here with me,—as he probably will know?'

'How should he know?'

'But if he did? Do you suppose that I want to have visits paid to me of which I am afraid to speak openly? What business have you here? Would you dare to tell Lady Mary that you had been sitting alone with me, out on the rocks at Grex?'

'Certainly I would.'

'Then it would be because you have not dared to tell her certain other things which have gone before.'

'I have told her nothing that was not true.'

'I do not care what you have told her. You have sworn to her no doubt that you love her better than all the world.'

'I have.'

'And you have taken the trouble to come here to tell me that;—to wound me to the core by saying so; to show me that, though I may still be sick, you have recovered,—that is if you ever suffered anything, and to do me all the harm in your power by being here to say it. It is unmanly in both ways,—unmanly, and unworthy of you. Go your way and let me go mine. I do not want you.'

'Mabel.'

'I do not want you. I know you will not help me, but you need not destroy me.'

'Surely you know that you are wronging me.'

'No! You understand it all though you look so calm. I hate your Lady Mary Palliser. There! But if by anything I could do I could secure her to you I would do it,—because you want it. But I hate her! Were she married to you I would never see her.'

'She would be your sister-in-law,—probably.'

'Never. It will never be so. But what has that to do with it?'

'Why do you hate her?'

'There again! You are so little of a man that you can ask me why!' Then she turned away, as though she intended to go down to the marge of the lake by a little path which descended through the rocks.

But he rose up and stopped her. 'Let us have this out, Mabel, before we go,' he said. 'Unmanly is a heavy word to hear from you, and you have used it about a dozen times.'

'It is because I have thought it a thousand times. Go and get her if you can get it,—but why tell me about it?'

'You said you would help me.'

'So I would,—as I would help you do anything you might want, though you ought not to want it. You can hardly think that after all that has passed I can wish to hear about her.'

'It was you spoke of her.'

'I told you you should not be here,—because of her and because of me. And I tell you again I hate her. Do you think I can hear you speak of her as though she were the only woman you had ever seen without feeling it? Did you ever swear that you loved anyone else?'

'Certainly I have so sworn.'

'And have so sworn it that—that——! Have you ever said that nothing could alter that love?'

'Indeed I have.'

'But it is altered. It has all gone. It has been transferred to one who has more advantages of beauty, youth, wealth, and position!'

'Oh Mabel, Mabel!'

'But it is so.'

'Can you attack me in this savage fashion and not think of yourself?'

'Yes,—because I have never been false to anyone. You are false to me.'

'Have I not offered half-a-score of times to face all the world with you,—whatever it might be?'

'You would not offer it now?'

'No,' he said, after a pause,—'not now. Were I to do so I should be false. You bade me take my love elsewhere, and I did so.'

'With the greatest ease.'

'We agreed it should be so,—for both of us; and you have done the same.'

'That is false. Look me in the face and tell me whether you do not know it to be false.'

'And yet I am told that I am injuring you with Silverbridge!'

'Oh,—so unmanly again! Of course I have to marry. Who does not know it? Do you want to see me begging my bread about the streets? But you! You have bread, at any rate;—or if not you might earn it. If you marry for money——'

'The accusation is altogether unjustifiable,' he said indignantly.

'Allow me to finish what I have to say. If you marry for money you will do that which is in itself bad, and which is also unnecessary. What other course would you recommend me to take? No one goes into the gutter while there is a clear path open, though it be ever so narrow. If there be no escape but through the gutter one has to take it.'

'Then you mean that my duty to you should have kept me from marrying all my life.'

'Not that;—but a little while, Frank; just a little while. Your bloom is not fading; your charms are not running from you. Have you not a strength which I cannot have? Do you not feel that you are a tree, standing firm in the ground, from which leaves and fruit will come though they may be long in coming; while I am a bit of ivy that will be trodden in the dirt unless it can be made to cling to something? Of course I put out my feelers. I have to cling to something. You should not liken yourself to me, Frank.'

'If I could do you any good——'

'Good! What is the meaning of good? If you love, it is good to be loved again. It is good not to have your heart torn in pieces. You know that I love you.' He was standing close to her, and put out his hand as though he would twine his arm round her waist. 'Not for worlds,' she said. 'It belongs to that Palliser girl. And, beyond that, as I have taught myself to think that what there is left of me may perhaps belong to some other one, worthless as it is, I will keep it for him. I love you,—but there can be none of that softness of love between us. I am beginning to think that we had better make up our minds to live apart.' These last words she spoke with a smile on her lips.

'I hope not that, Mabel.'

'But remember, Frank,—our position is not equal. You have got over your little complaint. It probably did not go deep with you and you have found a cure. For aught I know there may be a certain satisfaction in feeling that two young women love you.'

'You are trying to be cruel to me.'

'Why else should you be here? You know I love you,—with all my heart, with all my strength; and that I would give the world to cure myself. Knowing this you come and talk to me of your passion for this other girl!'

'I had hoped we might both talk rationally, as friends, of our future hopes.'

'Friends! Frank Tregear, I have been bold enough to tell you I love you; but you are not my friend, and cannot be my friend. If I have before asked you to help me in this mean catastrophe of mine, in my attack upon that poor boy, I now withdraw my request. But I may as well show you this.' Then she drew a purse from her pocket, and taking a ring out of it handed it to Tregear.

'Whence does that come?' he asked.

'Don't you remember the diamond? It is that which Silverbridge always wore and which the old Duke gave him.'

'I thought he would never have parted with that.'

'He has had the setting altered and has sent it to me. Poor dear fellow! I wish he had kept it. I think I will go back to the house now. Miss Cass will think, else, that you have drowned me in the lake.'

'I will walk back to Ledburgh if you wish it without going to the house again.'

'No; I will have nothing that looks like being ashamed. Miss Cass shall not be made to think that I have regretted your company. You ought not to have come, but you need not tell her that I said so.' Then they walked back to the house together and found Miss Cassewary on the terrace. 'We have been to the lake,' said Mabel, 'and have been thinking and talking of old days. I have but one ambition now in the world.' Of course Miss Cassewary asked what the remaining ambition was. 'To get a lot of money by hook and crook and purchase this place from the ruins of the Grex property. If I could own the house and the lake, and the paddocks about, and have enough income to keep one servant, and bread for us to eat,—of course including you, Miss Cass——'

'Thank'ee, my dear; but I am not sure I should like it.'

'Yes; you would. Frank would come and see us perhaps once a year. I don't suppose anybody else cares about the place, but to me it is the dearest spot in the world. It would lose half its charms if it were well kept and in good repair.' So she went on in almost high spirits, though alluding to the general decadence of the Grex family, till Tregear took his leave. He had walked over from Ledburgh, and there he intended to sleep the night, and to return to Kendal on the following morning on his way to Scotland.

'I wish he had not come,' said Miss Cassewary when he was gone.

'Why should you wish that? There is not so much here to amuse me that you should begrudge me a stray visitor.'

'I don't think that I grudge you anything in the way of pleasure, my dear; but still he should not have come. My Lord, if he knew it, would be angry.'

'Then let him be angry. Papa does not do so much for me that I am bound to think of him at every turn.'

'But I am,—or rather I am bound to think of myself. If I take his bread——'

'Bread!'

'Well;—I do take his bread, and I take it on the understanding that I will be to you what a mother might be,—or an aunt.'

'I do not know what a mother might have been, but I do not fancy that I could ever have liked an aunt so well.'

'And if so,——'

'Well,—and if so! Had I a mother living would not Frank Tregear have come to visit her, and in visiting her, would he not have seen me,—and should we not have walked out together?'

'Not after all that has come and gone.'

'But you are not a mother nor yet an aunt, and you have to do just what I tell you. And don't I know that you trust me in all things? And am I not trustworthy?'

'I think you are trustworthy.'

'I know what my duty is and I mean to do it. No one shall ever have to say of me that I have given way to self-indulgence. I couldn't help his coming, you know.'

That same night, after Miss Cassewary had gone to bed, when the moon was high in the heavens and the world around her was all asleep, Lady Mabel again wandered out to the lake, and again seated herself on the same rock. She knew the place well enough to find her way thither by a fainter light than that which now prevailed. And there she sat thinking of her past life and trying to think of her future life for more than an hour. It is so much easier to think of the past than of the future,—to remember what has been than to resolve what shall be! She had reminded him of the offer which he had made and repeated to her more than once,—to share with her all his chances in life, such as they were, and to make her at any rate equal to himself. When she had refused that, many obstacles had occurred to her, any one of which seemed then to be sufficient to induce her to reject this proposal as insane. She must have consented to run off with him and get herself married, where and how she did not know. There would have been almost no income for them. All the world would have been against her. She would have caused his ruin. Her light on the matter had been so clear that it had not taken her very long to decide that such a thing must not be thought of. 'They had been foolish,' she said; 'but let them not add to their folly.' She had at last been quite stern in her decision, and he had left her for a while almost in anger.

Now she was broken-hearted because she found that he had left her in very truth. Oh yes;—she would marry the boy, if she could so arrange it. She thought that she could arrange it. She was to meet him down in Scotland within a week or two from the present time. Mrs. Montacute Jones had managed that. He had all but offered to her a second time at Richmond. Nothing but a little encouragement from her would be wanting. But all that, if it were arranged, would not serve to make her happy. She declared to herself that she did not wish to see Frank Tregear again; but still it was a misery to her that his heart should in truth be given to another woman.

CHAPTER 38

CRUMMIE-TODDIE

As soon as the session was over the Duke with his daughter started for the Continent. The arrangement was at last made simply because there seemed for the moment nothing else to be done. The Duke in truth did not know how to occupy himself, so much astray was he still in consequence of the death of his wife. When he first entertained the idea of taking Lady Mary to the Continent, it had been with the notion that he would remain there probably for the next twelvemonth,—that being thought at the time to be the medicine most apt to cure her of her love. But other counsels now prevailed, and a different treatment was to be adopted. She was to be taken to Custins in October in order that she might be induced to marry Lord Popplecourt. There was not much danger that she should see Tregear in the intervening two months. But as something had to be done, they went abroad, first to the Tyrol, with a plan of going on from there to the salt-mines and to Vienna. The Duke had asked Lord Gerald to accompany them with his tutor, but Lord Gerald begged that he might join his brother at a Scotch shoot-ing, and as Scotch shooting in August is supposed to be a proper amusement for young lords, and as Lord Gerald was supposed to have passed a few weeks down in Devonshire in a rather exemplary manner, his request was granted, and the tutor was to have leave of absence for a week or two. He was to be taken in as a gentleman-commoner at Lazarus, of which college, as all the world knows, old Dr. Gwynne* is still the warden. At Lazarus they think a good deal of birth, and when that story of the races was told it was considered at that exemplary college to have been rather hard that Lord Gerald should not have been allowed to see his brother's horse run for the Derby.

Almost at the last moment Silverbridge and his brother were induced to join Lord Popplecourt's shooting-party in Scotland. The party perhaps might more properly be called the party of Reginald Dobbes, who was a man knowing in such matters. It was he who made the party up. Popplecourt and Silverbridge were to share the expense between them, each bringing three guns and each making what arrangement he pleased with his own adherents. Silverbridge brought his brother and Frank Tregear,—having absolutely had to refuse a most piteous petition on the subject from Major Tifto. With Popplecourt of course came Reginald Dobbes, who was, in truth, to manage everything, and Lord Nidderdale, whose wife had graciously permitted him this recreation. They paid their own shares.* Tregear and Lord Gerald no doubt were more fortunate. The shooting was in the west of Perthshire, known as Crummie-Toddie, and comprised an enormous acreage of so-called forest and moor. Mr. Dobbes declared that nothing like it had as yet been produced in Scotland. Everything had been made to give way to deer and grouse. The thing had been managed so well that the tourist nuisance had been considerably alleviated. There was hardly a potato patch left in the district, nor a head of cattle to be seen. There were no inhabitants remaining, or so few that they could be absorbed in game-preserving or cognate duties. Reginald Dobbes, who was very great at grouse, and supposed to be capable of outwitting a deer by venatical wiles more perfectly than any other sportsman in Great Britain, regarded Crummie-Toddie as the nearest thing there was to a Paradise on earth. Could he have been allowed to pass one or two special laws for his own protection,—laws which he thought would have been in consonance with perfect practice,—there might still have been improvement. He would like to have had the legal right to have all intruders thrashed by the gillies* within an inch of their lives; and he thought that there should be a clause in his lease for such shootings against the making of any new roads, opening of footpaths, or building of bridges. There was one matter, however, which did rob him of much of his happiness, and perturbed his mind with a fear of which he hardly liked to speak to his most intimate friends. He had seen somewhere in print a plan for running a railway from Callender to Fort Augustus right through Crummie-Toddie! If this were done in his time the beauty of the world would be over. Reginald Dobbes was a man of about forty, strong, active, well made, about five feet ten in height, with broad shoulders and greatly developed legs, of whom his friends were accustomed to boast that he was all muscle. He was not a handsome man, having a protrusive nose, high cheek-bones, and long upper lip; but there was a manliness about his face which redeemed it. Anyone by looking at him could say, and say truly, that in all that he did he was determined to do it vigorously. Sport was the business of his life, and he thoroughly despised all who were not sportsmen. He fished and shot and hunted during nine or ten months of the year, filling up his time as best he might with recreations which he rather despised, such as bicycling, tennis, polo, and pigeon-shooting. He regarded it as a great duty to keep his body in the firmest possible condition, and it was a duty which he never neglected. All his eating and all his drinking was done upon a system, and he would consider himself to be guilty of much weak self-indulgence if he ever allowed himself to break through sanitary rules in which he had found that he could trust. But it never occurred to him that his whole life was one of self-indulgence. He could walk his thirty miles with his gun on his shoulder as well now, at forty, as he could ten years ago; and being sure of this, was thoroughly contented with himself, thinking that he had lived better than others around him. He had a patrimony amounting to perhaps one thousand pounds a year, which he husbanded so as to enjoy all his amusements to perfection. No one had ever heard of his sponging on his friends, or of his being short of money. Of money he rarely spoke, sport being in his estimation the only subject worthy of a man's words. Such was Reginald Dobbes, who was now to be the master of the shooting at Crummie-Toddie.

Crummie-Toddie was but twelve miles from Killancodlem, Mrs. Montacute Jones's highland seat; and it was this vicinity which probably first induced Lord Silverbridge to join the party. Mabel Grex was to be at Killancodlem, and, determined as he still was to ask her to be his wife, he would make this his opportunity. Of real opportunity there had been none at Richmond. How is a man to say what he really means at a dinner-party,—or afterwards in the drawing-room, when everyone is looking at him? He had said as much as he could, but she had not taken it rightly. Since he had had his ring altered and had sent it to her there had come but a word or two of answer. 'What am I to say? You unkindest of men! To keep it or to send it back would make me equally miserable. I shall keep it till you are married and then give it to your wife.' This affair of the ring had made him more intent than ever. After that he heard that Isabel Boncassen would also be at Killancodlem, having been induced to join Mrs. Montacute Jones's swarm of visitors. Though he was dangerously devoid of experience, still he felt that this was unfortunate. He intended to marry Mabel Grex, the marriage having been assented to, as being in all respects fit and proper, by his father. And he could assure himself that he thoroughly loved her. Nevertheless he liked making love to Isabel Boncassen. He was quite willing to marry and settle down, and looked forward with perfect satisfaction to having Mabel Grex for his wife. But it would be pleasant to have a six-months' run of flirting and love-making before this settlement, and he had certainly never seen anyone with whom this would be so delightful as with Miss Boncassen. But that the two ladies should be at the same house was unfortunate. There were moments as he travelled down in which he almost made up his mind that he would not go over to Killancodlem at all.

He and Gerald reached Crummie-Toddie late on the evening of August 11th, and found Reginald Dobbes alone. That was on Wednesday. Popplecourt and Nidderdale ought to have made their appearance on that morning, but had telegraphed to say that they would be detained two days on their route. Tregear, whom hitherto Dobbes had never seen, had left his arrival uncertain. At this very moment he was on his way down to Kendal, thinking much more of his visit to Grex than of Reginald Dobbes and the grouse. This carelessness on such matters was very offensive to Mr. Dobbes, who loved discipline and exactitude. He ought to have received the two young men with open arms because they were punctual; but he had been somewhat angered by what he considered the extreme youth of Lord Gerald. Boys who could not shoot were, he thought, putting themselves forward before their time. And Silverbridge himself was by no means a first-rate shot. Such a one as Silverbridge had to be endured because from the nature of his position and his wealth he could facilitate such arrangements as these. It was much to have to do with a man who would not complain if an extra fifty pounds were wanted. But he ought to have understood that he was bound in honour to bring down competent friends. Of Tregear's shooting Dobbes had been able to learn nothing. Lord Gerald was a lad from the Universities; and Dobbes hated University lads. This was man's work. Popplecourt and Nidderdale were known to be efficient. They were men who could work hard and do their part of the required slaughter. Dobbes proudly knew that he could make up for some deficiency by his own prowess; but he could not repair the evil which would be done by three bad guns. What was the use of so perfecting Crummie-Toddie as to make it the best bit of ground for grouse and deer in Scotland, if the men who came there failed by their own idleness and incapacity to bring up the grand total of killed to a figure which would render Dobbes and Crummie-Toddie famous through the whole shooting world? He had, too, been hard at work on other matters. Dogs had perhaps gone amiss,—or guns, and he had been made angry by the champagne which Popplecourt caused to be sent down. He knew what champagne meant. Whisky-and-water, and not much of it, was the liquor which Reginald Dobbes loved in the mountains. In this way he was hardly in a good humour when the two young men arrived.

'Don't you call this a very ugly country?' Silverbridge asked almost as soon as he arrived. Now it certainly is the case that the traveller who travels into Argyllshire, Perthshire, and Inverness expects to find lovely scenery; and it was also true that the country through which they had passed for the last twenty miles before reaching Crummie-Toddie lodge had been not only bleak and barren, but uninteresting and ugly. It was all rough open moorland, never rising into mountains, and graced by no running streams, by no forest scenery, almost by no foliage. The lodge itself did indeed stand close upon a little river, and was reached by a bridge that crossed it; but there was nothing pretty either in the river or the bridge. It was a placid black little streamlet, which in that portion of its course was hurried by no steepness, had no broken rocks in its bed, no trees on its low banks, and played none of those gambols which make running water beautiful. The bridge was a simple low construction with a low parapet, carrying an ordinary roadway up to the hall door. The lodge itself was as ugly as a house could be, white, of two stories, with the door in the middle and windows on each side, with a slate roof, and without a tree or a picturesque outhouse near it. To a man whose mind was intent simply on sport, as was the mind of Reginald Dobbes, it seemed a most desirable residence. It was in the middle of the shooting, and did not create a town around itself as do sumptuous mansions, to the great detriment of that seclusion which is favourable to game. 'Look at Killancodlem,' he had been heard to say—'a very fine house for ladies to flirt in; but if you find a deer within six miles of it I will eat him first, and shoot him afterwards.' There was a Spartan simplicity about Crummie-Toddie which pleased the Spartan mind of Reginald Dobbes.

'Ugly do you call it?'

'Infernally ugly,' said Lord Gerald.

'What did you expect to find? A big hotel and a lot of cockneys looking at a lake? If you come after grouse you must come to what the grouse think pretty.'

'Nevertheless it is ugly,' said Silverbridge, who did not choose to be 'sat upon.' 'I have been at shootings in Scotland before, and sometimes they are not ugly. This I call beastly.' Whereupon Reginald Dobbes turned upon his heel and walked away.

'Can you shoot?' he said afterwards to Lord Gerald just before they were going to bed.

'I can fire off a gun, if you mean that,' said Gerald.

'You have never shot much?'

'Not what you call very much. I'm not so old as you are, you know. Everything must have a beginning.' Mr. Dobbes wished 'the beginning' might have taken place elsewhere; but there had been some truth in the remark. Even he had once been a beginner. He felt as one does with a cabdriver who is too evidently only just learning his business. It is a misfortune for the horse, but the horseman has to learn. Thinking of this Reginald Dobbes went to bed.

'What on earth made you tell him crammers like that?' asked Silverbridge, as the brothers sat together smoking on the wall of the bridge.

'Because he made an ass of himself;—asking me whether I could shoot!'

On the next morning they started at seven, Dobbes having been very eager as to the early hour, having determined to be cross because, as he thought, the young men would certainly keep him waiting; and being in fact cross because by their punctuality they robbed him of any just cause for crossness. During the morning on the moor they were hardly ever near enough to each other for much conversation, and very little was said. According to arrangement made they returned to the house for lunch, it being their purpose not to go far from home till their numbers were complete. As they came over the bridge and, putting down their guns near the door, wiped the perspiration from their brows, Mr. Dobbes spoke the first good-humoured word they had heard from his lips. 'Why did you tell me such an infernal—I would say lie only perhaps you mightn't like it.'

'I told you no lie,' said Gerald.

'You've only missed two birds all the morning, and you have shot forty-two. That's uncommonly good sport.'

'What have you done?'

'Only forty.' And Mr. Dobbes seemed for the moment to be quite gratified by his own inferiority. 'You are a deuced sight better than your brother.'

'Gerald's about the best shot I know,' said Silverbridge.

'Why didn't he tell?'

'Because you were angry when we said the place was ugly.'

'I see all about it,' said Dobbes. 'Nevertheless when a fellow comes to shoot he shouldn't complain because a place isn't pretty. What you want I suppose is a decent house as near as you can have it to your ground. If there is anything in Scotland to beat Crummie-Toddie in that way I don't know where to find it. Shooting is shooting, you know, and touring is touring.'

Upon that he took very kindly to Lord Gerald, who, even after the arrival of the other men, was second in skill only to Dobbes himself. With Nidderdale, who was an old companion, he got on very well. Nidderdale ate and drank too much, and refused to be driven beyond a certain amount of labour, but was in other respects obedient and knew what he was about. Popplecourt was disagreeable, but he was a fairly good shot and understood what was expected of him. Silverbridge was so good-humoured, that even his manifest faults,—shooting carelessly, lying in bed, and wanting his dinner,—were, if not forgiven, at least endured. But Tregear was an abomination. He could shoot well enough and was active, and when he was at the work seemed to like it;—but he would stay away whole days in the house by himself, reading or writing, and when spoken to would answer in a manner which seemed to Reginald Dobbes to be flat mutiny. 'We are not doing it for our bread,' said Tregear.

'I don't know what you mean.'

'There's no duty in killing a certain number of these animals.' They had been driving deer on the day before and were to continue the work on the day in question. 'I'm not paid fifteen shillings a week for doing it.'

'I suppose if you undertake to do a thing, you mean to do it. Of course you're not wanted. We can make the double party without you.'

'Then why the mischief should you growl at me?'

'Because I think a man should do what he undertakes to do. A man who gets tired after three days' work of this kind would become tired if he were earning his bread.'

'Who says I am tired? It's like the insanity of a man who keeps china cups and saucers and thinks that every moment of life is lost in which he is not looking after cups and saucers. I came here to amuse myself.'

'Amuse yourself!'

'And as long as it amuses me I shall shoot, and when it does not I shall give it up.'

This vexed the governor of Crummie-Toddie much. He had learned to regard himself as the arbiter of the fate of men while they were sojourning under the same autumnal roof as himself. But a defalcation which occurred immediately afterwards was still worse. Silverbridge declared his intention of going over one morning to Killancodlem. Reginald Dobbes muttered a curse between his teeth, which was visible by the anger on his brow to all the party. 'I shall be back to-night, you know,' said Silverbridge.

'A lot of men and women who pretend to come there for shooting,' said Dobbes angrily, 'but do all the mischief they can.'

'One must go and see one's friends, you know.'

'Some girl!' said Dobbes.

'Two or three I should think,' said Nidderdale.

But worse happened than the evil so lightly mentioned. Silverbridge did go over to Killancodlem; and presently there came back a man with a cart, who was to return with a certain not small proportion of his luggage.

'It's hardly honest, you know,' said Reginald Dobbes.

CHAPTER 39

KILLANCODLEM

MR. DOBBES was probably right in his opinion that a large concourse of people, that hotels, tourists, and congregations of men made for purposes of comfort and luxury are detrimental to shooting. Crummie-Toddie was in all respects suited for sport. Killancodlem, though it had the name of a shooting-place, certainly was not so. Men going there took their guns. Gamekeepers were provided and gillies,—and, in a moderate quantity, game. On certain grand days a deer or two might be shot,—and would be very much talked about afterwards. But a glance at the place would suffice to show that Killancodlem was not intended for sport. It was a fine castellated mansion, with beautiful though narrow grounds, standing in the valley of the Archay River, with a mountain behind and the river in front. Between the gates and the river there was a public road on which a stage-coach ran, with loud-blown horns and the noise of many tourists. A mile beyond the Castle was the famous Killancodlem hotel which made up a hundred and twenty beds, and at which half as many more guests would sleep on occasions under the tables. And there was the Killancodlem post-office half-way between the two. At Crummie-Toddie they had to send nine miles for their letters and newspapers,—which was done but twice a week when Mr. Dobbes was allowed to have his own way. At Killancodlem there was lawn-tennis and a billiard-room and dancing every night. The costumes of the ladies were lovely, and those of the gentlemen, who were wonderful in knickerbockers, picturesque hats, and variegated stockings, hardly less so. And then there were carriages and saddle-horses, and paths had been made hither and thither through the rocks and hills for the sake of the scenery. Scenery! To hear Mr. Dobbes utter the single word was as good as a play. Killancodlem was near enough to him to be a matter of importance, and he hated the place. Was it for such cockney purposes as those that Scotland had been created, fit mother for grouse and deer?

Silverbridge arrived just before lunch, and was soon made to understand that it was impossible that he should go back that day. Mrs. Jones was very great on that occasion. 'You are afraid of Reginald Dobbes,' she said severely.

'I think I am rather.'

'Of course you are. How came it to pass that you of all men should submit yourself to such a tyrant?'

'Good shooting, you know,' said Silverbridge, putting forward his best plea.

'But you know you dare not call an hour your own,—or your soul. Mr. Dobbes and I are sworn enemies. We both like Scotland and unfortunately we have fallen into the same neighbourhood. He looks upon me as the genius of sloth. I regard him as the incarnation of tyranny. He once said there should be no women in Scotland,—just an old one here and there, who would know how to cook grouse. I offered to go and cook his grouse!'

'Great power,—hasn't he?' said a man in knickerbockers who had been endeavouring to make himself agreeable to Lady Mabel. 'A kind of sporting Bismarck, I should say.'

'Any friend of mine,' continued Mrs. Jones, 'who comes down to Crummie-Toddie without staying a day or two with me—will never be my friend any more. I do not hesitate to tell you, Lord Silverbridge, that I call for your surrender in order that I may show my power over Reginald Dobbes. Are you a Dobbite?'

'Not thorough-going,' said Silverbridge.

'Then be a Montacute Jonesite;—or a Boncassenite, if, as is possible, you prefer a young woman to an old one.' At this moment Isabel Boncassen was standing close to them.

'Killancodlem against Crummie-Toddie for ever,' said Miss Boncassen, waving her handkerchief. As a matter of course a messenger was sent back to Crummie-Toddie for the young Lord's wearing apparel, et cetera.

The whole of that afternoon he spent playing lawn-tennis with Miss Boncassen.* Lady Mabel was asked to join the party, but she refused, having promised, as she said, to take a walk to a distant waterfall where the Codlem falls into the Archay. The gentleman in knickerbockers was to have gone with her, and two other young ladies; but when the hour came for the walk she was weary, she said,—and she sat almost the entire afternoon looking at the game from a distance. Silverbridge played well, but not so well as the pretty American, who had made herself very skilful at it. With them were joined two others somewhat inferior, so that Silverbridge and Miss Boncassen were on different sides. They played game after game, and Miss Boncassen's side always won. During such occupations there is not in truth much opportunity for conversation. If there be any reality in the game,—as there was on this occasion,—the energies of the players are too fully employed to allow of attention to other things. Hours spent thus give rise to intimacies which lead to moments of more ecstatic bliss;—but the moments are not then. Very little was said between Silverbridge and Miss Boncassen which did not refer absolutely to the game. But Lady Mabel, looking on, told herself that they were making love to each other before her eyes. And why shouldn't they? She asked herself that question in perfect good faith. Why should they not be lovers? Was ever anything prettier than the girl in her country dress, active as a fawn and as graceful in every motion,—and apparently as young? Or could anything be more handsome, more attractive to a girl, more good-humoured, or better bred in his playful emulation than Silverbridge?

'When Youth and Pleasure meet,* To chase the glowing hours with flying feet!' she said to herself over and over again, trying to take a pleasure from the prettiness of what she saw.

But why had he sent her the ring? She would certainly give him back the ring and bid him bestow it at once upon Miss Boncassen. Inconstant boy! Then she would get up and wander away for a time and rebuke herself. What right had she even to think of inconstancy? Inconstancy indeed! Could she be so irrational, so unjust, so un-human as to be sick for his love, as to be angry with him because he seemed to prefer another, or to be irritated at his fickleness? Was she not well aware that she herself did not love him;—but that she did love another man? She had made up her mind to marry him in order that she might be a duchess, and because she could give herself to him without any of that horror which would be her fate in submitting to matrimony with one or another of the young men around her who had been suggested to her. There might be disappointment if he escaped her. She now felt almost sure that there would be disappointment,—bitter disappointment. There could be no longer any question of sparing him. But seeing how it was with him, had she further ground for hope? She certainly had no ground for anger!

It was thus, within her own bosom, she put questions to herself. And yet all this before her was simply a game of play in which the girl and the young man were as eager for victory as though they were children or players of the same sex. They were thinking neither of love nor love-making. That the girl should be so lovely was no doubt a pleasure to him;—and perhaps to her also that he should be joyous to look at and sweet of voice. But he, could he have been made to tell all the truth within him, would have still owned that it was his purpose to make Mabel his wife. And Isabel was certainly free from any purpose to make him her husband.

When the game was over, and the colloquies after the game,—the propositions made for further matches and the like,—Miss Boncassen said that she would betake herself to her own room. 'I never worked so hard in my life before,' she said. 'And I feel like a navvie. I could drink beer out of a jug and eat bread and cheese. I won't play with you any more, Lord Silverbridge, because I am beginning to think it is unlady-like to exert myself.' And yet he thought, as she went away, that her exercise had only added to her charms.

'Are you not glad you came over?' said Lady Mabel to him as he was going off the ground without seeing her.

'Pretty well,' he said. 'I am half sick of the grouse;—but we should have been stalking to-morrow.'

'Is not that better than stalking?'

'Lawn-tennis?'

'Yes;—lawn-tennis,—with Miss Boncassen.'

'She plays uncommonly well.'

'And so do you.'

'Ah,—she has such an eye for distances.'

'And you,—what have you an eye for? I say you play better than she does.'

'No.'

'Yes;—at the game you were playing at. Will you answer me a question?'

'Well;—yes; I think so.'

'Truly.'

'Certainly;—if I do answer it.'

'Do you not think her the most beautiful creature you ever saw in your life?' He pushed back his cap and looked at her without making any immediate answer. 'I do. Now tell me what you think.'

'I think that perhaps she is.'

'I knew you would say so. You are so honest that you could not bring yourself to tell a fib,—even to me about that. Come here and sit down for a moment. I want to speak to you.' Of course he sat down by her. 'You know,' she said, 'that Frank came to see me at Grex.'

'He never mentioned it.'

'Dear me;—how odd!'

'It was odd,' said he in a voice which showed that he was angry. She could hardly explain to herself why she told him this at the present moment. It came partly from jealousy, as though she had said to herself, 'Though he may neglect me, he shall know that there is someone who does not';—and partly from an eager half-angry feeling that she would have nothing concealed. For,—though there were moments with her in which she thought that she could do all things politically, that she could arrange her future life in accordance with certain wise rules over which her heart should have no influence,—there were others, many others, in which her feelings completely got the better of her. And now at this very moment she told herself that she would be afraid of nothing. There should be no deceit, no lies!

'He went to see you at Grex!' said Silverbridge.

'Why should he not have come to me at Grex?'

'Only it is so odd that he did not mention it. It seems to me that he is always having secrets with you of some kind.'

'Poor Frank! There is no one else who would come to see me at that tumble-down old place. He looks at it as a kind of pilgrimage, and pilgrimages are sacred;—not to be talked about to anyone.'

'I don't care, you know,' said he, not knowing very well what he meant.

'I don't suppose you do. But I have another thing to say to you. You have behaved badly to me.'

'Have I?'

'Yes, sir. After my folly about that ring you should have known better than to send it to me. You must take it back again.'

'You shall do exactly what you said you would. You shall give it to my wife,—when I have one.'

'That did all very well for me to say in a note. I did not want to send my anger to you over a distance of two or three hundred miles by the postman. But now that we are together you must take it back.'

'I will do no such thing,' said he sturdily.

'You speak as though this were a matter in which a man like you was to be allowed to have his own way.'

'I mean to have mine about that.'

'Any lady then must be forced to take any present that a gentleman may send her! Allow me to assure you that the usages of society do not run in that direction. Here is the ring. I knew that you would come over to see——; well, to see someone here, and I have kept it ready in my pocket.'

'I came over to see you.'

'Lord Silverbridge! But we know that in certain employments all things are fair.' He looked at her not knowing what were the employments to which she alluded. 'At any rate you will oblige me by—by—by not being troublesome, and putting this little trinket into your pocket.'

'Never! Nothing on earth shall make me do it.'

At Killancodlem they did not dine till half-past eight, in order, as the lady of the house said, that they might get as much out of the day as was possible. Twilight was now stealing on these two, who were still out in the garden, all the others having already gone in to dress. She looked round, however, to see that no other eyes were watching them as she still held the ring. 'It is there,' she said, putting it on the bench between them, where he would not touch it. Then she prepared to rise from the seat so that she might leave it with him.

But he was too quick for her, and was away at a distance before she had collected her dress. And from a distance he spoke again. 'If you choose that it shall be lost, so be it.'

'You had better take it,' said she, following him slowly. But he would not turn back;—nor would she. They met again in the hall for a moment. 'I should be sorry it should be lost,' said he, 'because it belonged to my great-uncle. And I had hoped that I might live to see it very often.'

'You can fetch it,' she said, as she went to her room. He however would not fetch it. She had accepted it, and he would not take it back again, let the fate of the gem be what it might.

But to her feminine and more cautious mind the very value of the trinket made its position out there on the bench, within the grasp of any dishonest gardener, a burden to her. She could not reconcile it to her conscience that it should be so left. The diamond was a large one, and she had heard it spoken of as a stone of great value,—so much so, that Silverbridge had been blamed for wearing it ordinarily. She had asked for it in joke, regarding it as a thing which could not be given away. She could not go down herself and take it up again; but neither could she allow it to remain. As she went to her room she met Mrs. Jones already coming from hers. 'You will keep us all waiting,' said the hostess.

'Oh no;—nobody ever dressed so quickly as I do. But, Mrs. Jones, will you do me a favour?'

'Certainly.'

'And will you let me explain something?'

'Anything you like,—from a hopeless engagement down to a broken garter.'

'I am suffering neither from one or the other. But there is a most valuable ring lying out in the garden. Will you send for it?' Then of course the story had to be told. 'You will, I hope, understand how I came to ask for it foolishly. It was because it was the one thing which I was sure he would not give away.'

'Why not take it?'

'Can't you understand? I wouldn't for the world. But you will be good enough,—won't you,—to see that there is nothing else in it?'

'Nothing of love?'

'Nothing in the least. He and I are excellent friends. We are cousins, and intimate, and all that. I thought I might have had my joke, and now I am punished for it. As for love, don't you see he is over head and ears in love with Miss Boncassen?'

'I wish it were so,' said the match-making old woman.

'Of course he is.' This was very imprudent on the part of Lady Mabel, who, had she been capable of clinging fast to her policy, would not now in a moment of strong feeling have done so much to raise obstacles in her own way. 'But you will send for it,—won't you; and have it put on his dressing-table to-night?' This Mrs. Jones promised to do. She even walked across the park herself before dinner, and picked up the ring, and ate her dinner with it safe in her pocket. That evening when he went to bed Lord Silverbridge found it on his table.

But before that time came he had twice danced with Miss Boncassen, Lady Mabel having refused to dance with him. 'No,' she said, 'I am angry with you. You ought to have felt that it did not become you as a gentleman to subject me to inconvenience by throwing upon me the charge of that diamond.' She would not any longer speak of it as a ring. 'You may be foolish enough to be indifferent about its value, but as you have mixed me up with it I cannot afford to have it lost.'

'It is yours.'

'No, sir; it is not mine; nor will it ever be mine. But I wish you to understand that you have offended me.' Then she persisted in refusing to dance with him.

This made him so unhappy for the time that he almost told the story to Miss Boncassen. 'If I were to give you a ring,' he said, 'would not you accept it?'

'What a question!' she said laughing.

'What I mean is don't you think all those conventional rules about men and women are very absurd?'

'As a progressive American of course I am bound to think all conventional rules are an abomination.'

'If you had a brother and I gave him a stick he'd take it.'

'Not across his back, I hope.'

'Or if I gave your father a book?'

'He'd take books to any extent, I should say; but I would not advise you, because he'd want to draw you into a learned correspondence about it.'

'And why not you a ring?'

'Who said I wouldn't? But after all this you mustn't try me.'

'I was not thinking of it.'

'I'm so glad of that! Well;—if you'll promise that you'll never offer me one, I'll promise that I'll take it when it comes. I can't say fairer than that;—can I? But what does all this mean?'

'It isn't worth talking about.'

'Of course you have offered somebody a ring and somebody hasn't taken it. May I guess?'

'I had rather you did not.'

'I could, you know. I shouldn't want to have a second try.'

'Never mind about that. Now come and have a turn. I am bound not to give you a ring. But you are bound to accept anything else I may offer.'

'No, Lord Silverbridge;—not at all. Nevertheless we'll have a turn.' And so they went off.

That night before he went up to his room he had told Isabel Boncassen that he loved her. And when he spoke he certainly was telling her the truth. It had seemed to him that Mabel had become hard to him, and had over and over again rejected the approaches to tenderness which he had attempted to make in his intercourse with her, and had meant him to understand that she could not love him. Even though she were to accept him, what would that be worth to him if she did not love him? So many things had been added together! Why had Tregear gone to Grex, and having gone there why had he kept his journey a secret?

Tregear he knew was engaged to his sister;—but for all that, there was a closer intimacy between Mabel and Tregear than between Mabel and himself. This also had distressed him. And surely she might have taken his ring!

And then Isabel Boncassen was so perfect in every respect! Since he had first met her he had heard her loveliness talked of on all sides. It seemed to be admitted everywhere that so beautiful a creature had never been seen in London before,—at any rate not by the eyes of men now living. There is ever a certain dignity attached to that which is praised by all lips. Miss Boncassen as an American girl,—had she been merely an American girl, and been judged to be beautiful only by his own eyes,—might perhaps have seemed to him to be beneath his serious notice. In such a case he might have felt that he could find no sufficient ground on which to justify so extraordinary a choice. But there was an acclamation of assent as to this girl which taught him to think unconsciously that to possess her would be to possess the best thing that was to be had. Then came the dancing,—the one dance after another; the pressure of the hand, the entreaty that she would not, just on this occasion, dance with any other man, the attendance on her when she took her glass of wine, the whispered encouragement of Mrs. Montacute Jones, the half-resisting and yet half-yielding conduct of the girl. 'I shall not dance at all again,' she said when he asked her to stand up for another. 'Think of all that lawn-tennis. I am so tired that I can hardly stand.'

'But you will play to-morrow?'

'I thought you were going.'

'Of course I shall stay now,' he said, and as he said it he put his hand on her hand, which was on his arm. She drew it away at once. 'I love you so dearly,' he whispered to her,—'so dearly.'

'Lord Silverbridge!'

'I do. I do. Can you say that you will love me in return?'

'I cannot,' she said slowly. 'Certainly not to-night. I have never dreamed of such a thing. I hardly know now whether you are in earnest.'

'Indeed, indeed I am.'

'Then I will say good-night, and think about it. Everybody is going. We will have our game to-morrow at any rate, if I am rested.'

When he went to his room he found the ring on his dressing-table, and as he put it away all regrets as to its return to him seemed to have vanished.

CHAPTER 40

'AND THEN?'

ON the next morning Miss Boncassen did not appear at breakfast,—a meal which at Killancodlem made its appearance between ten and eleven o'clock. Word came that she had been so fatigued by the lawn-tennis and by the dancing as not to be able to leave her bed. 'I have been to her,' said Mrs. Montacute Jones, whispering to Lord Silverbridge, as though he were particularly interested in the lady's health. 'There's nothing really the matter. She will be down to lunch.'

'I was afraid she might be ill,' said Silverbridge, who was now hardly anxious to hide his admiration from others.

'Oh no;—nothing of that sort; but she will not be able to play lawn-tennis again to-day. It was your fault. You should not have made her dance last night.' After that Mrs. Jones said a word about it all to Lady Mabel. 'I hope the Duke will not be angry with me.'

'Why should he be angry with you?'

'I don't suppose he will approve of it, and perhaps he'll say I brought them together on purpose. It's not my fault that Crummie-Toddie is only twelve miles from Killancodlem.'

Soon afterwards Mabel asked Silverbridge to walk with her to the waterfall. Of course he professed himself glad to go. She had worked herself into such a state of mind that she hardly knew what to do, what to wish, or how to act. At one moment she would tell herself that it was better in every respect that she should cease to think of being Duchess of Omnium. It was not fit that she should think of it. She herself cared but little for the young man, and he,—she would tell herself,—now appeared to care as little for her. Under such circumstances why should she want to catch him? And yet—to be Duchess of Omnium! But was it not clear to her that he was absolutely in love with this other girl? She had, at any rate, played her cards so badly that the game was now beyond her powers, even though she should wish to win it. But then there would come other thoughts. Was it beyond her powers? Had he not told her in London that he loved her? Had he not given her the ring which she well knew he valued beyond anything else? Had he not come over from the shooting on purpose to see her? For she thought she was aware that he had not known of Miss Boncassen's presence. Ah;—if she could but have been aware of all that had passed between Silverbridge and the Duke, how different would have been her feelings!

And then would it not be so much better for him that he should marry her, one of his own class, than this American girl, of whom nobody knew anything? Would it not be well that she should interfere, if only that she might free him from that entanglement? And then,—to be the daughter of the Duke of Omnium, to be the future Duchess, to escape from all the cares which her father's vices and follies had brought upon her, to have come to an end of all her troubles! Would it not be sweet? Thoughts such as these forced themselves upon her again and again.

But she had made her mind up to nothing when she asked him to walk up to the waterfall. There was present to her only the glimmer of an idea that she ought to caution him not to play with the American girl's feelings. She knew herself well enough to be aware that when the time for her own action came, let her make up her mind as firmly as she might to be strategetical, her feminine feelings would get the better of her purpose. She could not craftily bring him to the necessity of bestowing himself upon her. Had that been within the compass of her powers, opportunities had not been lacking to her. On such occasions she had always—'spared him,' as she had explained the matter to Miss Casseary. And should the opportunity come again, again she would spare him. She was in truth aware of that. But she might perhaps do some good,—not to herself, that was now out of the question,—but to him by showing him how wrong he was in trifling with this girl's feelings. In all of which, though she did not herself know it, there was a germ of spite against the girl.

And so they started for their walk. He of course would have avoided it had it been possible. When men in such matters have two strings to their bow,—a state of things which is not uncommon,—much inconvenience is felt when the two become entangled. Silverbridge no doubt had come over to Killancodlem for the sake of making love to Mabel Grex, and instead of doing so he had made love to Isabel Boncassen. And during the watches of the night, and as he had dressed himself in the morning, and while Mrs. Jones had been whispering to him her little bulletin as to the state of the young lady's health, he had not repented himself of the change. Though he had loved Mabel he had not found that making love to her was easy or pleasant. She had been, he thought, so little gracious to him that he would have given up that notion earlier, but for his indiscreet declaration to his father. On the other hand, making love to Isabel Boncassen seemed to him to possess some divine afflatus of joy which made it of all imaginable occupations the sweetest and most charming. She had promised him nothing. She had acceded to no request. She had admitted of no embrace. Indeed he had attempted none unless that touch of the hand might be so called, from which she had immediately withdrawn. Her conduct had been such that he had felt it to be incumbent on him, at the very moment, to justify the touch by a declaration of love. Then she had told him that she would not promise to love him in return. And yet it had been so sweet, so heavenly sweet!

During the morning he had almost forgotten Mabel. When Mrs. Jones told him that Isabel would keep her room, he longed to ask for leave to go and make some inquiry at the door. He did not quite dare to do this; but comforted himself by thinking that perhaps the message had come express from her to him. She would not play lawn-tennis with him. Well;—he did not now care much for that. There was a game better than lawn-tennis, at which perhaps she might be willing to play. After what he had said to her she must at any rate give him some answer. She had told him that she would think about it. She had been so gracious to him that his hopes ran very high. It never occurred to him to fancy that she might be still more gracious because he was heir to the Dukedom of Omnium. She herself was so infinitely superior to all wealth, to all rank, to all merely sublunary acquirements, conventions, and considerations, that there was no room for confidence of that nature. But he was confident because her smile had been so sweet, and her eyes so bright,—and because he was conscious, though unconsciously conscious, of something of the sympathy of love. In this condition of course he was not very anxious to go to the waterfall with Mabel.

But he had to go. The sweet things of the world must have become very common with him if he had not thought her sweet to look at when they started. Lady Mabel was always dressed perfectly,—having great gifts of her own in that direction. But there was a freshness about her which made her morning costume more charming than that of the evening, and never did she look so well as when arrayed for a walk. And on this occasion she had certainly done her best. But he, poor blind idiot, saw nothing of this. The white gauzy fabric which had covered Isabel's satin petticoat on the previous evening still filled his eyes. Those perfect boots, the little glimpses of parti-coloured stockings* above them, the looped-up skirt, the jacket fitting but never binding that lovely body and waist, the jaunty hat with its small fresh feathers, all were nothing to him. Nor was the bright honest face beneath the hat anything to him now;—for it was an honest face, though misfortunes which had come had somewhat marred the honesty of the heart.

At first the conversation was about indifferent things,—Killancodlem and the merits of Mrs. Jones, Crummie-Toddie and the tyranny of

Reginald Dobbes. They had gone along the high-road as far as the post-office, and had turned up through the wood and reached a seat whence there was a beautiful view down upon the Archay before a word was said affecting either Miss Boncassen, or the ring, or their own standing in reference to each other. 'You got the ring safe,' she said.

'Oh, yes.'

'How could you be so foolish as to risk it?'

'I did not regard it as mine. You had accepted it,—I thought.'

'But if I had, and then repented of my fault in doing so, should you not have been willing to help me in setting myself right with myself? Do you understand me?'

'I think I do.'

'I am sure you do. Of course, after what had passed, it was a trouble to me when it came. What was I to do? For a day or two I thought I would take it,—not as liking to take it, but as getting rid of the trouble in that way. Then I remembered its value, its history, the fact that all who knew you would want to know what had become of it,—and I felt that it should be given back. There is only one person to whom you must give it.'

'Who is that?' he said quickly.

'Your wife;—or to her who is to become your wife. No other woman can be justified in accepting such a present, nor would you be justified in giving it to any other woman.'

'There has been a great deal more said about it than it's worth,' said he, not anxious at the present moment to discuss any matrimonial projects with her. 'Shall we go on to the Fall?' Then she got up and led the way till they came to the little bridge looking over which they could see the Falls of the Codlem below them. 'I call that very pretty,' he said.

'I thought you would like it.'

'I never saw anything of that kind more jolly. Do you care for scenery, Mabel?'

'Very much. I know no pleasure equal to it. You have never seen Grex.'

'Is it like this?'

'Not in the least;—but it is very lovely, and I think I have got my taste for scenery from being there so much alone. It is wilder than this, and there are not so many trees; but to my eyes it is very beautiful. I wish you had seen it.'

'Perhaps I may some day.'

'That is not likely now,' she said. 'The house is in ruins, and nothing is ever done to it. If I had just money enough to keep it up for myself, I think I could live alone there and be always happy.'

'You;—alone. Of course you mean to marry.'

'Mean to marry! Do persons marry because they mean it? With nineteen men out of twenty the idea of marrying them would convey the idea of hating them,—almost of murdering them.'

'Dear me! How disagreeable for them!'

'You can mean to marry. No doubt you do mean it.'

'I suppose I shall,—some day. How very well the house looks from here.' It was incumbent upon him at the present moment to turn the conversation away from the matter of marrying.

But when she had a project in her head it was not so easy to turn her away. 'Yes, indeed,' she said;—'very well. But, as I was saying,—you can mean to marry.'

'Anybody can mean it.'

'Or mean not to do it. But you can carry out a purpose. What are you thinking of doing now?'

'Upon my honour, Mabel, that is unfair. A fellow shouldn't be cross-questioned.'

'Are we not friends?'

'I think so.'

'Dear friends?'

'I hope so.'

'Then may I not tell you what I think? If you do not mean to marry that American young lady you should not raise false hopes.'

'False—hopes!' He had hopes, but he had never thought that Isabel could have any.

'False hopes,—certainly. Do you not know that everyone was looking at you last night?'

'Certainly I do not.'

'And that that old woman is going about, talking of it as her doing, pretending to be afraid of your father's displeasure, whereas nothing would in truth please her better than to humble a family standing so high as yours.'

'Humble!' exclaimed Lord Silverbridge.

'Do you think your father would like it? Looking at it as though the same thing had occurred to any other young man in your own position, would you think that that other man would be doing well for himself by marrying Miss Boncassen?'

'I do,' said he energetically.

'Then you must be very much in love with her.'

'I say nothing about that.'

'If you are so much in love with her that you have resolved to face the displeasure of all your friends——'

'Why should anyone be displeased?'

'But you mean it?'

'I do not say what I mean. It is a sort of question which no man would answer. I could talk more freely to you than to anyone else, but I won't talk about that even to you. As regards Miss Boncassen I think that any man might marry her, let him be he who he might, without discredit. I won't have it said that she can be inferior to me,—or to anybody.'

There was a steady manliness in this which took Lady Mabel rather by surprise. She was of course convinced that he intended to offer his hand to the girl, and now was actuated chiefly by a feeling that his doing so would be an outrage to all English propriety. What could she do to prevent it? But if a word might have an effect it would be her duty to speak that word. 'I think you are wrong there, Lord Silverbridge.'

'I am sure I am right.'

'What have you yourself felt about your sister and Mr. Tregear?'

'It is altogether different,—altogether. Frank's wife will be simply his wife. Mine will be Lady Silverbridge,—and, should I outlive my father, will be Duchess of Omnium. She could not be more so, let her have been what she might before.'

'But your father? I have heard you speak with bitter regret of this affair of Lady Mary's, because it vexes your father. Would your marriage with an American lady vex him less?'

'Why should it vex him at all? Is she vulgar, or ill to look at, or stupid?'

'Think of her mother.'

'I am not going to marry her mother. Nor, for the matter of that,'—added he, remembering himself,—'am I going to marry her. You are taking all that for granted in a most unfair way.'

'How can I help it after what I saw yesterday?'

'You forget that she is an American, and not like one of us.'

'Indeed, indeed, I do not, Lord Silverbridge.'

'At any rate I will not talk any more about it. We had better go down or we shall get no lunch. It is two o'clock now.' Lady Mabel sighed as she followed him. She tried to make herself believe that all her sorrow came from regret that so fine a scion of the British nobility should throw himself away upon an American adventuress.

The guests were still at lunch when they entered the dining-room, and Isabel was seated close to Mrs. Jones. Silverbridge at once went up to her and asked after her health,—and place was made for him as though he had almost a right to be seated next to her. Miss Boncassen herself bore her honours very well, seeming to regard the little change at table as though it was of no moment. 'I became so eager about that game,' she said, 'that I went on too long. And then I could not bring myself to give up the dancing.'

'I hope you are now none the worse.'

'I'm just like a schoolboy who overeats himself. The boy is so strong that he probably is not much the worse. But the third helping and the pudding and the jelly and then the cakes ought to have killed him. At six o'clock this morning I thought I should never use my legs again.'

'Were you awake at six?' said Silverbridge, with pitying voice.

'That was it. I could not sleep. Now I begin to hope that sooner or later I shall unstiffen. But I won't play lawn-tennis again for a long time.'

During every moment, at every word that he uttered, he was thinking of the declaration of love which he had made to her. But it seemed to him as though the matter had not dwelt on her mind. When they drew their chairs away from the table he thought that not a moment was to be lost before some further explanation of their feelings for each other should be made. Was not the matter which had been so far discussed of vital importance for both of them? It was to him! He was sure of that. And, glorious as she was above all other women, the offer which he had made to her must have some weight with her. He did not think that he proposed to give more than she deserved, but still he could not but feel that that which he was so willing to give was not a little. Or was it possible that she had not understood his full meaning? If so, he would not willingly lose a moment before he made it plain to her. But she seemed content to hang about with the other women, and when they all sauntered out into the grounds she seated herself on a garden-chair with Lady Mabel, and, within his hearing,—as he stood by,—discussed with great eloquence the general beauty of Scotch scenery. An hour went on in this way before he could find his opportunity. Could it possibly be that she knew that he had offered to make her his wife? During this time he went away and returned more than once, but still she was there, on the same garden-seat, talking to Lady Mabel and to others who came in her way.

Then on a sudden she got up and put her hand on his arm. 'Come and take a turn with me,' she said. The motion was so unexpected that he felt his own awkwardness, his own inability to speak at ease, as he did as he was desired. 'Lord Silverbridge,' she said, 'do you remember anything of last night?'

'Remember!'

'I thought for a while this morning that I would let it all pass as though it had been mere trifling.'

'It would have wanted two to let it pass in that way,' he said, almost indignantly.

On hearing this she looked up at him, and there came over her face that brilliant smile, which to him was perhaps the most potent of her spells. 'What do you mean by—wanting two?'

'I must have a voice in that, as well as you.'

'And what is your voice?'

'My voice is this. I told you last night that I loved you. This morning I ask you to be my wife.'

'It is a very clear voice,' she said,—almost in a whisper; but in a tone so serious that it startled him.

'It ought to be clear,' he said doggedly.

'Do you think I don't know that? Do you think that if I liked you well last night, I don't like you better now?'

'But do you—like me?'

'That is just the thing I am going to say nothing about.'

'Isabel!'

'Just the one thing I will not allude to. Now you must listen to me.'

'Certainly.'

'I know a great deal about you. We Americans are an inquiring people, and I have found out pretty much everything.' His mind misgave him as he felt she had ascertained his former purpose respecting Mabel. 'You,' she said, 'among young men in England are about the foremost, and therefore,—as I think,—about the foremost in the world. Nothing can excel your rank and your wealth. And you have all personal gifts;—youth and spirits and——; well, I will not go on and name the others. You are, no doubt, supposed to be entitled to the best and sweetest of God's feminine creatures.'

'You are she.'

'Whether you be entitled to me or not I cannot yet say. Now I will tell you something of myself. My father's father came to New York as a labourer from Holland and worked upon the quays in that city. Then he built houses, and became rich, and was almost a miser;—with the good sense, however, to educate his only son. What my father is you see. To me he is sterling gold, but he is not like your people. My dear mother is not at all like your ladies. She is not a lady in your sense,—though, with her unselfish devotion to others she is something infinitely better. For myself I am,—well, meaning to speak honestly I will call myself pretty and smart. I think I know how to be true.'

'I am sure you do.'

'But what right have you to suppose I shall know how to be a duchess?'

'I am sure you will.'

'Now listen to me. Go to your friends and ask them. Ask that Lady Mabel;—ask your father;—ask that Lady Cantrip. And above all ask yourself. And allow me to require you to take three months to do this. Do not come to see me for three months.'

'And then?'

'What may happen then I cannot tell, for I want three months also to think of it myself. Till then, good-bye. And, remember this;—if you change your mind, as I think you ought to do, no one will impute blame to you.' She gave him her hand and left it in his for a few seconds. He tried to draw her to him; but she resisted him, still smiling. Then she left him, and when on the following morning he went back to Crummie-Toddie there had not been another word between them.

CHAPTER 41

ISCHL

It may be remembered that the Duke of Omnium did at last find himself compelled by a sense of honour to write a letter of apology to Mrs. Finn in reference to his erroneous and too plainly expressed opinion of her conduct. The apology had not been very ample, but nevertheless the writing of it had been terribly bitter to him. There had been that between them which made the writing of such a letter more painful than it would have been to almost anyone else. There had been obligations between them, but they had all flowed from her to him and his. He had had many doubts respecting her,—regretting, when he so doubted, the intimacy which circumstances had created. Then his doubts would recede, and at such times he had endeavoured to open his heart to her. Now, on this occasion, he had not only doubted but had felt certain,—and had allowed this certainty to work within him to the expression of a most heavy accusation. To whom in such circumstances would not the necessity for an apology be most bitter? But to no one could it be more bitter than to him! He had, however, written it,—not with a free hand or a free heart, but with such thoroughness as his feelings in the moment made possible to him.

She, when she received it, had been contented, acknowledging to herself how great the effort to him must have been. Had she, indeed, so sinned against a friend, she would have knelt at that friend's feet and implored forgiveness in sackcloth and ashes; but she could not expect that from such a nature as his. Nor did she wish it. At the first moment she told herself that the Duke's letter sufficed. Anything like intimate friendship must of course be over. She had said as much as that in her letter to him. Such thoughts as he had entertained respecting her, and such a feeling of injury as had been hot in her bosom, were not compatible with renewed friendship. And the Duchess, whom she had really loved and who had really loved her, was gone. The Duke had apologised, and there might well be an end of everything between them. But when, as the season rolled on and she knew that he was living in town,—when she was aware that he had resumed his duties in the House of Lords, and was again spoken of as likely to take a part in some new Liberal Ministry,—when he had as it were thus come back to the world, and yet had never paid her the compliment of leaving a card at her door, then she again became sore and told herself that the man's nature had been altered by those three years of ministerial power.

When the apology had reached her, so that there was no longer any ground for absolute quarrel, then she had told the whole story to her husband. He at first was very indignant. What right had the Duke to expect that any ordinary friend should act duenna over his daughter in accordance with his caprices? This was said and much more of the kind. But any humour towards quarrelling which Phineas Finn might have felt for a day or two was quieted by his wife's prudence. A man, she said, can do no more than apologise. After that there is no room even for reproach. Former relations need not be re-established. This she said alluding to those former relations which had been so close between herself and the Duchess. But the affair must not be allowed to have any bearing on political matters,—as to which it would be monstrous, she declared, if the public service were made to suffer by reason of private bickerings. She spoke so well that there was no possibility of an answer. But, through the entire session, he was averse to meeting the Duke;—and she too was indignant though her indignation was hidden.

After a while there came to be a tacit agreement between them that nothing should be said about the Duke, and for many weeks neither the Duke's name nor that of Lady Mary was mentioned between them. It was her custom almost every autumn to go off to Vienna, where she possessed considerable property, and there to inspect the circumstances of her estate. Sometimes her husband would accompany her, and he did so on this occasion. One morning in September they were together at an hotel at Ischl,* whither they had come from Vienna, when as they went through the hall into the courtyard to get into a carriage, they came, in the very doorway, upon the Duke of Omnium and his daughter.

The Duke and Lady Mary had just arrived, having passed through the mountains from the salt-mine district, and were about to take up their residence in the hotel for a few days. They had travelled very slowly, for Lady Mary had been ill, and the Duke had expressed his determination to see a doctor at Ischl.

There is no greater mistake than in supposing that only the young blush. But the blushes of middle-life are luckily not seen through the tan which has come from the sun and the gas and the work and the wiles of the world. Both the Duke and Phineas blushed; and though their blushes were hidden, that peculiar glance of the eye which always accompanies a blush was visible enough from one to the other. The elder lady kept her countenance admirably, and the younger one had no occasion for blushing. She at once ran forward and kissed her friend, who received her embraces with admirable grace. The Duke stood with his hat off waiting to give his hand to the lady, and then with apparent cordiality took that of his late colleague. 'How odd that we should meet here,' he said, turning to Mrs. Finn.

'Odd enough to us that your Grace should be here,' she said, 'because we had heard nothing of your intended coming. I am here nearly every year.'

'It is so nice to find you,' said Lady Mary. 'We are this moment come. Don't say that you are this moment going.'

'At this moment we are only going as far as Halstadt.'

'And are coming back to dinner? Of course they will dine with us. Will they not, papa?' The Duke said that he hoped they would. To declare that you are engaged at an hotel, unless there be some real engagement, is almost an impossibility. Phineas would have avoided it if he could, for anger still rankled in his heart. She would not willingly have put herself in the way of them; but accident had now done all that. There was no escape, and before they were allowed to get into their carriage they had promised they would dine with the Duke and his daughter.

'I don't know that it is especially a bore,' Mrs. Finn said to her husband in the carriage. 'You may be quite sure of this,—that of whatever trouble there may be in it all, he has much more than his share.'

'His share should be the whole,' said her husband. 'No one else has done anything wrong.'

At dinner the conversation turned at first on British politics, in which Mrs. Finn was quite able to take her part. Phineas was decidedly of opinion that Sir Timothy Beeswax and Lord Drummond could not live another session. 'In the first place,' said he, 'Beeswax himself is determined to break up everything unless he be put at the head of affairs.'

'How is he to do that? They can't dismiss Drummond like a drunken butler.'

'Not like a drunken butler,—but after another fashion.'

'What fashion?' asked the Duke.

'If they were all to resign now, and then we were to fail,—as we might fail——'

'I think we should.'

'Then they would be recalled in a different form. In such an event Sir Timothy might make his demands. He could hardly do so without a crisis of some sort.'

'And he would bring about the crisis with such an object?' asked Mrs. Finn.

'He is clever enough for anything.'

'Do you call that cleverness, Mr. Finn?' said the Duke.

'I call it something else also,—of course. But really, Duke, we are getting so used to that something else that it need hardly surprise us. It is a game of chess in which though three or four may play on the same side one will want to have all the honour of winning the game.'

'If it be so, then it has become a work no longer fit for gentlemen.'

'If the gentlemen desert it what will become of the country? No, Duke; you, I think, will be the last man in England to agree to an idea that the honest men ought to run away from the rogues. If the honest men will only be sufficiently alive to their duty then the rogues will not have a chance.'

'But you tell me that in this Sir Timothy will prevail.'

'I have not even said that. I think he will fail. But if he does prevail it will be because the second-class men of his party, who are in fact the aristocracy of the country——'

'A part of the aristocracy, Mr. Finn.'

'Because they have been too idle to restrain the ambition of a partisan whose diligence has saved them so much trouble. To a fainéant politician,—to one who, though he has all his heart in it, has too many delights in the world or too large a stake of his own to be able to devote himself to party purposes,—such a man as Sir Timothy is a great godsend. It is like having a steward who can manage everything for you. Though you see him growing rich, too rich, you do not begrudge him his plunder because he is such a comfort! I can imagine that there are some to whom Sir Timothy is very comfortable, though I hardly think that Lord Drummond be one of them.'

Later in the evening the Duke found himself sitting with Mrs. Finn in the broad verandah over the hotel garden, while Lady Mary was playing to Phineas within. 'How do you think she is looking?' asked the father.

'Of course I see that she has been ill. She tells me that she was far from well at Salzburg.'

'Yes, indeed. For three or four days she frightened me much. She suffered terribly from headaches.'

'Nervous headaches?'

'So they said there. I feel quite angry with myself because I did not bring a doctor with us. The trouble and ceremony of such an accompaniment is no doubt disagreeable.'

'And I suppose seemed when you started to be quite unnecessary.'

'Quite unnecessary!'

'Does she complain again now?'

'She did to-day,—a little. And she is so good about it that she will hardly speak till she is driven to show that she is suffering.'

The next morning Lady Mary could not leave her bed; and the Duke in his sorrow was obliged to apply to Mrs. Finn. After what had passed on the previous day Mrs. Finn of course called, and was shown at once up to her young friend's room. There she found the girl in great pain, lying with her two thin hands up to her head, and hardly able to utter more than a word. Shortly after that Mrs. Finn was alone with the Duke, and then there took place a conversation between them which the lady thought to be very remarkable.

'Had I better send for a doctor from England?' he asked. In answer to this Mrs. Finn expressed her opinion that such a measure was hardly necessary, that the gentleman from the town who had been called in seemed to know what he was about very well, and that the illness, lamentable as it was, did not seem to be in any way dangerous. 'One cannot tell what it comes from,' said the Duke dubiously,—almost meaning to imply that though 'one' might not tell absolutely, 'one' might be able to make a very shrewd guess.

'Young people, I fancy, are often subject to such maladies.'

'I don't know why they should be. It must come from something wrong.'

'That may be said of all sickness.'

'And therefore one tries to find out the cause. She says that she is unhappy.' These last words he spoke slowly and in a very low voice. To this Mrs. Finn could make no reply. She did not doubt but that the girl was unhappy, and she knew well why; but the source of Lady Mary's misery was one to which she could not very well allude. 'You know all the misery about that young man.'

'That is a trouble that requires much time to cure it,' she said,—not meaning to imply that time would cure it by enabling the girl to forget her lover; but because in truth she had not known what else to say.

'If time will cure it!'

'Time they say cures all sorrows.'

'But what should I do to help time? There is no sacrifice I would not make;—no sacrifice! Of myself I mean! I would devote myself to her,— leave everything else on one side. We purpose being back in England in October; but I would remain here if I thought it better for her comfort.'

'I cannot tell, Duke.'

'Neither can I. But you are a woman and might know better than I do. It is so hard that a man should be left with a charge, of which from its very nature and from his own he cannot understand the duties.' Then he paused, but she, though she taxed herself hard for words to say, could find none which would suit at the moment. It was almost incredible to her that after what had passed he should speak to her at all as to the condition of his daughter. 'I cannot, you know,' he said very seriously, 'encourage a hope that she should be allowed to marry that man.'

'I do not know.'

'You yourself, Mrs. Finn, felt that when she told you about it at Matching.'

'I felt that you would certainly disapprove of it.'

'Disapprove of it! How could it be otherwise? Of course you felt that. If there is to be any propriety in such things, any law, any restraint, I could not but disapprove of it. There are ranks in life in which the first comer that suits a maiden's eye may be accepted as a fitting lover. I will not say but that they who are born to such a life as that may be the happier. They are, I am sure, free from many troubles to which they are incident whom fate has called to a different sphere. But duty is— duty;—and whatever pangs it may cost, duty should be performed. Is it not so, Mrs. Finn?'

'Certainly.'

'Certainly;—certainly; certainly,' he said, re-echoing her word as though he found some comfort in doing so.

'But then, Duke, one has to be so sure what duty requires. In many matters this is easy enough, and the only difficulty comes from temptation. One goes astray because to go astray is pleasant. But there are cases in which it is so hard to know.'

'Is this one of them?'

'I think so.'

'Then the maiden should—in any class of life—be allowed to take the man—that just suits her eye?' As he said this his mind was intent on his Glencora and on Burgo Fitzgerald.

'I have not said so. A man may be bad, vicious, a spendthrift,—eaten up by bad habits.' Then he frowned, thinking that she also had her mind intent on his Glencora and on that Burgo Fitzgerald, and being most unwilling to have the difference between Burgo and Frank Tregear pointed out to him. 'Nor have I said,' she continued, 'that even were none of these faults apparent in the character of a suitor, the lady should in all cases be advised to accept a young man because he has made himself agreeable to her. There may be discrepancies.'

'There are,' said he, still with a low voice but with infinite energy,— 'insurmountable as those which kept Lazarus apart from the rich man.'* It was an odd illustration for him to use, but it is certain that he did not intend to signify himself or his daughter by the rich man.

'I only said that this was a case in which it might be difficult for you to see your duty plainly.'

'Why should it be?'

'You would not have her—break her heart.' Then he was silent for a while, turning over in his mind the proposition in all its hardness which now seemed to have been made to him. If the question came to that,—should she be allowed to break her heart and die, or should he save her from that fate by sanctioning her marriage with Tregear? If the choice could be put to him plainly by some supernal power whose word in putting it he could not doubt, what then would he choose? If duty required him to prevent this marriage, his duty could not be altered by the fact that his girl would avenge herself upon him by dying! If such a marriage were in itself wrong, that wrong could not be made right by the fear of such a catastrophe as was now presented to his mind. Was it not often the case that duty required that someone should die? And yet as he thought of it,—thought that the someone whom his mind had suggested to itself was the one female creature now left belonging to him,—he put his hand up to his brow and trembled with agony. He had to tell himself that duty could not carry him as far as that. If he knew, if in truth he believed that such would be the result of firmness on his part,—then he would be infirm, then he must yield. Sooner than that, he must welcome this Tregear to his house. But why should he think that she would die? This woman had now asked him whether he would be willing to break his girl's heart. It was a frightful question; but he could see that it had come naturally in the sequence of the conversation which he had forced upon her. But why should the girl's heart be broken? Did girls break their hearts in such emergencies? Was it not all romance? 'Men have died and worms have eaten them,—but not for love.'* He remembered it all and carried on the argument in his mind, though the pause was but for a minute. There might be suffering no doubt, and in such matters there must be suffering. Who could hope to live and not suffer? The higher the duties the keener the pangs! But would it become him to be deterred from doing right because she for a time might find that she had made the world bitter to herself? And were there not feminine wiles,—tricks by which women learn to have their way in opposition to the experience and judgment of their lords and masters? He did not think that his Mary was or could be wilfully guilty of any dishonest scheme. The suffering he knew was true suffering. But not the less did it become him to be on his guard against attacks of this nature. How weak would he think another man who should yield in such a case because a girl had a headache!

'No,' he said at last; 'I would not have her break her heart,—if I understand what such words mean. They are generally, I think, used fantastically.'

'You would not wish to see her overwhelmed by continued sorrow?'

'Wish it! What a question to ask a father!'

'I must be more plain in my language, Duke. Though such a marriage be distasteful to you it might perhaps be preferable to seeing her sorrowing always.'

'Why should it? I have to sorrow always. We are told that man is born to sorrow as surely as the sparks fly upwards.'

'Then I can say nothing further.'

'You think I am cruel.'

'If I am to say what I really think I shall offend you.'

'No;—not unless you mean offence.'

'I shall never do that to you, Duke. When you talk as you do now you hardly know yourself. You think you could see her suffering and not be moved by it. But were it to be continued long you would give way. Though we know that there is an infinity of grief in this life, still we struggle to save those we love from grieving. If she be steadfast enough to cling to her affection for this man, if she be of a nature so little prone to change as not to be driven off from it either by absence or by her submission to you, then, at last, you will have to yield.' He looked at her frowning, but did not say a word. 'Then it will perhaps be a comfort for you to know that the man himself is good and trustworthy and honest.'

There was a terrible rebuke in this; but still, as he had called it down upon himself, he would not resent it, even in his heart. 'Thank you,' he said, rising from his chair. 'Perhaps you will see her again this afternoon.' Of course she assented, and as the interview had taken place in his rooms she took her leave. She felt that she was turned out; but, as he had bidden her come again to Lady Mary, this could not have been done in anger.

'Of course I will,' she said, 'and if I can be of service pray command me. Our time is quite our own.'

Then he was left alone. This which Mrs. Finn had said to him was all to the same effect as that which had come from Lady Cantrip; only it was said with a higher spirit and a stronger assurance. Both the women saw the matter in the same light. There must be a fight between him and his girl; but she, if she could hold out for a certain time, would certainly be the conqueror. He might take her away and try what absence would do, or he might have recourse to that specific which had answered so well in reference to his own wife, and put another lover in her way; but if she continued to sorrow during absence, and if she would have nothing to do with this other lover,—then he must at last give way! He had declared that he was willing to sacrifice himself,—meaning thereby that if it were thought that a lengthened visit to the cities of China or a prolonged sojourn in the Western States of America would wean her from her lover, he would go to China or to the Western States, clearly bound as his heart might be to the Houses of Parliament at Westminster. At present his self-banishment had been carried no farther than Vienna and had not hitherto achieved anything. During their travels hitherto Tregear's name had not once been mentioned. The Duke had come away from home resolved not to mention it,—and she was minded to keep it in reserve till some seeming catastrophe should justify a full declaration of her settled purpose. But from first to last she had been sad, and latterly she had been ill. When asked as to her complaint she would simply say that she was not happy. To go on with this through the Chinese cities could hardly be good for either of them. She would not wake herself to any enthusiasm either in regard to scenery, costumes, habits, pictures, or even discomforts. Wherever she was taken it was all barren to her. Even her little burst of pleasure at seeing Mrs. Finn only seemed to have been something gained.

As their plans stood at present they were to return to England so as to enable her to be at Custins by the middle of October. Had he taught himself to believe or even to hope that any good could be done by prolonged travelling he would readily have thrown over Custins and Lord

Popplecourt. He could not bring himself to trust much to the Popplecourt scheme. He almost felt that he should despise his girl if she fell
into the Popplecourt trap. But the same contrivance had answered on
that former occasion. And now he did not know what else to do. When
he spoke to her about their plans, she expressed herself quite ready to
go back to England. When he suggested those Chinese cities, her face
became very long and she was immediately attacked by paroxysms of
headache.

'I think I should take her to some place on the seashore in England,'
said Mrs. Finn.

'Custins is close to the sea,' he replied. 'I am told you can see it from
the house.' Mrs. Finn however had never heard of Custins, or had forgotten it. 'It is Lord Cantrip's place in Dorsetshire. It was partly settled
that she was to go there.'

'I suppose she likes Lady Cantrip.'

'Why should she not? No one could possibly have been more kind
to her.'

'She has not said a word to me to the contrary. I only fear she would
feel that she was being sent there,—as to a convent.'

'A convent! The house will be full of people.'

'As being out of the way.'

'What ought I to do then?'

'How can I venture to answer that? What she would like best I think
would be to return to Matching with you, and to settle down in a quiet
way for the winter.' The Duke shook his head. That would be worse
even than travelling abroad. She would still have headaches and still tell
him that she was unhappy, till in some outburst of womanly pity he
would himself feel disposed to send for the objectionable lover. 'Of
course I do not know what your plans are, and pray believe me that
I should not obtrude my advice if you did not ask me.'

'I know it,' he said. 'I know it. I know how good you are and how reasonable. I know how much I owe you, and how much you have to forgive.'

'Oh, no.'

'And if I have not said so as I should have done it has not been from
want of feeling. I do believe you did what you thought best when Mary
told you that story at Matching.'

'I did what was best.' There was a self-assurance about this which
startled him, but he soon recovered himself. 'The object being,' continued she, 'to place the whole matter as it really stood within your
knowledge as quickly as possible. But why should your Grace go back
to that?'

'Only that I may acknowledge my indebtedness to you, and say to you somewhat fuller than I could do in my letter that I am sorry for the pain which I gave you.'

'All that is over now,—and shall be forgotten.'

Then he spoke of his immediate plans. He would at once go back to England by slow stages,—by very slow stages,—staying a day or two at Salzburg, at Ratisbon, at Nuremberg, at Frankfort, and so on. In this way he would reach England about the 10th of October, and Mary would then be ready to go to Custins by the time appointed. This, however, must depend in some degree on her health, as at this moment she was still lying ill in her bed. The Finns when they heard all this determined to stay another fortnight at Ischl, as, notwithstanding their renewed intimacy with the Duke, they did not wish to join his party on their return home.

In a day or two Lady Mary was better,—or, as she declared herself, quite well. 'It is terrible while it lasts,' she said, speaking to Mrs. Finn of her headache, 'but when it has gone, then I am quite well. Only,'—she added after a pause,—'only I can never be happy again while papa thinks as he does now.' Then there was a party made up before they separated for an excursion to the Hintersee and the Obersee, two most lovely little lakes within a drive of Ischl,—within a drive, that is, if the carriage be supplemented by ponies for the mountain track. On this occasion Lady Mary seemed to enjoy herself, and in truth she did so, as she liked the companionship of Mrs. Finn. Against Lady Cantrip she never said a word,—nor could she have said a word with reason. But Lady Cantrip was always a duenna to her, whereas Mrs. Finn was a friend. While the Duke and Phineas were discussing politics together, thoroughly enjoying the weakness of Lord Drummond, the iniquity of Sir Timothy, and the vanity of Sir Orlando Drought, which they did with augmented vehemence from their ponies' backs, the two women in lower voices talked over their own affairs. 'I dare say you will be happy at Custins,' said Mrs. Finn.

'No; I shall not. There will be people there whom I don't know, and I don't want to know. Have you heard anything about him, Mrs. Finn?'

Mrs. Finn turned round and looked at her,—for a moment almost angrily. Then her heart relented. 'Do you mean—Mr. Tregear?'

'Yes,—Mr. Tregear.'

'I think I heard that he was shooting with Lord Silverbridge.'

'I am glad of that,' said Mary.

'It will be pleasant for both of them.'

'I am very glad they should be together. While I know that, I feel that we are not altogether separated. I will never give it up, Mrs. Finn,—never; never. It is no use taking me to China.' In that Mrs. Finn quite agreed with her.

The Duke was so pleasantly excited by the political views expressed by Phineas that he proposed that they should all travel back home together and offered to wait a day or two;—but of this project both Mr. and Mrs. Finn entertained some fears; and it was not carried out.

CHAPTER 42

AGAIN AT KILLANCODLEM

SILVERBRIDGE stayed a couple of days at Killancodlem and then, as we know, went back to Crummie-Toddie. There he remained under the dominion of Reginald Dobbes till the second week of September. Popplecourt, Nidderdale, and Gerald Palliser were there all the time, very obedient, and upon the whole very efficient. Tregear, who when he was there shot well, was intractable, occasional, and untrustworthy. He was the cause of much trouble and of very angry words to Mr. Dobbes,—which however were seldom spoken before his face. He would entertain a most heterodox and injurious idea that as he had come to Crummie-Toddie for amusement, he was not bound to do anything that did not amuse him. He could not be made to understand that in sport as in other matters there was an ambition, driving a man on to excel always and be ahead of others. This was a great vexation to Mr. Dobbes,—but still he had cause for much triumph. It was going to be, he had just ground for thinking, the greatest thing ever done by six guns in Scotland. As for Gerald, whom he had first regarded as a boy, and who had offended him by saying that Crummie-Toddie was ugly,—he was ready to go round the world for him. He had thoroughly indoctrinated Gerald with all his ideas of a sportsman,—even to a contempt for champagne and a conviction that tobacco should be moderated. The three Lords too had proved themselves efficient guns, and the thing was going to be a success. But just when a day was of such vital importance, when it was absolutely essential that there should be a strong party for a drive, Silverbridge found it absolutely necessary that he should go over to Killancodlem.

'She has gone,' said Nidderdale. The whole party was prepared to join with Reginald Dobbes in his remonstrance.

'Who the —— is "she?" ' asked Silverbridge almost angrily.

'Everybody knows who "she" is,' said Popplecourt.

'It will be a good thing when some "she" has got hold of you, my boy, so as to keep you in your proper place.'

'If you cannot withstand that sort of attraction you ought not to go in for shooting at all,' said Dobbes.

'Attraction be ——! I've been here for a fortnight without speaking to a soul but one of you fellows and haven't seen a meal on the table fit for a Christian to sit down to.'

'I never had better grub in my life,' said Gerald.

'I suppose you'd like to have a French cook,' said Dobbes.

'I shouldn't wonder at his going,' continued Nidderdale, 'if we didn't all know that the American is no longer there. Of course we understand that attraction;—but she has gone to—Bath I think they say.'

'I suppose it's Mrs. Jones herself,' said Popplecourt.

'My dear boys,' said Silverbridge, 'you may be quite sure that when I say that I am going to Killancodlem I mean to go to Killancodlem and that no confounded chaff about young ladies,—which I think very disgusting,—will stop me. I shall be sorry if Dobbes's roll of the killed should be lessened by a single head, seeing that his ambition sets that way. Considering the amount of slaughter we have perpetrated, I really think that we need not be so over-anxious.' After this nothing further was said. Tregear, who knew that Mabel Grex was still at Killancodlem, had not spoken.

In truth Mabel had sent for Lord Silverbridge, and this had been her letter:

'DEAR LORD SILVERBRIDGE,

'Mrs. Montacute Jones is cut to the heart because you have not been over to see her again and she says that it is lamentable to think that such a man as Reginald Dobbes should have so much power over you. "Only twelve miles," she says, "and he knows that we are here!" I told her that you knew Miss Boncassen was not here and that she had no right to expect you to come again.

'But though Miss Boncassen has left us we are a very pleasant party and surely you must be tired of such a place as Crummie-Toddie, with Mr. Reginald Dobbes for tyrant. If only for the sake of getting a good dinner once in a way do come over again. I shall be here yet for ten days. As they will not let me go back to Grex I don't know where I could be more happy. I have been asked to go to Custins and suppose I shall turn up there some time in the autumn.

'And now shall I tell you what I expect? I do expect that you will come over to—see me. "I did see her the other day," you will say, "and she did not make herself very pleasant." I know that. How was I to make myself pleasant when I found myself so completely snuffed out by your American beauty? Now she is away, and Richard will be himself again.* Do come because in truth I want to see you.

'Yours always sincerely,
'MABEL GREX.'

On receiving this he at once made up his mind to go to Killancodlem, but he could not make up his mind why it was that she had asked him. He thought he was sure of two things; sure in the first place that she had intended to let him know that she did not care about him; and then sure that she was well aware of his intention in regard to Miss Boncassen. She had absolutely told him that she was aware of it, and he had almost told her that she was right. Everybody at Killancodlem had seen it,—to his disgust; but still that it was so had been manifest to him. And he had consoled himself by saying that it would matter nothing should he be accepted. She had made one attempt to talk him out of his purpose. Could it be that she thought it possible a second attempt might be successful? If so, she did not know him.

She had in truth thought not only that this, but that something also further than this might be possible. Or rather she had buoyed herself with hopes in that direction in opposition to her thoughts. Of course the prize loomed larger before her eyes as the prospects of obtaining it became less. When alone at Grex she had thought much of her own condition and her prospects. She could not doubt,—did not in the least doubt that he had intended to offer her his hand when he had spoken to her of his love in London. Then she had stopped him,—she hardly knew why; had 'spared him,' as she had told her friend Miss Cassewary. Certainly she had then been swayed by some feeling that it would be ungenerous in her to seize greedily the first opportunity he had given her. But he had again made an effort. He surely would not have sent her the ring had he not intended her to regard him as her lover. When she received the ring, though she was half ashamed of the mock request which she had herself made, her heart had beat very high. Then she had sent that little note, saying that she would keep it till she could give it to his wife. When she wrote that, she had certainly intended that the ring should be her own. And then other things pressed upon her mind. Why had she been asked to the dinner at Richmond? Why was she invited to Custins? Little hints had reached her,—had reached her even from Silverbridge himself,—of the Duke's good-will towards her. If on that side the marriage were approved, why should she by her folly destroy her own hopes?

Then she had seen him with Miss Boncassen, and in her pique had forced the ring back upon him. During that long game on the lawn her feelings had been sad rather than very bitter. Of course the girl was the lovelier of the two. All the world was raving of her beauty. And there was no doubt as to the charm of her wit and manner. And then she had no touch of that blasé used-up way of life of which Lady Mabel was conscious herself. It was natural that it should be so. And was she, Mabel Grex, the girl to stand in his way and to force herself upon him, if he loved another? Certainly not,—though there might be a triple ducal coronet to be had. So she forced the ring back upon him.

But were there not other considerations? Could it be well that the heir of the house of Omnium should marry an American girl, as to whose humble birth whispers were already being uttered? As his friend,—for she was his friend,—would it not be right that she should tell him what the world would say? As his friend, therefore, she had given him her counsel;—but with very little avail.

When he was gone the whole thing as it came nearer to herself weighed heavily upon her mind. Why should she lose the prize if it might still be won? To be Duchess of Omnium! She had read of many of the other sex and of one or two of her own who by settled resolution had achieved greatness in opposition to all obstacles. Was this thing altogether beyond her reach? To hunt him, and catch him, and marry him to his own injury,—that would be impossible to her. Not for any reward, not for any prize, would she treat him after that fashion. She was sure of herself there. But how infinitely better would this be for him! Would she not have all his family with her,—and all the world of England? In how short a time would he not repent his marriage with Miss Boncassen? Whereas, were she his wife, she would so stir herself for his joys, for his good, for his improvement, for his honour, that there should be no possibility of repentance. And he certainly had loved her. Loved her! Why else had he followed her, and spoken such words to her? Of course he had loved her! But then there had come this blaze of beauty and had carried off,—not his heart, but his imagination. Because he had yielded to such fascination, fascination from which no man can altogether escape, was she to desert him, and also to desert herself? From day to day she thought of it, and then she wrote that letter. She hardly knew what she would do, what she might say; but she would trust to the opportunity to do and say something. She was successful at any rate in bringing him to Killancodlem.

'If you have no room for me,' he said to Mrs. Jones, 'you must scold Lady Mab. She has told me that you told her to invite me.'

'Of course I did. Do you think I would not go and sleep in the stables myself and give you up my bed if there were no other rooms? It is so good of you to come!'

'So good of you, Mrs. Jones, to ask me.'

'So very kind to come when all the attraction has gone.' Then he blushed and stammered, and was just able to say that his only object in life was to pour out his adoration at the feet of Mrs. Montacute Jones herself.

Soon afterwards the man in knickerbockers who had made one of the party at lawn-tennis accosted him. 'I'm afraid we shan't make up such a game as we had when you were here before.'

'I've had enough of that for this year,' said Silverbridge.

'Yes;—certainly. That's just what I feel. Only if Miss Boncassen were here——' Then Lord Silverbridge turned on his heel and would not speak to the man in knickerbockers again.

There was also there a certain Lady Fawn,—a pretty mincing married woman of about twenty-five, with a husband much older, who liked very mild flirtations with very mild young men. 'I am afraid we've lost your great attraction,' she whispered to him.

'Certainly not as long as Lady Fawn is here,' he said, seating himself close to her on a garden-bench, and seizing suddenly hold of her hand. She gave a little scream and a jerk, and so relieved herself from him. 'You see,' said he, 'people do make such mistakes about a man's feelings.'

'Lord Silverbridge!'

'It's quite true, but I'll tell you all about it another time,' and so he left her. All these little troubles, his experience in the 'House,' the necessity of snubbing Tifto, the choice of a wife, and his battle with Reginald Dobbes, were giving him by degrees age and flavour. There are affairs in life which ripen a man's wits abnormally, as a journey to Calcutta will ripen a hogshead of sherry. He certainly did not like having Miss Boncassen thrown at his head by everybody that spoke to him.

Lady Mabel had fluttered about him on his first coming, and had been very gracious, doing the part of an old friend,—of one intimate enough to be able to express her joy at seeing a friend. 'There is to be a big shooting to-morrow,' she said, in presence of Mrs. Jones.

'If it is to come to that,' he said, 'I might as well go back to Dobbesdom.'*

'What a glorious new word,' exclaimed Mrs. Jones.

'You may shoot if you like,' said Lady Mabel, explaining.

'I haven't even brought a gun with me.'

'Then we'll have a walk,—a whole lot of us,' she said. 'Can't we make up a sort of picnic, Mrs. Jones?'

This, however, was not practicable, as the other men were going to shoot; but there remained with them the idea that on the following day there was to be a walk in some direction among the mountains.

In the evening, about an hour before dinner, Silverbridge and Lady Mabel were seated together on the bank of a little stream which ran on the other side of the road from the house, but on a spot not more than a furlong from the hall-door. She no doubt had brought him there, but she had done so without any definite scheme. She had made no plan of campaign for the evening, having felt relieved when she found herself able to postpone the project of her attack till the morrow. Of course there must be an attack, but how it should be made she had never had the courage to tell herself. The great women of the world, the Semiramises, the Pocahontases, the Ida Pfeiffers, and the Charlotte Cordays,* had never been wanting to themselves when the moment for action came. Now, at this very time, she was pleased to have this opportunity added to her, this pleasant minute in which some soft preparatory word might be spoken; but the great effort should be made on the morrow.

'Is not this nicer than shooting with Mr. Dobbes?' she asked.

'A great deal nicer. Of course I am bound to say so.'

'But in truth! I want to find out what you really like. Men are so different! Of course you need not pay me any compliment. You know that well enough.'

'I like you better than Dobbes,—if you mean that.'

'Even so much is something.'

'But I am fond of stalking, and fond of shooting too.'

'Only a man may have enough of it.'

'Too much, if he is subject to Dobbes, as Dobbes likes them to be. Gerald likes it. But Dobbes, seeing his way to a follower, has flattered Gerald into strict obedience.'

'Poor boy!'

'It has given him a bent for life. He'll do nothing but shoot now.'

'And you?'

'I shall be a jack of all trades.'

'Did you think it odd,' she said after a pause, 'that I should ask you to come over again?'

'Was it odd?' he replied.

'That is as you may take it. There is certainly no other man in the world to whom I would have done it.'

'Not to Tregear?'

'Yes,' she said after pausing. 'Yes,—to Tregear, could I have been as sure of a welcome for him as I was for you. Frank is in all respects the

same as a brother to me. That would not have seemed to be odd,—
I mean to myself.'

'And has this been—odd,—to yourself?'

'Yes. Not that anybody else has felt it so. Only I,—and perhaps you.
You felt it so?'

'Not especially. I thought you were a very good fellow. I have always
thought that,—except when you made me take back the ring.'

'Does that still fret you?'

'No man likes to take back a thing. It makes him seem to have been
awkward and stupid in giving it. There is a reproach in having to take
a present back.'

'It was the value,—and the fact that it had come from your uncle.'

'You should have left me to judge of that.'

'If I have offended you I will beg your pardon. Give me anything
else, anything but that, and I will take it.'

'But why not that?' said he.

'Now that you have fitted it for a lady's finger it should go to your
wife. No one else should have it.' Upon this he brought the identical
ring once more out of his pocket and again offered it to her. 'No;—anything but that. That your wife must have.' Then he put the ring back
again. He certainly would not tell her now that she might take it in that
capacity.

'It would have been nicer for you had Miss Boncassen been here,'
she said. In saying this she followed no plan. It came rather from pique.
It was almost as though she had asked him whether Miss Boncassen was
to have the ring.

'What makes you say that?'

'But it would?'

'Yes, it would,' he replied stoutly, turning round as he lay on the
ground and facing her.

'Has it come to that?'

'Come to what? You ask me a question and I answer you truly.'

'You cannot be happy without her?'

'I did not say so. You ask me whether I should like to have her
here,—and I say yes. What would you think of me, if I said no?'

'My being here is not enough?' This should not have been said,
of course, but the little speech came from the exquisite pain of the
moment. She had meant to have said hardly anything just at the
time;—she had intended to be happy with him, just touching lightly on
things which might lead to that attack which must be made on the morrow. But words will often lead whither the speaker has not intended. So

it was now, and in the soreness of her heart she spoke. 'My being here is not enough?'

'It would be enough,' he said, jumping on his feet, 'if you understood all, and would be kind to me.'

'I will at any rate be kind to you,' she replied, as she sat upon the bank looking at the running water, and picking a lily to pieces which she had brought there in her hand.

'I have asked Miss Boncassen to be my wife.'

'And she has accepted?'

'No; not as yet. She is to take three months to think of it. Of course I love her best of all. Now you understand. If you will sympathise with me in that, then I will be as happy with you as the day is long.'

'No,' said she, 'I cannot. I will not.'

'Very well.'

'There should be no such marriage. If you have told me in confidence——!'

'Of course I have told you in confidence.'

'It will go no further;—but there can be no sympathy between us. It,—it,—it is not,—is not——' Then she burst into tears.

'Mabel!'

'No, sir, no; no! What did you mean——? But never mind. I have no questions to ask,—not a word to say. Why should I? Only this,—that such a marriage will disgrace your family. To me it is no more than to anybody else. Of—course—not. But it will disgrace your family.'

How she got back to the house she hardly knew; nor did he. That evening they did not again speak to each other, and on the following morning there was no walk to the mountains. Before dinner he drove himself back to Crummie-Toddie, and when he was taking his leave she shook hands with him with her usual pleasant smile.

CHAPTER 43

WHAT HAPPENED AT DONCASTER

THE Leger this year was to be run on the 14th September, and while Lord Silverbridge was amusing himself with the deer at Crummie-Toddie and at Killancodlem with the more easily pursued young ladies, the indefatigable Major was hard at work in the stables. As he frequently remarked to his faithful friend Captain Green, this did come a little hard on him. There was the cub-hunting to be looked after, which of course made his presence at Runnymede necessary, and then that 'pig-headed fellow Silverbridge' would not have the horses trained any-where but at Newmarket. How was he to be in two places at once? Yet he was in two places almost at once, cub-hunting in the morning at Egham and Bagshot, and sitting on the same evening at the stable-door at Newmarket, with his pipe in his mouth and his eyes fixed upon Prime Minister.

Gradually, but very gradually, had he and the Captain come to under-stand each other. And though they did at last understand each other, Tifto would often talk as though there were no such correct intelligence between them;—when for instance he would abuse Lord Silverbridge for being pig-headed. On such occasions the Captain's remarks would generally be very short. 'That be blowed!' he would say, implying thereby that all that state of things between the two partners, in which such complaints might be natural and perhaps just, had now been brought to an end. But on one occasion, about a week before the race, he spoke out a little plainer. 'What's the use of your going on with all that before me? It's all settled what you've got to do.'

'I don't know that anything is settled,' said the Major.

'Ain't it? I thought it was. If it ain't you'll find yourself in the wrong box. You've as straight a tip as a man need wish for, if you'll only mind your p's and q's. But if you back out, you'll come to grief. Your money's all on the other way already.'

On the Friday before the race Silverbridge was up in town to take as it were a preparatory canter. At the Beargarden, which was now almost destitute of customers, he met Tifto and dined with him, the two alone. On the next morning they went down to Newmarket together to see the horse get a gallop, and came back the same evening. During all this time, Tifto was more than ordinarily pleasant and courteous to his patron. No allusion was made to any of the wrongs that had been done him. The horse and the certainty of the horse's success were the only subjects mooted. 'It isn't what I say,' repeated Tifto for the third or fourth time, 'but look at the betting. You can't get five to four against him. They tell me that if you want to do anything on the Sunday, the pull will be the other way. I've got on as much as I can well manage. But if I did mean to go further I shouldn't wait.'

'I stand to lose over twenty thousand pounds already,' said Silverbridge, almost frightened by the amount as he thought of what his plight would be if he had to call on Mr. Moreton for such a sum of money.

'But how much are you on to win?' said Tifto,—'and then look at the chances. I suppose you could sell your bets for five thousand pounds down.'

'I wish I knew how to do it,' said Silverbridge. But this was an arrangement which, if made just now, would not suit the Major's views. Captain Green thought it expedient that his lordship should yet risk some further sum of money on his favourite horse.

They went to Newmarket, and there of course they met Captain Green. 'Tifto,' said the young Lord, 'I won't have that fellow with us when the horse is galloping.'

'There isn't an honester man or a man who understands a horse's paces better in all England,' said Tifto.

'I won't have him standing alongside of me on the Heath,' said his lordship.

'I don't know how I'm to help it.'

'If he's there I'll send the horse in,—that's all.' Then Tifto found it best to say a few words to Captain Green, and the Captain did not obtrude himself. But the Captain also said a few words to himself. 'D—— young fool; he don't know what he's dropping into.' Which assertion, if you lay aside the unnecessary expletive, was true to the letter. Lord Silverbridge was a young fool, and did not at all know into what a mess he was being dropped by the united experience, perspicuity, and energy of the man whose company on the Heath he had so rudely declined.

The horse was quite a 'picture to look at.' Mr. Pook the trainer assured his lordship that for health and condition he had never seen anything better. 'Stout all over,' said Mr. Pook, 'and not an ounce of what you may call flesh. And bright! Just feel his coat, my Lord! That's 'ealth,—that is; not dressing, nor yet macassar!'*

And then there were various evidences produced of his pace,—how he had beaten that horse, giving him two pounds; how he had been beaten by that, but only on a mile course; the Leger distance was just the thing for Prime Minister; how by a lucky chance that marvellous quick rat of a thing that had won the Derby had not been entered for the autumn race; how Coalheaver was known to have had bad feet; moreover Coalheaver could not at any time have covered this distance within ten seconds of the time in which Prime Minister would certainly do it. 'He's a stout 'orse no doubt,—is the 'Eaver,' said Mr. Pook, using the new favourite name for that celebrated horse, 'and that's why the betting men have stuck to him. But he'll be nowhere on Wednesday. They're beginning to see it now, my Lord. I wish they wasn't so sharp-sighted.'

In the course of the day, however, they met a gentleman who was of a different opinion. He said somewhat loudly that he looked on the

Heaver as the best three-year-old in England. Of course as matters stood he wasn't going to back the Heaver at even money;—but he'd take twenty-five to twenty in hundreds between the two. Major Tifto was quite surprised when he found that his friend Silverbridge did not know this gentleman. He had thought that Gilbert Villiers had been known to every racing man in England. All this ended in the bet being accepted and duly booked by Lord Silverbridge. 'He's done it for a 'edge, my Lord,' said Mr. Pook. 'Otherwise he'd not be so free. He's been putting a lot on our 'orse, and in this way he gets a turn in his favour. I don't know nothing, you know, my Lord; but that's the way I look at it.' So spoke Mr. Pook, who was quite as confident in his horse as he pretended to be. And in this way Silverbridge added two thousand five hundred pounds to his responsibilities.

But there was worse than this coming. On the Sunday afternoon he went down to Doncaster, of course in company with the Major. He was quite alive to the duty incumbent on him of ridding himself of the Major; but it had been as it were acknowledged that that duty could not be performed till after this race had been run. He was quite determined to be open with the Major after that event. 'Whether I race or not,' he would say to the Major, 'I mean to separate myself from you. I know that you have worked hard for our joint interests, and in our arrangements that shall be considered. But—you must go one way and I another.' As he sat opposite to his friend on their journey to Doncaster, he thought of this in the train. It should be done immediately on their return to London after the race. But the horse, his Prime Minister, was by this time so dear to him that he intended if possible to keep possession of the animal. If they won the race there would be ample means to enable him to do so.

When they reached Doncaster the racing men were all occupied with Prime Minister. The horse and Mr. Pook had arrived that day from Newmarket, via Cambridge and Peterborough, and the dangers of the journey had been surmounted without an accident. Tifto, Silverbridge, and Mr. Pook visited him together three times that afternoon and evening;—and the Captain also visited the horse, though not in company with Lord Silverbridge. To do Mr. Pook justice, no one could be more careful. When the Captain came round with the Major,—to whom the stable was open at all times as being the owner of the horse,—Mr. Pook was there. But Captain Green did not enter the box,—had no wish to do so, was of opinion that on such occasions no one whose business did not carry him there should go near a horse. His only object seemed to be to compliment Mr. Pook as to his care, skill, and good fortune.

It was on the Tuesday evening that the chief mischief was done. There was a club at which many of the racing men dined, and there Lord Silverbridge spent his evening. He was considered to be the hero of the hour, and everybody flattered him. I fear it must be acknowledged that his head was turned. They dined at eight and a good deal of wine was drunk. No one was probably tipsy, but many were elated; and much confidence in their favourite animals was imparted to men who had been sufficiently cautious before dinner. Then cigars and soda-and-brandy and other 'restoratives' became common, and our young friend was not more abstemious than others. Large sums were named, and at last in three successive bets Lord Silverbridge backed his horse for more than forty thousand pounds. As he was making the second bet Mr. Lupton, who in a moderate way was a racing man, came across to him and begged him to hold his hand. 'It will be a nasty sum for you to lose, and winning it will be nothing to you,' he said. Silverbridge took it good-humouredly, but said that he quite knew what he was about. 'These men will pay,' whispered Lupton, 'but you can't be quite sure what they're at.' The young man's brow was covered with perspiration. He was smoking quick and had already smoked more than was good for him. 'All right,' he said. 'I'll mind what I'm about.' Mr. Lupton could do no more, and retired. Before the night was over bets had been booked to the amount stated, and the Duke's son, who had promised that he would never plunge, who had been fully determined in his own mind that he would never commit to any folly of that kind, stood to lose about seventy thousand pounds* upon the race. What he might stand to win is a matter of no moment to this story.

While this was going on Tifto sat not far from his patron, but completely silent. During the day and early in the evening a few sparks of the honour which scintillated from the favourite horse flew in his direction. But he was on this occasion very unlike himself, and though the horse was to be run in his name had very little to say in the matter. Not a boast came out of his mouth during dinner or after dinner. He was so moody and apparently absent that his partner, who was generally anxious to keep him quiet, more than once endeavoured to encourage him. But he was unable to rouse himself. It was still within his power to run straight; to be on the square, if not with Captain Green, at any rate with Lord Silverbridge. But to do so he must make a clean breast with his lordship and confess the intended sin, and get his lordship to take off his hands those bets he had made against the horse. As he heard all that was being done, his conscience troubled him sorely. With pitch of this sort he had never soiled himself before. He was to have three thousand pounds from Green, and then there would be the bets he himself had laid against the horse,—by Green's assistance! It would be the making of him. Of what use had been all his 'square' work to him, seeing that he was still a poor indebted man? And then Silverbridge had behaved so badly to him! But still, as he sat there during the evening, he would have given a hand to have been free from the whole attempt. He had had no conception before that he could become subject to such misery from such a cause. He would make it straight with Silverbridge this very night,—but that Silverbridge was ever lighting fresh cigars and ever having his glass refilled. It was clear to him that on this night Silverbridge could not be made to understand anything about it. And the deed in which he himself was to be the chief actor was to be done very early in the following morning. At last he slunk away to bed. He had obeyed Captain Green's behest at any rate in this,—that he himself was completely sober.

On the following morning, the morning of the day on which the race was to be run, the Major tapped at his patron's door about seven o'clock. Of course there was no answer;—though the knock was repeated again and again there was no answer. When young men over-night drink as much brandy-and-water as Silverbridge had done, and smoke as many cigars, they are apt not to hear knocks at their door made at seven o'clock. Nor was his lordship's servant up,—so that Tifto had no means of getting at him except by personal and uninvited invasion of the sanctity of his bedroom. But there was no time, not a minute, to be lost. Now, within this very five minutes that was pressing on him, Tifto must choose his course. He opened the door and was standing at the young man's head.

'What the d—— does this mean?' said his lordship angrily, as soon as his visitor had succeeded in waking him. Tifto muttered something about the horse which Silverbridge altogether failed to understand. The young man's condition was by no means pleasant. His mouth was hot and furred by the fumes of tobacco. His head was aching sorely. He was still heavy with sleep, and this intrusion seemed to him to be a final indignity offered to him by the man whom he had now learned to hate. 'What business have you to come in here?' he said, leaning on his elbow. 'I don't care a straw for the horse. If you have anything to say why don't you send my servant? Get out!'

'Oh;—very well,' said Tifto;—and Tifto got out.

It was about an hour afterwards that Tifto returned, and on this occasion a groom from the stables, and the young Lord's own servant, and two or three other men were with him. Tifto had been made to understand that the news now to be communicated, must be communicated to his lordship by himself, whether his lordship were angry or not. Indeed, after what had now been done his lordship's anger was not an affair of much moment. In his present visit he was only carrying out, successfully as far as he could judge at present, the pleasant little plan which had been arranged for him by Captain Green. 'What the mischief is up?' said Silverbridge, rising suddenly in his bed.

Then Tifto told his story, sullenly, doggedly, but still in a perspicuous manner, and with words which admitted of no doubt. But before he told the story he had excluded all but himself and the groom. He and the groom had taken the horse out of the stable, it being the animal's nature to eat his corn better after slight exercise, and while doing so a nail had been picked up.

'Is it much?' asked Silverbridge, jumping still higher in his bed. Then he was told that it was very much,—that the iron had absolutely driven itself into the horse's frog, and that there was actually no possibility that the horse should run on that day.

'He can't walk, my Lord,' said the groom in that authoritative voice which grooms use when they desire to have their own way, and to make their masters understand that they at any rate are not to have theirs.

'Where is Pook?' asked Silverbridge. But Mr. Pook was, alas, still in bed. Mr. Pook, too, whose habit it had been of late to be with the horse almost at every moment, had enjoyed himself on the previous evening a little too freely.

It was soon known to Lord Silverbridge as a fact, long before he was dressed, that in very truth the horse could not run. Then, sick with headache, with a stomach suffering unutterable things from yesterday's cigars, he had, as he dressed himself, to think of his seventy thousand pounds. Of course the money would be forthcoming. He knew that. But how would his father look at him? How would it be between him and his father now? After such a misfortune as this how would he be able to break that other matter to the Duke, and say that he had changed his mind about his marriage,—that he was going to abandon Lady Mabel Grex and give his hand and his prospects and a future duchess's coronet to an American girl whose grandfather had been a porter?

A nail in his foot! Well! He had heard of such things before. He knew that such accidents had happened. What an ass must he have been to risk such a sum on the well-being and safety of an animal who might any day pick up a nail in his foot! Then he thought of the caution which Lupton had given him. What good would the money have done him had he won it? What more could he have than he now enjoyed through his father's liberality? But to lose such a sum of money;—oh, how terrible was the misfortune! How much there had been to lose, and how nearly nothing to gain! He had not calculated before how bad it might be with him! With all his advantages of wealth he felt himself to be as forlorn and wretched as though he had nothing left in the world before him.

CHAPTER 44

HOW IT WAS DONE

THE story was soon about the town, and was of course the one matter for discussion in all racing quarters. About the town! It was about England, about all Europe. It had travelled to America and the Indies, to Australia and the Chinese cities before two hours were over. Before the race was run the causes of the accident were being discussed and something like the truth was surmised in Cairo, Calcutta, Melbourne, and San Francisco. But at Doncaster it was so all-pervading a matter that down to the tradesmen's daughters and the boys at the free-school the town was divided into two parties, one party believing it to have been a 'plant,' and the other holding that the cause had been natural. It is hardly necessary to say that the ring, as a rule, belonged to the former party. The ring always suspects.* It did not behove even those who would win by the transaction to stand up for its honesty,—except for such as Tifto and Green, whose winnings would of course be secret,—as whatever treatment the horse might have received, the bets would have to be paid.

The intention had been,—so the story went,—to take the horse round a portion of the outside of the course near to which his stable stood. A boy rode him and the groom and Tifto went with him. At a certain spot on their return Tifto had exclaimed that the horse was going lame in his off fore-foot. As to this exclamation the boy and the two men were agreed. The boy was then made to dismount and run for Mr. Pook; and as he started Tifto commenced to examine the horse's foot. The boy saw him raise the off fore-leg. He himself had not found the horse lame under him, but had been so hustled and hurried out of the saddle by Tifto and the groom that he had not thought on that matter till he was questioned. So far the story told by Tifto and the groom was corroborated by the boy,—except as to the horse's actual lameness. So far the story was believed by all men,—except in regard to the actual lameness. And so far it was true. Then, according to Tifto and the groom, the other foot was looked at, but nothing was seen. This other foot, the near fore-foot, was examined by the groom, who declared himself to be so flurried by the lameness of such a horse at such a time, that he hardly knew what he saw or what he did not see. At any rate then in his confusion he found no cause of lameness, but the horse was led into the stable as lame as a tree. Here Tifto found the nail inserted into the very cleft of the frog of the near fore-foot, and so inserted that he could not extract it till the farrier came. That the farrier had extracted the nail from the part of the foot indicated was certainly a fact.

Then there was the nail. Only those who were most peculiarly privileged or most nearly interested were allowed to see the nail. But it was buzzed about the racing quarters that the head of the nail,—an old, rusty, straight, and well-pointed nail,—bore on it the mark of a recent hammer. In answer to this it was alleged that the blacksmith in extracting the nail with his pincers, had of course operated on its head, had removed certain particles of rust, and might easily have given it the appearance of having been struck. But in answer to this the farrier, who was a sharp fellow, and quite beyond suspicion in the matter, declared that he had very particularly looked at the nail before he extracted it,—had looked at it with the feeling on his mind that something base might too probably have been done,—and that he was ready to swear that the clear mark on the head of the nail was there before he touched it with his tools. And then not in the stable, but lying under the little dung-heap away from the stable-door, there was found a small piece of broken iron bar, about a foot long, which might have answered for a hammer,—a very old and rusty bit of iron; and amidst the rust of this was found such traces as would or might have been left had it been used in striking such a nail. There were some who declared that neither on the nail nor on the iron could they see anything. And among these was the Major. But Mr. Lupton brought a strong magnifying-glass to bear, and the world of examiners was satisfied that the marks were there.

It seemed however to be agreed that nothing could be done. Silverbridge himself would not lend himself at all to those who suspected mischief. He was miserable enough, but in this great trouble he would not separate himself from Tifto. 'I don't believe a word of all that,' he said to Mr. Lupton, who took a leading part in the endeavours made to discover the truth.

'It ought to be investigated at any rate,' said Lupton.

'Mr. Pook may do as he likes, but I will have nothing to do with it. I won't go near the horse. If I can help it I will never see him again.'

Then Tifto came to him swaggering. Tifto, as the reader will understand, had to go through a considerable amount of acting, for which perhaps he was not very well adapted. The Captain would have done it better. He would have endeavoured to put himself altogether into the same boat with his partner, and would have imagined neither suspicion or enmity on his partner's part till suspicion or enmity had been shown. But Tifto, who of course had not expected that the matter would be allowed to pass over without some inquiry, began by assuming that Silverbridge would think evil of him. Tifto, who at this moment would have given all that he had in the world not to have done the deed, who now hated the instigator of the deed with all the bitterness of his heart, and felt something almost akin to love for the young gentleman from whom he would now, too probably, be estranged for ever, found himself to be forced by circumstances to defend himself by swaggering. 'I don't understand all this that's going on, my Lord,' he said.

'Neither do I,' replied Silverbridge.

'Any horse is subject to an accident. I am, I suppose, as great a sufferer as you are, and a deuced sight less able to bear it.'

'Who has said anything to the contrary? As for bearing it, we must take it as it comes,—both of us. You may as well know now as later that I have done with racing—for ever.'

'What do you tell me that for? You can do as you like and I can do as I like about that. If I had had my way about the horse this never would have happened. Taking a horse out at that time in the morning;—before a race!'

'Why, you went with him yourself.'

'Yes;—by Pook's orders. You allowed Pook to do just as he pleased. I should like to know what money Pook has got on it, and which way he laid it.' This disgusted Silverbridge so much that he turned away and would have no more to say to Tifto.

Before one o'clock, at which hour it was stated nominally that the races would commence, general opinion had formed itself,—and general opinion had nearly hit the truth. General opinion declared that the nail had been driven in wilfully,—that it had been done by Tifto himself, and that Tifto had been instigated by Captain Green. Captain Green, though a very clever man and endowed with peculiar gifts in this direction, perhaps overacted his part a little. His intimacy with the Major was well known, and yet, in all this turmoil, he kept himself apart as though he had little or no interest in the matter. 'I have got my little money on, and what little I have I lose,' he said in answer to inquiries. But everyone knew that he could not but have a great interest in a race, as to which the half owner of the favourite was a peculiarly intimate friend of his own. Had he come down to the stables and been seen about the place with Tifto it might perhaps have been better. As it was, though he was very quiet, though he expressed no opinion either in favour of Tifto or against him, early in the day,—at any rate before the Leger was run,—his name had been mixed up in the matter. There was one man who asserted it as a fact known to himself that Green and Villiers,—one Gilbert Villiers,—were in partnership together. It was very well known that Gilbert Villiers would win two thousand five hundred pounds from Lord Silverbridge.

Then minute investigation,—as minute as the circumstances of the day allowed,—was made into the betting of certain individuals. Of course there would be great plunder, and where would the plunder go? Who would get all the money which poor Silverbridge would lose? It was said that one at least of the large bets made on that Tuesday evening could be traced to the same Villiers though not actually made by him. There would of course be more of this as time went on,—when the settling-day should come. But there was quite enough of it already to show that there were many men determined to get to the bottom of it all if possible. Among whom however Silverbridge would take no action.

There seemed to come to him in his trouble a keen sense of his position and a feeling of the dignity which he ought to support. He clung during a great portion of the morning,—as soon as he had thrown off the nausea of the last evening's excess,—to Mr. Lupton. Mr. Lupton was very much his senior and they had never been peculiarly intimate; but now there was comfort in his society. 'I am afraid you are hit heavily,' said Mr. Lupton.

'Something over seventy thousand pounds!'

'Looking at what will be your property it is of course nothing. But if——'

'If what?'

'If you go to the Jews for it, then it will become a great deal.'

'I shall certainly not do that.'

'Then you may regard it as a trifle,' said Lupton.

'No, I can't. It is anything but a trifle. I must tell my father. He can find the money.'

'There is no doubt about that.'

'And I think he will. But I feel at present that I would rather change places with the poorest gentleman I know than have to tell him. I have done with races, Lupton.'

'If so, this will have been a happy day for you. A man in your position can hardly make money by it, but he may lose so much! If a man really likes the amusement,—as I do,—and risks no more than what he has in his pocket, that may be very well. But you, I think, are too excitable for the turf.'

'At any rate I have done with it.'

Nevertheless he went to see the race run, and everybody seemed to be touched with pity for him. He carried himself well, saying as little as he possibly could of his own horse, and taking, or at any rate affecting to take, great interest in the race. When Coalheaver won he congratulated the winner with a pretty grace, and went down to look at the horse when he was stripped. After the race he managed to see all those to whom he had lost heavy stakes,—having to own to himself as he did so that not one of them was a gentleman to whom he should like to give his hand. To them he explained that his father was abroad,—that probably his liabilities could not be settled till after his father's return. He however would consult his father's agent and would then appear on settling-day. They were all full of the blandest courtesies. There was not one of them who had any doubt as to getting his money,—unless the whole thing might be disputed on the score of Tifto's villainy. Even then payment could not be disputed unless it was proved that he who demanded the money had been one of the actual conspirators. After having seen his creditors he went up alone to London. To Major Tifto he had not spoken a word since the little scene which has been narrated;—but he would have spoken with kindness had Tifto come in his way.

When in London he went to Carlton Terrace and spent the night there in solitude. He did not even show himself at the Beargarden. It had been his plan to join Gerald and one or two others for some partridge-shooting at Matching, and then to go yachting till such time as he should be enabled to renew his suit to Miss Boncassen. Early in November, when if not the entire three months at least ten weeks would have run by,—and he had thought that ten weeks might be allowed to stand for three months,—she with her father would be in London, and then he would again ask her to be his wife. These had been his plans. But now it seemed that everything was changed. Partridge-shooting and yachting must be out of the question till this terrible load was taken off his shoulders. So at least he thought at the moment. Soon after his arrival at the house two telegrams followed him from Doncaster. One was from Gerald. 'What is all this about Prime Minister? Is it a sell?* I am so unhappy.' The other was from Lady Mabel,—for among other luxuries Mrs. Montacute Jones had her own telegraph-wire* at

Killancodlem. 'Can this be true? We are all so miserable. I do hope it is not much!' From which he learned that his misfortune was already known to all his friends. Probably his father, in Germany, had by this time heard it.

And now what was he to do? It was about ten o'clock when he reached his house, and having telegraphed his coming, he found his supper ready for him. As in his misery he had eaten no dinner, this was not thrown away upon him. He ate heartily; but as he jumped up from the table he felt almost ashamed of himself for doing so, and manfully resolved that he would not allow himself a single cigar. Then, without hesitating for a moment,—feeling that if he did hesitate the task would certainly not be done on that night,—he sat down and wrote the following letter:

'Carlton Terrace, Sept. 14, 187—.

'MY DEAR MR. MORETON,

'I have just come up from Doncaster. You have probably heard already by the wire what has been Prime Minister's fate. I don't know whether any horse has ever been such a favourite for the Leger. Early in the morning he was taken out and picked up a nail. The consequence was he could not run.

'Now I must come to the bad part of my story. I have lost—seventy thousand pounds! It is no use beating about the bush. The sum is something over that. What am I to do? If I tell you that I shall give up racing altogether, I dare say you will not believe me. It is a sort of thing a young man always says, I suppose, when he wants money. But I feel now I cannot help saying it.

'But what shall I do? Perhaps, if it be not too much trouble you will come up to town and see me. This will go down to Silverbridge by the day mail to-morrow. You can send me a word by the wires. Of course I will wait here for you.

'You may be sure of this. I shall make no attempt to raise the money elsewhere, unless I find that my father will not help me. You will understand that of course it must be paid. You will understand also what I must feel about telling my father. But I shall do so at once. I only wait till I can hear from you,—or perhaps see you. I am very sorry to give you so much trouble.

'Yours faithfully,
'SILVERBRIDGE.'

During the next day two despatches reached Lord Silverbridge at his father's house in London, both of them coming as he sat down to his solitary dinner. The first consisted of a short but very civil note.

'Messrs. Comfort and Criball present their compliments to the Earl of Silverbridge.

'Messrs. C & C beg to offer their apologies for interfering, but desire to inform his lordship that should cash be wanting to any amount in consequence of the late races they will be happy to accommodate his lordship on most reasonable terms, at a moment's notice, upon his lordship's simple bond,* and to any amount.

'Lord Silverbridge may be quite sure of absolute secrecy, and may rest assured that such a loan as Messrs. C & C propose may be effected without the slightest trouble to his lordship.

'Crasham Court, Crutched Friars, Sept. 15, 187—.'

The other despatch consisted of a telegram from Mr. Moreton, saying that he would be in Carlton Terrace by noon on the following day.

CHAPTER 45

'THERE SHALL NOT BE ANOTHER WORD SAID ABOUT IT'

EARLY in October the Duke was at Matching with his daughter, and Phineas Finn and his wife were both with them. On the day after they parted at Ischl the first news respecting Prime Minister had reached him,—namely, that his son's horse had lost the race. This would not have annoyed him at all, but that the papers which he read contained some vague charge of swindling against somebody, and hinted that Lord Silverbridge had been a victim. Even this would not have troubled him,—might in some sort have comforted him,—were it not made evident to him that his son had been closely associated with swindlers. In these narrations, perforce, pity was expressed for Silverbridge. Now he did not wish that his son should be subject to pity. If it were a mere question of money, that might be settled without difficulty. Even though the sum lost might have grown out of what he might have expected into some few thousands,—which would in a sense be serious,—still he would bear it without a word, if only he could separate his boy from bad companions. Then came Mr. Moreton's letter telling the whole.

At the meeting which took place between Silverbridge and his father's agent at Carlton Terrace it was at last settled that Mr. Moreton should write the letter. Silverbridge tried and found that he could not do it. He did not know how to humiliate himself sufficiently, and yet could not keep himself from making attempts to prove that according to all recognised chances his bets had been good bets. But when he read what was written he found that it would not do,—nor, as it seemed, could he write what would do. At last he resigned the attempt in despair to Mr. Moreton.

Mr. Moreton was in truth much better able to accomplish the task. He knew the Duke's mind on the matter better than the son did, and was able to say more in the young man's favour than the young man could say himself. A very large discretion had been left in Mr. Moreton's hands in regard to moneys which might be needed on behalf of that dangerous heir!—so large that he had been able to tell Lord Silverbridge that if the money was in truth lost according to Jockey Club* rules, it should all be forthcoming on the settling-day,—certainly without assistance from Messrs. Comfort and Criball. The Duke had been, almost nervously, afraid of such men of business as Comfort and Criball, and from the earliest days of his son's semi-manhood had endeavoured to be on his guard against them. Let any sacrifice be made so that his son might be kept clear from the ready aid of Comforts and Criballs. He had not said all this to his son,—though much of it he had said. But to Mr. Moreton he had been very explicit. His own pecuniary resources were so great that they could bear some ravaging without serious detriment. It was for his son's character and standing in the world, for his future respectability and dignity that his fears were so keen, and not for his own money. By one so excitable, so fond of pleasure as Lord Silverbridge, some ravaging would probably be made. Let it be met by ready money. At any rate let it not be resisted by the assistance of the Criballs and Comforts of the metropolis. Such had been the Duke's instructions to his own trusted man of business, and, acting on these instructions, Mr. Moreton was able to tell the heir that the money should be forthcoming.

Mr. Moreton, after detailing the extent and the nature of the loss, and the steps which he had decided upon taking, went on to explain the circumstances as best he could. He had made some inquiry himself, and felt in his own mind no doubt that a gigantic swindle had been perpetrated by Major Tifto and others with the view of extracting a huge sum of money out of the young Lord's pocket. The swindle had been successful. Mr. Moreton had consulted certain gentlemen of high character well versed in affairs of the turf. He mentioned Mr. Lupton among others,—and had been assured by them that though the swindle was undoubted, the money had better be paid. It was thought to be impossible to connect the men who had made the bets with the perpetrators of the fraud;—and if such a man as Lord Silverbridge were to abstain from paying his bets because his own partner had ruined the animal which belonged to them jointly, the feeling would be against him rather than in his favour. In fact the Jockey Club could not sustain him in such refusal. Therefore the money would be paid. Mr. Moreton, with some expressions of doubt, trusted that he might be thought to have exercised a wise discretion in this matter. Then he went on to express his own opinion very favourably in regard to the lasting effect which the whole matter would have upon the young man. 'I think,' said he, 'that his lordship is heartily sickened of racing and that he will never return to it.'

The Duke was of course very wretched when these tidings first reached him. Though he was a rich man, and of all men the least careful of his riches, still he could not but feel that seventy thousand pounds was a large sum of money to throw away among a nest of swindlers. And then it was excessively grievous to him that his son should in any way have been mixed up with such men. Wishing to screen his son, even from his own anger, he was careful to remember that the promise made that Tifto should be dismissed was not to take effect till after this race had been run. There had been no deceit in that. But then Silverbridge had promised that he would not 'plunge.' There are, however, promises which from their very nature may be broken without falsehood. If a man says that he will drink nothing and then drinks, he is certainly false. But if he confines himself to promising that he will never again drink hard, he may fall into a bout of hard drinking and yet not be subject to the charge of lying. Plunging is a doubtful word, and the path down to it,—like all doubtful paths,—is slippery and easy! If that assurance with which Mr. Moreton ended his letter could only be made true, he could bring himself to forgive this offence, and could soon learn to forget the money. The boy must be made to settle himself in life. The Duke resolved that his only revenge should be to press on that marriage with Mabel Grex.

At Coblenz, on their way home, the Duke and his daughter were caught up by Mr. and Mrs. Finn, and the matter of the young man's losses was discussed by them. Phineas had heard all about it, and was loud in denunciations against Tifto, Captain Green, Gilbert Villiers, and one or two others whose names had reached him. The money he thought should never have been paid. The Duke however declared that the money would not cause a moment's regret, if only the whole thing could be got rid of at that cost. It had reached Finn's ears,—or rather his eyes, as the information had come by letter,—that Tifto was already at loggerheads with his associates as to his share of the plunder. There was some hope that the whole thing might be brought to light by this means. For all that the Duke cared nothing. If only Silverbridge and Tifto could for the future be kept apart, as far as he and his were concerned, good would have been done rather than harm. While they were in this way together on the Rhine it was decided that very soon after their return to England Phineas and Mrs. Finn should go down to Matching.

When the Duke arrived in London his sons were not there. Gerald had gone back to Oxford, and Silverbridge had merely left an address. There was a little note too. If his father wished to see him, he would come at once,—either to London or to Matching or elsewhere. Then his sister wrote him a very short letter. 'Papa will be so glad if you will come to Matching. Do come.' Of course he came, and presented himself some few days after the Duke's arrival.

He had suffered much since the fatal day. In the first place he had been urged by members of the Jockey Club to take steps to unravel the fraud, whereas, whether there had been fraud or not, he was very anxious to have nothing more to do with the matter. The money had been paid, and his father had been told. He had no more care about the money, though he was very anxious as to his father. Then it was pressed upon him that he should take a leading step in punishing Tifto. Tifto should be expelled from the Beargarden. A representation must be made to the members of the Runnymede hunt, so that he might be deposed from his Mastership. He should be expelled from all race meetings,— and as far as possible from all race-courses. He was not very solicitous as to what they might do to Tifto, but he was most unwilling to do anything himself. Even yet he did not feel sure that Tifto and the groom had driven the nail into the horse's foot. But his great trouble was the meeting with his father which, let it be postponed for ever so long, must come at last. In reference to this he made a great resolution,—that he would go instantly to his father as soon as he might be sent for. When the summons came he started; but, though he was by courtesy an earl, and by fact was not only a man but a member of Parliament, though he was half engaged to marry one young lady and ought to have been engaged to marry another, though he had come to an age at which Pitt was a great minister and Pope a great poet,* still his heart was in his boots, as a schoolboy's might be, when he was driven up to the house at Matching.

In two minutes, before he had washed the dust from his face and hands, he was with his father. 'I am glad to see you, Silverbridge,' said the Duke, putting out his hand.

'I hope I see you well, sir.'

'Fairly well, thank you. Travelling I think agrees with me on the whole. I miss, not my comforts, but a certain knowledge of how things are going on which comes to us I think through our skins when we are at home. A feeling of absence always pervades me. Otherwise I like it. And you;—what have you been doing?'

'Shooting a little,' said Silverbridge, in a mooncalf tone.*

'Shooting a great deal if what I see in the newspapers be true about Mr. Reginald Dobbes and his party. I presume it is a religion to offer up hecatombs to the autumnal gods,—who must surely take a keener delight in blood and slaughter than those bloodthirsty gods of old.'

'You should talk to Gerald about that, sir.'

'Has Gerald been so great at his sacrifices? How will that suit with Plato? What does Mr. Simcox say?'

'Of course they were all to have a holiday just at that time. But I think Gerald is reading. I fancy that Gerald is clever.'

'And he is a great Nimrod?'*

'As to hunting?'

'Nimrod I fancy got his game in any way that he could compass it. I do not doubt but that he trapped foxes if there were foxes in those parts.'

'With a rifle at deer, say for four hundred yards, I would back Gerald against any man of his age in England or Scotland.'

'As for backing, Silverbridge, do not you think that we had better have done with that?' This was said hardly in a tone of reproach, with something even of banter in it; and as the question was asked the Duke was smiling. But in a moment all that sense of joyousness which the young man had felt in singing his brother's praises was expelled. His face fell, and he stood before his father almost like a culprit. 'We might as well have it out, about this racing,' continued the Duke. 'Something has to be said about it. You have lost an enormous sum of money.' The Duke's tone in saying this became terribly severe. Such at least was its sound in his son's ears. He certainly did not mean to be severe. He would not have said a word on the subject had he not felt that propriety demanded it of him. But when he did speak of that which displeased him his voice naturally assumed that tone of indignation with which in days of yore he had been wont to denounce the public extravagance of his opponents in the House of Commons. Silverbridge, who had been standing, immediately seated himself, his knees almost giving way beneath him. The father paused, but the son could not speak at the moment. 'And worse than that,' continued the Duke; 'you have lost it in about as bad company as you could have found had you picked all England through.'

'Mr. Lupton and Sir Henry Playfair and Lord Stirling were in the room when the bets were made.'

'Were the gentlemen you name concerned with Major Tifto?'

'No, sir.'

'Who can tell with whom he may be in a room? Though rooms of that kind are I think best avoided.' Then the Duke paused again, but Silverbridge was now sobbing so that he could hardly speak. 'I am sorry that you should be so grieved,' continued the father, 'but such delights cannot I think lead to much real joy.'

'It is for you, sir,' said the son, rubbing his eyes with the hand which supported his head.

'My grief in the matter might soon be cured.'

'How shall I cure it? I will do anything to cure it.'

'Let Major Tifto and the horses go.'

'They are gone,' said Silverbridge energetically, jumping from his chair as he spoke. 'I will never own a horse again, or a part of a horse. I will have nothing more to do with races. You will believe me;—will you not?'

'I will believe anything that you tell me.'

'I won't say I will not go to another race, because——'

'No; no, I would not have you hamper yourself in that way for worlds. Nor shall you bind yourself by any further promises. You have done with racing?'

'Indeed, indeed I have, sir.'

Then the father came up to the son and put his arm round the young man's shoulders and embraced him. 'Of course it made me unhappy.'

'I knew it would. I knew it would.'

'But if you are cured of this evil, the money is nothing. What is it all for but for you and your brother and sister? It was a large sum, but that shall not grieve me. The thing itself is so dangerous that if with that much of loss we can escape, I will think that we have made not a bad market. Who owns the horse now?'

'The horses shall be sold.'

'For anything they may fetch so that we may get clear of this dirt. And the Major?'

'I know nothing of him. I have not seen him since that day.'

'Has he claims on you?'

'Not a shilling. It is all the other way.'

'Let it go then. Be quit of him, however it may be. Send a messenger so that he may understand that you have abandoned racing altogether. Mr. Moreton might, perhaps, see him.'

Lord Silverbridge was more moved to outward signs of contrition and sorrow by his father's generosity than he would have been by any severity. That his father should forgive so readily and yet himself suffer so deeply, affected the son's feelings so strongly that for a time he could hardly repress his sobs. 'And now there shall not be a word more said about it,' said the Duke suddenly. 'But I would have you always remember that such a one as you can gain nothing by gambling. Had you won this money, would not the very possession of money so obtained have been a disgrace to you? All money won by gambling should be a reproach;—yet what am I to say of money extracted by such a one as you out of the pockets of such as they? Would it not stink when you handled it?' Silverbridge in his confusion could make no answer. 'There shall not be another word said about it,' said the Duke again. 'And now, what do you mean to do with yourself immediately?'

'I'll stay here, sir, as long as you do. Finn and Warburton and I have still a few coverts* to shoot.' Mr. Warburton had been the Duke's private secretary when the Duke was Prime Minister and was now at Matching.

'That's a good reason for staying anywhere.'

'I meant that I would remain while you remained, sir.'

'That at any rate is a good reason as far as I am concerned. But we go to Custins next week.'

'There's a deal of shooting to be done at Gatherum,' said the heir.

'You speak of it as if it were a necessary task; the business of your life,—on which your bread depended.'

'One can't expect game to be kept up if nobody goes to shoot it.'

'Can't one? I didn't know. I should have thought that the less was shot the more there would be to shoot; but I am ignorant in such matters.' Silverbridge then broke forth into a long explanation as to coverts, gamekeepers, poachers, breeding, and the expectations of the neighbourhood at large, in the middle of which he was interrupted by the Duke. 'I am afraid, my dear boy, that I am too old to learn. But as it is so manifestly a duty, go and perform it like a man. Who will go with you?'

'I will ask Mr. Finn to be one.'

'He will be very hard upon you in the way of politics, I should think.'

'I can answer him better than I can you, sir. There is I think something to be said about it. Mr. Lupton said he would come for a day or two. He'll stand to me.'

After that his father stopped him as he was about to leave the room. 'One more word, Silverbridge. Do you remember what you were saying to me when you walked down to the House with me from your club that night?' Silverbridge remembered very well what he had said. He had undertaken to ask Mabel Grex to be his wife, and had received his father's ready approval to the proposition. But at this moment he was very unwilling to refer to that matter. 'I have thought about it very much since that,' said the Duke. 'I may say that I have been thinking of it every day. If there were anything to tell me, you would let me know;—would you not?'

'Yes, sir.'

'Then there is nothing to be told? I hope you have not changed your mind.'

Silverbridge paused a moment, trusting that he might be able to escape the making of any answer;—but the Duke evidently intended to have an answer. 'It appeared to me, sir, that it did not seem to suit her,' said the hardly-driven young man. He felt himself to be very hardly driven,—not by his father's pertinacity but by the unfortunate complexity of his own circumstances. He could not now say that Mabel had shown a disposition to reject his offer, because as they had been sitting by the brook-side at Killancodlem, even he, with all his self-diffidence and want of knowledge of the world, had been forced to see what were her wishes. Her confusion, and too evident despair when she heard of the offer that had been made to the American girl, had plainly told her tale. He could not now plead to his father that Mabel Grex, whom he had professed to love so dearly, would refuse his offer. But his self-defence, when first he found that he had lost himself in love for the American, had all been based on that idea. He had done his best to make Mabel understand him. If he had not actually offered to her, he had done the next thing to it. And he had run after her,—so he told himself,—till he was ashamed of such running. She had given him no encouragement;—and therefore he had been justified. No doubt he must have been mistaken as to her intentions. That he now perceived; but still he felt himself to be justified. It was impossible that he should explain all this to his father. He had, however, to say something. One thing he certainly could not say,—just at present. After his folly and misconduct in regard to those heavy bets he could not at once risk his father's renewed anger by proposing to him an American daughter-in-law. That must stand over, at any rate till the girl had accepted him positively. 'I am afraid it won't come off, sir,' he said at last.

'Then I am to presume that you have changed your mind?'

'I told you when we were speaking of it that I was not at all confident.'

'She has not——'

'I can't just explain it all, sir;—but I fear it won't come off.'

Then the Duke, who had been sitting, got up from his chair and with his back to the fire made a final little speech. 'We decided just now, Silverbridge, that nothing more should be said about that unpleasant racing business, and nothing more shall be said by me. But you must not be surprised if I am anxious to see you settled in life. No young man could ever have been more bound by duty to marry early than you are. In the first place you have to repair the injury done by my inaptitude for society. You have explained to me that it is your duty to have the Barsetshire coverts properly shot, and I have acceded to your views. Surely it must be equally your duty to see your Barsetshire neighbours. And you are a young man every feature of whose character would be improved by matrimony. As far as means are concerned you are almost as free to make arrangements as though you were already the head of the family.'

'No, sir.'

'I could never bring myself to dictate to a son in regard to his choice of a wife. But I will own that when you told me that you had chosen, I was much gratified. Try and think again, when you are pausing amidst your sacrifices at Gatherum, whether that be possible. If it be not, still I would wish you to bear in mind what is my idea as to your duty.' Silverbridge said that he would bear this in mind, and then escaped from the room.

The next two or three days passed quietly and pleasantly enough,—with a good deal of light political skirmishing in which the Duke took but little part, as Phineas Finn demolished one after another the juvenile arguments of the young deserter. 'He'll come back to us, Duke, before long,' said Phineas one morning.

'I hope it will not be when we are in power,' said the Duke. 'Nobody should ever go over to a winning side.'

'But I am not a candidate for office,' said Silverbridge.

'You don't know what you are. If a young man be asked to take office he cannot always very well refuse. I don't think Sir Timothy will make you an offer.'

'I shall have him for my under-secretary some day,' said Phineas.

'You must be secretary first before you can have a secretary under you. Sir Timothy means to do wonderful things next session. He'll have quite a new set round him. Perhaps you may be one of them, Silverbridge. You wait till you get to Gatherum and hear what Lupton has to say about it all.' This went on till the end of the second week in October, and then the party was broken up. The Duke and Lady Mary started for Custins. Lord Silverbridge went to Gatherum to prepare for his guests,—and Mr. and Mrs. Finn returned to London, whence she was to proceed in one direction, while he went in another to the Barsetshire shooting.

CHAPTER 46

LADY MARY'S DREAM

WHEN the Duke and his daughter reached Custins they found a large party assembled there. Lady Cantrip was accustomed to have her house full in October, and after talking the matter over carefully with her husband had resolved that the time had come in which the Duke and his daughter ought to be able to mingle again in the world. The Duchess had now been dead more than six months; and though a widow may be supposed to find it necessary to seclude herself for a longer time than that, a widower is generally thought to be made of stronger fibre. And as for Lady Mary, seeing that she was expected not only to fall in love but to get rid of a former love in order that she might do so, Lady Cantrip felt that further allusions to the girl's mourning would be unnecessary. And there was something of an idea present to the minds both of Lord and Lady Cantrip that they were doing for this restive young woman almost more than friendship required. They both of them felt the greatest regard for the Duke, and Lady Cantrip was really attached to the girl;—but there are limits. The Duke's feeling on the matter of his daughter's unfortunate love had been so strong that he had almost thought that the whole world ought to be moved by it. Some shadow of an idea of this kind made its way into the minds of the Cantrips;—not altogether justly, as the Popplecourt idea had been almost altogether her own. 'I'll bring them together, and then they must just settle it among themselves,' she said to the Earl. Now she was as good as her word, for Popplecourt was at Custins when the Duke and his daughter arrived.

The Duke was a little surprised and Lady Mary very much surprised to find such a crowd. Lord and Lady Nidderdale were there, which might have been expected as they were part of the family. And with Lord Popplecourt had come his recent friend Adolphus Longstaffe. That too might have been natural. Mr. and Miss Boncassen were there also, who at this moment were quite strangers to the Duke; and Mr. Lupton, who had not yet gone to assist Silverbridge in performing his duty among the Barsetshire coverts. The Duke also found a very old friend of his, Lady Rosina de Courcy; and Mr. and Mrs. Grey, who were also old and valued friends; and Lady Chiltern, whose father-in-law had more than once sat in the same Cabinet with himself and Lord Cantrip; and Mr. Monk, who was generally spoken of as the head of the coming Liberal Government, and the Ladies Adelaide and Flora FitzHoward, the still unmarried but not very juvenile daughters of the Duke of St. Bungay. These with a few others who need not be named made a large party, and rather confounded the Duke, who had hardly reflected that discreet and profitable love-making was more likely to go on among numbers, than if the two young people had been thrown together in big desolate rooms with no other companions than their elders. The St. Bungay girls, as they were generally called, were gay young women, though they were not clever, and understood the indescribable art of keeping up a chatter about nothing. Mr. Lupton and Lady Chiltern were both very lively people, and Dolly Longstaffe, though he had not often as much to say for himself as on those two last occasions when we saw him in company with Miss Boncassen, nevertheless had a way of his own of adding something to the cheeriness of a party.

Lord Popplecourt had been made to understand what was expected of him, and after some little hesitation had submitted himself to the conspiracy. There would not, he understood, be less at any rate than two hundred thousand pounds;—and then the connection would be made with one of the highest families in Great Britain. Though Lady Cantrip had said very few words, those words had been expressive; and the young bachelor peer had given in his adhesion. Some vague half-defined tale had been told him,—not about Tregear, as Tregear's name had not been mentioned,—but respecting some dream of a young man who had flitted across the girl's path during her mother's lifetime. 'All girls have dreams of that nature,' Lady Cantrip had suggested. Whereupon Lord Popplecourt said that he supposed it was so. 'But a softer, purer, more unsullied flower never waited on its stalk till the proper fingers should come to pluck it,' said Lady Cantrip, rising to unaccustomed poetry on behalf of her friend the Duke. Lord Popplecourt accepted the poetry and was ready to do his best to pluck the flower.

It so happened that soon after the Duke's arrival Lord Popplecourt found himself in one of the drawing-rooms with Lady Cantrip and his proposed father-in-law. A hint had been given him that he might as well be home early from shooting, so as to be in the way. As the hour in which he was to make himself specially agreeable, both to the father and to the daughter, had drawn nigh, he became somewhat nervous, and now, at this moment, was not altogether comfortable. Though he had been concerned in no such matter before, he had an idea that love was a soft kind of thing which ought to steal on one unawares and come and go without trouble. In his case it came upon him with a rough demand for immediate task-work. This might, for aught he knew, be customary; but he had not previously thought that he was to be subjected to such labours, and at this moment almost resented the interference with his ease. He was not sure but that he would have escaped from it if he could. He was already a little angry with Lady Cantrip, but at the same time felt himself to be so much in subjection to her that he could not rebel.

The Duke himself when he saw the young man was hardly more comfortable. He had brought his daughter to Custins, feeling that it was his duty to be with her; but he would infinitely have preferred, had his conscience permitted it, to leave the whole operation to the care of Lady Cantrip. He hardly liked to look at the fish whom he wished to catch,—or to have caught,—for his daughter. Whenever this aspect of affairs presented itself to him, he would endeavour to console himself by remembering the past success of a similar transaction in regard to his own wife. He often thought of his own first interview with her,—the first interview at least in which he had uttered a word to her of any moment. 'You have heard,' he had said, 'what our friends wish?' She had pouted her lips, and when gently pressed had at last muttered, with her shoulder turned to him, that she supposed it was to be so. Very much more coercion had been used to her then than either himself or Lady Cantrip had dared to apply to his daughter,—and much harder words spoken. Of that he had no doubt. He did not think that his girl in her present condition of mind would signify to Lord Popplecourt that 'she supposed it was to be so.' He knew,—in his heart he knew,—that she would signify quite something else. Now that the time for making the transaction was present he felt almost sure it would never be transacted. But still as he was there for the purpose he must go on with it. Were he now to abandon his scheme in reference to Lord Popplecourt, would it not be tantamount to abandoning everything in reference to Mr. Tregear? So he wreathed his face in smiles,—or made some attempt at it,—as he greeted the young man.

'I hope you and Lady Mary had a pleasant journey abroad,' said Lord Popplecourt. Lord Popplecourt, being aware that he had already been adopted or at any rate chosen as a son-in-law, felt himself called upon to be familiar as well as pleasant. The Duke hardly realised the feeling. The young man was to him one who, perhaps, might be a son-in-law, but probably would not, and with whom he was already almost prepared to be angry as being a matter of annoyance,—a thorn to him. 'I often thought of you and Lady Mary, and wondered what you were about,' continued Popplecourt.

'We were visiting lakes and mountains, churches and picture galleries, cities and salt-mines,' said the Duke.

'Does Lady Mary like that sort of thing?'

'I think she was pleased with what she saw.'

'She has been abroad a great deal before, I believe. It depends so much on whom you meet when abroad.'

This was unfortunate, because it recalled Tregear to the Duke's mind, and set him thinking on the impropriety of allowing young people to converse freely with whomever they might meet. 'We saw very few people whom we knew,' said the Duke.

'I've been shooting in Scotland with Silverbridge, and Gerald, and Reginald Dobbes, and Nidderdale,—and that fellow Tregear who is so thick with Silverbridge.'

'Indeed!'

'I'm told that Lord Gerald is going to be the great shot of his day,' said Lady Cantrip.

'It is a distinction,' said the Duke bitterly.

'He did not beat me by so much,' continued Popplecourt. 'I think Tregear did the best with his rifle. One morning he potted three. Dobbes was so disgusted. He hated Tregear.'

'Isn't it very stupid,—half-a-dozen men getting together in that way?' asked Lady Cantrip.

'It depends on how they get on together. Nidderdale is always jolly.'

'I am glad to hear that,' said the mother-in-law.

'And Gerald is a regular brick.' The Duke bowed. 'Silverbridge used always to be going off to Killancodlem where there were a lot of ladies. He is very sweet, you know, on this American girl whom you have here, Lady Cantrip.' Again the Duke winced. 'Dobbes is awfully good as to making out the shooting, but then he is a tyrant. Nevertheless I agree with him. If you mean to do a thing you should do it.'

'Certainly,' said the Duke. 'But you should make up your mind first whether the thing is worth doing.'

'Just so,' said Popplecourt. 'And as grouse and deer together are about the best things out, most of us made up our minds that it was worth doing. But that fellow Tregear would argue it out. He said a gentleman oughtn't to play billiards as well as a marker.'*

'I think he was right,' said the Duke.

'Nidderdale always says that a man should do a little of everything, and Nidderdale has a great deal of common sense.' This of course came from Lady Cantrip.

'Do you know Mr. Tregear, Duke?'

'I have met him,—with my son.'

'Do you like him?'

'I have seen very little of him,' said the Duke, preparing to escape from this irrational and untoward conversation.

'I cannot say I do. He thinks so much of himself, and as far as I can hear he is nobody. Of course he is very intimate with Silverbridge and that is all that anyone knows of him.' The Duke bowed almost haughtily, though why he bowed he could hardly have explained to himself. Lady Cantrip bit her lips in disgust. Why was the young man such a fool as to go on talking about Tregear? 'He's just the fellow,' continued Popplecourt, 'to think that some princess has fallen violently in love with him.' Then the Duke muttered some excuse and left the room.

'You had better not talk to him about Mr. Tregear,' said Lady Cantrip.

'Why not?'

'I don't know whether he approves of the intimacy between him and Lord Silverbridge.'

'I should think not;—a man without any position or a shilling in the world. I did not say any good of him.'

'The Duke is peculiar. If a subject is distasteful to him he does not like it to be mentioned. And though he does not easily take offence he is liable to impressions. You had better not mention Mr. Tregear.' Lady Cantrip as she said this blushed inwardly at her own hypocrisy.

It was of course contrived at dinner that Lord Popplecourt should take out Lady Mary. It is impossible to discover how such things get wind, but there was already an idea prevalent at Custins that Lord Popplecourt had matrimonial views, and that these views were looked upon favourably. Lady Adelaide FitzHoward had spread this report, and Lady Adelaide knew everything of that kind. 'You may be quite sure of it, Mr. Lupton,' she had said. 'I'll make you any bet you like they're married before this time next year.'

'It will be a terrible case of Beauty and the Beast,' said Lupton.

'I declare he is very good-looking,' said Lady Adelaide.

Lady Chiltern had whispered a suspicion of the same kind to Mrs. Grey, and both of them had expressed a hope that the lover would be worthy of the girl. 'He is hardly the sort of man,' said Mrs. Grey, 'that I should have thought her mother's daughter would have chosen.' In answer to this Lady Chiltern had explained that Lord Popplecourt had a very large estate entirely at his own command,—that he was reputed to be a careful young man, and that girls situated as was Lady Mary could not quite be allowed to choose for themselves in such matters.

And our old friend Dolly Longstaffe had chaffed his friend Popplecourt on the subject, Popplecourt having laid himself open by indiscreet allusions to Dolly's very manifest love for Miss Boncassen. 'Everybody can't have it as easily arranged for him as you, old fellow,—a duke's daughter and a pot of money without so much as the trouble of asking for it!'

'What do you know about the Duke's daughter?'*

'That's what it is to be a lord and not to have a father. Upon the whole fathers are mistakes. I don't want to get rid of mine, but I never could see that he was of any good to me. If I hadn't had a father perhaps some feminine swell would have jumped down my throat.' Popplecourt tried to show that he was disgusted; but he felt himself all the more strongly bound to go on with his project.

It was therefore a matter of course to almost everybody assembled that these should-be lovers would be sent out of the room together. 'You'll give your arm to Mary,' Lady Cantrip said, dropping the ceremonial prefix as she gave her instructions to her guest. Lady Mary of course went out as she was bidden. Though everybody else knew it, no idea of what was intended had yet come across her mind. Had she been told that she was to be locked up in a dungeon all her life it would have seemed to her a more probable exercise of parental authority than an attempt to make her marry Lord Popplecourt.

The should-be lover immediately reverted to the Austrian tour, expressing a hope that his neighbour had enjoyed herself. 'There's nothing I like so much myself,' said he, remembering some of the Duke's words, 'as mountains, cities, salt-mines, and all that kind of thing. There's such a lot of interest about it.'

'Did you ever see a salt-mine?'

'Well,—not exactly a salt-mine; but I have coal-mines on my property in Staffordshire and I suppose it is the same kind of thing. I'm very fond of coal. I hope you like coal.'

'I like salt a great deal better,—to look at.'

'But which do you think pays best? I don't mind telling you,—though it's a kind of thing I never talk about to strangers;—the royalties from the Blogownie and Toodlem mines go up regularly two thousand pounds every year. That's better than falling off, you know.'

'I thought we were talking about what was pretty to look at.'

'So we were. I'm as fond of pretty things as anybody. Do you know Reginald Dobbes?'

'No, I don't. Is he pretty?'

'Not exactly;—but he used to be so angry with Silverbridge because Silverbridge would say Crummie-Toddie was ugly.'

'Was Crummie-Toddie ugly?'

'Not particularly;—just a plain house on a moor.'

'That sounds ugly.'

'I suppose your family like pretty things.'

'I hope so.'

'I do, I know.' Lord Popplecourt when he said this endeavoured to look as though he intended her to understand that she was the pretty thing which he most particularly liked. She partly conceived his meaning,—thought it possible that he was endeavouring to attempt some unmeaning and vulgar compliment,—and was disgusted accordingly. On the other side of her sat Mr. Boncassen, to whom she had been introduced in the drawing-room,—and who had said a few words to her about some Norwegian poet equal, as he had declared, either to Homer or Dante. She turned round to him, and as he was at the moment disengaged she asked him some question about the Skald,* and so, getting into conversation with him, managed to turn her shoulder to her suitor. On the other side of him sat Lady Rosina de Courcy, to whom, as being an old woman and an old maid and altogether out of the world, he felt very little inclined to be courteous. She said a word to him, asking him whether he did not think the weather was treacherous. He answered her very curtly, and sat bolt upright, looking forward on the table, and taking his dinner as it came to him. He had been put there in order that Lady Mary Palliser might talk to him, and he regarded interference on the part of that old American as being ungentlemanlike and not at all the proper thing. But the old American disregarded him, and went on with his quotations from the Scandinavian bard.

But Mr. Boncassen, again, sat next to Lady Cantrip, who divided her favours equally between him and the Duke on her other hand. And when at last he was called upon to give his ear to the Countess, Lady Mary was again vacant for Popplecourt's attentions. 'Are you fond of poetry?' he asked.

'Very fond.'

'So am I. Which do you like best, Tennyson or Shakespeare?'

'They are so very unlike.'

'Yes;—they are unlike. Or Moore's elegies?* I am very fond of "When in death I shall calm recline." I think this equal to anything. We had a great deal of talk about poetry at Crummie-Toddie. Reginald Dobbes would have it that it's all bosh.'

'Then I think that Mr. Reginald Dobbes must be all bosh himself.'

'There was a man there named Tregear who had brought some books.' Then there was a pause; but Lady Mary, of course, had not a word to say. 'Dobbes used to declare that he was always pretending to read poetry.'

'Mr. Tregear never pretends anything.'

'Do you know him?' asked the rival.

'He is my brother's most particular friend.'

'Ah; yes. I dare say Silverbridge has talked to you about him. I think he's a stuck-up sort of fellow.' To this there was not a word of reply. 'Where did your brother pick him up?'

'They were at Oxford together.'

'I must say I think he gives himself airs;—because, you know, he's nobody.'

'I don't know anything of the kind,' said Lady Mary, becoming very red in the face, 'and as he is my brother's most particular friend,—his very friend of friends,—I think you had better not abuse him to me, Lord Popplecourt.'

'I don't think the Duke is very fond of him.'

'I don't care who is fond of him. I am very fond of Silverbridge, and I won't hear his friend ill spoken of. I dare say he had some books with him. It is just what I should expect from what Silverbridge has told me. He is not at all the sort of a young man to go to a place and satisfy himself with doing nothing but killing animals.'

'Do you know him, Lady Mary?'

'I have seen him, and of course I have heard a great deal of him from Silverbridge. I would rather not talk any more about him. I don't like having such ill-natured things said.'

'What did I say?'

'You were very ill-natured.'

'You seem to be very fond of Mr. Tregear,' he said almost angrily.

'It is no business of yours, Lord Popplecourt, whether I am fond of anybody or not. I have told you that Mr. Tregear is my brother's friend, and that ought to be enough.' Then, for the next half-hour there was almost a quarrel between them so that nothing more was said till the ladies had left the room.

Lord Popplecourt was a young man possessed of a certain amount of ingenuity. It was his custom to think over things as they passed, and to make deductions. The process was slow with him and did not always produce correct results. But it required a considerable amount of mental application, and produced a certain sharpness in his character for which among his friends he had credit. It was said of him that he knew on which side his bread was buttered, and that if you wished to take him in you must get up early. After dinner that day and during the night he pondered a good deal on what he had heard, and putting two and two together in different places made a certain number of fours. Lady Cantrip had told him there had been a—dream. Well! What was he to believe about that dream? Had he not better, he said to himself, avoid the error of putting too fine a point upon it, and tell himself at once that a dream in this instance meant a—lover! Lady Mary had already been troubled by a lover! He was not at all disposed to throw her over on that account. He was disposed to believe that young ladies often do have objectionable lovers, and that things get themselves right afterwards. Young ladies can be made to understand the beauty of coal-mines almost as readily as young gentlemen. There would be the two hundred thousand pounds; and there was the girl, beautiful, well born, and thoroughly well mannered. All might come right in spite of the dream,—only that the dream must be made to pass away. But what if this Tregear and the dream were one and the same? If so, had he not received plenty of evidence to show him that the dream had not yet passed away? A remnant of affection for the dream would not have been a fatal barrier, had not the girl been so fierce with him,—with him, the dream's rival,—in defence of her dream. He remembered too what the Duke had said about Tregear, and Lady Cantrip's advice to him to be silent before his future father-in-law in respect to this young man. There must have been some reason for such an injunction. And then do girls generally defend their brothers' friends as she had defended Tregear? He thought not. Putting all these things together, by eleven o'clock on the following morning he had come, not quite to a conviction, but to an uncomfortable belief that Tregear was the dream, and that the dream had not as yet been made to vanish.

Soon after that hour he found himself near to Dolly Longstaffe as they were shooting. 'You know that fellow, Tregear; don't you?'

'Oh, lord yes. He is one of the Beargarden men; Silverbridge brought him there.'

'Did you ever hear anything about him?'

'What sort of thing?'

'Was he ever—ever in love with anyone?'

'What makes you ask that?'

'Sometimes there are stories about.'

'I fancy he used to be awfully spooney on Mab Grex. I remember hearing that they were to have been married, only that neither of them had sixpence.'

'Oh—Lady Mabel Grex! That's a horse of another colour.'

'And which is the horse of your colour?'

'I haven't got a horse,' said Lord Popplecourt, going away to his own corner.

CHAPTER 47

MISS BONCASSEN'S IDEA OF HEAVEN

IT was very generally known that Dolly Longstaffe had been heavily smitten by the charms of Miss Boncassen; but the world at large hardly gave him credit for the earnestness of his affection. Dolly had never yet been known to be in earnest in anything;—but now he was in very truth in love. He had agreed to be Popplecourt's companion at Custins only because he had heard that Miss Boncassen would be there. He had thought over the matter with more painful consideration than he had ever before given to any subject. He had gone so far as to see his own man of business, a very peculiar man named Squercum, who had chambers in a little court leading out of Holborn, with a view of ascertaining what settlements he could make and what income he might be able to spend. He had told himself over and over again that he was not the 'sort of fellow' that ought to marry; but it was all of no avail. He confessed to himself that he was completely 'bowled over,'—'knocked off his pins'; and he had almost gone so far as to declare to himself that if the girl would not have him he must take to drinking.

'Is a fellow to have no chance?' he said to Miss Boncassen at Custins.

'If I understand what a fellow means, I am afraid not.'

'Of course you understand.'

'I suppose I do.'

'No man alive was ever more in earnest than I am.'

'Well, Mr. Longstaffe, I do not suppose that you have been trying to take me in all this time. I do not think so ill of you as that.'

'Why should you think ill of me at all?'

'Why should you imagine that I do? I may think well of a great many gentlemen without wishing to marry them.'

'But does love go for nothing?' said Dolly, putting his hand upon his heart. 'Perhaps there are so many that love you!'

'Not above half-a-dozen or so.'

'You can make a joke of it, when I——! But I don't think, Miss Boncassen, you at all realise what I feel. I am in such a condition that if I give it up, I shall give up,—oh, curses, everything. As to settlements and all that, your father could do what he likes with me.'

'My father has nothing to do with it, and I don't know what settlements mean. We never think of anything of that kind in our country. If two young people love each other they go and get married.'

'Let us do the same here.'

'But the two young people don't love each other. Look here, Mr. Longstaffe;—it's my opinion that a young woman ought not to be pestered!'

'Pestered!'

'You force me to speak in that way. I've given you an answer ever so many times. I will not be made to do it over and over again.'

'It's that d—— fellow, Silverbridge,' he exclaimed almost crying,— 'a young swell who doesn't mean what he's about, any more than I mean to marry the cookmaid!' On hearing this Miss Boncassen left the room without speaking another word, and poor Dolly found himself alone. He saw what he had done as soon as she was gone. He had compared the lady to a cookmaid,—implying at any rate that as was the distance between him, Adolphus Longstaffe, and a cookmaid, so was that between the Duke's heir and her, Isabel Boncassen. After that he could hardly venture to persevere again,—at any rate not here at Custins. For aught he knew she might demand the protection of the whole household against him. He weighed it over in his mind for a long time, almost coming to a resolution in favour of hard drink. He certainly had never felt anything like this before. He was so uncomfortable that he couldn't eat his luncheon, though in accordance with his usual habit he had breakfasted off soda-and-brandy and a morsel of devilled toast. He did not know himself in his changed character, and did not at all know what to do with himself. 'I wonder whether she understands that I have four thousand pounds a year of my own, and shall have twelve thousand pounds more when my governor goes!' He blamed himself that he had not made all that sufficiently clear. But then she was so headstrong that it was impossible to explain anything to her.

'I'm off to London,' he said to Popplecourt that afternoon.

'Nonsense! You said you'd stay for ten days.'

'All the same I'm going at once. I've sent to Bridport for a trap, and I shall sleep to-night at Dorchester.'

'What's the meaning of all that?'

'I've had some words with somebody. Don't mind asking any more.'

'Not with the Duke?'

'The Duke! No;—I haven't spoken to him.'

'Or Lord Cantrip?'

'I wish you wouldn't ask questions.'

'If you've quarrelled with anybody you ought to consult a friend.'

'It's nothing of that kind.'

'Then it's a lady. It's the American girl!'

'Don't I tell you, I don't want to talk about it. I'm going. I've told Lady Cantrip that my mother wasn't well and wants to see me. If I'd said that I was going to hang myself it would have been just the same to her. You'll stop your time out, I suppose.'

'I don't know.'

'You've got it all square, no doubt. I wish I'd had a handle to my name. I never cared for it before.'

'I'm sorry you're so down in the mouth about it. Why don't you try again? The thing is to stick to 'em like wax. If ten times of asking won't do, go in twenty times.' Dolly shook his head despondently. 'I didn't think you were the man to be put down so easily.'

'What can you do when a girl walks out of the room and slams the door in your face? She'll get it hot and heavy before she has done. I know what she's after. She might as well cry for the moon. Let me know when you've fixed it all and I will meet you wherever you please.' And so Dolly got into the trap and went to Bridport and slept that night at the hotel at Dorchester.

Lord Popplecourt, though he was able to give such excellent advice to his friend, explaining to him that in a matter of honest love nothing was so efficient as persistency, and recommending him to 'stick like wax,'—which really is the best advice which can be given in such circumstances, though it was not likely to be of service in the present instance,—though he could tell his friend that if ten times had been of no use, yet twenty times might succeed, he had been able as yet to do very little in his own case. He had been a week at Custins, and had found no opportunity for saying a word to denote his passion. Day after day he had prepared himself for the encounter, but the lady had never given him the opportunity. When he sat next to her at dinner she would be very silent. If he stayed at home on a morning she was not visible. During the short evenings after the gentlemen had left the dining-room he could never get her attention. And he made no progress with the Duke. The Duke had been very courteous to him at Richmond and during that drive up to London, but here he was monosyllabic and almost sullen.

Once or twice Lord Popplecourt had a little conversation with Lady Cantrip. 'Dear girl!' said her ladyship. 'She is so little given to seeking admiration.'

'I dare say. That is, I'm sure she's all that.'

'Girls are so different, Lord Popplecourt. With some of them it seems that a gentleman need have no trouble in explaining what it is that he wishes.'

'I don't think Lady Mary is like that at all.'

'Not in the least. Anyone who addresses her must be prepared to explain himself fully. Nor do I think that he ought to hope to get very much encouragement at first. I do not think that Lady Mary will bestow her heart till she is sure she can give it with safety.' There was an amount of falsehood in this which was proof at any rate of very strong friendship on the part of Lady Cantrip. But still Lord Popplecourt could not find the hour for explaining himself fully.

After a few days Lady Mary seemed to have become more intimate with the American and his daughter than with any others of the party assembled at Custins. Perhaps she liked to talk about the Scandinavian poets, of whom Mr. Boncassen was so fond. Perhaps she felt sure that her new transatlantic friend would not at any rate make love to her. Perhaps it was that she unconsciously yielded to the various allurements of Miss Boncassen. Miss Boncassen saw the Duke of Omnium for the first time at Custins, and there had the first opportunity of asking herself how such a man as that would receive from his son and heir such an announcement as Lord Silverbridge would have to make him, should she at the end of three months be pleased to accept the offer which had been made to her. She was quite aware that Lord Silverbridge need not repeat the offer unless he were so pleased. Her answer to him had given him a complete release should he wish to be released. But she thought it probable that he would come again. He had so spoken that she was sure of his love; and had so spoken as to obtain hers. Yes;—she was very sure that she loved him. She had never seen anything like him before;—so glorious in his beauty, so gentle in his manhood, so powerful and yet so little imperious, so great in condition, and yet so little confident in his own greatness, so bolstered up with external advantages, and yet apparently so little apt to trust to anything but his own heart and his own voice, his own personal entreaties, his own youth. My reader, I fear, will not have by any means so exalted an idea of the young man who had coloured the Dean's house at Oxford and had been cheated out of his money at Doncaster as that entertained by Miss Boncassen;—but then no reader can have had the same opportunity of falling in love with him. In asking for her love he had put forward no claim but his own love. He had not even looked at her as though he had felt himself to be the son and heir to a duke. She was glad enough that he was what he was. She counted at their full value all his material advantages. To be an English duchess! Oh—yes; her ambition understood it all! But she loved him, because in the expression of his love no hint had fallen from him of the greatness of the benefits which he could confer upon her. Had he been that bank clerk of whom she had once talked to him he could not have spoken of his love with less of self-assurance. Yes, she would like to be a duchess; but not to be a duchess would she become the wife of a man who should begin his courtship by assuming a superiority.

She had told him to consult his friends before he should come to her again. Now the chances of society had brought her into the company of his nearest friends. She was in the house with his father and with his sister. Now and again the Duke spoke a few words to her, and always did so with a peculiar courtesy. But she was quite sure that the Duke had heard nothing of his son's courtship. And she was equally sure that the matter had not reached Lady Mary's ears. She perceived that the Duke and her father would often converse together, and would generally spend some part of the afternoon in each other's company. Mr. Boncassen would discuss republicanism generally, and the Duke would explain that theory of monarchy as it prevails in England, which but very few Americans have ever been made to understand. All this Miss Boncassen watched with pleasure, venturing to entertain some hope that the Duke's natural objections to such a marriage might be made to disappear. She was still of opinion that it would not become her to force her way into a family which would endeavour to repudiate her, and to encounter perhaps the ill-will of all those among whom she ought to assume her new rank with grace and ease. She would not become this young man's wife if all connected with the young man were resolved to reject the contact. But if she could conquer them,—then,—then she thought that she could put her little hand into that young man's grasp with a happy heart. But they should all know the story of her grandfather, the porter.

It was in this frame of mind that she laid herself out not unsuccessfully to win the esteem of Lady Mary Palliser. 'I do not know whether you approve it,' Lady Cantrip said to the Duke; 'but Mary has become very intimate with our new American friend.' At this time Lady Cantrip had become very nervous,—so as almost to wish that Lady Mary's difficulties might be unravelled elsewhere than at Custins.

'They seem to be very sensible people,' said the Duke. 'I don't know when I have met a man with higher ideas on politics than Mr. Boncassen.'

'His daughter is popular with everybody.'

'A nice ladylike girl,' said the Duke, 'and appears to have been well educated.' After this there was nothing further to be said. Lady Cantrip, though she feared something, hardly knew what she feared. But day by day her faith in the Popplecourt cure was becoming weaker and more weak.

It was now near the end of October, and the weather was peculiarly fine. Perhaps in our climate, especially in the South of England, October would of all months be the most delightful if something of its charms were not detracted from by the feeling that with it will depart the last relics of the delights of summer. The leaves are still there with their gorgeous colouring, but they are going. The last rose still lingers on the bush, but it is the last,—the very last. The woodland walks are still pleasant to the feet, but caution is heard on every side as to the coming winter. Gentlemen are looking to their top-boots and breeches, and old ladies are already beginning to air their furs.

The park at Custins, which was spacious, had many woodland walks attached to it, from which, through vistas of the timber, distant glimpses of the sea were caught. No more charming spot for easy walking would be found in any British county. Within half a mile of the house the woods were reached, and within a mile the open sea was in sight,—and yet the wanderers might walk for miles without going over the same ground. Here, without other companions, Lady Mary and Miss Boncassen found themselves one afternoon, and here the latter told her story to her lover's sister. 'I so long to tell you something,' she said.

'Is it a secret?' asked Lady Mary.

'Well; yes; it is,—if you will keep it so. I would rather you should keep it a secret. But I will tell you anyway. I think you will keep it as a secret, but you shall judge yourself.' Then she stood still, looking into the other's face. 'I wonder how you will take it!'

'What can it be?'

'Your brother has asked me to be his wife.'

'Silverbridge!'

'Yes;—Lord Silverbridge. You are astonished?'

Lady Mary was very much astonished,—so much astonished that words escaped from her which she regretted afterwards. 'I thought there was someone else.'

'Who else?'

'Lady Mabel Grex. But I know nothing.'

'I think not,' said Miss Boncassen slowly. 'I have seen them together and I think not. There might be somebody, though I think not her. But why do I say that? Why do I malign him, and make so little of myself? There is no one else, Lady Mary. I am sure that when he spoke to me he was in earnest. I did not doubt him, and I do not doubt him;—not in the least. Is he not true?'

'I think he is true.'

'I am sure he is true. And he has asked me to be his wife.'

'What did you say?'

'Well;—what do you think? What is it probable that such a girl as I would say when such a man as your brother asks her to be his wife? Is he not the sort of man that a girl would love?'

'Oh, yes.'

'Is he not handsome as a god?' Mary stared at her with all her eyes. 'And sweeter than any god those pagan races knew? And is he not good-tempered, and loving;—and has he not that perfection of manly dash and indifference without which I do not think I could give my heart to any man?'

'Then you have accepted him.'

'And his rank, and his wealth! The highest position in all the world in my eyes!'

'I do not think you should take him for that.'

'Does it not all help? Can you put yourself in my place and say you would not be lifted off your legs? Why should I refuse him? No, not for that. I would not take him for that. But if I love him,—because he is all that my imagination tells me that a man ought to be;—if to be his wife seems to me to be the greatest bliss that could happen to a woman;—if I feel that I could die to serve him, that I could live to worship him, that his touch would be sweet to me, his voice music, his strength the only support in the world on which I would care to lean;— what then?'

'Is it so?'

'Yes;—it is so. It is after that fashion that I love him. He is my hero;—and not the less so because there is none higher than he among the nobles of the greatest land under the sun. Would you have me for a sister?' Lady Mary could not answer all at once. She had to think of her father;—and then she thought of her own lover. Why should not Silverbridge be at any rate as well entitled to his choice as she considered herself to be? And yet how would it be with her father?

Silverbridge would in process of time be the head of the family. Would it be proper that he should marry an American?

'You would not like me for a sister?'

'I was thinking of my father,' said Lady Mary. 'For myself, I like you very much.'

'Shall I tell you what I said to him?'

'If you will.'

'I told him that he must ask his friends;—that I would not be his wife to be rejected among them all. Nor will I. Though it be heaven I will not creep there through a hole. If I cannot go in with my head upright, I will not go even there.' Then she turned round as though she were prepared in her emotion to walk back to the house alone. But Lady Mary ran after her, and having caught her put her arm round her waist and kissed her.

'I at any rate will love you,' said Lady Mary.

'I will do as I have said,' continued Miss Boncassen energetically. 'I will do as I have said. I will tell his father everything. My father's father was a labouring man,—a porter on the quays. I suppose a young man in this country can marry without his father's leave. But though I love your brother down to the ground, he shall not marry me without his father's consent.' Then they returned arm-in-arm close together; but very little more was said between them on that occasion.

When Lady Mary entered the house she was told that Lady Cantrip wished to see her in her own room.

CHAPTER 48

THE PARTY AT CUSTINS IS BROKEN UP

THE message was given to Lady Mary by the old housekeeper after so solemn a fashion that she was sure some disagreeably important communication was about to be made to her. Her mind at that moment had of course been filled with her new friend's story. She felt that she required some time to think of it before she could determine what she herself would wish. This American girl seemed to her to be a very grand creature. That she was preeminently beautiful everyone allowed. That she was very clever no one could doubt. Every word that she had spoken in telling her own story and in speaking of her love had been, to Mary's thinking, noble and attractive. But then all this would be another trouble to the family,—another sorrow to that heavily burdened head of the family! Mary was by no means sure but that her elder brother, as being her elder brother, owed a peculiar duty to the Pallisers generally in this matter of his marriage. With his great privileges he ought, perhaps, to be alive to his great duties. Would it be well that the mother of the future Duke should be the granddaughter of an American porter? Mary, who was firm as a rock as to her own rights and who was quite resolved that no parental authority, no ducal pride, no family pretensions should separate her from her own lover, was almost disposed to think that her elder brother should in this matter obey her father. Had it been Gerald who was in love with the American it might have been different. But when she was going to her own room, in order that she might think it over and make up her mind, she was summoned to Lady Cantrip. 'My dear,' said the Countess, 'I wish you to do something to oblige me.'

'Of course I will.'

'Lord Popplecourt wants to speak to you.'

'Who?'

'Lord Popplecourt.'

'What can Lord Popplecourt have to say to me?'

'Can you not guess, my dear? Lord Popplecourt is a young nobleman, standing very high in the world, possessed of ample means, unmarried, but just in that position in which it behoves such a man to look about for a wife.' Lady Mary pressed her lips together, and clenched her two hands, and prepared herself for fighting. 'Can you not imagine what such a gentleman may have to say?' But the time for fighting did not seem to her to have come quite yet, and, though there was a pause, she made no immediate answer. 'I am to tell you, my dear, that your father would approve of it.'

'Approve of what?'

'He approves of Lord Popplecourt as a suitor for your hand.'

'How can he?'

'Why not, Mary? Of course he has made it his business to ascertain all particulars as to Lord Popplecourt's character and property.'

'Papa knows that I love somebody else.'

'My dear Mary, that is all vanity.'

'I don't want to talk about it, Lady Cantrip.'

'Of course your papa would be glad to see you properly settled in life.'

'I don't think that papa can want to see me married to another man when he knows that with all my heart and soul——'

'Oh, Mary!'

'When he knows,' continued Mary, who would not be put down, 'that I love another man with all my heart. What will Lord Popplecourt say if I tell him that? If he says anything to me, I shall tell him. Lord Popplecourt! He is the very last man in all the world that I should think of. He cares for nothing but his coal-mines. Of course if you bid me see him I will; but it can do no good. I despise him, and if he troubles me I shall hate him. As for marrying him,—I would sooner die this minute. Of course you can say that it is all vanity; but I shall never marry anybody unless they let me marry Mr. Tregear.'

After this Lady Cantrip did not insist on the interview. She expressed her regret that things should be as they were,—explained in sweetly innocent phrases, of which she perfectly understood the use, that in a certain rank of life young ladies could not always marry the gentlemen to whom their fancies might attach them, but must, not unfrequently, postpone their youthful inclinations to the will of their elders,—or in less delicate language, that though they might love in one direction they must marry in another; and then expressed a hope that her dear Mary would think over these things and try to please her father. 'Why does he not try to please me?' said Mary as she left the room. Then Lady Cantrip was obliged to see Lord Popplecourt also, a necessity which was a terrible nuisance to her. 'Yes;—she understands what you mean. But she is not prepared for it yet. You must wait awhile.'

'I don't see why I am to wait.'

'She is very young;—and so are you, indeed. There is plenty of time! She has not known you so very long.'

'There is somebody else I suppose.'

'I told you,' said Lady Cantrip, in her softest voice, 'that there has been a dream across her path.'

'It's that Tregear!'

'I am not prepared to mention names,' said Lady Cantrip, rather astonished that he should know so much. 'But indeed you must wait.'

'I don't see it, Lady Cantrip.'

'What can I say more? If you think that such a girl as Lady Mary Palliser, the daughter of the Duke of Omnium, possessed of fortune, beauty and every good gift is to come like a bird to your call, you will find yourself very much mistaken. All that her friends can do for you will be done in your favour. The rest must remain with yourself.' During that evening Lord Popplecourt endeavoured, and apparently with success, to make himself pleasant to one of the FitzHoward young ladies, and on the next morning he took his leave of Custins without saying anything further to Lady Mary beyond the coldest adieu.

'I will never interfere again in reference to anybody else's child as long as I live,' Lady Cantrip said to her husband that night. 'Of course she'll marry this man,'—meaning Tregear,—'and the sooner the Duke gives way the quicker he'll get over the annoyance.'

Lady Mary was very much tempted to open her heart to Miss Boncassen but could not quite make up her mind to do so. It would be delightful to her to have a friend; but were she to engage Miss Boncassen's sympathies on her own behalf, she must of course sympathise with Miss Boncassen in return, and she was hardly prepared to do this at present. She would require to hear something on this matter at any rate from her brother before she would do that. What if, after all, Silverbridge were not devoted to the American beauty! What if it should turn out that he was going to marry Lady Mabel Grex! Therefore she kept her own secret, though on various occasions she was sorely tempted. 'I wish you would call me Isabel,' her friend said to her. 'It is so odd;—since I have left New York I have never heard my name from any lips except father's and mother's.'

'Has not Silverbridge ever called you by your Christian name?'

'I think not. I am sure he never has.' But he had, though it had passed by her at the moment without attention. 'It all came from him so suddenly. And yet I expected it. I knew it was coming. But it was too sudden for Christian names and pretty talk of that kind. I do not even know what his name is.'

'Plantagenet.'

'Oh, how grand!'

'But we always call him Silverbridge.'

'Plantagenet is very much prettier. I shall always call him Plantagenet. But I recall that. You won't remember that against me, will you?'

'I will remember nothing that you do not wish.'

'I mean that if,—which is perhaps impossible,—if all the grandeurs of all the Pallisers could consent to put up with poor me, if heaven were opened to me with a strait gate, so that I could walk out of our republic into your aristocracy with my head erect, with the Stars and Stripes waving proudly round me till I had been accepted into the shelter of the Omnium griffins,—then I would call him—— But I need not think about all that, need I?'

'There is one Palliser would welcome you.'

'Would you, dear? Then I will love you so dearly. May I call you Mary?'

'Of course you may.'

'Mary is the prettiest name under the sun. But Plantagenet is so grand! Which of the kings did you branch off from?'

'I know nothing on earth about it. From none of them I should think. There is some story about a Sir Guy who was a king's friend.* I never trouble myself about it. I hate aristocracy.'

'Do you, dear?'

'Yes,' said Mary, full of her own grievances, of which, however, she was not prepared to speak openly. 'It is an abominable bondage, and I do not see that it does any good at all. Yet it has to be kept up,' she said, thinking of her brother and of future possible difficulties.

'I think it is so glorious,' said the American. 'There is no such mischievous nonsense in all the world as equality. That is what father says. What men ought to want is liberty. An aristocrat should be a real aristocrat,—like your father.'

'It is terrible to be tied up in a small circle,' said the Duke's daughter.

'What do you mean, Lady Mary?'

'I thought you were to call me Mary. What I mean is this. Suppose that Silverbridge loves you better than all the world.'

'I hope he does. I think he does. There!'

'And suppose he cannot marry you,—because of his—aristocracy.'

'But I know he can. What is to hinder him?'

'I thought you were saying yourself——'

'Saying what? That he could not marry me! No indeed! But that under certain circumstances I could not marry him. You don't suppose that I think he would be disgraced? If so I would go away at once, and he should never again see my face or hear my voice. Indeed, indeed, I think nothing of the kind. I think myself good enough for the best man God ever made,—if only that best man could love me and I could love him. But if others think differently, and those others are so closely concerned with him, and would be so closely concerned with me as to trouble our joint lives,—then will I neither subject him to such sorrow nor will I encounter it myself.'

'It all comes from what you call aristocracy.'

'No, dear,—but from the prejudices of an aristocracy. A thing may be very good, but not perfect. To tell the truth, Mary, the more difficult a place is to get into, the more the right of going in is valued. If everybody could be a duchess and a Palliser, I should not perhaps think so much about it.'

'I thought it was because you loved him.'

'So I do. Do you doubt it?'

'Oh, no!'

'If you do, you wrong me foully,—and do not in the least understand how it is. I love him entirely. I have said not a word of that to him,—but

I do. If I know at all what love is, I love him as a girl ought to love the man she means to marry. But if you love a star the pride you have in your star will enhance your love. The difficulty,—even the impossibility,—will enhance your love. Though you know that you must die of your love, still you must love your star the more.'

And yet Mary could not tell her tale in return. She could not show the reverse picture;—that she being a star was anxious to dispose of herself after the fashion of poor human rushlights. It was not that she was in the least ashamed of her own love, but that she could not bring herself to yield altogether in reference to the great descent which Silverbridge would have to make. It certainly was true that a future duke ought not to marry the granddaughter of a street porter. It would be as bad as some of those unnatural love affairs which take place in the *Arabian Nights.**

On the day after this,—the last day of the Duke's sojourn at Custins, the last also of the Boncassens' visit,—it came to pass that in the afternoon the Duke and Mr. Boncassen, with Lady Mary and Isabel, were all walking in the woods together. It is not impossible that this may have been arranged by the latter young lady with some view to creating an intimacy, or at any rate producing good humour, between herself and her possible future father-in-law. And it so happened when they were at a little distance from the house, each of the girls was walking with the other girl's father. Mr. Boncassen was no doubt eloquent, and satisfied Lady Mary's wishes in regard to conversation. But the Duke was much struck, first with the grace and wit of his companion,—and then with her good sense. Isabel had calculated what she would say to him should a time for speaking come to her. She could not tell him of his son's love. She could not ask his permission. She could not explain to him all her feelings, or tell him what she thought of the proper way of getting into heaven. That must come afterwards if it should ever come at all. But there was something that she could tell. 'We are so different from you,' she said, speaking of her own country.

'And yet so like,' said the Duke smiling;—'your language, your laws, your habits!'

'But still there is such a difference! I do not think there is a man in the whole Union more respected than father.'

'I dare say not.'

'Many people think that if he would only allow himself to be put in nomination by the New England and eastern Republicans he might be the next President.'

'The choice, I am sure, would do your country honour.'

'And yet his father was a poor labourer who came over from Holland and earned his bread among the shipping at New York. That kind of thing would be impossible here.'

'My dear young lady, there you wrong us.'

'Do I?'

'Certainly. A Prime Minister with us might as easily come from the same class.'

'Here you think so much of rank. You are—a duke.'

'But a Prime Minister can make a duke, and if a man can raise himself by his own intellect to that position, no one will think of his father or his grandfather. The sons of merchants have with us been Prime Ministers more than once, and no Englishmen ever were more honoured among their countrymen. Our peerage is being continually recruited from the ranks of the people, and hence it gets its strength. Half our peers are men whose grandfathers were commoners.'

'Is it so?'

'There is no greater mistake than to suppose that inferiority of birth is a barrier to success in this country.' She listened to this and to much more on the same subject with attentive ears,—not much shaken in her ideas as to the English aristocracy in general by what the Duke said, but thinking that she was perhaps learning something of his own individual opinions. If he were more liberal than others, on that liberality might perhaps be based her own future happiness and fortune.

He in all this was quite unconscious of the working of her mind. Nor in discussing such matters generally did he ever mingle his own private feelings, his own pride of race and name, his own ideas of what was due to his ancient rank and to his superior nobility with the political creed by which his conduct in public life was governed. The peer who sat next to him in the House of Lords, whose grandmother had been a washerwoman and whose father an innkeeper, was to him every whit as good a peer as himself. If not, how could they be peers? And he would as soon sit in counsel with Mr. Monk, whose father had risen from a mechanic to be a merchant, as with any nobleman who could count ancestors against himself. But there was an inner feeling in his bosom as to his own family, his own name, his own children, and his own personal self, which was kept altogether apart from his grand political theories. It was a subject on which he never spoke; but the feeling had come to him as a part of his birthright, not communicated by words from others but yet perfectly understood. And he conceived that it would pass through him to his children after the same fashion. It was this which made the idea of a marriage between his daughter and Tregear so intolerable to him, and which would operate as strongly in regard to any marriage which his son might contemplate. Lord Grex was not a man with whom he would wish to form any intimacy. He was, we may say, a wretched unprincipled old sinner, bad all round; and such the Duke knew him to be. But the blue blood and the rank were there; and as the girl was good herself he would have been quite contented that his son should marry the daughter of Lord Grex. That one and the same man should have been in one part of himself so unlike the other part,—that he should have one set of opinions so contrary to another set,—poor Isabel Boncassen did not at all understand.

As he and his daughter came together at the end of the walk, Isabel having for the moment gone off with her father, the Duke expressed great admiration for the American girl's manners and intellect.

CHAPTER 49

THE MAJOR'S FATE

THE affair of Prime Minister and the nail was not allowed to fade away into obscurity by the sporting world. Through the latter part of September and the whole of October it was made matter for pungent inquiry. The Jockey Club was alive. Mr. Pook was very instant,—with many Pookites all anxious to free themselves from suspicion and blame. Everybody concerned and many who were not at all concerned declared that the honour of the turf required that every detail of the case should be laid open to the light. But by the end of October, though almost every detail had been surmised and was all but known, nothing had in truth been discovered. Nobody doubted but that Tifto and the groom between them had driven the nail into the horse's foot, and that Green and Gilbert Villiers between them had shared the bulk of the plunder. As to those two gentlemen, there could be no doubt. They had gone off on their travels together, and the fact that each of them had been in possession of about twenty thousand pounds was absolutely proved. But then there is no law against two gentlemen having such a sum of money, nor even against their winning it on a race-course. Nor is there a law to keep such gentlemen from leaving the country after they have won it. It was notorious that Captain Green and Mr. Gilbert Villiers had enriched themselves to this extent by the failure of Prime Minister. But yet nothing was proved!

And it was notorious that the groom had gone off to Australia,—as people said, with five thousand pounds. Considerable blame was thrown upon the gentlemen who were managing the inquiry because they had not detained the groom. He no doubt could have told everything, and if sufficiently bribed would probably have done so. Some said that he might have been detained by a warrant. But the matter was not brought before the magistrates, and the man went before any sufficient bribe was offered to him. He had left the country, indeed, within a week of the day on which the race was run.

But the Major remained. Which of the culprits had with his own hand hammered the nail no one could take upon himself to decide; but that the Major must either have done it or seen it done, all racing men were agreed. He had been out with the horse in the morning and had been the first to declare that the animal was lame. The boy's evidence, which even he did not dispute, went so far as that. And he had been with the horse till the farrier had come,—till indeed the nail had been extracted. But he had concocted a story for himself. He did not in the least dispute that the horse had been lamed by the machinations of Green and Villiers,—and with the assistance of the groom. No doubt, he said, these men, who had been afraid to stay and face an inquiry, had contrived and had carried out the iniquity. How the original lameness had been caused he could not pretend to say. The groom, who was at the horse's head, and who evidently knew how these things were done, might have struck a nerve in the horse's foot with his boot. But when the horse was got into the stable he, Tifto,—so he declared,—at once ran out to send for the farrier. It was some minutes before he had found a messenger,—the boy having been sent for Mr. Pook. During those minutes so occupied the operation must have been made with the nail. That was Tifto's story,—and as he kept his ground and told it himself, there were some few who believed it.

But though the story was so far good, he had at moments been imprudent, and had talked when he should have been silent. The whole matter had been a torment to him from the moment in which he had been induced by Green to lend himself to the scheme. In the first place his conscience made him miserable. As long as it had been possible to prevent the evil he had hoped to make a clean breast of it to Lord Silverbridge and to confess his intentions. Up to this period of his life everything had been 'square' with him. He had betted 'square,' and had ridden 'square,' and had run horses 'square.' Even when Silverbridge had been most offensive to him he had been careful of his partner's interests. He had taken a pride in this, as though it had been a great virtue, often telling himself that he did for Silverbridge much more than Silverbridge deserved, and regarding himself as almost a miracle of virtue. It was not without great inward grief that he had deprived himself of the consolations of these reflections. He was going to do that which would take from him all his squareness! But when he had approached his noble partner, his noble partner snubbed him at every turn,—and he did the deed.

His reward was to be three thousand pounds, paid in hard cash by Captain Green,—and he got his money. The money was very much to him,—would perhaps have been almost enough to comfort him in his misery, had not those other rascals got so much more. When he heard that the groom's fee was higher than his own,—of which in truth he knew nothing, but such was the rumour which reached him,—it almost broke his heart. And Green and Villiers, men of infinitely lower standing than himself in the world,—men at whom the Beargarden would not have looked, and who had never been regarded as gentlemen,—had absolutely netted fortunes on which they could live in comfort for the rest of their lives! No doubt they had run away while Tifto still stood his ground;—but he soon began to doubt whether to have run away with twenty thousand pounds, to have gone to some Island of the Blest* where every luxury might have been obtained, was not better than to remain with such small plunder as had fallen to his lot, among such faces as those which now looked upon him! Then when he had drunk a few glasses of whisky-and-water, he said something very foolish as to his power of punishing that swindler Green. But still there were a few who believed that he had been made a victim, and among those few Lord Silverbridge for a long time was one.

An attempt had been made at the first moment to induce Silverbridge to delay the payment of his bets;—but he, and Mr. Moreton on his behalf, had been very eager that they should be paid. Whatever might be the result it was considered right that he should be extricated from the matter. Under the joint auspices of Mr. Lupton and Mr. Moreton the horses were sold, and the bets were paid, and the whole establishment was annihilated,—with considerable loss, but with great despatch. The Duke when he returned from the Continent was very urgent that there should be no delay. The Jockey Club, and the racing world, and the horsey fraternity generally, might do whatever seemed to them good,—so that Silverbridge was extricated from the matter. Silverbridge was extricated,—and the Duke cared nothing as to what the Jockey Club might do with Messrs. Tifto, Green, Villiers & Co.

But Silverbridge could not get out of the mess quite so easily, or at any rate not so entirely, as his father wished. Two questions arose about

Major Tifto, outside the exclusively racing world, but within the domain of the world of sport and pleasure generally, as to one of which it was almost impossible that Silverbridge should not express an opinion. The first question had reference to the Mastership of the Runnymede hounds. In this our young friend was not bound to concern himself. The other affected the Beargarden Club; and as Lord Silverbridge had introduced the Major to this society, he could hardly forbear from the expression of an opinion.

In these two matters the Major, wretched as he was, exhibited more pluck than his friends or enemies had expected. There was a meeting of the subscribers to the hunt in the last week of October,—just before the season commenced. At that meeting Major Tifto told his story. There he was, to answer any charge which might be brought against him. If he had made more money by losing the race than he would have done by winning it,—where was it and whence had it come? Was it not clear to anyone that a conspiracy might have been made and carried out without his knowledge;—and clear also that the real conspirators in this case had levanted? He had not levanted! The hounds, he believed, were his own,—at any rate his property in them was greater than that of any other person. He had undertaken to hunt the country for this season, and they had undertaken to pay him a certain sum of money. He should expect and demand that sum of money. If they chose to make any other arrangement for the year following they could do so. Then he sat down, and after a little while the meeting was adjourned,—the secretary having declared that he would not act in that capacity any longer, and that he would not collect the funds. A farmer had also asserted that he and his friends had resolved that Major Tifto should not ride over their fields. On the next day the Major had his hounds out, and some of the London men, with a few of the neighbours, joined him. Gates were locked in some places; but the hounds ran, and those who chose to ride with the Major managed to follow them. There are men who will stick to their sport though Apollyon* himself should carry the horn, who will declare that they want hunting and care nothing for the character of the Master so long as he is able to keep his hounds on to a fox. They come out for hunting, not for society. Who cares whether the lady who fills a theatre be or be not a moral young woman, or whether the bandmaster who keeps such excellent time in a ball-room has or has not paid his debts? There were men of this sort who supported Major Tifto;—but then there was a general opinion that the Runnymede hunt would have to come to an end unless a new Master could be found.

Then in the first week in November a special meeting was called at the Beargarden, at which Lord Silverbridge was asked to attend. 'It is impossible that he should be allowed to remain in the club.' This was said to Lord Silverbridge by Mr. Lupton, who had indeed summoned the society. 'Either he must go or the club must be broken up.'

Silverbridge was very unhappy on the occasion. He had at last been reasoned into believing that the horse had been made the victim of foul play, and had consented to credit Green, Villiers, and the groom with the villainy; but had persisted in saying that there was no conclusive evidence against Tifto. The matter was argued with him over and over again. Tifto had laid bets against the horse; Tifto had been hand and glove with Green; Tifto could not have been absent from the horse above two minutes, if so long; the thing could not have been arranged without Tifto's connivance. As he had been the means of bringing Tifto into the club, and had been his partner on the turf, it was his business to look into the matter and to express himself firmly. 'But for all that,' said he, 'I'm not going to jump on a man when he's down, unless I feel sure that he's guilty.'

Then the meeting was held, and Tifto himself appeared. When the accusation was made against him by Mr. Lupton, who proposed that he should be expelled from the club, he burst into tears;—and perhaps no course which he could have pursued would have told more in his favour. The whole story was repeated,—the nail, and the hammer, and the lameness, unreal when first declared, and afterwards so dreadfully real; and the moments of time were counted up, and poor Tifto's bets and friendship with Green were made apparent,—and the case was submitted to the club. An old gentleman who had been connected with the turf all his life, and who would not have scrupled, by square betting, to rob his dearest friend of the last shilling he had in the world, seconded the proposition,—telling all the story over again. Then Major Tifto was asked whether he wished to say anything.

'I've got to say that I'm here,' said Tifto, still crying, 'and if I'd done anything of that kind of course I'd have gone with the rest of 'em. I put it to Lord Silverbridge to say whether I'm that sort of fellow.' Then he sat down.

Upon this there was a pause, and the club was manifestly of opinion that Lord Silverbridge ought to say something. But Mr. Lupton, understanding the difficulty, came to his assistance. 'The position of Lord Silverbridge in the matter is peculiarly painful,' he said. 'I do not see why he should be called upon either to defend or to accuse you.'

'I think that Major Tifto should not have betted against the horse,' said Silverbridge.

'I can explain that,' said the Major. 'Let me explain that. Everybody knows that I'm a man of small means. I wanted to make my book safe, thinking I was sure to win half the stakes.'

Mr. Lupton shook his head. 'Why have you not shown us your book?'

'I told you before that it was stolen. Green got hold of it, I have no doubt. I did win a little. I never said I didn't. I hedged my bets in that way against the stakes. But what has that to do with hammering a nail into a horse's foot? I have always been true to you, Lord Silverbridge, and you ought to stick up for me now.'

'I will have nothing further to do with the matter,' said Silverbridge, 'one way or the other,' and he walked out of the room,—and out of the club soon after that. The affair was ended by a magnanimous declaration on the part of Major Tifto that he would not remain in a club in which he was suspected, and by a consent on the part of the meeting to receive the Major's instant resignation. The meeting, however, would not dissolve itself till the resignation was written. The letter, as it came from the hand of the unfortunate man, was not a credit to his scholarship.

After this the Major's name sank for a time almost into forgetfulness. That quarrel in the Runnymede hunt was carried on no doubt with great vehemence, much to the injury of sport in that neighbourhood; but the world generally did not for a time hear very much about it. It came to be acknowledged in the racing world that the terrible crime with which the Major was charged could not be absolutely proved against him; and, though he was debarred from certain race-courses and certain precincts, still he continued to show his face. 'If ever there was a fellow infernally treated, I am the man,' he would say, till he almost believed the story he told so often on his own behalf. And he wrote sundry letters to his late partner,—as to which, however, Silverbridge was wise enough to take advice from Mr. Lupton. But through it all there were some who declared that poor Tifto had been more sinned against than sinning.

CHAPTER 50

THE DUKE'S ARGUMENTS

THE Duke before he left Custins had an interview with Lady Cantrip, at which that lady found herself called upon to speak her mind freely about Lady Mary. 'I don't think she cares very much about Lord Popplecourt,' Lady Cantrip said.

'I'm sure I don't know why she should,' said the Duke, who in his own ill humour could be very aggravating even to his friends.

'But as we had thought——'

'She ought to do as she is told,' said the Duke, remembering how obedient his Glencora had been when she had been separated from her lover. 'Has he spoken to her?'

'I think not.'

'Then how can we tell?'

'I have spoken to her. I asked her to see him, but she expressed so much dislike that I could not press it. I am afraid, Duke, that you will find it very difficult to deal with her.'

'I have found it difficult;—extremely difficult.'

'As you have trusted me so much——'

'Yes;—I have trusted you, and do trust you. You have been a true friend,' said the Duke, remembering how great a debt of gratitude he owed to her. 'I hope you understand that I appreciate your kindness.'

'Perhaps then you will let me say what I think.'

'Certainly, Lady Cantrip.'

'Mary is a very peculiar girl,—with great gifts,—but——'

'But what?'

'She is obstinate. It is impossible to turn her. Perhaps it would be fairer to her to say that she has great firmness of character. It will no doubt be within your power to separate her from Mr. Tregear. I think it would be foreign to her character to—to—leave you, except with your approbation.'

'You mean, she will not run away.'

'She will do nothing, I think, without your permission. But she will remain unmarried unless she be allowed to marry Mr. Tregear.'

'What do you advise then?'

'That you should yield. If you ask me I must say so. As regards money you could give them what they want. Let him go into public life. You could manage that for him.'

'He is Conservative.'

'What does that matter when the question is one of your daughter's happiness? Everybody tells me that he is clever and well conducted. Knowing what I do of her character I think that you should give way to her.'

He betrayed nothing by his face as this was said to him. He smiled as he heard it, so that Lady Cantrip almost thought that she had prevailed. But as he got into the carriage he was a miserable man. It is all very well to tell a man that he should yield, but in truth there is nothing so wretched as yielding. Young people and women have to yield,—but for a man, and such a man as this, to yield is in itself a misery. A man, when he has a firm opinion, is of course sure that he is right. In this matter the Duke was quite certain of the propriety of his judgment. To yield would be not only to mortify himself, but to do wrong at the same time. He had convinced himself that the Popplecourt arrangement would come to nothing. The young man might be very well in his way, but there were no qualities in him by which the obstinacy of such a girl as his daughter could be overcome. Nor had he and Lady Cantrip combined been able to exercise over her the sort of power to which Lady Glencora had been subjected by her pastors and masters. In his case, if he persevered,—and he still was sure, almost sure, that he would persevere,—his object must be achieved after a different fashion. There must be infinite suffering,—suffering both to him and to her. Of Tregear's sufferings he of course took no thought. Could she have been made to consent to marry someone else, terrible as the rupture might have been to her at the time, still, when the thing was done, she would have reconciled herself to her new life. So it had been with his Glencora,—after a time. There would have been the new house, the new friends, the new interests, and probably children. Now the misery must go on from day to day beneath his eyes, with the knowledge on his part that he was crushing all joy out of her young life, and the conviction on her part that she was being treated with continued cruelty by her father! It was a terrible prospect for the coming years! But if it was manifestly his duty to act after this fashion, must he not do his duty? Is a man to be debarred from doing that which he knows to be right by any feeling that the right course will cause pain to him and to others?

But would it be right? If he were to find that by persevering in this course he would doom her to death, or perchance to madness,—what then? If it were right, he must still do it. He must still do it, if the weakness incident to his human nature did not rob him of the necessary firmness. A man has to act, not only on his own behalf, but as an example to others. If every foolish girl who chose to throw away her affections unworthily were indulged, all restraint would be lost, and there would be an end to those rules as to rank, birth, and position by which he thought his world was kept straight. If he were to allow such a marriage, what father could be expected to disallow any marriage in which any daughter might set her foolish heart?

And then, mixed with all this,—most illogically mixed with it,—was his feeling of the young man's arrogance and craft in looking for such a match. Here was a man without a shilling, so to say, with nothing to recommend him, whose manifest duty it was to go to work in some manner so that he might earn his bread, who instead of doing so, had hoped to raise himself to wealth and position by entrapping the heart of an unwary girl! There was something to the Duke's thinking thoroughly base in this, and much more base because the unwary girl was his own daughter. Heavens and earth! That such a man as Tregear should make an attack upon him and select his rank, his wealth, and his child as the stepping-stones by which he intended to rise in the world! What could be so mean as that a man should seek to live by looking out for a wife with money? But what so impudent, so arrogant, so unblushingly disregardful of all propriety, as that he should endeavour to select his victim from such a family as that of the Pallisers, and that he should lay his impious hand on the very daughter of the Duke of Omnium? All this, however,—which would mingle itself with his thoughts and which served to instigate him to firmness,—was most illogical. Seeing that he was prepared to justify himself in condemning his daughter to misery, and if necessary to death, because it was his duty to support his order, surely he could not add any rational strength to that justification by a desire to punish Tregear for arrogance and covetousness!

But together with all this, as he travelled home with his daughter to Matching, there came upon him moments of ineffable tenderness. He felt as though he longed to take her in his arms and tell her, as he pressed her to his heart, that if she were unhappy, so would he be unhappy too,—to make her understand that a hard necessity had made this sorrow common to them both. He thought that, if she would only allow it, he could speak of her love as a calamity which had befallen them, as from the hand of fate, and not as a fault; that he could sacrifice all his remaining life to hers, if only he could teach her to believe that what he did, he did from duty. If he could make a partnership in misery with her, so that each might believe that each was acting for the best, then, he thought, he could endure all that might come. But, as he was well aware, she regarded him as being simply cruel to her. She did not at all understand that he was merely performing an imperative duty.

She had set her heart upon a certain object, and having taught herself that in that way happiness might be reached, had no conception that there should be something in the world, some idea of personal dignity, more valuable to her than the fruition of her own desires! And yet every word he spoke to her at the time was tender and affectionate. He knew that she was bruised, and if it might be possible he would pour oil into her wounds,—even though she would not recognise the hand which relieved her.

They slept one night in town,—where they encountered Silverbridge soon after his retreat from the Beargarden. 'I cannot quite make up my mind, sir, about that fellow Tifto,' he said to his father.

'I hope you have made up your mind that he is no fit companion for yourself.'

'That's over of course. Everybody understands that, sir.'

'Is anything more necessary?'

'I don't like feeling that he has been ill-used on my account. They have made him resign the club, and I fancy they won't have him at the hunt. I don't know what is to become of him.'

'He has lost no money by you?'

'Oh, no.'

'Then I think you may be indifferent. From all that I hear I think he must have won money,—which will probably be a consolation to him. In such a matter such a man as Mr. Lupton probably knows what ought to be done.'

'I think they have been hard upon him, all the same,' continued Silverbridge. 'Of course he is not a good man, nor a gentleman, nor possessed of very high feelings. Of course he was a trouble, and I am very sorry that I ever had anything to do with him. But a man is not to be sacrificed altogether for that. There are so many men who are not gentlemen, and so many gentlemen who are very bad fellows!'

'I have no doubt Mr. Lupton knew what he was about,' replied the Duke.

On the next morning the Duke and Lady Mary went down to Matching. During the railway journey the Duke occupied himself with his newspapers and parliamentary documents,—blue-books and returns, with the contents of which he thought it necessary that he should be familiar before the next session. But after the railway journey there was a drive of seven miles, and as they sat together in the carriage the father endeavoured to make himself pleasant to his daughter. 'I suppose we shall stay at Matching now till Christmas,' he said.

'I hope so.'

'Whom would you like to have here?'

'I don't want anyone, papa.'

'You will be very sad without somebody. Would you like the Finns?'

'If you please, papa. I like her. He never talks anything but politics.'

'He is none the worse for that, Mary. When a man has taken up politics as the occupation of his life, the subject should always be present to his mind. I wonder whether Lady Mabel Grex would come.'

'Lady Mabel Grex!'

'Do you not like her?'

'Oh yes, I like her;—but what made you think of her, papa?'

'Perhaps Silverbridge would come to us then?'

Lady Mary thought that she knew a great deal more about that than her father did. But why was her father so anxious that Silverbridge and Lady Mabel should be brought together, if all that Miss Boncassen had said was true? 'Is he fond of Lady Mabel, papa?'

'Well,—I don't know. There are secrets which should not be told. I think they are very good friends and, perhaps, if she were at Matching, he would come too. I would not have her asked unless it would please you.'

'I like her very much, papa.'

'And perhaps we might get the Boncassens to come to us. I did say a word to him about it.' Now, as Mary felt, difficulty was heaping itself upon difficulty. 'I have seldom met a man in whose company I could take more pleasure than in that of Mr. Boncassen; and the young lady seems to be worthy of her father.' Mary was silent, feeling the complication of the difficulties, and looking about her to see whether there was any way out of them to be found. 'Do you not like her?' asked the Duke.

'Very much indeed,' said Mary.

'Then let us fix a day and ask them. I do not think that solitude can be at all good for you. If you will come to me after dinner with an almanac we will arrange it all. Of course you will invite that Miss Cassewary too. I rather fancy that she has been very good to Lady Mabel. I suppose we shall find Warburton here. Or if not he will come soon.'

The complication seemed to be very bad indeed. In the first place was it not clear that she, Lady Mary, ought not to be a party to asking Miss Boncassen to meet her brother at Matching? Would it not be imperative on her part to tell her father the whole story, rather than allow such a meeting as that to take place at Matching? And yet how could she do that? Had it not been told to her in confidence, and did she not remember what her own feelings had been when Mrs. Finn had suggested the propriety of telling the Duke the story which had been told to her? And how would it be possible to ask Lady Mabel to come to Matching to meet Miss Boncassen in the presence of Silverbridge? Perhaps Silverbridge would not come. Silverbridge was not peculiarly fond of Matching. If the party could be made up without Silverbridge then things might run smoothly.

As she was thinking of all this in her own room, thinking also how very happy she could be if one other name might be added to the list of guests, the Duke had gone alone into his library. There a pile of letters reached him, among which Mr. Warburton had not yet gone to work so as to separate the private wheat from the official chaff. Here, when he had opened two or three which had first attracted him,—one from Mr. Monk, written after that gentleman had left Custins, in which he very anxiously suggested certain political combinations, a second from Mr. Moreton giving in detail the expenditures of Lord Silverbridge in the last twelvemonth, and a third from Lord Chiltern full of trouble about foxes in the Brake country,—a country hunted by his lordship in which the Duke possessed much property,—when he had opened and read these, he pitched upon a fourth one marked 'Private,' and addressed in a hand which he did not recognise. This he opened suddenly,—with a conviction that it would contain a thorn,—and, turning over the page, found that the signature to it was 'Francis Tregear.' Mr. Monk's combinations, his son's follies, and the Brake foxes,—which he despised from the bottom of his heart,—had failed to ruffle the serenity which he had determined to assume on his daughter's behalf; but that man's name was wormwood to him. He at once felt that he would wish to have his dinner, his fragment of a dinner, brought to him in that solitary room, and that he might remain there secluded for the rest of the evening. But still he must read the letter;—and he read it. The letter was as follows.

'My Dear Lord Duke,

'If my mode of addressing your Grace be too familiar I hope you will excuse it. It seems to me that if I were to use one more distant, I should myself be detracting something from my right to make the claim which I intend to put forward. You know what my feelings are in reference to your daughter. I do not, however, pretend to suppose that they should have the least weight with you. But, I think, you know also what her feelings are for me. A man seems to be vain when he expresses his own conviction of a woman's love for himself. But this matter is so important to her as well as to me, that I feel myself compelled to lay aside all pretence. If she do not love me, even as I love her, then the whole thing drops to the ground. Then of course it will be for me to take myself off from out of your notice,—and from hers, and to keep to myself whatever heart-breaking I may have to undergo. But if, as I believe, she be as steadfast in this matter as I am,—if her happiness be fixed on marrying me as mine is on marrying her,—then, I think, I am entitled to ask you, as her father, whether you are justified in keeping us apart.

'I know well what are the discrepancies. Speaking from my own feeling I regard very little those of rank. I believe myself to be as good a gentleman as though my father's forefathers had sat for centuries past in the House of Lords. I believe that you would have thought so also had you and I been brought in contact on any other subject than this. The discrepancy in regard to money is, I own, a great trouble to me. Having no wealth of my own I wish that your daughter were so circumstanced that I could go out into the world and earn bread for her. I know myself so well that I dare say positively that her money,—if it be that she will have money, as to which I have never made inquiry,—had no attraction for me when I first became acquainted with her, and adds nothing now to the persistency with which I claim her hand. Should I ever be happy enough to receive your sanction to my claim, I should feel disposed to follow any advice you might give me as to my future life.

'But I venture to ask whether you can dare to keep us apart if her happiness depends, as I believe it does, on her love for me. It is now more than six months since I called upon you in London and explained my wishes. I am sure you will understand me when I say that I cannot be contented to sit idle, trusting simply to the assurance which I have of her affection. Did I doubt it, my way would be, not easier, but more simple. I should feel in that case that she would yield to your wishes, and I should then, as I have said before, just take myself out of the way. But if it be not so, then I am bound to do something,—on her behalf as well as my own. What am I to do? Any endeavour to meet her clandestinely is against my instincts, and would certainly be rejected by her. A secret correspondence would be equally distasteful to both of us. Whatever I do in this matter, I wish you to know that I do it. Therefore it is that I write to you; pleading my own cause,—and as I believe hers.

'Yours always,

'Most faithfully, and with the greatest respect,

'Francis Tregear.'

He read the letter very carefully, and at first was simply astonished by what he considered to be the unparalleled arrogance of the young man. In regard to rank this young gentleman thought himself to be as good as anybody else,—let that anybody else be what he might! In regard to money he did, indeed, acknowledge some inferiority. But that was a misfortune, and could not now be helped! Not only was the letter arrogant;—but the fact that he should dare to write any letter on such a subject was proof of most unpardonable arrogance. The Duke walked about the room thinking of it in this way till he was almost in a passion. Then he read the letter again and was gradually pervaded by a feeling of its manliness. Its arrogance remained, but with its arrogance there was a certain boldness of argument which induced respect. 'Whether I am such a son-in-law as you would like or not, it is your duty to accept me, if by refusing to do so you will render your daughter miserable.' That was Mr. Tregear's argument. He himself might be prepared to argue in answer that it was his duty to reject such a son-in-law, even though by rejecting him he might make his daughter miserable. Though he might be sure of the truth of his own argument, still there was something to be said on the other side, and this young man had said it well. He was not shaken; but with his condemnation of the young man there was mingled something of respect.

He continued to digest the letter before the hour of dinner, so that he might revert to his original tenderness, and when the almanac was brought to him he fixed on certain days. The Boncassens he knew would be free from engagements in ten days' time. Mr. Boncassen would be then at work in the British Museum; but he had half promised that he would come for a week if he might be allowed to bring a trunk full of books with him. As to Lady Mabel, he seemed to think it almost certain that she would come. 'I believe she is always going about from one house to another at this time of the year,' said Mary, who was aware that the Earl did not himself inhabit the family mansion at Grex.

'I think she will come to us if it be possible,' said the Duke. 'And you must write to Silverbridge.'

'And what about Mr. and Mrs. Finn?'

'She promised she would come again, you know. They are at their own place in Surrey. They will come unless they have friends with them. They have no shooting, and nothing brings people together now except shooting. I suppose there are things here to be shot. And be sure you write to Silverbridge.' Mary of course intended to write to Silverbridge; but she was determined to tell her brother that both Lady Mabel and Miss Boncassen had been invited. He must then do as he pleased about coming to meet them.

CHAPTER 51

THE DUKE'S GUESTS

'THE DUKE OF OMNIUM presents his compliments to Mr. Francis
Tregear and begs to acknowledge the receipt of Mr. Tregear's letter
of———. The Duke has no other communication to make to Mr. Tregear,
and must beg to decline any further correspondence.' This was the
reply which the Duke wrote to the applicant for his daughter's hand.
And he wrote it at once, on the night of the day in which the application
had reached him, after he had given his instructions to his daughter as
to the invitations to be sent out to their friends, but while his feeling of
anger was still hot upon him. He had acknowledged to himself that
Tregear had shown a certain manliness in his appeal; but not on that
account was such a man to have all that he demanded! Let the merits of
the letter be what they might, that which was right before was right still.
It seemed to the Duke that there was no alternative between such a note
as that given above and a total surrender,—unless indeed he could reconcile himself to the want of ordinary courtesy which would be displayed by sending no answer at all.

But the post did not go out during the night, and the note lay hidden
in the Duke's private drawer till the morning. There was still that *locus
poenitentiae** which should be accorded to all letters written in anger.
Nor was he in a hurry to despatch it on the next morning, feeling that
as far as expedition was concerned the post of that evening would
answer all necessary purposes. During the day he thought over it all
constantly, not in any spirit of yielding, not regarding it as possible that
he should surrender his daughter to such a claim, not descending a single step from that altitude of conviction which made him feel that it
might be his duty absolutely to sacrifice his daughter,—but asking
himself whether it might not be well that he should explain the whole
matter at length to a young man who was evidently capable of understanding an argument. He thought that he could put the matter
strongly. It was not by his own doing that he belonged to an aristocracy
which, if all exclusiveness were banished from it, must cease to exist.
But being what he was, having been born to such privileges and such
limitations, and thinking that the welfare of the country depended
much on the preservation of its aristocracy, was he not bound in duty to
maintain a certain exclusiveness? He would appeal to the young man
himself to say whether marriage ought to be free between all classes of

the community. And if not between all, who was to maintain the limits but they to whom authority in such matters was given? So much in regard to rank! And then he would ask this young man whether as a rule he thought it fitting that a young man, whose duty according to all known principles it must be to earn his bread by his daily work, should avoid that manifest duty by looking for a wife who could maintain him in idleness? As he roamed about his park alone he felt that he could write such a letter as would make an impression even upon a lover. But when he had come back to his study, and had seated himself with pen and ink before him, other reflections came to his aid. Though he might write the most appropriate letter in the world,—a letter which ought so to convince the young man to whom it would be addressed as to put an end to this courtship altogether,—would there not certainly be a reply? Did he not know that an opponent, let him be ever so much confounded by an argument, would always argue in reply? As to conviction, had he ever known an instance of a man who had been convinced by an adversary? Of course there would be a reply,—and replies. And then to such a correspondence there would be no visible end. Though he half wrote his letter, and felt that all that he had said and all that he was about to say was as true as gospel, still he did not dare to say it. It behoved him, above all things, to be secure. Words when once written remain, or may remain, in testimony for ever. So at last when the moment came he sent off those three lines, with his uncourteous compliments and his demand that there should be no further correspondence.

At dinner on that day he endeavoured to make up for this harshness by increased tenderness to his daughter, who was altogether ignorant of the correspondence between her father and her lover. 'Have you written your letters, dear?' She said she had written them all. 'I hope the people will come.'

'If it will make you comfortable, papa!'

'It is for your sake I wish them to be here. You ought to have friends of your own age. I think that Lady Mabel and Miss Boncassen are just such girls as you would like.'

'I do like them; only——'

'Only what?'

'Miss Boncassen is an American.'

'Is that an objection? According to my ideas it is very desirable to become acquainted with persons of various nations. I have heard, no doubt, many stories of the awkward manners displayed by American ladies,—stories which, I am bound to say, I have never quite believed. If you look for them you may probably find American women who are not polished. I do not think I shall calumniate my own country if I say the same of English women. It should be our object to select for our own acquaintances the best we can find of all countries. It seems to me that Miss Boncassen is a young lady with whom any other young lady might be glad to form an acquaintance.'

This was a little sermon which Mary was quite contented to endure in silence if only she could carry her point. She was, in truth, fond of the young American beauty, and had felt a real pleasure in the intimacy which the girl had proposed to her. But she thought it inexpedient that Miss Boncassen, Lady Mabel, and Silverbridge should be at Matching together. Therefore she made a reply to her father's sermon which hardly seemed to go to the point at issue. 'She is so beautiful!' she said.

'Very beautiful!' said the Duke. 'But what has that to do with it? Is that an objection? My girl need not be jealous of any girl's beauty.' Mary laughed and shook her head. 'What is it then?'

'Perhaps Silverbridge might admire her.'

'I have no doubt he would,—or does, for I am aware that they have met.' This the father said with an easy heart, not at all anxious on that head, remembering his son's confidential communication about Mabel, which had been made to him, as it seemed, but the other day. 'But why should he not admire her?'

'I don't know,' said Lady Mary sheepishly.

'I fancy that there is no danger in that direction. I think Silverbridge understands what is expected from him.' Had not Silverbridge plainly shown that he understood what was expected from him when he selected Lady Mabel? Had he not given evidence of his understanding by the arguments he had used in defending the choice which he had made? Nothing could have been more proper, and the Duke had been altogether satisfied. That in such a matter there should have been such a change in so short a time did not seem to him to be possible! And poor Mary was now completely silenced. She had been told that Silverbridge understood what was expected from him; and of course could not fail to carry home to herself an accusation that she failed to understand what was expected from her. The Duke had been innocent of any such intention; but Mary was completely silenced. She had no further argument to use against the congregation of the persons whom the Duke had selected.

When this conversation took place, she had written her letters but had not as yet sent them. Those to Mrs. Finn and to the two young ladies had been easy enough. Could Mr. and Mrs. Finn come to Matching on the 20th of November? 'Papa says that you promised to return and thinks this time will perhaps suit you.' And then to Lady Mabel: 'Do come if you can; and papa particularly says that he hopes Miss Cassewary will come also. Pray tell her from me that I do so hope we shall see her.' To Miss Boncassen she had written quite a long letter, but that too had been written very easily. 'I write to you instead of your mamma because I know you. You must tell her that, and then she will not be angry. I am only papa's messenger, and I am to say how much he hopes that you will come on the 20th. Mr. Boncassen is to bring the whole British Museum if he wishes.' Then there was a little postscript which showed that there was already considerable intimacy between the two young ladies. 'We won't have either Mr. L. or Lord P.' But not a word was said about Lord Silverbridge. There was not even an initial to indicate his name.

But the letter to her brother was much more difficult. In her epistles to those others she had so framed her words as if possible to bring them to Matching. But in writing to her brother, she was anxious so to write as to deter him from coming. She was bound to obey her father's commands. He had desired that Silverbridge should be asked to come,—and he was asked to come. But she craftily endeavoured so to word the invitation that he should be induced to remain away. 'It is all papa's doing,' she said; 'and of course I am very glad that he should like to have people here. I have asked the Finns, with whom papa seems to have made up everything so as to be more friendly with them than ever. Mr. Warburton will be here of course and I think Mr. Moreton is coming, though papa arranges that himself. He seems to think that a certain amount of shooting ought to be done. Then I have invited Lady Mabel Grex and Miss Cassewary,—all of papa's choosing,—and the Boncassens. I don't know whether Lady Mabel and Miss Boncassen will get on well together, but they must take their chance. Now you will know whether the set will suit you. Papa has particularly begged that you will come,—apparently because of Lady Mabel. I don't at all know what that means. Perhaps you do. As I like Lady Mabel very much, I hope she will come.' Mary as she read this over thought that it must be effective. Surely Silverbridge would not run himself into the jaws of the lion. When he heard that he was specially expected by his father to come to Matching in order that he might make himself agreeable to one young lady, he would hardly venture to come, seeing that he would be bound to make love to another young lady! It was thus that Lady Mary argued with herself when she sent her letter off to the post.

After this was a lull for a few days at Matching till the answers came,—during which some few additions were made to the party, invited by the Duke himself. He answered Mr. Monk's letter by asking him to come to Matching, and he also wrote to an old political adherent, one Mr. Barrington Erle, begging him also to become one of the guests. Which facts became known very speedily,—in some occult manner, the nature of which is not at all understood by the world at large,—to the editor of the *People's Banner*,* who explained at considerable length in a leading article that the Duke was collecting together at his country seat the future Cabinet which was to walk into power over the prostrate corpses of Sir Timothy Beeswax and Lord Drummond. As the *People's Banner* always rankled with animosity against the Duke, for reasons which it is not now necessary to explain, the article went on to assert that any such attempt on the part of the Duke and his party was simply a sign of arrogance only equalled by the ignorance displayed,—that Sir Timothy was stronger than ever and the Duke weaker,—that the adherence of Mr. Phineas Finn would damn any party, and that Mr. Monk as a popular politician was altogether 'played out.' All this was expressed in very strong language;—but not the less did the gentlemen named accept the invitations which had been sent to them.

And, to Mary's great horror, all the other invitations were accepted also. Mr. and Mrs. Finn were quite at the Duke's disposal. That she had expected. Mr. and Mrs. and Miss Boncassen would all come. This was signified in a note from Isabel, which covered four sides of the paper and was full of fun. But under her signature had been written a few words,—not in fun,—words which Lady Mary perfectly understood. 'I wonder. I wonder. I wonder!' Lady Mary well knew the cause of her wondering. Did the Duke when inviting her know anything of his son's inclinations? Would he be made to know them now, during this visit? And what would he say when he did know them? There was quite enough in the proposed visit to excite her feelings; and to induce her, as she said, to 'wonder.'

That the Boncassens would come was to Mary a matter of course; but she had thought that Lady Mabel would perhaps have refused. She had taken care to let Lady Mabel know that the Boncassens had been asked, and to her thinking it had not been improbable that the young lady would be unwilling to meet her rival at Matching. But the invitation was accepted in a very short note. Both Lady Mabel and Miss Cassewary were delighted, and ever so much obliged to the Duke!

But it was her brother's ready acquiescence which troubled Mary chiefly. He wrote as though there were no doubt about the matter,—adding very little about the two young ladies. 'Of course there is a deal of shooting to be done,' he said, 'and I consider myself bound to look after it. There ought not to be less than four guns,—particularly if Warburton is to be one of them. I like Warburton very much, but I think he shoots badly on purpose to ingratiate himself with the governor. I wonder whether the governor would get leave for Gerald for a week. He has been sticking to his work like a brick ever since he has been up. If not would he mind my bringing someone? I haven't anyone I care about, only we can't do it with three guns. You ask the governor, and let me know. I'll be there on the 20th. I wonder whether they'll let me hear what goes on among them about politics. I'm sure there's not one of them hates Sir Timothy worse than I do. If they'll give me something good, perhaps I'll rat. Lady Mab is a brick and I'm glad you have asked her. I don't think she'll come as she likes shutting herself up at Grex. Miss Boncassen is another brick. And if you can manage about Gerald, I will say that you are a third.'

This would have been all very well had she not known that secret;—but knowing it, what was she to think? Could it be that Miss Boncassen had been mistaken? She was forced to write again to say that her father did not think it right that Gerald should be brought away from his studies for the sake of shooting, and that the necessary fourth gun would be there in the person of Barrington Erle. Then she added: 'Lady Mabel Grex is coming, and so is Miss Boncassen.' But to this she received no reply. As the matter stood, he would meet both the girls there on Saturday 20th November.

Though Silverbridge had written to his sister in his usual careless style, he had considered the matter much. The three months were over,—the three months at the expiration of which he was to receive his answer from Miss Boncassen. He had no idea of any hesitation on his part. He had asked her to be his wife, and he was fully determined to go on with his suit. Had he ever been enabled to make the same request to Mabel Grex, or had she answered him when he did half make such a request in a manner to make him think that she had received his proposition with favour, he would have been true to her. At present he was quite resolved. He had not told his father, or his sister, or his friends, as Isabel had suggested. He had determined that he would not do so till he should have received some more certain answer from her. But in respect to his love he was prepared to be quite as obstinate as his sister. It was a matter for his own consideration, and he would choose for himself. The three months were over, and it was now his business to present himself to the lady again. Upon the whole he was glad to have the opportunity of doing so at Matching.

That Lady Mabel should also be at Matching would certainly be a misfortune. He thought it probable that she, knowing that Isabel Boncassen and he would be there together, would refuse the invitation. Surely she ought to do so. He had told her what were his intentions. If she was disappointed, that was not his fault. Why had she sent him away when he had shown himself willing to kneel at her feet? It might be that his father would have ground of complaint, but surely she would have none. He thought that she would not show herself at Matching. That was his opinion when he wrote to his sister. When he heard afterwards that she intended to be there, he could only suppose that she was prepared to accept the circumstances as they stood.

CHAPTER 52

MISS BONCASSEN TELLS THE TRUTH

EVERYTHING was very tranquil at Matching till the 20th. Mr. Warburton arrived, and Mr. Moreton; but their business was with the Duke and they did not disturb Lady Mary's quiet. On the 20th all the guests came rattling in, one after another,—some from the north, some from the south, and some from the west. The Boncassens were the first, but Lady Mabel with Miss Cassewary followed them very quickly. Then came the Finns, who had had to pass through London, and with them Barrington Erle. Lastly came Lord Silverbridge himself. He arrived by a late express which reached the station at 7 p.m., and only entered the house as his father was taking Mrs. Boncassen into the dining-room. He dressed himself in ten minutes, and joined the party as they had finished their fish. 'I am awfully sorry,' he said, rushing up to his father, 'but I thought that I should just hit it.'

'There is no occasion for awe,' said the Duke, 'as a sufficiency of dinner is left for you. But how you should have hit it, as you say,—seeing that the train is not due at Bridstock till 7:05, I do not know. You can hardly drive seven miles, have your things unpacked, and dress for dinner in fifty-five minutes.'

'I've done it often, sir,' said Silverbridge, walking around the room and then taking the seat left vacant for him next to Lady Mabel. 'We've had a political caucus of the party,—all the members who could be got together in London,—at Sir Timothy's, and I was bound to attend. I only just got away in time.'

'We've all heard of that,' said Phineas Finn.

'And we pretty well know all the points of Sir Timothy's eloquence,' said Barrington Erle.

'I am not going to tell any of the secrets, I can assure you. I have no doubt that there were reporters present, and you will see the whole of it in the papers to-morrow; but you won't hear a word from me,—unless Mr. Monk has something very good to offer me.'

'I think we can combat Sir Timothy and all his wiles without treachery,' said Mr. Monk laughing.

Then Silverbridge turned to his neighbour. 'Well, Lady Mab, and how are you this long time?'

'But how are you? Think what you have gone through since we were at Killancodlem together!'

'Don't talk of it.'

'I suppose it is not to be talked of.'

'Though upon the whole it has happened very luckily. I have got rid of the accursed horses, and my governor has shown what a brick he can be. He always was a brick, but I don't think there is another man in England who would have done as he did.'

'There are not many who could.'

'There are a great deal fewer who would. When they came into my bedroom that morning and told me that the horse could not run I thought I should have broken my heart. Such a day I had of it. Seventy thousand pounds gone!'

'Seventy thousand pounds!'

'And the honour and glory of winning the race! And then the feeling that one had been so awfully swindled! Of course I had to look as though I did not care a straw about it, and to go and see the race run, with a jaunty air and a cigar in my mouth,—just as though I were as jolly as a sandboy.* That is what I call hard work.'

'But you did it?'

'Well;—I tried. And then, after the race, I started off to London by myself. I wish I could explain to you my state of mind as I went. In the first place the money had to be got. Though it was to go into the hands of swindlers, still it had to be paid. I don't know how your father and Percival get on together;—but I felt uncommonly like the prodigal son.'

'It is very different with papa.'

'I suppose so. I almost felt like hanging myself when I was alone in London that evening. And now everything is right again.'

'I am glad that everything is right,' she said, with a strong emphasis on the 'everything.'

'Everything of that sort, I mean. I have done with racing at any rate. I don't think I'd own a horse if all the best animals in England were offered me for nothing. The feeling of being in the power of a lot of low blackguards is so terrible! I did love the poor brute so dearly. I went to see him in his stable when I first heard about the nail, but I have not put my eyes upon him since. And now what have you been doing?'

'Just nothing;—and have seen nobody. I went back to Grex after leaving Killancodlem, and shut myself up in my misery.'

'Why misery?'

'Why misery! What a question for you to ask! As you are an old friend, I tell you everything. Though I love Grex, I am not altogether fond of living alone. And though Grex has its charms, they are of a melancholy kind. I do not know that a half-furnished barrack exactly suits my taste. And when I think of the state of our family affairs, that is not reassuring. Your father has just paid seventy thousand pounds for you. My father has been good enough to take something less than a quarter of that sum from me;—but still it was all that I was ever to have.'

'Girls don't want money.'

'Don't they? When I look forward it seems to me that a time will soon come when I shall want it very much. Altogether my prospects are not comfortable.'

'You will marry,' he said. She turned round for a moment and looked at him, full in the face, after such a fashion that he did not dare to promise her further comfort in that direction. 'Things always do come right, somehow.'

'Let us hope so. Only nothing has ever come right with me yet. What has become of Frank?'

'I haven't seen him since he left Crummie-Toddie. I suppose he is in Cornwall.'

'And your sister?' she whispered.

'I know nothing about it at all. It never can come to any good; I am sure of that.'

'And you? I have told you everything about myself.'

'As for me, I think of nothing but politics now. I have told you about my racing experiences. Just at present shooting is up. Before Christmas I shall go into Chiltern's country for a little hunting.'

'You can hunt here.'

'I shan't stay long enough to make it worth while to have my horses down. If Tregear will go with me to the Brake, I can mount him for a day or two. But I dare say you know more of his plans than I do. He went to see you at Grex.'

'And you did not.'

'I was not asked.'

'Nor was he.'

'Then all I can say is,' replied Silverbridge, speaking in a low voice, but with considerable energy, 'that he can use a freedom with Lady Mabel Grex upon which I cannot venture.'

'I believe you begrudge me his friendship. If you had no one else belonging to you with whom you could have any sympathy, would not you find comfort in a relation who could be almost as near to you as a brother?'

'I do not grudge him to you.'

'Yes, you do;—although we knew each other as children. And what business have you to interfere?'

'None at all;—certainly. I will never do it again.'

'Don't say that, Lord Silverbridge. You ought to have more mercy on me. Yes, you ought. You ought to put up with anything from me,—knowing how much I suffer.'

'I will put up with anything,' said he.

'Do, do. And now I will try to talk to Mr. Erle.' Mr. Erle was sitting on the other side of her, and her endeavours soon seemed to be crowned with perfect success.

Miss Boncassen was sitting on the other side of the table, between Mr. Monk and Phineas Finn, and throughout the dinner talked mock politics with the greatest liveliness. Silverbridge when he entered the room had gone round the table and had shaken hands with everyone, regarding them almost as being his own guests. But there had been no other greeting between him and Isabel, nor had any sign passed from one to the other. No such greeting or sign had been possible. Nothing had been left undone which she had expected, or hoped, or even conceived. But, though she was very lively in her political badinage with her neighbours, nevertheless she kept her eye upon her lover and Lady Mabel. Lady Mary had said that she thought her brother was in love with Lady Mabel. Could it be possible? In her own land she had heard absurd stories,—stories which at the moment had seemed to her to be absurd,—of the treachery of lords and countesses, of the baseness of aristocrats, of the iniquities of high life in London. But her father had told her that go where she might, she would find people in the main to be very like each other; and she had believed her father. It had seemed to her, in her intercourse with him, that nothing could be more ingenuous than this young man had been in the declaration of his love. No simplest republican could have spoken more plainly. But now, at this moment, seeing what she did see, she could not doubt but that her lover was very intimate with this other girl. Of course he was at liberty to do as he pleased. When she had refused to say a word to him of her own love or want of love, she had necessarily given him that liberty. When she had put him off for three months, of course he was to be his own master. If he never said another word, neither would she. But what must she think of him if it were so? And how could he have the courage to come and face her in his father's house if he intended to treat her in such a fashion? But of all this she showed nothing in her face, nor was there a tone in her voice which betrayed any want of equanimity. When she got up to leave the room, she said her last word to Mr. Monk with so sweet a smile that that old bachelor almost wished he were somewhat younger for her sake.

'If it is considered desirable, sir,' said Silverbridge when the ladies were gone, 'I'll take my glass and a bottle of wine, and go and sit alone in the billiard-room. I don't want to hear any secrets.'

The Duke shook his head. 'Is it not a pity that there should be secrets between you and me?'

'What are the secrets?' asked Phineas. 'I am sure it is no secret that we all want to get rid of Sir Timothy Beeswax. But we have nothing to do with it. We have only got to wait till our time comes. That there are secrets between him and Lord Drummond, and between him and Lord Ramsden, and him and Sir Orlando, no one can doubt. Very disagreeable secrets I should think they must be. But I don't suppose that we have any secrets.'

'I have none,' said Mr. Monk.

'Perhaps I rather meant counsels,' said the Duke sadly. But after that the conversation turned rather on shooting than on politics. There was very little spoken which even the ingenuity of the editor of the *People's Banner* could have made the subject of sterling political denunciation. Afterward, during the evening, music prevailed. It was discovered that Miss Boncassen sang divinely, and both Lady Mabel and Lady Mary accompanied her. Mr. Erle, and Mr. Warburton, and Mr. Monk, all of whom were unmarried, stood by enraptured. But Lord Silverbridge kept himself apart, and interested himself in a description which Mrs. Boncassen gave him of their young men and their young ladies in the States. He hardly came forward,—had hardly spoken to Miss Boncassen,—till he offered her sherry or soda-water before she retired for the night. She refused his courtesy with her usual smile, but showed no more emotion than though they two had now met for the first time in their lives.

He had quite made up his mind as to what he would do. When the opportunity should come in his way he would simply remind her that the three months were passed. But though he was fully resolved as to this, nevertheless he was shy of talking to her in the presence of Lady Mabel and his father. He was quite determined that the thing should be done, and done at once, but he certainly wished that Lady Mabel had not been there. In what she had said to him at the dinner-table she had made him understand that she would be a trouble to him. He remembered her look when he told her she would marry. It was as though she had declared to him that it was he who ought to be her husband. That look could have meant nothing else. It referred back to that proffer of love which he had once made to her,—just as though she had not rejected the proffer. Of course all this was disagreeable. Of course it made things difficult for him. But not the less was it a thing quite assured that he would press his suit to Miss Boncassen. When he was talking to Mrs. Boncassen he was thinking of nothing else. When he was offering Isabel the glass of sherry he was telling himself that he would find his opportunity on the morrow,—though now, at that moment, it was impossible that he should make a sign. She, as she went to bed, asked herself whether it were possible that there should be such treachery;—whether it were possible that he should pass it all by as though he had never said a word to her!

During the whole of the next day, which was Sunday, he was equally silent. Immediately after breakfast, on the Monday, shooting commenced, and though he was in the house for a couple of hours before dinner he could not find a moment in which to speak. It seemed to him that she purposely kept out of his way. With Mabel he did find himself for a few minutes alone, and was then interrupted by his sister and Isabel. 'I hope you have killed a lot of things,' said Miss Boncassen.

'Pretty well, among us all.'

'What an odd amusement it seems, going out to commit wholesale slaughter. However it is the proper thing no doubt.'

'Quite the proper thing,' said Lord Silverbridge, and that was all.

On the next morning he dressed himself for shooting,—and then sent out the party without him. He had heard, he said, of a young horse for sale in the neighbourhood, and had sent to desire that it might be brought to him to be looked at. And now he found his occasion.

'Come and play a game of billiards,' he said to Isabel, as the three girls with the other ladies were together in the drawing-room. She got up very slowly from her seat, and very slowly crept away to the door. Then she looked round as though expecting the other ladies to follow her. None of them did follow her. Mary felt that she ought to do so; but, knowing all that she knew, did not dare to do it. And what good could she have done by one such interruption as that? Lady Mabel would fain have gone too;—but neither did she quite dare. Had there been no special reason why she should or should not have gone with them, the thing would have been easy enough. When two people go to play billiards, a third may surely accompany them. But now, on this occasion, Lady Mabel found that she could not stir. Mrs. Finn, Mrs. Boncassen, and Miss Cassewary were all in the room, but none of them moved. Silverbridge led the way quickly across the hall, and Isabel Boncassen followed him very slowly. When she entered the room she found him standing with a cue in his hand. He at once shut the door, and walking up to her dropped the butt of the cue on the floor and spoke one word. 'Well!' he said.

'What does "well" mean?'

'The three months are over.'

'Certainly they are "over." '

'And I have been a model of patience.'

'Perhaps your patience is more remarkable than your constancy. Is not Lady Mabel Grex in the ascendant just now?'

'What do you mean by that? Why do you ask that? You told me to wait for three months. I have waited and here I am.'

'How very—very—downright you are.'

'Is not that the proper thing?'

'I thought I was downright,—but you beat me hollow. Yes, the three months are over. And now what have you got to say?' He put down his cue, and stretched out his arms as though he were going to take her and hold her to his heart. 'No;—no; not that,' she said laughing. 'But if you will speak, I will hear you.'

'You know what I said before. Will you love me, Isabel?'

'And you know what I said before. Do they know that you love me? Does your father know it, and your sister? Why did they ask us to come here?'

'Nobody knows it. But say that you love me and everyone shall know it at once. Yes;—one person knows it. Why did you mention Lady Mabel's name? She knows it.'

'Did you tell her?'

'Yes. I went again to Killancodlem after you were gone, and then I told her.'

'But why her? Come, Lord Silverbridge; you are straightforward with me, and I will be the same with you. You have told Lady Mabel. I have told Lady Mary.'

'My sister!'

'Yes;—your sister. And I am sure she disapproves it. She did not say so, but I am sure it is so. And then she told me something.'

'What did she tell you?'

'Has there never been reason to think that you intended to offer your hand to Lady Mabel Grex?'

'Did she tell you so?'

'You should answer my question, Lord Silverbridge. It is surely one which I have a right to ask.' Then she stood waiting for his reply, keeping herself at some little distance from him as though she were afraid that he would fly upon her. And indeed there seemed to be cause for such fear from the frequent gestures of his hands. 'Why do you not answer me? Has there been reason for such expectations?'

'Yes,—there has.'

'There has!'

'I thought of it,—not knowing myself; before I had seen you. You shall know it all if you will only say that you love me.'

'I should like to know it all first.'

'You do know it all,—almost. I have told you that she knows what I said to you at Killancodlem. Is not that enough?'

'And she approves?'

'What has that to do with it? Lady Mabel is my friend, but not my guardian.'

'Has she a right to expect that she should be your wife?'

'No;—certainly not. Why should you ask all this? Do you love me? Come, Isabel, say that you love me. Will you call me vain if I say that I almost think you do? You cannot doubt about my love;—not now.'

'No;—not now.'

'You needn't. Why won't you be as honest to me? If you hate me, say so;—but if you love me——!'

'I do not hate you, Lord Silverbridge.'

'And is that all?'

'You asked me the question.'

'But you do love me? By George, I thought you would be more honest and straightforward.'

Then she dropped her badinage and answered him seriously enough. 'I thought I had been honest and straightforward. When I found that you were in earnest at Killancodlem——'

'Why did you ever doubt me?'

'When I felt that you were in earnest, then I had to be in earnest too. And I thought so much about it that I lay awake nearly all that night. Shall I tell you what I thought?'

'Tell me something that I should like to hear.'

'I will tell you the truth. "Is it possible," I said to myself, "that such a man as that can want me to be his wife; he an Englishman, of the highest rank and the greatest wealth, and one that any girl in the world would love?" '

'Psha!' he exclaimed.

'That is what I said to myself.' Then she paused, and looking into her face he saw that there was a glimmer of a tear in each eye. ' "One that any girl must love when asked for her love;—because he is so sweet, so good, and so pleasant." '

'I know that you are chaffing.'

'Then I went on asking myself questions. "And is it possible that I, who by all his friends will be regarded as a nobody, who am an American,—with merely human work-a-day blood in my veins,—that such a one as I should become his wife?" Then I told myself that it was not possible. It was not in accordance with the fitness of things. All the dukes in England would rise up against it, and especially that Duke whose good-will would be imperative.'

'Why should he rise up against it?'

'You know he will. But I will go on with my story of myself. When I had settled that in my mind, I just cried myself to sleep. It had been a dream. I had come across one who in his own self seemed to combine all that I had ever thought of as being lovable in man——'

'Isabel!'

'And in his outward circumstances soared as much above my thoughts as the heaven is above the earth. And he had whispered to me soft, loving, heavenly words. No;—no. You shall not touch me. But you shall listen to me. In my sleep I could be happy again and not see the barriers. But when I woke I made up my mind. "If he comes to me again," I said—"if it should be that he should come to me again, I will tell him that he shall be my heaven on earth,—if,—if,—if the ill-will of his friends would not make that heaven a hell to both of us." I did not tell you quite all that.'

'You told me nothing but that I was to come again in three months.'

'I said more than that. I bade you ask your father. Now you have come again. You cannot understand a girl's fears and doubts. How should you? I thought perhaps you would not come. When I saw you whispering to that highly born well-bred beauty, and remembered what I was myself, I thought that—you would not come.'

'Then you must love me.'

'Love you! Oh, my darling! No, no, no,' she said, as she retreated from him round the corner of the billiard-table, and stood guarding herself from him with her little hands upon the cushion. 'You ask if I love you. You are entitled to know the truth. From the sole of your foot to the crown of your head I love you as I think a man would wish to be loved by the girl he loves. You have come across my life, and have swallowed me up, and made me all your own. But I will not marry you to be rejected by your people. No;—nor shall there be a kiss between us till I know that it will not be so.'

'May I speak to your father?'

'For what good? I have not spoken to father or mother because I have known that it must depend upon your father. Lord Silverbridge, if he will tell me that I shall be his daughter I will become your wife,—oh, with such perfect joy, with such perfect trust! If it can never be so, then let us be torn apart,—with whatever struggle, still at once. In that case I will get myself back to my own country as best I may, and will pray to God that all this may in time be forgotten.' Then she made her way round to the door, leaving him fixed to the spot in which she had been standing. But as she went she made a little prayer to him. 'Do not delay my fate. It is all in all to me.' And so he was left alone in the billiard-room.

CHAPTER 53

'THEN I AM AS PROUD AS A QUEEN'

DURING the next day or two the shooting went on without much interruption either from politics or from love-making. In politics there was not in truth very much to be done. The general conclusion among the politicians assembled seemed to be that if sufficient rope were allowed to that chief enemy, Sir Timothy Beeswax, he would probably hang himself, and that therefore it was desirable to give him as much rope as possible. Nothing could be done till the next spring. There was no chance that either Sir Timothy or Lord Drummond would resign till they had encountered the accidents of another session. Should the accidents of the session drive Sir Timothy from his position, then, it was thought, Mr. Monk must be selected as the only person in the House capable of forming a Government. In that event the Duke would, if at the moment he found it possible, lend his cooperation to any arrangements that might be made. The meaning of this was that in the event of the party coming into power he would consent to be President of the Council* and to fill the office which his old friend the Duke of St. Bungay positively refused to occupy again. In achieving this Mr. Monk,

Phineas Finn, and Barrington Erle thought that they had achieved very much. The nucleus of a Liberal Cabinet was again made. There was no doubt that Lord Cantrip would join such a party. Barrington Erle and Phineas Finn, as they walked about the grounds on the second Sunday, previous to their departure on the Monday following, were able to fill up nearly all the important offices. Mr. Monk and the Duke were, perhaps, more intent upon the measures which they thought ought to be proposed to Parliament.

Such were the political achievements of the Duke's guests, but the love-making was not quite so prosperous. Poor Lady Mary had nothing to comfort her. Could she have been allowed to see the letter which her lover had written to her father,—could she have been made to know but a few of the words which had there been written,—the comfort would have been, if not ample, still very great. In regard to any matter that is of importance to us, though we may not doubt that the facts are as we desire them to be, still to be assured that they are so is always a comfort. Mary told herself again and again that she was quite sure of Tregear;—but it was hard upon her that she could not be made certain that her certainty was well grounded. Had she known that Tregear had written, though she had not seen a word of his letter, it would have comforted her for a time. But she had heard nothing of the letter, and nothing of her father's reply. In June last she had seen him, by chance, for a few minutes, in Lady Mabel's drawing-room. Since that she had not heard from him or of him. That was now more than five months since. During all those five months she had not heard his name mentioned. How could her love serve her,—how could her very life serve her, if things were to go on like this? It might be for years,—or it might be for ever! How was she to bear it? Thinking of this she resolved, she almost resolved, that she would go boldly to her father and desire that she might be given up to her lover.

Her brother, though infinitely more triumphant,—for how could he fail to triumph after such words as Isabel had spoken to him?—still felt his own difficulties very seriously. She had imbued him with a strong sense of her own firmness, and she had declared to him that she would go away and leave him altogether if the Duke should be unwilling to receive her. He knew very well that the Duke would be unwilling. The Duke, who was not crafty in managing either his family or his political adherents, and who certainly was not handy in those duties of match-making which seemed to have fallen upon him at the death of his wife, showed by a hundred little signs his anxiety that his son and heir should arrange his affairs with Lady Mabel. These signs were manifest to Mary,—were disagreeably manifest to Silverbridge,—were unfortunately manifest to Lady Mabel herself. They were manifest to Mrs. Finn, who was clever enough to perceive that the inclinations of the young heir himself were turned quite in another direction. And gradually they became manifest to Isabel Boncassen. The host himself, as host, was courteous to all his guests. They had been of his own selection, and he did his best to make himself pleasant to them all. But he selected two for his peculiar notice,—and those two were Miss Boncassen and Lady Mabel. But while he would himself walk, and talk, and argue after his own peculiar fashion with the American beauty,—explaining to her matters political and social, till he absolutely persuaded her to promise to read his pamphlet upon decimal coinage,—he was always making awkward efforts to throw Silverbridge and Lady Mabel together. The two girls saw it all and knew well how the matter was,—knew that they were rivals, and knew each the ground on which she herself and on which the other stood. But neither was satisfied with her advantage, or nearly satisfied. Isabel would not take the prize without the Duke's consent;—and Mabel could not have it without that other consent, which she feared would be the more difficult to attain. 'If you want to marry an English duke,' she once said to Isabel in that anger which she was unable to restrain, 'there is the Duke himself. I never saw a man more absolutely in love.' 'But I do not want to marry an English duke,' said Isabel, 'and I pity any girl who has any idea of marriage except that which comes from a wish to give back love for love.'

Through it all the father never suspected for a moment the real state of his son's mind. He was too simple to think it possible that the purpose which Silverbridge had declared to him as they walked together from the Beargarden to the Houses of Parliament had already been thrown to the winds. He did not like to ask directly why the thing was not settled. Young men, he thought, were sometimes shy, and young ladies not always ready to give immediate encouragement. But, when he saw them together,—and they often were together,—he concluded that matters were going in that direction as he would have them. It was, however, an opinion which he had all to himself.

During the three or four days which followed that scene in the billiard-room Isabel kept herself as much as she could out of her lover's way. She had explained to him that which she wished him to do, and she left him to do it. Day by day she watched the circumstances of the life around her, and knew that it had not been done. She was sure that it could not have been done while the Duke was explaining to her the beauty of quints,* and expatiating on the horrors of twelve pennies, and twelve inches, and twelve ounces,—variegated in some matters by sixteen and fourteen! He could not know that she was ambitious of becoming his daughter-in-law, while he was opening out to her the mysteries of the British House of Peers, and explaining how it came to pass that while he was a member of one House of Parliament, his son should be sitting as a member of another;—how it was that a nobleman could be a commoner, and how a peer of one part of the Empire could sit as the representative of a borough in another part. She was an apt scholar, intent no doubt on proving to him that however different she might be as to birth, she was in intellect equal to any position that might be offered to her. In this she altogether succeeded. Had there been a question of any other young man marrying her, he would probably have thought that no other young man could have done better. But, during these days, Isabel never deluded herself into feeling that she was overcoming the one difficulty which stood in her way.

Silverbridge was of course discontented with himself. The greatest misfortune was that Lady Mabel should be there. While she was present to his father's eyes he did not know how to declare his altered wishes. Every now and then she would say to him some little word indicating her feelings of the absurdity of his passion. 'I declare I don't know whether it is you or your father that Miss Boncassen most affects,' she said. But to this and to other little speeches of the same kind he would make no answer. She had extracted his secret from him at Killancodlem, and might use it against him if she pleased. In his present frame of mind he was not at all disposed to joke with her upon the subject.

On that second Sunday,—it having been then decided that the Boncassens were to return to London on the following Tuesday,—he found himself by chance alone with Isabel's father. The American had been brought out at his own request to see the stables and coach-houses, and had been accompanied round the premises by Silverbridge, Mr. Warburton, by Isabel herself, and by Lady Mary. As they got out into the park the party had become divided, and Silverbridge found himself with Mr. Boncassen. Then it occurred to him that the proper thing for a young man in love was to go, not to his own father, but to the lady's father. Why should not he do as others always did? Isabel no doubt had suggested a different course. But that which Isabel had suggested was at the present moment impossible to him. He might do it when he found himself alone with his father. He might do it when Mabel was gone. At the present moment it was impossible,—and yet it was indispensably necessary that something should be done. He could not allow her to leave Matching without taking some steps towards the declaration of his purpose. Now at this instant, without a moment's forethought, he determined to tell his story to Isabel's father,—as any other lover might tell it to any other father.

'I am very glad to find ourselves alone, Mr. Boncassen,' he said. Mr. Boncassen bowed and showed himself prepared to listen. Though so many at Matching had seen the whole play, Mr. Boncassen had seen nothing of it. When the young Lord told him that this opportunity for private conversation was very fortunate, his mind was quite a blank as to what might be the subject of conversation. 'I don't know whether you are aware of what I have got to say.'

'I cannot quite say that I am, my Lord.' The American was perhaps a little too demonstrative in his title. 'But whatever it is, I am sure I shall be delighted to hear it.'

'I want to marry your daughter,' said Silverbridge. Isabel had told him that he was downright, and in such a matter he had hardly as yet learned how to express himself with those paraphrases in which the world delights. Mr. Boncassen stood stock still, and in the excitement of the moment pulled off his hat. 'The proper thing is to ask your permission to go on with it.'

'You want to marry my daughter!'

'Yes. That is what I have got to say.'

'Is she aware of your—intention?'

'Quite aware. I believe I may say that if other things go straight, she will consent.'

'And your father—the Duke?'

'He knows nothing about it,—as yet.'

'Really, Lord Silverbridge, this takes me quite by surprise. You want to marry my daughter!'

'Certainly I do.'

'I am afraid you have not given enough thought to the matter.'

'I have been thinking about it for the last three months,' said Lord Silverbridge.

'Marriage is a very serious thing.'

'Of course it is.'

'And men generally like to marry their equals.'

'I don't know about that. I don't think that counts for much. People don't always know who are their equals.'

'That is quite true. If I were speaking to you or to your father theoretically I should perhaps be unwilling to admit superiority on your side simply because of your rank and wealth. I could make an argument in favour of my equality with the best Briton that ever lived,—as would become a true-born republican.'

'That is just what I mean.'

'But when the question becomes one of practice,—a question for our lives, for our happiness, for our own conduct, then, knowing what must be the feelings of an aristocracy in such a country as this, I am prepared to admit that your father would be as well justified in objecting to a marriage between a child of his and a child of mine as I should be in objecting to one between my child and the son of some mechanic in our native city.'

'He wouldn't be a gentleman,' said Silverbridge, using the argument with which his sister had always supported her cause.

'That is a word of which I don't quite know the meaning.'

'I do,' said Silverbridge confidently.

'But you could not define it. If a man be well educated and can keep a good house over his head perhaps you may call him a gentleman. But there are many such with whom your father would not wish to be so closely connected as you propose.'

'But I may have your sanction?' Mr. Boncassen again took off his hat and walked along thoughtfully. 'I hope you don't object to me personally.'

'My dear young Lord, what ought I to say if one of your royal princes were to be imprudent enough to make to me the same offer? Your father has gone out of his way to be civil to me. Am I to return his courtesy by bringing a great trouble upon him?'

'He seems to be very fond of Miss Boncassen.'

'Will he continue to be fond of her when he has heard this? What does Isabel say herself?'

'She says the same as you, of course.'

'Why "of course";—except that it is evident to you as it is to me that she could not with propriety say anything else?'

'I think she would,—would like it, you know.'

'She would like to be your wife!'

'Well;—yes. I don't mean to boast about it; but if it were all serene, I think she would consent.'

'I dare say she would consent,—if it were all serene. Why should she not? Do not try her too hard, Lord Silverbridge. You say you love her.'

'I do indeed.'

'Then think of the position in which you are placing her. You are struggling to win her heart.' Silverbridge as he heard this assured himself that there was no need for any further struggling in that direction.

'Perhaps you have won it, or at any rate made some impression which cannot be removed without a pang. And yet she may feel that she cannot with due regard to her own dignity become your wife. She may well say to herself that all this that is offered to her is so great that she does not know how to refuse it; and may yet have to say, at the same time, that she cannot accept it without disgrace. You would not put one that you love into such a position?'

'As for disgrace,—that is nonsense. I beg your pardon, Mr. Boncassen.'

'Would it be no disgrace that she should be known here, in England, to be your wife, and that none of those of your rank,—of what would then be her own rank,—should welcome her into her new world? From what you have seen of her, do you think she would bear that easily?'

'That would be out of the question.'

'If your own father refused to welcome her would not others follow suit, do you think?'

'You don't know my father.'

'You seem to know him well enough to fear that he would object.'

'Yes;—that is true.'

'What more do I want to know?'

'If she were once my wife he could not reject her. Of all human beings he is in truth the kindest and most affectionate. My father could not be harsh. He might object, but then he would accept her.'

'And therefore you would try him after this fashion? No, my Lord; I cannot see my way through these difficulties. You can say what you please to him as to your own wishes. But you must not tell him that you have any sanction from me.'

That evening the whole story was told to Mrs. Boncassen, and the matter was discussed among the family. Isabel in talking to them made no scruple of declaring her own feelings; and though in speaking to Lord Silverbridge she had spoken very much as her father had done afterwards, yet in this family conclave she took her lover's part,—and in doing so perhaps her own. 'That is all very well, father,' she said; 'and I told him the same thing myself. But if he is man enough to be firm I shall not throw him over,—not for all the dukes in Europe. I shall not stay here to be pointed at. I will go back home. If he follows me, then I shall choose to forget all about his rank. If he loves me well enough to show that he is really in earnest I shall not disappoint him for the sake of pleasing his father.' To this neither Mr. nor Mrs. Boncassen were able to make any efficient answer. Mrs. Boncassen, dear good woman, could see no reason why two young people who loved each other should not be married at once. Dukes and duchesses were nothing to her.

If they couldn't be happy in England, then let them come and live in New York. She didn't understand that anybody could be too good for her daughter. Was there not an idea that Mr. Boncassen would be the next President? And was not the President of the United States as good as the Queen of England? Mr. Boncassen listened to his daughter without rebuke. It was her affair and not his. When asked his advice he could give it, but that was all.

Lord Silverbridge when he left Mr. Boncassen wandered about the park awhile by himself. King Cophetua* married the beggar's daughter. He was sure of that. King Cophetua probably had not a father; and the beggar, probably, was not high-minded. But the discrepancy in that case was much greater. He intended to persevere, trusting much to a belief that when once he was married his father would surely 'come round.' His father always did come round. But the more he thought of it the more impossible it seemed to him that he should ask his father's consent now at the present moment. Lady Mabel's presence in the house was an insuperable obstacle. He thought that he could do it if he and his father were alone together, or comparatively alone. He must be prepared for an opposition, at any rate of some days, which opposition would make his father quite unable to entertain his guests while it lasted. At the present moment the Duke was doing his best to make himself pleasant,—as Silverbridge understood. It would be cruel to disturb him at such a period.

But as he could not declare his wishes to his father, and by not doing so was already disobeying Isabel's behests, he must explain the difficulty to her. He could not allow her to leave Matching without further words between them. He felt already that she would despise him for his cowardice,—that she would not perceive the difficulties in his way, or understand that he might injure his cause by precipitation. He had hoped that Mr. Boncassen might assist him, but Mr. Boncassen had only made fresh difficulties. Then he considered whether he might not possibly make some bargain with his father. How would it be if he should consent to go back to the Liberal party on being allowed to marry the girl he loved? As far as his political feelings were concerned he did not think that he would much object to make such a change. But then he must give up his seat,* and his father, he was sure, would not approve of that. There was only one thing certain,—that he must explain his condition to Miss Boncassen before she went.

He found no difficulty now in getting the opportunity he desired. She was equally anxious, and as well disposed to acknowledge her anxiety. After what had passed between them she was not at all desirous of pretending that the matter was one of small moment to herself. She had told him that it was all the world to her, and had begged him to let her know her fate as quickly as possible. On that last Monday morning they were in the grounds together, and Lady Mabel, who was walking with Mrs. Finn, saw them pass through a little gate which led from the gardens into the Priory ruins. 'It all means nothing,' Mabel said with a little laugh to her companion.

'If so, I am sorry for the young lady,' said Mrs. Finn.

'Don't you think that one always has to be sorry for the young ladies? Young ladies generally have a bad time of it. Did you ever hear of a gentleman who had always to roll a stone to the top of a hill; but it would always come back upon him, and then he would have to begin again?'*

'That gentleman I believe never succeeded,' said Mrs. Finn. 'The young ladies I suppose do sometimes.'

In the meantime Isabel and Silverbridge were among the ruins together. 'This is where the old Pallisers used to be buried,' he said.

'Oh,—indeed. And married, I suppose?'

'I dare say. They had a priest of their own, no doubt, which must have been convenient. This block of a fellow without any legs left is supposed to represent Sir Guy. He ran away with half-a-dozen heiresses they say. I wish things were as easily done now.'

'Nobody should have run away with me. I have no idea of going on such a journey except on terms of perfect equality,—just step and step alike.' Then she took hold of his arm and put out one foot as though she were going to march away with him. 'Are you ready?'

'I am very willing.'

'But are you ready,—for a straightforward walk off to church before all the world? None of your private chaplains, such as Sir Guy had at his command. Just the registrar, if there is nothing better,—so that it be public, before all the world.'

'I wish we could start this instant.'

'But we can't,—can we?'

'No, dear. So many things have to be settled.'

'And what have you settled on since you last spoke to me?'

'I have told your father everything.'

'Yes;—I know that. What good does that do? Father is not a Duke of Omnium. No one supposed that he would object.'

'But he did,' said Silverbridge.

'Yes;—as I do; for the same reason; because he would not have his daughter creep in at a hole, as I told you. But to your own father you have not ventured to speak.' Then he told his story, as best he knew how. It was not that he feared his father, but that he felt that the present moment was not fit. 'He wishes you to marry that Lady Mabel Grex,' she said. He nodded his head. 'And you will marry her?'

'Never! I might have done so, had I not seen you. I should have done so, if she had been willing. But now I never can,—never, never.' Her hand had dropped from his arm, but now she put it up again for a moment, so that he might feel the pressure of her fingers. 'Say that you believe me.'

'I think I do.'

'You know I love you.'

'I think you do. I am sure I hope you do. If you don't, then I am— a miserable wretch.'

'With all my heart I do.'

'Then I am as proud as a queen. You will tell him soon?'

'As soon as you are gone. As soon as we are alone together. I will,—and then I will follow you to London. Now shall we not say, good-bye?'

'Good-bye, my own,' she whispered.

'You will let me have one kiss?'

Her hand was in his, and she looked about as though to see that no eyes were watching them. But then, as the thoughts came rushing to her mind, she changed her purpose. 'No,' she said. 'What is it but a trifle! It is nothing in itself. But I have bound myself to myself by certain promises, and you must not ask me to break them. You are as sweet to me as I can be to you, but there shall be no kissing till I know that I shall be your wife. Now take me back. There were eyes looking at us when you brought me through the gate, and I do not care if they be there to look at us again.'

VOLUME 3

CHAPTER 54

'HE MUST BE MADE TO PLEASE SOMETHING ELSE'

ON the following day, Tuesday, the Boncassens went, and then there were none of the guests left but Mrs. Finn and Lady Mabel Grex,—with of course Miss Cassewary. The political gathering had dispersed itself. Mr. Moreton had gone back to his duties at Gatherum, and even Mr. Warburton had been relieved from his duties. The Duke had especially asked both Mrs. Finn and Lady Mabel to remain, the former, through his anxiety to show his repentance for the injustice he had formerly done her, and the latter in the special hope that something might be settled as soon as the crowd of visitors should have gone. He had never spoken quite distinctly to Mabel. He had felt that the manner in which he had learned his son's purpose,—that which once had been his son's purpose,—forbade him to do so. But he had so spoken to her as to make Lady Mabel herself quite aware of his wish. He would not have told her how sure he was that Silverbridge would keep no more race-horses, how he trusted that Silverbridge had done with betting, how he believed that the young member would take a real interest in the House of Commons, and much more of the same kind, had he not intended that she should take some special interest in the young man. And then he had spoken about the house in London. It was to be made over to Silverbridge as soon as Silverbridge should marry. And there was Gatherum Castle. Gatherum no doubt was rather a trouble than otherwise. He had ever felt it to be so, but had nevertheless always kept it open perhaps for a month in the year. His uncle had always resided there for a fortnight at Christmas. When Silverbridge was married it would become the young man's duty to do something of the same kind. Gatherum was the White Elephant* of the family, and Silverbridge must enter in upon his share of the trouble. He did not know that in saying all this he was offering his son as a husband to Lady Mabel, but she understood it as thoroughly as though he had spoken the words plainly.

But she knew the son's mind as well as she did the father's. He had indeed himself told her all his mind. 'Of course I love her best of all,' he had said. No doubt he had done so then, and she had perceived that his love had in no degree diminished. When he told her of it she had been so overcome that she had wept in her despair;—had wept in his presence. She had declared to him her secret,—that it had been her intention to become his wife, if she could compass it. Then he had rejected her! And since that, though they had been frequently together here at Matching, he had not said a word from which she could get encouragement. It had all been shame, and sorrow, and disappointment to her. And she could not but remember that there had been a moment when she might have secured him by a word. A look would have done it; a touch of her finger on that morning. She had known then that he had intended to be in earnest,—that he only waited for such encouragement as she might easily have given him. She had not given it because she had not wished to grasp too eagerly at the prize,—and now the prize was gone! She had said that she had spared him;—but then she could afford to joke, thinking that he would surely come back to her. But this American had crossed his path, and hers, and now all the world was a blank to her.

It was indeed a sad blank. She had begun her world with so fatal a mistake! When she was quite young, when she was little more than a child but still not a child, she had given all her love to a man whom she soon found that it would be impossible she should ever marry. He had offered to face the world with her, promising to do his best to smooth the rough places, and to soften the stones for her feet. But she, young as she was, had felt that both he and she belonged to a class which could hardly endure poverty with contentment. The grinding need for money, the absolute necessity of luxurious living, had been pressed upon her from her very childhood. She had seen it and acknowledged it, and had told him, with precocious wisdom, that that which he offered to do for her sake would be a folly for them both. She had not stinted the assurance of her love, but had told him that they must both turn aside and learn to love elsewhere. He had done so, with too complete a readiness,—with a sincerity which was hardly gratifying to her. She had dreamed of a second love, which should not, however, obliterate the first,—of something which might satisfy her aspirations for a home and a position, but which might still leave to her the memory of the romance of her early passion. Then this boy had come in her way;—for when he had first come across her path, he had been little more than a boy. With him all her ambition might have been satisfied. She desired high rank, and great wealth, and all that fashion could give her. With him she might have had it all. And then, too, though there would always be the memory of that early passion, though that romance, she thought, would never die out of her heart, yet she could in another fashion love this youth. He was pleasant to her, and gracious;—and she had told herself that if it should be so that this great fortune might be hers, she would atone to him fully for that past romance by the wife-like devotion of her life. The cup had come within the reach of her fingers, but she had not grasped it. Her happiness, her triumphs, her great success had been there, present to her, and she had dallied with her fortune. There had been a day on which he had been all but at her feet, and on the next he had been altogether prostrate at the feet of another. He had even dared to tell her so,—saying of that American that 'of course he loved her the best!'

Over and over again since that she had asked herself whether there was no chance. She must put up with things now which she had once thought she could never have endured. Though he had loved that other one best she would take him if it were possible. When the invitation came from the Duke, though Mary had told her that Miss Boncassen would be there, she would not lose a chance. She had told him that it was impossible that he, the heir to the Duke of Omnium, should marry an American, and she almost thought that she had told him the truth. All his family, all his friends, all his world would be against him. And then he was so young,—and, as she thought, so easily led. He was lovable and prone to love;—but surely his love could not be very strong, or he would not have changed so easily, straying from her to this American girl as a bee strays from one flower to another. She hoped now that his affections might not be strong, that he might be prone to change, so that in his vacillations he might come back to her.

She did not hesitate to own to herself that this American was very lovely. She too, herself, was beautiful. She too had a reputation for grace, loveliness, and feminine high-bred charm. She knew all that, but she knew also that her attractions were not so bright as those of her rival. She could not smile or laugh and throw sparks of brilliance around her as did the American girl. Miss Boncassen could be graceful as a nymph in doing the awkwardest thing! When she had pretended to walk stiffly along, to some imaginary marriage ceremony, with her foot stuck out before her, with her chin in the air, and one arm akimbo, Silverbridge had been all afire with admiration. Lady Mabel understood it all. The American girl must be taken away,—from out of the reach of the young man's senses,—and then the struggle must be made. Then all the family, all the friends, all the world must combine to teach him how impossible it was that he should marry an American,—and an American so meanly born.

Lady Mabel had not been long at Matching before she learned that she had very much in her favour. She soon perceived that the Duke himself had no suspicion of what was going on, and she perceived also that he was strongly disposed in her favour. She unravelled it all in her own mind as well as she knew how. There must have been some accord, some agreement, between the father and the son, when the son had all but made his offer to her. More than once she was half-minded to speak openly to the Duke, to tell him what she feared and what she hoped,—to tell him all that Silverbridge had said to her and all that he had not said, and to ask the father's help in scheming against that rival. But she did not quite dare to do it. She could not find the words with which to begin. And then, might he not despise her, and despising her reject her, were she to declare her desire to marry a man who, as she knew, had given his heart to another woman? And so, when the Duke asked her to remain after the departure of the other guests, and seemed to signify that her time would then come, she decided that it would be best to bide her time. Of course she would remain. The Duke, as she assented, kissed her hand, and she knew that this sign of grace was given to his intended daughter-in-law. Surely among them they might be too strong for that boy!

In all this she half confided her thoughts and half confided her prospects to her old friend, Miss Cassewary. 'That creature has gone at last,' she said to Miss Cass in her own room on that Tuesday morning.

'I fear she has left her spells behind her, my dear.'

'Of course she has. The venom out of the snake's tooth will poison all the blood; but still the poor bitten wretch does not always die.'

'I don't think she is a snake.'

'Don't be moral, Cass. She is a snake in my sense. I have not a word to say against her character. She has got her weapons and of course it is natural enough that she should use them. If I want to be Duchess of Omnium, why shouldn't she?'

'I hate to hear you talk of yourself in that way.'

'Because you have enough of the old school about you to like conventional falsehood and make-believe proprieties. This young man did in fact ask me to be his wife. Of course I meant to accept him,—but I didn't. Then comes this convict's granddaughter.'

'Not a convict's!'

'You know what I mean. Had he been a convict it would have been all the same. I take upon myself to say that had the world been informed that an alliance had been arranged between the eldest son of the Duke of Omnium and the daughter of Earl Grex,—the world would have been quite satisfied. Every unmarried daughter of every peer in England would have envied me,—and perhaps some of the young men might have envied him. But it would all have been *comme il faut*.'

'Certainly, my dear.'

'But what would be the feeling as to the convict's granddaughter? Looking all round it don't you know that such a thing ought not to be?'

'You don't suppose that I would approve it;—but it seems to me that in these days young men do just what they please.'

'He shall do what he pleases, but he must be made to please something else.' So much she said to Miss Cassewary; but she did not divulge any plan. Indeed at that moment her plans were hardly formed. The Boncassens had just gone off to the station, and Silverbridge was out shooting with one or two gentlemen of the neighbourhood. If anything could be done here at Matching, it must be done quickly, as Silverbridge, no doubt, would soon take his departure. That which had attracted him was gone, and it could hardly be expected that he would remain. She did not know it, but, in truth, he was remaining in order that he might, as he said, 'have all this out with the governor.'

She tried to realise for herself some plan,—something that might be done at once. But when the evening came nothing was fixed as yet. For a quarter of an hour, just as the sun was setting, the Duke joined her in the gardens,—and then spoke to her more plainly than he had ever spoken before. 'Has Silverbridge come home?' he asked.

'I have not seen him.'

'I hope you and Mary get on well together.'

'I think so, Duke. I am sure we should if we saw more of each other.'

'I hope you may do so. I sincerely hope you may. There is nothing I wish for Mary so much as that she should have a sister. And there is no one whom I would be so glad to hear her call by that name as yourself.' How could he have spoken plainer? Lady Mabel looked up into his face blushing,—with a purposed blush, and, without speaking a word, had thus told him that she also wished that it might be so.

The ladies were all together in the drawing-room when Silverbridge came bursting in rather late. 'Where's the governor?' he asked, turning to his sister.

'Dressing I should think;—but what is the matter?'

'The Duke was in his study two minutes ago,' said Mrs. Finn.

'I want to see him. I must be off to Cornwall to-morrow morning.'

'To Cornwall!' said Miss Cassewary and Mrs. Finn together. 'Why to Cornwall?' asked Lady Mabel. But Mary, connecting Cornwall with Frank Tregear, held her peace.

'I can't explain it all now, but I must start very early to-morrow.' Then he went off to his father's study, and finding the Duke still there explained the cause of his intended journey. The member for Polpenno had died, and Frank Tregear had been invited to stand for the borough. He had written to his friend to ask him to come and assist in the struggle.

'I did not know that he could afford that kind of thing,' said the Duke with a frown on his brow.

'Of course his father will have to see to that. Years ago there used to be always a Tregear in for Polpenno,' said Silverbridge.

'But he is a younger son.'

'I don't know anything about it,' said Silverbridge; 'but as he has asked me to go I think I ought to do it.' The Duke, who was by no means the man to make light of the political obligations of friendship, raised no objection, and the question of the journey was thus settled.

'I wish,' said he, 'that something could have been arranged between you and Mabel before you went.' The young man stood in the gloom of the dark room aghast. This was certainly not the moment for explaining everything to his father. 'I have set my heart very much upon it. I had her here because of what you said to me, and you ought to be gratified by knowing that I quite approve your choice.'

All that had been years ago,—in last June. It had occurred under an altogether different set of human circumstances,—before Mrs. Montacute Jones's garden-party, before that day in the rain at Maidenhead, before the brightness of Killancodlem had shone upon him, before the glories of Miss Boncassen had been revealed to his eyes. But how could he now, at this moment, make all that intelligible to his father? 'There is no time for that kind of thing now,' he said weakly.

'I thought that when you were here together——'

'I must dress now, sir;—but I will tell you all about it when I get back from Cornwall. I will come back direct to Matching, and will explain everything.' So he escaped, leaving the Duke altogether in doubt as to what there might be to be explained.

It was clear to Lady Mabel that there was no opportunity now for any scheme. Whatever there might be to be done, whatever might be possible, must be postponed till after this Cornish business had been completed. Perhaps it might be better so. She had thought that she would appeal to himself, that she would throw herself upon his mercy, that she would tell him of his father's wishes, of her love for him,—of the authority which he had once given her for loving him,—and of the absolute impossibility of his marriage with the American. She thought that she could do it, if not efficiently at any rate effectively. But it could not be done on the very day on which the American had gone. There must be some interval.

It came out in the course of the evening that he was going to assist Frank Tregear in his canvass. The matter was not spoken of openly, as Tregear's name could hardly be mentioned before the Duke and Lady Mary together. But everybody knew it, and the matter gave occasion to Mabel for a few words apart with Silverbridge, which words could be spoken in confidence but without any reference to their own peculiar affairs. 'I am so glad you are going to him,' she said in a little whisper.

'Of course I go when he wishes me. I don't know that I can do him any good.'

'The greatest good in the world. Your name will go so far! It will be everything to him to be in Parliament. He will do well there, and that will force your father to respect him.'

'I hope he'll succeed. We'll make a good fight for it at any rate.'

Then there was a pause. 'And when are we to meet again?' she said.

'I shall turn up somewhere,' he replied as he gave her his hand to wish her good-bye.

On the following morning the Duke sent for Lady Mabel and proposed to her that she should stay at Matching for yet another fortnight,—or even for a month if it might be possible. It would be a great kindness, he said, to Lady Mary. Lady Mabel, whose father was still abroad, was not sorry to accept the invitation.

CHAPTER 55

POLPENNO

POLPENNO was a borough on the northern coast of Cornwall as to which most politicians were agreed that it ought to have been abolished by some Reform Bill. It had been spared, so the Tories said, at the first Great Reform Bill, because at that time it was under the influence of that mighty Whig nobleman the Earl of Camborne. As certain small boroughs certainly were spared, apparently in the interests of magnates both on one side and on the other, the allegation in this respect may not improbably have been true. At the second Reform Bill* it was still spared because when that moderate measure became law, no existing borough was sent out actually into the cold. Polpenno at that time returned but one member, and that one it retained.

But there had been changes since the days in which the old Earl of Camborne had been so powerful. He had always sent up to Parliament some Liberal selected by himself,—choosing his member just as though there had never been a whisper of reform in the county of Cornwall. But there had come other earls less efficient, and there had been sales of property, and gradually the Camborne interest had dwindled. But still there had been something of a Camborne interest, and the Liberals had at any rate retained their hold on the borough down to the present date. There had been a rapid succession of members, and various contests. It was thought by many that a good deal of money had been spent at Polpenno, and that certainly Sir Simon Carstairs, the late member, who had once been Lord Mayor of London and certainly had no special connection with Cornwall, had paid very dear for his whistle.* Poor Sir Simon had now died suddenly, and it was immediately decided that there should be another struggle. Mr. Carbottle, coming whence nobody knew, or recommended by whom very few understood, was on his way down from London very soon after the death of Sir Simon. But it was known that Mr. Carbottle was a man of means. It was soon whispered about that he had made a large fortune in the indigo trade, and that he did not very much care what he spent so that he could get into Parliament.

Polwenning, the seat of Mr. Tregear, Frank's father, was close to Polpenno,—so close that the gates of the grounds opened into the town. Many years ago the Tregears had owned many houses in the little borough, and had professed almost as strong an interest as the Camborne family had afterwards consolidated. As Silverbridge had told his father, many of the Tregear family had sat for the borough. Then there had come changes, and the Camborne interest had been consolidated. Since those days strange Conservatives* had been brought down,—as Sir Simon and Mr. Carbottle were brought,—but they had never succeeded. When the vacancy now occurred a deputation waited upon Squire Tregear and asked him to stand. The deputation would guarantee that the expense should not exceed—a certain limited sum. Mr. Tregear for himself had no such ambition. His eldest son was abroad and was not at all such a man as one would choose to make into a member of Parliament. After much consideration in the family, Frank was invited to present himself to the constituency. Frank's aspirations in regard to Lady Mary Palliser were known at Polwenning, and it was thought that they would have a better chance of success if he could write the letters M.P. after his name. Frank acceded, and as he was starting wrote to ask the assistance of his friend Lord Silverbridge.

At that time there were only nine days more before the election, and Mr. Carbottle, the Liberal candidate, was already living in great style at the Camborne Arms.

Mr. and Mrs. Tregear and an elder sister of Frank's, who now quite acknowledged herself to be an old maid, were very glad to welcome Frank's friend. On the first morning of course they discussed the candidates' prospects. 'My best chance of success,' said Frank, 'arises from the fact that Mr. Carbottle is fatter than the people here seem to approve.'

'If his purse be fat,' said old Mr. Tregear, 'that will carry off any personal defect.' Lord Silverbridge asked whether the candidate was not too fat to make speeches. Miss Tregear declared that he had made three speeches daily for the last week, and that Mr. Williams, the rector, who had heard him, declared him to be a godless dissenter in favour of women's rights and republican institutions. Mrs. Tregear thought that it would be much better that the place should be disfranchised altogether than that such a horrid man should be brought into the neighbourhood. 'A godless dissenter!' she said, holding up her hands in dismay. Frank thought that they had better abstain from allusion to their opponent's religion. Then Mr. Tregear made a little speech. 'We used,' he said, 'to endeavour to get someone to represent us in Parliament, who would agree with us on vital subjects, such as the Church of England and the necessity of religion. Now it seems to be considered ill-mannered to make any allusion to such subjects! A Turk or a Mohammedan if he had made money enough to be called an enlightened man would be just the member for Polpenno.' From which it may be seen that this old Tregear was very conservative indeed.

When the old people were gone to bed the new member of Parliament and the expectant member betook themselves to the servants' hall in order that Silverbridge might smoke his pipe. 'I hope you'll get in,' said Silverbridge.

'Well—yes; I suppose I may trust to you for as much as that.'

'And if I can do anything for you, of course I will.'

'It is always good to have a real member along with one,' said Tregear.

'But I begin to think I am a very shaky Conservative myself.'

'I am sorry for that.'

'I almost repent what I have done. Sir Timothy is such a beast,' said Silverbridge.

'Is that your notion of a political opinion? Are you to be this or that in accordance with your own liking or disliking for some particular man? One is supposed to have opinions of one's own.'

'Your father would be down on a man because he is a dissenter.'

'Of course my father is old-fashioned.'

'It does seem so hard to me,' said Silverbridge, 'to find any difference between the two sets. You who are a true Conservative are much more like to my father who is a Liberal than to your own who is on the same side as yourself.'

'It may be so, and still I may be a good Conservative.'

'It seems to me in the House to mean nothing more than choosing one set of companions or choosing another. There are some awful cads who sit along with Mr. Monk;—fellows that make you sick to hear them, and whom I couldn't be civil to. But I don't think there is anybody I hate so much as old Beeswax. He has a contemptuous way with his nose which makes me long to pull it.'

'And you mean to go over in order that you may be justified in doing so?'

'Not quite that,—but I declare I do spend my time thinking whether I'd rather sit behind Beeswax or Ratler.'

'I think I soar a little higher,' said Tregear.

'Oh, of course. You're a clever fellow,' said Silverbridge, not without a touch of sarcasm.

'A man may soar higher than that without being very clever. If the party that calls itself Liberal were to have all its own way, who is there that doesn't believe that the Church would go at once, then all distinction between boroughs and counties, the House of Lords immediately afterwards, and after that the Crown?'

'Those are not my governor's ideas.'

'Your governor couldn't help himself. A Liberal party,—what you call a Liberal party,—with plenipotentiary power, must go on right away to the logical conclusion of those arguments. It is only the conservative feeling of the country which saves such men as your father from being carried headlong to ruin by their own machinery. You have read Carlyle's *French Revolution.*'*

'Yes, I have read that.'

'Wasn't it so there? There were a lot of honest men who thought they could do a deal of good by making everybody equal. A good many were made equal by having their heads cut off. That's why I mean to be member for Polpenno and to send Mr. Carbottle back to London. Carbottle, probably, doesn't want to cut anybody's head off.'

'I dare say he's as conservative as anybody.'

'But he wants to be a member of Parliament; and, as he hasn't thought much about anything, he is quite willing to lend a hand to communism, radicalism, socialism, chopping people's heads off, or anything else.

These are my ideas,' said Tregear, getting up, 'and I regard myself as a philanthropic patriot.'*

'That's all very well,' said Silverbridge, as he followed his friend, 'but where should we have been if there had been no Liberals? Robespierre and his pals cut off a lot of heads, but Louis XIV and Louis XV locked up more in prison.'* And so he had the last word in the argument.

But in spite of the repentance which the future head of the Pallisers felt as to the first step which he had taken in political life, he was prepared to do the best he could to assist his friend's canvass. It would be a grand thing that Tregear should be in Parliament. He too thought that, were it to be so, the Duke's opposition might be in some degree softened by the fact, and he was essentially loyal in his nature and fond of action. He was ready to do anything,—except, as he said at Polwenning, to make a speech. And even that he declared himself ready to do if it could be assured to him that there should be such a row that nobody could hear him. The whole of the next morning was spent in canvassing, and the whole of the afternoon. In the evening there was a great meeting at the Polpenno Assembly Room, which at the present moment was in the hands of the Conservative party. Here Frank Tregear made an oration, in which he declared his political convictions. The whole speech was said at the time to be very good; but the portion of it which was apparently esteemed the most had direct reference to Mr. Carbottle. Who was Mr. Carbottle? Why had he come to Polpenno? Who had sent for him? Why Mr. Carbottle rather than anybody else? A great man he certainly was, but surely not great enough for Polpenno. This very bad joke, referring to the candidate's personal dimensions, seemed to be very popular. Did not the people of Polpenno think that it might be as well to send Mr. Carbottle back to the place from whence he had come? These questions, which seemed to Silverbridge to be as easy as they were attractive, almost made him desirous of making a speech himself.

Then Mr. Williams, the rector, followed, a gentleman who had many staunch friends and many bitter enemies in the town. He addressed himself chiefly to that bane of the whole country,—as he conceived them,—the godless dissenters; and was felt by Tregear to be injuring the cause by every word he spoke. But in such positions a man has to endure the blows, not only of his enemies,—which are generally endurable without much suffering,—but of his friends also; and such blows are sometimes excruciating. It was necessary that Mr. Williams should liberate his own mind, and therefore he persevered with the godless dissenters at great length,—not explaining, however, how a man who thought enough about his religion to be a dissenter could be godless, or how a godless man should care enough about religion to be a dissenter.

Mr. Williams was heard with impatience, and then there was a clamour for the young Lord. He was the son of an ex-Prime Minister, and therefore of course he could speak. He was himself a member of Parliament, and therefore of course he could speak. He had boldly severed himself from the faulty political tenets of his family, and therefore on such an occasion as this was peculiarly entitled to speak. When a man goes electioneering, he must speak if he be called for. At a dinner-table to refuse is possible;—or in any assembly convened for a semi-private purpose, a gentleman may declare that he is not prepared for the occasion, and there are generally so many anxious for the honour that to escape is not difficult. But in such an emergency as this, a man,—and a member of Parliament,—cannot plead that he is not prepared. A son of a former Prime Minister who had already taken so strong a part in politics as to have severed himself from his father, not prepared to address the voters of a borough whom he had come to canvass! The plea was so absurd, that he was thrust off his chair and onto his feet before he knew what he was about.

It was in truth his first public speech. At Silverbridge he had attempted to repeat a few words which he had imperfectly learned by rote, and in his failure had been covered by the Sprugeons and the Sprouts. There had been no contest at Silverbridge, and everything had been made very easy;—but now he was on his legs in a great room, in an unknown town, with all the aristocracy of the place before him! His eyes at first swam a little, and there was a moment in which he thought he would run away. But, on that morning, as he was dressing, there had come to his mind the idea of the possibility of such a moment as this, and a few words had occurred to him. 'My friend Frank Tregear,' he began, rushing at once at his subject, 'is a very good fellow and I hope you'll elect him.' Then he paused, not remembering very well what was to come next; but the sentiment which he had uttered appeared to his auditors to be so good in itself and so well delivered, that they filled up a very long pause with continued clappings and such acclamations. 'Yes,' continued the young member of Parliament, encouraged by the kindness of the crowd before him and around him, 'I have known Frank Tregear ever so long, and I don't think you could find a better member of Parliament anywhere.' There were a great many ladies present and they thought that the Duke's son was just the person who ought to come electioneering among them. His voice was much pleasanter to their ears than that of old Mr. Williams. The women waved their handkerchiefs and the men stamped their feet. Here was an orator come among them. 'You all know all about it just as well as I do,' continued the orator, 'and I am sure you feel that he ought to be member for Polpenno.' There could be no doubt about that as far as the opinion of the audience went. 'There can't be a better fellow than Frank Tregear and I ask you all to give three cheers for the new member.' Ten times three cheers were given, and the Carbottleites outside the door who had come to report what was going on at the Tregear meeting were quite of opinion that this eldest son of the former Prime Minister, who had political ideas of his own, was a tower of strength. 'I don't know anything about Mr. Carbottle,' continued Silverbridge, who was almost growing to like the sound of his own voice. 'Perhaps he's a good fellow too.' 'No; no; no.' 'A very bad fellow indeed,' was heard from different parts of the room. 'I don't know anything about him. I wasn't at school with Carbottle.' This was taken as a stroke of the keenest wit, and was received with infinite cheering. Silverbridge was in the pride of his youth, and Carbottle was sixty at the least. Nothing could have been funnier. 'He seems to be a stout old party, but I don't think he's the man for Polpenno. And I don't think you'll return him. I think you'll return Frank Tregear. I was at school with him;—and I tell you, that you can't find a better fellow anywhere than Frank Tregear.' Then he sat down, and I am afraid he felt that he had made the speech of the evening. 'We are so much obliged to you, Lord Silverbridge,' Miss Tregear said as they were walking home together. 'That's just the sort of thing that the people like. So reassuring, you know. What Mr. Williams says about the dissenters is of course true; but it isn't reassuring.'

Mr. Williams, who came back with them all to supper, was not quite so well contented. There had been but faint applause after his speech. 'I hope, my Lord,' said he severely, 'that you agreed with the few remarks I ventured to make regarding the religion of this country.'

'I'm not sure that all the dissenters are so very bad,' said Silverbridge. 'There is Lord Drummond, the Prime Minister. He's a Presbyterian.' This happened to be a fact,—which would have been explained away at great length by Mr. Williams, who was beginning to show that a Presbyterian in Scotland was not a dissenter,* when Mrs. Tregear took them all into supper.

'I hope I didn't make a fool of myself to-night,' Silverbridge said when he was alone with Tregear,—probably with some little pride in his heart.

'Perhaps I ought to say that you did, seeing that you praised me so violently. But, whatever it was, it was well taken. I don't know whether they will elect me; but had you come down as a candidate I am quite sure they would have elected you.' Silverbridge was hardly satisfied with this. He wished to have been told that he had spoken really well. He did not, however, resent his friend's coldness. 'Perhaps after all I did make a fool of myself,' he said to himself as he went to bed.

On the next day, after breakfast, it was found to be raining heavily, and to be raining after such a fashion that they who knew the weather in that part of the world declared that it would rain all day. Canvassing was of course the business of the hour, and canvassing is a business which cannot very well be done indoors. It was, therefore, very soon decided that the rain should go for nothing. Could an agreement have been come to with the Carbottleites it might have been decided that both parties should abstain, but as that was impossible the Tregear party could not afford to lose the day. As Mr. Carbottle, by reason of his fatness and natural slowness, would perhaps be specially averse to walking about in the slush and mud, it might be that they would gain something; so after breakfast they started with umbrellas,—Tregear, Silverbridge, Mr. Newcomb the curate, Mr. Pinebott the Conservative attorney, with four or five followers who were armed with books and pencils, and who ticked off on the lists of the voters the names of the friendly, the doubtful, and the inimical.

Canvassing under heavy rain in December is not a pleasant occupation. Perhaps nothing more disagreeable, more squalid, more revolting to the senses, more opposed to personal dignity, can be conceived. And if at all times, so especially is it abominable and degrading in such weather in December. The same words have to be repeated over and over again in the cottages, hovels, and lodgings of poor men and women who only understand that the time has come round in which they are to be flattered by, instead of being the flatterers of, their superiors. 'I think I am right in supposing that your husband's principles are conservative, Mrs. Bubbs.' 'I don't know nothing about it. You'd better call again and see Bubbs hissel.' 'Certainly I will do so. I shouldn't at all like to leave the borough without seeing Mr. Bubbs. I hope we shall have your influence, Mrs. Bubbs.' 'I don't know nothing about it. My folks at home allays vote buff;* and I think Bubbs ought to go buff too. Only mind this; Bubbs don't never come home to his dinner. You must come arter six. And I hope he's to have some'at for his trouble. He won't have my word to vote unless he have some'at.' Such is the conversation in which the candidate takes a part, while his cortège at the door is criticising his very imperfect mode of securing Mrs. Bubbs's good wishes. Then he goes on to the next house, and the same thing with some slight variation is endured again. Some guide, philosopher, and friend, who accompanies him, and who is the chief of the cortège, has calculated on his behalf that he ought to make twenty such visitations an hour, and to call on two hundred constituents in the course of the day. As he is always falling behind in his number, he is always being driven on by his philosopher, till he comes to hate the poor creatures to whom he is forced to address himself, with a most cordial hatred.

It is altogether a nuisance to which no man should subject himself in any weather. But when it rains there is superadded a squalor and an ill humour to all the party which makes it almost impossible for them not to quarrel before the day is over. To talk politics to Mrs. Bubbs under any circumstances is bad, but to do so with the conviction that the moisture is penetrating from your greatcoat through your shirt to your bones, while you hold your umbrella away from you, while you feel that you are breathing the steam from those seven other wet men at the door, is very bad indeed. To have to go through this is enough to take away all the pride which a man might otherwise take from becoming a member of Parliament. But to go through it and then not to become a member is base indeed!* To go through it and to feel that you are probably paying at the rate of a hundred pounds a day for the privilege is most disheartening. Silverbridge, as he backed up Tregear in the uncomfortable work, congratulated himself on the comfort of having a Mr. Sprugeon and a Mr. Sprout who could manage his borough for him without a contest.

They worked on that day all the morning till one, when they took luncheon, all reeking with wet, at the King's Head,—so that a little money might be legitimately spent in the cause. Then, at two, they sallied out again, vainly endeavouring to make their twenty calls within the hour. About four, when it was beginning to be dusk, they were very tired, and Silverbridge had ventured to suggest that as they were all wet through, and as there was to be another meeting in the Assembly Room that night, and as nobody in that part of the town seemed to be at home, they might perhaps be allowed to adjourn for the present. He was thinking how nice it would be to have a glass of hot brandy-and-water and then lounge till dinner-time. But the philosopher received the proposition with stern disdain. Was his lordship aware that Mr. Carbottle had been out all day from eight in the morning, and was still at work; that the Carbottleites had already sent for lanterns and were determined to go on till eight o'clock among the artisans who would then have returned from their work? When a man had put his hand to the plough, the philosopher thought that that man should complete the furrow!

The philosopher's view had just carried the day, the discussion having been held under seven or eight wet umbrellas at the corner of a dirty little lane leading into the High Street, when suddenly, on the other side of the way, Mr. Carbottle's cortège made its appearance. The philosopher at once informed them that on such occasions it was customary that the rival candidates should be introduced. 'It will take ten minutes,' said the philosopher; 'but then it will take them ten minutes too.' Upon this Tregear, as being the younger of the two, crossed over the road, and the introduction was made.

There was something comfortable in it to the Tregear party, as no imagination could conceive anything more wretched than the appearance of Mr. Carbottle. He was a very stout man of sixty, and seemed to be almost carried along by his companions. He had pulled his coat-collar up and his hat down till very little of his face was visible, and in attempting to look at Tregear and Silverbridge he had to lift up his chin till the rain ran off his hat onto his nose. He had an umbrella in one hand and a stick in the other, and was wet through to his very skin. What were his own feelings cannot be told, but his philosopher, guide, and friend would allow him no rest. 'Very hard work, Mr. Tregear,' he said, shaking his head.

'Very hard indeed, Mr. Carbottle.' Then the two parties went on, each their own way, without another word.

CHAPTER 56

THE NEWS IS SENT TO MATCHING

THERE were nine days of this work, during which Lord Silverbridge became very popular and made many speeches. Tregear, who was really in earnest in his politics, did not win half so many hearts, or recommend himself so thoroughly to the political predilections of the borough;—but nevertheless on the ninth day he was returned. It would probably be unjust to attribute this success chiefly to the young Lord's eloquence. It certainly was not due to the strong religious feelings of the rector. It is to be feared that even the thoughtful political convictions of the candidate did not altogether produce the result. It was that chief man among the candidate's guides and friends, that leading philosopher who would not allow anybody to go home from the rain, and who kept his eyes so sharply open to the pecuniary doings of the Carbottleites that Mr. Carbottle's guides and friends had hardly dared to spend a shilling;—it was he who had in truth been efficacious. In every attempt they had made to spend their money they had been looked into and circumvented. As Mr. Carbottle had been brought down to Polpenno on purpose that he might spend money,—as he had nothing but his money to recommend him, and as he had not spent it,—the free and independent electors of the borough had not seen their way to vote for him. Therefore the Conservatives of the neighbourhood were very elate with their triumph. Here and there about the borough vast plac- ards were exhibited declaring the great Conservative reaction which had taken place among the thoughtful men of Polpenno,—a reaction which would no doubt spread itself through all Cornwall and probably communicate itself to the neighbouring county! But the electioneering guide, philosopher, and friend, in the humble retirement of his own home,—he was a tailor in the town, whose assistance at such periods had long been in requisition and whose time was not given up without some slender remuneration,—knew very well how the seat had been secured. Ten shillings a head would have turned three hundred voters to liberalism,—would at any rate have sent a great majority of them as true Liberals to the ballot-boxes! The mode of distributing the money with absolute secrecy had been arranged; but the Conservative tailor had been too acute, and not a half-a-sovereign could be passed. Tregear won by one hundred and fifteen votes, and would never have won but for the tailor's sharpness. The tailor only got twenty-five pounds for his work, and that was smuggled in among the bills for printing.

Mr. Williams, however, was quite sure that he had so opened out the iniquities of the dissenters as to have convinced the borough. Yes; there had been a great reaction, and he allowed himself to hope that every Salem and Zion and Ebenezer* in his large parish would be closed,—forgetting probably that he would have had no seats in his own church to offer to this bulk of the parishioners who would thus have become converted to his religious views. But who is there that would not think it better that the world should remain prayerless, than that it should say its prayers after any fashion but his own? 'It is a great thing for the country,' said Mr. Williams in Mr. Tregear's dining-room on the eve of the departure of the two young men.

'He'll make a capital member,' said Silverbridge, clapping his friend on the back.

'I hope he'll never forget,' said Mr. Williams, 'that he owes his seat to the Protestant and Church of England principles which have sunk so deeply into the minds of the thoughtful portion of the inhabitants of this borough.'

'I am thoroughly attached to the Church,' said Tregear, who knew that friends, even when indiscreet, must be conciliated.

'Any man who wishes to hold the seat for Polpenno,' continued the clergyman, 'must show that he is in earnest about the Church of the State.'

'Whom should they elect but a Tregear?' said the proud mother, feeling that her rector took too much of the praise to himself.

'I think you have done more for us than anyone else,' whispered Miss Tregear to the young Lord. 'What you said was so reassuring!' The father before he went to bed expressed to his son, with some trepidation, a hope that all this would lead to no great permanent increase of expenditure. 'I did not like to stand in your way,' said the father, 'when the offer came. And yet I felt that I was hardly justified.'

That evening before he went to bed Lord Silverbridge wrote to his father an account of what had taken place at Polpenno.

'Polwenning, 15th December.

'MY DEAR FATHER,

'Among us all we have managed to return Tregear. I am afraid you will not be quite pleased because it will be a vote lost to your party. But I really think that he is just the fellow to be in Parliament. If he were on your side I'm sure he's the kind of man you'd like to bring into office. He is always thinking about those sort of things. He says that if there were no Conservatives such Liberals as you and Mr. Monk would be destroyed by the Jacobins. There is something in that. Whether a man is a Conservative or not himself I suppose there ought to be Conservatives.' The Duke as he read this made a memorandum in his own mind that he would explain to his son that every carriage should have a drag to its wheels, but that an ambitious soul would choose to be the coachman rather than the drag.

'It was beastly work.' The Duke made another memorandum to instruct his son that no gentleman above the age of a schoolboy should allow himself to use such a word in such a sense. 'We had to go about in the rain up to our knees in mud for eight or nine days, always saying the same thing. And of course all that we said was bosh.' Another memorandum,—or rather two, one as to the slang, and another as to the expediency of teaching something to the poor voters on such occasions. 'Our only comfort was that the Carbottle people were quite as badly off as us.' Another memorandum as to the grammar. The absence of Christian charity did not at the moment affect the Duke. 'I made ever so many speeches, till at last it seemed to be quite easy.' Here there was a very grave memorandum. Speeches easy to young speakers are generally very difficult to old listeners. 'But of course it was all bosh.' This required no separate memorandum but was too probably true.

'I have promised to go up to town with Tregear for a day or two. After that I will stick to my purpose of going to Matching again. I will be there about the 22nd and will then stay over Christmas. After that I am going into the Brake country for some hunting. It is such a shame to have a lot of horses and never to ride them.

'Your most affectionate Son,
'SILVERBRIDGE.'

The last sentence gave rise in the Duke's mind to the necessity of a very elaborate memorandum on the subject of amusements generally. It was becoming, he thought, the great fault of the higher ranks in England to seek the means of expending their energy in useless play rather than in useful labour. Men such as his son could not be idle. Life was not pleasant to them unless they could work hard. To toil was a necessity to them. But, under the dominion of fashion, they sacrificed themselves to employments which could have no beneficial results. His son could not forgive himself because he had not hunted so many days,—as another young man might be angry with himself because he had not read so many hours! In this way the best energies of the country were being wasted. The Duke made a very strong memorandum within his own mind on this subject.

By the same post another letter went from Polpenno to Matching, which also gave rise to some mental memoranda. It was as follows:

'MY DEAR MABEL,

'I am a member of the British House of Commons. I have sometimes regarded myself as being one of the most peculiarly unfortunate men in the world, and yet now I have achieved that which all commoners in England think to be the greatest honour within their reach, and have done so at an age at which very few achieve it but the sons of the most wealthy and the most powerful.

'I now come to my misfortunes. I know that as a poor man I ought not to be a member of Parliament. I ought to be earning my bread as a lawyer or a doctor, or perhaps as a magistrate a thousand miles up the country in India.* I have no business to be what I am, and when I am forty I shall find that I have eaten up all my good things instead of having them to eat. You will understand this thoroughly,—you, who have your good things still to come.

'I have one chance before me. You know very well what that is. Tell her, unless you feel that you will be breaking confidence by doing so, that my pride in being a member of Parliament is much more on her behalf than on my own. The man who dares to love her ought at any rate to be something in the world. If it might be,—if ever it may be,— I should wish to be something for her sake. You will tell her this from me,—if you think you can do so honestly.

'I am sure you will be glad of my success yourself, for my own sake.

'Your affectionate Friend and Cousin,

'FRANCIS TREGEAR.'

The first mental memorandum in regard to this came from the writer's assertion that he at forty would have eaten up all his good things. No! He being a man might make his way to good things though he was not born to them. He surely would win his good things for himself. But what good things were in store for her? Had not everything slipped from her? What chance of success was there for her? Oh,—if she also could have been born a man, then too she might have fought her own battle. But the reflection which was the most bitter to her of all came from her assurance that his love for that other girl was so genuine. Even when he was writing to her there was no spark left of the old romance! Some hint of a recollection of past feelings, some half-concealed reference to the former passion might have been allowed to him! She as a woman,—as a woman all whose fortune must depend on marriage,—could indulge in no such allusions; but surely he need not have been so hard! There was, however, no hardness in it. It was not that he refrained from the expression of the feeling, but that the feeling itself no longer existed. From his heart all regard for her had been quite banished. She had bade him go and love elsewhere, and he had taken her absolutely at her word. Her memorandum on this matter was at last to the effect that a time should come when she would exact some penalty for his absolute desertion.

But still there was another memorandum. At the present moment she would do all that he desired as far as it was in her power. She was anxious that he should marry Lady Mary Palliser, though so anxious also that something of his love should remain with herself! She was quite willing to convey that message,—if it might be done without offence to the Duke. She understood well what Tregear meant when he asked her to convey it,—if she could do so honestly. She was there with the object of ingratiating herself with the Duke. She must not imperil her favour with the Duke by making herself the medium of any secret communications between Mary and her lover. Tregear had seen all that and had understood it as well as herself.

But how should she serve Tregear without risk of offending the Duke? She read the letter again and again, and thinking it to be a good letter she determined to show it to the Duke. Now that Miss Boncassen was gone,—and Silverbridge gone also,—the Duke devoted some period of his afternoons to Lady Mabel, and instructed her also in the beauty of tenths, and in the hideous deformity of dozens.* 'Mr. Tregear has got in at Polpenno,' she said on the day on which she and the Duke had received their letters.

'So I hear from Silverbridge.'

'It will be a good thing for him, I suppose.'

'I do not know,' said the Duke coldly.

'He is my cousin and I have always been interested in his welfare.'

'That is, no doubt, natural.'

'And a seat in Parliament will give him something to do.'

'Certainly it ought,' said the Duke.

'I do not think that he is an idle man.' To this the Duke made no answer. He did not wish to be made to talk about Tregear. 'May I tell you why I say all this?' she asked softly, pressing her hand on the Duke's arm ever so gently. To this the Duke assented, but still coldly. 'Because I want to know what I ought to do. Would you mind reading that letter? Of course you will remember that Frank and I have been brought up almost as brother and sister.'

The Duke took the letter in his hand and did read it, very slowly. 'What he says about young men without means going into Parliament is true enough.' This was not encouraging, but as the Duke went on reading, Mabel did not think it necessary to argue the matter. He had to read the last paragraph twice before he understood it. He did read it twice, and then folding the letter very slowly gave it back to his companion.

'What ought I to do?' asked Lady Mabel.

'Your correspondent talks of breaking confidence. What does he mean?'

'Breaking confidence with you. I certainly shall not do that.'

'I think he was right to put that in. It would have been better that he should not have written at all about my daughter. But as he has done so, he was right to put that in.'

'What am I to do, Duke?'

'As you and I, my dear, are friends, I think that any carrying of a message to Mary would be breaking confidence. I think that you should not

speak to Mary about Mr. Tregear.' Then he changed the subject. Lady
Mabel of course understood that after that she could not say a word to
Mary about the election at Polpenno.

CHAPTER 57

THE MEETING AT THE BOBTAILED FOX

IT was now the middle of December, and matters had not been going
on at all comfortably in the Runnymede country. The Major, with more
pluck than some had given him the credit of possessing, had carried on
his operations in opposition to the wishes of the majority of the resi-
dent members of the hunt. The owners of coverts had protested that
they would not preserve foxes for him,* and farmers had sworn that he
should not ride over their lands. There had even been some talk among
the younger men of thrashing him if he persevered. But he did persevere, and, as it had happened, had managed to have one or two good
runs. Now it was the fortune of the Runnymede hunt that many of
those who rode with the hounds were strangers to the country,—men
who came down by train from London in the morning and went back
in the evening, gentlemen of perhaps no great distinction, who could
ride hard, and were popular enough while they kept the creatures in
their proper places, but as to whom it was thought that as they did not
provide the land to ride over, or the fences to be destroyed, or the crops
to be injured, or the coverts for the foxes, or the greater part of the
subscription, they ought not to oppose those by whom all these things
were supplied. But the Major, knowing where his strength lay, had
managed to get a party to support him. The contract to hunt the country had been made with him in last March, and was good at any rate
for one year. Having the kennels and the hounds under his command
he did hunt the country; but he did so amidst a storm of contumely
and ill-will.

At last it was decided that a general meeting of the members of the
hunt should be called together with the express object of getting rid of
the Major. The gentlemen of the neighbourhood felt that the Major
was not to be borne, and the farmers were very much stronger against
him than the gentlemen. It had now become a settled belief among
almost all sporting men in England that the Major had with his own
hands driven the nail into the horse's foot. The groom, it was said, had
confessed so much to a friend who had seen him off in the emigrant

ship from Plymouth. Gradually there had come to be very little doubt about the matter; and was it to be endured that the Runnymede farmers should ride to hounds under a Master who had been guilty of such an iniquity as that? 'He is doing the thing uncommonly well,' said some of the hard riders down from London. No doubt! A man who could make ever so many thousand pounds by such a trick as that could afford to do the thing well. But what honest man would choose to participate in the results of such rascality? *The Staines and Egham Gazette*, which had always supported the Runnymede hunt, declared in very plain terms that all who rode with the 'Major,'—for at this time poor Tifto's majority became the subject of many unpleasant remarks,—were enjoying their sport out of the plunder which had been extracted from Lord Silverbridge. Then a meeting was called for Saturday, the 18th December, to be held at that well-known sporting little inn The Bobtailed Fox, within a mile and a half of Egham. All those who were really members of the hunt were earnestly called upon to attend. It was,—so said the printed document which was issued,—the only means by which the hunt could be preserved. If gentlemen who were interested did not put their shoulders to the wheel, and probably also their hands into their pockets, then,—so said the document,—the Runnymede hunt must be regarded as a thing of the past. One of the documents was sent to the Major with an intimation that if he wished to attend no objection would be made to his presence. The chair would be taken at half-past twelve punctually by that very popular and well-known old sportsman Mr. Mahogany Topps.

Was ever the Master of a hunt treated in such a way! His presence not objected to! As a rule the Master of a hunt never does attend hunt meetings, because the matter to be discussed is generally that of the money to be subscribed for him, as to which it is as well that he should not hear the pros and cons. But it is presumed that he is to be the hero of the hour, and that he is to be treated to his face, and spoken of behind his back, with love, admiration, and respect. But now this Master was told that his presence—would be allowed! And then this fox-hunting meeting was summoned for half-past twelve on a hunting day;—when, as all the world knew, the hounds were to meet at eleven, twelve miles off! This was done with the intention of securing the absence of the hard-riding London men, who though they had no interest in a single acre of land were still members of the hunt. Was ever anything so base? said the Major to himself as he read the letter in the seclusion of Tally-ho Lodge. But he resolved that he would be equal to the occasion. He immediately issued cards to all the members, stating that on that day the meet had been changed from Croppingham Bushes, which was ever so much on the other side of Bagshot, to The Bobtailed Fox,—for the benefit of the hunt at large, said the card,—and that the hounds would be there at half-past one. There would not after that be much time for hunting on the 18th December; but on such an occasion as this the Major felt that he must be 'high-spirited.' Whatever might happen, he must show a spirit. In all this there were one or two of the London brigade who stood fast to him. 'Cock your tail, Tifto,' said one hard-riding supporter, 'and show 'em you ain't afraid of nothing.' So Tifto cocked his tail and went to the meeting in his best new scarlet coat, with his whitest breeches, his gayest waistcoat, his pinkest boots, his neatest little bows at his knees, and with his biggest breast-pin in his most gorgeous scarf. He entered the room with his horn in his hand, as a symbol of authority, and took off his hunting-cap to salute the assembly generally with a jaunty air. He had taken two glasses of cherry brandy, and as long as the stimulant lasted would no doubt be able to support himself with audacity.

Two stout young farmers had been placed at the door to prevent any from entering who were not members of the hunt. Their duty was difficult because no one knew exactly who were members and who were not. Anyone who paid, though he paid no more than a five-pound note, was a member. Farmers who paid nothing were supposed to be members. That excellent old sportsman, the parson from Croppingham, was certainly a member, though he had never paid a shilling. The object was to exclude any rough attendants from London who might be able to mount a pair of breeches and a hunting-whip, and, so equipped, might possibly come down to assist the Major. When the time came very few who sought admittance were excluded. On one occasion there was a little noise. 'You ain't paid a penny these two years and I'm blowed if you shall go in,' said one of the young farmers at the door, and then the impecunious sportsman was thrust rather rudely down the stairs. But this was not the Major's doing. The Major knew that he could not support his position by such means as that. The Major had one great argument on which he would depend, and his object was to have that supported by a majority of votes. His argument and his appeal would be, he thought, so just that even his enemies would support it.

Old Mr. Topps, in rising from his chair, did not say very much. He had been hunting in the Runnymede country for nearly fifty years, and had never seen anything so sad as this before. It made him, he knew, very unhappy. As for foxes, there were always plenty of foxes in his coverts. His friend Mr. Jawstock, on the right, would explain what all this was about. All he wanted was to see the Runnymede hunt properly kept up. Then he sat down, and Mr. Jawstock rose to his legs.

Mr. Jawstock was a gentleman very well known in the Runnymede country, who had himself been instrumental in bringing Major Tifto into these parts. There is often someone in a hunting country who never becomes a Master of Hounds himself, but who has almost as much to say about the business as the Master himself. Sometimes at hunt meetings he is rather unpopular, as he is always inclined to talk, and gentlemen who wish to be hunting do not care to be detained by eloquence, however excellent. But there are occasions on which his services are felt to be valuable,—as were Mr. Jawstock's at present. He was a gentleman about forty-five years of age who was not much given to riding, who owned no coverts himself, and was not a man of wealth; but he understood the nature of hunting, knew all its laws, and was a judge of horses, of hounds,—and of men; and could say a thing when he had to say it. Therefore the conduct of this matter had been placed in his hands.

Mr. Jawstock sat on the right hand of Mr. Topps, and a place was left for the Master opposite. The task to be performed was certainly neither easy nor pleasant. It was necessary that the orator should accuse the gentleman opposite to him,—a man with whom he himself had been very intimate,—of iniquity so gross and so mean, that nothing worse can be conceived. 'You are a swindler, a cheat, a rascal of the very deepest dye,—a rogue so mean, that it is revolting to be in the same room with you!' That was what Mr. Jawstock had to say. And he said it. Looking round the room, occasionally appealing to Mr. Topps, who on these occasions would lift up his hands in horror, but never letting his eye fall for a moment on the Major, Mr. Jawstock told the whole story. And he told it very well. 'I did not see it done,' said he. 'I know nothing about it. I never was at Doncaster in my life, and I don't pay much attention to races. But you have evidence of what the Jockey Club thinks. The Master of our hunt has been banished from race-courses!' Here there was considerable opposition, and a few short but excited little dialogues were maintained;—throughout all which Tifto restrained himself like a Spartan. But Jawstock held his own. If not banished from race-courses, he had been banished from this and that special enclosure. 'At any rate he has been thoroughly disgraced,' continued Mr. Jawstock, 'as a sporting man. He has been driven out of the Beargarden Club.' 'He resigned in disgust at their treatment,' said a friend of the Major's. 'Then let him resign in disgust at ours,' said Mr. Jawstock, 'for we won't have him here. Caesar wouldn't keep a wife* who was suspected of infidelity, nor will the Runnymede country endure a Master of Hounds who is supposed to have driven a nail into a horse's foot.' When the matter was discussed afterwards it was thought that this little studied peroration might have been spared.

Two or three other gentlemen had something to say before the Major was allowed to speak,—the upshot of the discourse of all of them being the same. The Major must go. If he didn't go, nobody should be allowed to ride across the country at all.

Then the Major got up, and certainly as far as attention went he had full justice done him. Every word that he said was listened to in silence. However clamorous they might intend to be afterwards, that amount of fair play they were all determined to accord him. The Major was not excellent at speaking, but he did perhaps better than might have been expected. 'This is a very disagreeable position,' he said,—'very disagreeable indeed. As for the nail in the horse's foot I know no more about it than the babe unborn. But I've got two things to say, and I'll say what ain't the most consequence first. These hounds belong to me.' Here he paused, and a loud contradiction came from many parts of the room. Mr. Jawstock, however, proposed that the Major should be heard to the end before opinion was expressed on that subject or on any other. 'I say they belong to me,' repeated the Major. 'If anybody tries his hand at anything else the law will soon set that to rights. But that ain't of much consequences. What I've got to say is this. Let the matter be referred. If that 'orse had a nail run into his foot, and I don't say he hadn't, who was the man most injured? Why, Lord Silverbridge. Everybody knows that. I suppose he dropped well on to eighty thousand pounds, and I don't think he was best pleased. I propose to leave it to him. Let him say. He ought to know more about it than anyone else. He and I were partners in the horse. His lordship ain't very sweet upon me just at present. Nobody need fear that he'd do me a good turn. I say leave it to him. If he says I did it, I'll walk out of the country. As to the hounds we can settle that afterwards. If you'll agree to leave it to Lord Silverbridge,—so will I.'

In this matter the Major had certainly been very well advised. A rumour had become prevalent among sporting circles that Silverbridge had positively refused to condemn the Major. It was known that he had paid his bets without delay, and that he had, to some extent, declined to take advice from the leaders of the Jockey Club. The Major's friends were informed that the young Lord had refused to vote against him at the club. Was it not more than probable that if this matter were referred to him he would refuse to give a verdict against his late partner? Tifto might more probably get evidence in his favour from that quarter than from any other. And then how strong would such evidence be!

The Major sat down, put on his cap, and folded his arms akimbo, with his horn sticking out from his left hand. For a time there was general silence, broken, however, by murmurs in different parts of the room. Then Mr. Jawstock whispered something into the ear of the Chairman, and Mr. Topps, rising from his seat, suggested to Tifto that he should retire. 'I think so,' said Mr. Jawstock. 'The proposition you have made is one that can be discussed only in your absence.' Then the Major held a consultation with one of his friends, and after that did retire. As he went, very glorious in his pink top boots and white leather breeches, one or two of his adherents attempted to express some applause, but that was quickly stopped by the joint efforts of Mr. Topps and Mr. Jawstock. The poor Major went down to the bar, regaled himself with another glass of cherry brandy, and then sat on horseback disconsolate among his hounds.

When he was gone the real hubbub of the meeting commenced. There were some there, and among them Mr. Jawstock, who well understood the nature of Lord Silverbridge's feelings in the matter. 'He would be the last man in England to declare him guilty,' said Mr. Jawstock. 'Whatever my Lord says, he shan't ride across my land,' said a farmer in the background. 'I don't think any gentleman ever made a fairer proposition,—since anything was anything,' said a friend of the Major's, a gentleman who kept livery stables in Long Acre. 'We won't have him here,' said another farmer,—whereupon Mr. Topps shook his head sadly. 'I don't think any gentleman ought to be condemned without a 'earing,' said one of Tifto's admirers, 'and where you're to get anyone to hunt the country like him, I don't know as anybody is prepared to say.' 'We'll manage that,' said a young gentleman from the neighbourhood of Bagshot, who thought that he could hunt the country himself quite as well as Major Tifto. Then another Londoner expressed an opinion that fair was fair, and that nothing fairer could be said than Tifto had spoken himself. 'He must go from here; that's the long and the short of it,' said Mr. Jawstock. 'Put it to the vote, Mr. Jawstock,' said the livery-stable keeper. 'That is what it must come to at last.'

Mr. Topps, who had had great experience in public meetings, and thought that a counting of hands was better than any eloquence in the world for hurrying a meeting to a decision, and who was aware, moreover, that if the matter were protracted much longer his lunch would interfere most prejudicially with his dinner, hereupon expressed an opinion that they might as well go to a vote. No doubt he was right if the matter was one which must sooner or later be decided in that manner. In an assembly of Britons who ever knew an opinion to be swayed by any amount of eloquence? Very much may be said, and the speakers may take great delight in what they say;—but the gentlemen who vote all vote at last as they would have voted had not a speech been made. So it would be, no doubt, on this occasion.

Mr. Jawstock looked round the room trying to calculate what might be the effect of a show of hands. The majority was with him; but he was well aware that of this majority some few would be drawn away, not in favour of Tifto, but in favour of the apparent justice of Tifto's proposition. And what was the use of voting? Let them vote as they might, it was out of the question that Tifto should remain Master of the hunt. But the Chairman had acceded, and on such occasions it is difficult to go against the Chairman. Therefore with much doubting Mr. Jawstock proposed to take the votes of the meeting.

Then there came a show of hands,—first for those who desired to refer the matter to Lord Silverbridge, and afterwards for Tifto's direct enemies,—for those who were anxious to banish Tifto out of hand, without reference to anyone. Here again there was squabbling; one man was alleged to have held up two hands, and another to have attempted to oblige both parties by holding up the same hand twice. At last the matter was settled. To the great annoyance of Mr. Jawstock and the farmers the meeting voted that Lord Silverbridge should be invited to give his opinion as to the innocence or guilt of his late partner.

The Major's friends carried the decision out to him as he sat on horseback, as though he had altogether gained the battle and was secure in his position as Master of the Runnymede hunt for the next dozen years. But at the same time there came a message with compliments from Mr. Mahogany Topps. It was now half-past two, and Mr. Topps ventured to express a hope that Major Tifto would not attempt to draw* the country round on the present occasion. The Major, thinking that it might be as well to conciliate his enemies, rode solemnly and slowly home to Tally-ho Lodge in the middle of his hounds.

CHAPTER 58

THE MAJOR IS DEPOSED

WHEN Silverbridge undertook to return with Tregear to London instead of going off direct to Matching, it is to be feared that he was simply actuated by a desire to postpone his further visit to his father's house. He had thought that Lady Mabel would surely be gone before his task at Polpenno was completed; but, while he was there, he learned from Tregear that she

was still at Matching, and likely to stay for yet a few days longer. As soon
as he should again find himself in his father's presence he would at once
declare his intention of marrying Isabel Boncassen. He had postponed
this too long, and now it must be done. But he could not see his way to
doing it at all while Lady Mabel should be in the house. He had understood that Lady Mabel was to spend Christmas with a brother of Miss
Cassewary's who was a clergyman. As he did not leave Polwenning till the
16th December he might still avoid her if he could find excuses for staying
a week in London. It was on this account chiefly that he agreed to return
thither with the newly elected member. 'I suppose you will find Mabel still
at Matching,' said Tregear as they were on their journey up to town.

'I thought she was going to Stogpingum.' Stogpingum was the name
of the Rev. Mr. Cassewary's parish.

'I suppose she will sooner or later, but I think you will find her at
Matching. She will wait for you, I fancy.'

'I don't know why she should wait for me,' said Silverbridge almost
angrily.

'I thought that you and she were fast friends.'

'I suppose we are—after a fashion. She might wait for you perhaps.'

'I think she would,—if I could go there.'

'You are much thicker with her than I ever was. You correspond with
her. You went to see her at Grex,—when nobody else was there.'

'Is Miss Cassewary nobody?'

'Next door to it,' said Silverbridge, half jealous of the favours shown to
Tregear, though he did not now want to have any favours shown to himself.

'I thought,' said Tregear, 'that there would be a closer intimacy
between you and her.'

'I don't know why you should think so.'

'Had you never any such idea yourself?'

'I haven't any now,—so there may be an end of it. I don't think a fellow ought to be cross-questioned on such a subject.'

'Then I am very, very sorry for Mabel,' said Tregear. This was uttered
solemnly, so that Silverbridge found himself debarred from making any
flippant answer. He could not altogether defend himself. But then neither could she have defended herself. She had not blushed, and been
soft and gentle to him, when he had said soft words to her. He had been
quite justified, he thought, in changing his mind, but he did not like to
own that he had changed it so quickly.

'I think we had better not talk any more about it,' he said, after pausing for a few moments. After that nothing more was said between them
on the subject.

Up in town Silverbridge found a few friends and spent two or three days pleasantly enough, while a thunderbolt was being prepared for him, of which at the time he knew nothing;—or rather, in truth, two thunderbolts. During these days he was very much with Tregear; and though he could not speak freely of his own matrimonial projects,—though he did not dare to say anything of Isabel Boncassen because of Mabel Grex,—still he was brought round to give some sort of assent to the engagement between Tregear and his sister. No doubt this new position which his friend had won for himself did in some degree operate on his judgment. It was not perhaps that he himself imagined that Tregear as a member of Parliament would be worthier to be his brother-in-law than before, but that he fancied that such would be the Duke's feelings. The Duke had declared that Tregear was nobody,—was nothing. That could hardly be said of a man who had a seat in the British House of Commons;—certainly could not be said by so staunch a politician as the Duke. Silverbridge at any rate gave in his adherence.

But had he known of those two thunderbolts he would not have enjoyed his time at the Beargarden. The thunderbolts fell upon him in the shape of two letters which reached his hands at the same time, and were as follows:

'The Bobtailed Fox. Egham. 18th December.

'MY LORD,

'At a meeting held in this house to-day in reference to the hunting of the Runnymede country, it was proposed that the management of the hounds should be taken out of the hands of Major Tifto in consequence of certain conduct of which it is alleged that he was guilty at the last Doncaster races.

'Major Tifto was present at that meeting and requested that your lordship's opinion should be asked as to his guilt. I do not know myself that we are warranted in troubling your lordship on the subject. I am, however, commissioned by the majority of the gentlemen who were present to ask you whether you think that Major Tifto's conduct on that occasion was of such a nature as to make him unfit to be the depositary of that influence, authority, and intimacy which ought to be at the command of a Master of Hounds.

'I feel myself bound to inform your lordship that the hunt generally will be inclined to place great weight upon your opinion; but that it does not undertake to reinstate Major Tifto even should your opinion be in his favour.

'I have the honour to be,

'My Lord,
'Your lordship's most obedient Servant,
'JEREMIAH JAWSTOCK.
'Juniper Lodge, Staines.'

Mr. Jawstock, when he had written this letter in obedience to what was called the sense of the meeting, was proud of his own language, but still felt that the application was a very lame one. Why ask any man for an opinion, and tell him at the same time that his opinion might probably not be taken! And yet no other alternative had been left to him. The meeting had decided that the application should be made; but Mr. Jawstock was well aware that let the young Lord's answer be what it might, the Major would not be endured as Master of Hounds in the Runnymede country. Mr. Jawstock felt that the passage in which he explained that a Master of Hounds should be a depositary of influence and intimacy was good;—but yet the application as a whole was lame, and was, he thought, hardly fair to Lord Silverbridge.

Lord Silverbridge as he read it alone in the morning-room of his club became red in the face, and thought that it was very unfair. It was a most disagreeable thunderbolt. Then he opened the second letter, of which he well knew the handwriting. It was from the Major. Tifto's letters were very legible, but the writing was stiff and cramped, showing that the operation had been performed with difficulty. Silverbridge had hoped that he might never receive another epistle from his late partner,—but now that this epistle had come he was bound to read it. It was dated from Tally-ho Lodge on the 19th December,—which day was a Sunday; but it was written in the evening, and during the morning the Major had been up to London and had received advice from his friends. The letter itself was, indeed, drawn out for Tifto in rough by the livery-stable keeper in Long Acre. It was as follows:

'MY DEAR LORD SILVERBRIDGE,

'I venture respectfully to appeal to your lordship for an act of justice. Nobody has more of a true-born Englishman's feeling of fair play between man and man than your lordship; and as you and me have been a good deal together and your lordship ought to know me pretty well by this time, I venture to appeal to your lordship for a good word.

'All that story from Doncaster has got down into the country where I am M.F.H.' The livery-stable keeper had particularly pressed upon the Major the expediency of using the talismanic initials. It is possible, however, that some imperfectly educated reader may not know that the words indicated are Master of Foxhounds. 'Nobody could have been more sorry than me that your lordship dropped your money. Would not I have been prouder than anything to have a horse run in my name win the race! Was it likely I should lame him? Anyways I didn't; and I don't think your lordship thinks it was me. Of course your lordship and me is two now;—but that don't alter the facts.

'What I want is your lordship to send me a line, just stating your lordship's opinion that I didn't do it, and didn't have nothing to do with it,—which I didn't. There was a meeting at The Bobtailed Fox yesterday, and the gentlemen was all of one mind to go by what your lordship would say. I couldn't desire nothing fairer. So I hope your lordship will stand to me now, and write something that will pull me through.

'With all respects I beg to remain,
'Your lordship's most dutiful Servant,
'T. TIFTO.'

There was something in this letter which the Major himself did not quite approve. There was an absence of familiarity about it which annoyed him. There was no bounce,*—barring that little allusion to the glory he would have had in winning the race, which had been inserted in compliance with his earnest prayers. He would have liked to call upon his late partner to declare that a more honourable man than Major Tifto had never been known on the turf. But he felt himself to be so far down in the world that it was not safe for him to hold an opinion of his own, even against the livery-stable keeper; and therefore he copied exactly the document which his friend had prepared for him.

Silverbridge when he had read the two letters was for a time in great doubt whether he should answer them at all, and if so how he should answer them. In regard to Mr. Jawstock and the meeting at large, he regarded the application as an impertinence. It was clear to him that they had no right to send to him for a character of their Master of Hounds. But as to Tifto himself he vacillated much between pity, contempt, and absolute condemnation. Everybody had assured him that the man had certainly been guilty. The fact that he had made bets against their joint horse,—bets as to which he had said nothing till after the race was over,—had been admitted by himself. He hardly doubted now but that Tifto was a rascal. And yet it was possible that the man might not be a rascal,—not such a rascal as to be unfit to manage the Runnymede hounds. Having himself got rid of Tifto, he would have been glad that the poor wretch should have been left with his hunting honours. But he did not think that he could write to his late partner any letter that would preserve those honours for him.

It was at Tregear's advice that he referred the matter to Mr. Lupton, who was kind enough to come up to London to see Lord Silverbridge on the subject. Mr. Lupton was of opinion that both the letters should be answered, but that the answer to each should be very short. 'There is a prejudice about the world just at present,' said Mr. Lupton, 'in favour of answering letters. I don't always see the reason of it myself, but one very often has to do what other people think right. I don't see why I am to be subjected to an annoyance because another man has taken a liberty. But it is better to submit to public opinion. Public opinion thinks that letters should be answered, and therefore you had better answer them.' Then Mr. Lupton dictated the answers.

'Lord Silverbridge presents his compliments to Mr. Jawstock and begs to say that he does not feel himself called upon to express any opinion as to Major Tifto's conduct at Doncaster.' That was the first. The second was rather less simple, but not much longer.

'SIR,

'I do not feel myself called upon to express any opinion either to you or to others as to your conduct at Doncaster. Having received a letter on the subject from Mr. Jawstock I have written to him to this effect.

'I am obliged to decline any further correspondence with you on this subject,—and perhaps I had better say, on any other.

'Your obedient Servant,

'SILVERBRIDGE.

'To T. Tifto, Esq.,

'Tally-ho Lodge.'

Poor Tifto, when he got this very curt epistle from his late noble friend, was broken-hearted. He did not dare to show it. Day after day he told the livery-stable keeper that he had received no reply, and at last asserted that his appeal had remained altogether unanswered. Even this he thought was better than acknowledging the rebuff which had reached him. As regarded the meeting which had been held,—and any further meetings which might be held,—at The Bobtailed Fox, he did not see the necessity, as he explained to the livery-stable keeper, of acknowledging that he had written any letter to Lord Silverbridge. The desired inference had of course been made by the hunt, and he might keep his peace.

He did keep his peace,—with the consent of the livery-stable keeper;—but the letter to Mr. Jawstock was of course brought forward.

Another meeting at The Bobtailed Fox was convened. But in the meantime hunting had been discontinued in the Runnymede country. The Major with all his pluck, with infinite cherry brandy, could not do it. Men who had a few weeks since been on very friendly terms, and who had called each other Jones and Brown,—or perhaps Dick and Harry,—when the squabble first began, were now talking of 'punching' each other's heads. Special whips had been procured by men who intended to ride, and special bludgeons by the young farmers who intended that nobody should ride over their land as long as Major Tifto kept the hounds. It was said that the police would interfere and that anybody who trespassed would be arrested. It was whispered that the hounds would be shot,—though Mr. Topps, Mr. Jawstock, and others declared that no crime so heinous as that had ever been contemplated in the Runnymede country. The difficulties at any rate were too many for poor Tifto, and the hounds were not brought out again after that day on which they had been kept standing for two hours in the cold on the little green before The Bobtailed Fox.

A second meeting was summoned, and an invitation was sent to the Major similar to that which he had before received;—but on this occasion he did not appear. Nor were there many of the gentlemen down from London. They had fought their fight, and had made up their minds among themselves that they were beaten.

This second meeting might almost have been called select. Mr. Mahogany Topps was there of course, in the chair, and Mr. Jawstock took the place of honour and of difficulty on his right hand. There was the young gentleman from Bagshot, who considered himself quite fit to take Tifto's place if somebody else would pay the bills and settle the money, and there was the sporting old parson from Croppingham. Three or four other members of the hunt were present, and perhaps half-a-dozen farmers, ready to declare that Major Tifto should never be allowed to cross their fields again.

But there was no opposition. Mr. Jawstock read the young Lord's note, and declared that it was quite as much as he expected. He had never thought well of applying to Lord Silverbridge, and had written the letter only on the instructions of the meeting. He considered that the note, short as it was, must be decisive. Major Tifto, in appealing to Lord Silverbridge, had agreed to abide by his lordship's answer, and that answer was now before them. Mr. Jawstock ventured to propose that Major Tifto should be declared to be no longer Master of the Runnymede Hounds. The parson from Croppingham seconded the proposition, and Major Tifto was formally deposed from his high position.

Then, however, came the great difficulty,—as Mr. Jawstock soon perceived. There is nothing so dangerous to meddle with as a pack of hounds. It is very well for an enterprising man to put himself forward, to make speeches, to show that he knows all about it, and to take quite a leading part, when he is sure that he has a tower of strength behind him in the shape of a real Master who can and will pay for everything. But when a country has got rid of its Master then the eloquent gentleman who knows all about it is expected to put his hand in his pocket. In such emergencies the hand must often go very deep.

'One thing was quite impossible.' So said Mr. Topps. The Runnymede country had not been without a pack of hounds since his father was a little boy and couldn't be so left now.

'The country must be hunted of course,' said the parson from Croppingham, who, however good he might be to ride, was unfortunately not able to give assistance in the way of money.

'I shall be glad to do anything,' said the young man from Bagshot, blushing deeply.

'I suppose we must have a committee,' said Mr. Jawstock. And there was a committee, which consisted at last of Mr. Topps, Mr. Jawstock, and the young gentleman. Among them they had to buy the Major's horses, and to pay the Major one hundred and fifty pounds for his interest in the hounds, and to hire a huntsman,—the young man from Bagshot being found on trial to be inefficient for the duty, which is in truth one of the most difficult operations that a man can have to learn. Mr. Topps and Mr. Jawstock had many consultations, and before the season was over had, I fear, spent more money than they had intended. The new huntsman, too, did not at first know the country. He had been hired at a cheap rate,—having not been found to be quite sober in his last place. All of which was so inconvenient, that before the season was over some of the Runnymede men were heard to say that though Tifto was undoubtedly a rascal, they wished that he were back again among them at Tally-ho Lodge.

Poor Tifto in the meantime had skulked away, no one quite knew whither.

CHAPTER 59

'NO ONE CAN TELL WHAT MAY COME TO PASS'

HAVING thus, with the assistance of Mr. Lupton, got through the troubles of his correspondence, Lord Silverbridge returned to Matching.

He made his journey with a heavy heart, knowing well that Lady Mabel was still there. He did not leave London till the 24th, the eve of Christmas Day, and he knew that even then she would not have taken her departure. The visit to Stogpingum had been postponed. That he had learned from Tregear.

Why should she have postponed her visit? No doubt it might be very pleasant for her to be his father's guest at Matching, but she had been there above a month! It certainly had not been intended that she should stay so long when she first came. He could understand that his father should ask her to remain. His father,—who must, Lord Silverbridge thought, be very blind to things around him,—was still brooding over that foolish communication which had been made to him on the night of the dinner at the Beargarden. His father was still thinking that he should soon be able to take Mabel to his arms as a daughter-in-law. But Lady Mabel herself knew that it could not be so! The whole truth had been told to her very precisely. Why should she remain at Matching for the sake of being mixed up in a scene the acting of which could not fail to be disagreeable to her? That she should still hope, after all that had passed, to win her way to be his wife did not seem to be possible to him. He could not imagine that she would take further trouble in making any such attempt.

He found the house very quiet and nearly empty. Mrs. Finn was there with the two girls, and Mr. Warburton had come back. Miss Cassewary had already gone to her brother's house. Other guests to make Christmas merry there were none. As he looked round at the large rooms he reflected that he himself was there only for a special purpose. It was his duty, his very disagreeable duty, to break the news of his intended marriage to his father. As he stood before the fire, thinking how best he might do this, it occurred to him that a letter from a distance would have been the ready and the simple way. But then it had occurred to him also, when at a distance, that a declaration of his purpose face to face was the simplest and readiest way. The truth is that when you have to be flogged there is no pleasant way of receiving the lashes. The flogging had to be endured, and thus he was at Matching for the sake of undergoing it. If you have to go headlong into the water you should take your plunge without hesitating. So he told himself, making up his mind that he would have it all out with his father that evening.

At dinner Lady Mabel sat next to his father, and he sat between Mrs. Finn and his sister. As he did so he could watch the special courtesy with which the Duke treated the girl whom he was so desirous of introducing to his house. Silverbridge could not talk about the election at

Polpenno because all conversation about Tregear was interdicted in the presence of his sister. He could say nothing as to the Runnymede hunt and the two thunderbolts which had fallen on him in London, as Major Tifto and his sins was not a subject on which he could expatiate in the presence of his father. He asked a few questions about the shooting,—which had been altogether neglected in his absence,—and referred with great regret to his absence from the Brake country, in which Phineas was reported to have been doing great things under the auspices of Lord Chiltern. 'He and I once had an adventure there out hunting,*—before we were married,' said Mrs. Finn. Then she told the adventure,—how they had both been left behind in a wood by all the hunt because Mr. Finn's horse had refused to jump a fence; but Silverbridge cared but little for the story, giving all his ears to the conversation between his father and Lady Mabel.

'I am sure Mr. Cassewary could spare you for another fortnight.'

'If so he would have to spare me altogether,' said Mabel laughing, 'for I must meet my father in London in the middle of January.'

'Could you not put off Stogpingum to another year?'

'You would think I had taken root, and was growing at Matching.'

'Of all our products you would be the most delightful, and the most charming,—and we would hope the most permanent,' said the courteous Duke.

'After being here so long I need hardly say that I like Matching better than almost any place in the world. I suppose it is the contrast to Grex.'

'Grex was a palace,' said the Duke, 'before a wall of this house had been built.'

'Grex is very old, and very wild,—and very uncomfortable. Nobody can live there and it looks as though it were devoted to ghosts. But I love it dearly. Matching is the very reverse of Grex.'

'Not I hope in your affections.'

'I did not mean that. I think one likes a contrast. But I must go to Stogpingum,—say on the first of January, if it were only to pick up Miss Cassewary. You don't know what Miss Cassewary has been to me.'

'I have the greatest possible respect for Miss Cassewary,' said the Duke.

It was certain, therefore, that she was going on the first of January. How would it be if he put off the telling of his story for yet another week, till she should be gone? Then he looked around and bethought himself that the time would hang very heavy with him. And his father would daily expect from him a declaration exactly opposed to that which he had to make. During the whole week he would be thrust together with Mabel, with whom he could now find no possible subject that would be common to both of them. He had no horses to ride, and had become sick of shooting at Matching. As he went on listening he almost convinced himself that the proper thing to do would be to go back to London and thence write to his father a letter that should be explanatory and conclusive. At any rate he made no confession to his father on that night.

On the next morning there was a heavy fall of snow, but nevertheless everybody managed to go to church. The Duke, as he looked at Lady Mabel tripping along over the swept paths in her furs and short petticoats and well-made boots, thought that his son was a very lucky fellow to have the chance of winning the love of such a girl. No remembrance of Miss Boncassen came across his mind as he saw them close together. It was so important that Silverbridge should marry and thus be kept from further follies! And it was so momentous to the fortunes of the Palliser family generally that he should marry well! There were so many girls about, said the Duke to himself, from an alliance with whom he himself would recoil. In so thinking it did not occur to him that the granddaughter of an American labourer might be offered to him. The girls who were present to his mind were perhaps a little too fast, too fond of admiration, perhaps too old, unattractive in manner, and, not improbably, of birth if not ignoble, still not sufficiently ennobled. A young lady fit to be Duchess of Omnium was not to be found everywhere. But this girl, he thought as he saw her walking briskly and strongly through the snow, with every mark of health about her, with every sign and certainty of high breeding, very beautiful, exquisite in manner, gracious as a goddess, was fit to be a duchess! She wanted but one thing, money; and to that one thing he was indifferent. Silverbridge at this moment was walking close to her side,—in good looks, in gracious manner, in high breeding at any rate her equal,—in worldly gifts infinitely her superior. Surely she would not despise him! Silverbridge at the moment was expressing a hope that the sermon would not be very long.

After lunch Mabel came suddenly behind the chair on which Silverbridge was sitting and asked him to take a walk with her. He inquired whether she were not afraid of the snow. 'Perhaps you are,' she said laughing. 'I do not mind it in the least.' Of course he went with her. She looped up her petticoats, he put on a pair of knickerbockers, and away they went. When they were but a few yards from the front door, she put her hand upon his arm, and spoke to him as though she had arranged the walk with reference to that special question, 'And now tell me all about Frank.'

She had arranged everything with this intention. She had a plan before her now, and had determined in accordance with that plan that she would say nothing to disturb him on this occasion. If she could succeed

in bringing him into good humour with herself, that should be sufficient for to-day. 'Now tell me everything about Frank! Of course there
are reasons why nothing can be said in there.'

'Frank is member of Parliament for Polpenno. That is all.'

'That is so like a man and so unlike a woman. What did he say? What
did he do? How did he look? What did you say? What did you do? How
did you look?'

'We looked very miserable, when we got wet through, walking about
all day in the rain.'

'Was that necessary?'

'Quite necessary. We looked so mean and draggled that nobody would
have voted for us, only that poor Mr. Carbottle looked meaner and more
draggled.'

'The Duke says you made ever so many speeches.'

'I should think I did. It is very easy to make speeches down at a place
like that. Tregear spoke like a book.'

'What did he say?'

'All manner of things. You wouldn't care to hear.'

'It is just what I should care to do. If I were a man and could go to
places of that sort myself, then perhaps I shouldn't care. But he
spoke well?'

'Awfully well. He told them that all the good things that had ever
been done in Parliament had been carried by the Tories. He went back
to Pitt's time, and had it all at his fingers' ends.'

'And quite true.'

'That's just what it was not. It was all a crammer.* But it did as well.
As for being true, when you say a thing like that who is to know the
difference? Nobody contradicts you.'

'I am glad he is a member. Don't you think the Duke will come round
a little now?'

When Tregear and the election had been sufficiently discussed, they
got round by degrees to Major Tifto and the two thunderbolts.
Silverbridge, when he felt that no disagreeable allusions were to be
made, when he perceived that nothing was to be said about Isabel
Boncassen or his own freedom in the matter of love-making, was not
sorry to have a friend from whom he could find sympathy for himself in
his own troubles. Tregear was always a little hard with him about Tifto.
Mr. Lupton had been extremely useful; but he had been perhaps somewhat sententious and dictatorial. To his father he had not dared to speak
about that correspondence. But with some encouragement from Mabel
the whole story was told. 'Was it not a great impertinence?' she asked.

'It was an awful bore. What could I say? I was not going to pronounce judgment against the poor wretch. I dare say he was good enough for Mr. Jawstock.'

'But I suppose he did cheat horribly.'

'I dare say he did. A great many of them do cheat. But what of that? I was not bound to give him a character, bad or good.'

'Certainly not.'

'He had not been my servant. It was such a letter. I'll show it you when we get in;—asking whether poor Tifto was fit to be the—'depositary of the intimacy of the Runnymede hunt'! And then Tif's letter! I almost wept over that.'

'What could he say to you? How could he have had the audacity to write at all?'

'He said that "him and me had been a good deal together." Unfortunately that was true. I do feel a pity for him. And even now I am not quite sure that he lamed the horse himself.'

'Everybody thinks he did. Percival says there is no doubt about it.'

'Percival knows nothing about it,—nor anybody else for the matter of that. Three of the gang ran away, and he stood his ground. That's about all we do know.'

'What did you say to him?'

'I had to address him as Sir, and beg him not to write to me any more. Of course they mean to get rid of him, and I couldn't do him any good. Poor Tifto! Upon the whole I think I hate Jawstock worse than Tifto.'

In this way there came up between the two something like a renewal of confidence, and this was done altogether without reference to the subject which was nearest to the hearts of each of them. Silverbridge had feared that he would be asked about Miss Boncassen, and had therefore wished to avoid Lady Mabel's company; but when he found that no unpleasant allusions were to be made he enjoyed his walk well enough. 'Mind you show me Mr. Jawstock's letter,' she said as she entered the house,—'and the unfortunate Major's.'

'Poor Tifto!'

Lady Mabel was content with her afternoon's work. When they had been at Matching before the Polpenno election, there had apparently been no friendship between them,—at any rate no confidential friendship. Miss Boncassen had been there, and he had had neither ears nor eyes for anyone else. But now something like the feeling of old days had been restored. She had not done much towards her great object, certainly;—but then she had known that nothing could be done towards her great object till he should again be in good humour with her. There could be no chance for her till they should be on intimate terms of friendship,—and that she thought she had achieved.

As Christmas fell on a Saturday, there were two church-going days together, to the disgust of Lord Silverbridge, who was not carried by the ladies to hear the second service without some trouble. On that day, and the Monday and the Tuesday, he again found himself thrown together with Mabel. In some of these interviews Silverbridge described the Polpenno people, and told her how Miss Tregear had been reassured by his eloquence. He also read to her the whole Jawstock and Tifto correspondence, and was complimented by her as to his prudence and foresight. 'To tell the truth I consulted Mr. Lupton,' he said, not liking to take credit for wisdom which had not been altogether his own. Then they talked about Grex, and Killancodlem, about Gerald and the shooting, about Mary's unconquerable love for Tregear, and about the work of the coming session. On all these subjects they were comfortable and confidential,—Miss Boncassen's name never having been as yet so much as mentioned since his return to Matching.

But still the real work was all before her. She had never ventured to think that she could bring him round to kneel once more at her feet by such gentle measures as these. She had not dared to dream that he could in this way be brought to forget the past autumn and all its charms. She knew well that there was something very difficult before her. But, if that difficult thing might be done at all, these were the preparations which must be made for the doing of it.

It was arranged that she should leave Matching on Saturday, the first day of the new year. Things had gone on in the manner described till the Thursday had come. The Duke had been impatient but had restrained himself. He had seen that they were much together and that they were apparently friends. He too told himself that there were two more days, and that before the end of those days everything might be pleasantly settled. It was a matter in which it was so hard for a father to interfere!

During the last four or five days it had become a matter of course that Silverbridge and Mabel should walk together in the afternoon. He himself had felt that there was danger in this,—not danger that he should be untrue to Isabel, but that he should make others think that he was true to Mabel. But he excused himself to himself on the plea that he and Mabel had been intimate friends,—were still intimate friends, and that she was going away in a day or two. Mary, who watched it all without saying a word, was sure that misery was being prepared for someone. She was well aware that by this time her father was anxious to welcome Mabel as his daughter-in-law. She strongly suspected that something had been said, that some agreement had been made between her father and her brother on the subject. But then she had Isabel Boncassen's direct assurance that Silverbridge was engaged to her! Now when Isabel's back was turned, Silverbridge and Mabel were always together. The Duke, however, was almost satisfied. Surely the matter would now be settled.

On the Thursday after lunch they were again out together. It had become so much a habit that the walk repeated itself without an effort. It had been part of Mabel's scheme that it should be so. During all this morning she had been thinking of her scheme. It was all but hopeless. So much she had declared to herself. But forlorn hopes do sometimes end in splendid triumphs. Men will face almost certain death, and then live as heroes for many after years. That which she might gain was so much! And what could she lose? The sweet bloom of her maiden shame? That, she told herself, with bitterest inward tears, was already gone from her. Frank Tregear at any rate knew where her heart had been given, and that, having been given, it had never been recovered. Frank Tregear knew that having lost her heart to one man she was anxious to marry another. He knew that she was willing to accept the coronet of a duchess as her consolation for that early misfortune. That bloom of her maiden shame, of which she quite understood the sweetness, the charm, the value,—its ineffable superiority to all other feminine charms,—was gone when she had brought herself to such a state that any human being should know that, loving one man, she should be willing to marry another. She had fought all that out with Miss Cass, who knew quite as much as did Frank Tregear. The sweet treasure was gone from her. Its aroma was fled. It behoved her now to be ambitious, cautious,—and if possible successful.

When first she had so resolved, success seemed to be easily within her reach. Of all the golden youths that crossed her path no one was so pleasant to her eye, to her ear, to her feelings generally as this Duke's young heir. There was a coming manliness about him which she liked,—and she liked even the slight want of present manliness. Putting aside Frank Tregear she could go nearer to loving him than any other man she had ever seen. She could feel sure that with him she would not be turned from her duties by disgust, by dislike, or dismay. She could even think that the time would come when she might really love him. Then she had all but succeeded. She might certainly have succeeded altogether had she been but a little more prudent,—in some slight degree better acquainted with the game which she was playing. But she had allowed her great prize to escape from her fingers.

But the prize was not yet utterly beyond her grasp. To recover it,—to recover even the smallest chance of recovering it, there would be need of great exertion. She must be bold, sudden, unwomanlike,—and yet with such display of woman's charm that he at least should discover no want. She must be false, but false with such perfect deceit that he must regard her as a pearl of truth. If anything could lure him back it must be his conviction of her passionate love. And she must be strong;—so strong as to overcome not only his weakness, but all that was strong in him. She knew that he did love that other girl,—and she must overcome even that. And to do this she must prostrate herself at his feet,—as, since the world began, it has been man's province to prostrate himself at the feet of the woman he loves.

To do this she must indeed bid adieu to the sweet bloom of her maiden shame! But had she not done so already when, by the side of the brook at Killancodlem, she had declared to him plainly enough her despair at hearing that he loved that other girl? Though she were to grovel at his feet she could not speak more plainly than she had spoken then. She had coyed it with him a little when he had first come to her, meaning that he should not think that his suit was to be too easily won, meaning to use a fair girl's privilege of perversity for a day or two;—and then, when the other fair girl had come between them, she had told her story all too plainly. She could not tell her story now more plainly than she had done then; but,—though the chances were small,—perchance she might tell it more effectively.

'Perhaps this will be our last walk,' she said. 'Come down to the seat over the river.'

'Why should it be the last? You'll be here to-morrow.'

'There are so many slips in such things,' she said laughing. 'You may get a letter from your constituents that will want all the day to answer. Or your father may have a communication to make to me. You can't think how many political secrets he has taught me. I am beginning to tremble in my shoes lest he should make me a Liberal. But at any rate come.' So they went to the seat.

It was a spot in the park from whence there was a fine distant view over many lands, and low beneath the bench, which stood on the edge of a steep bank, ran a stream which made a sweeping bend in this place, so that a reach of the little river might be seen both to the right and to the left. It was known to be a favourite spot with the Duke himself,—but not in such weather as this. For, though the sun was shining, the snow under their feet was hard with frost. It was an air such as one sometimes finds in England, and often in America. Though the cold was very perceptible, though water in the shade was freezing at this moment, there was no feeling of damp, no sense of bitter wind. It was a sweet and jocund air, such as would make young people prone to run and skip, and old people prone to think themselves young. 'Now you are here,' said Silverbridge, 'you are not going to sit down with all the snow on the bench?'

On their way thither she had not ventured to say a word that would disturb him. She had spoken to him of the coming session, and had managed to display to him the great interest which she took in his parliamentary career. In doing this she had flattered him to the top of his bent.* If he would return to his father's politics, then would she certainly become a renegade. Would he speak in the next session? She hoped he would speak. And if he did, might she be there to hear him? She was cautious not to say a word of Frank Tregear, understanding something of that strange jealousy which could exist even when he who was jealous did not love the woman who caused it. She was very clever, and by the time they had reached the spot had certainly made him think that she now, at least, respected him as a man. It had been a ground of complaint with him that she had treated him like a boy.

'No,' she said, 'I do not think we can sit. But still I like to be here with you. All that some day will be your own.' Then she stretched her hands out to the far view.

'Some of it, I suppose. I don't think it is all ours. As for that, if one cared for extent of acres all around, one ought to go to Barsetshire.'

'Is that larger?'

'Twice as large, I believe. And yet none of the family like being there. The rental is very well.'

'And the borough,' she said, leaning on his arm and looking up into his face.

'And the borough,—for the present.'

'What a happy fellow you ought to be!'

'Bar Tifto,—and Mr. Jawstock.'

'You have got rid of Tifto and all those troubles very easily.'

'Thanks to the governor.'

'Yes indeed. I do love your father so dearly.'

'So do I,—rather.'

'May I tell you something about him?' As she asked the question she was standing very close to her companion, leaning upon his arm, with her left hand crossed upon her right. Had others been there, of course she would not have stood in such a guise. She knew that,—and he knew it too. Of course there was something in it of declared affection,—of that kind of love which most of us have been happy enough to give and receive, without intending to show more than true friendship will allow at special moments. Her feelings at the moment were tender to him, and he certainly made no effort to reject them, as they stood there together looking down upon the views.

'Don't tell me anything about him I shan't like to hear,' said Silverbridge.

'Ah;—that is so hard to know. I wish you would like to hear it.'

'What can it be?'

'I cannot tell you now.'

'Why not? And why did you offer?'

'Because—— Oh, Silverbridge!'

He certainly as yet did not understand it. It had never occurred to him that she would know what were his father's wishes. Perhaps he was slow of comprehension as he urged her to tell him what this was about his father. 'What can you tell me about him that I should not like to hear?'

'You do not know?' said she, leaning heavily on his arm. 'Oh, Silverbridge, I think you know.' Then there came upon him a glimmering of the truth. 'You do know.' And she stood apart looking him full in the face.

'I do not know what you can have to tell me.'

'No;—no. It is not I that should tell you. But yet it is so. Silverbridge, what did you say to me when you came to me that morning in the Square?'

'What did I say?'

'Was I not entitled to think that you—loved me?' To this he had nothing to reply, but stood before her silent and frowning. 'Think of it, Silverbridge. Was it not so? And because I did not at once tell you all the truth, because I did not then say that my heart was all yours, were you right to leave me?'

'You only laughed at me.'

'No;—no; no; I never laughed at you. How could I laugh when you were all the world to me? Ask Frank; he knew. Ask Miss Cass;—she knew. And can you say you did not know; you, you, you yourself? Can any girl suppose that such words as these are to mean nothing when they have been spoken? You knew I loved you.'

'No;—no.'

'You must have known it. I will never believe but that you knew it. Why should your father be so sure of it?'

'He never was sure of it.'

'Yes, Silverbridge; yes. There is not one in the house who does not see that he treats me as though he expected me to be his son's wife. Do you not know that he wishes it?' He fain would not have answered this; but she paused for his answer and then repeated her question. 'Do you not know that he wishes it?'

'I think he does,' said Silverbridge;—'but it can never be so.'

'Oh, Silverbridge;—oh my loved one. Do not say that to me! Do not kill me at once!' Now she placed her hands one on each arm as she stood opposite to him and looked up into his face. 'You said you loved me once. Why do you desert me now? Have you a right to treat me like that? When I tell you that you have all my heart?' The tears were now streaming down her face, and they were not counterfeit tears. In this prayer that she was making, she was asking for all that she valued in the world, and at this moment she did believe that she loved him.

'You know,' he said, submitting to her hands, but not lifting his arm to embrace her.

'What do I know?'

'That I have given all I have to give to another.' As he said this he looked away sternly, over her shoulder, to the distance.

'That American girl!' she exclaimed starting back, with some show of sternness also on her brow.

'Yes;—that American girl,' said Silverbridge.

Then she recovered herself immediately. Indignation, natural indignation, would not serve her turn in the present emergency. 'You know that cannot be. You ought to know it. What will your father say? You have not dared to tell him. That is so natural,' she added, trying to appease his frown. 'How possibly can it be told to him? I will not say a word against her.'

'No; do not do that.'

'But there are fitnesses of things which such a one as you cannot disregard without preparing for yourself a whole life of repentance and sorrow.'

'Look here, Mabel.'

'Well!'

'I will tell you all the truth.'

'Well!'

'I would sooner lose all, the rank I have; the rank that I am to have; all these lands that you have been looking on; my father's wealth, my seat in Parliament,—everything that Fortune has done for me,— I would give them all up, sooner than lose her.' Now at any rate he was a man. She was sure of that now. This was more, very much more, not only than she had expected from him, but more than she had thought it possible that his character should have produced.

His strength reduced her to weakness. 'And I am nothing,' she said.

'Yes, indeed. You are Lady Mabel Grex,—whom all women envy, and whom all men honour.'

'The poorest wretch this day under the sun!'

'Do not say that. You should take shame to say that.'

'I do take shame;—and I do say it. Sir, do you not feel what you owe me? Do you not know that you have made me the wretch I am? How did you dare to talk to me as you did talk when you were in London? You tell me that I am Lady Mabel Grex;—and yet you come to me with a lie on your lips,—with such a lie as that? You must have taken me for some nursemaid on whom you had condescended to cast your eye! It cannot be that even you should have dared to treat Lady Mabel Grex after such a fashion as that! And now you have cast your eye on this other girl. You can never marry her!'

'I shall endeavour to do so.'

'You can never marry her,' she said, stamping her foot. She had now lost all the caution which she had taught herself for the prosecution of her scheme,—all the care with which she had burdened herself. Now she was natural enough. 'No,—you can never marry her. You cannot look your father in the face and tell him that you will. You could not show yourself after it in your clubs, or in Parliament, or in the world. Come home, do you say? No, I will not go to your home. It is not my home. Cold;—of course I am cold;—cold through to the heart!'

'I cannot leave you here alone,' he said, for she had now turned from him, and was walking with hurried steps and short turns on the edge of the bank, which at this place was almost a precipice.

'You have left me,—utterly in the cold, more desolate than I am here, even though I should spend the night among the trees. But I will go back, and will tell your father everything. If my father were other than he is,—if my brother were better to me, you would not have done this.'

'If you had a legion of brothers it would have been the same,' he said, turning sharp upon her.

They walked on together, but without a word till the house was in sight. Then she looked round at him, and stopped him on the path as she caught his eye. 'Silverbridge!' she said.

'Lady Mabel.'

'Call me Mabel. At any rate call me Mabel. If I have said anything to offend you—I beg your pardon.'

'I am not offended,—but unhappy.'

'If you are unhappy, what must I be? What have I got to look forward to? Give me your hand, and say that we are friends.'

'Certainly we are friends,' he said, as he gave her his hand.

'Who can tell what may come to pass?' To this he would make no answer, as it seemed to imply that some division between himself and Isabel Boncassen might possibly come to pass. 'You will not tell anyone that I love you.'

'I tell such a thing as that!'

'But never forget it yourself. No one can tell what may come to pass.'

After that they entered the house without another word, and Lady Mabel at once went up to her room. She had played her scene, but was well aware that she had played it altogether unsuccessfully.

CHAPTER 60

LORD GERALD IN FURTHER TROUBLE

WHEN Silverbridge got back to the house he was by no means well pleased with himself in regard to what had passed between him and Lady Mabel. In the first place it pained him greatly to think that she was unhappy, and that he had contributed anything to her unhappiness. And then she had told him that he would not have dared to have acted as he had done, but that her father and brother were careless to defend her. He had replied fiercely that a legion of brothers ready to act on her behalf would not have altered his conduct; but not the less did he feel that he had behaved badly to her. It could not now be altered. He could not now be untrue to Isabel. But certainly he had said a word or two to Mabel which he could not remember without regret. He had not thought that a word from him could have been so powerful. He remembered well that he had gone away from that interview with a feeling that she had laughed at him, rebuffed him,—almost scorned him. No doubt he had afterwards thought it probable that she might accept him, and, acting on that, had made that indiscreet communication to his father. Now, when that word was recalled to his memory by the girl to whom it had been spoken, he could not quite acquit himself. And in truth he was too fond of Mabel to be able to see her sorrow without grieving himself. He was very, very sorry that it should be as it was;—but not on that account could he sever himself from Isabel Boncassen.

And Mabel had declared to him that she would at once appeal to his father. There was an absurdity in this at which he could not but smile,—that the girl should complain to his father because he would not marry her! But even in doing this she might cause him great vexation. Of course it was to be expected that he should be the first to communicate his engagement to his father,—and especially as that engagement would imply a change in a declared intention. But he could not bring himself to ask her not to tell her story to the Duke. He must take all that as it might come. Even now, at this moment, Mabel might be telling her story. He was, however, strong in his determination that nothing should stand between him and Isabel.

While he was thinking of all this in his own room, postponing the disagreeable moment in which he would begin to dress for dinner, a servant brought him two letters. The day mail arrived at Matching at this hour, and the letters were generally distributed over the house while people were dressing. From the first which he opened he soon perceived that it contained an account of more troubles. It was from his brother Gerald, and was written from Auld Reikie, the name of a house in Scotland belonging to Lord Nidderdale's people. Gerald, while at Crummie-Toddie, had made an engagement to go there for the Christmas, thus postponing his visit to Matching,—not altogether in conformity with his father's wishes. This was Gerald's letter.

'DEAR SILVER,

'I have got into a most awful scrape. That fellow Percival is here, and Dolly Longstaffe, and Nidderdale, and Popplecourt, and Jack Hindes, and Perry who is in the Coldstreams,* and one or two more, and there has been a lot of cards, and I have lost ever so much money. I wouldn't mind it so much but Percival has won it all,—a fellow I hate; and now I owe him—three thousand four hundred pounds! He has just told me he is hard up and that he wants the money before the week is over. He can't be hard up because he has won from everybody;—but of course I had to tell him that I would pay him.

'Can you help me? Of course I know that I have been a fool. Percival knows what he is about and plays regularly for money. When I began I didn't think that I could lose above twenty or thirty pounds. But it got on from one thing to another, and when I woke this morning I felt I didn't know what to do with myself. You can't think how the luck went against me. Everybody says that they never saw such cards.

'And now do tell me how I am to get out of it. Could you manage it with Mr. Moreton? Of course I will make it all right with you some day. Moreton always lets you have whatever you want. But perhaps he couldn't do this without letting the governor know. I would rather anything than that. There is some money owing at Oxford also which of course he must know.

'I was thinking that perhaps I might get it from some of those fellows in London. There are people called Comfort and Criball who let men have money constantly. I know two or three up at Oxford who have had it from them. Of course I couldn't go to them as you could do, for, in spite of what the governor said to us up in London one day, there is nothing that must come to me. But you could do anything in that way, and of course I would stand to it.

'I know you won't throw me over because you always have been such a brick;—but above all things don't tell the governor. Percival is such a nasty fellow, otherwise I shouldn't mind it. He spoke this morning as though I was treating him badly,—though the money was only lost last night; and he looked at me in a way that made me long to kick him. I told him not to flurry himself and that he should have his money. If he speaks to me like that again I will kick him.

'I will be at Matching as soon as possible, but I cannot go till this is settled. Nid,'—meaning Lord Nidderdale,—'is a brick.

'Your affectionate Brother,
'GERALD.'

The other was from Nidderdale, and referred to the same subject.

'DEAR SILVERBRIDGE,
'Here has been a terrible nuisance. Last night some of the men got to playing cards and Gerald lost a terribly large sum to Percival. I did all that I could to stop it because I saw that Percival was going in for a big thing. I fancy that he got as much from Dolly Longstaffe as he did from Gerald;—but it won't matter much to Dolly; or at any rate, if it does, nobody cares. Gerald told me he was writing to you about it, so I am not betraying him.

'What is to be done? Of course Percival is behaving badly. He always does. I can't turn him out of the house, and he seems to intend to stick to Gerald till he has got the money. He has taken a cheque from Dolly dated two months hence. I am in an awful funk for fear Gerald should pitch into him. He will in a minute if anything rough is said to him. I suppose the straightest thing would be to go to the Duke at once; but Gerald won't hear of it. I hope you won't think me wrong to tell you. If I could help him I would. You know what a bad doctor I am for that sort of complaint.

'Yours always,
'NIDDERDALE.'

The dinner-bell had rung before Silverbridge had come to an end of thinking of this new vexation, and he had not as yet made up his mind what he had better do for his brother. There was one thing as to which he was determined that it should not be done by him,—nor, if he could prevent it, by Gerald. There should be no dealings with Comfort and Criball. The Duke had succeeded, at any rate, in filling his son's mind

with a horror of aid of that sort. Nidderdale had suggested that the
'straightest' thing would be to go direct to the Duke. That no doubt
would be straight,—and efficacious. That sure fount of love and
assistance would certainly pour forth the needed waters at once. The
Duke would not have allowed a boy of his to be a debtor to Lord Percival
for a day, let the debt have been contracted how it might. But Gerald
had declared against this course,—and Silverbridge himself would
have been most unwilling to adopt it. How could he have told that story
to the Duke, while there was that other infinitely more important story
of his own, which must be told at once,—which not improbably must
be told that very night, which perhaps at that very moment was being
told by Mabel Grex?

In the midst of all these troubles he went down to dinner, and soon
perceived that nothing had been told as yet. 'Lady Mabel,' said the
Duke, 'tells me that you two have been to see Sir Guy's look-out.'

She was standing close to the Duke and whispered a word into his
ear. 'You said you would call me Mabel.'

'Yes, sir,' said Silverbridge, 'and I have made up my mind that Sir
Guy never stayed there very long in winter. It was awfully cold.'

'I had furs on,' said Mabel. 'What a lovely spot it is, even in this
weather.' Then dinner was announced. She knew that she had not been
cold. She could still feel the tingling heat of her blood as she had implored
him to love her.

Silverbridge when he went up to his room felt that he must write to
his brother by the first post. The communication was of a nature that
would bear no delay. If his hands had been free he would himself have
gone off to Auld Reikie and have made some arrangement with Percival.
At last he made up his mind, and sat down to his writing-table. The
first letter he wrote was neither to Nidderdale nor to Gerald, but to
Lord Percival himself.

'DEAR PERCIVAL,

'Gerald writes me word that he has lost to you at cards £3,400 and he
wants me to get him the money. It is a terrible nuisance, and he has
been an ass. But of course I shall stand to him for anything he wants.
I haven't got £3,400 in my pocket, and I don't know anyone who
has,—that is among our set. But I send you my I.O.U. for the amount,
and will promise to get you the money in two months. I suppose that
will be sufficient and that you will not bother Gerald any more about it.

'Yours truly,

'SILVERBRIDGE.'

Then he copied this letter and enclosed the copy in another which he wrote to his brother.

'DEAR GERALD,

'What an ass you have been! But I don't suppose you are worse than I was at Doncaster. I will have nothing to do with such people as Comfort and Criball. That is the sure way to the d——! As for telling Moreton, that is only a polite and roundabout way of telling the governor. He would immediately ask the governor what was to be done. I think he has orders to pay any amount for me because I am understood to be such an utter donkey;—but I don't think that as yet you are supposed to be bad enough for such treatment.

'You will see what I have done. Of course I must tell the governor before the end of February, as I cannot get the money in any other way. But that I will do. It does seem hard upon him. Not that the money will hurt him much; but that he would so like to have a steady-going son.

'I suppose Percival won't make any bother about the I.O.U. He'll be a fool if he does. I wouldn't kick him if I were you,—unless he says anything very bad. You would be sure to come to grief somehow. He is a beast,—and I am very sorry for it on Lady Mab's account.

'Your affectionate Brother,

'SILVERBRIDGE.'

With these letters that special grief was removed from his mind for a while. Looking over the dark river of possible trouble which seemed to run between the present moment and the time at which the money must be procured, he thought that he had driven off this calamity of Gerald's to infinite distance. But into that dark river he must now plunge almost at once. On the next day, the Friday, he managed to be out among the coverts, or in the stables, or about the park the entire day, so that there should be no walk with Mabel. In the evening he could see that the Duke was uneasy;—but not a word was said to him. On the following morning Lady Mabel took her departure. When she went from the door, both the Duke and Silverbridge were there to bid her farewell. She smiled and was as gracious as though everything had gone according to her heart's delight. 'Dear Duke, I am so obliged to you for your kindness,' she said, as she put out her cheek for him to kiss. Then she gave her hand to Silverbridge. 'Of course you will come and see me in town.' And she smiled upon them all,—having courage enough to keep down all her sufferings.

'Come in here a moment, Silverbridge,' said the father as they returned into the house together. 'How is it now between you and her?'

CHAPTER 61

'BONE OF MY BONE'

'How is it now between you and her?' That was the question which the Duke put to his son as soon as he had closed the door of the study, to which he had led the way. Lady Mabel had just been dismissed from the front door on her journey to Stogpingum, and there could therefore be no doubt as to the 'her' intended. Nor could there be any doubt as to the meaning of the question. No such question would have been asked had not Silverbridge himself declared to his father his purpose of making Lady Mabel his wife. On that subject the Duke, without such authority, would not have interfered, even with his son. But he had been consulted, had acceded, and had encouraged the idea by excessive liberality on his part. He had never dropped it out of his mind for a moment. He had hardly doubted but that the event would be as he wished. But when he found that the girl was leaving his house without any explanation, then he became restless and inquisitive. As soon as she was in truth gone he asked the question which had often before been almost on his tongue.

Silverbridge was certainly afraid of his father. They say that perfect love casteth out fear.* If it be so the love of children to their parents is seldom altogether perfect,—and perhaps had better not be quite perfect. With this young man it was not that he feared anything which his father could do to him, that he thought that his father would exercise severity, that he believed that in consequence of the declaration which he had to make his comforts and pleasures would be curtailed or his independence diminished. He knew his father too well to dread such punishment as that. But he feared that what he had to say would make his father unhappy, and he was conscious that he had so often sinned in that way. He had stumbled so frequently! Though he was apparently thoughtless, though in action he would sometimes be absolutely thoughtless,—yet he understood perfectly the effect which had been produced on his father's mind by his conduct. He had it at heart 'to be good to the governor,' to gratify that most constant and loving of all possible friends, who, as he knew well, was always thinking of his welfare. And yet he had never been 'good to the governor';—nor had Gerald;—and to all this was added his sister's determined perversity. He was afraid that his father had a 'bad time of it' with his children, and now he was going to add to these troubles. It was thus he feared his father.

He paused a moment, while the Duke stood with his back to the fire looking at him. 'I'm afraid that it is all over, sir,' he said.

'All over!'

'I am afraid so.'

'Why is it all over? Has she refused you?'

'Well, sir;—it isn't quite that.' Then he paused again. It was so difficult to begin about Isabel Boncassen.

The Duke also hesitated for a few moments before he went on with his cross-examination. 'I am sorry for that,' he said; 'very sorry. You will understand, I hope, that I should make no inquiry in such a matter unless I had felt myself warranted in doing so by what you had yourself told me in London.'

'I understand all that.'

'I have been very anxious about it, and have even gone so far as to make some preparations for what I had hoped would be your early marriage.'

'Preparations!' exclaimed Silverbridge, thinking of church bells, bride cake, and wedding presents.

'As to the property. I am so anxious that you should enjoy all the settled independence which can belong to an English gentleman! I never plough, or sow. I know no more of sheep and bulls than of the extinct animals of earlier ages. I would not have it so with you. I would fain see you surrounded by those things which ought to interest a nobleman in this country. Why is it all over, as you say, with Lady Mabel Grex?'

The young man looked imploringly at his father, as though earnestly begging that nothing more might be said about Mabel. The story as far as Mabel was concerned certainly could not be told. 'I had changed my mind before I found out that she was really in love with me!' He could not say that. He could not even hint that he might have had, might still have, Mabel if he would. The only thing for him was to tell everything about Isabel Boncassen with as little delay as possible. He felt that in doing this he must begin with himself. 'I have rather changed my mind, sir,' he said, 'since we were walking together in London that night.'

'Changed your mind! Have you quarrelled with Lady Mabel?'

'Oh dear no. I am very fond of Mabel;—only not just like that.'

'Not just like what?'

'I had better tell the whole truth at once.'

'Certainly tell the truth, Silverbridge. I cannot say that you are bound in duty to tell the whole truth even to your father in such a matter. There may be secrets.'

'But I mean to tell you everything. Mabel did not seem to care about me much—in London. And then I saw someone,—someone I liked better.' Then he stopped, but as the Duke did not immediately ask any questions he plunged on. 'It was Miss Boncassen.'

'Miss Boncassen!'

'Yes, sir,' said Silverbridge, with a little access of decision, feeling that the moment was coming in which he would have to adhere to his own purpose in opposition to anything his father would say to him.

'The American young lady.'

'Yes, sir.'

'Do you know anything of her family?'

'I think I know all about her family. It is not much in the way of—family.'

'You have not spoken to her about it?'

'Yes, sir;—I have settled it all with her, on condition———'

'Settled it with her that she is to be your wife!'

'Yes, sir,—on condition that you will approve.'

'Did you go to her, Silverbridge, with such a stipulation as that;—and did she accept you on those terms?'

'It was not like that.'

'How was it then?'

'She stipulated. She will marry me if you will consent.'

'It was she then who thought of my wishes and my feelings;—not you?'

'I knew that I loved her. What is a man to do when he feels like that? Of course I meant to tell you.' The Duke was standing with his hands behind his back, looking very black and unpropitious. 'I thought you liked her, sir.'

'Liked her! I did like her. I do like her. What has that to do with it? Do you think I like none but those with whom I should think it fitting to ally myself in marriage? Is there to be no duty in such matters, no restraint, no feeling of what is due to your own name, and to others who bear it? The lad out there who is sweeping the walks can marry the first girl that pleases his eye if she will take him. Perhaps his lot is the happier because he owns such liberty. Have you, do you think, the same freedom?'

'I suppose I have,—by law.'

'Do you recognise no duty but what the laws impose upon you? Should you be disposed to eat and drink in bestial excess, the laws would not hinder you! Should you lie and sleep all the day, the law would say nothing! Should you neglect every duty which your position imposes on you, the law could not interfere! To such a one as you the law can be no guide. You should so live as not to come near the law,—or to have the law come near to you. From all evil against which the law bars you, you should be barred, at an infinite distance, by honour, by conscience, and nobility. Does the law require patriotism, philanthropy, self-abnegation, public service, purity of purpose, devotion to the needs of others who have been placed in the world below you? The law is a great thing,—because men are poor and weak, and bad. And it is great, because where it exists in its strength, no tyrant can be above it. But between you and me there should be no mention of law as the guide of your conduct. Speak to me of honour, of duty, and of nobility; and tell me what they require of you.'

Silverbridge listened in silence and with something of true admiration in his heart. He agreed with his father on his premises,—so as to repent himself of having unfortunately pleaded that the law would allow him to marry Isabel Boncassen; but he did not agree with the deduction which his father had drawn, and which went to show that he, Silverbridge, was debarred by duty, by honour, and by nobility from marrying the girl he loved. And he felt the strong necessity of declaring his own convictions on that point here, at once, in this very crisis of the conversation. That accident in regard to the colour of the Dean's lodge had stood in the way of his logical studies,—so that he was unable to put his argument into proper shape; but there belonged to him a certain natural astuteness which told him that he must put in his rejoinder at this particular point. 'I think I am bound in honour and in duty to marry Miss Boncassen,' he said; 'and, if I understand what you mean, by nobility just as much.'

'Because you have promised?'

'Not only from that. I have promised and therefore I am bound. She has——; well, she has said that she loves me and therefore of course I am bound. But it is not only that.'

'What do you mean?'

'I suppose a man ought to marry the woman he loves,—if he can get her.'

'No;—no; not so; not always so. Do you think that love is a passion that cannot be withstood?'

'But here we are both of one mind, sir. Of course I am very sorry if it makes you unhappy. When I saw how you seemed to take to her——'

'Take to her! Can I not interest myself in human beings without wishing to make them flesh of my flesh, bone of my bone? What am I to think of you? It was but the other day that all that you are now telling me of Miss Boncassen you were telling me of Lady Mabel Grex.' Here poor Silverbridge bit his lips and shook his head, and looked down upon the ground with a thorough feeling of being disconcerted. This, as he well knew, was the weak part of his case. He could not tell his father the whole story about Mabel,—that she had coyed her love, and that he had misunderstood her,—that he had been justified in thinking himself quite free from any claim in that direction when he had encountered the infinitely sweeter charms of Isabel Boncassen. 'You are weak as water!' said the unhappy father.

'I am not weak in this.'

'Did you not say exactly the same about Lady Mabel? When I questioned you, did you not assure me that you knew your own mind? Was it not so?'

There was a pause, so that he was driven to reply. 'I found her as I thought indifferent, and then—I changed my mind.'

'Indifferent! What does she think about it now? Does she know of this? How does it stand between you two at the present moment? How did you regard each other when she went away half an hour ago?'

'She knows that I am engaged to—Miss Boncassen.'

'Does she approve of it?'

'Why should I ask her, sir? I have not asked her.'

'Then why did you tell her? She could not but have spoken her mind when you told her. There must have been much between you when this was talked of. I think that I have a right to ask because you had prepared me to accept her as a daughter-in-law.'

The unfortunate young man was obliged to take some time for thought before he could answer this appeal. He had to own that his father had some justice on his side, but at the same time he was called upon to strengthen himself in his determination to tell nothing of Mabel's secret.

'I told her because we were friends. I did not ask her approval;—but she did disapprove. She thought that your son should not marry an American girl without family.'

'Of course she would feel that.'

'Now I have told you what she said, and I hope that you will ask me no further questions about her. I cannot make Lady Mabel my wife;—though for the matter of that, I ought not to presume to think that she would take me if I wished it. If you had not called me I had intended to ask you to-day to consent to my marriage with Miss Boncassen.'

'I cannot give you my consent.'

'Then I am very unhappy.'

'How can I believe as to your unhappiness when you would have said the same about Lady Mabel Grex a few weeks ago?'

'Nearly eight months,' said Silverbridge, trying to make the best of it.

'What is the difference? It is not the time, but the disposition of the man with which I have to deal. I cannot give you my consent. It seems that the young lady sees it in the right light, and that will make your escape easy for you.'

'I do not want to escape.'

'She has indicated the cause which will necessarily separate you.'

'I will not be separated from her,' said Silverbridge, who was beginning to feel that he was being subjected to tyranny. That argument as to the law seemed again to have considerable strength in it. If he chose to marry Isabel, no one could have a right to hinder him,—and he certainly did choose to do so.

'I can only hope that you will think better of it, and that when next you speak to me on that or any other subject you will answer me with less arrogance.'

This rebuke was terrible to the son, whose mind at the present moment was filled with two ideas, that of constancy to Isabel Boncassen, and then of respect and affection for his father. 'Indeed, sir,' he said, 'I am not arrogant; and if I have answered improperly, I beg your pardon. But my mind is made up about this, and I thought you had better know how it is.'

'I do not see that I can say anything else to you now.'

'I think of going to Harrington this afternoon.' Then the Duke, with further very visible annoyance, asked where Harrington was. Silverbridge was in the habit of announcing his goings and comings in this sudden way and, as it seemed to his father, without any adequate reason for coming and going. Matching was naturally his home at this time of the year, but he never came to Matching except as a visitor. It was now explained that Harrington was Lord Chiltern's seat, Lord Chiltern being the Master of the Brake Hounds. Then the young man had to explain, on being interrogated, that it was his purpose to remain six weeks among the Brake hounds, but that he should stay only a day or two with Lord and Lady Chiltern. A great many more questions were asked, and when it appeared that Silverbridge intended to put himself up for the greater part of the time at a hunting inn in the neighbourhood, the Duke did not at all like the plan. To his idea an inn was a place at which travellers stayed, under compulsion, when their journeys compelled them to dwell one or more nights upon the road. That his son should choose to live at an inn, when the comforts of a first-class English country-house were open to him, was distasteful and almost offensive to the Duke. And the matter was not improved when he was made to understand that all this was to be done for the sake of hunt-ing,—that all the duties and comforts of life were to be made to yield to the prosecution of an amusement. There had been the shooting in Scotland; then the racing,—ah, alas! yes,—the racing, and the betting at Doncaster! Then, as it seemed to him, the shooting at Matching had been made to appear to be the chief reason why he himself had been living in his own house! And now his son was going away to live at an inn in order that another large portion of the year might be devoted to hunting! 'Why can't you hunt here at home, if you must hunt?'

'It is all woodland,' said Silverbridge.

'I thought you wanted woods. Lord Chiltern is always troubling me about Trumpeton Wood. What is the use of going, when Lord Chiltern himself says that there are no foxes?'

This little breeze about the hunting enabled the son to escape from his father, however, without any further allusion to Miss Boncassen. He did escape, and proceeded to turn over in his mind all that had been said, so that he might judge how far he had done well by his morning's work, and how far evil. At any rate, his tale had been told. A great bur-den was thus taken off his shoulders. He could now tell Isabel so much, and thus free himself from any injurious suspicion that he had been afraid to declare his own purpose. She should know what he had done, and should be made to understand also that he had been very firm in the declaration of his intentions. He had, he thought, been very firm and gave himself some credit on that head. His father, no doubt, had been very firm too, but that he had expected. His father had said a good deal, but could hardly have been expected to say less. All that about honour and duty had been very good; but this was certain to all the world,—that when a young man had promised a young woman he ought to keep his word. And he thought that there were certain changes going on in the management of the world which his father did not quite understand. Fathers never do quite understand the changes which are manifest to their sons. Some years ago it might have been improper that an American girl should be elevated to the rank of an English duchess; but now all that was altered! He was sure at any rate of this,—that he would alter it.

He was to leave home that afternoon about three, but before he went he managed to see his sister alone. After leaving his father he made up his mind that he would now tell her also of his engagement,—so that it might be, as it were, the more strongly riveted. 'I have been with the governor this morning,' he said.

'I hope there is nothing wrong.'

'It seems to me that nothing ever is right. I am always in hot water, and suppose I always shall be. I dare say you know what I had to tell him.'

'Indeed I don't.'

'Don't you know that I have engaged myself to Isabel Boncassen?' To this she made no reply. 'I don't believe that you can have been so blind as not to have seen that.'

'She told me,' said Mary,—'when we were at Custins together.'

'I know she did. But you have kept it very dark.'

'It is you that have kept it dark. How could I speak of it to you when you did not tell me? What will papa say?'

'I have just told him. Of course he does not like it. I knew that before. But it has got to be.'

'What will she say when she knows that papa will not welcome her? I liked her so much;—but I was afraid there would be difficulties. I fancied once that it would have been Mabel Grex.'

'But it won't be Mabel Grex, you see. I am going off now, but I thought that I would tell you first. And there is another trouble,—about Gerald. He has lost a lot of money.'

'Gerald!'

'Yes;—why not Gerald as well as another? But don't you whisper a word of that to anybody. It seems to me that everything comes to grief. We are all in the black books now and I don't see how we are ever to get out again. I shall emigrate to the States and set up there as a politician.' Then he started on his way to the Brake country.

The Duke spent the rest of that day alone, and was not happy in his solitude. All that Silverbridge had told him was very sad to him. He had taught himself to think that he could love Lady Mabel as an affectionate father wishes to love his son's wife. He had set himself to wish to like her from the moment in which he had assented to his son's proposition, and had been altogether successful. Being most anxious that his son should marry and settle himself in the world he had prepared himself to be more than ordinarily liberal,—to be in every way gracious to the young people. His children were now everything to him, and of course among his children his son and heir was the chief. From the moment in which he had heard from Silverbridge that Lady Mabel was his chosen one he had given himself up to considering how he might best promote their interests,—how he might best enable them to live, with that personal dignity and splendour which he himself had unwisely despised. That the son who was to come after him should be worthy of the high place assigned to his name had been, of personal objects, the one nearest to his heart. There had been many failures, but still there had always been left room for hope. The boy had been unfortunate at Eton;—but how many unfortunate boys had become great men! He had disgraced himself by his folly at college,—but, though some lads will be men at twenty, others are then little more than children. The fruit that ripens the soonest is seldom the best. Then had come Tifto and the racing mania. Nothing possibly could be worse than Tifto and race-horses. But from that evil Silverbridge had seemed to be made free by the very disgust which the vileness of the circumstances had produced. Perhaps Tifto driving a nail into his horse's foot had been a better colleague for him than some interfering young brother nobleman. That apostasy from the recognised political creed of the Pallisers had been a sore blow,—very much more keenly felt than the loss of the seventy thousand pounds;—but even under that blow he had consoled himself by thinking that a conscientious, well-thinking, patriotic nobleman may serve his country,—even as a Conservative. In the midst of much of this he had felt that the surest recourse for his son against evil would be in an early marriage. If he would marry becomingly, then might everything still be made pleasant. If his son would marry becomingly nothing which a father could do should be wanting to add splendour and dignity to his son's life.

In thinking of all this he had by no means regarded his own mode of living as a proper example for a nobleman to follow. He knew now very well how jejune his life had been,—how devoid of other interests than that public service to which he had in his early youth devoted himself. He was thinking of this when he told his son that he himself had neither ploughed and sowed or been the owner of sheep or oxen. He often thought of this, when he heard those around him talking of those sports which, though he condemned them as the employments of a life, he now regarded wistfully, hopelessly as far as he himself was concerned, as proper recreations for a man of wealth. Silverbridge should have it all, if he could so arrange it. He would have been happy to have talked politics by the hour to the young man, but he would content himself in hoping that that might come gradually. Gradually that would come, if those meaner things could be abolished. He had allowed himself to think that the meaner things were being abolished, and that the better things were coming. The one thing necessary was a fitting wife;—and the fitting wife had been absolutely chosen, been chosen by Silverbridge himself.

It may be conceived, therefore, that he was again unhappy when he was left to ponder over the last communication that had been made to him. He had already been driven to acknowledge that these children of his,—thoughtless, reckless though they seemed to be,—still had a will of their own. In all which how like they were to their mother! With her, however, he had felt that his word, though it might be resisted, and even disobeyed, had never altogether lost its authority. When he had declared that a thing should not be done, she had never persisted in saying that she would do it. But with his children it was otherwise. What power had he over Silverbridge,—or, for the matter of that, even over his daughter? They had proposed to him, the one a daughter-in-law, and the other a son-in-law, altogether against his taste; but he was beginning to be aware that his taste must yield to theirs. They had only to be firm and he knew that he must be conquered.

'I thought that you liked her,' Silverbridge had said to him. How utterly unconscious, thought the Duke, must the young man have been of all that his position required of him when he used such an argument as that! Liked her! He did like her. She was clever, accomplished, beautiful, well mannered,—as far as he knew endowed with all good qualities! Would not many a noble old Roman, in the old days, have said as much for some favourite Greek slave,—for some freedman whom he would admit not only to his friendship but to his very heart? But what noble old Roman ever dreamed of giving his daughter to the son of a Greek bondsman! Had he done so, what would have become of the name of a Roman citizen? And was it not as much his duty to fortify and maintain that higher, smaller, more precious pinnacle of rank on which Fortune had placed him and his children, that lofty summit of ancestral nobility, by the maintenance of which alone could that democratic progress be safely made which it had been the pride and the business of his life to expedite?

Like her! Yes! he liked her certainly. He had by no means always found that he best liked the companionship of his own order. He had liked to feel around him the free bustle of the House of Commons. He liked the power of attack and defence in carrying on which an English politician cares nothing for rank. He liked to remember that the son of any tradesman might, by his own merits, become a peer of Parliament. He liked to see around him, at his own table, such men as Mr. Monk and Phineas Finn. He would have liked to think that his son should share all these tastes with him. Yes,—he liked Isabel Boncassen. But how different was that liking from a desire that she should be bone of his bone, and flesh of his flesh! But to all that Silverbridge was, alas, impervious!

CHAPTER 62

THE BRAKE COUNTRY

'WHAT does your father mean to do about Trumpeton Wood?' That was the first word that Lord Chiltern spoke to his guest after he had shaken hands with him. Silverbridge had arrived some hours before his host's return from hunting, and had been made welcome by Lady Chiltern.

'Isn't it all right yet?'

'All right? No! How can a wood like that be all right without a man about the place who knows anything of the nature of a fox? In your grandfather's time——'

'My great-uncle you mean.'

'Well;—your great-uncle! They used to trap the foxes there. There was a fellow named Fothergill who used to come there for shooting. Then the Duchess interfered and we were nearly right for a year or two.* Now it is worse than ever. Nobody shoots there because there is nothing to shoot. There isn't a keeper. Every scamp about the place is allowed to go where he pleases, and of course there isn't a fox in the whole covert. My huntsman laughs at me when I ask him to draw it just for the appearance of the thing.' As the indignant Master of the Brake Hounds said this the very fire seemed to flash from his eyes.

'My dear,' said Lady Chiltern, expostulating, 'Lord Silverbridge hasn't been in the house above half an hour.'

'What does that matter? When a thing has to be said it had better be said at once.'

'The truth is,' pleaded Silverbridge, 'my governor knows as much about hunting as I do of financial arrangements.'

'You knew something about them, I fancy, last September,' said Lord Chiltern. After that the stranger was allowed to go to his own room.

Phineas Finn was staying at Harrington with his specially intimate friends the Chilterns, as were also a certain Mr. and Mrs. Maule, both of whom were much addicted to hunting,—the lady, whose maiden name had been Palliser, being a cousin to Lord Silverbridge. They were guests staying in the house, but on that day also a certain Mr. and Mrs. Spooner dined at Harrington. Mr. and Mrs. Spooner were both very much given to hunting, as seemed to be necessarily the case with every-body admitted to that house. Mr. Spooner was a gentleman who might be on the wrong side of fifty, with a red nose, very uxorious,* and sub-missive in regard to all things but port-wine. His wife was perhaps something more than half his age, a stout, hard-riding, handsome woman, all whose exterior appanages* seemed to be adapted to horse exercise. How Mrs. Spooner spent her time when there was no hunting,—during those unfortunate days from the middle of April to the middle of September, at which time she would begin to go out early in the morning with the young hounds,—nobody knew in those parts, except perhaps her husband. She had been the penniless daughter of a retired officer,—but yet had managed to ride on whatever animal anyone would lend her. Then Mr. Spooner, who had for many years been part and parcel of the Brake hunt, and who was much in want of a wife, had, luckily for her, cast his eyes upon Miss Leatherside. It was thought that upon the whole she made him a good wife. She hunted four days a week, and he could afford to keep horses for her. She never flirted, and wanted no one to open gates for her. Tom Spooner himself was not always quite so forward as he used to be; but his wife was always there and she would tell him all that he did not see himself. And she was a good housewife, taking care that nothing should be spent lavishly, except upon the stable. Of him, too, and of his health, she was very careful, never scrupling to say a word in season when she thought he was likely to hurt himself, either among the fences or among the decanters. 'You ain't so young as you were, Tom. Don't think of doing it.' This she would say to him with a loud voice when she would find him pausing doubtfully at a fence. Then she would hop over herself and he would go round. She was 'quite a Providence to him,' as her mother, old Mrs. Leatherside, would say when she was anxious to praise her daughter.

She was hardly the woman that one would have expected to meet as a friend in the drawing-room of Lady Chiltern. Lord Chiltern was perhaps a little rough, but Lady Chiltern was all that a mother, a wife, and a lady ought to be. She probably felt that some little apology ought to be made for Mrs. Spooner when Lord Silverbridge and she were alone in the dining-room before dinner. 'I hope you like hunting,' she said.

'Better than anything;—best of all things,' said he enthusiastically.

'Because you know this is Castle Nimrod in which no other subject is ever allowed to interfere for a moment with the one great business of life.'

'It's like that;—is it?'

'Quite like that. Lord Chiltern has taken up hunting as his duty in life, and, being naturally energetic, he does it with his might and main. Not to have a good day is a misery to him;—not for himself but because he feels that he is responsible to others. But to have a blank confounds him! We had one blank last year, and I thought that he never would recover it. It was that unfortunate Trumpeton Wood.'

'How he will hate me!'

'Not if you will praise the hounds judiciously. And then there is a Mr. Spooner coming here to-night. He is the first-lieutenant. He understands all about the foxes, and all about the farmers. He has got a wife.'

'Does she understand anything?'

'She understands him, I hope. She is coming too. They have not been married long and he never goes anywhere without her.'

'Does she ride?'

'Well; yes. I never go out myself now,* because I hear so much of it all at home. But I fancy she does ride a good deal. She will talk hunting too. If Chiltern were to leave the country, I think they ought to make her Master. Perhaps you'll think her rather odd; but, really, she is a very good woman.'

'I am sure I shall like her.'

'I hope you will. You know Mr. Finn? He is here. He and my husband are very old friends. And Adelaide Maule is your cousin. She hunts too. And so does Mr. Maule,—only not quite so energetically. He came into his property last year,* and now they have quite a string of horses. I think that is all we shall have. I hope you will get on with them;—but I am afraid you will find that it is hunting, hunting, hunting from morning till night.'

Immediately after that all the guests came in at once. Chiltern and Phineas Finn met in the hall, and while they were there Mr. and Mrs. Spooner arrived. Then Mrs. Maule joined them, and so they were crowding in together. Mr. Maule was not there, but nobody ever waited for him and he seldom appeared till the middle of dinner. 'No;—that wasn't it,' Mrs. Spooner was saying loudly as she entered. 'I don't care what Dick said.' Dick Rabbit was the first whip,* and seemed to have been much exercised with the matter now under dispute. 'The fox never went into Grobby Gorse at all. I was there and saw Sappho give him a line* down the bank, and she is the best bitch in the pack.'

'I think he must have gone into the gorse,* my dear,' said her husband. 'They always do, and the earth was open, you know.'

'I tell you she didn't. You weren't there, and you can't know. I'm sure it was a vixen by her running. We ought to have killed that fox, my Lord.' Then Mrs. Spooner made her obeisance to her hostess. Perhaps she was rather slow in doing this, as Lady Chiltern was standing up to welcome her, but the greatness of the subject, and no want of courtesy, had been the cause. There are matters so important, that the ordinary civilities of the world should not stand in their way.

'What do you say, Chiltern?' asked the husband who had been contradicted.

'I say that Mrs. Spooner isn't very often wrong, and that Dick Rabbit isn't very often right about a fox. I wasn't there myself.'

'It was a pretty run at any rate,' said Phineas.

'Just thirty-four minutes,' said Mr. Spooner.

'Thirty-two up to Grobby Gorse,' asserted Mrs. Spooner with great authority. 'The hounds never hunted a yard after that. Dick hurried them into the covert, and the old hound wouldn't stick to her line when she found that no one believed her.' Then they all went in to dinner.

This was on a Monday evening, and the Brake hounds went out generally five days a week. 'You'll hunt to-morrow, I suppose,' Lady Chiltern said to her neighbour, Lord Silverbridge.

'I hope so.'

'You must hunt to-morrow or you will be held to have disgraced yourself. Indeed there is nothing else to do. Chiltern has taken such a dislike to shooting-men that he won't shoot any pheasants himself. We don't hunt on Wednesdays or Sundays, and then everybody lies in bed. Here is Mr. Maule. He lies in bed on other mornings as well, and then spends the rest of his day riding about the country looking for the hounds.'

'Does he ever find them?'

'Not often I believe;—and then Chiltern has to look after Mrs. Maule,—which is hard, as his own work is quite enough for him.'

'What did become of you all to-day?' said Mr. Maule, as he took his place at the dinner-table. 'You can't have drawn any of the coverts regularly.'

'Then we found our foxes without drawing them,' said the Master.

'We chopped one* at Bromleys,' said Mr. Spooner.

'I went there.'

'Then you ought to have known better,' said Mrs. Spooner. 'When a man loses the hounds in that country he ought to go direct to Brackett's Wood. He is sure to be right then. If you had come on to Brackett's you'd have seen as good a thirty-two minutes as ever you wished to ride. Another time always make for Brackett's.' When the ladies went out of the room Mrs. Spooner gave a parting word of advice to her husband, and to the host. 'Now, Tom, don't you drink port-wine. If you do, your nerves won't be worth so much brown paper to-morrow. Lord Chiltern, look after him, and don't let him have port-wine.'

Then there began an altogether different phase of hunting conversation. As long as the ladies were there it was all very well to talk of hunting as an amusement. Good sport, a fast thirty minutes or so, the delight of leaving a friend in a ditch,* or the glory of a stiff-built rail* were fitting subjects for a lighter hour. But now the business of the night was to begin. The difficulties, the animosities, the enmities, the precautions, the resolutions, the resources of the Brake hunt were to be brought under discussion. And from thence not unnaturally the conversation of these devotees strayed away to the perils at large to which hunting in these modern days is subjected;—not the perils of broken necks and crushed ribs, which can be reduced to an average, and so an end made of that small matter; but the perils from outsiders, the perils from new-fangled prejudices, the perils from more modern sports, the perils from slighted vanity, the perils from over-cultivation, the perils from extended population, the perils from encroaching railroads, the perils from literary ignoramuses,* the perils from intruding cads, the perils from indifferent magnates,—the Duke of Omnium, for instance;—and that peril of perils, the peril of decrease of funds and increase of expenditure! The jaunty gentleman who puts on his one pair of breeches and his one pair of boots, and on his single horse rides out on a pleasant morning to some neighbouring meet, thinking himself a sportsman, has but a faint idea of the troubles which a few staunch workmen endure in order that he may not be made to think that his boots, and his breeches, and his horse, have been altogether thrown away.

A word or two further was at first said about that unfortunate wood for which Silverbridge at the present moment felt himself to be responsible. Mr. Spooner declared that in all his memory he had never known anything like it before;—and as he did so he filled a bumper of port. 'You've got to think of your nerves, you know,' said Maule. Spooner winked his eye, and poked his thumb near his shoulder, thereby intimating the fact that his wife wasn't 'here,' but 'there.' Phineas Finn said that he was sure the Duke would look to it, if Silverbridge would mention it. Chiltern simply groaned. Silverbridge said nothing, remembering how many troubles he had on hand at this moment. Then by degrees the solicitude of the assembled sportsmen worked itself round to the cares of a neighbouring hunt. The U.R.U.* had lost their Master,—who had not been regarded as being very much in the way of a Master,—one Captain Glomax, and had been driven to the necessity of advertising for a successor. 'When hunting comes to that,' said Lord Chiltern, 'one begins to think that it is in a bad way.' It may always be observed that

when hunting men speak seriously of their sport, they speak despond-
ingly. Everything is going wrong. Perhaps the same thing may be
remarked in other pursuits. Farmers are generally on the verge of ruin.
Trade is always bad. The Church is in danger. The House of Lords
isn't worth a dozen years' purchase. The constitution has been under-
mined. The throne totters. The Pope of Rome seems to be the only
institution which understands how far self-assertion goes towards
self-preservation.*

'An itinerant Master with a carpet-bag never can carry on a country,'
said Mr. Spooner, speaking with great authority.

'You ought really to have a gentleman of property in the county,'
said Lord Chiltern, in a self-deprecating tone. His father's acres lay
elsewhere.

'It should be someone who has a real stake in the country,' replied
Mr. Spooner,—'whom the farmers can respect, a man who is or will
be a landlord. Glomax understood hunting no doubt, but the farmers
didn't care for him. If you don't have the farmers with you, you can't
have hunting.' Then he filled another glass of port.

'If you don't approve of Glomax what do you think of a man like
Major Tifto?' asked Mr. Maule.

'That was in the Runnymede,' said Spooner contemptuously. The
Brake was in the Shires,* and men who hunt in the Shires despise those
who are outside this Elysium, as the member of a first-rate club at his
well-served table despises the poor fellow who is obliged to eat his dinner in a chop-house.

'Who is Major Tifto?' asked Lord Chiltern.

'He is the man,' said Silverbridge boldly, 'who owned Prime Minister
with me when he didn't win the Leger last September.' Then Lord
Chiltern whistled. 'At that time he was Master of the Runnymede Hounds.
I think they have got rid of him now.'

'There was a deuce of a row,' said Maule. Then Mr. Spooner, who
read his *Land and Water*, and *Bell's Life*, and *Field* very religiously, and
who never missed an article in *Bayley's*,* proceeded to give them an
account of everything that had taken place in the Runnymede hunt.
It mattered but little that he was wrong in all his details. Narrations
always are. The result to which he came was nearly right when he
declared that the Major had been turned off, that a committee had been
formed to buy his horses and his share of the hounds, and that now
Messrs. Topps and Jawstock had been threatened with a lawsuit as to
the sum of money promised to the Major for hunting the country that
season.

'That comes,' said Lord Chiltern solemnly, 'of employing men like Major Tifto in places for which they are radically unfit. I dare say Major Tifto knew how to handle a pack of hounds,—perhaps almost as well as my huntsman, Fowler. Fowler, though he is getting a little slow now, understands hunting I believe as well as any man in England. But I don't think a country would get on very well which appointed Fowler Master of Hounds. He is an honest man, and therefore would be better than Tifto. He would not pretend to be what he is not, and therefore would be better than Tifto. But—it would not do. It is a position in which a man should at any rate be a gentleman. If he be not, all those who should be concerned in maintaining the hunt will turn their backs upon him. When I take my hounds over this man's ground and that man's ground, certainly without doing him any good, I have to think of a great many things. I have to understand that those whom I cannot compensate by money, I have to compensate by courtesy. When I shake hands with a farmer and express my obligation to him because he does not lock his gates, or destroy the foxes, or make a row about his crops, his fences, and his poultry, he is perhaps in some degree gratified. I don't think any decent farmer would care much for shaking hands with Major Tifto. If we fall into that kind of thing there must soon be an end of hunting. Major Tiftoes are cheap no doubt; but in hunting as in most other things, cheap and nasty go together. If men don't choose to put their hands in their pockets they had better say so, and give the thing up altogether. If you won't take any more wine, we'll go to the ladies. Silverbridge, the trap will start from the door to-morrow morning precisely at 9.30 a.m. Grantingham Cross is fourteen miles.' Then they all left their chairs,—but as they did so Mr. Spooner finished the bottle of port-wine.

'I never heard Chiltern speak so much like a book before,' said Spooner to his wife as she drove him home that night.

The next morning everybody was ready for a start at half-past nine, except Mr. Maule,—as to whom his wife declared that she had left him in bed when she came down to breakfast at nine. 'He can never get there if we don't take him,' said Lord Chiltern, who was in truth about the most good-natured man in the world. Five minutes were allowed him, during which his wife went up to his room. Five minutes more were allowed, and then he came down with a large sandwich in one hand and a button-hook in the other, with which he was prepared to complete his toilet. 'What the deuce makes you always in such a hurry?' were the first words he spoke as Lord Chiltern got on the box. The Master knew him too well to argue the point. 'Well;—he always is in a hurry,' said the sinner, when his wife accused him of ingratitude.

In spite of the lost ten minutes they were at Grantingham Cross by eleven. 'Where's Spooner?' asked the Master when he saw Mrs. Spooner without her husband at the meet.

'I knew how it would be when I saw the port-wine,' she said in a whisper that could be heard all round the meet. 'He has got it this time, sharp,—in his great toe. We shan't find at Grantingham. They were cutting wood there last week. If I were you, my Lord, I'd go away to the Spinnies at once.'

'I must draw the country regularly,' muttered the Master, as he proceeded to give directions to Fowler, the huntsman.

The country was drawn regularly, but in vain till about two o'clock. Not only was there no fox at Grantingham Wood, but none even at the Spinnies. One or two coverts beyond that were equally inauspicious, and at two o'clock, Fowler, with an anxious face, held a consultation with his more anxious Master. Trumpeton Wood lay on their right, and that no doubt would have been the proper draw. 'I suppose we must try it,' said Lord Chiltern. Silverbridge was standing by and could not fail to hear what was being said.

Old Fowler looked very sour. 'You might as well look for a fox under my wife's bed, my Lord.'

'I dare say we should find one there,' said one of the wags of the hunt. Fowler shook his head, feeling that this was no time for joking.

'It ought to be drawn,' said Chiltern.

'Of course you know best, my Lord. I wouldn't touch it,—never no more. Let 'em all know what the Duke's Wood is.'

'This is Lord Silverbridge, the Duke's son,' said Chiltern laughing.

'I beg your lordship's pardon,' said Fowler, taking off his cap. 'We shall have a good time coming, some day. Let me trot 'em off to Michaelmas Daisies, my Lord. I'll be there in thirty minutes.' In the neighbouring parish of St. Michael de Dezier there was a favourite little gorse which among hunting men had acquired this unseasonable name.* After a little consideration the Master yielded, and away they trotted.

'I was thinking what I could best do in honour of you,' said the Master to Silverbridge;—'whether I would pay you the compliment of drawing your covert, or give you the best chance I can of a run.' Silverbridge of course declared that he would prefer the run to the compliment, and so away they went.

'You'll cross the ford, Fowler?' asked Mrs. Spooner.

'Oh yes, ma'am; we couldn't draw the Daisies this afternoon if we didn't.'

'It'll be up to the horses' bellies.'

'Those who don't like it can go round.'

'They'd never be there in time, Fowler.'

'There's a many, ma'am, as don't mind that. You won't be one to stay behind.' The water was up to the horses' bellies, but, nevertheless, Mrs. Spooner was at the gorse side when the Daisies were drawn.

They found and were away in a minute. It was all done so quickly that Fowler, who had alone gone into the gorse, had hardly time to get out with his hounds. The fox ran right back, as though he were making for the Duke's pernicious Wood. In the first field or two there was a succession of gates, and there was not much to do in the way of jumping. Then the fox, keeping straight ahead, deviated from the line by which they had come, making for the brook by a more direct course. The ruck of the horsemen, understanding the matter very well, left the hounds, and went to the right, riding for the ford. The ford was of such a nature that but one horse could pass it at a time, and that one had to scramble through deep mud. 'There'll be the devil to pay there,' said Lord Chiltern, going straight with his hounds. Phineas Finn and Dick Rabbit were close after him. Old Fowler had craftily gone to the ford; but Mrs. Spooner, who did not intend to be shaken off, followed the Master, and close with her was Lord Silverbridge. 'Lord Chiltern hasn't got it right,' she said. 'He can't do it among these bushes.' As she spoke the Master put his horse at the bushes and then—disappeared. The lady had been right. There was no ground at that spot to take off from, and the bushes had impeded him. Lord Chiltern got over, but his horse was in the water. Dick Rabbit and poor Phineas Finn were stopped in their course by the necessity of helping the Master in his trouble.

But Mrs. Spooner, the judicious Mrs. Spooner, rode at the stream where it was, indeed, a little wider, but at a place in which the horse could see what he was about, and where he could jump from and to firm ground. Lord Silverbridge followed her gallantly. They both jumped the brook well, and then were together. 'You'll beat me in pace,' said the lady as he rode up alongside of her. 'Take the fence ahead straight, and then turn sharp to your right.' With all her faults Mrs. Spooner was a thorough sportsman.

He did take the fence ahead,—or rather tried to do so. It was a bank and a double ditch,—not very great in itself, but requiring a horse to land on the top and go off with a second spring. Our young friend's nag, not quite understanding the nature of the impediment, endeavoured to 'swallow it whole,' as hard-riding men say, and came down in the further ditch. Silverbridge came down on his head, but the horse pursued his course,—across a heavily ploughed field.

This was very disagreeable. He was not in the least hurt, but it became his duty to run after his horse; and perhaps of the many troubles which occur to hunting men there is nothing worse than the necessity of running across a ploughed field in top boots. A very few furrows of that work suffice to make a man think that hunting altogether is a 'beastly sort of thing.' Mrs. Spooner's horse, who had shown himself to be a little less quick of foot than his own, had known all about the bank and the double ditch, and had, apparently of his own accord, turned down to the right, either seeing or hearing the hounds, and knowing that the ploughed ground was to be avoided. But his rider soon changed his course. She went straight after the riderless horse, and when Silverbridge had reduced himself to utter speechlessness by his exertions, brought him back his steed.

'I am,—I am,—I am—so sorry,' he struggled to say,—and then as she held his horse for him he struggled up into the saddle.

'Keep down this furrow,' said Mrs. Spooner, 'and we shall be with them in the second field. There's nobody near them yet.'

CHAPTER 63

'I'VE SEEN 'EM LIKE THAT BEFORE'

IF Miss Boncassen had cause to be jealous of any other woman, that woman, after the occurrences recorded in the last chapter, was Mrs. Spooner. 'Upon my word,' Silverbridge said to Lady Chiltern that evening, 'I don't think I ever came across such a thorough brick in all my life.'

'Doesn't she ride well?'

'I should think she did! She coached me through the whole run. But I didn't quite like having my horse caught by a woman. Just at that moment I wished she had left me in the ploughed field.'

On this occasion he stayed only a few days at Harrington, having promised Tregear to entertain him at The Baldfaced Stag, the hunting inn of which the Duke had so strongly disapproved. It was here that his horses were standing, and he now intended, by limiting himself to one horse a day, to mount his friend for a couple of weeks. 'I've got five of them,' he said when Tregear found him, 'and we'll see if we can't stretch a point and make four days a week out of them.* If the worst comes to the worst we can always hire from the fellow here.' It was settled at last that Tregear should ride his friend's horse one day, hire the next, and so on. 'I wonder what you'll think of Mrs. Spooner,' he said.

'Why should I think anything of her?'

'Because I doubt whether you ever saw such a woman before. She does nothing but hunt.'

'Then I certainly shan't want to see her again.'

'And she talks as I never heard a lady talk before.'

'Then I don't care if I never see her at all.'

'But she is the most plucky and most good-natured human being I ever saw in my life. After all, hunting is very good fun.'

'Very;—if you don't do it so often as to be sick of it.'

'Long as I have known you I don't think I ever saw you ride yet.'

'We used to have hunting down in Cornwall, and thought we did it pretty well. I suppose we were mistaken.'

'Why shouldn't you hunt in Cornwall?'

'And I have ridden in South Wales, which I can assure you isn't an easy thing to do. But you mustn't expect much from me. Now that I am a member of Parliament I am bound to preserve my life for the sake of my constituents.'

They were both out the Monday and Tuesday in that week, and then again on the Thursday without anything special either in the way of sport or of accidents. Lord Chiltern, who had found Silverbridge to be a young man after his own heart,—in spite of the hereditary sin accruing to him from Trumpeton Wood,—was anxious that he should come back to Harrington and bring Tregear with him. But to this Tregear would not assent, alleging that he should feel himself to be a burden both to Lord and Lady Chiltern. On the Friday Tregear did not go out, saying that he would avoid the expense, and on that day there was a good run. 'It is always the way,' said Silverbridge. 'If you miss a day, it is sure to be the best thing of the season. We killed one fox just at the brook where Chiltern got the cropper;—an hour and a quarter with hardly anything you could call a check.* It is the only very good thing I have seen since I have been here. Mrs. Spooner was with them all through.'

'And I suppose you were with Mrs. Spooner.'

'I wasn't far off. I remembered the brook well, and when I was thinking whether there was enough left in old Peacock to carry me over, I saw Dick bustle down off his horse and tumble in among the bushes. I wasn't sorry, I can tell you, to hear "whoo-whoop."* I wish you had been there.'

On the next day the meet was at the kennels, close to Harrington, and Silverbridge drove his friend over in a gig. The Master and Lady

Chiltern, Spooner and Mrs. Spooner, Maule and Mrs. Maule, Phineas Finn, and a host of others condoled with the unfortunate young man because he had not seen the good thing yesterday. 'We've had it a little faster once or twice,' said Mrs. Spooner with deliberation, 'but never for so long. Then it was straight as a line, and a real open kill. No changing, you know. We did go through the Daisies, but I'll swear to its being the same fox.' All of which set Tregear wondering. How could she swear to her fox? And if they had changed, what did it matter? And if it had been a little crooked, why would it have been less enjoyable? And was she really so exact a judge of pace as she pretended to be? 'I'm afraid we shan't have anything like that to-day,' she continued. 'The wind's in the west and I never do like a westerly wind.'

'A little to the north,' said her husband, looking round the compass.

'My dear,' said the lady, 'you never know where the wind comes from. Now don't you think of taking off your comforter. I won't have it.'

Tregear was riding his friend's favourite hunter, a thoroughbred bay horse, very much more than up to his rider's weight, and supposed to be peculiarly good at timber, water, or any well-defined kind of fence, however high or however broad. 'I am not quite so sure of him at those wicked places which require an animal to have three or four legs to spare,' Silverbridge had said; 'but he has never brought me down yet.' Tregear had mounted the animal with perfect satisfaction, and in the early part of the day rode him over a few places with great ease. He was a man who liked his amusements as well as another, though he seldom talked about them;—and whatever he did he generally did well. He was in truth a very good horseman, though he never gave himself or obtained from others special credit for the accomplishment. They found at a covert near the kennels, and killed their fox after a burst of a few minutes. Then they found again, and having lost their fox, all declared that there was not a yard of scent. 'I always know what a west wind means,' said Mrs. Spooner.

Then they lunched, and smoked, and trotted about with an apparent acknowledgment that there wasn't much to be done. It was not right that they should expect much after so good a thing as they had had yesterday. At half-past two Mr. Spooner had been sent home by his Providence, and Mrs. Spooner was calculating that she would be able to ride her horse again on the Tuesday,—when on a sudden the hounds were on a fox. It turned out afterwards that Dick Rabbit had absolutely ridden him up among the stubble, and that the hounds had nearly killed him before he had gone a yard. But the astute animal, making the best use of his legs till he could get the advantage of the first ditch, ran, and crept, and jumped absolutely through the pack. Then there was shouting, and yelling, and riding. The men who were idly smoking threw away their cigars. Those who were loitering at a distance lost their chance. But the real sportsmen, always on the alert, always thinking of the business on hand, always mindful that there may be at any moment a fox just before the hounds, had a glorious opportunity of getting 'well away.' Among these no one was more ready, more intent, or, when the moment came, 'better away' than Mrs. Spooner.

Silverbridge had been talking to her, as he very generally did in the hunting field, and had the full advantage of her care. Tregear was riding behind with Lord Chiltern, who had been pressing him to come with his friend to Harrington for a few days before they left the country. As soon as the shouting was heard Chiltern was off like a rocket. It was not only that like others there he was anxious to 'get well away,' but that a sense of duty compelled him to see how the thing was being done. Old Fowler certainly was a little slow, and Dick Rabbit, with the true bloody-minded instinct of a whip, was a little apt to bustle a fox back into covert with the view of making certain of his death. And then, when a run commences with a fast rush, riders are apt to over-ride the hounds, and then the hounds will over-run the fox. All of which has to be seen to by a Master who knows his business.

Tregear followed, and being mounted on a fast horse was soon in as good a place and as forward as a judicious rider would desire. 'Now, Runks, don't you press on and spoil it all,' said Mrs. Spooner to the hard-riding objectionable son of old Runks, the vet from Rufford. But young Runks did press on till the Master spoke a word. The word shall not be repeated, but it was efficacious,—and then young Runks slunk away.

At that moment there had been a check,—as there is generally after a short burst, when fox, hounds, and horsemen get off together, and not always in the order in which they have been placed here. There is too much bustle from steady business, and the pack becomes disconcerted. But it enabled Fowler to get up, and by dint of growling at the men and conciliating his hounds, he soon picked up the scent. 'If they'd all stand still for two minutes and be —— to them,' he muttered aloud to himself, 'they'd 'ave some'at to ride arter. They might go then, and there's some of 'em 'd soon be nowhere.'

But in spite of Fowler's denunciations there was, of course, another rush. Runks had slunk away, but by making a little detour was now again ahead of the hounds. And unfortunately there were perhaps half-a-dozen with him. Fowler was in a very bad humour, and Lord Chiltern was very wrath. 'When he's like that,' said Mrs. Spooner to Tregear, 'it's always well to give him a wide berth. I get the rough side of his tongue sometimes myself.' But as the hounds were now running fast it was necessary that even in taking this precaution due regard should be had to the fox's line. 'He's back for Harrington bushes,' said Mrs. Spooner. 'That's his favourite.' And as she said so, she rode at a bank, with a rail at the top of it perhaps a foot and a half high, with a deep drop into the field beyond. It was not a very nice place, but it was apparently the only available spot in the fence. She seemed to know it well, for as she got close to it she brought her horse almost to a stand and so took it. The horse cleared the rail, seemed just to touch the bank on the other side, while she threw herself back almost onto his crupper,* and so came down with apparently the most perfect ease. But she, knowing that it would not be easy to all horses, paused a moment to see what would happen.

Tregear was next to her and was intending to 'fly' the fence,—as he had thought she would do before him. But when he saw Mrs. Spooner pull her horse and pause, he also had to pull his horse. This he did so effectually as to enable her to take her leap without danger or encumbrance from him, but hardly so completely as to bring his horse to the bank in the same way. It may be doubted whether the animal he was riding would have known enough and been quiet enough to have performed the acrobatic manoeuvre which had carried Mrs. Spooner so pleasantly over the peril. He had some idea of this, for the thought occurred to him that he would turn and ride fast at the jump. But almost before he could move he saw that Silverbridge was pressing on him. It was thus his only recourse to do as Mrs. Spooner had done, and get out of the way. He was too close to the rail, but still he tried it. The horse attempted to jump, caught his feet against the bar, and of course went over head-foremost. This might have been nothing, probably would have been nothing, had not Silverbridge with his rushing beast been immediately after them. When the young Lord saw that his friend was down it was too late for him to stop his course. His horse was determined to have the fence,—and did have it. He touched nothing, and would have skimmed in glory over the next field had he not come right down on Tregear and Tregear's steed. There they were, four of them, two men and two horses in one confused heap.

The first person with them was Mrs. Spooner, who was off her horse in a minute. And Silverbridge too was very soon on his legs. He at any rate was unhurt, and the two horses were up before Mrs. Spooner was out of her saddle, and were standing perfectly quiet on the scene of this disaster. But Tregear did not move. 'What are we to do?' said Lord Silverbridge, kneeling down over his friend. 'Oh, Mrs. Spooner, what are we to do?'

The hunt had passed on and no one else was immediately with them. But at this moment Dick Rabbit, who had been left behind to bring up his hounds who had strayed at the check, appeared above the bank. 'Leave your horse and come down,' said Mrs. Spooner. 'Here is a gentleman who has hurt himself.' Dick wouldn't leave his horse, but was soon on the scene, having found his way through another part of the fence.

'No; he ain't dead,' said Dick—'I've seen 'em like that before, and they wurn't dead. But he's had a hawful squeege.' Then he passed his hand over the man's neck and chest. 'There's a lot of 'em is broke,' said he. 'We must get him into farmer Tooby's.'

After a while he was got into farmer Tooby's, where that surgeon came who is always in attendance on a hunting field. The surgeon declared that he had broken his collar-bone, two of his ribs, and his left arm. In point of fact he had been doubled up under the horse. And then one of the animals had struck him on the cheek as he raised himself, and had given him a very ugly wound. A little brandy was poured down his throat, but even under that operation he gave no sign of life. 'No, missis; he ain't dead,' said Dick to Mrs. Tooby; 'no more he won't die this bout; but he's got it very nasty. I must be making for the hounds.' They were now not above a mile or two from the kennel, and Dick was desired to send a carriage from Harrington.

That night Silverbridge was sitting by his friend's bedside at ten o'clock in Lord Chiltern's house. Tregear had spoken a few words, and the bones had been set. But the doctor had not as yet felt himself justified in speaking with that assurance which Dick had expressed. It was, he said, a very nasty case. The man's whole body had been bruised by the horse which had fallen on him. The agony of Silverbridge was extreme, for he knew that it had been his doing. Nor was it lessened when Tregear, almost in his first conscious moment, gently pressed the fingers of his friend's hand, which was lying on the bed close to his own. The motion was intended to express forgiveness;—but forgiveness itself declares that wrong has been sustained.

'You were a little too close,' Mrs. Spooner had said to him; 'but nobody saw it and we'll hold our tongues.' Silverbridge however would not hold his tongue. He told everybody how it had happened, how he had been unable to stop his horse, how he had jumped upon his friend, and perhaps killed him. 'I don't know what I am to do, I am so miserable,' he said to Lady Chiltern with the tears running down his face.

The two of them of course remained at Harrington and their luggage was brought over from The Baldfaced Stag. The accident had happened on a Saturday. On the Sunday there was no comfort. On the Monday the patient's recollection and mind were re-established, and the doctor ventured to say that perhaps, with great care, his constitution would pull him through. On that day the consternation at Harrington was so great that neither Lord Chiltern nor Mrs. Spooner went to the meet. She came over from Spoon Hall, and spent a considerable part of the day in the sick man's room. 'It's sure to come right if it's above the vitals,' she said, expressing an opinion which had no doubt come from much experience. 'That is,' she added, 'unless the neck's broke. When poor old Jack Stubbs drove his head into his cap and dislocated his wertibry of course, it was all up with him.' The patient heard this, and was seen to smile.

On the Tuesday there arose the question of family communication. As the accident would of course make its way into the papers, a message had been sent early on Monday to Polwenning to say that various bones had been broken, but that the patient was upon the whole doing well. Then there had been different messages backwards and forwards, in all of which there had been an attempt to comfort old Mrs. Tregear,—and perhaps to prevent the coming of the anxious parents. But on the Tuesday letters were written. Silverbridge, sitting in his friend's room, sent a long account of the accident to Mrs. Tregear, giving a list of the injuries done, and adding an assurance that in spite of all those injuries, Frank in a couple of months would be himself again. 'Is there anyone else?' asked Silverbridge when that letter was finished.

'Your sister!' whispered the poor fellow from his pillow.

'Yes,—yes; yes, I will.'

'And Mabel Grex.' Silverbridge nodded assent and again went to the writing-table. He did write to his sister, and in plain words told her everything. 'The doctor says he is not now in danger.' Then he added a postscript. 'As long as I am here I will let you know how he is.' Then he gave a long account of the whole affair to Lady Mabel, confessing entirely his own fault. And after that he wrote a third letter, of which he did not say a word to Tregear. This was to his father,—and it was written chiefly with the purpose of letting the Duke know that he had sent tidings of the accident to his sister.

CHAPTER 64

'I BELIEVE HIM TO BE A WORTHY YOUNG MAN'

LADY MARY and Mrs. Finn were alone together at Matching when the tidings came from Silverbridge as to Tregear's accident. The Duke had been absent for two or three days, having gone to spend an unpleasant week in Barsetshire. Gatherum Castle on this Christmas had not been opened, and the Duke had excused to himself this breach of his accustomed hospitality by the recent death of his wife. It was the first Christmas since he had been a widower, and therefore Gatherum was closed,—not at all to the delight of the neighbours. But there were matters of business which he thought required his presence. He had been gone two or three days, and intended to remain in Barsetshire for a week. Mrs. Finn, with whom he was now on more friendly terms than ever, had promised to stay with Mary till his return.

Mary had taken the opportunity of his absence to discuss her own prospects at full length. 'My dear,' said Mrs. Finn, 'I will not express an opinion. How can I after all that has passed? I have told the Duke the same. I cannot be heart and hand with either without being false to the other.' But still Lady Mary continued to talk about Tregear, and forced her companion to listen to her.

'I don't think papa has a right to treat me in this way,' she said. 'He wouldn't be allowed to kill me, and this is killing me.'

'While there is life there is hope,' said Mrs. Finn, saying almost more than she intended.

'Yes;—while there is life, there is hope. That is just it. But one doesn't want to grow old first.'

'There is no danger of that yet, Mary.'

'I feel very old. What is the use of life without something to make it sweet? Everything is blank to me now. I am not even allowed to hear anything that he is doing. If he were to ask me I think I would go away with him to-morrow.'

'That would be to destroy everything. He would not be foolish enough for that.'

'Because he does not suffer as I do. He has his borough, and his public life, and a hundred things to think of. I have got nothing but him. I know he is true;—quite as true as I am. I should despise myself if I doubted him for a moment. But it is I that have the suffering in all this. A man can never be like a girl. Papa ought not to make me suffer like this.'

That took place on the Monday. On the Tuesday Mrs. Finn received a letter from her husband giving his account of the accident in the hunting field. 'As far as I can learn,' he said, 'Silverbridge will write about it to-morrow.' Then he went on to give a by no means good account of the state of the patient. The doctor had declared him to be out of immediate danger, and had set the broken bones, but had not given a cheerful view of his patient's condition. Perhaps, he added, as tidings would be sent on the next day, she had better say nothing about the accident to Lady Mary. This letter reached Matching on Tuesday and of course made the position of Mrs. Finn very disagreeable. She was bound to carry herself as though nothing was amiss, knowing, as she did so, the condition of Mary's lover.

On the evening of that day Lady Mary was more lively than usual, though her liveliness was hardly of a happy nature. 'I don't know what papa can expect. I've heard him say a hundred times that to be in Parliament is the highest place a gentleman can fill, and now Frank is in Parliament.' Mrs. Finn looked at her with beseeching eyes, as though begging her not to speak of Tregear. Knowing what she knew, it was impossible for her to speak of him. 'And then to think of their having that Lord Popplecourt there! I shall always hate Lady Cantrip, for of course it was her plan.* That she should have thought it possible! Lord Popplecourt! Such a creature. I suppose you have seen him?' Mrs. Finn said that she had seen him. 'Hyperion to a satyr! Isn't it true? Look on that picture and on this.* Oh, that papa should have thought it possible.'

'My dear, I cannot talk about it.' Then Lady Mary got up, and walked about the room, beating her hands together. And all this time Mrs. Finn knew that Tregear was lying at Harrington with half his bones broken, and in danger of his life!

On the next morning Lady Mary received her letter. At Matching the letters in the morning were always laid upon the breakfast-table, and on this occasion Mrs. Finn was in the room before her hostess. There were two lying before her plate when Mary came in, one from her father and the other from Silverbridge. She read that from the Duke first while Mrs. Finn was watching her. 'Papa will be home on Saturday,' she said. 'He declares that the people in the borough are quite delighted with Silverbridge for a member,—and he is quite jocose. "They used to be delighted with me once," he says, "but I suppose everybody changes!" ' Then she began to pour out the tea before she opened her brother's letter. Mrs. Finn's eyes were still on her anxiously. 'What will you have? I ought to offer you everything, only I know you will take nothing. Though I am a disconsolate female, yet I am hungry. I mean to have some cold pheasant. I wonder what Silverbridge has got to say about the Brake hunt.' Then she opened her letter.

'Oh;—oh,' she exclaimed,—'Frank has killed himself.'

'Killed himself! Not that! It is not so bad as that,' said Mrs. Finn, rising from her chair.

'You had heard it before?'

'How is he, Mary?'

'Oh, heavens! I cannot read it. Do you read it. Read it and tell me. Tell me all. Tell me the truth. What am I to do? Where shall I go?' Then she threw up her hands, and with a loud scream fell on her knees with her head upon the chair. In the next moment Mrs. Finn was down beside her on the floor; but the girl had not fainted, and was still sensible to her suffering. 'Read it,' she said. 'Why do you not read it? If you will not read it, give it to me.'

Mrs. Finn did read the letter, which was very short,—hardly perhaps quite considerate, as dealing with such a subject and written to such a purpose, but still giving on the whole by no means an unfavourable account of the patient. 'I am sorry to say he has broken ever so many bones, and we were all very much frightened about him.' Then the writer went into details, from which a reader who did not read the words carefully might well imagine that the man's life was still in imminent danger.

Mrs. Finn did read it all, and then did her best to comfort her friend. 'It has been a very bad accident,' she said; 'but it is quite clear that he is getting better. Men do so often break their bones, and then seem to think nothing of it afterwards. He has broken two of his ribs and his arm. Of course that is very bad; but I do not think that such accidents are often fatal.'

'Silverbridge says it was his fault. What does he mean?'

'I suppose he was riding too close to Mr. Tregear, and that they both came down together. Of course it is distressing, but I do not think you need make yourself positively unhappy about it.'

'Would not you be unhappy if it were Mr. Finn?' said Mary, jumping up from her knees. 'I shall go to him. I can't stay here. I should go mad if I were to remain here and know nothing about it but what Silverbridge will tell me.'

'I will telegraph to Mr. Finn, who is staying there.'

'Mr. Finn won't care. Men are so heartless. They write about each other just as though it did not signify in the least whether anybody were dead or alive. I shall go to him.'

'You cannot do that.'

'I don't care now what anybody may say or what anybody may think. I choose to be considered as belonging to him, and if papa were here I would say the same.' It was of course not difficult to make her understand that she could not go to Harrington, and that no one would so thoroughly disapprove of such a step as Frank Tregear himself; but it was by no means an easy thing to keep her tranquil. She would send a telegram herself. This was debated for a long time between her and Mrs. Finn, till at last Lady Mary insisted that she was not subject to Mrs. Finn's authority, and that if she were driven to do so, she would have herself taken to the post-office at Bridstock and would herself send the telegram from there. 'If papa were here, even then I would send it,' she said. And she did send it, in her own name, quite regardless of the fact pointed out to her by Mrs. Finn, that the people at the post-office would thus know her secret. 'It is no secret,' she said. 'I don't want it to be a secret.' Mrs. Finn knew that it was wrong, but she could not stop it;—and the telegram went in the following words: 'I have heard it. I am so wretched. Send me one word to say how you are.' Matching was seven miles from the nearest telegraph-office, and Harrington was nine; but nevertheless she got an answer back, with Tregear's own name to it, on that afternoon. 'Do not be unhappy. I am doing well. Silverbridge is with me.'

That was on the Wednesday. About midday on the Thursday Gerald came home from Scotland. He had arranged his little affair with Lord Percival, not however without some difficulty. Lord Percival had declared that he did not understand having an I.O.U. tendered to him in an affair of that kind. That was not the way in which money won at cards should be paid. He had always thought that gentlemen did not play for stakes which they could not pay at once, either in cash or by cheques on their bankers. This was not said to Gerald himself;—or the result would have been very calamitous indeed. Nidderdale was the go-between, and at last arranged it,—not however till he had pointed out that Percival, having won so large a sum of money from a lad under twenty-one years of age, was very lucky in receiving such substantial security for its payment as that offered by Lord Silverbridge. Upon that Lord Percival took himself off with the I.O.U. in his pocket.

Gerald, who felt that he ought to have been home much before this time, had stayed away the longer because he knew that he had already caused his father to be angry. Then he had chosen the period of his father's absence for his return. It was absolutely necessary that the story of the gambling debt should be told the Duke in February! Silverbridge had explained that to him, and he had quite understood that in making use of his father's name and his brother's security he had assented to this necessity. He, indeed, would be up at Oxford in February, and, in that case, the first horror of the thing would be left to poor Silverbridge! Thinking of all this, Gerald felt that he was bound to tell his father himself. He resolved that he would do so. But still he was most anxious to postpone the evil day. He lingered therefore in Scotland till he knew that his father was absent in Barsetshire.

On his arrival he was immediately told of Tregear's accident. 'Oh, Gerald; have you heard?' said his sister. He had not as yet heard, and then the history was repeated to him. Mary in telling it did not make any attempt to conceal her own feelings. She was quite as open with her brother as she had been with Mrs. Finn.

'I suppose he'll get over it,' said Gerald.

'Is that all you say?' she asked.

'What can I say better? I suppose he will. Fellows always do get over that kind of thing. Herbert de Burgh smashed both his thighs, and now they say he can move about again,—of course with crutches.'

'Gerald! How can you be so unfeeling!'

'I don't know what you mean. I always liked Tregear, and I am very sorry for him. All the same if you would take it a little quieter, I think it would be better.'

'I could not take it quietly. I don't mean to take it quietly. How can I take it quietly when he is more than all the world to me?'

'You should keep that to yourself.'

'Yes,—and so let people think that I didn't care, till I broke my heart! I don't mean to be like that. And I don't see what business you have to find fault with me. I shall say just the same to papa when he comes home.' After that the brother and sister were not on very good terms with each other for the remainder of the day.

On the Saturday there was a long letter from Silverbridge to Mrs. Finn. Tregear was better; but was unhappy because it had been decided that he could not be moved for the next month. This entailed two misfortunes on him;—first that of being the enforced guest of persons who were not,—or hitherto had not been his own friends,—and then his necessary absence from the first meeting of Parliament. When a gentleman has been in Parliament some years and has perhaps been attending regularly for a month or two of the session, then he may be able to reconcile himself to an obligatory vacation with a calm mind. But when the honours and the glory and the importance are new, and the tedium of the benches has not yet been experienced, then such an accident as this is felt to be a grievance. Tregear perfectly understood that he must serve an apprenticeship before he could make himself conspicuous as a brilliant or even as a useful member,—and now that very apprenticeship must be delayed! But the young member was out of danger, and was, as Silverbridge declared, in the very best quarters which could be provided for a man in such a position.

Phineas Finn told him all the politics; Mrs. Spooner related to him, on Sundays and Wednesdays, all the hunting affairs down to the particulars of every find, of every run, of every kill, and of every escape; while Lady Chiltern read to him light literature, because he was not allowed to hold a book in his hand or to turn upon his side. 'I wish it were me,' said Gerald. 'I wish I were there to read to him,' said Mary.

Then the Duke came home. 'Mary,' said he, 'I have been distressed to hear of this accident.' This seemed to her to be the kindest word she had heard from him for a long time. She took his hand and, pressing it, looked up into his face. 'I believe him to be a worthy young man. I am sorry that he should be the cause of so much sorrow to you—and to me.'

'Of course I was sorry for his accident,' she replied, after pausing awhile; 'but now that he is better I will not call him a cause of sorrow—to me.' Then the Duke said nothing further about Tregear; nor did she.

'So you have come at last,' he said to Gerald. That was the first greeting,—to which the son responded only by an awkward smile. But in the course of the evening he walked straight up to his father. 'I have something to tell you, sir,' said he.

'Something to tell me.'

'Something that will make you very angry.'

CHAPTER 65

'DO YOU EVER THINK WHAT MONEY IS?'

GERALD told his story, standing bolt upright, and looking his father full in the face as he told it. 'You lost three thousand four hundred pounds at one sitting to Lord Percival—at cards!'

'Yes, sir.'

'In Lord Nidderdale's house.'

'Yes, sir. Nidderdale wasn't playing. It wasn't his fault.'

'Who were playing?'

'Percival and Dolly Longstaffe and Jack Hindes,—and I. Popplecourt was playing at first.'

'Lord Popplecourt!'

'Yes, sir. But he went away when he began to lose.'

'Three thousand four hundred pounds! How old are you?'

'I am just twenty-one.'*

'You are beginning the world well, Gerald! What is the engagement which Silverbridge has made with Lord Percival?'

'To pay him the money at the end of next month.'

'What had Silverbridge to do with it?'

'Nothing, sir. I wrote to Silverbridge because I didn't know what to do. I knew he would stand to me.'

'Who is to stand to either of you if you go on thus, I do not know.' To this Gerald of course made no reply, but an idea came across his mind that he knew who would stand both to himself and his brother. 'How did Silverbridge mean to get the money?'

'He said he would ask you. But I thought that I ought to tell you.'

'Is that all? Is there any more?'

'All what, sir?'

'Are there other debts?' To this Gerald made no reply. 'Other gambling debts?'

'No, sir;—not a shilling of that kind. I have never played before. I don't know what made me play then.'

'Does it ever occur to you that going on at that rate you may very soon lose all the fortune that will ever come to you? You were not yet of age and you lost three thousand four hundred pounds at cards to a man whom you probably knew to be a professed gambler!' The Duke seemed to wait for a reply, but poor Gerald had not a word to say. 'Can you explain to me what benefit you proposed to yourself when you sat down to play for such stakes as that?'

'I hoped to win back what I had lost.'

'*Facilis descensus Averni!*' said the Duke, shaking his head. '*Noctes atque dies patet atri janua Ditis.*'* No doubt he thought that as his son was at Oxford, admonitions in Latin would serve him better than in his native tongue. But Gerald, when he heard the grand hexameter rolled out in his father's grandest tone, entertained a comfortable feeling that the worst of the interview was over. 'Win back what you had lost! Do you think that that is the common fortune of young gamblers when they fall among those who are more experienced than themselves?'

'One goes on, sir, without reflecting.'

'Go on without reflecting! Yes; and, where to? Where to? Oh Gerald, where to? Whither will such progress without reflection take you?' 'He means—to the devil,' the lad said inwardly to himself, without moving his lips. 'There is but one goal for such going on as that. I can pay three thousand four hundred pounds for you certainly. I think it hard that I should have to do so; but I can do it,—and I will do it.'

'Thank you, sir,' murmured Gerald.

'But how can I wash your young mind clean from the foul stain which has already defiled it? Why did you sit down to play? Was it to win the money which these men had in their pockets?'

'Not particularly.'

'It cannot be that a rational being should consent to risk the money he has himself,—to risk even the money which he has not himself,—without a desire to win that which as yet belongs to his opponents. You desired to win? You were anxious to win?'

'I suppose I did hope to win.'

'And why? Why did you want to extract their property from their pockets, and to put it into your own? That the footpad* on the road should have such desire when, with his pistol, he stops the traveller on his journey, we all understand. And we know what we think of the foot-pad,—and what we do to him. He is a poor debased creature, who from his youth upwards has had no good thing done for him, uneducated, an outcast from society, whom we should pity more than we despise him. We take him, as a pest which we cannot endure, and lock him up where he can harm us no more. On my word, Gerald, I think that the so-called gentleman who sits down with the deliberate intention of extracting if he can the money from the pockets of his antagonists, who lays out for himself that way of repairing the shortcomings of fortune, who looks to that recourse as an aid to his means,—I look upon that man, Gerald, as worse, much worse, than the public robber! He is meaner, more cowardly, and has I think in his bosom less of the feelings of an honest man. And he probably has been educated,—as you have been. He calls himself a gentleman. He should know black from white. It is considered terrible to cheat at cards.'

'There was nothing of that, sir.'

'All cheating is terrible,—very terrible. But the man who sits down to play cards with the distinct purpose of winning money, even though he play fairly as the rules go, is to my thinking further removed from the condition of a true gentleman than is the man who cheats from his own. Do you understand me?'

'Not quite,' said Gerald, who in truth had not at all understood this last denunciation.

'The man who plays and cheats has fallen low indeed.'

'I understand that, sir.'

'He who plays that he may make an income, but does not cheat, has fallen nearly as low. Do you ever think what money is?'

The Duke paused so long, collecting his own thoughts and thinking of his own words, that Gerald found himself obliged to answer. 'Cheques, and sovereigns, and bank-notes,' he replied with much hesitation.

'Money is the reward of labour,' said the Duke, 'or rather in the shape in which it presents itself to you, it is your representation of that reward. You may earn it yourself, or, as is, I am afraid, more likely to be the case with you, you may possess it honestly as prepared for you by the labour of others who have stored it up for you. But it is a commodity of which you are bound to see that the source is not only clean but noble. You would not let Lord Percival give you money.'

'He wouldn't do that, sir, I am sure.'

'Nor would you take it, I hope, from anyone but from me. There is nothing so comfortable as money,—but nothing so defiling if it be come by unworthily; nothing so comfortable, but nothing so noxious if the mind be allowed to dwell upon it constantly. As a man should use his horse, and not spend his voice in praising him, or his time in fostering him, or his mind in thinking of him,—so it should be with his money. If he have enough let him spend it freely. If he wants it, let him earn it honestly. Let him do something for it, so that the man who pays it to him may get its value. But to think that it may be got by gambling, to hope to live after that fashion, to sit down with your fingers put almost in your neighbour's pockets, with your eye on his purse, trusting that you may know better than he some studied calculations as to the pips* concealed in your hands, praying to the only god you worship that some special card may be vouchsafed to you,—that I say is to have left far, far behind you all nobility, all gentleness, all manhood! Write me down Lord Percival's address and I will send him the money.'

The poor lad was too crushed to write the words then, in his father's presence. Whether he had understood all that had been said may be doubted;—but he felt the weight of it if he did not understand it. As he went out to seek pen and ink elsewhere he declared to himself that whatever might be the pleasures of his future life, gambling should not be one of them.

In a few moments he returned to the Duke with Lord Percival's direction* written on an envelope. Lord Percival belonged to the Beargarden and the address was given there. Then the Duke wrote a cheque for the money claimed and sent it with a note, as follows:—'The Duke of Omnium presents his compliments to Lord Percival. The Duke has been informed by Lord Gerald Palliser that Lord Percival has won at cards from him the sum of three thousand four hundred pounds. The Duke now encloses a cheque for that amount, and requests that the document which Lord Percival holds from Lord Silverbridge, as security for the amount, may be returned to Lord Gerald.' Though he had expressed very clearly to his own son his opinion of Lord Percival's conduct and his opinion also of his son's folly, he would make no anim- adversions of any kind in writing on the subject to a stranger. Let the noble gambler have his prey. He was little solicitous about that. If he could only so operate on the mind of this son,—so operate on the minds of both his sons, as to make them see the foolishness of folly, the ugliness of what is mean, the squalor and dirt of ignoble pursuits, then he could easily pardon past faults. If it were half his wealth, what would it signify if he could teach his children really to accept those lessons without which no man can live as a gentleman, let his rank be the high- est known, let his wealth be as the sands, his fashion and popularity unrivalled?

This happened late on Saturday evening; and the Duke, when he had enclosed the cheque, remained late in his room, walking up and down from corner to corner, thinking of it all. He had that morning, before he had left Gatherum, received a letter from Mr. Monk anxiously begging him to be in his place in Parliament at the beginning of the session so as to take the lead for the Liberal party in the House of Lords. During the last session there had seemed to be so general a disruption of political affairs that no peers had filled this position with adequate authority. The world generally would have said that the Duke of St. Bungay had been the leader, though he himself would hardly have admitted it. Many things, but chiefly the death of his wife, had precluded our Duke from putting himself sufficiently forward; but now, as Mr. Monk argued, and as Lord Cantrip and the old Duke had both assured him, he was bound to take the first place in his own House. On the receipt of Mr. Monk's letter he had almost made up his mind to assent uncondi- tionally. He was certainly gratified by this strong testimony to his polit- ical merits. But the word or two which his daughter had said to him, declaring that she still took pride in her lover's love, and then this new misfortune on Gerald's part, upset him greatly. He almost sickened of politics when he thought of his domestic bereavement and his domestic misfortunes. How completely had he failed to indoctrinate his children with the ideas by which his own mind was fortified and controlled! Nothing was so base to him as a gambler, and they had both com- menced their career by gambling. From their young boyhood nothing had seemed so desirable to him as that they should be accustomed by early training to devote themselves to the service of their country and to fit themselves for such work by thoughtful study. He saw other young noblemen around him who at eighteen were known as debaters at their colleges, or at twenty-five were already deep in politics, social science, and educational projects. Hitherto the careers of his boys had been—almost disgraceful. And, though utter disgrace had been warded off, partly by money and in some degree by rank, though Silverbridge after his escapade at Oxford was already in Parliament, and though Gerald had been allowed a second chance at Oxford, what good would all his wealth or all his position do for his children if their minds could rise to nothing beyond the shooting of deer and the hunting of foxes? There was young Lord Buttercup,* the son of the Earl of Woolantallow, only a few months older than Silverbridge,—who was already a junior lord, and as constant at his office, or during the session as persistent on the Treasury bench, as though there were neither a pack of hounds, or a deer forest, or a card-table in Great Britain! Lord Buttercup, too, had already written an article in *The Fortnightly*,—Conservative young Lord as he was,*—on the subject of Turkish finance. How long would it be before Silverbridge would write an article, or Gerald sign his name in the service of the public?

And then those proposed marriages,—as to which he was beginning to know that his children would be too strong for him! Anxious as he was that both his sons,—that his girl as well as his sons,—should be permeated by Liberal politics, studious as he had ever been to teach them that the highest duty of those high in rank was to use their authority, their wealth, and their power to elevate those beneath them, still he was hardly less anxious to make them understand that their second duty required them to defend and fortify their own position. It was by feeling this second duty,—by feeling it and performing it,—that they would be enabled to perform the first. And now both Silverbridge and his girl were bent upon marriages by which they would depart out of their own order,—almost as far as it was possible that they should depart. Let Silverbridge marry whom he might, he could not be other than heir to all the honours of his family. But by his marriage he might either support or derogate from these honours. And now, having at first made a choice that was good,—having proposed to ally himself with a name as noble and as old as any in the kingdom,—he had altered his mind from simple freak, captivated by a pair of bright eyes and an arch smile; and without a feeling in regard to his family, was anxious to take to his bosom the granddaughter of an American day-labourer!

And then his girl,—of whose beauty he was so proud, from whose manners, and tastes, and modes of life he had expected to reap those good things, in a feminine degree, which his sons as young men seemed so little fitted to give him,—his girl who could read books and be happy without the excitement of some riotous pleasure, from whose marriage he had been entitled to expect so much, had determined to give herself to a man who could lend no aid in supporting the glories of the house of Palliser. By slow degrees he had been brought round to acknowledge that the young man was worthy. Tregear's conduct in all this matter had been felt by the Duke to be manly. The letter he had written was a good letter. And then he had won for himself a seat in the House of Commons. He was not an adventurer, as the Duke had at first thought. When forced to speak of him to his girl he had been driven by justice to call him worthy. But how could he serve to support and strengthen that nobility, the endurance and perpetuation of which should be the peculiar care of every Palliser? He was a younger son, without any fortune, who, if he married, must take his very means of living from his wife!

And yet as the Duke walked about his room he almost acknowledged to himself that his opposition either to the one marriage or to the other was vain. Of course they would marry according to their wills,—unless indeed Silverbridge should again change his purpose, as was not impossible. But when all these troubles were so heavy upon him, when he found himself so thoroughly disappointed and crushed in his own household, he could hardly bring himself back to that desire for public service which a few years since had been the mainspring of almost all his actions. While acknowledging that it was so, he knew that he was wrong; but he told himself that the steel had been taken out of his heart by the troubles he had endured.

That same night Gerald wrote to his brother before he went to bed; and as he wrote in an unusually serious frame of mind the letter should be given here.

'DEAR SILVER,

'I was awfully obliged to you for sending me the I.O.U. for that brute Percival. He only sneered when he took it, and would have said something disagreeable but that he saw that I was in earnest. I know he did say something to Nid, only I can't find out what. Nid is an easy-going fellow, and, as I saw, didn't want to have a rumpus. And Lady Nid would not have liked it.

'But now what do you think I've done? Directly I got home I told the governor all about it! As I was in the train I made up my mind that I would. I went slap at it. If there is anything that never does any good, it's craning.* I did it all at one rush, just as though I was swallowing a dose of physic. I wish I could tell you all that the governor said, because it was really tip-top sound good sense. What is a fellow to get by playing high,—a fellow like you and me? I didn't want any of that beast's money. I don't suppose he had any. But one's dander gets up, and one doesn't like to be done, and so it goes on. I shall cut that kind of thing altogether. You should have heard the governor spouting Latin! And then the way he sat upon Percival without mentioning the fellow's name! I do think it mean to set yourself to work to win money at cards,—and it is awfully mean to lose more than you have got to pay.

'Then at the end the governor said he'd send the beast a cheque for the amount. You know his way of finishing up, just like two fellows fighting;—when one has awfully punished the other he goes up and shakes hands with him. He did pitch into me,—not abusing me, nor even saying a word about the money which he at once promised to pay; but laying it on to gambling with a regular cat-o'-nine-tails.* And then there was an end of it. He just asked the fellow's address and said that he would send him the money. I will say this;—I don't think there's a greater brick than the governor out anywhere.

'I am awfully sorry about Tregear. I can't quite make out how it happened. I suppose you were too near him and Melrose always does rush at his fences. One fellow shouldn't be too near another fellow,—only it so often happens that it can't be helped. It's just like anything else, if nothing comes of it then it's all right. But if anybody comes to grief then he has got to be pitched into. Do you remember when I nearly cut over old Sir Simon Slobody? Didn't I hear about it!

'I am awfully glad you didn't smash up Tregear altogether,—because of Mary. I am quite sure it is no good anybody setting up his back against that. It's one of the things that have got to be. You always have said that he is a good fellow. If so what's the harm? At any rate it has got to be.

'Your affectionate Brother,

'GERALD.

'I go up in about a week.'

CHAPTER 66

THE THREE ATTACKS

DURING the following week the communications between Harrington and Matching were very frequent. Silverbridge was still a guest at Lord

Chiltern's house, as was also Tregear, perforce. Phineas Finn was also
still staying there. He of course wrote to his wife, as did Silverbridge to
his brother and sister. There were no further direct communications
between Tregear and Lady Mary, but she heard daily of his progress,
and did at last succeed in inducing Gerald to send him one word of
a message through his brother. The Duke was conscious of the special
interest which existed in his house as to the condition of the young
man, but, after his arrival, not a word was spoken for some days between
him and his daughter on the subject. Then Gerald went back to his
college, and the Duke made his preparations for going up to town. At
last he had consented to obey Mr. Monk. To do something would at any
rate be better than idleness. The session of Parliament would commence on Friday the 11th of February, and it was expedient that he
should be in town a few days before that time. Then the day for his
departure was settled. He would go on Monday the 31st. Phineas Finn
was to be in London about the same time;—but Mrs. Finn agreed to
remain at Matching for yet a fortnight with Lady Mary.

It was by no concert that an attack was made upon him from three
quarters at once as he was preparing to leave Matching. On the Sunday
morning before church time,—or rather during church time, for on
that day Lady Mary went to her devotions alone,—Mrs. Finn was
closeted for an hour with the Duke in his study. It was natural enough
that she should ask to see him, as she was to be left, not perhaps in
charge of his house, but altogether in charge of his daughter. And yet
she had been made to understand that, should there come between
them any difference of opinion, Lady Mary did not consider herself
bound to obey her guardian. 'I think you ought to be aware,' she said
to the Duke, 'that though I trust Mary implicitly and know her to be
thoroughly high-principled, I cannot be responsible for her, if I remain
with her here.'

'I do not quite follow your meaning.'

'Of course there is but one matter on which there can, probably, be
any difference between us. If she should choose to write to Mr. Tregear,
or to send him a message, or even to go to him, I could not prevent it.'

'Go to him!' exclaimed the horrified Duke.

'I think I may say that she certainly will not do that.' Mrs. Finn in
saying this did not consider herself bound to tell the Duke that his
daughter had threatened even to take this step. 'I merely suggest such
a thing in order to make you understand that I have absolutely no control over her.'

'What control have I?'

'Nay;—I cannot define that. You are her father, and she acknowledges your authority. She regards me as a friend,—and as such treats me with the sweetest affection. Nothing can be more gratifying than her manner to me personally.'

'It ought to be so.'

'She has thoroughly won my heart. But still I know that if there were a difference between us, she would not obey me. Why should she?'

'Because you hold my deputed authority.'

'Oh, Duke, that goes for very little anywhere. No one can depute authority. It comes too much from personal accidents, and too little from reason or law. Could any word of yours make Mr. Warburton subject to another, as he is subject to you? Besides I fear——' Then she paused. But the Duke only smiled. It was an expression of countenance which was peculiar to him but which she had known him long enough to understand. It expressed his regret, perhaps sorrow, at what he was hearing. It augured opposition on his part. But it declared at the same time that he would hear what was to be said to him without displeasure. 'Besides I fear,' she continued, 'that on one matter concerning her you and I are not agreed.'

'I shall be sorry if it be so.'

'I feel that I am bound to tell you my opinion.'

'Oh, yes.'

'You think that in the end Lady Mary will allow herself to be separated from Mr. Tregear. I think that in the end they will become man and wife.'

This seemed to the Duke to be not quite so bad as it might have been. Any speculation as to results was very different from an expressed opinion as to propriety. Had Mrs. Finn told him that according to her views they ought to be allowed to become man and wife, he would have continued to smile indeed, but the smile would have become harder. Were he to tell the truth as to his own mind,—which he certainly did not think that he was called upon to do,—he might perhaps have said the same thing. But one is not to relax in one's endeavours to prevent that which is wrong, because one fears that that wrong may be ultimately perpetrated. 'Let that be as it may,' he said, 'it cannot alter my duty.'

'Nor mine, Duke, if I may presume to think that I have a duty in this matter.'

'That you should encounter the burden of a duty in such a matter binds me to you for ever.'

'If it be that they will certainly be married one day,——'

'Who has said that? Who has admitted that?'

'If it be so;—if it seems to me that it must be so,—then how can I be anxious to prolong her sufferings?' The Duke still smiled, but his smile had become much harder. 'She does suffer terribly.' Upon this the Duke frowned, but there was more of tenderness in his frown than in his smile. 'I do not know whether you see it all.' He well remembered all that he had seen when he and Mary were travelling together. 'I see it; and I do not pass half an hour with her without sorrowing for her from the very bottom of my heart.' On hearing this he sighed and turned his face away. 'Girls are so different! There are many who though they be genuinely in love, though their natures are sweet and feminine and affectionate, are not strong enough to support their own feelings in resistance to the will of those who have authority over them.' Had it been so with his wife? At this moment all the former history passed through his mind. 'They yield to that which seems to them to be inevitable, and allow themselves to be fashioned by the purposes of others. It is well for them often that they are so plastic, so prone to obedience! Whether it would be better for her that she should be so, I will not say.'

'It would be better,' said the Duke doggedly.

'But such is not her nature. In the teeth of all that you have said, in spite of all opposition, she is as determined as ever.'

'I may be determined too,' said the Duke;—but there was doubt in his voice, though his words were meant to be very firm.

'But if at last it will be of no use,—if it be her fate either to be married to this man or die of a broken heart——'

'What justifies you in saying that? How can you torture me by such a threat?'

'If I think so, Duke, surely I am justified. Of late I have been with her daily,—almost hourly. I do not say that this will kill her, now—in her youth. It is not often, I fancy, that women die after that fashion,—none, perhaps, do to whom nature has given the constitution and vitality which she possesses. But a broken heart may bring the poor sufferer to the grave after a lapse of many years. How will it be with you if she should live like a ghost beside you for the next twenty years, and you should then see her die, faded and withered before her time,—all her life gone without a joy,—because she had loved a man whose position in life was displeasing to you? Would the ground on which the sacrifice had been made then justify itself to you? In thus performing your duty to your order would you feel satisfied that you had performed that to your child? In such a matter I need hardly say that there is very much for you to think of as a father!'

She had come there determined to say it all,—to liberate her own soul as it were,—but had very much doubted the spirit in which the Duke would listen to her remonstration. That he would listen to her she was sure,—and then if he chose to cast her out, she would endure his wrath. It would not be to her now as it had been when he accused her of treachery. But, nevertheless, bold as she was and independent, there was a certain awe mixed with her feelings in regard to him;—he had imbued her, as he did all those around him, with so strong a sense of his personal dignity, that when she had finished her speech she almost trembled as she looked in his face. Since he had asked her how she could justify to herself the threats which she was using he had sat perfectly still with his eyes fixed upon her. Now, when she had done, he was in no hurry to speak. He rose slowly and walking towards the fireplace stood with his back towards her, looking down upon the fire. She was the first to speak again. 'Shall I leave you now?' she said, hardly daring to trust her own voice.

'Perhaps it will be better,' he answered. His voice, too, was very low. In truth he was so moved that he hardly knew how to speak at all. Then she rose and was already on her way to the door when he followed her. 'One moment if you please,' he said almost sternly. 'I am under a debt of gratitude to you of which I cannot express my sense in words. How far I may agree with you, and where I may disagree, I will not attempt to point out to you now. Nor will you expect it.'

'Oh no.'

'But all that you have troubled yourself to think and to feel in this matter, and all that true friendship has compelled you to say to me, shall be written down in the tablets of my memory as acts of friendship which no efforts on my part can repay.'

'Duke!'

'My poor child has at any rate been fortunate in securing the friendship of such a friend.' Then he turned back to the fireplace, and she was constrained to leave the room without another word.

She had thought it not improbable that her departure from Matching would be very much expedited by what she had resolved to do. She had determined to make the best plea in her power for Mary; and while she was making the plea had been almost surprised by her own vehemence; but the greater had been her vehemence, the stronger, she thought, would have been the Duke's anger. And as she had watched the workings of his face she had felt, from moment to moment, that the vials of his wrath were about to be poured out upon her. Even when she left the room she almost believed that had he not taken those moments for consideration at the fireplace his parting words would have been different in their nature. But, as it was, there could be no question now of her departure. No power was left to her of separating herself from Lady Mary. Though the Duke had not as yet acknowledged himself to be conquered, there was no doubt to her now but that he would be conquered. And she, either here or in London, must be the girl's nearest friend up to the day when she should be given over to Mr. Tregear. 'Where is papa?' Mary asked when she and Mrs. Finn went into lunch together. Mrs. Finn replied that she believed the Duke was busy and that she thought he would have his lunch taken into his own room. Neither of them saw him again that day till dinner-time;—and after dinner he soon disappeared. Yet this was to be his last night at Matching! That was one of the three attacks which were made upon the hostile father before he went up to his parliamentary duties.

The second was as follows. Among the letters on the following morning one was brought to him from Tregear. It is hoped that the reader will remember the lover's former letter and the very unsatisfactory answer which had been sent to it. Nothing could have been colder, less propitious, or more inveterately hostile than the reply. When writing it the Duke had not been as yet at all shaken in his opposition. Tregear had taken it much to heart, though he had been sensible enough hardly to expect anything else. He had written because he had felt that he was bound to do something. If he took no steps whatever towards the accomplishment of his wishes, the girl might indeed be true to him and the engagement might remain in force between them, but months,—nay, years,—might go by without bringing them any nearer to each other. He had therefore written his letter to the Duke,—and he had received his reply. As he lay in bed with his broken bones at Harrington he had ample time for thinking over all this. He knew every word of the Duke's distressing note by heart, and had often lashed himself to rage as he had repeated it. But he was well aware that he could effect nothing by showing his anger. He must go on and still do something. Since the writing of that letter he had done something. He had got his seat in Parliament, which he knew could not fail to recommend him in some degree to the Duke. And he had secured the interest of his friend Silverbridge. This had been partially done at Polwenning; but the accident in the Brake country had completed the work. Silverbridge, having very nearly killed his friend by his own imprudent riding, had felt himself compelled to make some amends. The consequence was that the brother had at last declared himself in his friend's favour. 'Of course I should be glad to see it,' he had said while sitting by Tregear's bedside. 'The only thing is that everything does seem to go so against the poor governor. I shall go back to the other side. It's the only thing I can do for him.'

Then Tregear made up his mind that he would write another letter to the Duke. Personally he was not in the best condition for doing this as he was lying in bed with his left arm tied up, and with straps and bandages all round his body. But he could sit up in bed, and his right hand and arm were free. So he declared to Lady Chiltern his purpose of writing a letter. She tried to dissuade him gently and offered to be his secretary. But when he assured her that no secretary could write this letter for him,—that the matter was of such a nature that it could not be confided to anyone else,—then she understood pretty well what would be the subject of the letter. How such private matters become public nobody knows. But they do become public, and Lady Chiltern was quite aware that her guest aspired to the hand of the only daughter of the Duke of Omnium. With considerable difficulty Tregear wrote his letter.

'MY LORD DUKE,'—On this occasion he left out the epithet which he had before used,—

'Your Grace's reply to my last letter was not encouraging, but in spite of your prohibition I venture to write to you again. If I had the slightest reason for thinking that your daughter was estranged from me, I would not persecute either you or her. But if it be true,—and I know it is true,—that she is as devoted to me as I am to her, can you think that I am wrong in pleading my cause? Is it not evident to you that she is made of such stuff that she will not be controlled in her choice,—even by your will? And in pleading my cause do I not plead hers also?

'I have had an accident in the hunting field and am now writing from Lord Chiltern's house where I am confined to bed. But I think you will understand me when I say that even in this helpless condition I feel myself constrained to do something. Of course I ask for nothing from you on my own behalf,—but on her behalf may I not add my prayers to hers?

'I have the honour to be,
'Your Grace's very faithful Servant,
'FRANCIS TREGEAR.'

This coming alone would perhaps have had no effect. The Duke had desired the young man not to address him again; and the young man had disobeyed him. No mere courtesy would now have constrained him to send any reply to this further letter. But coming as it did while his heart was still throbbing with the effects of Mrs. Finn's words, it was allowed to have a certain force. The only argument used was at any rate a true argument. His girl was devoted to the man who sought her hand. Mrs. Finn had told him that sooner or later he must yield,—unless he was prepared to see his child wither and fade at his side. He had once thought that he would be prepared even for that. He had endeavoured to strengthen his own will by arguing with himself that when he saw a duty plainly before him, he should cleave to that let the results be what they might. Even though she should die,—he had said to himself then,—he must do his duty. But that picture of her face withered and worn after twenty years of sorrowing had had more effect upon his heart than his own rapid thought that possibly she might die while he was performing his duty.

He even made excuses within his own breast in the young man's favour. Since this was first discussed the young man had certainly bettered his own condition. He was in Parliament now, and what may not be done for a young man in Parliament? And then he had heard good things of him. The young man was now a guest at Lord Chiltern's house, and Silverbridge was certainly staunch in his friendship. Altogether the young man appeared to him in a light different from that through which he had viewed the presumptuous, arrogant, utterly unjustifiable suitor who had come to him, now nearly a year since, in Carlton Terrace, asking him for his daughter's hand.

He went that morning to breakfast with Tregear's letter in his pocket, and was then very gracious to Mrs. Finn, and very tender to his daughter. 'When do you go, papa?' Mary asked.

'I shall take the 11:45 train. I have ordered the carriage at a quarter before eleven.'

'May I go to the train with you, papa?'

'Certainly. I shall be delighted. I suppose they'll send my things in the cart. Joseph will be on the box. When shall we see you in town, Mrs. Finn?'

'Mary and I will go together, I suppose.'

'I hope Mary feels how good you are to her. But what does Mr. Finn say to all this?'

'Mr. Finn is like your Grace, I take it;—very full of politics at the present moment. He is thinking a great deal more of Sir Timothy Beeswax than of his wife. If he only loved me as thoroughly as he hates him it would be well. But I suppose we shall all be up by Valentine's Day.'

'I will have everything ready for Mary.'

'Of course we will write and settle the hour,—and all that. I will bring her to Carlton Terrace myself on the way. As you will be in a hurry

I will say good-bye, Duke, now till then.' Then the Duke with formal courtesy kissed her hand and again told her, in his daughter's presence, that he felt himself to be under a heavy load of obligation to her. It was thus he bore the second attack. And the third was made as follows.

'Papa!' Mary said as soon as she found herself seated beside her father in the carriage.

'My dear!'

'Oh, papa!' And she threw herself onto his breast. He put his arm round her and kissed her,—as he would have had so much delight in doing, as he would have done so often before, had there not been this terrible ground of discord between them. She was very sweet to him. It had never seemed to him that she had disgraced herself by loving Tregear;—but that a great misfortune had fallen upon her from which it was impossible that he should relieve her by the only remedy which she would accept. Silverbridge when he had gone into a racing partnership with Tifto, and Gerald when he had allowed himself to be lured in to play for sums of money which he did not possess, had—degraded themselves in his estimation. He would not have used such a word in reference to them; but such was his feeling. They were less noble, less pure than they might have been, had they kept themselves free from such meanness. But this girl,—whether she should live and fade by his side as Mrs. Finn had foretold, or whether she should consent to give her hand to some fitting noble suitor,—or even though she might at last become the wife of this man who loved her,—would be and would always have been pure. It was very sweet to him to have something to caress. Now, in the comparative solitude of his life, as years were coming on him, and as his hair was turning grey, he felt how necessary it was that he should have someone to love and who would love him. Since he had been alone, since his wife had left him, he had been debarred from these caresses by the necessity,—as it had seemed to him the necessity,—of showing his antagonism to her dearest wishes. It had been his duty to be stern to her. In all his words and actions to his daughter he had been governed by a conviction that never for a moment should he allow to be absent from his mind the duty which was incumbent on him of separating her from her lover. He was not at all prepared to acknowledge that that duty had now ceased;—but yet there had crept over him a feeling that as he was half conquered, why should he not seek some recompense in his daughter's love? He allowed her now to lie for a minute on his shoulder while he pressed her to his heart.

'Papa,' she said, 'you do not hate me?'

'Hate you, my darling?'

'Because I am so disobedient. Oh, papa, I cannot help it. He should not have come. He should not have been let to come. But now——' He had not a word to say to her. He could not tell her,—he could not as yet bring himself to tell her,—that it should all be as she desired. He had not told himself so. Much less could he now argue with her as to the impossibility of such a marriage as he had done on all former occasions when the matter had been discussed between them. He could only press his arm more tightly round her waist, and be silent. 'It cannot be altered now, papa. Look at me. Tell me that you love me.'

'Have you doubted my love?'

'No, papa;—but I would do anything to make you happy;—anything that I could do. Papa, you do not want me to marry Lord Popplecourt?'

'I would not have you marry any man without loving him.'

'I certainly shall never love Lord Popplecourt. I never can love any-body else. That is what I wanted you to know, papa.'

To this he made no reply, nor was there anything else said upon the subject before the carriage drove up to the railway station. 'Do not get out, dear,' he said, seeing that her eyes had been filled with tears. 'It is not worth while. God bless you, my child. You will be up in London I hope in a fortnight, and we must try to make the house a little less dull for you. Make the most one can of Mrs. Finn, because she has been very good to you.'

'You may be sure of that, papa. I am very fond of Mrs. Finn.' When left alone he could not but feel that Mary, in declaring her partiality for Mrs. Finn, had expressed a different sentiment in regard to Lady Cantrip. And yet, as he told himself, Lady Cantrip had done her best. It was all that unfortunate Lord Popplecourt!

And so he had encountered the third attack.

Lady Mary, as she was driven home, recovered her spirits wonder-fully. Not a word had fallen from her father which she could use hereafter as a refuge from her embarrassments. He had made her no promise. He had assented to nothing. But there had been something in his manner, in his gait, in his eye, in the pressure of his arm, which taught her at any rate to hope that her troubles would soon be at an end.

'I do love you so much,' she said to Mrs. Finn late on that afternoon.

'I am glad of that, dear.'

'I shall always love you,—because you have been on my side all through.'

'No, Mary;—that is not so.'

'I know it is so. Of course you have to be wise because you are older. And papa would not have you here with me if you were not wise. But

I know you are on my side,—and papa knows it too. And someone else shall know it some day.'

CHAPTER 67

'HE IS SUCH A BEAST'

LORD SILVERBRIDGE remained hunting in the Brake country till a few days before the meeting of Parliament, staying chiefly at Harrington, but also paying a short visit to Spoon Hall. Thither he went at the special request of both Mr. and Mrs. Spooner, who made up a grand dinner-party for the occasion. The popularity of our hero among the Brake sportsmen was very great, and by no means the less because of Tregear's accident. It was acknowledged that the horse was a rusher, that Silverbridge was young and ardent, and that his subsequent behaviour to his friend had been perfect. 'We shall be so proud if you'll stay two or three days with us,' said Mrs. Spooner imploringly. 'Spoon Hall is better situated for the meets than any house in the country, and I'll drive you over to all of them myself.' Who could resist that? 'Chiltern is the best fellow in the world,' said Spooner, 'and Harrington is a very comfortable house. But he hasn't lived there long enough to have a cellar, and a man doesn't go in for that kind of thing in a house that is not his own. I can give you such a glass of wine as he hasn't got.' The lady's offer was perhaps the more tempting of the two; but, between them both, he was tempted. It was all very well when he was there, but he afterwards owned to Lady Chiltern that a certain word of warning which she had spoken to him was true. 'I don't know whether Mrs. Spooner doesn't shine most on horseback,' Lady Chiltern had said. 'You were quite right about her shining,' Silverbridge said afterwards. 'When she is showing a lead after the hounds she is bright. She doesn't quite know what she's about so well when she's at home.' But, on the whole, he had a pleasant time of it, and when he went up to join his father in Carlton Terrace a week before Parliament met, he felt that he was already a martyr to the public service. Who does not know that February is the best month for hunting in the whole year? He at any rate swore that it was so to Lady Chiltern when he complained of his hard fate. 'What's the good of having horses?' he said to this new friend. 'Of course while it has lasted here nothing could be more jolly. But what with having to be at Matching with the governor, and then going up to this beastly session, you see it comes to so little. I really do think they ought to put off Parliament till the first of April.' Lady Chiltern remarked that the grouse were too imperative in August to allow the foxes to plead their cause properly in February or March.* But Silverbridge seemed to think that if such fellows as Sir Timothy Beeswax stuck to it properly, four months would be quite enough for all that there was to do.

Tregear's grumbling was quite of another kind. He did not say a word before Silverbridge lest he should seem to complain of him who had caused the accident;—but to Lady Chiltern he also poured out his woes. 'It does seem hard,' he said. 'Since I was a boy just going up to school it has been the dream of my life to have a seat in Parliament. And now that I've got it, I can't go there.'

'It won't be for long, Mr. Tregear.'

'I know that I'm foolishly impatient, and that I must seem to you to be ungrateful in showing it.'

'Indeed not that.'

'But of course one fancies that the very days when one is laid up will be the most important days of the year. It won't be so, I dare say, but the idea that it may be so makes one fretful.'

Had Silverbridge been left to himself he would have had another week or two in the country and might not improbably have overstayed the opening day; but he had not been left to himself. In the last week in January a very important despatch reached his hands, from no less important a person than Sir Timothy Beeswax himself, suggesting to him that he should undertake the duty of seconding the address in the House of Commons. When the proposition first reached him it almost made his hair stand on end. He had never yet risen to his feet in the House of Commons. He had spoken at those election meetings in Cornwall, and had found it easy enough. After the first or second time he had thought it very good fun. But he knew that standing up in the House of Commons would be different from that. Then there would be the dress! 'I should so hate to fig myself out and look like a guy,'* he had said to Tregear, to whom of course he had confided the offer that had been made to him. Tregear was very anxious that he should accept it. 'A man should never refuse anything of that kind which comes in his way,' Tregear had said.

'It is only because I am the governor's son,' Silverbridge had pleaded.

'Partly so, perhaps. But if it be altogether so, what of that? Take the goods the gods provide you,* whencesoever they may come. Of course all those things which our ambition covets are easier to dukes' sons than to others. But not on that account should a duke's son refuse them. A man should be continuously taking steps upwards, and when he sees a rung vacant on the ladder should always put his foot there.'

'I'll tell you what,' said Silverbridge. 'If I thought this was all fair sailing, I'd do it. I should feel pretty certain that I should come a cropper, but still I'd try it. As you say, a fellow should try. But it's all meant as a blow at the governor. Old Beeswax thinks that if he can get me up to swear that he and his crew are real first-chop hands at carrying on the Government, that will hit the governor hard. If it wasn't for that he wouldn't have asked me. It's as much as saying to the governor,—"This chap belongs to me, not to you." That's a thing I won't go in for.' Then Tregear counselled him to write to his father for advice, and at the same time to ask Sir Timothy to allow him a day or two for consideration. This counsel he took, and he wrote both to his father and to Sir Timothy. The letter reached his father two days before he left Matching. In answer to it there came first a telegram begging Silverbridge to be in London on the Monday, and then a letter, in which the Duke expressed himself as being very anxious to see his son before giving a final answer to the question. Thus it was that Silverbridge had been taken away from his hunting so soon, a week before the day which he had himself appointed.

Isabel Boncassen, however, was now in London, and from her he thought it possible that he might find consolation. He had written to her soon after reaching Harrington, telling her in his own phraseology that he had had it all out with the governor, and that though he could not say that his father had at once assented to his views, he did not anticipate any prolonged opposition. 'There is a good deal that I can only tell you when I see you,' he said. Then he assured her with many lover's protestations that he was and always would be till death altogether her own most loving S. To this he had received an answer by return of post. She would be delighted to see him up in town,—as would her father and mother. They had now got a comfortable house in Brook Street. And then she signed herself his sincere friend, Isabel. Silverbridge thought that it was rather cold, and remembered certain scraps in another feminine handwriting in which more passion was expressed. Perhaps this was the way with American young ladies when they were in love. At any rate he would soon see her, and with that he comforted himself.

'Yes,' said the Duke, 'I am glad that you have come up at once as Sir Timothy should have his answer without further delay. You should take care that it is in his hands early to-morrow.'

'But what shall I say?'

The Duke, though he had already considered the matter very seriously, nevertheless took a few minutes to consider it again. 'The offer,'

said he, 'must be acknowledged as very flattering. Under usual circumstances, it certainly would be so.'

'But the circumstances are not usual?'

'It cannot often be the case that a minister should ask the son of his
keenest political opponent to render him such a service. But, however,
we will put that aside.'

'Not quite, sir.'

'For the present we will put that on one side. Not looking at the party
which you may be called upon to support, having for the moment no
regard to this or that line in politics, there is no opening to the real
duties of parliamentary life which I would sooner see accorded to you
than this.'

'But if I were to break down?' Talking to his father he could not quite
venture to ask what might happen if he were to 'come a cropper.'

' "None but the brave deserve the fair," ' said the Duke, slapping his
hands upon the table with unusual briskness. 'Why, if we fail, "We fail!
But screw your courage to the sticking place, And we'll not fail." What
high point would ever be reached, if caution such as that were allowed
to prevail? What young men have done before, cannot you do? I have no
doubt of your capacity. None.'

'Haven't you, sir?' said Silverbridge, considerably gratified by his
father's assurance,—and also surprised.

'None in the least. But, perhaps, some of your diligence.'

'I could learn it by heart, sir,—if you mean that.'

'But I don't mean that;—or rather I mean very, very much more
than that. You have first to realise in your mind the thing to be said, and
then the words in which you should say it, before you come to learning
by heart.'

'Some of them I suppose would tell me what to say.'

'No doubt with your inexperience it would be unfit that you should
be left entirely to yourself. But I would wish you to know,—perhaps
I should say to feel,—that the sentiments to be expressed by you were
just. You should at any rate hold the opinions which you are to recommend to others as just and proper.'

'I should have to praise Sir Timothy?'

'Not that necessarily. But you would have to advocate that course in
Parliament which Sir Timothy and his friends have taken and propose
to take. In that way you must certainly praise him.'

'But I hate him like poison.'

'There need be no personal feeling in the matter. I remember that
when I moved the address in your House Mr. Mildmay was Prime

Minister,—a man for whom my regard and esteem were unbounded, — who had been, in political matters, the preceptor of my youth, whom as a patriotic Statesman I almost worshipped, whom I now remember as a man whose departure from the arena of politics left the country very destitute. No one has sprung up since like to him,—or hardly second to him. But in speaking on so large a subject as the policy of a party, I thought it beneath me to eulogise a man. The same feeling reversed may keep you silent respecting Sir Timothy.'*

'I needn't of course say what I think about him. That wouldn't do at all.'

'I would not have you make any words that you may utter on such an occasion a thing of course. I suppose you do agree with Sir Timothy as to his general policy?' This was put in the form of a question and certainly required an answer; but Silverbridge had no answer ready. 'On no other condition can you undertake such a duty.'

'Of course I have voted with him.'

'So I have observed,—not so regularly perhaps as Mr. Roby would have desired.' Mr. Roby was the Conservative whip.*

'And I suppose the people at Silverbridge expect me to support him.'

'I hardly know how that may be. They used to be contented with my poor services. No doubt they feel they have changed for the better.'

'You shouldn't say that, sir.'

'I am bound to suppose that they think so, because when the matter was left in their own hands they at once elected a Conservative. You, at any rate, need not fear that you will offend them by seconding the address. They will probably feel proud to see their young member brought forward on such an occasion. As I shall be proud to see my son.'

'You would if it were on the other side, sir.'

'Yes, Silverbridge; yes; I should be very proud if it were on the other side. But there is a useful old adage which bids us not cry for spilt milk. You have a right to your opinions, though perhaps I may think that in adopting what I must call new opinions you were a little precipitate. We cannot act together in politics. But not the less on that account do I wish to see you take an active and useful part on that side to which you have attached yourself.' As he said this he rose from his seat and spoke with emphasis, as though he were addressing some imaginary Speaker or a house of legislators around him. 'I shall be proud to hear you second the address. If you do it as gracefully and as fitly as I am sure you may if you will give yourself the trouble, I shall hear you do it with infinite satisfaction even though I shall feel at the same time anxious to answer all your arguments and to disprove all your assertions. I should be listening no doubt to my opponent;—but I should be proud to feel that I was listening also to my son. My advice to you is to do as Sir Timothy has asked you.'

'He is such a beast, sir,' said Silverbridge.

'Pray do not speak in that way on matters so serious.'

'I do not think you quite understand it, sir.'

'Perhaps not. Can you enlighten me?'

'I believe he has done this only to annoy you.' The Duke, who had again seated himself, and was leaning back in his chair, raised himself up, placed his hands on the table before him, and looked his son hard in the face. The idea which Silverbridge had just expressed had certainly occurred to himself. He remembered well all the circumstances of the time when he and Sir Timothy Beeswax had been members of the same Government;—and he remembered how animosities had grown, and how treacherous he had thought the man who was now offering this honour to his son. From the moment in which he had read the minister's letter to the young member, he had felt that the offer had too probably come from a desire to make the political separation between himself and his son complete. But he had thought that in counselling his son he was bound to ignore such a feeling; and it certainly had not occurred to him that Silverbridge would be astute enough to perceive the same thing.

'What makes you fancy that?' said the Duke, striving to conceal by his manner, but not altogether successful in concealing, the gratification which he certainly felt.

'Well, sir; I am not sure that I can explain it. Of course it is putting you in a different boat from me.'

'You have already chosen your boat.'

'Perhaps he thinks I may get out again. I dislike the skipper so much that I am not sure that I shall not.'

'Oh, Silverbridge;—that is such a fault! So much is included in that which is unstatesmanlike, unpatriotic, almost dishonest! Do you mean to say that you would be this or that in politics according to your personal liking for an individual?'

'When you don't trust the Leader you can't believe very firmly in the followers,' said Silverbridge doggedly. 'I won't say, sir, what I may do. Though I dare say that what I think is not of much account, I do think a good deal about it.'

'I am glad of that, at any rate.'

'And as I think it not at all improbable that I may go back again, if you don't mind it, I will refuse.'

Of course after that the Duke had no further arguments to use in favour of Sir Timothy's proposition. 'Now that you have explained yourself I think that you are right,' he said, 'and I am confirmed in my opinion that it was desirable that we should talk this matter over before you arrived at any conclusion. But you should remember two things;—first, that no man should change his side in politics lightly. Such changes are permissible, and are often evidence of honesty; but they are apt to be deleterious to the man himself, and are sometimes taken as showing a vague and vacillating character. And secondly I would have you bear in mind that I have never expected from you such a step. Before you had declared yourself it was fit that I should use my influence to keep you in the path that I thought right. My influence was insufficient. But now I would not raise my little finger to induce you to come back. If conviction brings you back, then I will welcome you with all my heart.'

After that Silverbridge was left alone to write his letter to Sir Timothy, the Duke absolutely refusing to assist his son in the composition. It should never be truly said of him that he had stood between his son and the performance of a public duty because of his own animosity to the existing Leader of the House of Commons. The letter was not at last written with much ease; but when completed it was decisive, explicit, and at the same time courteous. Silverbridge said that he felt the honour very much; that he knew himself to be incompetent, but would not on that account have thought himself justified in opposing the wishes of the Leader of his party; but that as his own political opinions were on certain subjects unfortunately in a state of doubt, he could not venture to undertake a task by which he would feel himself bound to support the Ministry in everything.

'I can trace the Duke's hand in every word of it,' Sir Timothy said to Mr. Roby as he showed the letter to that worthy colleague.

CHAPTER 68

BROOK STREET

SILVERBRIDGE had now a week on his hands which he felt that he might devote with considerable satisfaction to the lady of his love. It certainly was a comfort to him that he need have nothing to do with the address. To have to go, perhaps day after day, to the Treasury in order that he might learn his lesson, would have been very disagreeable to him. He did not quite know how the lesson would have been communicated, but fancied it would have come from 'old Roby,' whom he did not love much better than Sir Timothy. Then the speech must have been composed, and afterwards submitted to someone,—probably to old Roby again, by whom no doubt it would be cut and slashed, and made quite a different speech than he had intended. If he had not praised Sir Timothy himself, Roby,—or whatever other tutor might have been assigned to him,—would have put the praise in for him. And then how many hours would it have taken him to learn 'the horrid thing' by heart? The whole week would have been little enough for the work,—which week he was bound to devote to Isabel. He proudly felt that he had not been prompted by idleness to decline the task; but not the less was he glad to have shuffled the burden from off his shoulders.

Early the next morning he was in Brook Street, having sent a note to say he would call, and having even named the hour. And yet when he knocked at the door, he was told with the utmost indifference by a London footman that Miss Boncassen was not at home;—also that Mrs. Boncassen was not at home;—also that Mr. Boncassen was not at home. When he asked at what hour Miss Boncassen was expected home, the man answered him, just as though he had been anybody else, that he knew nothing about it. He almost fancied that the man was predetermined not to give him any information. He turned away in disgust, and getting into his own private hansom had himself driven to the Beargarden. It was then past two, and he proceeded to eat his lunch. After having told Isabel that he would call in Brook Street at two, he had of course expected to lunch there. In his misery he had recourse to game-pie and a pint of champagne. 'Halloa, old fellow, what is this I hear about you?' said Nidderdale, coming in and sitting opposite to him.

'I don't know what you have heard.'

'You are going to second the address. What on earth made them pick you out from the lot of us?'

'It is just what I am not going to do.'

'I saw it in all the papers.'

'I dare say;—and yet it isn't true. I shouldn't wonder if they ask you.' At this moment a waiter handed a large official letter to Lord Nidderdale, saying that the messenger who had brought it was waiting for an answer in the hall. The letter bore the important signature of T. Beeswax on the corner of the envelope, and so disturbed Lord Nidderdale that he called at once for a glass of soda-and-brandy. When opened it was found to be very nearly a counterpart of that which Silverbridge had received down in the country. There was, however, added a little prayer that Lord Nidderdale would at once come down to the Treasury Chambers, as time was pressing.

'They must be very hard up,' said Lord Nidderdale, 'when they apply to me. But I shall do it. Cantrip is always at me to do something, and you see if I don't butter them up properly.' Then having fortified himself with game-pie and a glass of brown sherry he went away at once to the Treasury Chambers.

Silverbridge felt himself a little better after his lunch,—better still when he had smoked a couple of cigarettes walking about the empty smoking-room. And as he walked he collected his thoughts. She could hardly have meant to slight him. No doubt her letter down to him at Harrington,—if it could be called a letter,—had been very cold. No doubt he had been ill-treated in being sent away so unceremoniously from the door. But yet she could hardly intend that everything between them should be over. Even an American girl could hardly be so unreasonable as that. He remembered the passionate way in which she had assured him of her love. All that could not have been forgotten so soon,—could not be altogether laid aside! He had done nothing to offend her; nothing by which he could have forfeited her esteem. She had desired him to tell the whole affair to his father, and he had done so. Mr. Boncassen might perhaps have objected. It might be that this American was so prejudiced against English aristocrats as to desire no commerce with them at all. He, Silverbridge, was well aware that there were not many Englishmen who would not have welcomed him as a son-in-law, but Americans might be different. Still,—still Isabel would hardly have shown her obedience to her father in this way. He did indeed believe her to be too independent to obey her father at all in a matter concerning her own heart. And if he had not been the possessor of her heart at that last interview, then she must have been false indeed! So he got once more into his hansom and had himself taken back to Brook Street.

Mrs. Boncassen was in the drawing-room alone,—a circumstance which Silverbridge at first regarded as a bad omen. 'I am so sorry,' said the lady, 'but Mr. Boncassen has, I think, just gone out.'

'Indeed! And where is Isabel?'

'Isabel is downstairs;—that is if she hasn't gone out too. She did talk of going with her father to the Museum. She is getting quite bookish,—is Isabel. She has got a ticket, and goes there, and has all the things brought to her just like the other learned folks. Mr. Boncassen says she'll turn out a literary spinster* after all.'

'I am anxious to see her, Mrs. Boncassen.'

'My! If she has gone out it will be a pity. If she'd have known I'm sure she'd've stayed. She was only saying yesterday she wouldn't wonder if you shouldn't turn up.'

'Well;—no. Of course I've turned up, Mrs. Boncassen. I was here an hour ago.'

'Was it you who called and asked all them questions? My! We couldn't make out who it was. The man said it was a flurried young gentleman who wouldn't leave a card,—but who wanted to see Mr. Boncassen most especial.'

'It was Isabel I wanted to see. Didn't I leave a card? No; I don't think I did. But I thought she would have expected me. I felt so—almost at home, that I didn't think of a card.'

'That's very kind of you, Lord Silverbridge.'

'I hope you are going to be my friend, Mrs. Boncassen.'

'I am sure I don't know, Lord Silverbridge. Isabel is most used to having her own way, I guess. I think when hearts are joined almost nothing ought to stand between them. But Mr. Boncassen does have doubts. He don't wish as Isabel should force herself anywhere as she won't be welcome. But here she is and now she can speak for herself.' Whereupon not only did Isabel enter the room, but at the same time Mrs. Boncassen most discreetly left it. It must be confessed that American mothers are not afraid of their daughters.

Silverbridge, when the door was closed, stood looking at the girl for a moment and thought that she was more lovely than ever. She was dressed for walking, with thick boots, and her frock somewhat looped up. She still had on her fur jacket, but she had taken off her hat. 'I was in the parlour downstairs,' she said, 'when you came in, with papa; and we were going out together; but when I heard who was here, I made him go alone. Was I not good?'

He felt himself at the moment to be, as folks say, all in a quiver. The blood was tingling at his fingers' ends, and he knew that it reached to his face. He had made up his mind as to nothing,—nothing for that special occasion. He had not thought of a word to say, or a thing to do;—but he felt as he looked at her that the only thing in the world worth living for, was to have her for his own. For a moment he was half abashed, conscious of a certain longing, but unconscious how he might best gratify it. Then, in the next moment, she was close in his arms with his lips pressed to hers. He had been so sudden that she had been unable, or at any rate thought that she had been unable, to repress him. Had it been any other man she might, probably, have been quicker. 'Lord Silverbridge,' she said, 'I told you I would not have it. You have offended me.'

'Isabel!'

'Yes; Isabel! Isabel is offended with you. Why did you do it?'

Why did he do it? It seemed to him to be the most unnecessary question. 'I want you to know how I love you.'

'Will that tell me? That only tells me how little you think of me.'

'Then it tells you a falsehood;—for I am thinking of you always. And I always think of you as being the best and dearest and sweetest thing in the world. And now I think you dearer and sweeter than ever.' Upon this she tried to frown; but her frown at once broke out into a smile. 'When I wrote to say that I was coming why did you not stay at home for me this morning?'

'I got no letter, Lord Silverbridge.'

'Why didn't you get it?'

'That I cannot say, Lord Silverbridge.'

'Isabel, if you are so formal you will kill me.'

'Lord Silverbridge, if you are so forward you will offend me.' Then it turned out that no letter from him had reached the house; and as the letter had been addressed to Bruton Street instead of Brook Street, the failure on the part of the post-office was not surprising.

Whether or no she were offended or he were killed he remained with her nearly the whole of that afternoon. 'Of course I love you,' she said. 'Do you suppose I should be here with you if I did not, or that you could have remained in the house after what you did just now? I am not given to run into rhapsodies quite so much as you are,—and being a woman perhaps it is as well that I don't. But I think I can be quite as true to you, as you are to me.'

'I am so much obliged to you for that,' he said, grasping at her hand.

'But I am sure that rhapsodies won't do any good. Now I'll tell you my mind.'

'You know mine,' said Silverbridge.

'I will take it for granted that I do. Your mind is to marry me will ye nill ye, as the people say.' He answered this by merely nodding his head and getting a little nearer to her. 'That is all very well in its way, and I am not going to say but what I am gratified by your devotion.' Then he did grasp her hand. 'If it pleases you to hear me say so, Lord Silverbridge——'

'Not Lord!'

'Then I shall call you Plantagenet;—only it sounds so horribly historical. Why are you not Thomas or Abraham? But, if it will please you to hear me say so, I am ready to acknowledge that nothing in all my life ever came near to the delight I have in your love.' Hereupon he almost succeeded in getting his arm round her waist. But she was strong, and seized his hand and held it. 'And I speak no rhapsodies. I tell you a truth which I want you to know and to keep in your heart,—so that you may be always, always sure of it. There can never be any doubt about that.'

'I never will doubt it.'

'But that marrying will ye nill ye, will not suit me. It will not suit me even though the choice be between that and not marrying at all. There can be no other marriage for me now, but yet I will not have that. There is so much wanted for happiness in life.'

'I will do all that I can.'

'Yes. Even though it be hazardous, I am willing to trust you. If you were as other men are, if you could do as you please as lower men may do, I would leave father and mother and my own country,—all my friends whom I have known from my youth upwards,—that I might be your true wife. I would do that because I love you, down to the very bottom of my heart. But what will my life be here, if they who are your friends turn their backs upon me? What will your life be, if through all that you continue to love me?'

'That would all come right very soon.'

'And what will your life be, or mine,' she said, going on with her own thoughts without seeming to have heard his last words, 'if in such a condition as that you did not continue to love me?'

'I should always love you.'

'It might be very hard;—and if once felt to be hard, then impossible. You have not looked at it as I have done. Why should you? Even with a wife that was a trouble to you——'

'Oh, Isabel!'

His arm was now round her waist, but she continued speaking as though she were not aware of the embrace. 'Yes, a trouble! I shall not be always just what I am now. Now I can be bright and pretty and hold my own with others because I am so. But are you sure,—I am not,—that I am such stuff as an English lady should be made of? If in ten years' time you found that others did not think so,—that those who are near-est to you did not think so,—that, worse again, you did not think so yourself, would you be true to me then?'

'I will always be true to you.'

She gently extricated herself, as though she had done so that she might better turn round and look into his face. 'Oh, my own one, who can say of himself that it would be so? How could it be so, when you would have all the world, all your own world, against you? You would still be what you are,—with a clog round your leg, indeed, while at home,—but still, in Parliament, among your friends, at your clubs, you would be just what you are. You would be that Lord Silverbridge who had all good things at his disposal,—except that he had been unfortunate in his marriage! But what should I be?' Though she paused he could not answer her,—not yet. There was a solemnity in her speech which made it necessary that he should hear her to the end. 'I, too, have my friends in my own country. It is no disgrace to me there that my grandfather worked on the quays. No one holds her head higher there than I do, or is more sure of being able to hold it. I have there that assurance of esteem and honour which you have here. I would lose it all—to do you a good. But I will not lose it to do you an injury.'

'I don't know about injuries,' he said, getting up and walking about the room. 'But I am sure of this. You will have to be my wife.'

'If your father will take me by the hand and say that I shall be his daughter, I will risk all the rest. Even then it might not be wise; but we love each other too well not to run some peril. Do you think that I want anything better, that I can imagine anything more heavenly than to preside in your home, to soften your cares, to welcome your joys, to be the mother perhaps of your children,—and to know that you are proud that I should be so? No, my darling. I can see a Paradise;—only, only, I may not be fit to enter it. I must use some judgment better than my own, sounder, dear, than yours. Tell the Duke what I say;—tell him with what language a son may use to his father. And remember that all you ask for yourself you will ask doubly for me.'

'I will ask him so that he cannot refuse me.'

'If you do I at any rate shall be contented. And now go. I have said ever so much, and I am tired.'

'Isabel! Oh, my love.' And he stretched out his arms to her.

'Yes; Isabel;—your love! I am that, at any rate for the present,—and proud to be so as a queen. Well; if it must be, this once,—as I have been so hard to you.' Then she gave him her cheek to kiss, but of course he took more than she gave.

When he got out into the street it was dark and there was still standing the faithful cab. But he felt that at the present moment it would be impossible to sit still, and he dismissed the equipage. No; he would not want it again that evening. He would send word to the stables in the morning. He could think nothing now either of cabs or carriages. He walked rapidly along Brook Street into Park Lane, and from thence to the park, hardly knowing whither he went in the enthusiasm of the moment. He walked back to the Marble Arch, and thence round by the drive to the Guard House and the bridge over the Serpentine, by

the Knightsbridge Barracks to Hyde Park Corner. And as he walked he
hardly knew what he was doing in the fury of his love. Though he
should give up everything and go and live in her own country with her,
he would marry her. His politics, his hunting, his address to the Queen,
his horses, his guns, his father's wealth, and his own rank,—what were
they all to Isabel Boncassen? In meeting her he had met the one human
being in all the world who could really be anything to him either in
friendship or in love. When she had told him what she would do for him
to make his home happy, it had seemed to him that all other delights
must fade away from him for ever. How odious were Tifto and his race-
horses, how unmeaning the noise of his club, how terrible the tedium of
those parliamentary benches! He could not tell his love as she had told
hers! He acknowledged to himself that his words could not be as her
words,—nor his intellect as hers. But his heart could be as true. She had
spoken to him of his name, his rank, and all his outside world around
him. He would make her understand at last that they were nothing to
him in comparison with her. When he had got round to Hyde Park
Corner, he felt that he was almost compelled to go back again to
Brook Street. In no other place could there be anything to interest
him;—nowhere else could there be light, or warmth, or joy! But what
would she think of him? He must at any rate take care that she should
not despise him! To go back hot, and soiled with mud, in order that he
might say one more adieu,—that possibly he might ravish one more
kiss,—would hardly be manly. He must postpone all that for the morrow. On the morrow of course he would be there. Then as he thought of
the ecstasy of that first embrace he plunged down Constitution Hill.

But his work was all before him! That prayer had to be made to his
father; or rather some wonderful effort of eloquence must be made by
which his father might be convinced that this girl was so infinitely
superior to anything of feminine creation that had ever hitherto been
seen or heard of, that all ideas as to birth, country, rank, or name ought
in this instance to count for nothing. He did believe himself that he
had found such a pearl, that no question of setting need be taken into
consideration. Set the pearl as you might, it would show itself to be
superior to all other pearls that had ever yet been found. All this the
Duke must be made to see. If the Duke would not see it the fault would
be in the Duke's eyes, or perhaps in his own words,—but certainly not
in the pearl.

Then he compared her to poor Lady Mabel, and in doing so did
arrive at something near the truth in his inward delineation of the two
characters. Lady Mabel with all her grace, with all her beauty, with all

her talent, was a creature of efforts, or, as it might be called, a manufactured article. She strove to be graceful, to be lively, to be agreeable and clever. Isabel was all this and infinitely more without any struggle. When he was most fond of Mabel, most anxious to make her his wife, there had always been present to him a feeling that she was—old. Though he knew her age to a day,—and knew her to be younger than himself,—yet she was old. Something had gone of her native bloom, something had been scratched and chipped from the first fair surface, and this had been repaired by varnish and veneering. He knew nothing of that early passion which had made his friend Tregear so dear to her, but, without knowing it, he had felt its effects. Though he had loved her he had never been altogether satisfied with her. But Isabel was as young as Hebe.* He knew nothing of her actual years, but he did know that to have seemed younger, or to have seemed older,—to have seemed in any way different from what she was,—would have been to be less perfect. He certainly would never have thought of marrying Mabel Grex, if he had, at that time, seen Isabel Boncassen.

CHAPTER 69

'PERT POPPET!'

A COUPLE of days after the occurrences told in the last chapter, on a Sunday morning,—while Lord Silverbridge was alone in a certain apartment in the house in Carlton Terrace which was called his own sitting-room, and which was profusely ornamented with whips, foils, sticks, guns, and spurs,—the name was brought him of a gentleman who was very anxious to see him. He was at the moment not in the best spirits. He had seen his father and had used all the eloquence of which he was master,—but not quite with the effect which he had desired. His father had been very kind, but he, too, had been eloquent;—and had, as is often the case with orators, been apparently more moved by his own words than by those of his adversary. If he had not absolutely declared himself as irrevocably hostile to Miss Boncassen he had not said a word that might be supposed to give token of assent. But he had said many words showing the extreme indiscretion of such a marriage.

Silverbridge, therefore, on this Sunday morning was moody, contemplative, and desirous of solitude. Nothing that the Duke had said had at all shaken him. He was still sure of his pearl, and quite determined that he would wear it. Various thoughts were running through his brain. What if he were to abdicate the title and dukedom to Gerald, and go out and become a republican? He was inclined to think that he could not abdicate,* but he was quite sure that no one could prevent him from going to America and calling himself Mr. Palliser if he chose it. Or might it not be well that he should simply threaten to do this, with a conviction that the Duke might thus be brought round to reason? That his father would forgive him and accept the daughter-in-law brought to him, were he in the first place to marry without sanction, he felt quite sure. What was there that his father would not forgive? But then Isabel would not assent to this. Isabel required a distinct acceptance from the Duke in person. The hardship was that the Duke, knowing all this, might on that very account remain firm.

He was turning all this in his head and ever and anon trying to relieve his mind by *Clarissa*, which he was reading in conformity with his father's advice,—since Macaulay's enthusiasm in India all Liberal Statesmen have recommended the reading of *Clarissa*,*—when the gentleman's card was put into his hand. 'Whatever does he want here?' he said to himself; and then he ordered that the gentleman might be shown up. The gentleman in question was our old friend Dolly Longstaffe. Dolly Longstaffe and Silverbridge had for the last year or two been intimate;—intimate as young men are. But they certainly were not friends, nor, as far as Silverbridge knew, had Dolly ever set foot in that house before. 'Well, Dolly,' said he. 'What's the matter now?'

'I suppose you are surprised to see me.'

'I didn't think you were ever up so early.' It was at this time almost noon.

'Oh, come now; that's nonsense. I can get up as early as anybody else. Don't go and say that, or it will do me a mischief. I have changed all that for the last four months. I was at breakfast this morning very soon after ten.'

'What a miracle! Is there anything I can do for you?'

'Well;—yes, there is. Of course you are surprised to see me.'

'You never were here before;—and therefore of course it is odd.'

'It is odd; I felt that myself. And when I tell you what I have come about you will think it more odd. I know I can trust you with a secret?'

'That depends, Dolly.'

'What I mean is I know you are good-natured. There are ever so many fellows that are one's most intimate friends that would say anything on earth they could that was ill-natured.'

'I hope they are not my friends.'

'Oh yes, they are. Think of Glasslough, or Popplecourt, or Hindes! If they knew anything about you that you didn't want to have known,—about a young lady or anything of that kind,—don't you think they'd tell everybody? I suppose a man may light a cigar here, Silverbridge?' The permission was given and the cigar was lighted. 'I have a sort of idea that you wouldn't tell.'

'I can't tell anything I don't know.'

'That's true. I had thought of that myself. But then there's a particular reason for my telling you this. It is about a young lady. You won't tell;—will you?'

'No, I won't. But I can't see why on earth you should come to me. You are ever so many years older than I am.'

'I had thought of that too. But you are just the person that I must tell. Nobody else can have anything to do with it. I want you to help me.'

These last words were said in a whisper, and Dolly as he said them had drawn nearer to his friend. Silverbridge remained in suspense, saying nothing by way of encouragement, but still looking as though he were ready to listen. Dolly, either in love with his own mystery or doubtful of his own purpose, sat still, looking eagerly at his companion. 'What the mischief is it?' asked Silverbridge impatiently.

'I have quite made up my own mind.'

'That's a good thing at any rate.'

'Well;—I had a deal of difficulty about it. I'm not what you would have called a marrying sort of man.'

'I should have said,—no. But I suppose most men do marry sooner or later.'

'That's just what I said to myself. It has to be done, you know. There are three different properties coming to me. At least one has come already.'

'You're a lucky fellow.'

'I've been horribly cheated.* I suppose you've heard that. But still,—I've made up my mind; and when I say a thing I mean to do it.'

'But what can I do?'

'That's just what I'm coming to. If a man does marry I think he ought to be attached to her.' To this, as a broad proposition, Silverbridge was quite ready to accede. But, regarding Dolly as a middle-aged sort of fellow, one of those men who marry because it is convenient to have a house kept for them when they have become tired of bachelor looseness, he simply nodded his head. He could not become enthusiastic about the lady of Dolly's heart,—at any rate not till he had heard her name. 'I am awfully attached to her,' Dolly went on to say.

'That's all right.'

'Of course there are fellows who marry girls for their money. I've known men who have married their grandmothers.'

'Not really!'

'That kind of thing, I mean. When a woman is old it does not much matter who she is. But my one——! She's not old!'

'Nor rich?'

'Well; I don't know about that. I shouldn't wonder if she did have something tidy. But I'm not after her money. Pray understand that. It's because I'm downright fond of her. She's an American.'

'A what!' said Silverbridge, startled.

'You know her. That's the reason I've come to you. It's Miss Boncassen.' A dark frown came across the young man's face, but with the anger expressed there was mingled much of doubt. That all this should be said to him was disgusting. That an oaf* like that should dare to talk of loving Miss Boncassen was offensive to him. But in such a crisis he must be careful not to make a fool of himself. Before he ventured to speak he warned himself that as her name was in question he must be very careful. Therefore at the moment he said nothing. 'It's because you know her that I've come to you. She thinks that you're after her.' Dolly as he said this lifted himself quickly up in his seat, and nodded his head mysteriously as he looked into his companion's face. It was as much as though he should say, 'I see you are surprised; but so it is.' And so he sat, nodding his head for some seconds before he continued his address. 'She does; the pert poppet!' This was almost too much for Silverbridge; but still he contained himself, and in order that he might do so he got up and poked the fire, and altered the position of half-a-dozen things on the chimney-piece. 'She won't look at me because she has got it into her head that perhaps some day she may be Duchess of Omnium! That of course is out of the question.'

'Upon my word all this seems to me to be so very odd,—so very, I may say, distasteful that I think you had better say nothing more about it.'

'It is distasteful,' said Dolly; 'but the truth is I am so downright,—what you may call enamoured——!'

'Don't talk such stuff as that here,' said Silverbridge, jumping up. 'I won't have it.'

'But I am. There is nothing I wouldn't do to get her. Now you've got it all. Of course it's a good match for her. I've got three separate properties; and when the governor goes off, I shall have a clear fifteen thousand a year.'

'Oh; bother!'

'Of course that's nothing to you. I dare say the Duke allows you as much as that already; but it is a very tidy income for a commoner. And how is she to do better?'

'I don't know how she could do much worse,' said Silverbridge in a transport of rage. Then he pulled his moustache in vexation, angry with himself that he should have allowed himself to say even a word on so preposterous a supposition as this that had been set before him. Isabel Boncassen and Dolly Longstaffe! It was Titania and Bottom* over again. It was absolutely necessary that he should get rid of this intruder, and he began to be afraid that he could not do this without using language which would be very uncivil indeed. 'Upon my word,' he said, 'I think you had better not talk about it any more. The young lady is one for whom I have a very great respect, and I don't like to have her name mentioned in this absurd way.'

'I mean to marry her,' said Dolly, thinking thus to vindicate himself.

'You might as well think of marrying one of the stars.'

'One of the stars!'

'Or a royal princess;—anything you can think of that is most absolutely out of your reach.'

'Well! Perhaps that is your opinion, but I can't say that I agree with you. I don't see why she shouldn't take me. I can give her a position which you may call A1 out of the peerage. I can bring her into society. I can make an English lady of her.'

'You can't make anything of her,—except to insult her,—and me too by talking of her.'

'I don't quite understand all this,' said the unfortunate lover, getting up from his seat. 'Very likely she won't have me. Perhaps she has told you so.'

'She never mentioned your name to me in her life. I don't suppose she remembers your existence.'

'But I say that there can be no insult in such a one as me asking such a one as her to be my wife. She needn't take me, but to say that she doesn't remember my existence is absurd.'

'Why should I be troubled with all this? Why do you come here? Why do you tell me?'

'Because I think you're making a fool of her, and because I'm honest. That's why,' said Dolly with much energy. There was something in this which partly reconciled Silverbridge to his despised rival. There was a touch of truth about the man, though he was so utterly mistaken in his ideas. 'I want you to give over,' said Dolly, 'in order that I may try again.

I don't think you ought to keep a girl from her promotion, merely for the fun of a flirtation. Perhaps you're fond of her;—but you won't marry her. I am fond of her, and I shall.'

After a minute's pause Silverbridge resolved that he would be magnanimous. 'Miss Boncassen is going to be my wife,' he said, drawing himself into some unintended assumption of dignity.

'Your wife!'

'Yes;—my wife. And now I think you will see that nothing further can be said about this matter.'

'Duchess of Omnium!'

'She will be Lady Silverbridge.'

'Oh;—of course. She'll be that first. Then I've got nothing further to say. I'm not going to enter myself to run against you. Only I shouldn't have believed it if anybody else had told me.'

'Such is my good fortune.'

'Oh, ah,—yes; of course. That is one way of looking at it. Well, Silverbridge, I'll tell you what I shall do; I shall hook it.'*

'No; no; not you.'

'Yes, I shall. I dare say you won't believe me, but I've got such a feeling about me here,'—as he said this he laid his hand upon his heart,—'that if I stayed here I should go in for hard drinking. I shall take the great Asiatic tour. I know a fellow that wants to go, but he hasn't got any money. I dare say I shall be off before the end of next month. You don't know any fellow that would buy a half-a-dozen hunters; do you?' Silverbridge shook his head. 'Good-bye,' said Dolly in a melancholy tone. 'I am sure I am very much obliged to you for telling me;—because you know it puts an end to it all, and settles a fellow. I shall see her once more,—once more before I go. If I'd known you'd meant it, I shouldn't have meddled of course. Duchess of Omnium!'

'Look here, Dolly,' said the object of all this worship when the other man was already at the door. 'I have told you what I should not have told anyone, but I wanted to screen the young lady's name.'

'It was so kind of you! I shall never forget it.'

'Do not repeat it. It is a kind of thing that ladies are particular about. They choose their own time for letting everybody know.' Then Dolly promised to be as mute as a fish, and took his departure, having evidently experienced much mental relief.

Silverbridge, when he was alone, walked about his room in anger with himself. He had felt, towards the end of the interview, that he had been arrogant to the unfortunate man,—particularly in saying that the young lady would not remember the existence of such a suitor,—and had also recognised a certain honesty in the man's purpose, which had not been the less honest because it was so absurd. Actuated by the consciousness of this, he had swallowed his anger, and had told the whole truth. Nevertheless certain things had been said which were horrible to him. This buffoon of a man had called his Isabel a—pert poppet! How was he to get over the remembrance of such an offence as that? And then the wretch had declared that he was—enamoured! There was sacrilege in the term when applied by such a man to Isabel Boncassen. He had thoughts of days to come, when everything would be settled, when he might sit close to her, and call her by pretty names,—when he might in sweet familiarity tell her that she was a little Yankee and a fierce republican, and 'chaff' her about the Stars and Stripes; and then she would lean upon him,—all those joys being prepared in his mind for the delight of some time yet to come, the picture at present having only been painted by his imagination,—and she would give him back his chaff, and would call him an aristocrat and would laugh at his titles. And he the while would hold her close in his arms! As he thought of all this he would be proud with the feeling that such privileges would be his own. And now this wretched man had called her a pert poppet!

There was a sanctity about her,—a divinity which had greatly grown in his conception since the scene in the drawing-room in Brook Street,—which had made it almost a profanity to have talked about her at all to such a one as Dolly Longstaffe. She was his Holy of Holies, at which vulgar eyes should not even be allowed to gaze. It had been a most unfortunate interview. But this at any rate was clear,—was clear at least to his eyes,—that, as he had announced his engagement to such a one as Dolly Longstaffe, the matter now would admit of no delay. He had of course cautioned Dolly Longstaffe to hold his peace, but he was, he told himself, very sure that such a caution would have no effect. In this he was, in truth, unjust to Dolly, who kept the secret like a man and a martyr. But as the conviction implied the expediency of despatch in the matter of his desired marriage, he was determined to hold fast by it. He would explain to his father that as tidings of the engagement had got abroad, honour to the young lady would compel him to come forward openly as her suitor at once. If this argument might serve him, then perhaps this intrusion on the part of Dolly would not have been altogether a misfortune.

The interview had taken an hour and he was engaged to lunch in Brook Street at two. Unfortunately time did not admit of his rushing to his father with this new argument at once, so as to enable him to declare on his arrival at Mr. Boncassen's house that all impediments had now been happily removed. But still, as he was going to enjoy the happiness of being in her presence, he recovered himself quickly after the departure of his rival, and having put on his frock coat and gloves with something more than his ordinary care, he got into his cab and was taken quickly by the route with which his servant had become already intimately acquainted.

CHAPTER 70

'LOVE MAY BE A GREAT MISFORTUNE'

SILVERBRIDGE when he reached Brook Street that day was surprised and hardly well pleased to find that a large party was going to lunch there. Isabel had asked him to come,—when he had seen her only for a moment at the door of the house on the Saturday,—and he had thought her the dearest girl in the world for doing so. But now his gratitude for that especial favour was considerably abated. He did not care just now for the honour of eating his lunch in the presence of Mr. Gotobed, the American minister, whom he found there already in the drawing-room with Mrs. Gotobed, nor with Ezekiel Sevenkings,* the great American poet from the far West, who sat silent and stared at him in an unpleasant way. Nor was he made happy by meeting on this occasion his friend Mr. Lupton. When Sir Timothy Beeswax was announced, with Lady Beeswax and her daughter, his gratification certainly was not increased. And the last comer,—who did not arrive indeed till they were all seated at the table,—almost made him start from his chair and take his departure suddenly. That last comer was no other than Mr. Adolphus Longstaffe. Then he understood that mysterious announcement that the loved one was sure to be seen once more. As it happened he was seated next to Dolly, with Lady Beeswax on the other side of him. Whereas his Holy of Holies was on the other side of Dolly! The arrangement made seemed to him to have been monstrous. He had endeavoured to get next to Isabel; but she had so manoeuvred that there should be a vacant chair between them. He had not much regarded this because a vacant chair may be easily pushed on one side. But before he had quite made all his calculations there was Dolly Longstaffe sitting there! There never had been such a 'sell' as this since lovers were lovers, since Brook Street had been built, since America had become a country. He almost thought that Dolly winked at him in triumph,—that very Dolly who an hour ago had promised to take himself off upon his Asiatic travels! He wished that the man were already there, but had no wishes as to the man's safe return.

Sir Timothy and the minister kept up the conversation very much between them, Sir Timothy flattering everything that was American, and the minister finding fault with very many things that were English. Now and then Mr. Boncassen would put in a word to soften the severe honesty of his countryman, or to correct the euphemistic falsehoods of Sir Timothy. The poet seemed always to be biding his time for saying something pungent, but, though he even made preparation with his thumb, the pungent thing did not come. Dolly ventured to whisper a word to his neighbour. It was but to say that the frost had broken up. But Silverbridge heard it and looked daggers at everyone. Then Lady Beeswax expressed to him a hope that he was going to do great things in Parliament this session. 'I don't mean to go near the place,' he said, not at all conveying any purpose to which he had really come, but driven by the stress of the moment to say something that should express his general hatred of everything around him. 'You are not going to accept the Chilterns?'* asked Lady B. with intense interest. 'I have been staying with them, and I think I shall go back again to-morrow,' said Silverbridge. Lady Beeswax told her husband that afternoon that Lord Silverbridge was the most incoherent young nobleman she had ever met. She was very glad that the address was altogether out of his hands. Mr. Lupton was on the other side of Isabel, and soon seemed to be engaged with her in a pleasant, increasingly familiar conversation. Then Silverbridge remembered that he had always thought Lupton to be a most conceited prig. Nobody gave himself so many airs or thought himself so clever,—or was so careful as to the dyeing of his whiskers. It was astonishing that Isabel should allow herself to be amused by such an antiquated coxcomb as that. When they had finished eating they moved about and changed their places, Mr. Boncassen being rather anxious to stop the flood of American eloquence which came from his friend Mr. Gotobed. British viands had become subject to his criticism, and Mr. Gotobed had declared to Mr. Lupton that he didn't believe that London could produce a dish of squash or tomatoes all the year through. He was quite sure you couldn't have sweet corn. Then there had been a moving of seats in which the minister was shuffled off to Lady Beeswax, and the poet found himself by the side of Isabel. 'Do you not regret our mountains and our prairies,' said the poet;—'our great waters and our green savannahs?' 'I think more perhaps of Fifth Avenue,' said Miss Boncassen. Silverbridge, who at this moment was being interrogated by Sir Timothy, heard every word of it.

'I was so sorry, Lord Silverbridge,' said Sir Timothy, 'that you could not accede to our little request about the address.'

'I did not quite see my way,' said Silverbridge, with his eye upon Isabel.

'So I understood, but I hope that things will make themselves clearer to you shortly. There is nothing that I desire so much as the support of young men such as yourself,—the very cream I may say of the whole country. It is to the young conservative thoughtfulness and the truly British spirit of our springing aristocracy that I look for that reaction which I am sure will at last carry us safely over the rocks and shoals of communistic propensities.'

'I shouldn't wonder if it did,' said Silverbridge. They didn't think that he was going to remain down there talking politics to an old humbug like Sir Timothy when the sun, and moon, and all the stars had gone up into the drawing-room! For at that moment Isabel was making her way to the door.

But Sir Timothy had buttonholed him. 'Of course it is too late now to say anything further about the address. We have arranged that. Not quite as I would have wished, for I had set my heart upon initiating you into the rapturous pleasure of parliamentary debate. But I hope that a good time is coming. And pray remember this, Lord Silverbridge;—there is no member sitting on our side of the House, and I need hardly say on the other, whom I would go further to oblige than your father's son.'

'I'm sure that's very kind,' said Silverbridge, absolutely using a little force as he disengaged himself. Then he at once followed the ladies upstairs, passing the poet on the stairs. 'You have hardly spoken to me,' he whispered to Isabel. He knew that to whisper to her now, with the eyes of many upon him, with the ears of many open, was an absurdity; but he could not refrain himself. His heart was so full of her, his thoughts had been so intent upon her, that he was unable to carry himself with that indifference which is expected from a man even in love.

'There are so many to be—entertained, as people say! I don't think I ought to have to entertain you,' she answered, laughing. No one heard her but Silverbridge, yet she did not seem to whisper. She left him, however, at once, and was soon engaged in conversation with Sir Timothy.

There can, I think, be no doubt that, as an opportunity for social gatherings, lunches are a mistake. It may be that nature requires that such a meal should be made; and if so, it is of course convenient that the inhabitants of one and the same house should eat it in company. But it should never become a convivial gathering, and should be partaken only by those who use it as the simple mode of obtaining the nourishment necessary to them. Who has not felt the disagreeable nature of its attributes when other purposes have been intended? When you dine out you know how to get away from your host's house without difficulty. He dictates to you with easy confidence the moment at which you shall leave his dining-room, and when the half-hour of subsequent conversation is over your departure from the precincts of your hostess is as little embarrassing. But who ever knew how to get away from a convivial lunch? What to do, what to say, when to move, and when to go, is always a matter of uneasy thought. At dinner one takes three or four glasses of champagne, and perhaps as many more of claret afterwards. Added to this there may be a little drop of cognac together with an opening and concluding modicum of sherry. And who is the worse for it? Who after it is conscious that either he himself or anyone else has drunk any wine? But when you have taken the very minimum at lunch which the circumstances of the case will allow, when you have passed that unhappy hour in a continually broken resolve not to eat a morsel, or drink a drop, you feel nevertheless so permeated with strong liquors, so overcome by a sense of victuals through the whole subsequent afternoon, that you do not know what to do with yourself; and when you see others who have gone through the same damnable struggle, you are scandalised by their red faces and uncomfortable grins.

But the worst of it all is that vacillating unsteady mind which does not know when to take its owner off. Silverbridge was on this occasion quite determined not to take himself off at all. As it was only lunch the people must go, and then he would be left with Isabel. But the vacillation of the others was very distressing to him. Mr. Lupton went, and poor Dolly got away apparently without a word. But the Beeswaxes and the Gotobeds would not go, and the poet sat staring immovably, as though that immortality for which his sort sighed was to be found in the permanence of his present abode. In the meanwhile Silverbridge endeavoured to make the time pass lightly by talking to Mrs. Boncassen. He had been so determined to accept Isabel with all her adjuncts that he had come almost to like Mrs. Boncassen, and would certainly have taken her part violently had anyone spoken ill of her in his presence. But still it was not easy to talk to her for an hour.

Then suddenly he found that the room was nearly empty. The Beeswaxes and the Gotobeds were gone; and at last the poet himself, with a final glare of admiration at Isabel, had taken his departure. When Silverbridge looked round, Isabel also was gone. Then too Mrs. Boncassen had left the room as though but for a moment, going to the door as though she had meant to return, and then escaping. At the same instant Mr. Boncassen entered by another door, and the two men were alone together. 'My dear Lord Silverbridge,' said the father, 'I want to have a few words with you.' Silverbridge stood bolt upright, and then sat down again. Of course there was nothing for him but to submit. 'You remember what you said to me down at Matching?'

'Oh yes; I remember that.'

'You did me the great honour of expressing a wish to make my child your wife.'

'I was asking for a very great favour.'

'That also;—for there is no greater favour that I could do to any man than to give him my daughter. Nevertheless, you were doing me a great honour,—and you did it, as you do everything, with an honest grace that went far to win my heart. I am not at all surprised, sir, that you should have won hers.' The young man as he heard this could only blush and look foolish. 'If I know my girl neither your money nor your title would go for anything. I have always felt that manly earnestness with outside grace would prevail with her,—if anything ever did prevail.'

'I think much more of her love, Mr. Boncassen, than I do of anything else in the world.'

'But love, my Lord, may be a great misfortune.' As he said this the tone of his voice was altered, and there was a melancholy solemnity not only in his words but in his countenance. 'I take it that young people when they love rarely think of more than the present moment. It is not perhaps natural that they should contemplate all the vicissitudes of a joint life. If they did so the bloom would be gone from their romance. But others have to do this for them. If Isabel had come to me saying that she loved a poor man, there would not have been much to disquiet me. A poor man may earn bread for himself and his wife,—the happiest lot which a man can have. And if he failed I could have found them bread. Nor, had she loved somewhat below her own degree, should I have opposed her. So long as her husband had been an educated man, there might have been no future punishment to fear.'

'I don't think she could have done that,' said Silverbridge.

'At any rate she has not done so. But how am I to look upon this that she has done?'

'I'll do my best for her, Mr. Boncassen.'

'I believe you would. But even your love can't make her an Englishwoman. You can make her a duchess.'

'Not that, sir.'

'But you can't give her a parentage fit for a duchess,' he continued, not noting the interruption,—'not fit at least in the opinion of those with whom you will pass your life, with whom,—or rather perhaps without whom,—she will be destined to pass her life if she becomes your wife. It does not matter whether I may think it fit. Unfortunately it does not suffice that even you should think it fit. Though you loved each other as well as any man and woman that ever were brought into each other's arms by the beneficence of God, you cannot make each other happy,—you at least cannot make her happy,—unless you can ensure her the respect of those around her.'

'All the world will respect her.'

'Her conduct,—yes. I think the world, your world, would learn to do that. I do not think it could help itself. But that would not suffice. I may respect the man who makes my boots,—or him who cleans them. But he would be a wretched man if he were thrown on me for society. I would not give him my society. Will your duchesses and your countesses give her theirs?'

'Certainly they will.'

'I do not ask for it as thinking it to be of more value than that of others; but were she to become your wife she would be so abnormally placed as to require it for her comfort. She would have become a lady of high rank,—not because she loves rank but because she loves you.'

'Yes, yes, yes,' said Silverbridge, hardly himself knowing why he became impetuous at the moment.

'But having removed herself into that position, being, as she would be, a countess or a duchess or what not, how could she be happy if she were excluded from the community of countesses and duchesses?'

'They are not like that,' said Silverbridge.

'I will not say that they are, but I do not know. Having Anglican tendencies* I have been wont to contradict my countrymen when they have told me of the narrow exclusiveness of your nobles. Having come here and been received here with open arms, having found your nobles and your commoners all alike in their courtesy,—which is a cold word; in their hospitable friendships,—I would now not only contradict but would laugh to scorn any such charge,'—so far he spoke somewhat loudly, and then dropped his voice as he concluded,—'were it anything less than the happiness of my child that is in question.'

'What am I to say, sir? I only know this;—I am not going to lose her.'

'You are a fine fellow. I was going to say that I wished you were an American, so that Isabel need not lose you. But, my boy, I have told you that I do not know how it might be. Of all whom you know, who could best tell me the truth on such a subject? Who is there whose age will have given him experience, whose rank will have made him familiar with this matter, who from friendship to you would be least likely to decide against your wishes, who from his own native honesty would be most sure to tell the truth? Can you name such a man to whom I may trust for an opinion?'

'You mean my father,' said Silverbridge.

'I do mean your father. He must know, and, happily, he seemed to have taken no dislike to the girl herself. I have seen enough of him to feel sure that he is devoted to his own children.'

'Indeed he is.'

'A just and a liberal man;—one I should say not carried away by prejudices!' Here Silverbridge put up his hand and passed it uneasily backwards and forwards across his head. He did not feel so certain as to that absence of all prejudice on the part of his father. 'Well;—my girl and I have just put our heads together, and we have come to a conclusion. If the Duke of Omnium will tell us that she would be safe here as your wife,—safe from the contempt of those around her,—you shall have her. And I shall rejoice to give her to you, not because you are Lord Silverbridge, not because of your rank and wealth; but because you are—that individual human being whom I now hold by the hand.'

When the American had come to an end of what he had to say, Silverbridge was too much moved and too deeply concerned to make him any immediate answer. He had an idea in his own mind that the appeal was not altogether fair. His father was no doubt a just man,—just, affectionate, and liberal. But then it will so often happen that fathers do not want their sons to marry those very girls on whom the sons have set their hearts. In this case there was that additional difficulty about Lady Mabel! He could not tell the story to Mr. Boncassen. He could not explain that before he had really known his own mind he had thought of marrying the daughter of Lord Grex. The story would not have recommended itself to Isabel's father. But if properly understood it would have gone to show that his father might have a reason of his own for opposing this marriage,—which reason, however, would have been a very bad reason. But he could only say that he would speak to his father again on the subject. 'Let him tell me that he is contented,' said Mr. Boncassen, 'and I will tell him I am contented. If it does not suit him to come to me, I will willingly go to him. And now, my friend, good-bye.' Silverbridge asked piteously that he might be allowed to see Isabel before he was turned out; but Isabel had left the house in company with her mother.

CHAPTER 71

'WHAT AM I TO SAY, SIR?'

WHEN Lord Silverbridge left Mr. Boncassen's house after his lunch banquet on Sunday afternoon, he was resolved to go to his father without an hour's delay and represent to the Duke exactly how the whole case stood. This he would do with all the powers of supplication which were at his command. He would be urgent, piteous, submissive, and eloquent. In any other matter he would promise to make whatever arrangements his father might desire,—or if sacrifices were necessary, whatever sacrifices;—by which latter assurance to himself he intended to signify that he would be ready to tell his constituents that they must either allow him to sit as a Liberal or to vacate the seat. He would make his father understand that all his happiness depended on this marriage, that it was everything to him; that, having married, he would settle down, even at Gatherum Castle if the Duke should wish it;—that as a married man he would not think of race-horses, that he would desert the Beargarden, that he would learn blue-books by heart, and only do as much shooting and hunting as would become a young nobleman in his position. All this he would say as eagerly and as pleasantly as it might be said. But he would add to all this an assurance of his unchangeable intention. It was his purpose to marry Isabel Boncassen. If he could do this with his father's good-will,—so best. But at any rate he would marry her! How this was to be done in the teeth of what Mr. Boncassen had said to him he had not as yet made up his mind; but he had distant ideas of a temporary but prolonged emigration to the United States in case he should be driven to emergencies. He conceived that neither Isabel nor her father would be able to withstand such a test of his love; and he also, perhaps, conceived that a father, with a father's usual weakness, would yield rather than succumb to so great an evil. The system of primogeniture, which is salutary to the prosperity and permanence of the country at large, is sometimes detrimental to the authority of fathers;—a fact of which elder sons become aware at an early age. When a most respectable and very Protestant Irish nobleman had positively refused to pay his son's debts for the third or fourth time, he was reduced to compliance by a threat on his son's part of conversion to the Church of Rome. There was perhaps some malice in this; whereas Silverbridge certainly bore no malice against his father. But he was determined that Isabel Boncassen should be his wife.

On that Sunday afternoon when the fever heat of his love was upon him, he went at once in search of his father; but unluckily the Duke was not to be found. At the house it was only known that he was dining out. On the following morning, though the lover's ardour was not diminished, his discretion was increased. This thing which he had to do was difficult, and he was not now so sure of his eloquence as when he had just left Mr. Boncassen's house. Might it perhaps be better that he should write a letter? He absolutely did write a letter in which, to the best of his abilities, he poured out all his heart and all his wishes. But, when it was written, he found that his father had left town. No notice had been left for him as to the Duke's departure; but the butler had understood from the Duke's own man that the Duke had gone with Mr. Monk down to Longroyston. Now Longroyston was the country seat of the Duke of St. Bungay; and it was manifest to Silverbridge that such a journey at such a time of year to such a place with such a companion could have been made only in reference to political expectations. Under these circumstances he did not send his letter, but again changed his mind, resolving that he would await his father's return.

The world at the time was altogether busy with political rumours; and it was supposed that Sir Timothy Beeswax would do something very clever. It was supposed also that he would sever himself at any rate from some of his present companions. On that point everybody was agreed,—and on that point only everybody was right. Lord Drummond, who was the titular Prime Minister, and Sir Timothy had, during a considerable part of the last session, and through the whole vacation, so belauded each other in all their public expressions that it was quite manifest that they had quarrelled. When any body of Statesmen make public asseverations, by one or various voices, that there is no discord among them, not a dissentient voice on any subject, people are apt to suppose that they cannot hang together much longer. It is the man who has no peace at home that declares abroad that his wife is an angel. He who lives on comfortable terms with the partner of his troubles can afford to acknowledge the ordinary rubs of life. Old Mr. Mildmay, who was Prime Minister for so many years, and whom his party worshipped, used to say that he had never found a gentleman who had quite agreed with him all round; but Sir Timothy has always been in exact accord with all his colleagues,—till he has left them, or they him. Never had there been such concord as of late,—and men, clubs, and newspapers now predicted that as a natural consequence there would soon be a break-up.

But not on that account would it perhaps be necessary that Sir Timothy should resign,—or at any rate not necessary that his resignation should be permanent. The Conservative majority had dwindled,—but still there was supposed to be a majority. It certainly was the case that Lord Drummond could not get on without Sir Timothy. No one supposed that he would attempt to do so. But might it not be possible that Sir Timothy should get on without Lord Drummond? If so he must begin his action in this direction by resigning. He would have to place his resignation, no doubt with infinite regret, in the hands of Lord Drummond. But if such a step were to be taken now, just as Parliament was about to assemble, what would become of the Queen's speech, of the address, and of the noble peers and noble and other commoners who were to propose and second it in the two Houses of Parliament? There were those who said that such a trick played at the last moment would be very shabby. But then again there were those who foresaw that the shabbiness would be made to rest anywhere rather than on the shoulders of Sir Timothy. If it should turn out that he had striven manfully to make things run smoothly, and had only given way at last when his conscience and his loyalty were no longer comfortable;—if it should turn out that anyone was in fault rather than Sir Timothy;—that the Premier's incompetence, or the Chancellor's obstinacy, or this or that Secretary's peculiarity of temper had done it all;—might not Sir Timothy then be able to emerge from the confused flood, and swim along pleasantly with his head higher than ever above the waters?

In these great matters parliamentary management goes for so much! If a man be really clever and handy at his trade, if he can work hard and knows what he is about, if he can give and take and be not thin-skinned or sore-boned,* if he can ask pardon for a peccadillo and seem to be sorry with a good grace, if above all things he be able to surround himself with the prestige of success, then so much will be forgiven him! Great gifts of eloquence are hardly wanted, or a deep-seated patriotism which is capable of strong indignation. A party has to be managed, and he who can manage it best, will probably be its best Leader. The subordinate task of legislation, if there must be legislation, and of executive government, may well fall into the inferior hands of less astute practitioners. It was admitted on both sides that there was no man like Sir Timothy for managing the House or for coercing a party, and there was therefore a general feeling that it would be a pity that Sir Timothy should be squeezed out. He knew all the little secrets of the business;—could always arrange, let the cause be what it might, to get a full House for himself and his friends, and empty benches for his opponents,—could foresee a thousand little things to which even a Walpole

would have been blind, which a Pitt would not have condescended to
regard, but with which his familiarity made him a very comfortable
Leader of the House of Commons for those who chose to go along with
him. There were various ideas prevalent as to the politics of the coming
session; but the prevailing idea was probably in favour of Sir Timothy.

The Duke was absent from Sunday the 6th till the morning of Friday
the 11th, on which day Parliament was to meet. On that morning at
about noon a letter came to the son saying that his father had returned
and would be glad to see him if he were disengaged. Silverbridge too
was of course going to the House on that day and was not without his
own political anxieties. If Lord Drummond remained in, he thought
that he must, at any rate for the present, stand by the party which he
had adopted. If, however, Sir Timothy should become Prime Minister
there would be a loophole for escape. There were some three or four
besides himself who detested Sir Timothy, and in such case he thought
that he might perhaps have company in his desertion. All this was on
his mind; but through all this he was aware that there was a matter of
much deeper moment which required his energies. When his father's
message was brought to him, and he thus heard of his father's return,
he told himself at once that now was the time for his eloquence.

'Well, Silverbridge,' said the Duke, 'and how are matters going on
with you?' There seemed to be something in his father's manner more
than ordinarily jocund and good-humoured,—as it might have been
had he heard that Sir Timothy had been banished into private life
for ever.

'With me, sir?'

'I don't mean to ask any party secrets. If you and Sir Timothy understand each other, of course you will be discreet.'

'I can't be discreet, sir, because I don't know anything about him.
I suppose you have, all of you, been arranging something.'

'No, indeed. We have been discussing matters which do not as yet
seem to admit of any arrangement. So your friend Lord Nidderdale
seconds the address.'

'Two hours after I had written my refusal he had the offer brought to
him in my presence. That was droll.'

'I hope you had not told him.'

'He had heard all about it. But that would not worry him, sir. He has
no conceit of that kind.'

'When I heard afterwards,' said the Duke smiling, 'of your being in
close conference with Sir Timothy——'

'I, sir!'

'Yes, you. Mr. Boncassen told me that you and he were so deeply taken up with each other at his house, that nobody could get a word with either of you.'

'Have you seen Mr. Boncassen?' asked the son, whose attention was immediately diverted from his father's political badinage.

'Yes;—I have seen him. I happened to meet him where I was dining last Sunday, and he walked home with me. He was so intent upon what he was saying that I fear he allowed me to take him out of his way.'

'What was he talking about?' said Silverbridge. All his preparations, all his eloquence, all his method, now seemed to have departed from him. He knew that that one peculiar subject must be discussed now, at this moment; but he could not stop to think how he might best word his request. He felt sure that it had been discussed already between his father and Mr. Boncassen. The fact that the American had come out of his way would never have been mentioned to him had there not been some such cause. But he could form no judgment from his father's manner of the result of that conversation.

'He was talking about you,' said the Duke.

'He had told me that he wanted to see you. I should have asked you to go to him, but when I inquired for you, you had left town. What did he say, sir?'

'I suppose you can guess what he said. He wished to know what I thought of the offer you have made to his daughter.'

The subject had come up so easily, so readily,—this question as to which he had thought that it must be introduced by him with the greatest care,—that he was almost aghast when he found himself in the middle of it before it had been introduced at all. And yet he must speak on the matter, and that at once. He paused, expecting that his father would probably tell him what reply had been made to Mr. Boncassen; but the Duke seemed to think that it was now his son's turn to make some remark.

'I hope you raised no objection, sir,' he said.

'The objection came mainly from him; and I am bound to say that every word that fell from him was spoken with great good sense.'

'But still he asked you to consent?'

'By no means. He made no request to me of any kind. He told me his opinion,—and then he asked me a question.'

'I am sure he did not say that we ought not to be married.'

'He did say that he thought you ought not to be married, if——'

'If what, sir?'

'If there were any probability that his daughter would not be well received as your wife. Then he asked me what would be my reception of her.' Silverbridge looked up into his father's face with beseeching, imploring eyes as though everything now depended on the next few words that he might utter. 'I shall think it an unfortunate marriage,' continued the Duke. Silverbridge when he heard this at once knew that he had gained his cause. His father had spoken of the marriage as a thing that was to happen, a thing which, not might be, but which was in the future. A joyous light dawned in his eyes, and the look of pain went from his brow, all which the Duke was not slow to perceive. 'I shall think it an unfortunate marriage,' he continued, repeating his words; 'but I was bound to tell him that were Miss Boncassen to become your wife she would also become my daughter.'

'Oh, sir.'

'I told him why the marriage would be distasteful to me. Whether I may be wrong or right I think it to be for the good of our country, for the good of our order, for the good of our own individual families, that we should support each other by marriage. It is not as though we were a narrow class, already too closely bound together by family alliances. The room for choice might be wide enough for you without going across the Atlantic to look for her who is to preside over your home, and be the mother of your children.'

'It was she that came. I did not go.'

'It is the same. To this Mr. Boncassen replied that he was bound to look solely to his daughter's happiness,—and to yours, of course, as bound up with hers.'

'Of course it will be, sir.'

'He meant me to understand that he cared nothing for my feelings. Why should he? That which to me is deep wisdom is to him an empty prejudice. He asked me then how others would receive her.'

'I am sure that everybody would like her,' said Silverbridge.

'That is a very strong word. I like her. I like her very much.'

'I am so glad!' shouted Silverbridge.

'But still all this is a sorrow to me. When, however, he put that question to me about the world around her,—as to those among whom her lot would be cast, I could not say that I thought she would be rejected.'

'Oh, no!' The idea of rejecting Isabel! Had he not already seen enough of her to know that, go where she might, she would be the chosen companion of all with whom she chose to associate?

'She has a brightness and a grace all her own,' continued the Duke, 'which will ensure her acceptance in all societies.'

'Yes, yes;—it is just that, sir.'

'You will be a nine days' wonder,—the foolish young nobleman who chose to marry an American!'

'I think it will be just the other way up, sir,—among the men. I don't know what the women may say.'

'But her place will I think be secure to her. That is what I told Mr. Boncassen.'

'It is all right with him then,—now?'

'If you call it all right. You will understand of course that you are acting in opposition to my advice,—and my wishes.'

'What am I to say, sir?' exclaimed Silverbridge, almost in despair. 'When I love the girl better than my life, and when you tell me that she can be mine if I choose to take her; when I have asked her to be my wife, and have got her to say that she likes me; when her father has given way, and all the rest of it, would it be possible that I should say now that I will give her up? What would you think of it yourself? Is it not impossible?'

'My opinion is to go for nothing,—in anything!' The Duke as he said this knew that he was expressing aloud a feeling which should have been restrained within his own bosom. It was natural that there should have been such plaints. The same suffering must be encountered in regard to Tregear and his daughter. In every way he had been thwarted. In every direction he was driven to yield. In all that he had done he had been tender-hearted, honest, and forbearing. In what had he ever consulted pleasures or even tastes of his own? And yet now he had to undergo rebuke, to undergo deserved rebuke from his own son, because one of these inward plaints would force itself from his lips. Of course this girl was to be taken in among the Pallisers and treated with an almost idolatrous love,—as perfect as though 'all the blood of all the Howards'* were running in her veins. What further inch of ground was there for a fight? And if the fight were over, why should he rob his boy of one sparkle from off the joy of his triumph? Silverbridge was now standing before him abashed by that plaint, inwardly sustained no doubt by the conviction of his great success, but subdued by his father's wailing. 'However,—perhaps we had better let that pass,' said the Duke, with a long sigh. Then Silverbridge took his father's hand, and looked up in his face. 'I most sincerely hope that she may make you a good and loving wife,' said the Duke, 'and that she may do her duty by you in that not very easy sphere of life to which she will be called.'

'I am quite sure she will,' said Silverbridge, whose ideas as to Isabel's duties were confined at present to a feeling that she would now have to give him kisses without stint.

'I am bound to say that what I have seen of her personally recommends her to me,' said the Duke. 'Some girls are fools——'

'That's quite true, sir.'

'Who think that the world is to be nothing but laughing, dancing, and going to parties.'

'Many have been doing it for so many years,' said Silverbridge, 'that they can't understand that there should be an end of it.'

'A wife ought to feel the great responsibility of her position. I hope she will.'

'And the sooner she begins the better,' said Silverbridge stoutly.

'But there is one thing, Silverbridge,' said the Duke very gravely, 'which I cannot understand. I hope you will give me credit for a desire to make you happy.'

'Indeed I do.'

'And that you do not think that I would willingly say a word to trouble you. What am I to understand about Lady Mabel?' Upon hearing Lady Mabel's name Silverbridge looked rather blank. 'It was you yourself who suggested it.'

'I thought I had explained all that, sir.'

'It is a pity that you should have spoken to me, as you did last year. I am afraid she will have been made to suffer.' There was, however, nothing more to be said upon that less fortunate branch of the subject; and as Silverbridge was dumb the father did not press it.

'And now,' said the Duke, looking at his watch, 'we might as well have lunch and go down to the House. I will walk with you if you please. It will be about time for each of us.' Then the son was forced to go down and witness the somewhat faded ceremony of seeing Parliament opened by three lords sitting in commission before the throne. Whereas but for such stress as his father had laid upon him, he would have disregarded his parliamentary duties and have rushed at once up to Brook Street with the good news. As it was he was so handed over from one political pundit to another, was so buttonholed by Sir Timothy, so chaffed as to the address by Phineas Finn, and at last so occupied with the whole matter that he found himself compelled to sit in his place till he had heard Nidderdale make his speech. This the young Scotch Lord did so well, and received so much praise for the doing of it, and looked so well in his uniform, and was altogether so great a man on the occasion, that Silverbridge almost regretted the opportunity he had lost. And then, when Mr. Monk got up to give his reasons for not opposing the address at the present moment, following as he did so Sir Timothy, who had been eloquent, good-humoured, and enigmatic,—for up to this moment the expected rupture had not taken place,—Silverbridge heard him to the end. The crisis was an interesting one, and Isabel would be more probably at home at half-past six than at half-past five.

At seven the sitting was over, the speeches, though full of interest, having been shorter than usual. They had been full of interest, but nobody understood in the least what was going to happen. 'I don't know anything about the Prime Minister,' said Mr. Lupton as he left the House with our hero and another not very staunch supporter of the Government, 'but I'll back Sir Timothy to be the Leader of the House on the last day of the session,—against all comers. I don't think it much matters who is Prime Minister nowadays.' In the evening that was the opinion at most of the political clubs.

At half-past seven Silverbridge was at the door in Brook Street. Yes; Miss Boncassen was at home. The servant thought that she was upstairs dressing. Then Silverbridge, who had by this time called at the house often enough to be very well known to all the servants, made his way without further invitation into the drawing-room. There he remained alone for ten minutes. At last the door opened, and Mrs. Boncassen entered. 'Dear, dear, Lord Silverbridge, who ever dreamed of seeing you? I thought all you Parliament gentlemen were going through your ceremonies. Isabel had a ticket, and went down, and saw your father.'

'Where is Isabel?'

'She's gone.'

'Gone! Where on earth has she gone to?' asked Silverbridge, as though fearing lest she had been already carried off to the other side of the Atlantic. Then Mrs. Boncassen explained. Within the last three minutes Mrs. Montacute Jones had called and carried Isabel off to the play. Mrs. Jones was up in town for a week and this had been a very old engagement. 'I hope you did not want her very particularly,' said Mrs. Boncassen.

'But I did,—most particularly,' said Lord Silverbridge. The door was opened and Mr. Boncassen entered the room. 'I beg your pardon for coming at such a time,' said the lover, 'but I did so want to see Isabel.'

'I rather think she wants to see you,' said the father.

'I shall go to the theatre after her.'

'That might be awkward,—particularly as I doubt whether anybody knows what theatre they are gone to. Can I receive a message for her, my Lord?' This was certainly not what Lord Silverbridge had intended,—to send the last loving word which was to settle everything between them as a message by her father! 'You know, perhaps, that I have seen the Duke.'

'Oh yes;—and I have seen him. Everything is settled.'

'That is the only message she will want to hear when she comes home. She is a happy girl, and I am proud to think that I should live to

call such a grand young Briton as you my son-in-law. I like all that
I have seen of you, sir, and I think that she is a lucky girl.' Then the
American took the young man's two hands and shook them cordially,
while Mrs. Boncassen bursting into tears insisted on kissing his
forehead.

'Indeed she is a happy girl,' said she; 'but I hope Isabel won't be carried away too high and mighty.' Lord Silverbridge as he went away to
dine at his club was not quite contented with the results of the evening.

CHAPTER 72

CARLTON TERRACE

THREE days after this, on the Sunday afternoon, it was arranged that
Isabel should be taken to Carlton Terrace to be accepted there into the
full good graces of her future father-in-law, and to go through the
pleasant ceremony of seeing the house in which it was to be her destiny
to live as mistress. What can be more interesting to a girl than this first
visit to her future home? Some matter-of-fact critic will say that the
first word of assurance from the man who is to give her the home must
be much more interesting. No doubt. The man is more than the
house,—or ought to be; as heaven is,—or ought to be,—more than
earth. But among earthly things, of all mere material comforts, the
house to the woman must stand first. It is to be the scene of her joys, her
labours, and her troubles. To a man his house is, comparatively, but as
a kennel to a dog. It is a convenience and he likes to have it well arranged.
But to the woman it is a temple sacred to the gods;—her own temple
sacred to her own gods. And then the change to be made is so great,—so
sudden! Hitherto she has probably had other shrines, her own sacred
places, her own Penates,*—which she has shared with her mother;
which have grown into her heart, unconsciously, from early years;
which she has loved without knowing that she has loved them,—and
which now must be her own no longer! These new altars are to be prepared for her with all a lover's care, and are to be doubly dear to her
because they are to be given to her by her lover. But everything will be
strange to her, and though it is probable that her taste may be consulted, she will be too abashed by the novelty of her position to do
much more than assent to all that he proposes. There can be no corner
in the house, no closet, no little coign* of vantage or of discomfort, no
charm of colour, no dark receptacle for hidden properties, which will

not have an interest of its own. Every chair and every table has to be a friend,—or perhaps an enemy. There will be no morsel of china, no little gilded ornament, no book, no domestic article with which it will not be her duty and her delight to become familiar. Everything must be of moment, either to please or to displease.

And now Isabel Boncassen was to make her first visit to the house in Carlton Terrace, which the Duke had already declared his purpose of surrendering to the young couple. She was going among very grand things,—so grand that those whose affairs in life are less magnificent may think that her mind should have soared altogether above chairs and tables, and reposed itself among diamonds, gold and silver ornaments, rich necklaces, the old masters, and alabaster statuary. But dukes and duchesses must sit upon chairs,—or at any rate on sofas,—as well as their poorer brethren, and probably have the same regard for their comfort. Isabel was not above her future furniture, or the rooms that were to be her rooms, or the stairs which she would have to tread, or the pillow on which her head must rest. She had never yet seen even the outside of the house in which she was to live, and was now prepared to make her visit with as much enthusiasm as though her future abode was to be prepared for her in a small house in a small street beyond Islington.*

But the Duke was no doubt more than the house, the father-in-law more than the tables. Isabel, in the ordinary way of society, had already known him with quite as close an intimacy as will generally take place between a host and one of his younger guests,—for her host had distinguished her by his personal attention. She, the while, had been well aware that if all things could possibly be made to run smoothly with her, this lordly host, who was so pleasantly courteous to her, would become her father-in-law. But she had known also that he, in his courtesy, had been altogether unaware of any such intention on her part, and that she would now present herself to him in an aspect very different from that in which she had hitherto been regarded. She was well aware that the Duke had not wished to take her into his family,—would not himself have chosen her for his son's wife. She had seen enough to make her sure that he had even chosen another bride for his heir. She had been quite clever enough to perceive that Lady Mabel Grex had been not only selected,—but almost accepted as though the thing had been certain. She had learned nearly the whole truth from Silverbridge, who was not good at keeping a secret from one to whom his heart was open. That story had been all but read by her with exactness. 'I cannot lose you now,' she had said to him, leaning on his arm;—this had occurred since that evening on which she had so wickedly taken herself off to the theatre with Mrs. Montacute Jones,—'I cannot afford to lose you now. But I fear that someone else is losing you.' To this he answered nothing, but simply pressed her closer to his side. 'Someone else,' she continued, 'who perhaps may have reason to think that you have injured her.' 'No,' he said boldly, 'no; there is no such person.' For he had never ceased to assure himself that in all that matter with Mabel Grex he had been guilty of no treachery. There had been a moment, indeed, in which she might have taken him; but she had chosen to let it pass from her. All of which,—or nearly all of which,—Isabel now saw, and had seen also that the Duke had been a consenting party to that other arrangement. She had reason therefore to doubt the manner of her acceptance. How could it be that such a one as the Duke of Omnium should receive her into his house with real good-will!

But she had been accepted. She had made such acceptance by him a stipulation in her acceptance of his son. She was sure of the ground on which she trod and was determined to carry herself, if not with pride, yet with personal dignity. There might be difficulties before her, but it should not be her fault if she were not as good a countess, and,—when time would have it so,—as good a duchess as another.

The visit at last was made not quite in the fashion which Silverbridge himself had wished. His idea had been to call for Isabel in his cab and take her down to Carlton Terrace. 'Mother must go with me,' she had said. Then he looked very blank,—as he could look when he was disappointed, as he had looked when she would not talk to him at the lunch, when she told him that it was not her business to entertain him. 'Don't be selfish,' she added, laughing. 'Do you think that mother will not want to have seen the house that I am to live in, and to feel that she knows something of my whereabouts?'

'She shall come afterwards as often as she likes.'

'What;—paying me morning visits from New York! She must come now, if you please. Love me, love my mother.'

'I am awfully fond of her,' said Silverbridge, who felt that he really had behaved well to the old lady.

'So am I—and therefore she shall go and see the house. Now you are as good as gold,—and do everything just as I tell you. But a good time is coming, when I shall have to do everything that you tell me.' Then it was arranged that Mrs. and Miss Boncassen were to be taken down to the house in their own carriage, and were to be received at the door by Lord Silverbridge.

Another arrangement had also been made. Isabel was to be taken to the Duke immediately upon her arrival and to be left for a while with him, alone, so that he might express himself as he might find fit to do to this newly adopted child. It was a matter to him of such importance that nothing remaining to him in his life could equal it. It was not simply that she was to be the wife of his son,—though that in itself was a consideration very sacred. Had it been Gerald who was bringing to him a bride, the occasion would have had less of awe. But this girl, this American girl, was to be the mother and grandmother of future Dukes of Omnium,—the ancestress, it was to be hoped, of all future Dukes of Omnium! By what she might be, by what she might have in her of mental fibre, of high or low quality, of true or untrue womanliness, were to be fashioned those who in days to come might be amongst the strongest and most faithful bulwarks of the constitution. An England without a Duke of Omnium,—or at any rate without any duke,—what would it be? And yet he knew that with bad dukes his country would be in worse stress than though she had none at all. An aristocracy;—yes; but an aristocracy that shall be of the very best! He believed himself thoroughly in his order; but if his order, or many of his order, should become as was now Lord Grex, then he thought that his order not only must go to the wall but that, in the cause of humanity, it had better do so. With all this daily, hourly, always in his mind, this matter of the choice of a wife for his heir was to him of solemn importance.

When they arrived Silverbridge was there to help them out of the carriage, and led them first of all into the dining-room. 'My!' said Mrs. Boncassen, as she looked around her. 'I thought that our Fifth Avenue parlours whipped everything,—in the way of city houses.'

'What a nice little room for Darby and Joan to sit down to eat a mutton-chop in,' said Isabel.

'It's a beastly great barrack,' said Silverbridge;—'but the best of it is that we never use it. We'll have a cosy little place for Darby and Joan;—you'll see.' Then he at once led her away to her destiny. 'Now come to the governor. I've got to leave you with him.'

'Oh me! I am in such a fright!'

'He can't eat you,' said Mrs. Boncassen.

'And he won't even bite,' said Silverbridge.

'I should not mind that because I could bite again. But if he looks as though he thought I shouldn't do, I shall drop.'

'My belief is that he's almost as much in love with you as I am,' said Silverbridge, as he took her to the door of the Duke's room. 'Here we are, sir.'

'My dear,' said the Duke, rising up and coming to her, 'I am very glad to see you. It is good of you to come to me.' Then he took her in both his hands and kissed her forehead and her lips. She, as she put her face up to him, stood quite still in his embrace, but her eyes were bright with pleasure.

'Shall I leave her?' said Silverbridge.

'For a few minutes.'

'Don't keep her too long, for I want to take her all over the house.'

'A few minutes;—and then I will bring her up to the drawing-room.' Upon this the door was closed, and Isabel was alone with her new father. 'And so, my dear, you are to be my child.'

'If you will have me.'

'Come here and sit down by me. Your father has already told you that,—has he not?'

'He has told me that you had consented.'

'And Silverbridge has said as much?'

'I would sooner hear it from you than from either of them.'

'Then hear it from me. You shall be my child. And if you will love me you shall be very dear to me. You shall be my own child,—as dear as my own. I must either love his wife very dearly or else I must be an unhappy man. And she must love me dearly, or I must be unhappy.'

'I will love you,' she said, pressing his hand.

'And now let me say some few words to you,—only let there be no bitterness in them to your young heart. When I say that I take you to my heart you may be sure that I do so thoroughly,—without any inward drawback. You shall be as dear to me and as near as though you had been all English.'

'Shall I?'

'There shall no difference be made. My boy's wife shall be my daughter in very deed. But I had not wished it to be so.'

'I knew that;—but could I have given him up?'

'He at any rate could not give you up. There were little prejudices. You can understand that.'

'Oh, yes.'

'We who wear black coats could not bring ourselves readily to put on scarlet garments; nor should we sit comfortably with our legs crossed like Turks.'

'I am your scarlet coat and your cross-legged Turk,' she said, with feigned self-reproach in her voice, but with a sparkle of mirth in her eye.

'But when I have once got into my scarlet coat I can be very proud of it, and when I am once seated in my divan I shall find it of all postures the easiest. Do you understand me?'

'I think so.'

'Not a shade of any prejudice shall be left to darken my mind. There shall be no feeling but that you are in truth his chosen wife. After all neither can country, nor race, nor rank, nor wealth make a good woman. Education can do much. But nature must have done much also.'

'Do not expect too much of me.'

'I will so expect that all shall be taken for the best. You know, I think, that I have liked you since I first saw you.'

'I know that you have always been very, very good to me.'

'I have liked you from the first. That you are lovely perhaps is no merit;—though, to speak the truth, I am well pleased that Silverbridge should have found so much beauty.'

'That is all a matter of taste, I suppose,' she said, laughing.

'But there is much that a young woman may do for herself which I think you have done.'

'I am glad of that.'

'A silly girl, though she had been a second Helen, would hardly have satisfied me.'

'Or perhaps him,' said Isabel.

'Or him; and it is in that feeling that I find my chief satisfaction,—that he should have had the sense to have liked such a one as you better than others. Now I have said it. As not being one of us I did at first object to his choice. As being what you are yourself, I am altogether reconciled to it. Do not keep him long waiting.'

'I do not think he likes to be kept waiting for anything.'

'I dare say not. I dare say not. And now there is one thing else.' Then the Duke unlocked a little drawer that was close to his hand, and taking out a ring put it on her finger. It was a bar of diamonds, perhaps a dozen of them, fixed in a little circlet of gold. 'This must never leave you,' he said.

'It never shall,—having come from you.'

'It was the first present that I gave to my wife, and it is the first that I give to you. You may imagine how sacred it is to me. On no other hand could it be worn without something which to me would be akin to sacrilege. Now I must not keep you longer or Silverbridge will be storming about the house. He of course will tell me when it is to be; but do not you keep him long waiting.' Then he kissed her again and led her up into the drawing-room. When he had spoken a word of greeting to Mrs. Boncassen, he left them to their own devices.

After that they spent the best part of an hour in going over the house; but even that was done in a manner unsatisfactory to Silverbridge. Wherever Isabel went, there Mrs. Boncassen went also. There might

have been some fun in showing even the back kitchens to his bride-
elect, by herself;—but there was none in wandering about those vast
underground regions with a stout old lady who was really interested
with the cooking apparatus and the washhouses. The bedrooms one
after another became tedious to him when Mrs. Boncassen would make
communications respecting each of them to her daughter. 'That is
Gerald's room,' said Silverbridge. 'You have never seen Gerald. He is
such a brick.' Mrs. Boncassen was charmed with the whips and sticks
and boxing-gloves in Gerald's room, and expressed an opinion that
young men in the States mostly carried their knick-knacks about with
them to the Universities. When she was told that he had another collection of knick-knacks at Matching, and another at Oxford, she thought
that he was a very extravagant young man. Isabel, who had heard all
about the gambling in Scotland, looked round at her lover and smiled.

'Well, my dear,' said Mrs. Boncassen, as they took their leave, 'it is
a very grand house, and I hope with all my heart you may have your
health there and be happy. But I don't know that you'll be any happier
because it's so big.'

'Or any unhappier,' said Isabel, 'if we only remember that a house is
no more than a house.'

'Wait till you see Gatherum,' said Silverbridge. 'That, I own, does
make me unhappy. It has been calculated that three months at Gatherum
Castle would drive a philosopher mad.'

In all this there had been a certain amount of disappointment for
Silverbridge; but on that evening, before dinner in Brook Street, he
received compensation. As the day was one somewhat peculiar in its
nature he decided that it should be kept altogether as a holiday, and he
did not therefore go down to the House. And not going to the House of
course he spent the time with the Boncassens. 'You know you ought to
go,' Isabel said to him when they found themselves alone together in
the back drawing-room.

'Of course I ought.'

'Then go. Do you think I would keep a Briton from his duties?'

'Not though the constitution should fall in ruins. Do you suppose that
a man wants no rest after inspecting all the pots and pans in that establishment? A woman, I believe, could go on doing that kind of thing all day long.'

'You should remember at least that the—woman—was interesting
herself about your pots and pans.'

'And now, Bella, tell me what the governor said to you.' Then she
showed him the ring. 'Did he give you that?' She nodded her head in
assent. 'I did not think he would ever have parted with that.'

'It was your mother's.'

'She wore it always. I almost think that I never saw her hand without it. He would not have given you that unless he had meant to be very good to you.'

'He was very good to me. Silverbridge, I have a great deal to do, to learn to be your wife.'

'I'll teach you.'

'Yes; you'll teach me. But will you teach me right? There is something almost awful in your father's serious dignity and solemn appreciation of the responsibilities of his position. Will you ever come to that?'

'I shall never be a great man,—as he is.'

'Why not? Or is it only because you are younger?'

'There is something in that I suppose.'

'It seems to me that life to him is a load,—which he does not object to carry, but which he knows must be carried with a great struggle.'

'I suppose it ought to be so with everyone.'

'Yes,' she said, 'but the higher you put your foot on the ladder the more constant should be your thought that your stepping requires care. I almost fear that I am climbing too high.'

'You can't come down now, my young woman.'

'I have to go on now,—and do it as best I can. I will try to do my best. I will try to do my best. I told him so, and now I tell you so. I will try to do my best.'

'Perhaps after all I am only a "pert poppet," ' she said half an hour afterwards, for Silverbridge had told her of that terrible mistake made by poor Dolly Longstaffe.

'Brute!' he exclaimed.

'Not at all. And when we are settled down in the real Darby and Joan way I shall hope to see Mr. Longstaffe very often. I dare say he won't call me a pert poppet, and I shall not remind him of the word. But I shall always think of it; and remembering the way in which my character struck an educated Englishman,—who was not altogether ill-disposed towards me,—I may hope to improve myself.'

CHAPTER 73

'I HAVE NEVER LOVED YOU'

IT was now nearly the end of February and Silverbridge had been in town three or four weeks. Lady Mabel Grex had also been in London all that time, as he was well aware; and yet he had not seen her. They certainly had not parted as enemies, though their last interview had been of such a nature as hardly to admit of an immediate renewal of friendship. She had told him that she loved him and had asked him plainly to make her his wife. He had told her that he could not and would not do so,—that he was altogether resolved to make another woman his wife. Then she had rebuked him, and had demanded from him how he had dared to treat her as he had done. His conscience was clear. He had his own code of morals as to such matters, and had, as he regarded it, kept within the law. But she thought that she was badly treated;—or at any rate had not scrupled to say that she thought so. And then, when he had told her that he was quite resolved,—that his destiny in regard to marriage was fixed,—she had declared that she was now left out in the cold for ever through his treachery. Then her last word had been almost the worst of all, 'Who can tell what may come to pass?'—showing too plainly that she would not even now give up her hope. In such circumstances as these, though he was still anxious to regard her as a friend, he could hardly go to see her. Of what could he talk to her,—he whose mind was now full only of Isabel Boncassen?

But she thought differently,—so differently that before the month was up she wrote to him as follows:

'DEAR LORD SILVERBRIDGE,

'Why do you not come and see me? Are friends so plentiful with you, that one so staunch as I may be thrown aside as unnecessary? But of course I know why you do not come. Put all that aside,—and come. I certainly cannot hurt you, nor will you hurt me. I have learned to feel that certain things which the world regards as too awful to be talked of,—except in the way of scandal,—such as the unfortunate aspirations of unfortunate maidens, may be discussed and then laid aside just like other subjects. What though I wear a wig or a wooden leg, I may still be fairly comfortable among my companions unless I crucify myself by trying to hide my misfortune. It is not the presence of the skeleton that crushes us,—not even that will hurt us much, if we let him go about the house as he lists. It is the everlasting effort which the horror makes to peep out of his cupboard in which we so vainly try to hide him that robs us of our ease. When all who know me know all my little troubles, then I think I shall be, not happy, but comfortable. At any rate come and see me.

'Of course I know that you are to be married to Miss Boncassen. Who does not know it? The trumpeters have been at work for the last week.

'Your very sincere Friend,
'MABEL.'

He very much wished that she had not written. Of course he must go to her. And though there was a word or two in her letter which angered him, his feelings towards her were kindly. Had not that American angel flown across the Atlantic to his arms he could have been well content to make her his wife. He would tell himself that over and over again, even now! But an interview at the present moment could hardly be other than painful. She could, she said, talk of her own misfortunes,—that is of her disappointed love for himself,—but the subject would be very painful to him. It was not to him exactly a skeleton, to be locked out of sight; but it had been a misfortune, and the sooner that such misfortunes could be buried and forgotten the better.

And then he was also angry with her. He knew what she meant about trumpeters. So at least he told himself. She had intended to signify that Isabel in her pride had boasted of her matrimonial prospects. Of course there had been trumpets. Are there not always trumpets when a marriage is contemplated magnificent enough to be called an alliance? As for that he himself had blown the trumpets. Asserting to himself in his own fashion that 'secrets are beastly bothers,' he had told everybody that he was going to be married to Miss Boncassen. Isabel had blown no trumpets. In her own straightforward way she had told the truth to whom it concerned. Of course he would go and see Lady Mabel, but he trusted that for her own sake nothing would be said about trumpets. He would be very gentle, very courteous, very kind, so long as no word was said imputing fault to Isabel.

'So you have come at last,' Mabel said when he entered the room. 'No;—Miss Cassewary is not here. As I wanted to see you alone I got her to go out this morning. Why did you not come before?'

'You said in your letter that you knew why.'

'But in saying so I was accusing you of cowardice;—was I not?'

'It was not cowardice.'

'What was it then? And why did you not come?'

'I thought you would hardly wish to see me so soon,—after what passed.'

'That is honest at any rate. You felt that I must be too much ashamed of what I said when we were last together to be able to look you in the face.'

'Not that exactly.'

'No;—not exactly, but very nearly. Any other man would have felt the same, but no other man would be honest enough to tell me so. I do not think that ever in your life you have constrained yourself to the civility of a lie.'

'I hope not.'

'To be civil and false is often better than to be harsh and true. I may be soothed by the courtesy and yet not deceived by the lie. But what I told you in my letter,—which I hope you have destroyed——'

'I will destroy it.'

'Do. It was not intended for the partner of your future joys. As I told you then I can talk freely, at any rate to you, about all that there has been between us. Why not? We know it,—both of us. How your conscience may be, I cannot tell; but mine is,—no, not clear; but clear from that soil with which you think it should be smirched.'

'I think nothing of the sort.'

'Yes, Silverbridge, you do. You have said to yourself this;—"That girl has determined to get me, and she has not scrupled as to how she would do it." '

'No such idea has ever crossed my mind. It is not in my nature to think like that.'

'But you have never told yourself of the encouragement which you gave me. You have never said to yourself that it was because you had invited me to love you that I found myself driven to appeal to you when you told me that I was to be—abandoned. Such condemnation as I have spoken of would have been just if my efforts had been sanctioned by no words, no looks, no deeds from you. Did you give me warrant for thinking that you were my lover?'

He did not know what to say to her. That theory by which he had justified himself so completely to himself seemed to fall away from him under her questioning. He could not now remember what had been his very words to her in those old days before Miss Boncassen had crossed his path; but he did know that in that very room he had once intended to make her understand that he loved her. She had not understood him;—or, understanding, had not accepted his words; and therefore he had thought himself free. But it now seemed that he had not been entitled so to regard himself. There she sat, looking at him, waiting for his answer; and he who had been so sure that he had committed no sin against her, had not a word to say to her. He could not assert that he had not given her the warrant of which she spoke.

'I want your answer to that, Lord Silverbridge. I have told you that I would have no skeleton in the cupboard. Down at Matching, and before that at Killancodlem, I appealed to you, asking you to take me as your wife. Did I not?'

'Hardly that.'

'Altogether that! I will have nothing denied that I have done,—nor will I be ashamed of anything. I did do so. And I did it the second time, even after I had heard of this infatuation.' Then he scowled at her because by that latter word she alluded to Isabel. But as Isabel was assuredly his own he did not find it necessary to interrupt her by a reproach. 'I thought then,' she continued, 'that one so volatile might perhaps fly back again.'

'I shall not do that,' said he.

'You need trouble yourself with no assurances, my friend. Let us understand each other at any rate as to that. I am not now supposing that you can fly back again. You have found your perch, and you must settle on it,—which you will do like a good domestic barn-door fowl.' Again he scowled. If she were too hard upon him he would certainly turn upon her. 'No; you will not fly back again now;—but was I, or was I not, justified when you came to Killancodlem in thinking that my lover had come there? Are you not man enough to answer that for me?'

'How can I tell? It is my own justification I am thinking of.'

'Just so. I see all that. But we cannot both be justified. Did you mean me to suppose that you were speaking to me words in earnest when there,—sitting in that very spot,—you spoke to me of your love?'

'Did I speak of my love?'

'Did you speak of your love! And now, Silverbridge,—for if there be an English gentleman on earth I think that you are one,—as a gentleman tell me this. Did you not even tell your father that I should be your wife?' He was struck dumb by the question, but his face gave a true reply. 'I know you did.'

'Did he tell you?'

'Men such as you and he, who cannot even lie with your eyelids, who will not condescend to cover up a secret by a moment of feigned inanimation, have many voices, and each as clear as the others. He did tell me;—but he broke no confidence. He told me, but did not mean to tell me. Now you also have told me,—so that all doubt is at an end.'

'I did. I told him so,—and then I changed my mind.'

'I know you changed your mind. Men often do. A pinker pink, a whiter white,—a finger that will press you just half an ounce the closer,—a cheek that will consent to let itself come just a little nearer——'

'No; no; no!' It was because Isabel had not easily consented to such approaches! He was sure of that.

'Trifles such as these will do it;—and some such trifles, I suppose, have done it with you. It would be beneath me to make comparisons where I might seem to be the gainer. I will grant her beauty. She is very lovely. She has succeeded.'

'I have succeeded.'

'But—at any rate, between you and me, I am justified and you are condemned. Is it not so? Tell me like a man.'

'You are justified certainly.'

'And you are condemned? When you told me that I should be your wife, and then told your father the same story, then I was still to think that it was all to go for nothing! Have you deceived me?'

'I did not mean it.'

'Have you deceived me? What; you cannot deny it, and yet have not the manliness to own it to a poor woman who can only save herself from humiliation by extorting the truth from you!'

'Oh, Mabel. I am so sorry it should be so.'

'I believe you are;—with a sorrow that will last till she is again sitting close to you. Nor, Silverbridge, do I wish it to be longer. No;—no;—no. Your fault after all has not been great. You deceived, but did not mean to deceive me.'

'Never; never.'

'And I fancy you have never known how much you bore about with you. Your modesty has been so perfect that you have never thought of yourself as more than other men. You have forgotten that you carried with you such a prize of prizes; that you have had in your hand the disposal to some one woman of a throne in Paradise.'

'I don't suppose you thought of that.'

'But I did. Why should I tell falsehoods now? Silverbridge, I have determined that you should know everything,—but I could better confess to you my own sins when I had shown that you too have not been innocent. Not think of it! Do not men think of high titles and great wealth and power and place? And if men, why should not women? Do not men try to get them;—and are they not even applauded for their energy? A woman has but one way to try. I tried.'

'I do not think it was all for that.'

'How shall I answer that without a confession which even I am not hardened enough to make? Nor in confessing all the truth, as I would fain do, can I make you understand quite everything. I have never loved you.'

He drew himself up slowly before he answered her, and as he did so he gradually assumed a look and attitude very different from that easy boyish smile and gait which were customary to him. 'I am glad of that,' he said at last.

'Why are you glad?'

'Now I can have no regrets.'

'You need have none. I am telling you this in order that you should have none. It was necessary to me that I should have my little triumph;— so poor a triumph! That I should show you that I knew how far you had wronged me. But now I wish that you should know everything. I have never loved you.'

'There is an end of it then.'

'But I have liked you so well,—so much better than all others! A dozen men, I suppose, have asked me to marry them. And though they might be nothing till they made that request, then they became— things of horror to me. But you were not a thing of horror. I could have become your wife, and I think that I could have learned to love you.'

'It is best as it is.'

'No doubt you think so,—and she no doubt thinks so. I ought to say that I think so too; but I have a doubt. I should have liked to be Duchess of Omnium,* and perhaps I might have fitted the place better than one who can as yet know but little of its duties or its privileges. I may perhaps think that that other arrangement would have been better even for you.'

'I can take care of myself in that.'

'You can be proud now when I seem to question the perfection of your goddess. I want you to know all that I had determined to do for you. I should have married you without loving you, but I should have done so determined to serve you with a devotion which no woman who does love you will perhaps think necessary. I would have so done my duty that you should never then have guessed that my heart had been in the keeping of another man.'

'Another man!'

'Well;—yes; of course. If there had been no other man, why not you? Am I so hard, do you think, that I can love no one? Are you not such a one that a girl would love down to the very ground—were she not preoccupied? To love a man seems to me to be so naturally the condition of a woman that I am lost in wonder when I see so many who love none. That a woman should love seems as necessary as that a man should not.'

'A man can love too, I suppose.'

'No;—hardly. He can admire, and he can like, and he can fondle and be fond. He can admire, and approve, and, perhaps, worship. He can know of a woman that she is part of himself, the most sacred part, and therefore will protect her from the very winds. She can be his Holy of Holies. But all that will not make love. It does not come to a man that to be separated from a woman is to be dislocated from his very self. A man has but one centre, and that is himself. A woman has two. Though the second may never be seen by her, may live in the arms of another, may do all for that other that man can do for woman,—still, still, though he be half the globe asunder from her, still he is to her the half of her existence. If she really love there is, I fancy, no end of it. To the end of time I shall love Frank Tregear.'

'Tregear!'

'Who else? You know enough of me at any rate to be sure that if there be any such man it must be he.'

'He is engaged to Mary.'

'Of course he is. Why not;—to her or whomsoever else he might like best? He is as true I doubt not to your sister as you are to your American beauty,—or as you would have been to me had fancy held. I used to think he loved me.'

'You were always friends.'

'Always;—dear friends. And he would have loved me if a man were capable of loving. He can do better and can be a good husband,—which is what your sister will want. I thought too that I could perhaps make a good wife. When he broke himself from me so easily,—just in compliance with the first word spoken,—and sundered himself from me, just as Messrs. Smith and Brown may go apart from each other when their partnership no longer exists, I thought that I could perhaps do the same. But I cannot. A jackal is born a jackal, and not a lion, and cannot help himself. So is a woman born—a woman. There are clinging, parasite things which cannot but adhere, though they destroy themselves by adhering. I have been such a thing. Do not suppose that I take a pride in it. I would give one of my eyes to be able to disregard him.'

'Time will do it.'

'Yes; time,—that brings wrinkles and rouge pots and rheumatism. Though I have so hated those men as to be unable to endure them, still I want some man's house, and his money, and his carriages,*—some man's bread and beef and wine,—some man's jewels and titles and woods and parks and gardens;—if I can get them. Time can help a man in his sorrow. If he begins at forty to make speeches, or to win races, or to breed oxen, he can yet live a prosperous life. Time is but a poor consoler for a young woman who has to be married. You will see perhaps now, my friend, that I was not altogether indifferent to your position as an eldest son. But you have escaped.'

'Oh, Mabel.'

'And now let there be not a word more about it. I know—that I can trust you.'

'Indeed you may.'

'Though you will tell her everything else, you will not tell her this.'

'No;—not this.'

'There will be something between us which will not be common to her. And surely you will not tell your sister!'

'I shall tell no one.'

'It is because you are so true that I have dared to trust you. I had to justify myself,—and then to confess. Had I at that one moment taken you at your word, you would never have known anything of all this. "There is a tide in the affairs of men——!"* But I let the flood go by! I shall not see you again now before you are married, but come to me afterwards sometimes. I dare say she and I may become friends.' Then he took his leave, almost without a word, and walked home, pondering what he had heard.

CHAPTER 74

'LET US DRINK A GLASS OF WINE TOGETHER'

SILVERBRIDGE pondered it all much as he went home,—so much that for the moment he forgot other things. It was Monday and he had intended to go down to the House as soon as he left Belgrave Square; but instead of doing so he turned up by the Duke of York's column to Carlton Terrace. What a terrible story was this that he had heard! The horror to him was chiefly in this,—that she should yet be driven to marry some man without even fancying that she could love him;—that she should have tried her hand upon him and that she had confessed that she must now seek some other victim, while she was conscious that her heart had been altogether given to Frank Tregear! And this was Lady Mabel Grex, who, on his own first entrance into London life, now not much more than twelve months ago, had seemed to him to stand above all other girls in beauty, charm, and popularity! Poor Lady Mabel Grex!

As he opened the door of the house with his latch-key, who should be coming out but Frank Tregear,—Frank Tregear with his arm in a sling and various outward signs of bandages about him, but still with an unmistakable look of general prosperity and satisfaction. 'When on earth did you come up?' asked Silverbridge. Tregear told him that he had arrived in London on the previous evening from Harrington. 'And why? I don't suppose the doctor would have let you come if he could have helped it.'

'When he found he could not help it, he did let me come. I am nearly all right;—and if I had been nearly all wrong I should have had to come.'

'And what are you doing here?' asked Silverbridge.

'Well;—if you'll allow me I'll go back with you for a moment.' Then they went together into the house. 'What do you think I have been doing?'

'Have you seen my sister?'

'Yes, I have seen your sister,—for a moment. And I have done better than that. I have seen your father. Lord Silverbridge,—behold your brother-in-law.'

'You don't mean to say that it is arranged?'

'I do. The Duke has yielded,—not with the very best grace.'

'What did he say?'

'He made me understand by most unanswerable arguments that I had no business to think of such a thing,—that I have not a leg to stand upon. I did not fight the point with him,—but simply stood there, as conclusive evidence that I had a leg. He told me that we should have nothing to live on unless he gave us an income, and that I had no right to expect him to give me anything. I assured him that I would never ask him for a shilling. "But I cannot allow her to marry a man without an income," he said.'

'I know his way so well.'

'I could only shrug my shoulders. I had just two facts to go upon,—that I would not give her up and that she would not give me up. When I pointed that out he tore his hair,—in a mild way, and said that he did not understand that kind of thing at all.'

'And yet he gave way.'

'Of course he did. When he consented to see me, that I knew was settled. They say that when a king of old would consent to see a petitioner for his life, he was bound by his royalty to mercy. So it was with the Duke. Then, very early in the argument, he forgot himself, and called her—Mary. I knew he had thrown up the sponge then. A father never calls his daughter Mary to the man he means to reject.'

'How did he give way at last?'

'He asked me what were my ideas about life in general. I said that I thought Parliament was a good sort of thing,—that I was lucky enough to have a seat, and that I should take lodgings somewhere in Westminster till—— "Till what?" he asked. "Till something is settled," I replied. Then he turned away from me and remained silent, I suppose for a minute or two. "May I see Lady Mary?" I asked. "Yes; you may see her," he replied, as he rang the bell. Then when he had sent his message and the servant was gone, he stopped me. "I love her too dearly to see her grieve," he said. "I hope you will show that you can be worthy of her." Then I made some sort of protestation and went upstairs. While I was with Mary there came a message to me, telling me to come to dinner to-day. Somebody will have to cut my food for me, but I shall come.'

'The Boncassens are all dining here.'

'Then we shall be a family party. So far I suppose I may say it is settled. When he will let us marry heaven only knows. Mary declares that she will not press him. I certainly cannot do so. It is all a matter of money.'

'He won't care about that.'

'But he may perhaps think that a little patience will do us good. You will have to soften him. I suppose you will be a married man soon.' Then Silverbridge told all that he knew about himself. He was to be married in May, was to go to Matching for a week or two after his wedding, was then to see the session to an end, and after that to travel with his wife in the United States through the autumn. 'I don't suppose we shall be allowed to run about the world together so soon as that,' said Tregear, 'but I am too well satisfied with my day's work to complain. Only remember this,—if you can put in a good word for me, do.'

'Did he say what he meant to give her?'

'Oh dear no;—nor even that he meant to give her anything further than I have told you. I should not dream of asking a question about it. Nor when he makes any proposition shall I think of having any opinion of my own. I feel, you know, now, the disgrace of being a pauper.'

'He'll make it all right.'

'I don't want him to make it very right.'

'For her sake, you know.'

'He will do at any rate as much as she wants. My chief object, as regards him, is that he should not think that I have been looking after her money. Well; good-bye. I suppose we shall all meet at dinner.'

So that was settled. There were two men to be made happy,—himself, and Frank Tregear; and two girls, also, were happy enough now,—his sister and Isabel. He flattered himself that Isabel was happy. But poor Mabel Grex! She could not be happy. She was altogether out in the cold! In the midst of his own joy, and even when startled by the sudden prosperity of his friend Tregear, he could not keep his mind from Mabel Grex. That her plight should be so wretched,—that she whom he had so nearly loved, whom he did regard with so dear a friendship, should be exempt from all their content, should be as it were left out from their festivities,—took away much from the thoroughness of his satisfaction. He and his friend Tregear were the heroes of the day; and it was through Tregear and through him that she had fallen to the ground. He had been wont to tell himself that he had committed no offence against her. But he could no longer comfort himself with that assurance. The very fact that she had found out that he and his father between them had at one time all but settled that she should be his wife seemed to cut that ground from under his feet. Poor Mabel Grex! It was, however, a great comfort to him that Isabel should have intervened just in time. Lady Mabel had many charms,—but there could be only one chief, one best, one loveliest of her sex!

When Tregear left him Silverbridge went to his father's room. He was anxious that they should understand each other as to Mary's engagement. 'I thought you were at the House,' said the Duke.

'I was going there, but I just met Tregear by chance at the door. I thought he was still down at Lord Chiltern's.'

'I wish he were.'

'Oh, sir!'

'Well;—what would you have me say?'

'He tells me you have accepted him for Mary. If that be true, is he not better here?'

'I wish that he had never been here. Do you think that a man can be thwarted in everything and not feel it? I had set my mind to judge as best I could for the welfare of my children, and they have crossed me in everything.'

'I thought—you had quite reconciled yourself—to Isabel.'

'If it were that alone I could do so the more easily because personally she wins upon me. And this man too;—it is not that I find any fault with him himself.'

'You will find him to be in all respects a high-minded gentleman.'

'I hope so. I do believe it. But yet, had he a right to set his heart there, where he could make his fortune,—having none of his own?'

'He did not think of that.'

'He should have thought of it. A man does not I suppose allow himself to love without any consideration of propriety.* He should have kept aloof from one so circumstanced. You say that he is a gentleman.'

'I certainly say that.'

'A gentleman should not look to live on means brought to him by a wife. You say that he did not.'

'He did not think of it.'

'A gentleman should do more than not think of it. He should think that it shall not be so with him. A man should own his means or should earn them. He should be beholden to no one for his bread.'

'How many men, sir——'

'Yes; yes; I know,' said the Duke. 'Such a doctrine nowadays is caviare to the general.* One must live as others live around one, I suppose. At any rate I could not see her suffer. It was too much for me. When I became convinced that this was no temporary passion, no romantic idea which time and other scenes might banish, that she was of such a temperament that she could not change,—then I had to give way. I have always to give way. Gerald I suppose will bring me some kitchen-maid for his wife.'

'Oh, sir, you should not say that to me.'

'No;—I should not have said it to you. I beg your pardon, Silverbridge. Isabel is certainly no kitchen-maid.' Then he paused a moment, turning over certain thoughts within his own bosom. 'Perhaps, after all, it is well that a certain pride of which I am conscious should be rebuked. And it may be that the rebuke has come in such a form that I should be thankful. I know that I can love Isabel.'

'That to me will be everything.'

'And this young man has nothing that should revolt me. I think he has been wrong. But now that I have said it I will let all that pass from me. I have told him that he shall have her, and I have made him welcome to my house. He will dine with us to-day.'

'So he has told me. Of course I shall come as soon as I can get away,' said Silverbridge, looking as though he would be unable to neglect his legislative duties even for the sake of sitting by Isabel Boncassen at dinner. 'I don't suppose they can be married as soon as we are,' he added.

'I know nothing about that,' said the Duke, 'but I should think not.'

Silverbridge then went up to see his sister. 'So you have settled your little business, Mary.'

'Oh, Silverbridge, you will wish me joy?'

'Certainly. Why not?'

'Papa is so stern with me. Of course he has given way, and of course I am grateful. But he looks at me as though I had done something wicked;—as though I were to be forgiven.'

'Take the good the gods provide you, Mary. That will all come right very soon now.'

'But I have not done anything wrong;—have I?'

'Well! That is a matter of opinion. How can I answer about you when I don't quite know whether I have done anything wrong or not myself? I am going to marry the girl I have chosen. That's enough for me.'

'But you did change.'

'We need not say anything about that. I've got what I want, and you are to have what you want. Surely that ought to be enough.'

'But I have never changed. Papa just told me that he would consent and that I might write to him. So I did write, and he came. But papa looks at me as though I had broken his heart.'

'I'll tell you what it is, Mary. You expect too much from him. Of course he has not had his own way with either of us, and of course he feels it. They say that a conqueror always ought to be good-humoured. You are the conqueror here. If you are gentle with him now, he will very soon be gentle with you,—and with Tregear.'

As Tregear had said, there was quite a family party dining that day in Carlton Terrace, though as yet the family was not absolutely bound together by family ties. All the Boncassens were there, the father, the mother, and the promised bride. Mr. Boncassen bore himself perhaps with more ease than anyone in the company, having at his command a certain gift of manliness which enabled him to regard this marriage exactly as he would have done any other with which, in regard to his daughter, he might have felt himself satisfied. Partly because rank was not much to him as an American, partly perhaps because it was not much to him as a man, he was not confounded by the success of his girl. America was not so far distant but what he would be able to see her occasionally. He liked the young man and he believed in the comfort of wealth. Therefore he was satisfied. But when the marriage was spoken of, or written of, as 'an alliance,' then he would say a hard word or two about dukes and lords in general. On such an occasion as this he was able to be, and apparently was, happy and at his ease.

So much perhaps could not be said for his wife, with whom the Duke, as he gave her his arm to take her out to dinner, attempted to place himself on terms of family equality. But in doing this he failed to hide the attempt even from her, and she broke down under it. Had he simply walked into the room with her as he would have done on any other occasion, and then remarked that the frost was very keen or the thaw very disagreeable, it would have been better for her. But when he told her that he hoped she would often make herself at home in that house, and looked, as he said it, as though he were asking her to take a place among the goddesses of Olympus, she was troubled as to her answer. 'Oh, my Lord Duke,' she said, 'when I think of Isabel living here and being called by such a name it almost upsets me.' He smiled and endeavoured to say something good-natured, but it was too evident that she was 'almost upset.'

Isabel had all her father's courage and sureness of purpose, but she was more sensitive; and though she would have borne her honours well, was somewhat oppressed by the feeling that the weight was too much for her mother. She had known that a struggle would be necessary to enable her not to seem oppressed, to save her from an appearance of thinking rather of the position of the man she was to marry than of the man himself. No one would have known by her manner that she was not the daughter of some other English magnate, a girl of that class from which Silverbridge might have been expected to choose his wife; but, as it was, she could not keep her ear from listening to her mother's words or her eye from watching her mother's motions. There was in this nothing of shame. She was prepared to carry her mother everywhere. 'As other girls have to be taken with their belongings, so must I, if I be taken at all.' This she had said plainly enough both to the Duke and to Silverbridge,—if not in those very words, still in words which were sufficiently intelligible. There should be no division between her and her mother. But still knowing that her mother was not quite at ease, she was hardly at ease herself.

Silverbridge came in at the last moment just as the others had taken their seats, and of course occupied a chair next to Isabel. As the House was sitting, and as he had not gone down till late, it was of course necessary that he should come up in a flurry. 'I left Phineas,' he said, 'pounding away in his old style at Sir Timothy. By-the-bye, Isabel, you must come down some day and hear Sir Timothy badgered. I must be back again I suppose about ten. Well, Gerald, how are they all at Lazarus?' He made an effort to be free and easy, and to whisper pleasant things to his sweet neighbour; but even he soon found that it was an effort.

Gerald had come up from Oxford for the occasion on purpose that he might make acquaintance with the Boncassens. He had taken Isabel in to dinner, but had been turned out of the place he was about to occupy when his brother came in. He had been a little confused by the first impression made upon him by Mrs. Boncassen, and had involuntarily watched his father. 'Silver is going to have an odd sort of a mother-in-law,' he said afterwards to Mary, who remarked in reply that this would not much signify, as the mother-in-law would generally be in New York.

Tregear's part was one very difficult to play. He could not but feel that though he had succeeded, though he had been accepted, still he was as yet looked upon askance. Silverbridge had told him that by degrees the Duke would be won round to gentleness and gracious courtesy, and that it was not to be expected that he should swallow at once all his regrets. The truth of this was so plain that it could not but be accepted. The immediate inconvenience, however, was not the less felt. Nothing had on this occasion been said to the Boncassens as to his peculiar position in the family; but of course it was known to them through Silverbridge. Each and everyone there knew the position of each and everyone;—but Tregear felt it difficult to act up to his. He could not play the well-pleased lover openly, as did Silverbridge. Mary herself was disposed to be very silent. The heart-breaking tedium of her dull life had been removed. Her determination had been rewarded. All that she had wanted had been granted to her, and she was happy. But she was not prepared to show off her happiness before the Boncassens,—not even before her brothers. Though she was proud of her lover, thinking him of course to be superior to all other men who had come in her way, yet she was aware that she was still thought to have done evil by introducing him as her lover into her august family.

But it was the Duke who made the greatest efforts, and with the least success. He had told himself again and again that he was bound by every sense of duty to swallow all regrets. He had taken himself to task on this matter. He had done so even out loud to his son. He had acknowledged that it was necessary that his pride should be rebuked. He had declared that he would 'let it all pass from him.' But who does not know how hard it is for a man in such matters to keep his word to himself? Who has not said to himself at the very moment of his own delinquency, 'Now,—it is now,—at this very instant of time, that I should crush, and quench, and kill the evil spirit within me; it is now that I should abate my greed, or smother my ill humour, or abandon my hatred. It is now, and here, that I should drive out the fiend, as I have sworn to myself that I would do';—and yet has failed?

That it would be done, would be done at last, by this man was very certain,—and also that it would be done quickly. When Silverbridge assured his sister that 'it would come all right very soon,' he had understood his father's character. But it could not be completed quite at once. Had he been required to take Isabel only to his heart, it would have been comparatively easy. So much indeed had been done. There are men, who do not seem at first sight very susceptible to feminine attractions, who nevertheless are dominated by the grace of flounces, who succumb to petticoats unconsciously, and who are half in love with every woman merely for her womanhood. So it was with the Duke. He had given way in regard to Isabel with less than half the effort that Frank Tregear was likely to cost him. And now had not Frank Tregear been at table, had he not felt himself compelled to acknowledge by the man's presence that the man had overcome him, he would have succeeded much better in talking easily with poor Mrs. Boncassen.

'You were not at the House, sir?' said Silverbridge when he felt that there was a pause.

'No, not to-day.' Then there was a pause again.

'I think that we shall beat Cambridge this year to a moral,'* said Gerald, who was sitting at the round table opposite to his father. Mr. Boncassen, who was next to him, with the other brother on his right hand, asked, in irony probably rather than in ignorance, whether the victory was to be achieved by mathematical or classical proficiency. Gerald turned and looked at him, and then looked round the table. 'Do you mean to say that you have never heard of the University boat-races?'*

'Papa, you have disgraced yourself for ever,' said Isabel.

'Have I, my dear? Yes, I have heard of them. But I thought Lord Gerald's protestation was too great for a mere aquatic triumph.'

'Now you are poking your fun at me,' said Gerald.

'Well he may,' said the Duke sententiously. 'We have made ourselves very open to having fun poked at us in this matter.'

'I think, sir,' said Tregear, 'that they are learning to do the same sort of thing at the American Universities.'

'Oh, indeed,' said the Duke in a solemn, dry, funereal tone. And then all the little life which Gerald's remark about the boat-race had produced, was quenched at once. The Duke was not angry with Tregear for his little word of defence, and had no wish on the occasion to give special honour to American institutions; but he was not able to bring himself into harmony with this one guest, and was almost savage to him without meaning it.

'I take it,' said Mr. Boncassen, 'that we are doing our best to copy you in most things.' The Duke remarked that the justification of the United States was to be found in their avoidance of what were supposed to be English faults. 'Nevertheless it is natural that we should copy even the faults. The healthy country gentleman who decries the fashionable absurdities of the city cannot save himself from their attraction. He ridicules you for dining at eight, but he allows his own hour to be gradually changed from five to six. We are becoming very English in our tastes.'

'With a tendency to Parisian proclivities,' said Tregear, who could not talk to Mary beside him, and was bound to assert his own position by a word or two now and then.

'I do like Paris,' said Mrs. Boncassen.

'I hate it,' said Silverbridge. 'I never know what to do there.'

'It is Paradise upon earth,' said Isabel. 'If I had my way I would live there always.'

'What would you do?' asked her lover.

'Drive up and down the Champs-Elysées, and wear the prettiest bonnet that the world could produce.'

'The Parisians at any rate would be the gainers,' said the Duke, striving to be gallant and pleasant. But even this was said in the same solemn voice, showing so plainly that his mind was elsewhere, and not at ease! He was continually asking himself why destiny had been so hard upon him as to force him to receive there at his table as his son-in-law a man who was distasteful to him; why he should be compelled to take this man by the hand and make this man's fortune;—and he was endeavouring to answer the question, and to persuade himself that his destiny had done him no injury, that his daughter had been entitled to please herself, and that the pride which had been wounded was a false pride. He was making a brave fight; but during the fight he was hardly fit to be the genial host and to shine as the happy father and father-in-law of young people who were going to be married to one another. But before the dinner was over he made a great effort. 'Tregear,' he said,—and even that was an effort, for he had never hitherto mentioned the man's name without the formal Mister,—'Tregear, as this is the first time you have sat at my table, let me be old-fashioned and ask you to drink a glass of wine with me.'

The glass of wine was drunk of course, and the ceremony afforded infinite satisfaction at least to one person there. Mary could not keep herself from some expression of joy by pressing her finger for a moment against her lover's arm. He, though not usually given to such manifestations, blushed up to his eyes as he acknowledged the Duke's courtesy. But the feeling produced on the company was solemn rather than jovial. Everyone there understood it all. Mr. Boncassen could read the Duke's mind down to the last line. Even Mrs. Boncassen was aware that an act of reconciliation had been intended. 'When the governor drank that glass of wine it seemed as though half the marriage ceremony had been performed,' Gerald said to his brother that evening after Tregear had left them. When the ceremony was over and the Duke's glass was replaced on the table, he himself was conscious of the solemnity of what he had done, and was half ashamed of it. It was not till afterwards that he could comfort himself by the reflection that though he had been perhaps almost ridiculous, still he had been honest and true to his purpose.

When the ladies had gone upstairs the conversation became political and lively. The Duke could talk freely about the state of things to Mr. Boncassen, and was able gradually to include Tregear in the badinage with which he attacked the conservatism of his son. And so the half-hour passed well. Upstairs the two girls immediately came together, leaving Mrs. Boncassen to chew the cud of the grandeur around her in the sleepy comfort of an arm-chair near the fire. 'And so everything is settled for both of us,' said Isabel.

'Of course I knew it was to be settled for you. You told me so at Custins.'

'I did not know it myself then. I only told you that he had asked me. And you hardly believed me.'

'I certainly believed you.'

'But you knew about—Lady Mabel Grex.'

'I only suspected something, and now I know it was a mistake.'

'I hope,—I hope there has been nothing wrong,—that he has not been—anything that he ought not to have been.'

'I have known nothing. It has never been more than a suspicion.'

'I don't think he has quite told me all. Perhaps he ought not to do so. At any rate I never ask him. And why, when we were at Custins, did you not tell me about yourself?'

'I had nothing to tell.'

'I suppose I can understand that. But is it not joyful that it should all be settled! Only poor Lady Mabel! You have got no Lady Mabel to trouble your conscience.' From which it was evident that Silverbridge had not told all.

Upon the whole the evening's entertainment had been useful. There had no doubt been periods in which some of those assembled had found themselves to be uncomfortable; but when it was over, all those who were concerned felt that good results had been achieved.

CHAPTER 75

THE MAJOR'S STORY

BY the end of March there was certainly no one in all the world who did not know both that Lord Silverbridge was going to be married to Isabel Boncassen and also that Frank Tregear had resolved all his difficulties and was to be made happy by the hand of Lady Mary Palliser. At this time Isabel herself was not in London, having gone for a few weeks with other Americans to Paris. She had thought that a short separation from her lover before her wedding would be good for him, and had insisted on absenting herself. He had rebelled and had threatened to follow her; but she at last had had her way, arguing, as she often did, that his time, his unlimited time for having his way, was fast coming. Silverbridge was therefore reduced to the shifts of a bachelor's life, in which his friends seemed to think that he ought now to take special delight as he would so soon be deprived of them. Perhaps he did not take much delight in them. He was no doubt impatient to commence that steady married life for which he had prepared himself. But nevertheless, just at present, he lived a good deal at the Beargarden. Where was he to live? The Boncassens were in Paris, his sister was at Matching with a houseful of other Pallisers, and his father was again deep in politics. He declared to one or two of his friends, to Tregear, to Lady Mabel Grex, and to Mrs. Finn that the Beargarden was the stupidest place he knew; but still he spent many of his hours there. When a marriage has been arranged there can be no doubt that as far as the man is concerned, it cannot take place too soon.

Of course he was much in the House of Commons, but that also was stupid. Indeed everything would be stupid till Isabel came back. Perhaps dinner was more comfortable,—what he would have called less stupid,—at the club than at the House. And then, as everybody knew, it was a good thing to change the scene. Therefore he dined at the club, and though he would keep his hansom and go down to the House again in the course of the evening, he spent many long hours at the Beargarden. 'There'll very soon be an end of this as far as you are concerned,' said Mr. Lupton to him one evening as they were sitting in the smoking-room after dinner. They were at the moment alone, having a corner of the room to themselves.

'The sooner the better as far as this place is concerned.'

'The place is as good as any other. For the matter of that I like the Beargarden since we got rid of two or three not very charming characters.'

'You mean my poor friend Tifto,' said Silverbridge.

'No;—I was not thinking of Tifto. There were one or two here at one time who were quite as bad as Tifto. I wonder what has become of that poor devil.'

'I don't know in the least. I haven't seen him since that horrid day at Doncaster. You heard of that row about the hounds?'

'And his letter to you.'

'He wrote to me,—and I answered him, as you know. But whither he vanished or what he is doing or how he is living, I have not the least idea.'

'Gone to join those other fellows abroad I should say. Among them they got a lot of money;—as the Duke ought to remember. There was quite enough for them all to live in what they would think luxury.'

'He is not with them,' said Silverbridge, as though he were in some degree mourning over the fate of his unfortunate friend. 'However it all was done, the poor devil didn't get his share of the plunder.'

'I suppose Captain Green was the leader in all that.'

'Now it is all done and gone I own to a certain regard for the Major. He was true to me till he thought I snubbed him. I would not let him go down to Silverbridge with me one day, and then I was angry with him when he asked to be introduced to the governor in the other room there. I always thought that I drove the poor Major to his malpractices.'

At this moment Dolly Longstaffe sauntered into the room and came up to them. It may be remembered that Dolly had some few weeks since declared his purpose of emigrating. As soon as he heard that the Duke's heir had serious thoughts of marrying the lady whom he loved himself, he withdrew at once from the contest, but, as he did so, he acknowledged to himself that there could be no longer a home for him in the country which Isabel was to inhabit as the wife of another man. Gradually, however, better thoughts had returned to him. He had told himself that a man should never run away. After all, what was she but a 'pert poppet'? He determined that marriage 'clips a fellow's wings confoundedly,' and so he set himself to work to enjoy life after his old fashion. There was perhaps a little swagger as he threw himself into a chair and addressed the happy lover. 'Who do you think I've just seen, Silverbridge?'

'I have not the least idea.'

'I'll give you three guesses;—and I'll give Lupton three.'

'You are very kind,' said Lupton, 'but I won't take advantage of your good nature.'

'I'll be shot if I didn't meet Tifto at the corner of the street just now.'

'Tifto!'

'Yes, Tifto. He looked awfully seedy, with a greatcoat buttoned up to his chin, a shabby hat and old gloves. I caught him just under the lamp-post.'

'Did he speak to you?' asked Silverbridge.

'No;—nor I to him. He hadn't time to think whether he would speak or not, and you may be sure I didn't wait.'

The coincidence was declared to be very singular, in that they should have been talking about the man and that he should have been seen just at the same moment. Then nothing further was said about him. But Silverbridge was uneasy and silent. When his cigar was finished he got up saying that he should go back to the House. As he left the club he looked about him as though expecting to see his old friend, and when he had passed through the first street and had got into the Haymarket there he was! The Major came up to him and, touching his hat, asked to be allowed to say a few words. 'I don't think it can do any good,' said Silverbridge, walking on quickly. The man had not attempted to shake hands with him, or affected familiarity; but seemed to be thoroughly humiliated. 'I don't think I can be of any service to you, and therefore I had rather decline,' said Silverbridge.

'I don't want you to be of any service, my Lord.'

'Then what's the good?'

'I have something to say. May I come to you to-morrow?'

Then Silverbridge allowed himself to make an appointment with the man for the next day, and an hour was named at which Tifto might call in Carlton Terrace. He repented himself that he had done so as soon as he was alone, and for a time had almost made up his mind that he would ask some friend, Mr. Lupton, probably, to be present at the interview. But he did not. He felt that he almost owed some reparation to the wretched man,—whom he had unfortunately admitted among his friends, whom he had used, and to whom he had been uncourteous. He did not think that there was anything to fear, and at last he resolved to see the Major alone. Exactly at the hour named the Major was shown into his room.

Dolly had said that he was shabby,—but the man was altered rather than shabby. He still had rings on his fingers and studs in his shirt-sleeves, and a jewelled pin in his cravat,—as was to be seen when he opened his greatcoat; but he had shaven off his moustache and the tuft

from his chin, and his hair had been cut short, and in spite of his jew-
ellery there was a hang-dog look about him. 'I've got something that
I particularly want to say to you, my Lord.' These were his first words
as soon as he had seated himself. Silverbridge would not shake hands
with him, but could not refrain from offering him a chair.

'Well;—you can say it now.'

'Yes; I can say it now,—but it isn't so very easy to be said. There are
some things, though you want to say them ever so, you don't quite know
how to do it.'

'You have your choice, Major Tifto. You can speak or hold your
tongue. It isn't because I want anything from you that you are here. You
understand that.'

'I know that, my Lord.' Then there was a pause, during which
Silverbridge sat with his hands in his pockets trying to look uncon-
cerned. 'But if you've got it here, and feel it,—as I do,'—the poor man
as he said this put his hand upon his heart,—'you can't sleep in your
bed till it's out. I did that thing that they said I did.'

'What thing?'

'Why, the nail! It was I lamed the horse,—out of sheer villainy.'

'I am sorry for it. I can say nothing else.'

'You ain't so sorry for it as I am,—oh, no. You can never be that, my
Lord. After all what does it matter to you?'

'Very little. I meant that I was sorry for your sake.'

'I believe you are, my Lord. For though you could be rough you was
always kind. Now I will tell you everything, and then you can do as you
please.'

'I wish to do nothing at all. As far as I am concerned the matter is
over. It made me sick of horses, and I do not wish ever to have to think
of it again if I can help it.'

'Nevertheless, my Lord, I've got to tell it. It was Green who put me
up to it. The man who calls himself Captain Green.'

'We all supposed so.'

'He did it just for the plunder,—that he and Villiers might have an
opportunity of robbing you. As God is my judge it was not for the
money I did it.'

'Then it was revenge.'

'It was the devil got hold of me, my Lord. Up to that I had always
been square,—square as a die! I got to think that your lordship was
upsetting to me,*—that you didn't give me just as much credit as you
ought to do. I don't know whether your lordship remembers, but you
did put me down once or twice rather uncommon.'

'I hope I was not unjust.'

'I don't say you was, my Lord. But I got a feeling on me that you wanted to get rid of me, and I all the time doing the best I could for the 'orses. I did do the best I could up to that very morning at Doncaster. Well;—it was Green put me up to it, and arranged it all. I don't say I was to get nothing; but it wasn't to say so much more than I could have got by the 'orse winning. And I've lost pretty nearly all that I did get!' Lord Silverbridge shrugged his shoulders, not liking to say out loud that thieves can never make a good use of their plunder. 'Do you remember, my Lord,'—and now the Major sank his voice to a whisper,— 'when I came up to your bedroom that morning?'

'I remember it.'

'The first time?'

'Yes; I remember it.'

'Because I came twice, my Lord. When I came first it hadn't been done. You turned me out.'

'That is true, Major Tifto.'

'You was very rough then. Wasn't you rough?'

'A man's bedroom is generally supposed to be private.'

'Yes, my Lord;—that's true. I ought to have sent your man in first, but I was so flustered then, I could hardly think of things properly. I came then,—to tell your lordship all about it;—to confess it all, before it was done.'

'Then why couldn't you let the horse alone?'

'I was in their hands. And then you was so rough with me! You was rough with me.'

'I was certainly. I remember it well.'

'So I said to myself I might as well do it,—and I did it.'

'What do you want me to say? As far as my forgiveness goes, you have it.'

'That's saying a great deal, my Lord,—a great deal,' said Tifto, now in tears. 'But I ain't said it all yet. He's here; in London!'

'Who's here?'

'Green. Green. He's here. He doesn't think that I know, but I could lay my hand on him to-morrow.'

'There is no human being alive, Major Tifto, whose presence or absence could be a matter of more indifference to me.'

'I'll tell you what I'll do, my Lord. I'll go before any judge or magistrate or police-officer in the country and tell the truth. I won't ask even for a pardon if they don't like to give it me. They shall punish me and him too. I'm in that state of mind that any change would be for the better. But he,—he ought to have it heavy.'

'It won't be done by me, Major Tifto.'

'But the club, my Lord? The Jockey Club would take it up at once.'

'Not if I can prevent it. Look here, Major Tifto. You have come here to confess that you have done me a great injury.'

'Yes, I have.'

'And you say you are sorry for it.'

'Indeed I am.'

'And I have forgiven you. There is only one way in which you can show your gratitude.'

'Tell me that, and I'll do it though I was to have to be hung for it.'

'Hold your tongue about all this. Let it be as a thing done and gone. The money has been paid. The race has been lost. The horse has been sold. The whole thing has clean gone out of my mind and I don't want to have it brought back again. If I can forgive you, you can forgive the other man, and so let it go round.'

'And nothing is to be done to Green!'

'I should say nothing—on that score.'

'And he has got they say five-and-twenty thousand pounds clear money!'

'It is a pity, but it cannot be helped. Look here, Major Tifto; I will have nothing further to do with it. Of course I cannot bind you, but I have told you my wishes.' The poor wretch was silent, but still it seemed as though he did not wish to go quite yet. 'If you have said what you have got to say, Major Tifto, I may as well tell you that my time is engaged.'

'And must that be all?'

'What else?'

'I am in such a state of mind, Lord Silverbridge, that it would be a satisfaction to tell it all even against myself.'

'I can't prevent you, of course.'

'I ain't going to do anything against your lordship,' he said whining. Then Tifto got up from his chair, as though he were going. 'I wish I knew what I was going to do with myself.'

'I don't know that I can help you, Major Tifto.'

'I suppose not, my Lord. I haven't twenty pounds left in all the world. I have that feeling that if they'd put me in prison it would be a relief. It's the only thing that wasn't square that ever I did in all my life.' Silverbridge could not help thinking that if this statement was true the delinquent had commenced his anti-squareness by a very strong measure of iniquity. 'Your lordship couldn't do anything for me I suppose. We was very much together at one time, my Lord.'

'Yes, Major Tifto; we were.'

'Of course I was a villain. But it was only once, and I was led on by my feelings. I had got to think that you owed me so much!'

'For being honest?'

'I suppose it was. And then your lordship was so rough to me! I'm not saying but what I was a villain. Think of what I did for myself, by that one piece of wickedness! Master of Hounds! Member of the club! And the horse would have run in my name and won the Leger! And everybody knew as your lordship and me was together in him! Think what I must think of myself, Lord Silverbridge! If I could get round any way again I wouldn't mind blacking shoes!' Then he burst out into a paroxysm of tears and sobbing.

The young Lord certainly could not take the man into partnership again, nor could he restore to him either the hounds or his club,—or his clean hands. Nor did he know in what way he could serve the man, except by putting his hand into his pocket,—which he did. Tifto accepted the gratuity, and ultimately became an annual pensioner on his former noble partner, living on the allowance made him in some obscure corner of South Wales.

Till a year or two had passed by Silverbridge told no one of the interview and its results except his brother; and even to him he found himself obliged to make an apology for his ill-judged generosity. 'I had been rough to him and I suppose I did drive him to it. I couldn't help being rough because he encroached; but then it was my fault all the same because I had encouraged him. Poor devil! If he can manage to live on a hundred a year I won't begrudge it him.' In process of time Tifto married a publican's daughter under the name of Henry Walker,* and, having inherited his father-in-law's business, lived to be able to tell his noble patron that the pension was no longer needed.

CHAPTER 76

ON DEPORTMENT

FRANK TREGEAR had come up to town at the end of February on hearing from Lady Mary that he was to be accepted into the family of the Pallisers, and had dined in Carlton Terrace and had been accepted. The Duke had drunk a special glass of wine with him and that matter was so far concluded. But he had not then been able to take his place in Parliament. Indeed on leaving Harrington he had done so in opposition to the advice both of the doctor and of Lady Chiltern;—though Lady Chiltern was obliged to acknowledge, when all the circumstances were explained to her, that the reasons for going were very strong indeed. He remained in London, with an understanding that he was not to see Lady Mary again till the Easter holidays, which would occur this year about the middle of April. He was then to pay a visit to Matching, and to enter in, it may be presumed, on the full fruition of his advantages as accepted suitor for Lady Mary's hand. All this had been arranged with a good deal of precision,—as though there had still been a hope left that Lady Mary might change her mind. Of course there was no such hope. When the Duke asked the young man to dine with him in London, when he invited him to drink that memorable glass of wine, when the young man was allowed, in the presence of the Boncassens, to sit next to Lady Mary, it was of course settled. But the father probably found some relief in yielding by slow degrees. 'I would rather that there should be no correspondence till then,' he had said both to Tregear and to his daughter. And of course they had promised there should be no correspondence. At that time it wanted only six weeks to Easter, and though the prohibition was felt to be a hardship, it was bearable. At Easter they would meet. After Easter Mary was to come up to London to be present at her brother's wedding, to which also Tregear had been formally invited; and it was hoped that then something might be settled as to their own marriage. But as yet no one had dared to ask the Duke a question on that subject.

On the last day of March, the very day on which Lord Silverbridge had heard the poor Major's story, Tregear, with the surgeon's permission, took his seat in Parliament. He was introduced by two leading members on the Conservative side, but immediately afterwards found himself seated next to his friend Silverbridge on the top bench behind the ministers. The House was very full, as there was a feverish report abroad that Sir Timothy Beeswax intended to make a statement. No one quite knew what the statement was to be; but every politician in the House and out of it thought that he knew that the statement would be a bid for higher power on the part of Sir Timothy himself. But if there had been, as there needs must have been, dissensions in the Cabinet, the secret of them had been well kept, for no one seemed quite to know what was to be done. To Tregear, who was not as yet familiar with the House, there was no special appearance of activity; but Silverbridge could see that there was more than wonted animation. That the Treasury bench* should be full at this time was a thing of custom. A whole broadside of questions would be fired off, one after another, like a rattle of musketry down the ranks, when as nearly as possible the report of each gun is made to follow close upon that of the gun before,—with this exception, that in such case each little sound is intended to be as like as possible to the preceding; whereas with the rattle of the questions and answers, each question and each answer becomes a little more authoritative and less courteous than the last. The Treasury bench was ready for its usual responsive firing, and so the questioners were of course in their places here and there. But the opposition front bench was also crowded, and those behind were nearly equally full. There were many peers in the peers' gallery, and a general feeling of sensation prevailed. All this Silverbridge had been long enough in the House to appreciate;—but to Tregear the House was simply the House.

'It's odd enough we should have a row the very first day you come,' said Silverbridge.

'You think there will be a row?'

'Beeswax has something special to say. He's not here yet you see. They've left about six inches for him there between Roby and Sir Orlando. You'll have the honour and glory of looking just down on the top of his head when he does come. I shan't stay much longer after that.'

'Where are you going?'

'I don't mean to-day. But I should not have been here now,—in this very place I mean,—but I want to stick to you just at first. I shall move down below the gangway; and not improbably creep over to the other side before long.'

'You don't mean it?'

'I think I shall. I begin to feel I've made a mistake.'

'In coming to this side at all?'

'I think I have. After all it is not very important.'

'What is not important? I think it very important.'

'Perhaps it may be to you, and perhaps you may be able to keep it up. But the more I think of it the less excuse I seem to have for deserting the old ways of the family. What is there in those fellows down there to make a fellow feel that he ought to bind himself to them neck and heels?'

'Their principles.'

'Yes, their principles! I believe I have some vague idea as to supporting property and rank and all that kind of thing. But the more I see of it all, the less I feel it. I don't know that anybody wants to attack anything.'

'Somebody soon would want to attack it if there were no defenders.'

'I suppose there is an outside power,—the people, or public opinion, or whatever they choose to call it. And the country will have to go very much as that outside power chooses. Here, in Parliament, everybody will be as conservative as the outside will let them. I don't think it matters on which side you sit;—but it does matter that you shouldn't have to act with those who go against the grain with you. I like the other set the best.'

'I never heard a worse political argument in my life.'

'I dare say not,—but perhaps that may be because I am unable to explain myself. However here's Sir Timothy. When he looks in that way, all buckram,* deportment, and solemnity, I know he's going to pitch into somebody or do something unhandsome.' At this moment the Leader of the House came in from behind the Speaker's chair and took his place between Mr. Roby and Sir Orlando Drought, those two gentlemen forcing themselves into smaller spaces in order that room might be made for the great man. Silverbridge had been right in saying that Sir Timothy's air was solemn, though perhaps he was carried away by personal feelings when he spoke of buckram and deportment. When a man has to declare a solemn purpose on a solemn occasion in a solemn place, it is needful that he should be solemn himself. And though the solemnity which befits a man best on such an occasion will be that which the importance of the moment may produce, without thought given by himself to his own outward person or dignity, still, who is there can refrain himself from some attempt? Who can boast, who that has been versed in the ways and duties of high places, that he has kept himself free from all study of grace, of feature, of attitude, of gait—or even of dress? For most of our bishops, for most of our judges, of our Statesmen, our orators, our generals, for many even of our doctors and our parsons, even our attorneys, our tax-gatherers, and certainly our butlers and our coachmen, Mr. Turveydrop, the great professor of deportment, has done much. But there should always be the art to underlie and protect the art;—the art that can hide the art. The really great and clever archbishop,—the really potent Chief Justice, the man who, as a politician, will absolutely succeed in becoming a king of men, should know how to carry his buckram without showing it. It was in this that Sir Timothy perhaps failed a little. There are men who look as though they were born to wear blue ribbons, and who can sit in raised chairs so easily as to make the spectator feel that chairs not raised would be out of place for them. It has come, probably, from study, but it seems to be natural. Sir Timothy did not impose on those who looked at him as do these men. You could see a little of the paint; you could hear the crumple of the starch and the padding; you could trace something of uneasiness in the would-be composed grandeur of the brow. 'Turveydrop!' the spectator would say to himself. But after all it may be a question whether a man be open to reproach for not doing that well which the greatest man among us,—if we could find one great enough,—would not do at all.

For I think we must hold that true personal dignity should be achieved,—must, if it be quite true, have been achieved,—without any personal effort. Though it be evinced, in part, by the carriage of the body, that carriage should be the fruit of the operation of the mind. Even when it be assisted by external garniture such as special clothes, and wigs, and ornaments, such garniture should have been prescribed and allotted by the Sovereign or by custom, and should not have been selected by the wearer. In regard to speech a man may study all that which may make him suasive, but if he go beyond that he will trench on* those histrionic efforts which he will know to be wrong because he will be ashamed to acknowledge them. It is good to be beautiful, but it should come of God and not of the hairdresser. And personal dignity is a great possession; but a man should struggle for it no more than he would for beauty. Many, however, do struggle for it, and with such success that, though they do not achieve quite the real thing, still they get something on which they can bolster themselves up and be mighty. As this was what Sir Timothy did he was not perhaps fairly subject to all the scorn which Lord Silverbridge threw upon him.

Others, older men than Silverbridge, perhaps saw quite as much as did our young friend, but they were more complaisant and probably more reasonable. They, too, heard the crackle of the buckram, and were aware that the last touch of awe had come upon that brow just as its owner was emerging from the shadow of the Speaker's chair;—but to them it was a thing of course. A real Caesar is not to be found every day, nor can we always have a Pitt to control our debates. That kind of thing, that last touch has its effect. Of course it is all paint,—but how would the poor girl look before the gaslights if there were no paint? The House of Commons likes a little deportment on occasions. If a special man looks very much bigger than you, you can console yourself by reflecting that he also looks very much bigger than your fellows. Sir Timothy probably knew what he was about, and did himself on the whole more good than harm by his little tricks.

As soon as Sir Timothy had taken his seat, with a certain amount of cheering which also showed that the occasion was a special one, Mr. Ratler got up from the opposition bench to ask him some question on a matter of finance. The brewers were very anxious about publican licences.* Could the Chancellor of the Exchequer say whether there was any truth in the rumours which suggested that an alteration in regard to the licences would be proposed in the budget? Notice had of course been given, and the questioner had stated a quarter of an hour previously that he would postpone his query till the Chancellor of the Exchequer was in the House.

Now Sir Timothy rose from his seat, and in his blandest manner began by apologising for his late appearance. He was sorry that he had been prevented by public business from being in his place to answer the honourable gentleman's question in its proper turn. And even now, he feared that he must for the present decline to give any answer which could be supposed to be satisfactory. It would probably be his duty to make a statement to the House on the following day,—a statement which he was not quite prepared to make at the present moment. But in the existing state of things he was unwilling to make any reply to any question by which he might seem to bind the Government to any opinion. Then he sat down. And rising again not long afterwards, when the House had gone through certain formal duties, he moved that it should be adjourned till the next day. Then all the members trooped out, and with the others Tregear and Lord Silverbridge. 'So that is the end of your first day of Parliament,' said Silverbridge.

'The work certainly has so far been neither difficult nor tedious. But what does it all mean?'

'Let us go to the Carlton and hear what the fellows are saying.' So they went to the Carlton and heard what the fellows were saying.

On that evening both the young men dined at Mr. Boncassen's house. Though Tregear had been cautioned not to write to Lady Mary, and though he was not to see her before Easter, still it was so completely understood that he was about to become her husband, that he was entertained in that capacity by all those who were concerned in the family. Isabel professed herself to be very fond of him, and had already desired him to call her by her Christian name,—almost to the dismay of her own lover. 'If Mary is to be my sister,' she said, 'I suppose he is to be my brother. And what is the good of a Christian name if nobody is to use it?' Silverbridge did not quite dare to say that it was intended for his own exclusive use and benefit.

'And so they will all go out,' said Mr. Boncassen.

'That seems to be the general idea,' said the expectant son-in-law. 'When two men want to be first and neither will give way, they can't very well get on in the same boat together.' Then he expatiated angrily on the treachery of Sir Timothy, and Tregear in a more moderate way joined in the same opinion.

'Upon my word, young men, I doubt whether you are right,' said Mr. Boncassen. 'Whether it can be possible that a man should have risen to such a position with so little patriotism as you attribute to our friend, I will not pretend to say. I should think that in England it was impossible. But of this I am sure, that the facility which exists here for a minister or ministers to go out of office without disturbance of the Crown is a great blessing. You say the other party will come in.'

'That is most probable,' said Silverbridge. 'The House is nearly evenly divided. This majority,—I suppose I ought to say our majority,—melted away at the last election.'

'With us the other party never comes in,—never has a chance of coming in,—except once in four years when the President is elected.* And that one event, which is so managed by wire-pullers that it hardly shows the real feeling of the country at that moment, binds us all for four years.'

'But you do change your ministers,' said Tregear.

'A secretary may quarrel with the President, or he may have the gout, or be convicted of peculation. No doubt we change our ministers, but we don't change our policy even though the country should be ever so determined.'

'And yet you think yourselves more nearly free than we are.'

'I am not so sure of that. We have had a pretty difficult task, that of carrying on a Government in a new country which is nevertheless more populous than almost any old country. The influxions are so rapid that every ten years the nature of the people is changed; and as they change we have got to fit our institutions to them. It isn't easy; and though I think on the whole we've done pretty well, I am not going to boast that Washington is as yet the seat of a political Paradise.'

'I cannot make your politics out at all,' said Silverbridge.

'If you behave yourself well you shall be taught before long,' said Isabel.

CHAPTER 77

'MABEL, GOOD-BYE'

WHEN Tregear first came to town with his arm in a sling, and bandages all round him, in order that he might be formally accepted by the

Duke,—when as far as his bones and limbs were concerned, he ought to have remained at Harrington subject to the soft custody of Lady Chiltern,—he had himself taken to one other house besides the house in Carlton Terrace. A few days after that dinner he went to Belgrave Square, in order that he might announce his fate to Lady Mabel Grex;—but Lady Mabel Grex was not there. The Earl was ill at Brighton, and Lady Mabel had gone down with Miss Cassewary to nurse him. The old woman who came to him in the hall and whom he had known for many years told him that the Earl was supposed to be very ill;—he had been attacked by the gout, but in spite of the gout, and in spite of the doctors, he had insisted on being taken to his club. Then he had been removed to Brighton, under the doctor's advice, chiefly in order that he might be kept out of the way of temptation. And now he was supposed to be very ill,—very ill indeed. The old woman hinted something as to gout in the stomach.* 'My Lord is so imprudent,' she said, shaking her old head in real unhappiness. For though the Earl had been a tyrant to everyone near him, yet when a poor woman becomes old it is something to have even a tyrant to protect her. 'My Lord' always had been imprudent. Tregear knew that it had been the theory of my Lord's life that to eat, drink, and die was better than to abstain and live.

Had he been in fair health, with his leisure at his own command, Tregear would have gone at once to Brighton himself. There had been that between him and Lady Mabel which would have justified that intrusion even in her father's present condition;—but he was afraid of the journey and of the exertion which would attend such a visit, and therefore he wrote to her announcing his own good fortune,—as follows. As soon as his good fortune was fixed he felt it to be imperative on him to announce it, at any rate to her.

'MY DEAR MABEL,

'I am up in town again as you will perceive, although I am still in a very helpless condition, and am hardly able to write even this letter. I called to-day in Belgrave Square and was very sorry to hear so bad an account of your father. Had I been able to travel I should have come down to you. When I am able I will do so if you would wish to see me. In the meantime pray tell me how he is, and how you are.

'My news is this. The Duke has accepted me. It is great news to me, and I hope will be acceptable to you. I do believe that if ever a friend has been anxious for a friend's welfare you have been anxious for mine,—as I have been and ever shall be for yours.

'Of course this thing will be very much to me. I will not speak now of my love for the girl who is to become my wife. In that respect I do not know that I am different from any other, and you might again call me Romeo. Nor do I like to say much of what may now be my pecuniary prospects. Most certainly I did not ask Mary to become my wife because I supposed she would be rich. But as certainly I could not have married her or anyone else who was not rich. I do not know whether you will understand me. My conscience is not quite clear,—and yet when I argue the matter with myself I think that it ought to be clear. I do at any rate so far trust myself as to think that I shall make her a good husband.

'What are the Duke's intentions I have not the slightest idea, nor shall I ask him. I am to go down to Matching at Easter, and shall of course endeavour to have some time fixed. I suppose the Duke will say something about money. If he does not I shall not.

'Pray write to me at once, and tell me when I shall see you.

'Your affectionate Cousin,

'F.O. TREGEAR.'

In answer to this there came a note in a very few words. She congratulated him,—not very warmly,—but expressed a hope that she might see him soon. But she told him not to come to Brighton. The Earl was better but very cross. She at any rate would be up in town before long. He was to understand that she did not write at length because she would see him soon. There were other notes which passed between them, but still he was desired not to go to Brighton. Then also towards the end of the month it became suddenly known in London that Lord Grex had died at Brighton. There was a Garter to be given away, and everybody was filled with regret that such an ornament to the peerage, to the turf, and to society generally should have departed from them. The Conservative papers remembered how excellent a politician he had been in his younger days, and the world was informed that the family of Grex was about the oldest in Great Britain of which authentic records were in existence. Then there came another note from Lady Mabel to Tregear. 'I shall be in town on the 31st, in the old house, with Miss Cassewary, and will see you if you can come on the 1st. Come early,—at eleven if you can.'

On the day named and at the hour fixed he was in Belgrave Square. He had known this house since he was a boy, and could well remember how, when he first entered it during his holidays, he had thought with some awe of the grandeur of the Earl, who was his cousin. The Earl had then not paid much attention to him, but he had become very much taken by the grace, and good nature, and general attractiveness of the girl who at once had owned him as a cousin, and who was about a year younger than himself. 'You are my cousin Frank,' she had said; 'I am so glad to have a cousin.' He could remember the words now as though they had been spoken to him only yesterday. Then there had quickly grown to be friendship between him and this, as he thought, sweetest of all girls. At that time he had just gone to Eton; but before he left Eton they had sworn to love each other, still as cousins. At that time she had been brought out to the world and should perhaps have known better than to have loved him so well. He was still a boy, though not a boyish boy, and he too ought to have known better. And so it had been and the thing had grown, till at last, just when he had taken his degree, two matters had been settled between them; the first was that each loved the other irretrievably, irrevocably, passionately; the second, that all this love was to go for nothing, and that it was altogether out of the question that they should ever marry each other.

It is but fair to Tregear to say that this last decision originated with the lady. He had told her that he certainly would marry her, or at any rate would hold himself engaged to marry her at some future time; but she had thrown this aside at once. 'How was it possible,' she said, 'that two such creatures as they were, brought up in luxury, and taught to expect that they were to enjoy all the good things of the world, should expect to live and be happy together without an income?' He offered to go to the bar;—but she asked him whether he really believed that he would succeed at the bar, and also whether he thought it well that such a one as she should wait say a dozen years for such success. 'When the time comes,' she said, 'I should be an old woman and you would be a wretched man.' She released him,—said that they would both be released and free; declared with apparent gaiety her own purpose of marrying well; and then, though there had been a moment in which her own assurance of her own love had been passionate enough, she went so far as to tell him that she was heart-whole. 'We have been two foolish children, but we cannot be children any longer,' she said. 'There must be an end of it.' Then she had, laughing, bade him to look for a rich wife, and had declared her purpose of finding for herself a rich husband, 'whom,' she had said, 'I shall love down to the ground.'

What had hitherto been the result of all this the reader knows,—and unfortunately Tregear knew also. He had taken the privilege given to him, and had found for himself a rich wife;—and had made so complete a use of the privilege that he had in truth transferred his heart as well as his allegiance. Where is the young man who cannot do so;—how few are there who do not do so when their first fit of passion has come on them at one-and-twenty? And at first he had thought that she would do the same. But gradually he found that she had not done so, did not do so, could not do so! When she first heard of Lady Mary she had not reprimanded him,—but she could not keep herself from showing the bitterness of her disappointment. Though she would still boast of her own strength and of her own purpose, and would speak of the world before her as an oyster which she would still open by a brilliant marriage, yet it was too clear to him that she was wounded and very sore. She would have liked him to remain single at any rate till she herself were married. But the permission had been hardly given before he availed himself of it. And then he talked to her not only of the brilliancy of his prospects,—which she could have forgiven,—but of his love—his love! He soon saw his mistake,—or rather that he had been mistaken as to her. As to himself, what he had said was true, and he thought it best that the truth should be known. The woman he loved now was not her, but Lady Mary.

Then she had refused one offer after another, and he had known it all. There was nothing in which she was concerned that she did not tell him,—not altogether with his approval. He did not wish to divide himself from her, but he did think that if the intercourse were less close it might be better for herself. But she told him everything. Then young Silverbridge had come across her, and she had determined that he should be her husband. Tregear would have been well pleased that it should have been so, but he had never quite trusted that it would be so. She had been very nearly successful,—so nearly that at moments she had felt sure of success. But the prize had slipped from her through her own fault. She knew well enough that it was her own fault. When a girl submits to play such a game as that, she should not stand on too nice scruples. She had told herself this many a time since;—but the prize was gone.

All this Tregear knew, and knowing it almost dreaded the coming interview. Of course he had sought it, but it was impossible that he should not seek it. He could not without actual cruelty have avoided her. Had he done so before he could not have continued to do so now, when she was left alone in the world. Her father had not been much to her, but still his presence had enabled her to be the mistress of a house in London, and to put herself before the world as being somebody. Now she would be almost nobody. And she had lost her rich prize, while he,—out of the same treasury as it were,—had won his! It would be difficult indeed to console her, and unreasonable to expect true congratulation.

The door was opened to him by the same old woman, by which he judged that the powder-headed footmen were already gone, and he was shown, at a funereal pace, up into the drawing-room which he had known so well. Then he was told that Lady Mabel would be down to him directly. As he looked about him he could see that already had been commenced that work of division of spoil which is sure to follow the death of most of us. Things were already gone which used to be familiar to his eyes, and the room, though not dismantled, had been deprived of many of its little prettinesses and was ugly. Any stranger entering it would have known that the family had been or was to be disturbed.

In about ten minutes she came down to him,—with so soft a step and hand that he would not have been aware of her entrance had he not seen her form in the mirror. Then, when he turned round to greet her, he was astonished by the blackness of her appearance. It seemed to him as though the milliner had altered even the colour of her countenance. She looked as though she had become ten years older since he had last seen her, and yet he thought that she had never been more handsome. As she came up to him she was grave and almost solemn in her gait, but there was no sign of any tears. Why should there have been a tear? Women weep, and men too, not from grief, but from emotion. Indeed, grave and slow as was her step, and serious, almost solemn, as was her gait, there was something of a smile on her mouth as she gave him her hand. And yet her face was very sad, seeming before she spoke a word to declare to him something of the hopelessness of her heart. 'And so the Duke has consented,' she said. These were her first words,—referring to the one matter on which he had determined that he would say as little as possible. He had told her that in his letter, but, since that, her father had died, and she had been left, he did not as yet know how far desolate or how far impoverished, but, he feared, with no pleasant worldly prospects before her. He certainly did not mean to sing a paean to his own glory. She had once called him Romeo because he had said that he dearly loved the girl whom he was now to marry. He had perceived that he had then made a mistake, and he certainly would not repeat it on this occasion.

'Yes, Mabel;—that I suppose will be settled. I have been so shocked to hear all this.'

'It has been very sad;—has it not? Sit down, Frank. You and I have a good deal to say to each other now that we have met. It was no good your going down to Brighton. Everything was so uncomfortable there! He would not have seen you, and at last I never left him.'

'Was Percival there?' She only shook her head. 'That was dreadful.'

'It was not Percival's fault. He would not see him. Nor till the last hour or two had come would he believe in his own danger. Nor was he ever frightened for a moment,—not even then.'

'Was he good to you?'

'Good to me! Well;—he liked my being there. And he liked to have Miss Cass there. But of course he scolded us always. Poor papa! It had gone so far with him that he could not be good to anyone. I think that he felt that it would be unmanly not to be the same to the end.'

'He would not see Percival?'

'When it was suggested he would only ask what good Percival could do him. I did send for him at last, in my terror, but he was not there in time to see his father alive. And when he did come he only told me how badly his father had treated him! It was very dreadful!'

'I did so feel for you!'

'I am sure you did, and will. After all, Frank, I think that the pious godly people have the best of it, at any rate in this world. Let them be ever so covetous, ever so false, ever so hard-hearted, the mere fact that they must keep up appearances, makes them comfortable to those around them. Poor papa was not comfortable to me;—nor I fear will Percival be so. A little hypocrisy, a little sacrifice to the feelings of the world, may be such a blessing!'

'I am sorry that you should feel it so.'

'Yes; it is sad to have to make such a confession. But you;—everything is smiling with you! Let us talk about your plans.'

But this was what he had determined that he would if possible avoid. 'Another time will do for that. I had come to hear about your own affairs.'

'There they are,' she said, pointing round the room. 'I have no other affairs. You see that I am going from here.'

'And where are you going?' She shook her head. 'With whom will you live?'

'With Miss Cass, I suppose. Two old maids together! I know nothing further. Both my aunts have asked me to go to them, but as I greatly dislike them both that does not sound comfortable. One is very high church, and the other very low. How could I live with either of them?'

'But about money? That is if I am justified in asking.'

'What would you not be justified in asking? Do you not know that I would tell you every secret of my heart,—if my heart had a secret? It seems that I have given up what was to have been my fortune. It never was much, a claim of twelve thousand pounds on Grex. But I have abandoned it.'

'And there is nothing.'

'There will be scrapings, they tell me,—unless Percival refuses to agree. This house is mortgaged,—but not for its value. And there are some jewels. But all that is detestable,—a mere grovelling among mean hundreds; whereas you,—you will soar among——'

'Oh Mabel!'

'Well;—what is it?'

'Do not say hard things to me.'

'No, indeed; why should I,—I who have been preaching that comfortable doctrine of hypocrisy? I will say nothing hard. But I would sooner talk of your good things than of my evil ones. And so I think would you.'

'No;—not so.'

'Then you must talk about them for my sake. How was it that the Duke came round at last?'

'I hardly know. She sent for me.'

'A fine high-spirited girl. These Pallisers have more courage about them than one expects from their outward manner. Silverbridge has plenty of it.'

'I remember telling you he could be obstinate.'

'And I remember it, and I remember that I did not believe you. Now I know it. He has that sort of pluck which enables a man to break a girl's heart,—or to destroy a girl's hopes,—without wincing. He can tell a girl to her face that she can go to the—mischief for him. There are so many men who can't do that,—from cowardice, though their hearts be ever so well inclined. "I have changed my mind." There is something great in the courage of a man who can say that to a woman, in so many words. The man who can do that will live to be great at last. All men are willing enough,—as far as any feeling of mercy is concerned. All men are willing enough,—though some are too poor-spirited to effect their escape at all. Most of them when they escape, escape by lies and subterfuges. Or they run away and won't allow themselves to be heard of. They trust to the chapter of accidents,* and leave things to arrange themselves. But when a man can look a girl in the face with those seemingly soft eyes, and say with that seemingly soft mouth,—"I have changed my mind,"—though she would look him dead in return if she could, or kill him in any other way, still she must admire him.'

He hardly dared to ask a question about this, and yet he was obliged to say something. 'Are you speaking of Silverbridge now?'

'Of course I am speaking of Silverbridge. I suppose I ought to hide it all and not to tell you. But, as you are the only person I do tell, you must put up with me. I cannot quite talk even to Cass about all this. Yes;—when I taxed him with his falsehood to me,—for he had been false,—he answered me with those very words. "I have changed my mind." He could not lie. To speak the truth was a necessity to him,—even at the expense of his gallantry, his courtesy, almost of his humanity.'

'Has he been false to you, Mabel?'

'Of course he has. But there is nothing to quarrel about, if you mean that. People do not quarrel now about such things. A girl has to fight her own battle with her own pluck and her own wits. As with these weapons she is generally stronger than her enemy, she succeeds sometimes although everything else is against her. I think I am courageous, but his courage beat mine. I craned at the first fence. When he was willing to swallow my bait my hand was not firm enough to strike the hook in his jaws. Had I not quailed then I think I should have—"had him." '

'It is horrid to hear you talk like this.' She was leaning over from her seat, looking, in black as she was, so much older than her wont, with something about her of that air of unworldly serious thoughtfulness which a mourning garb always gives. And yet her words were so worldly, so unfeminine, as Tregear said, 'so horrid'!

'I have got to tell the truth to somebody. It was so, just as I have said. Of course I did not love him. How could I love him after what has passed? But there need have been nothing much in that. I don't suppose that dukes' eldest sons often get married for love.'

'Miss Boncassen loves him.'

'I dare say the beggar's daughter loved King Cophetua. When you come to distances such as that, there can be love. The very fact that a man should have descended so far in quest of beauty,—the flattery of it alone,—will produce love. When the angels came after the daughters of men of course the daughters of men loved them. The distance between him and me, great as it is in all good things, is not great enough to have produced that sort of worship. There was no reason open to the world why Lady Mabel Grex should not be good enough wife for the son of the Duke of Omnium.'

'Certainly not.'

'And therefore I was not struck as by the shining of a light from heaven. No, I cannot say I loved him. I certainly shall not tell you that

I loved him. Frank,—I was gone beyond worshipping even a light from heaven.'

'Then I do not know that you could blame him,' he said very seriously.

'Just so;—and as I have chosen to be honest I have told him everything. But I had my revenge first.'

'I would have said nothing.'

'You would have recommended—delicacy, no doubt. You think that women should be delicate let them suffer what they may. Men are always in favour of hypocrisy and pretence for women. A woman should not let it be known that she has any human nature in her. I had him on the hip,* and for a moment I used my power. He had certainly done me a wrong. He had asked for my love,—and, with the delicacy which you all commend, I had not, at once, grasped at all that such a request conveyed. Then, as he told me so frankly, "he changed his mind!" Did he not wrong me?'

'He should not have raised false hopes.'

'False hopes!' she exclaimed, bursting out almost into anger. 'That comes from you so well!'

'What am I to say?'

'Well;—yes; false hopes! But, though I may call them so, you should not. He told me that he had changed his mind. I think I loved him then as nearly as ever I did,—because he looked me full in the face. Well,—then I told him I had never cared for him, and that he need have nothing on his conscience. His conscience had been wounded;—but I doubt whether he was glad to hear it. Men are so vain.'

'And so he went?'

'I told him more than that. But I have talked too much of myself. And so you are to be the Duke's son-in-law.'

'It seems so.'

'And she will have hundreds of thousands.'

'Thousands I should think;—but I do not in the least know.'

'Nor care?'

'I do not think very much about it. I feel that he will provide for her.'

'And that you, having secured her, can creep under his wing like an additional ducal chick. It is very comfortable. The Duke will be quite a Providence to you. I wonder that all young gentlemen do not marry heiresses;—it is so easy. And you have got your seat in Parliament too! Oh, your luck! When I look back upon it all it seems so hard to me! It was for you,—for you, that I used to be anxious, thinking it would be so hard for you to come with your feet upon the ground. Now it is I who have not an inch of ground to stand upon.' Then he approached her and put out his hand to her. 'No,' she said, putting both her hands behind her back, 'for God's sake let there be no tenderness,—no attempt at that. But is it not cruel? Think of my advantages at that moment when you and I agreed that our paths should be separate. My fortune then had not been made quite shipwreck by my father and brother. I had before me all that society could offer. I was called handsome and clever. Where was there a girl more likely to make her way to the top? And what am I now?'

'You may do so still.'

'No;—no;—I cannot. And you at least should not tell me so. I did not know then the virulence of the malady which had fallen on me. I did not know then that, because of you, other men would be abhorrent to me. I thought that I was as easy-hearted as you have proved yourself.'

'How cruel you can be!'

'Have I done anything to interfere with you? Have I said a word even to that young lad, when I might have said a word? Yes, to him I did say something; but I waited, and would not say it, while a word could hurt you. Shall I tell you what I told him? Just everything that has ever happened between you and me.'

'You did?'

'Yes;—because I saw that I could trust him. I told him because I wanted him to be quite sure that I had never loved him. But, Frank, I have put no spoke in your wheel. There has not been a moment since you told me of your love for this rich young lady in which I would not have helped you had help been in my power. Whomever I may have harmed or tried to harm, I have never harmed or tried to harm you.'

'Am I not as clear from blame towards you?'

'No, Frank, no; you are not. You have done me the terrible evil of ceasing to love me.'

'It was at your own bidding.'

'Certainly! But if I were to bid you to cut my throat, would you do it?'

'Was it not you who decided that we could not wait for each other?'

'And should it not have been for you to decide that you at any rate would strive to wait?'

'You also would have married!'

'It almost angers me that you should not see the difference. A girl unless she marries becomes nothing, as I have become nothing now. A man does not want a pillar on which to lean,—or ought not. A man, when he has done as you had done with me, and made a girl's heart all his own, even though his own heart had been flexible and plastic as yours is, should have been true to her, at least for a while. I at any rate might have been the first to show that I could make the change. Did it never occur to you that you owed something to me?'

'I have always owed you very much.'

'There should have been some touch of chivalry if not of love to make you feel that a second passion should have been postponed, at any rate for a year or two. You could wait without growing old. You might have allowed yourself a little space to dwell—I was going to say on the sweetness of your memories. But they were not sweet, Frank; they were not sweet to you.'

'These rebukes, Mabel, will rob them of their sweetness,—for a time.'

'It is gone; all gone,' she said, shaking her head,—'gone from me because I have been so easily deserted; gone from you because the change has been so easy to you. How long was it, Frank, after you had left me that day, before you were basking happily in the smiles of Lady Mary Palliser?'

'It was not very long,—as months go.'

'Say days, Frank.'

'I have to defend myself, and I will do so with truth. It was not very long,—as months go; but why should it have been long, whether for months or days? I had to cure myself of a wound, to cauterise a scar.'

'To put a plaster on a scratch, Frank.'

'And the sooner a man can do that the more manly he is. Is it a sign of strength, do you suppose, to wail under a sorrow that cannot be cured,—or of truth to perpetuate the appearance of a woe?'

'Has it been an appearance with me?'

'I am speaking of myself now. I am driven to speak of myself by the bitterness of your words. It was you who decided,—and your decision for the moment crushed me.'

'You accepted it very easily.'

'Because it was based not only on my unfitness for such a marriage, but on yours. When I saw that there would be perhaps some years of misery for you, of course I accepted your decision. That romance was over. The sweetness had been very sweet to me.'

'Oh Frank, was it ever sweet to you?'

'And the triumph of it had been very great. I had been assured of the love of her who among all the high ones of the world seemed to me to be the highest. There were moments in which I was almost drunk with the idea that Lady Mabel Grex was all my own.'

'What was that to Lady Mary Palliser? But you are hardened now to your own successes.'.

'Then came your decision. Do you really believe that I could abandon the sweetness, that I could be robbed of my triumph, that I could think I could never again be allowed to put my arm round your waist, never again to feel your cheek close to mine, that I should lose all that to me for a month or two had seemed to lift me among the gods, without feeling it?'

'Frank, Frank,' she said, rising to her feet, and stretching out her hands as though she were going to give him back all these joys.

'Of course I felt it. I did not then know what was before me.' When he said this she sank back immediately upon her seat. 'I was wretched enough,—very wretched. As most of us have to feel, I suppose, at some period of our lives, I felt then as though all my light had gone out. I had lost a leg and could not walk; my eyes, and must always hereafter be blind; my fitness to be among men, and must always hereafter be secluded. It is so that a man is stricken down when some terrible trouble comes upon him. But it is given to him to retrick his beams.'*

'You have retricked yours.'

'Yes;—and the strong man will show his strength by doing it quickly. Mabel, I sorrowed for myself greatly when that word was spoken,—sorrowed partly because I thought that your love could so easily be taken from me.'

'No;—no;—no!'

'And, since I have found that it has not been so, I have sorrowed for you also. But I do not blame myself, and,—and I will not submit to have blame even from you.' She stared him in the face as he said this. 'A man should never submit to blame.'

'But if he has deserved it?'

'Who is to be the judge? But why should we contest this? You do not really wish to trample on me.'

'No;—not that.'

'Nor to disgrace me;—nor to make me feel myself disgraced in my own judgment!' Then there was a pause for some moments as though he had left her without another word to say. 'Shall I go now?' he asked.

'Oh, Frank!'

'I fear that my presence only makes you unhappy.'

'Then what will your absence do? When shall I see you again? But, no; I will not see you again. Not for many days,—not for years. Why should I? Frank, is it wicked that I should love you?' He could only shake his head in answer to this. 'If it be so wicked that I must be punished for it eternally, still I love you. I can never, never, never love another. You cannot understand it. Oh, God,—that I had never understood it myself! I think, I think, that I would go with you now anywhere, facing all misery, all judgments, all disgrace. You know, do you not, that if it were possible, I should not say so. But as I know that you would not stir a step with me, I do say so.'

'I know it is not meant.'

'It is meant, though it could not be done. Frank, I must not see her, not for a while; not for years. I do not wish to hate her, but how can I help it? Do you remember when she flew into your arms in this room?'

'I remember it.'

'Of course you do. It is your great joy now to remember that, and such like. She must be very good! Though I hate her!'

'Do not say that you hate her, Mabel.'

'Though I hate her she must be very good. It was a fine and a brave thing to do. I have done it; but never before the world like that,—have I, Frank? Oh, Frank, I shall never do it again. Go now, and do not touch me. Let us both pray that in ten years we may meet as passionless friends;—but now you had better go.' He came to her hardly knowing what he meant, but purposing, as though by instinct, at any rate to take her hand as he parted from her. But she, putting both her hands before her face, and throwing herself onto the sofa, buried her head among the cushions.

'Is there not to be another word?' he said. Lying as she did, she still was able to make a movement of dissent, and he left her, muttering just one word between his teeth, 'Mabel, good-bye.'

CHAPTER 78

THE DUKE RETURNS TO OFFICE

THAT farewell took place on the Friday morning. Tregear as he walked out of the Square almost felt as though he could never put his feet in those precincts again without sacrilege,—at any rate till the years had passed by of which Mabel had spoken. He knew now that he had been the cause of a great shipwreck. All that he had said of himself in that interview had been perfectly true. At first when that passionate love had been declared,—he could hardly remember whether with the fullest passion by him or by her,—he had been as a god walking upon air. His triumph had been so great that all consequences had been as nothing to him. That she who seemed to be so much above him should have owned that she was all his own seemed then to be world enough for him. For a few weeks he lived a hero to himself, in that world of romance in which the hero is able to dispense for a while with all sublunary things, and to tell himself that for him, for him perhaps alone, the glory of a passion is sufficient. In those halcyon moments no common human care is allowed to intrude itself. To one who has thus entered in upon the heroism of romance his own daily work, his dinners, clothes, income, father and mother, sisters and brothers, his own street and house are nothing. Hunting, shooting, rowing, Alpine-climbing, football, even speeches in Parliament,—if they perchance have been attained to,—all become leather or prunella.* The heavens have been opened to him, and he walks among them like a god. So it had been with Tregear. Then had come the second phase of his passion,— a phase which is also not uncommon to young men who venture to soar high in their first assaults. He was told that it would not do; and was not so told by a hard-hearted parent,—who after the manner of parents might probably in time cease to be hard-hearted,—but by the young lady herself, who clearly had made up her mind. And she had spoken so reasonably of his and of her own future life, that he had yielded, and had walked away home with that sudden feeling of a vile return to his own mean belongings, to his father and mother, his lodgings, and his income which not a few ambitious young men have experienced. But she had absolutely convinced him. Then had come the journey to Italy, and the reader knows all the rest. He certainly had not derogated in transferring his affections from Lady Mabel Grex to Lady Mary Palliser,—but it may be doubted whether in this second love he had walked among the stars as in the first. A man can hardly mount twice among the stars. But he had been as eager in it as in the first,—and as true. And he had now succeeded, without any flaw on his conscience. It had been agreed, when that first disruption took place, that he and Mabel should be friends; and, as to a friend, he had told her of his hopes, his intentions, and his difficulties. When first she had mingled something of sarcasm with her congratulations, though it had annoyed him, it had hardly made him unhappy. When she called him Romeo and spoke of herself as Rosaline, he took her remark as indicating not an enduring love for him, but some petulance on her part that he should so soon have forgotten his for her. That had been womanly and he could forgive it. And when she added the assurance,—which perhaps had been womanly also, but which certainly he did not believe,—that she had in truth never loved him, though it had vexed him a little, it did not disturb him much. He had his other great and solid happiness to support him. Then he had believed that she would soon marry, if not Silverbridge, then some other fitting young nobleman, and that all would be well. But now things were very far from well. He still possessed the solid rock on which his own fortunes were to be built; but the storm which was howling round her afflicted him also.

Perhaps the bitterest feeling of all was that her love should have been so much stronger, so much more enduring than his own. He could not but remember how in his first agony he had blamed her because she had declared that she could cease to love him. He then told himself that such ceasing would be to him impossible, and that had her nature been as high as his, it would have been as impossible to her. Which nature must he now regard as the higher? She had done her best to rid herself of the load of her passion and had failed. But he had freed himself with convenient haste. All that he had said as to the manliness of conquering grief had been true enough,—wise enough at any rate. But still he could not quit himself of some feeling of disgrace in that he had changed and she had not.

As he walked to his lodgings and sat there, purposeless till the time should come in which he might walk down to the House, he tried to comfort himself with reflecting that Mary was all his own,—that in that matter he had been victorious and would soon reap the fruit of his victory;—but during that hour or two he thought more of Mabel than Mary.

When the time came in which he could employ himself he called for Silverbridge on his way, and they walked together across the park to Westminster. Silverbridge was gay and full of eagerness as to the coming ministerial statement, but Tregear could not turn his mind from the work of the morning. 'I don't seem to care very much about it,' he said at last, 'though of course I am anxious to see how these things are done.'

'I do care very much,' said Silverbridge.

'What difference will it make?'

'I breakfasted with the governor this morning, and I have not seen him in such good spirits since,—well, for a long time.' The date to which Silverbridge would have referred, had he not checked himself, was that of the evening on which it had been agreed between him and his father that Mabel Grex should be promoted to the seat of highest honour in the house of Palliser,—but that was a matter which must henceforward be buried in silence. 'He did not say as much but I feel perfectly sure that he and Mr. Monk between them have arranged a new Government.'

'I don't see any matter for joy in that to Conservatives like you and me.'

'He is my father,—and as he is going to be your father-in-law I should have thought that you also might have been pleased.'

'Oh yes;—if he likes it. But I have heard so often of the crushing cares of office, and I had thought that of all living men he had been the most crushed by them.'

'I don't suppose that one ought to think that what a man may feel about himself once, he will feel for ever.'

'I suppose not,' said Tregear.

'A man changes his idea. When I have a headache of a morning I swear that I will never smoke another cigar. But I go on afterwards. I believe the governor will like to go back, and if he does I don't think the country could have a better man whether he be Liberal or Conservative.'

'I quite agree with that,' said Tregear.

All that had to be done in the House of Commons on that afternoon was finished before five o'clock. By half-past five the House, and all the purlieus of the House, were deserted. And yet at four, immediately after prayers, there had been such a crowd that members had been unable to find seats! Tregear and Silverbridge having been early had both succeeded in getting possession of their accustomed places high up behind the ministers, but those who had been less careful were obliged to listen as best they could in the galleries. The stretching out of necks and the holding of hands behind the ears did not last long. Sir Timothy had not much to say, but what he did say was spoken with a dignity which certainly seemed to anticipate future exaltation rather than present downfall. There had arisen a question in regard to revenue,—he need hardly tell them that it was that question in reference to brewers' licences to which the honourable gentleman opposite had alluded on the previous day,—as to which unfortunately he was not in accord with his noble friend the Prime Minister. It was certainly to be regretted that a matter comparatively small should lead to a disruption, but as matters referring to the revenue of the country had been more especially transferred to his unworthy hands, he would not take blame to himself for not yielding in this matter. Under the circumstances it was hardly possible that they should at once proceed to business, and he therefore moved that the House should stand adjourned till Tuesday next. That was the whole statement.

Not very long afterwards the Prime Minister made another statement in the House of Lords. As the Chancellor of the Exchequer had very suddenly resigned and had thereby broken up the Ministry, he had found himself compelled to place his resignation in the hands of Her Majesty. Then that House was also adjourned till the Tuesday. On that afternoon all the clubs were alive with admiration at the great cleverness displayed by Sir Timothy in this transaction. It was not only that he had succeeded in breaking up the Ministry,—his determination to do which had been suspected by the political world for weeks,—and that he had done this without incurring violent disgrace; but he had so done it as to throw all the reproach upon his late unfortunate colleague. It was thus that Mr. Lupton explained it. Sir Timothy had been at the pains to ascertain on what matters connected with the revenue Lord Drummond,—or Lord Drummond's closest advisers,—had opinions of their own, opinions strong enough not to be abandoned; and, having discovered that, he also discovered arguments on which to found an exactly contrary opinion. But as the revenue had been, as he said, entrusted specially to his unworthy hands, he was entitled to his own opinion on this matter. 'The majority of the House,' said Mr. Lupton, 'and the entire public, will no doubt give him credit for great self-abnegation.' But then Mr. Lupton was in the habit of making sarcastic remarks.

All this happened on the Friday. During the Saturday it was considered probable that the Cabinet would come to terms with itself, and that these internal wounds would be healed. The general opinion was that Lord Drummond would give way. But on the Sunday morning it was understood that Lord Drummond at any rate would not yield. It was reported that Lord Drummond was willing to purchase his separation from Sir Timothy even at the expense of his office. That Sir Timothy should give way after what he had done seemed to be impossible. Had he done so it would have been impossible for him to recover the respect of the House. Then it was rumoured that two or three others had gone or would go with Sir Timothy. And on Monday morning it was proclaimed that the Prime Minister was not in a condition to withdraw his resignation. On the Tuesday the House met and Mr. Monk announced, still from the opposition benches, that he had that morning been with the Queen. Then there was another adjournment, and all the Liberals knew that the gates of Paradise were again about to be opened to them.

This, at the close of our story, is only interesting to us as affecting the happiness and the character of our Duke. He had now consented to assist Mr. Monk in forming a Government, and to take office under Mr. Monk's leadership. He had had many contests with himself before he could bring himself to this submission. A letter had been written to him,—it is hoped that the reader may remember it,—by a very old friend, the purport of which from that day to this he had not ceased to turn in his mind. He knew that if anything could once again make him contented it would be work; he knew that if he could serve his country it was his duty to serve it; and he knew also that it was only by the adhesion of such men as himself that the traditions of his party could be maintained and its authority preserved. But he had been Prime Minister,—and he was sure that he could never be Prime Minister again. There are in all matters certain little, almost hidden, signs, by which we can measure within our own bosoms the extent of our successes and our failures. A man, if he has been asked to take the lead in some affair, to act as Chairman at some meeting, will know when the duty has been performed, without a word of criticism from without, whether he will again be called on for similar service. Our Duke's friends had told him, especially that old Duke of St. Bungay, that his Ministry had been serviceable to the country; but no one had ever suggested to him that he would again be asked to fill the place which he had filled. He had stopped a gap; and that was all. He would beforehand have declared himself willing to serve his country even in this way; but having done so,—having done that and no more than that,—he felt that he had failed. He had in his soreness declared to himself again and again that he would never more take office. He had much to do to overcome his own scruples before he was able to depart from this promise to himself;—but when he had brought himself to submit to the advice of others he was certainly a happier man.

There was no going to see the Queen. That on the present occasion was done simply by Mr. Monk. But on the Wednesday morning his name appeared in the list of the new Cabinet as President of the Council. He was perhaps a little fidgety, a little fretful, a little too anxious to employ himself and to be employed, a little too desirous of immediate work;—but still he was happy and gracious to those around him. 'I suppose you like that particular office,' Silverbridge said to him that afternoon.

'Well; yes;—not best of all, you know,' and he smiled as he made this admission.

'You mean Prime Minister.'

'No, indeed I don't. Very far from that. I am almost inclined to think that the Premier should always sit in your House. It is certainly better for the country generally that he should be a commoner.* No, Silverbridge; if I could have my way,—which is of course impossible, for I cannot put off my honours,—I would return to my old place. I would return to the Exchequer again* where the work is hard and certain, where a man can do, or at any rate can attempt to do, some special thing. A man there, if he stick to that and does not travel beyond it, need not be popular, need not be a partisan, need not be eloquent, need not be a courtier. He should understand his profession, as should a lawyer or a doctor. If he does that thoroughly he can serve his country without recourse to that parliamentary strategy for which I know that I am unfit.'

'You can't do that in the House of Lords, sir.'

'No; no. I wish the title could have passed over my head, Silverbridge, and gone to you at once.* I think we both should have been suited better. But these are things which one should not consider. Even in this place I may perhaps do something. If it be nothing else, I can be loyal. Shall you attack us very bitterly?'

'I am the only man who does not mean to make any change.'

'How so?'

'I shall stay where I am,—on the Government side of the House.'

'Are you clear about that, my boy?'

'Quite clear.'

'Such changes as that should not be made without very much consideration.'

'I have already written to them at Silverbridge and have had three or four answers. Mr. Du Boung says that the borough is more than gratified. Mr. Sprout regrets it much, and suggests a few months' consideration. Mr. Sprugeon seems to think it does not signify.'

'That is hardly complimentary.'

'No,—not to me. But he is very civil to the family generally. As long as a Palliser represents the borough Mr. Sprugeon thinks that it does not matter much on which side he may sit. I have had my little vagary and I don't think that I shall change again.'

'I suppose it is your republican bride-elect that has done that,' said the Duke laughing.

To this the young man made no direct answer, but took advantage of the allusion to turn from his own projected marriage to that of his sister, and to ask whether anything could as yet be fixed as to its period. 'Mary has said nothing to me about it,' said the Duke.

'But she has asked me to do so. Frank of course can only urge her, and she can only answer by referring to you. I suppose that delay can do no good.'

'I will think about it,' said the Duke gravely. Then Silverbridge knew that a day would be fixed at no very distant date.

CHAPTER 79

THE FIRST WEDDING

As Easter Sunday fell on the 17th April, and as the arrangement of the new Cabinet, with its inferior offices, was not completed till the 6th of that month, there was only just time for the new elections before the holidays. Indeed it was all holiday up to Easter, though the House did once meet in order that the new ministers might take their new places. Mr. Monk sat on his bench so comfortably that he hardly seemed ever to have been off it. And Phineas Finn, in the few words which he was called upon to say, resumed the peculiar ministerial tone of voice just as though he had never allowed himself to use the free and indignant strains of opposition. As to a majority,—nothing as yet was known about that. Some few besides Silverbridge might probably transfer themselves to the Government. None of the ministers lost their seats at the new elections, at which indeed but very little effort was made to displace them. The opposite party seemed for a while to have been paralysed by the defection of Sir Timothy, and men who liked a quiet life were able to comfort themselves with the reflection that nothing could be done this session.

For our lovers this was very convenient. Neither of them would have allowed their parliamentary energies to have interfered at such a crisis with his domestic affairs; but still it was well to have time at command. The day for the marriage of Isabel and Silverbridge had been now fixed. That was to take place on the Wednesday after Easter, and was to be celebrated in some magnificent fashion by special royal favour in the chapel at Whitehall. All the Pallisers would be there, and all the relations of all the Pallisers, all the ambassadors, and of course all the Americans in London. It would be a 'wretched grind,' as Silverbridge said, but still it had to be done. One cannot be the heir to a dukedom without paying in some shape for the privilege. But in the meantime the whole party, including the new President of the Council, were down at Matching. Even Isabel, though it must be presumed that she had much to do in looking after her bridal garments, was able to be there for a day or two. But Tregear was the person to whom this visit was of the greatest importance.

He had been allowed to see Lady Mary in London, but hardly to do more than see her. Matters had so arranged themselves at that time that he had spent more time with the Duke than with the Duke's daughter.

With her he had been alone for about five minutes, and then cruel circumstances,—circumstances, however, which were not permanently cruel,—had separated them. All their great difficulties had been settled for them, and no doubt they were happy. But Tregear, though he had been as it were received into grace by that glass of wine, still had not entered into the intimacies of the house. This he felt himself,—and had felt so strongly that during the six weeks after that, while he remained in town, he hardly even spoke to the Duke. He had been told that he had better restrain himself from writing to Mary, and he had restrained himself. She was at Matching and he could not see her. He had therefore no immediate opportunity of gradually creeping into that perfect intimacy with the house and household which is generally accorded to a promised son-in-law.

On this occasion he travelled down alone, Silverbridge having gone on an earlier day than that fixed for his visit;—and as he approached the house he, who was not by nature timid in such conditions, felt himself to be somewhat cowed. That the Duke should not be cold to him was almost impossible. Of course he was there in opposition to the Duke's wishes. It was impossible that the Duke should as yet be genial with him. And everyone about the place, with the exception of the one person, would be more or less hostile to him. Even Silverbridge had never quite liked the match. Of course he was to have all that he desired. Of course he was the most fortunate of men. Of course no man had ever stronger reason to be contented with the girl he loved. But still his heart was a little low as he was driven up to the door.

The first person whom he saw was the Duke himself, who, as the fly from the station arrived, was returning from his walk and met his guest at the front of the house. 'You are welcome to Matching,' he said, taking off his hat with something of ceremony. This was said before the servants, but Tregear was then led into the study and the door was closed. 'I never do anything by halves, Mr. Tregear,' he said. 'Since it is to be so you shall be the same to me as though you had come under other auspices. Of yourself personally I hear all that is good. Consider yourself at home here, and in all things use me as your friend.' Tregear endeavoured to make some reply, but could not find words that were fitting. 'I think that the young people are out,' continued the Duke. 'I saw Silverbridge with Miss Boncassen and his sister about half an hour ago. Mr. Warburton will help you to find them if you like to go upon the search.' The words had been very gracious, but still there was something in the manner of the man which made Tregear find it almost impossible to regard him as he might have regarded another father-in-law.

He had often heard the Duke spoken of,—especially by Silverbridge and even by the Duchess herself,—as a man who could become awful if he pleased, almost without an effort. He had been told of the man's mingled simplicity, courtesy, and self-assertion against which no amount of impudence or raillery could prevail. And now he seemed to understand it. And yet nothing could have been kinder than the words which had been spoken to him.

He was not, however, driven to go under the private secretary's escort in quest of the young people. Mary had understood her business much better than that. 'If you please, sir, Lady Mary is in the little drawing-room,' said a well-arrayed young girl to him, as soon as the Duke's door was well and certainly closed. This was Lady Mary's own maid who had been on the look-out since he had entered the house. Lady Mary had known all details as to the arrival of the trains and the length of the journey from the station, and had not been walking with the other young people when the Duke had intercepted her lover at the door. Even that delay she had thought was hard, though she felt that it was not unfortunate that the first interview should thus be had between her lover and her father. The discreet maid opened the door of the little drawing-room,—and discreetly closed it instantly. 'At last!' she said, throwing herself into his arms.

'Yes,—at last.'

On this occasion time did not envy them. The long afternoons of spring had come, and as Tregear had reached the house between four and five they were able to go out together before the sun set. 'No,' she said when he came to inquire as to her life during the last twelve months; 'you had not much to be afraid of as to my forgetting.'

'But when everything was against me!'

'One thing was not against you. You ought to have been sure of that.'

'And so I was. And yet I felt that I ought not to have been sure. Sometimes in my solitude I used to think that I myself had been wrong.'

'That would be bad news for me, Frank,' she said laughing.

'Even though you would forgive me, still I might have been wrong.'

'If you had acted as though you thought so I could not have forgiven you.'

'I began to doubt whether under any circumstances I could have been justified in asking your father's daughter to be my wife.'

'Because of his rank!'

'Not so much his rank as his money.'

'Ought that to be considered?'

'Or rather my want of money. A poor man who marries a rich woman will always be suspected.'

'Because people are so mean and poor-spirited,—and because they think that money is more than anything else. It should be nothing at all in such matters. I don't know how it can be anything. They have been saying that to me all along,—as though one were to stop to think whether one was rich or poor.' Tregear, when this was said, could not but remember that at a time not very much prior to that at which Mary had not stopped to think, neither had he and Mabel, and that the results in that case had not been fortunate. 'I suppose it was worse for me than for you,' she added.

'I hope not.'

'But it was, Frank; and therefore I ought to have it made up to me now. Oh, yes, I dare say you will do your best. At any rate you will promise and I must trust you. It was very bad to be alone here, particularly when I felt that papa always looked at me as though I were a sinner. He did not mean it, but he could not help looking at me like that. At every glance, he threw you and all your iniquities in my teeth. And there was nobody to whom I could say a word.'

'It was pretty much the same with me.'

'Yes; but you were not offending a father who, though he would not say a word to reproach me, could not keep himself from looking at me. I was like a boy at school who had been put into Coventry.* And then they sent me to Lady Cantrip.'

'Was that very bad?'

'I do believe that if I were a young woman with a well-ordered mind, which I am not, I should feel myself very much indebted to Lady Cantrip. She had a terrible task of it; with no thanks, and nothing to get. But I could not teach myself to like her. I believe she knew all through that I should get my way at last.'

'That ought to have made you friends.'

'But yet she tried everything she could. And when I told her about that meeting up at Lord Grex's she was so shocked! Do you remember that?'

'Do I remember it?'

'Were not you shocked?' This question was not to be answered by any word. 'I was,' she continued. 'It was an awful thing to do; but I was determined to show them all that I was in earnest. I would not make a speech. Do you remember how Miss Cassewary looked? I don't think she can have recovered from it yet.'

'Miss Cassewary knew all about it.'

'I dare say she did. And so I suppose did Mabel Grex. I had thought that perhaps I might make Mabel a confidante, but——' Then she looked up into his face.

'But what?'

'You like Mabel, do you not? I do.'

'I like her very, very much.'

'Perhaps you have liked her too well for that; eh, Frank?'

'Too well for what?'

'That she should have heard all that I had to say about you with pleasure and sympathy. If so, I am so sorry.'

'You need not fear that I have ever for a moment been untrue either to her or you.'

'I am sure you have not to me. Poor Mabel! I almost wish that she and Silverbridge could have come together. Then they took me to Custins. That was worst of all. I cannot quite tell you what happened there.' Of course he asked her,—but, as she had said, she could not quite tell him about Lord Popplecourt and his suit. To her thinking Lady Cantrip's great sin had been in supposing that while one man had been entertained by her as a lover, another could be accepted as a husband.

The next morning the Duke asked his guest in a playful tone what was his Christian name. It could hardly be that he should not have known, but yet he asked the question. 'Francis Oliphant,' said Tregear.

'Those are two Christian names I suppose; but what do they call you at home?'

'Frank,' whispered Mary, who was with them.

'Then I will call you Frank if you will allow me. The use of Christian names is, I think, pleasant and hardly common enough among us. I almost forget my own boy's name because the practice has grown up of calling him by a title.'

'I am going to call him Abraham,' said Isabel.

'Abraham is a good name, only I do not think he got it from his god-fathers and godmothers.'

'Who can call a man Plantagenet? I should as soon think of calling my father-in-law Coeur de Lion.'

'So he is,' said Mary. Whereupon the Duke kissed the two girls and went his way,—showing that by this time he had adopted the one and the proposed husband of the other into his heart.

Isabel was the first to go back to London, intent no doubt upon furbelows and flounces. The trousseau for such a wedding is an important matter, and Isabel was not the girl to neglect her duties.

Then Silverbridge followed. He too had his own affairs to manage. The Duke and Mary with Tregear and Gerald, who had of course come home for the occasion, did not return to town till the day before the ceremony. And on the morning of that day the Duke sent for Frank. 'I suppose,' said he, 'that you would wish that some time should be fixed for your own marriage.' To this the accepted suitor of course assented. 'But before we can do that something must be settled about—money.' Tregear when he heard this felt that he became hot all over, and that he could not restrain his blushes. Such must be the feeling of a man when he finds himself compelled to own to a girl's father that he intends to live upon her money and not upon his own. 'I do not like to be trouble-some,' continued the Duke, 'or to ask questions which might seem to be impertinent.'

'Oh, no! Of course I feel my position. I can only say that it was not because your daughter might probably have money that I first sought her love.'

'It shall be so received. And now—— But perhaps it will be best that you should arrange all this with my man of business. Mr. Moreton shall be instructed. Mr. Moreton lives near my place in Barsetshire, but is now in London about this other marriage. If you will call on him he shall tell you what I would suggest. I hope you will find that your affairs will be comfortable. And now as to the time. Mary has been told by me that she may fix it. I suppose that you, like Silverbridge, must in some degree conform yourself to Mr. Speaker.'

The wedding on the next day was declared by the newspapers to have been one of the most brilliant remembered in the metropolis. There were six bridesmaids, of whom of course Mary was one,—and of whom poor Lady Mabel Grex was equally of course not another. Poor Lady Mabel was at this time with Miss Cassewary at Grex, paying what she believed would be a last visit to the old family home. Among the others were two American girls, brought into that august society for the sake of courtesy rather than of personal love. And there were two other Palliser girls and a Scotch M'Cluskie cousin. The breakfast was of course given by Mr. Boncassen at his house in Brook Street, where the bridal presents were displayed. And not only were they displayed; but a list of them, with an approximating statement as to their value,—prob-ably given at about four times the true amount,—appeared in one or two of the next day's newspapers;—as to which terrible sin against good taste neither was Mr. or Mrs. Boncassen guilty. But in these days, in which such splendid things are done on so very splendid a scale, a young lady cannot herself lay out her friends' gifts so as to be properly seen by her friends, by the breach of which practice, however, friends would be more honoured than by the observance. Some well-skilled and well-paid hand is needed even for that, and hence comes this public information on affairs which should surely be private. In our grand-mothers' time it may be presumed that the happy bride's happy mother herself compounded the cake which her guests were to eat for luck;—or at any rate the trusted housekeeper. But we all know that terrible tower of silver which now stands niddle-noddling* with its appendages of flags and spears on the modern wedding breakfast-table. It will come to pass with some of us soon that we must deny ourselves the pleasure of having many young friends, because their marriage presents are so costly.

Poor Mrs. Boncassen had not perhaps a happy time with her august guests on that morning; but when she retired to give Isabel her last kiss in privacy she did feel proud to think that her daughter would some day be an English duchess.

'Mother,' she said. 'It is but ten days across the Atlantic.* The years in which you won't come to us we will go to you.'

CHAPTER 80

THE SECOND WEDDING

NOVEMBER is not altogether an hymeneal month, but it was not till November that Lady Mary Palliser became the wife of Frank Tregear. It was postponed a little perhaps, in order that the Silverbridges,—as they were now called,—might be present. The Silverbridges, who were now quite Darby and Joan, had gone to the States instead of Scotland when the session had been brought to a close early in August, and had remained there nearly three months. Isabel,—she shall be so called in these last few pages, although the reader is well aware that even in such a chronicle as this, young ladies' Christian names should not be treated with freedom after marriage,—Isabel had no doubt taken infinite pleasure in showing her English husband to her American friends, and the American friends had no doubt taken a pride in seeing so glorious a British husband in the hands of an American wife. Everything was new to Silverbridge, and he was happy in his new possession. She too enjoyed it infinitely, and so it happened that they had been unwilling to curtail their sojourn. But in November they had to return, because Mary had declared that her marriage should be postponed till it could be graced by the presence of her elder brother.

The marriage of Silverbridge had been august. There had been a manifest intention that it should be so. Nobody knew with whom this originated. Mrs. Boncassen had probably been told that it ought to be so, and Mr. Boncassen had been willing to pay the bill. External forces had perhaps operated. The Duke certainly had simply been passive and obedient. There had however been a general feeling that the bride of the heir of the house of Omnium should be produced to the world amidst a blare of trumpets and a glare of torches. So it had been. But both the Duke and Mary were determined that this wedding should be very different. It was to take place at Matching, and none would be present but they who were staying in the house, or who lived around,—such as tenants and dependants. Four clergymen united their forces to tie Isabel to her husband, one of whom was a bishop, one a canon, and the two others royal chaplains; but there was only to be the vicar of the parish at Matching. And indeed there were no guests in the house except the two bridesmaids and Mr. and Mrs. Finn. As to Mrs. Finn Mary had made a request, and then the Duke himself had suggested that the husband should be asked to accompany his wife. The father had hesitatingly whispered the name of Lady Cantrip, but Mary, though she had replied only by a look, had resisted. The two brothers were of course there,—and the new sister.

It was very pretty. The church itself is pretty, standing in the park, close to the ruins of the old Priory, not above three hundred yards from the house. And they all walked, taking the broad path through the ruins, going under that figure of Sir Guy which Silverbridge had pointed out to Isabel when they had been whispering there together, in doubt as to their future happiness. The Duke led the way with his girl upon his arm. The two bridesmaids followed. Then Silverbridge and his wife, with Phineas and his wife,—and I grieve to say that Gerald and the bridegroom accompanied them, belonging as it were to the same party! It was very rustic;—almost improper! 'This is altogether wrong, you know,' said Gerald. 'You should appear coming from some other part of the world, as if you were almost unexpected. You ought not to have been in the house at all, and certainly should have gone under some disguise.' But though the circumstances were so unfortunate,—certainly so very un-ducal,—the marriage was solemnised, and Lady Mary became the wife of Frank Tregear.

There had been presents too on this occasion, and rich presents,—as was a matter of course. But they were shown to none except to Mrs. Finn and the bridesmaids,—and perhaps to the favoured servants of the house. At any rate there was nothing said of them in the newspapers.

One present there was,—given not to the bride but to the bride-groom,—which he showed to no one except to her. This came to him only on the morning of his marriage, and the envelope containing it bore the postmark of Sedbergh. He knew the handwriting well before he opened the parcel. It contained a small signet-ring with his crest, a ring such as young men customarily wear, and with it there were but a few words written on a scrap of paper. 'I pray that you may be happy. This was to have been given to you long ago, but I kept it back because of that decision.' He showed the ring to Mary and told her it had come from Lady Mabel;—but the scrap of paper no one saw but himself.

Perhaps the matter most remarkable in the wedding was the hilarity, or, at any rate, the good humour of the Duke. One who did not know him well might have said that he was a man with very few cares, and who now took special joy in the happiness of his children,—who was thoroughly contented to see them marry after their own hearts and make themselves happy in their own fashion. And yet, as he stood there on the altar-steps giving his daughter to that new son and looking first at his girl, and then at his married son, he was reminding himself of all he had suffered, and reflecting how seldom it had happened that he to whom so many good things had been given had been allowed to have his own way in the affairs of life.

After the breakfast,—which was by no means a grand repast and at which the cake did not look so like an ill-soldered silver castle as that other construction had done,—the happy couple were sent away in a modest chariot to the railway station, and not above half-a-dozen slippers were thrown after them. They were enough probably for luck,—or perhaps there might have been luck even without them, for the wife thoroughly respected her husband, as did the husband his wife. Mrs. Finn, when she was alone with Phineas, said a word or two about Tregear. 'When she first told me of her engagement I did not think it possible that she should marry him. The distance between them was so great. But after he had been with me I felt sure that he would succeed.* I could not tell him that I thought so, but there was that in his manner which convinced me.'

'Well, sir,' said Silverbridge to the Duke when they were out together in the park that afternoon, 'what do you think about him?' Silverbridge since his marriage seemed even to his father to be much more of a man than he had been before.

'I think he is a manly young man.'

'He certainly is that. And then he knows things and understands them. It was never a surprise to me that Mary should have been so fond of him.'

'I do not know that one ought to be surprised at anything. Perhaps what surprised me most was that he should have looked so high. There seemed to be so little to justify it. But now I will accept that as courage which I before regarded as arrogance. Who knows, he may live yet to be a much greater man than his father-in-law. I am certainly very glad that he has a seat in Parliament.'

'It will be my turn next,' said Gerald, as he was smoking with his brother that evening. 'After what you and Mary have done, I think he must let me have my own way whatever it is.'*

APPENDIX

SAMPLE OF CUTS TO THE MANUSCRIPT

TROLLOPE was averse to cutting. In his surviving manuscripts, one rarely finds even a single sentence crossed out (unless it is replaced by another sentence), let alone a series of sentences or a paragraph. And extensive cutting was inconceivable to him, as he explains in this passage about *Barchester Towers* from *An Autobiography* (written in 1876):

> When it was done, Mr. W. Longman required that it should be subjected to his reader; and he returned the MS to me, with a most laborious and voluminous criticism,—coming from whom I never knew. This was accompanied by an offer to print the novel on the half-profit system, with a payment of £100 in advance out of my half-profits,—on condition that I would comply with the suggestions made by his critic. One of these suggestions required that I should cut the novel down to two volumes. In my reply, I went through the criticisms, rejecting one and accepting another, almost alternately, but declaring at last that no consideration should induce me to put out a third of my work. I am at a loss to know how such a task could be performed. I could burn the MS., no doubt, and write another book on the same story; but how two words out of every six are to be withdrawn from a written novel, I cannot conceive. I believe such tasks have been attempted—perhaps performed; but I refused to make even the attempt. Mr. Longman was too gracious to insist on his critic's terms; and the book was published, certainly none the worse, and I do not think much the better, for the care that had been taken with it.[1]

Even if Trollope suggests that he was willing to make some cuts because of what the publisher 'required' ('I went through the criticisms, rejecting one and accepting another'), his distaste for any massive undertaking of this sort is unequivocal. Yet in April and May of 1878, Trollope chose not to 'burn' the MS of *The Duke's Children* but to chop it down extensively for *All the Year Round*, the periodical founded by Charles Dickens and edited by Charles Dickens Jr. after his father's death. Trollope eliminated roughly 65,000 words, or 22 per cent of the novel. It was not quite two out of six words, but still a reduction on a scale that he had never attempted previously and would never attempt again.

Though none of his letters about cutting *The Duke's Children* survive, one that Trollope wrote a few months later, in October 1878, helps us understand what happened—and how he felt about it. In the letter, Trollope addresses John Blackwood about possible changes to the latter

---

[1] Anthony Trollope, *An Autobiography* (Oxford: Oxford University Press, 1999), 103–4.

part of his novel *John Caldigate*, which since April had been appearing monthly in *Blackwood's Magazine*:

If you wish to have the matter reduced, that is a much more difficult, and is, indeed, a very difficult affair. Even in that case you would have to put 5 chapters each into 4 of the numbers; but I should have to reduce the amount of each chapter so as to bring them within the number of pages you could allow. In this case it will be much better done on the proof than on the MS.

If done on the MS it would have to be recopied for Chapman;—because the reduction of matter would not be carried on in the re-published form. If you cannot allow the full number of pages required for those numbers which are to have the 5 chapters, you had better, in sending me the proofs, tell me what reduction you require,—or how many pages you can allow. Then I will make the reduction accordingly,—but with an aching heart! (11 October 1878)

Trollope makes his stance clear: he does not want to cut but will do so if Blackwood insists. Now at a vulnerable moment in his career, especially after the disastrous reception *The Prime Minister* had received when it was published in 1876, Trollope was no longer inclined to resist potential editors in the manner that he had described in *An Autobiography*. As it turns out, Blackwood put a note on the letter saying, 'Trollope had misunderstood & I have written a line to him explaining that I intended the parts to be lengthened.'[2] If Trollope made a similar plea to Dickens Jr., it is evident that he received a different response.

Even if he had gone ahead to make the cuts on *John Caldigate*, Trollope stipulated that the full text would be published in book form by Chapman & Hall, as precautions would be taken to preserve the original text: either because the changes would be made on the proofs rather than the manuscript, or because the manuscript would be 'recopied' for the book with the deleted parts restored. Although the cuts would only be limited to *Blackwood's Magazine*, he says he would have 'an aching heart' regardless; thus we can easily imagine how he felt about the reduced version of *The Duke's Children* that would be appearing soon not only in *All the Year Round* (weekly from October 1879 to July 1880) but in the book edition (published by Chapman & Hall in May 1880). Yet he had already made extensive cuts on over a thousand pages of *The Duke's Children* manuscript, keeping in all eighty chapters but striking out paragraphs, sentences, phrases, and single words; he would even sometimes replace one word with a slightly shorter one. To recopy the text thereafter would be an extraordinarily laborious process; instead, Trollope chose to move on. (See the Introduction, pp. xxviii–xxix.)

[2] N. John Hall, *The Letters of Anthony Trollope: Volume Two, 1871–82* (Stanford: Stanford University Press, 1983), 795.

For over a century and a quarter, *The Duke's Children* could only be read in its truncated form. The complete edition (reconstructed and edited by Steven Amarnick, assisted by Robert F. Wiseman, with Susan Lowell Humphreys) was published in a limited fine edition by the Folio Society during the Trollope bicentenary in 2015, in trade hardcover by Everyman's Library in 2017, and now, with further minor emendations, for Oxford World's Classics.

Given how eager Trollope was to embrace new experiences—and thus to help keep his writing fresh—it is possible that the pain of cutting *The Duke's Children* was lessened slightly by the challenge of performing the task in a way that did not absolutely destroy the novel. But he would never have believed that he was doing anything other than weakening the book on the whole, even if on rare instances some of his changes happened to improve the text. What follows is a small sampling of cuts, with the deleted words in boldface, and brackets around any words that were put in to replace what had been deleted.

In Chapter 1 (p. 10), the Duke wishes he could summon Alice Grey (formerly Alice Vavasor, who in *Can You Forgive Her?* hesitates before agreeing to marry John Grey):

The friend whom he most trusted was a certain Mrs. Grey. She had been a distant cousin of his wife, and with her he had always maintained something like real friendship. He and his wife, who on such matters were often at variance, had agreed in valuing the society of this lady, and in the early days of the Duke's married life she had been much with them; but any close social intercourse with persons so far above him in rank had hardly suited Mr. Grey's views, and he had somewhat discouraged the near intimacy which the Duchess certainly would have liked. But the poor widower, when he looked about thinking where he might find assistance, turned his mind more frequently to Mrs. Grey than to any other female friend.

In Chapter 2 (p. 23), Mary tells Mrs. Finn about Frank's domestic arrangements:

... And this letter was directed to the Beargarden Club, that being the only address for her lover which the young lady knew. 'Of course he has a residence,' she said, with some touch of disdain in her voice. 'When he is at home he lives at Polwenning where the Tregears have lived from before the Conquest. But a young man isn't always under his mother's apron string. No;—I don't know where he sleeps when he is in London. The Tregears have no town house. They don't come to town. I suppose they are not rich enough. I don't think they are a bit inferior because of that.'

'Certainly not; only I did not know whether you might not have a better address than the gentleman's club.'

'I have no address, and had no intention of writing to him. But the name of the club is on the note which I got from him immediately after poor mamma's death.'

In Chapter 3 (pp. 25–26), we learn about Frank Tregear's refusal to find a way to earn a living:

When he had taken his degree his friends were urgent with him to enter some profession. At that time there was but one profession open to him. Were he to submit to work at all he must work as a barrister. The church was out of the question. The whole tone of his mind and his mode of life made medicine and surgery impossible to him. It was already too late with him for diplomacy,—which he told his friends he would have liked; or at any rate for that regular entrance into the lower ranks by which alone, we are given to understand though not always made to believe, can the good things of the Civil Service be reached. For the army and the navy he was also too old, and, as he himself thought, by far too well educated. But to the bar he made many objections. He did not, he said, like the duplicity. He did not, in truth, like the labour. He liked to be a gentleman at large, having certain vague ideas as to a future career in Parliament; and he tried, very much in vain, to satisfy himself by thinking that he could be content to live among gentlemen as a poor man.

In Chapter 6 (p. 48), we gain insight into Major Tifto's success:

. . . And it must be added also to the above good things that he had a way of making himself decidedly pleasant with young men. He could be authoritative about horses, as is required from a man who is a Master of Foxhounds and a pundit on race-courses, and at the same time could be short of speech, flattering in manner, and not dictatorial. He could yield when he knew himself to be right. At the same time, even when wrong, he could be very positive if he had the flower of his company with him. But whether yielding or insisting, he could do it with an easy air and with a certain amount of pleasant drollery.

In Chapter 9 (p. 76), Silverbridge and Frank talk about Lady Mabel Grex, after they have parted from her and her 'old brute' of a father:

'What an old brute he is!' said Frank as they were walking home together along Piccadilly.
'Yes;—he doesn't make himself pleasant when he's cross. I was afraid you were going to cut up rough.'
'I'm too fond of Mabel for that. We have known each other so long that she is almost like a sister to me. I sometimes fancy the Earl wants to quarrel with me, so that I should not go there any more;—but I don't

mean to let him. I can, perhaps, be of some service to her. Don't you call her very handsome?'

'Certainly I do.'

'I look at her just as I would at a picture, and in that way I think she is the most beautiful thing to be seen in London. And then how clever she is!'

'I wonder she is not married.'

'She never seems to think that she has found anybody good enough. Good-night, old fellow. No, I won't go down to the club now. I am a little out of sorts about my own affairs;—as you may understand.'

In Chapter 11 (pp. 88–89), the Duke, consumed by the news of Mary and Frank's secret engagement, turns his attention back to Silverbridge's politics:

It filled his mind so completely that he had hardly heart enough to be made additionally miserable by his son's apostasy. Of course he saw Lord Silverbridge when he was in town, and asked sundry questions about the coming election. It was quite arranged that the young man should stand for the borough. Mr. Fletcher, who had sat for it, was required down in Herefordshire, his own county,—so that nothing could possibly be more convenient. There was some talk of an opposition. Mr. Du Boung, the brewer, thought of coming forward again, and had declared himself to be a supporter of the Duke. But the general opinion in the borough was that on the day of nomination there would be no second candidate, and that any second candidate, should there be one, would find himself nowhere. 'You see,' said Lord Silverbridge, apparently thinking that he would receive all his father's sympathy, 'I have your influence and my own politics to support me.'

'My influence ought to be worth nothing,' said the angry Duke, 'and your politics worth less.'

'Less than nothing!' exclaimed the son.

'As belonging to you. The facts that you are my son and that being so you call yourself a Conservative ought, together, to debar you from receiving a single vote. But of course I shall not interfere.'

'I thought it so good of you, sir, to tell Moreton to pay the bills.'

'That is another matter entirely. It is right that you should go into Parliament and not right that your income should be crippled by doing so.' After that nothing further was said between them on the matter.

In Chapter 28 (p. 218), Silverbridge and Isabel talk charming 'nonsense' with one another:

'We are dining to-day with Sir Oliver Crumblewit, the president of the Phrenological Society. I suppose you don't go there.'

'Well; no; I don't think I know Sir Oliver.'

'And to-morrow with General Vansinoff, the great Dutch traveller.'

'I don't think I know the General either.'

'I dare say not. We always go to learned places;—never anywhere else. On the next evening there is a grand meeting of vivisectors. You won't be there I dare say.'

'My Lord, you mustn't believe all the nonsense that my girl talks,' said the father.

'Oh yes, I do,' said Lord Silverbridge cheerfully, as he made his way through the crowd. 'At any rate I shall be sure to come and call.' Then Miss Boncassen smiled and nodded to him familiarly. At that moment he saw that Lady Mabel was just at his other elbow. She also smiled and nodded, but it seemed to him that there was more of sarcasm than of good humour in her smile.

In Chapter 31 (pp. 233–34), Silverbridge makes three more attempts—or near attempts—to ask Mabel to marry him:

Twice before the expiration of that June month, and once early in July, did Lord Silverbridge sally forth from his own house, or from the club, or from the House of Commons with the full intention of asking Mabel Grex to be his wife; but on none of the occasions were either Venus or Hymen kind to him. On the first attempt he did not find the lady; on the second he could not at first secure her solitary ear for a moment, and, when he did so, had got into so strong an argument about his sister that it had become impossible to adapt himself to the other matter. 'Of course I was very sorry at first that he should have come in,' Lady Mabel had said. 'But I was glad of it afterwards, because I could see what sort of a girl she was. Of course she will marry him. Cart-ropes won't keep them apart.' Then Silverbridge had become angry and had expressed an opinion that they would have to be kept apart, whether by cart-ropes or other means. He had altogether taken his father's part and had become rather violent. 'It was monstrous.' he had said, 'that a girl like that should think that she was going to have her own way!' When there had been this difference between them he had found himself compelled to leave the house without pleading his own cause.

Then he tried again, but on the third attempt Miss Cassewary was with her, and did not leave the room,—as she had done on the former occasion, discreetly though to no purpose. And [Thrice within the next three weeks did Lord Silverbridge go forth to ask Mabel to be his wife, but thrice in vain. On one occasion she would talk on other things. On the second Miss Cassewary would not leave her. On the third] the conversation turned in a very disagreeable way on Miss Boncassen, as to whom he [Lord Silverbridge] could not but think that Lady Mabel said some very ill-natured things.

In Chapter 37 (p. 285), Lady Mabel continues to live with some luxuries, despite her family's growing impoverishment:

. . . She had her own maid, for an earl's daughter, even in poverty, must have her own maid. But in truth the ruin of the family was not as yet absolute ruin. There was a handsome house still maintained in

Belgrave Square. During the season there was a carriage and horses, and there were servants with white plastered heads. Lady Mabel dressed handsomely. Lord Percival lived luxuriously,—though of his living little was seen either by the father or sister. The old sinner himself always had money for gambling and had now taken himself off to some German baths,—so he said,—with his own valet and a courier. Lady Mabel presumed that he had gone to Monaco. Money could still be made to be forthcoming for such absolute needs as these. But still anyone who saw Grex would say that the family was ruined.

In Chapter 45 (pp. 354–55), Silverbridge persists in offering 'juvenile arguments' in favor of the Conservatives—but his behaviour indicates that it is only a matter of time before he joins the Liberals:

The next two or three days passed quietly and pleasantly enough,—with a good deal of light political skirmishing in which the Duke took but little part, as Phineas Finn demolished one after another the juvenile arguments of the young deserter. 'He'll come back to us, Duke, before long,' said Phineas one morning.

'I hope it will not be when we are in power,' said the Duke. 'Nobody should ever go over to a winning side.'

'But I am not a candidate for office,' said Silverbridge.

'You don't know what you are. If a young man be asked to take office he cannot always very well refuse. I don't think Sir Timothy will make you an offer'.

'I shall have him for my under-secretary some day,' said Phineas.

'You must be secretary first before you can have a secretary under you. Sir Timothy means to do wonderful things next session. He'll have quite a new set round him. Perhaps you may be one of them, Silverbridge. You wait till you get to Gatherum and hear what Lupton has to say about it all.' This went on till the end of the second week in October, and then the party was broken up. The Duke and Lady Mary started for Custins. Lord Silverbridge went to Gatherum to prepare for his guests,—and Mr. and Mrs. Finn returned to London, whence she was to proceed in one direction, while he went in another to the Barsetshire shooting.

In Chapter 46 (p. 355), Lady Cantrip considers the 'limits' of her friendship with the Duke:

... Lady Cantrip was accustomed to have her house full in October, and after talking the matter over carefully with her husband had resolved that the time had come in which the Duke and his daughter ought to be able to mingle again in the world. The Duchess had now been dead more than six months; and though a widow may be supposed to find it necessary to seclude herself for a longer time than that, a widower is generally thought to be made of stronger fibre. And as for Lady Mary, seeing that she was expected not only to fall in love but to get rid of a former love in order that she might do so, Lady Cantrip felt that further allusions to the girl's mourning would be unnecessary. And there was something of an idea present to the minds both of Lord and Lady Cantrip that they were doing for this restive young woman almost more than friendship required. They both of them felt the greatest regard for the Duke, and Lady Cantrip was really attached to the girl;—but there are limits. The Duke's feeling on the matter of his daughter's unfortunate love had been so strong that he had almost thought that the whole world ought to be moved by it. Some shadow of an idea of this kind made its way into the minds of the Cantrips;—not altogether justly, as the Popplecourt idea had been almost altogether her own. 'I'll bring them together, and then they must just settle it among themselves,' she said to the Earl. Now she was as good as her word, for Popplecourt was at Custins when the Duke and his daughter arrived.

In Chapter 53 (pp. 407–08), we are given an update on the political situation:

During the next day or two the shooting went on without much interruption either from politics or from love-making. In politics there was not in truth very much to be done. The general conclusion among the politicians assembled seemed to be that if sufficient rope were allowed to that chief enemy, Sir Timothy Beeswax, he would probably hang himself, and that therefore it was desirable to give him as much rope as possible. Nothing could be done till the next spring. There was no chance that either Sir Timothy or Lord Drummond would resign till they had encountered the accidents of another session. Should the accidents of the session drive Sir Timothy from his position, then, it was thought, Mr. Monk must be selected as the only person in the House capable of forming a Government. In that event the Duke would, if at the moment he found it possible, lend his cooperation to any arrangements that might be made. The meaning of this was that in the event of the party coming into power he would consent to be President of the Council and to fill the office which his old friend the Duke of St. Bungay positively refused to occupy again. In achieving this Mr. Monk, Phineas Finn, and Barrington Erle thought that they had achieved very much. The nucleus of a Liberal Cabinet was again made. There was no doubt that Lord Cantrip would join such a party. Barrington Erle and Phineas Finn, as they walked about the grounds on the second Sunday, previous to their departure on the Monday following, were able to fill up nearly all the important offices. Mr. Monk and the Duke were, perhaps, more intent upon the measures which they thought ought to be proposed to Parliament.

Such were the political achievements of the Duke's guests, but the love-making was not quite so prosperous [all round].

In Chapter 56 (p. 435), the Duke composes a stern 'memorandum' in his mind as he reads a letter from Silverbridge:

... It was becoming, he thought, the great fault of the higher ranks in England to seek the means of expending their energy in useless play rather than in useful labour. Men such as his son could not be idle. Life was not pleasant to them unless they could work hard. To toil was a necessity to them. But, under the dominion of fashion, they sacrificed themselves to employments which could have no beneficial results. His son could not forgive himself because he had not hunted so many days,—as another young man might be angry with himself because he had not read so many hours! In this way the best energies of the country were being wasted. The Duke made a very strong memorandum within his own mind on this subject.

In Chapter 57 (p. 440), members of the hunt gather to rid themselves of Tifto:

Two stout young farmers had been placed at the door to prevent any from entering who were not members of the hunt. Their duty was difficult because no one knew exactly who were members and who were not. Anyone who paid, though he paid no more than a five-pound note, was a member. Farmers who paid nothing were supposed to be members. That excellent old sportsman, the parson from Croppingham, was certainly a member, though he had never paid a shilling. The object was to exclude any rough attendants from London who might be able to mount a pair of breeches and a hunting-whip, and, so equipped, might possibly come down to assist the Major. When the time came very few who sought admittance were excluded. On one occasion there was a little noise. 'You ain't paid a penny these two years and I'm blowed if you shall go in,' said one of the young farmers at the door, and then the impecunious sportsman was thrust rather rudely down the stairs. But this was not the Major's doing. The Major knew that he could not support his position by such means as that. The Major had one great argument on which he would depend, and his object was to have that supported by a majority of votes. His argument and his appeal would be, he thought, so just that even his enemies would support it.

At the end of Chapter 58 (p. 451), members of the hunt realize that Tifto may not be so easy to replace:

Then, however, came the great difficulty,—as Mr. Jawstock soon perceived. There is nothing so dangerous to meddle with as a pack of hounds. It is very well for an enterprising man to put himself forward, to make speeches, to show that he knows all about it, and to take quite a leading part, when he is sure that he has a tower of strength behind him in the shape of a real Master who can and will pay for everything.

But when a country has got rid of its Master then the eloquent gentleman who knows all about it is expected to put his hand in his pocket. In such emergencies the hand must often go very deep.

'One thing was quite impossible.' So said Mr. Topps. The Runnymede country had not been without a pack of hounds since his father was a little boy and couldn't be so left now.

'The country must be hunted of course,' said the parson from Croppingham, who, however good he might be to ride, was unfortunately not able to give assistance in the way of money.

'I shall be glad to do anything,' said the young man from Bagshot, blushing deeply.

'I suppose we must have a committee,' said Mr. Jawstock. And there was a committee, which consisted at last of Mr. Topps, Mr. Jawstock, and the young gentleman. Among them they had to buy the Major's horses, and to pay the Major one hundred and fifty pounds for his interest in the hounds, and to hire a huntsman,—the young man from Bagshot being found on trial to be inefficient for the duty, which is in truth one of the most difficult operations that a man can have to learn. Mr. Topps and Mr. Jawstock had many consultations, and before the season was over had, I fear, spent more money than they had intended. The new huntsman, too, did not at first know the country. He had been hired at a cheap rate,—having not been found to be quite sober in his last place. All of which was so inconvenient, that before the season was over some of the Runnymede men were heard to say that though Tifto was undoubtedly a rascal, they wished that he were back again among them at Tally-ho Lodge.

Poor Tifto in the meantime had skulked away, no one quite knew whither.

In Chapter 61 (pp. 475–76), Silverbridge is in a temporarily dark mood after he tells his father he wishes to marry Isabel:

He was to leave home that afternoon about three, but before he went he managed to see his sister alone. After leaving his father he made up his mind that he would now tell her also of his engagement,—so that it might be, as it were, the more strongly riveted. 'I have been with the governor this morning,' he said.

'I hope there is nothing wrong.'

'It seems to me that nothing ever is right. I am always in hot water, and suppose I always shall be. I dare say you know what I had to tell him.'

'Indeed I don't.'

'Don't you know that I have engaged myself to Isabel Boncassen?' To this she made no reply. 'I don't believe that you can have been so blind as not to have seen that.'

'She told me,' said Mary,—'when we were at Custins together.'

'I know she did. But you have kept it very dark.'

'It is you that have kept it dark. How could I speak of it to you when you did not tell me? What will papa say?'

'I have just told him. Of course he does not like it. I knew that before. But it has got to be.'

'What will she say when she knows that papa will not welcome her? I liked her so much;—but I was afraid there would be difficulties. I fancied once that it would have been Mabel Grex.'

'But it won't be Mabel Grex, you see. I am going off now, but I thought that I would tell you first. And there is another trouble,—about Gerald. He has lost a lot of money.'

'Gerald!'

'Yes;—why not Gerald as well as another? But don't you whisper a word of that to anybody. It seems to me that everything comes to grief. We are all in the black books now and I don't see how we are ever to get out again. I shall emigrate to the States and set up there as a politician.' Then he started on his way to the Brake country.

In Chapter 67 (p. 523), after Silverbridge has given his reasons for turning down the chance to make a prestigious speech on behalf of the Conservatives, the Duke pronounces himself satisfied—and does *not* dictate the letter Silverbridge writes to the party leaders. If Silverbridge happens to sound much like his father, it is because he has been listening to him and learning from him:

. . . 'Now that you have explained yourself I think that you are right,' he said, 'and I am confirmed in my opinion that it was desirable that we should talk this matter over before you arrived at any conclusion. But you should remember two things;—first, that no man should change his side in politics lightly. Such changes are permissible, and are often evidence of honesty; but they are apt to be deleterious to the man himself, and are sometimes taken as showing a vague and vacillating character. And secondly I would have you bear in mind that I have never expected from you such a step. Before you had declared yourself it was fit that I should use my influence to keep you in the path that I thought right. My influence was insufficient. But now I would not raise my little finger to induce you to come back. If conviction brings you back, then I will welcome you with all my heart.'

After that Silverbridge was left alone to write his letter to Sir Timothy, the Duke absolutely refusing to assist his son in the composition. It should never be truly said of him that he had stood between his son and the performance of a public duty because of his own animosity to the existing Leader of the House of Commons. The letter was not at last written with much ease; but when completed it was decisive, explicit, and at the same time courteous. Silverbridge said that he felt the honour very much; that he knew himself to be incompetent, but would not on that account have thought himself justified in opposing the wishes of the Leader of his party; but that as his own political opinions were on certain subjects unfortunately in a state of doubt, he could not venture to undertake a task by which he would feel himself bound to support the Ministry in everything.

'I can trace the Duke's hand in every word of it,' Sir Timothy said to Mr. Roby as he showed the letter to that worthy colleague.

In Chapter 70 (pp. 540–41), the narrator argues against an elaborate lunch:

There can, I think, be no doubt that, as an opportunity for social gatherings, lunches are a mistake. It may be that nature requires that such a meal should be made; and if so, it is of course convenient that the inhabitants of one and the same house should eat it in company. But it should never become a convivial gathering, and should be partaken only by those who use it as the simple mode of obtaining the nourishment necessary to them. Who has not felt the disagreeable nature of its attributes when other purposes have been intended? When you dine out you know how to get away from your host's house without difficulty. He dictates to you with easy confidence the moment at which you shall leave his dining-room, and when the half-hour of subsequent conversation is over your departure from the precincts of your hostess is as little embarrassing. But who ever knew how to get away from a convivial lunch? What to do, what to say, when to move, and when to go, is always a matter of uneasy thought. At dinner one takes three or four glasses of champagne, and perhaps as many more of claret afterwards. Added to this there may be a little drop of cognac together with an opening and concluding modicum of sherry. And who is the worse for it? Who after it is conscious that either he himself or anyone else has drunk any wine? But when you have taken the very minimum at lunch which the circumstances of the case will allow, when you have passed that unhappy hour in a continually broken resolve not to eat a morsel, or drink a drop, you feel nevertheless so permeated with strong liquors, so overcome by a sense of victuals through the whole subsequent afternoon, that you do not know what to do with yourself; and when you see others who have gone through the same damnable struggle, you are scandalised by their red faces and uncomfortable grins.

In Chapter 71 (pp. 545–46), Silverbridge considers his options, just before his father relents and agrees to his marriage with Isabel:

... How this was to be done in the teeth of what Mr. Boncassen had said to him he had not as yet made up his mind; but he had distant ideas of a temporary but prolonged emigration to the United States in case he should be driven to emergencies. He conceived that neither Isabel nor her father would be able to withstand such a test of his love; and he also, perhaps, conceived that a father, with a father's usual weakness, would yield rather than succumb to so great an evil. The system of primogeniture, which is salutary to the prosperity and permanence of the country at large, is sometimes detrimental to the authority of fathers;—a fact of which elder sons become aware at an early age. When a most respectable and very Protestant Irish nobleman had positively refused to pay his son's debts for the third or fourth time, he was reduced to compliance by a threat on his son's part of conversion to the Church of Rome. There was perhaps some malice in this; whereas Silverbridge certainly bore no malice against his father. But he was determined that Isabel Boncassen should be his wife.

On that Sunday afternoon when the fever heat of his love was upon him, he went at once in search of his father; but unluckily the Duke was not to be found. At the house it was only known that he was dining out. On the following morning, though the lover's ardour was not diminished, his discretion was increased. This thing which he had to do was difficult, and he was not now so sure of his eloquence as when he had just left Mr. Boncassen's house. Might it perhaps be better that he should write a letter? He absolutely did write a letter in which, to the best of his abilities, he poured out all his heart and all his wishes. But, when it was written, he found that his father had left town. No notice had been left for him as to the Duke's departure; but the butler had understood from the Duke's own man that the Duke had gone with Mr. Monk down to Longroyston. Now Longroyston was the country seat of the Duke of St. Bungay; and it was manifest to Silverbridge that such a journey at such a time of year to such a place with such a companion could have been made only in reference to political expectations. Under these circumstances he did not send his letter, but again changed his mind, resolving that he would await his father's return.

In Chapter 72 (pp. 554–55), the narrator explains why a bride-to-be is more than merely curious about her new house:

Three days after this, **on the Sunday afternoon**, it was arranged that Isabel should be taken to Carlton Terrace to be accepted there into the full good graces of her future father-in-law, and to go through the pleasant ceremony of seeing the house in which it was to be her destiny to live as mistress. What can be more interesting to a girl than this first visit to her future home? Some matter-of-fact critic will say that the first word of assurance from the man who is to give her the home must be much more interesting. No doubt. The man is more than the house,—or ought to be; as heaven is,—or ought to be,—more than earth. But among earthly things, of all mere material comforts, the house to the woman must stand first. It is to be the scene of her joys, her labours, and her troubles. To a man his house is, comparatively, but as a kennel to a dog. It is a convenience and he likes to have it well arranged. But to the woman it is a temple sacred to the gods;—her own temple sacred to her own gods. And then the change to be made is so great,—so sudden! Hitherto she has probably had other shrines, her own sacred places, her own Penates,—which she has shared with her mother; which have grown into her heart, unconsciously, from early years; which she has loved without knowing that she has loved them,—and which now must be her own no longer! These new altars are to be prepared for her with all a lover's care, and are to be doubly dear to her because they are to be given to her by her lover. But everything will be strange to her, and though it is probable that her taste may be consulted, she will be too abashed by the novelty of her position to do much more than assent to all that he proposes. There can be no corner in the house, no closet, no little coign of vantage or of discomfort, no charm of colour, no dark receptacle for hidden properties, which will not have an interest of its own. Every chair and every table has to be a friend,—or perhaps an enemy. There will be no morsel of china, no little gilded ornament, no book, no domestic article with which it will not be her duty and her delight to become familiar. Everything must be of moment, either to please or to displease.

In Chapter 74 (pp. 577–78), the dinner guests banter about national differences—and similarities—soon before the Duke solemnly raises his glass to welcome Frank into the family:

'I take it,' said Mr. Boncassen, 'that we are doing our best to copy you in most things.' The Duke remarked that the justification of the United States was to be found in their avoidance of what were supposed to be English faults. 'Nevertheless it is natural that we should copy even the faults. The healthy country gentleman who decries the fashionable absurdities of the city cannot save himself from their attraction. He ridicules you for dining at eight, but he allows his own hour to be gradually changed from five to six. We are becoming very English in our tastes.'

'With a tendency to Parisian proclivities,' said Tregear, who could not talk to Mary beside him, and was bound to assert his own position by a word or two now and then.

'I do like Paris,' said Mrs. Boncassen.

'I hate it,' said Silverbridge. 'I never know what to do there.'

'It is Paradise upon earth,' said Isabel. 'If I had my way I would live there always.'

'What would you do?' asked her lover.

'Drive up and down the Champs-Elysées, and wear the prettiest bonnet that the world could produce.'

'The Parisians at any rate would be the gainers,' said the Duke, striving to be gallant and pleasant. But even this was said in the same solemn voice, showing so plainly that his mind was elsewhere, and not at ease!

In Chapter 75 (p. 586), Tifto gets a name change—and a new way of earning a living:

Till a year or two had passed by Silverbridge told no one of the interview and its results except his brother; and even to him he found himself obliged to make an apology for his ill-judged generosity. 'I had been rough to him and I suppose I did drive him to it. I couldn't help being rough because he encroached; but then it was my fault all the same because I had encouraged him. Poor devil! If he can manage to live on a hundred a year I won't begrudge it him.' In process of time Tifto married a publican's daughter under the name of Henry Walker, and, having inherited his father-in-law's business, lived to be able to tell his noble patron that the pension was no longer needed.

In Chapter 78 (p. 608), Silverbridge accounts for his father's change of mind about returning to work—and, implicitly, defends his own change of political loyalties:

'I don't suppose that one ought to think that what a man may feel about himself once, he will feel for ever.'

'I suppose not,' said Tregear.

'A man changes his idea. When I have a headache of a morning I swear that I will never smoke another cigar. But I go on afterwards. I believe the governor will like to go back, and if he does I don't think the country could have a better man whether he be Liberal or Conservative.'

'I quite agree with that,' said Tregear.

The longer cuts included above (along with several passages already quoted at length in the Introduction: from Chapter 26 (p. 199), about the Duke as widower now lacking a threshold that he could cross; from Chapter 76 (p. 591), about Isabel wanting Frank to call her by her Christian name; and of course from Chapter 80 (p. 621), the final paragraphs of the novel) are all of interest, often because of new information they contain about key characters (as in Chapter 3 and Chapter 75), or because of the lively details they add to the text (as in Chapter 28 and Chapter 31). But even more important are the thousands of words contained in smaller cuts that *cumulatively* enrich the novel. Some examples are in the Introduction. In Chapter 1 (p. 14), the Duke is victimized by **morbid self-debasement**; also (p. 13), soon after the Duchess's funeral, **the father and his eldest son had not parted altogether on pleasant terms with each other**, emphasizing how nearly estranged they are from one another. In Chapter 4 (p. 35), Frank is described as **one who prided himself on being the master of others in the great affairs of life and on submitting himself to no masterdom**, making us wonder from the start what kind of fate is in store for Mary if she marries him. In Chapter 7 (p. 57), the Duke tries to sway Silverbridge from the Conservatives by saying, '**You have never spoken to me on the subject in your life before**,' but Silverbridge has a swift retort that is polite but cutting: '**Nor you to me, sir**,' which was true, or very nearly so, and the Duke felt that the reproach was just. In Chapter 25 (p. 188), Silverbridge tells Gerald to 'stick to the Liberals. I've made an ass of myself. **I can see that already,**' suggesting that he has already been giving plenty of thought to the matter and is not just speaking off the cuff. In Chapter 28 (p. 211), rather than remark to Silverbridge only that 'You ought to have said you came to see me' when he arrives at her garden-party, Mrs. Montacute Jones adds, '**but you young men of the present day never will condescend to pay a compliment to an old woman.**' In Chapter 33 (p. 255), to deter Dolly Longstaffe, Isabel speaks with an American twang, **to be free from which had been one of the great labours of her life,** indicating that she will work just as hard—and successfully—to learn how to become a Duchess of Omnium. In Chapter 41 (p. 324), rather than respond meekly when the Duke says, 'I do believe you did what you thought best when Mary told you that story at Matching,' Mrs. Finn replies, '**I did what was best,**' with **a self-assurance . . . which startled him.** In Chapter 74 (p. 574), Silverbridge tries to give Mary wise advice: '**They say that a conqueror always ought to be good-humoured. You are the conqueror here. If you are gentle with him now, he will very soon be gentle with you,—and with Tregear.**' In Chapter 76 (p. 592), Silverbridge says, '**I cannot make your politics out at all**' and Isabel playfully replies, '**If you behave yourself well you shall be taught before long.**' In Chapter 77 (p. 598), Mabel considers her future living arrangements: '**Both my aunts have asked me to go to them, but as I greatly dislike them both that does not sound comfortable. One is very high church, and the other very low. How could I live with either of them?**' In Chapter 80 (p. 618), the narrator tells us that he will refer to Lady Silverbridge as Isabel **in these last few pages, although the reader is well aware that even in such a chronicle as this, young ladies' Christian names should not be treated with freedom after marriage.** And also in Chapter 80 (p. 620), after Silverbridge asks what his father now thinks about Frank, the Duke first observes silently that **Silverbridge since his marriage seemed . . . to be much more of a man than he had been before.**

There are numerous other examples. In Chapter 4 (p. 36), Tregear feels that if the Duke is 'propitiated' by Silverbridge leaving the Conservatives to become a Liberal, **the sacrifice made would not be very great,** suggesting his low opinion of the friend and schoolmate whom he has mentored politically. Also in Chapter 4 (p. 37), Mrs. Finn reads Frank's **stiff and almost uncivil note** and thinks to herself, '**Silly boy! . . . Even if he had money he would not be fit to marry her,**' an opinion that she later revises. In Chapter 27 (p. 207), Tifto is 'made supremely happy by what he considered to have been the Duke's joke. **To have had a joke made for his express behoof by the Duke of Omnium,—a fact of which he could talk in all societies without lying for the next two years,—was more than consolation to him for his friend's ill** nature.' Tifto could have made something up, but telling the truth is more satisfying here. In Chapter 31 (p. 236), we find out that Mrs. Boncassen **completely understood that it was her duty in life to be a sort of upper servant to Isabel**—showing her to be more self-aware than we might have thought. In Chapter 46 (p. 360), Dolly Longstaffe gives a colourful explanation for 'what it is to be a lord and not to have a father': **'Upon the whole fathers are mistakes. I don't want to get rid of mine, but I never could see that he was of any good to me. If I hadn't had a father perhaps some feminine swell would have jumped down my throat.'** In Chapter 59 (p. 459), Mabel displays some rare humour when she writes Silverbridge and says about the Duke, **'You can't think how many political secrets he has taught me. I am beginning to tremble in my shoes lest he should make me a Liberal.'** As is so often the case in this novel, the humour reveals more serious truths: at this stage, though she is a fervent Conservative, Mabel would become a Liberal partisan if necessary to marry Silverbridge. In Chapter 79 (p. 618), Isabel soothes her anxious mother by saying, **'It is but ten days across the Atlantic. The years in which you won't come to us we will go to you.'** And in Chapter 80 (p. 619), we learn that while the Duke **had hesitatingly whispered the name of Lady Cantrip** as a guest at his daughter's wedding, **Mary, though she had replied only by a look, had resisted**— a remarkably unforgiving gesture on her part.

The examples above contain roughly 6,000 out of the 65,000 words that were deleted from the manuscript. The complete manuscript cuts, along with commentary on over a thousand passages, can be found both at https://www.dukeschildrencomplete.com and at the Trollope Society website (https://www.trollopesociety.org/works/dukes-children).

EXPLANATORY NOTES

The present editor is grateful to Hermione Lee (Oxford, 1983), Dinah Birch (Penguin, 1995), and Katherine Mullin and Francis O'Gorman (Oxford, 2011), all previous editors of *The Duke's Children*. Notes carried over from the Oxford editions have been marked either [HL] or [M&O'G]. References to the *Oxford English Dictionary (OED)* are to the 3rd edition, electronic version.

7 *our old friend*: Trollope first introduced him as a young man, Plantagenet Palliser, in a comic sequence from *The Small House at Allington*, the fifth book in the Barsetshire series. He appears in *Can You Forgive Her?*, *Phineas Finn*, and *The Eustace Diamonds*; inherits the title of Duke of Omnium in *Phineas Redux*; and is the eponymous Prime Minister in the fifth novel of the Palliser series.

Duke of Omnium: a name probably inspired by nom de plume Jacob Omnium, 'the most forcible newspaper writer of my days' (*An Autobiography*, ch. 11). The elder Duke of Omnium dies in *Phineas Redux*; he is in many ways the opposite of his hard-working nephew who inherits the title: 'no man who had lived during the same period . . . had done less, or had devoted himself more entirely to the consumption of good things without the slightest idea of producing anything in return!' (*Phineas Redux*, Vol. 1, p. 215).

The other boy was to go to Cambridge: Trollope included a third son, Lord Maurice, in the first few pages of the manuscript, but changed his mind and eliminated all references to him.

Lady Mary, the only daughter: another daughter, Lady Glencora, had appeared in the previous Palliser novel, *The Prime Minister*, but there is no mention of her in this book. Trollope might have forgotten about her; or, given the high mortality rate of children at the time, she might have died. Or (see note on p. 8 below) Trollope decided to not be overly concerned with accuracy in depicting the children from book to book. He clearly wanted there to be only one daughter in *The Duke's Children* and might have felt it would be distracting to the reader if her name were Glencora.

8 *the early spring of 187—*: Trollope wrote *The Duke's Children* in 1876 and revised it in 1878. To keep dates from becoming chaotic, he worked with an 1869 and 1870 calendar, but the novel does not take place in 1869–70 or any other specific years. Had he insisted on being overly literal about the dates, he could never have written the novel with three children who are nineteen, twenty, and twenty-two, as Silverbridge is born at the end of *Can You Forgive Her?* (begun by Trollope in 1863).

Matching Priory: a gift from the old Duke to Plantagenet, together with the estate, at the time of the wedding; it is the couple's favourite residence throughout their marriage.

9 *the youngest of whom was now nineteen*: Trollope wrote this sentence when he still had four children in mind; the youngest would have been Lord Maurice, who was 'nearly nineteen'. When he changed four to three, he forgot to cut 'nearly' as well. It is clear, however, that Lady Mary is already nineteen (see p. 8, 'Lady Mary Palliser was at that time nineteen' and p. 15, 'The one was nineteen').

10 *The friend whom he most trusted was a certain Mrs. Grey*: Alice Vavasor from *Can You Forgive Her?*, who finally makes up her mind by the end of the novel and marries John Grey. This restored paragraph suggests that she was right to worry about losing her identity in marriage, as it is 'Mr. Grey's views'—not her own—that prevent her from having a closer relationship with the Duke and Duchess.

has been told elsewhere: see *Phineas Redux*, ch. 17, 'Madame Goesler's Story'. However, a reader of *The Duke's Children* who persists to ch. 13 will find a clear and concise explanation.

11 *M'Cluskies*: the inverted comma is Scottish; Trollope had included it in his manuscript, and it is printed in both *All the Year Round* and Chapman & Hall. Trollope uses the inverted comma again in ch. 24, but both *All the Year Round* and Chapman & Hall printed the name with a lower-case *c* instead. Our spelling here, M'Cluskie rather than the manuscript M'Closkie, matches the spelling in *Can You Forgive Her?*

15 *fifteen hundred a year*: a comfortable income but not enough to live as a wealthy man. Besides, when we meet Frank's mother later in the novel, we see that she is not very old and in seemingly fine health.

23 *Beargarden Club*: perhaps based on the Savage Club, founded in 1857 and still in existence today. See ch. 3, 'The Beargarden', in *The Way We Live Now*. In that novel, the club is heavily associated with the dissolute Felix Carbury and comes across as more pernicious than it does in *The Duke's Children*.

25 *ideas with which . . . her life*: though the Duchess becomes a fierce Liberal partisan after her marriage, she does not share her husband's political views (see note below, p. 58). In *An Autobiography*, Trollope says that Glencora compared to her husband 'is in all respects inferior to him' (ch. 10)—referring perhaps to her understanding of politics, too.

26 *Crim Tartary*: region on the Black Sea where Crimean Tartars lived; sometimes used to indicate a distant fantastical land ripe for adventure. Thackeray's 1854 Christmas book, *The Rose and the Ring*, is partially set there.

28 *Carlton Terrace*: shortened name for Carlton House Terrace, near St. James's Park.

29 *She used to be . . . grandfather*: Silverbridge is referring not to his grandfather but to his great-uncle, who was Duke of Omnium before Plantagenet Palliser inherited the title. Trollope most likely is misremembering at this point, though it is fascinating that in ch. 62, Silverbridge corrects Lord Chiltern for saying the same thing—raising the possibility that, as he matures, Silverbridge no longer wants to call his grandfather figure an actual grandfather.

fad: *OED*, 'a crotchety rule of action; a peculiar notion as to the right way of doing something.' Already in the nineteenth century, something could *become* a fad only by being shared by a group of people, whereas Silverbridge is saying the opposite about Mrs. Finn's refusal to accept the bequest—that it's an individual peculiarity. As Madame Max Goesler in *Phineas Finn*, she had turned down the elderly Duke's marriage proposal— and then, in *Phineas Redux*, the jewels that he bequeathed her in his will. Her thinking is finely tuned, and remains consistent in the years that the jewels lie in a vault—not a whim at all.

Ça va sans dire: 'That goes without saying.' We are told in the first paragraph of the novel that the Palliser children have 'perhaps perfected their French' when they went abroad after the Duke left office, and here Silverbridge gets a chance to show off some of that French.

30 *'None but the brave . . . fair'*: from the first stanza of John Dryden, 'Alexander's Feast': 'Happy, happy, happy pair! | None but the brave | None but the brave | None but the brave deserves the fair!' The Duke uses the quotation later (p. 520), and it is the title of ch. 53 of *Phineas Redux*.

'De l'audace, et encore . . . de l'audace': 'Dare, dare again, dare always.' From a speech by Georges Danton during the French Revolution. Frank has a harsh view of the revolution (see pp. 426–27), but the proverb was commonly used beyond its origins.

34 *'I have no sister, as it happens'*: as it turns out, he does have a sister; she emerges in ch. 55. Frank also says, 'I never had a sister' in ch. 14, in that case when he is lying to Silverbridge and claiming that Mabel Grex is 'more like a sister to me than anyone else' instead of the woman he not very long ago passionately loved. There is at least a slight possibility in ch. 4 that Frank is lying too in the face of Mrs. Finn's unwelcome questioning. It is also possible that he is being overly literal without fully lying, as his sister may actually be a half-sister (his elder brother has a different mother than his own; we are never told whether his older sister has a different mother as well). Or, because she is much older than he is, Frank may not think of her as a real sister—i.e. one he grew up with. Or Trollope might have erred.

36 *He wants me . . . a Conservative*: the county is the rural constituency of West Barsetshire and the borough is the market town of Silverbridge. Though Lord Silverbridge would almost certainly win either election, he is apparently more comfortable running as a Conservative for the borough.

I thought you were . . . Radicals: though Frank conflates the Radicals and Liberals (as does Silverbridge in ch. 7, and Mabel in ch. 9), Trollope himself does not do so. There are Radicals within the Liberal Party— including Mr. Monk, who is a more moderate figure in this novel (see note to p. 123)—but they are hardly a majority.

37 *a most chilly note*: not *chilling*; one of numerous obvious compositor errors that have previously always been reprinted. Frank writes a cold, indeed 'chilly' letter, but he does not aspire to scare the daylights out of Mrs. Finn.

39 *'Of course he ought . . . Parliament'*: though the Duke himself later expresses a wish that he could return to the House of Commons, the law forbids it. The 'Lord' before Silverbridge, however, is a courtesy title and thus he can run for office.

   The two seats are vacant together: this sentence was added in proofs, perhaps unwisely. The Duke is only speaking about one seat, in West Barsetshire; the second seat, in Silverbridge, is not mentioned until Mary speaks about it in the next paragraph.

   'You used to sit for Silverbridge, papa': Palliser had the seat in *The Small House at Allington*; John Grey, also a Liberal, was able to win it with Palliser's open support in *Can You Forgive Her?*

43 *Croesus*: king of Lydia in sixth century BC, known for his fabulous wealth.

45 *she-Pandarus*: Pandarus's machinations in bringing the lovers together in both Chaucer's *Troilus and Criseyde* and Shakespeare's *Troilus and Cressida* lead to tragedy for the couple. The word 'pander', derived from 'Pandarus', as a noun means 'a go-between in clandestine love affairs; a person who provides another with the means of sexual gratification; a pimp, a procurer, *esp.* a male one' (*OED*, 1a).

46 *Good-morning, sir*: it is past five o'clock in the afternoon; the Duke is either disoriented by the startling news, or Trollope has forgotten the time. See also note to p. 259, where both Silverbridge and Dolly Longstaffe say 'good-morning' in the afternoon.

   access of tenderness: an outburst of tenderness. Published erroneously as 'excess of tenderness' in *All the Year Round* and thereafter. See also 'access of decision' on p. 471.

47 *a former Carlist war*: there were three civil wars in nineteenth-century Spain involving Don Carlos's monarchical claims.

   M.F.H.: Master of Foxhounds, whose duties are explained later in the paragraph.

48 *only two blackballs*: members would vote with white balls (to accept the candidate) or black balls (to reject him).

   with his own hounds . . . Queen's: the King's or Queen's Hounds were bred to hunt stags in the royal forests but were disbanded before Trollope's era. Sir Robert Walpole, 'often viewed as the first British Prime Minister' (https://www.gov.uk), held the title of Master of the King's Staghounds in Windsor Forest in the mid-eighteenth century.

   flower of his company: similar to Thomas Macaulay's 1849 use of 'flower' in *The History of England from the Accession of James the Second* ('the flower of their profession') as cited in *OED*, 7: 'the choicest individual or individuals among a number of persons or things; "the pick".'

49 *Great Leamington handicap*: the Leamington handicap was run at Warwick. Trollope capitalized 'Great' in the manuscript and was likely intending the word to be part of his variant name rather than an adjective.

'straight tip': 'A tip for a bet that comes straight from an owner or trainer' (Adrian Room, *Dictionary of Sports and Games Terminology*, 2010).

50 *bark*: ship; more commonly spelled 'barque'.

of a colt and of a filly: though three-year-old colts and fillies were (and are) eligible to run the Derby, the Oaks is open only to fillies. During the late part of the seventeenth century and the early part of the eighteenth century, the five Group 1 flat horse races for three-year-olds, which were to become known as the British Classics, gradually came into existence. They were as follows:

The 2000 Guinea Stakes at Newmarket (first run spring 1809)
The 1000 Guinea Stakes at Newmarket (fillies only; first run spring 1814)
The Derby at Epsom (first run spring 1780)
The Oaks at Epsom (fillies only; first run spring 1779)
The St. Leger Stakes at Doncaster (first run 1776 in September)

loo . . . blind hookey: card games of chance, popular among the gambling fraternity.

53 *Mdlle. Stuffa was . . . the season*: opera singer Jenny Lind (1820–87) had become famous as the 'Swedish nightingale' in the 1840s. Her career had long since passed its peak, though she still occasionally sang in public at concerts.

54 *as a Tory or Conservative*: though there was no longer a Tory Party, then as now some have preferred to use the name.

58 *the greatest benefit of the greatest number*: echoing utilitarian Jeremy Bentham (1748–1832), who wrote, 'The greatest happiness of the greatest number is the foundation of morals and legislation.' The Duke's emphasis on 'benefit' rather than 'happiness' is perhaps intentional; in any case, he is far from a fervent Benthamite. See *The Prime Minister*, ch. 68 ('The Prime Minister's Political Creed') for a more detailed account of his views, which match Trollope's own from *An Autobiography*.

62 *Gatherum Castle*: principal property of the Dukes of Omnium, larger but far less comfortable than Matching. It is described in detail in ch. 19 of *Doctor Thorne*.

63 *Lucullus*: military and political leader of the Roman Republic; also well known for the lavish dinners he gave.

67 *because he has gone*: gone, presumably, because the private secretary doesn't need an assistant now that the Duke is no longer Prime Minister.

68 *in medias res*: Latin, in the middle of things. Though Trollope is willing to start Mabel's story *in medias res*, he only rarely began a novel this way—most notably *The Last Chronicle of Barset*. As Trollope explained in the first paragraph of *Is He Popenjoy?* (completed in 1875), if certain details must be included, they might as well be dealt with from the beginning: 'I hold that it is better to have the boiled mutton first, if boiled mutton there must be.'

69 *Lady Mabel Grex*: in the manuscript, Trollope named the family Burgundy before soon changing it to Grex.

Belgrave Square: in the manuscript, Trollope first placed the house in the older, though also upmarket, Berkeley Square before changing his mind.

70 *the Seven Dials*: still a slum area, notoriously unsafe to enter, at the time of this novel. In Gilbert & Sullivan's *Iolanthe* (1882), 'the lowly air of Seven Dials' is compared to the more rarefied surroundings a couple of miles away in Belgrave Square. The area got its name from the column with multiple sundials that stood at its centre, and was rumoured to be the site of a buried treasure. A new column was built in the 1980s as a replacement.

71 *perhaps did not require . . . specially*: the relation is distant enough that chaperonage would be appropriate. As Mabel says to Miss Casseway on p. 290, 'But you are not a mother nor yet an aunt, and you have to do just what I tell you.' We can assume that Mabel has told her that she wants to be alone with Silverbridge.

72 *the Beaufort*: perhaps a reference to Pratt's Club, established in 1857 and still in existence today. The founder, William Pratt, had been steward to Lord Beaufort.

the Garter: Most Noble Order of the Garter, the highest form of civil or military knighthood. Trollope writes of Glencora in *Phineas Redux*: 'With all her radical propensities and inclination to laugh at dukes and marquises, she thought very much of Garters and Lieutenancies;—but her husband would not think of them at all, and hence there were words between them.'

73 *ratting*: OED, 'desertion of a party, cause, principle, etc.'

78 *Rosaline*: Romeo is in love with Rosaline (whom we hear much about, but who never appears in the play) before he meets Juliet.

84 *treated humanly*: not 'humanely' as in previous editions; Trollope intended to highlight the contrast with 'inhuman' at the end of the paragraph.

The Horns: a wedding gift to Glencora from the old Duke.

90 *though she should die . . . produced*: this scenario—where the father is right to prevent the marriage to a scoundrel, and the girl dies of a broken heart—is played out in Trollope's short novel *Sir Harry Hotspur of Humblethwaite* (completed in early 1869).

91 *The pity of it! The pity of it*: Othello, Act 4, Scene 1, 'Nay, that's certain: But yet the pity of it, Iago!—O, Iago, the pity of it, Iago!' In *He Knew He Was Right* (ch. 45), Trollope uses the quotation in a more directly relevant way, as Trevelyan is a jealous husband falsely accusing his wife of infidelity.

the wife of Lord Nidderdale: in *The Way We Live Now*, Lord Nidderdale had tried hard to marry an heiress, setting his sights on Marie Melmotte.

99 *had submitted himself . . . taste*: though most of this paragraph reminds us of what happened in previous Palliser novels, this part is new. It is possible

that the Duke continued to have some misgivings about Mrs. Finn as she became close friends with his wife. It is also possible that, in his pique, he is misremembering.

101 *who had to . . . House of Commons*: Phineas held two different seats in *Phineas Finn*. At the end of the novel, he returns to Ireland, presumably forever, but comes back to England in *Phineas Redux* and wins a new seat in Tankerville.

103 *Silverbridge had been Liberal . . . course*: Silverbridge the borough, not the young man. For *All the Year Round* and thereafter, the sentence was changed to 'Silverbridge had been supposed to be a Liberal as a matter of course,' though in context (especially with the two following sentences restored) it is clear that the manuscript was correct.

   causes which have been described elsewhere: Fletcher's victory over the Liberal candidate, the nefarious Ferdinand Lopez, is described in *The Prime Minister*. Chapter 27, titled 'The Duke's Misery', captures the Duchess's frustrations too as she tries to get her husband to wield power more effectively: 'as for him,—he does not help me in the least. He wanders about among the clouds of the multiplication table, and thinks that a majority will drop into his mouth because he does not shut it.'

104 *Mr. Du Boung*: who 'used to be plain English as Bung before he got rich and made his name beautiful'. He offers only 'very cautious support' to the coalition Government that the Duke leads (*The Prime Minister*, ch. 34).

108 *George and Vulture*: in *The Last Chronicle of Barset* (ch. 20), it is first referred to as the George Inn, but then the narrator explains that it was 'properly called' the George and Vulture, and that it was 'the house in which the magistrates had sat when they committed Mr. Crawley for trial'. One actual George and Vulture is an eighteenth-century inn that is still in existence in twenty-first-century London. It features prominently in Dickens's *The Pickwick Papers* (serialized 1836–7).

110 *seemed to have cut his eye-teeth*: to have gained his first significant experience as a politician; as opposed to 'give' one's eye-teeth (to give away something significant).

111 *that other certain people ought . . . Whigs*: it makes sense for the elderly Dr. Tempest to use the older terms, rather than Conservative and Liberal, for allegiances that go back generations.

120 *law-lords*: officially, Lords of Appeal in Ordinary. 'Highly qualified, full-time judges, the Law Lords carried out the judicial work of the House of Lords until 30 July 2009. . . . The judicial role of the House of Lords as the highest appeals court in the UK has ended. From 1 October 2009, the Supreme Court of the UK assumed jurisdiction on points of law for all civil law cases in the UK and all criminal cases in England, Wales and Northern Ireland' (https://www.parliament.uk).

122 *had been treacherously false to him*: both had been members of the coalition Government in *The Prime Minister* but were glad to sabotage it.

123 *Mr. Monk who . . . the firmest*: in *Phineas Finn* (ch. 9), Mr. Monk is described as 'a Radical, much admired by the people, sitting in Parliament for that most Radical of all constituencies, the Pottery Hamlets.' Even in that novel, he is pragmatic about gradual change; after a defeat on a vote, he tells Phineas how Radical ideas can be absorbed into the mainstream (ch. 75): 'Such a debate and such a majority will make men think. But no;—think is too high a word; as a rule men don't think. But it will make them believe that there is something in it. Many who before regarded legislation on the subject as chimerical, will now fancy that it is only dangerous, or perhaps not more than difficult. And so in time it will come to be looked on as among the things possible, then among the things probable;—and so at last it will be ranged in the list of those few measures which the country requires as being absolutely needed. That is the way in which public opinion is made.' See also note to p. 36.

the baronet and the law-knight: Sir Orlando Drought and Sir Timothy Beeswax, respectively. As Solicitor-General in the Duke's Government, Sir Timothy would have been knighted—hence the derisive reference to him as a law-knight.

125 *When I was a child*: 'When I was a child, I spake as a child, I understood as a child, I thought as a child: but when I became a man, I put away childish things' (1 Corinthians 13:11, King James version).

128 *two pounds more*: the Jockey Club's weight-for-age scale had been devised by Admiral Henry John Rous (1795–1877) and, as is clear, was at this point still subject to some local adjustment: Silverbridge has been persuaded to allow Coalition to carry what has proved an unfair additional weight. [M&O'G]

129 *the young Lord's comb . . . long*: to cut one's comb, idiom for humbling a person who is arrogant.

130 *Prime Minister stood very . . . Derby*: a horse called the Prime Minister was strongly backed at 7–1 for the 1851 Derby but came nowhere. A famous horse called Plenipotentiary (known as 'Plenipo') won in 1834, beating a fine horse called Glencoe. (Could there be an echo of these names in 'Planty Pall' and 'Glencora'?) [HL]

132 *Mr. Lupton came in . . . racing*: described in *The Way We Live Now* as a 'young aristocrat' and Conservative member of Parliament who is 'inoculated with the idea' that the party would gain if the shady financier Melmotte could get a seat in the House of Commons, 'but who would have given up his Scotch shooting rather than have undergone Melmotte's company for a day' (ch. 54).

133 *Quousque*: Cicero, *Quo usque tandem abutere, Catilina, patientia nostra?*, 'How long, Catiline, will you abuse our patience?' In 1877, Trollope wrote about Cicero for *The Fortnightly Review*; his lengthy *Life of Cicero* was published in 1880.

136 *Eastern Counties Railway station*: the Eastern Counties Railway had been incorporated into the Great Eastern Railway in 1862—though that

wouldn't preclude Trollope from using the older, more familiar name for this station at Liverpool Street (see note below on p. 136).

hansom cab: first version patented by Joseph Hansom in the 1830s. One horse pulled a two-wheeled carriage meant to hold two people; the driver was in an elevated seat behind them.

Liverpool Street: mainline station opened in 1874 as terminus for the Great Eastern Railway. There was also a new Underground station at Liverpool Street that had just opened in 1875, but Gerald at this moment has no need for the Tube.

jump onto the guard's brake: Gerald tries to jump onto the last carriage, which would more properly be designated the 'guard's brake van', or merely 'brake van'.

'Why on earth . . . give me one': Silverbridge is naive to think that Gerald would be able to book a special train—especially without their father's knowledge—at the last minute, just for himself.

142 *Silverbridge is wanted to make a House*: to be among a quorum of forty in the House of Commons so that business can proceed.

144 *the punishment . . . the arrogant intruder*: the punishment for these three figures in Greek mythology was death—and in the satyr Marsyas's case, an especially gruesome death, as he is flayed alive. In his private thoughts, the Duke indulges in fantasies that he would never actually support.

152 *some star which had been accorded to him*: probably the star worn as part of the Order of the Garter (see note to p. 72), though it would not be common to wear this to a non-ceremonial occasion.

155 *Mrs. Montacute Jones's great ball*: originally, 'Mrs. Montgomery Jones' throughout the 1876 manuscript. While editing in 1878, Trollope crossed out 'Montgomery' and replaced it with 'Montacute' to correspond with the character he had created for *Is He Popenjoy?* (*All the Year Round* 1877–8; Chapman & Hall 1878).

158 *a fainéant Premier*: accomplishing little or nothing. In *Phineas Finn* (ch. 13), Lady Glencora advocates for the 'twenty schemes of reform' her husband has thought up as Chancellor of the Exchequer that the party leaders will not take up. She is told by one of them that 'a fainéant Government is not the worst Government that England can have. It has been the great fault of our politicians that they have all wanted to do something.'

a great Conservative reaction: though Disraeli had become Prime Minister again in 1874, it is doubtful that Trollope is referring to that real-world event. For the purposes of his fiction, the Conservatives hold power in *The Duke's Children*—with the Liberals gathering strength until they take control at the end.

159 *first man*: official Leader of the House.

160 *Elysium of creaminess*: in this case, the Elysium is a heaven on earth rather than any sort of afterlife.

162 *fisheries or frontiers*: the United States Commission of Fish and Fisheries was established in 1871 to investigate the decline of fish stocks in US waters. That same year American subjects had been given the right to fish off eastern Canada in return for permission for British subjects to fish off a portion of the east coast of the US. This was a source of argument until the treaty was overtaken in 1885. On the question of borders more generally, the growing power of the post-Civil War US was always a matter of interest for the British Parliament. [M&O'G]

   a Pitt or a Peel: William Pitt the Younger (1759–1806) and Sir Robert Peel (1788–1850), two of the UK's more highly regarded (and more liberal) Tory/Conservative Prime Ministers.

   made his way to the bench: 'bench' here is a metonym for 'the judiciary'; i.e. he could have been expected to be appointed to a judgeship.

163 *to a Conservative minister*: Mr. Daubeny, who in the opening pages of *Phineas Redux* has been Prime Minister for a year. 'Then Mr. Daubeny for twelve months had sat upon the throne distributing the good things of the Crown amidst Conservative birdlings, with beaks wide open and craving maws, who certainly for some years previous had not received their share of State honours or State emoluments' (ch. 1).

164 *a hot politician*: vigorous, enthusiastic.

165 *looking to their arms*: metaphorically, to arm themselves both for battle and for ruling.

166 *old Duke of St. Bungay*: close ally of Plantagenet; described in *Phineas Finn* (ch. 48) as 'a useful man' who 'had been so all his life, sitting in Cabinets and serving his country, constant as any peer in the House of Lords, always ready to take on his own shoulders any troublesome work required of him.'

   Solve senescentem: *Solve senescentem mature sanus equum, ne | peccet ad extremum ridendus et ilia ducat*, 'send the old horse out to pasture | Before he falls down while everybody jeers' (Horace, *Epistles*, I. i. 8, trans. David Ferry).

167 *the advice of Lord Grey . . . Mr. Huskisson*: Charles Grey, 2nd Earl Grey (1764–1845) and William Huskisson (1770–1830). Grey was Whig Prime Minister during the first Great Reform Act in 1832. Huskisson, a Tory, supported 'free trade, modernity and progress' and 'was a great supporter of the engineer George Stephenson. Ironically, he was run over and killed at the opening ceremony of Stephenson's Manchester and Liverpool Railway' (National Portrait Gallery, https://www.npg. org.uk).

   emancipation of the Roman Catholics: the Roman Catholic Relief Act of 1829 made it possible for Catholics to become members of Parliament.

   either by pride or by diffidence: published erroneously in *All the Year Round* and thereafter as 'either by pride or by indifference'. It is hard to imagine the Duke of St. Bungay accusing his friend of indifference.

177 *Faint heart*: 'faint heart never won fair lady,' old proverb best known from Robert Burns's adaptation in 'Epistle to Dr. Blacklock': 'faint heart ne'er wan | A lady fair.'

179 *in spite of . . . very soft within*: Trollope may have in mind something akin to *OED*, 17b: 'easily influenced or swayed; having little power of resistance to the influence of other persons or things; compliant; impressionable.' If he does mean 'soft-hearted', Frank's own use of the word is relevant, as it refers to someone with ordinary human feelings rather than someone especially kind or compassionate. As Frank says of the Duke, 'he's just as soft-hearted as other people. The man who holds out is not the man of the firmest opinion, but the man of the hardest heart' (p.108).

190 *dura ilia*: 'strong stomach', from Horace, *Epodes*, iii.4. In *The Bertrams*, Harcourt warns against heavy lunches, since 'one doesn't know what on earth to do when they're over.' When Twisleton suggests going straight to dinner, Harcourt says, 'That may do for the *dura ilia* of a freshman' but not for an older man. See pp. 540–41 of *The Duke's Children* for more on the hazards of a large lunch.

192 *Not though you build palaces out into the deep . . . . beautiful with exquisite boots*: the Duke is alluding to, and also quoting from, Horace's *Odes*, iii. i, with Gerald offering a translation of one line. (*Sed timor et Minae | Scandunt eodem quo dominus, neque | decedit aerata triremi et | post equitem sedet atra Cura*: 'But Fear and Foreboding | climb as high as the master. Black care | stays aboard the bronze-plated trireme, | and sits behind the Knight'; trans. David West).

193 *as Sinbad did of the Old Man*: in the *One Thousand and One Nights* (*Arabian Nights*), Sinbad avoids death on his fifth voyage by getting the Old Man of the Sea drunk and then killing him.

194 *two eldest sons*: though it is possible that Silverbridge exaggerates, the family's wealth is such that the Duke may be able to treat all his children more or less equally without the eldest son feeling deprived.

second reading: with the first reading, a bill is read out loud without debate; with the second reading, discussion begins.

195 *in a matter . . . very well*: see ch. 57 of *The Prime Minister*, when Phineas Finn makes a speech defending the Duke from unfair charges of corruption. The Duke thanks Phineas and is deeply grateful, but because 'gratitude with him always failed to exhibit itself readily,' Phineas perceives the Duke as being 'cold' to him.

196 *a royal concert would make the House empty*: the musical enthusiasm of Prince Albert, who started the concerts at Windsor Castle and Buckingham Palace in 1840, and arranged many of the programmes for the Philharmonic Society, was continued after his death in 1861. In 1876 there was a season of summer concerts at Buckingham Palace, known as 'State Concerts' or 'Her Majesty's Concerts'. The first, on 21 June 1876, was attended by most of the leading parliamentarians (Disraeli, Northcote, Bentinck,

Gladstone, etc.) as well as by visiting heads of state and diplomats. These concerts, which would certainly 'empty' the House, were announced in advance in *The Times*. [HL]

197 *fighting a duel*: see ch. 38 of *Phineas Finn*, where Phineas and Lord Chiltern duel over Violet Effingham.

198 *Turveydrop*: 'Master of Deportment' in Dickens's *Bleak House*. Trollope mentions him again later, in ch. 76, titled 'On Deportment'.

blue-books: parliamentary reports published with blue covers.

203 *she had behaved ... trying circumstances*: the 'circumstances' are presumably those mentioned elsewhere in this book, which Mabel refers to when she tells Frank how 'I have given up what was to have been my fortune' (p. 599). Mabel would have had to give her formal consent for any of her own potential dowry/inheritance to be used to settle family debts—something she has been doing in various stages over recent years.

209 *'All vanity; and vexation of spirit'*: 'I have seen all the works that are done under the sun; and, behold, all is vanity and vexation of spirit' (Ecclesiastes 1:14, King James Version).

211 *British Museum*: nowadays, the British Library, which became separate from the Museum in the British Library Act of 1972.

213 *speaking with no slightest twang*: as we discover later (p. 255), it is no accident that Isabel speaks without a twang, as she has worked hard to remove it.

the tender: OED, n.1, 3b, 'a small ship used to carry passengers, luggage, mails, goods, stores, etc., to or from a larger vessel (usually a liner), esp. when not otherwise accessible from shore.'

215 *the Langham ... that great American caravansary*: the Langham, a lavish hotel then and now, was built in the 1860s and thus still relatively new. Isabel jokes about it being a run-of-the-mill inn.

218 *the Phrenological Society*: George Combe's *The Constitution of Man Considered in Relation to External Objects* (1828) had helped to popularize phrenology, which argued that the size and shape of the skull could give deep insights into a person's character traits. Though the heyday of phrenology had passed after the 1830s, there was some revival of interest in the 1860s and beyond. The British Phrenological Society was founded in 1886 and operated until 1967.

223 *The Major is ... Strait Gate*: in *Pilgrim's Progress*, Worldly-Wiseman urges Christian to go to the town of Morality to find a man named Legality and his son Civility, rather than continue on what we are meant to see as the correct path—that is, his religious journey to the Wicket Gate.

237 *champagne-cup*: OED, 'a "cup" of which champagne is the basis or chief ingredient.'

sward: an expanse of short grass, such as a clipped lawn.

239 *Newport*: roughly two hundred miles from Manhattan. In *North America* (begun in 1861; completed and published in 1862), Trollope writes about

it at length, saying, 'All the world has heard of Newport in Rhode Island as being the Brighton, and Tenby, and Scarborough of New England.' As one of the 'summer haunts' that are popular in America, it 'is supposed to be in many ways the most captivating. In the first place it is certainly the most fashionable, and in the next place it is said to be the most beautiful' (ch. 2). As Trollope goes on to make clear, he was less impressed with Newport than others were.

243 *for a President of the United States*: Mr. Boncassen may evoke physical comparisons to Lincoln, but it is hard to imagine someone of his ilk— a man who spends his days in the British Museum and demonstrates no taste for political machinations—being seriously thought of as a presidential candidate. Still, Trollope might have enjoyed imagining a man of Mr. Boncassen's integrity in this role; in *An Autobiography*, he decries 'the infinite baseness of . . . public life' in America, and how 'the very men who are the least fit to occupy high places' rise to the top (ch. 17).

244 *Belgravia*: since the 1820s, a wealthy area of London.

Why, my Lord, . . . Lord Tybalt: though there is no attribution, Mr. Boncassen must be the one speaking here; it would be out of character for Mrs. Boncassen to make these references to *Romeo and Juliet*.

'*Laws!*': *OED*, 6a: 'used for "Lord" in various phrases, esp. *laws d'mercy* and variants'; 6b: 'expressing surprise, emphasis, dismay, etc.'

249 *Erebus*: *OED*, '*Mythology*. The proper name of "a place of darkness, between Earth and Hades" (Liddell and Scott); often used in phrase *dark as Erebus*.' In *A Summer in Western France* (1840) written by Trollope's brother Thomas Adolphus and edited by his mother, Frances, the former writes, 'I stumbled along a winding lane between two dead walls, as black as Erebus.'

treble-piled sofas: triple-pile velvet would be extremely luxurious.

253 *as plenty with her as blackberries*: Falstaff, *Henry IV, Part One*, Act Two, Scene Four: 'If reasons were as plenty as blackberries, I would give no man a reason upon compulsion.' Although they can be cultivated (and improved), blackberries grow wild all over the UK and are a free food supply. They are still collected to eat and make jam with.

255 *But new things are such ducks! . . . Trowsers may be*: Isabel is using 'ducks' as 'a term of endearment' (*OED*, 1, 3a) but her mention of clothing gets Dolly thinking about ducks in a different sense: trousers (or 'trowsers', a spelling which was not fully obsolete at the time that Trollope used it) made of 'a strong untwilled linen (or later, cotton) fabric, lighter and finer than canvas' (*OED*, n.3, 1). It is unlikely that he intends to be clever, though Isabel cannot be sure.

259 '*Good-morning*': it is already afternoon. Trollope himself may be forgetting what time it is, but given their leisurely schedules, it is more than possible that both Silverbridge and Dolly do feel as if it is still morning. See also note to p. 46.

267 *noble Duke who boasted in the House of Lords*: in a tribute to Sir Robert Peel
    after his death in 1850, the Duke of Cleveland talked about the two men
    riding together in 1806 to attend the trial of Lord Melville. For the Duke,
    'trivial as this travelling together in a postchaise might appear . . . it made
    an impression on his mind never to be effaced' (*Hansard's Parliamentary
    Debates*, vol. CXII, 866).

270 *Questions of rank . . . have two sides*: at any formal dinner, the host would
    lead out the woman of the highest rank and the hostess would be led out
    by the highest-ranking man. A duchess would precede a countess, a peer
    would precede a commoner, and a married sister would precede her
    unmarried elder sibling. Titles of equal rank would be arranged by their
    date of creation. Women, such as Lizzie Eustace in *The Eustace Diamonds*,
    were allowed to retain their position and title even if they contracted
    another later marriage of lower rank. Lady Cantrip faces challenges in
    putting together her preferred seating arrangements, but is able to get
    what she wants since each lady has another side in addition to the side
    where her dining escort will be seated.

272 *murder a man*: the accusation, trial, and exoneration of Phineas Finn on
    a charge of murder are narrated in *Phineas Redux*, chs. 47–67.

273 *Home Rule*: self-government, in particular for Ireland. In *An Autobiography*
    Trollope writes, 'Home Rule no doubt is a nuisance,—and especially
    a nuisance because the professors of the doctrine do not at all believe it
    themselves. There are probably no other twenty men in England or Ireland
    who would be so utterly dumbfounded and prostrated were Home Rule to
    have its way as the twenty Irish members who profess to support it in the
    House of Commons' (ch. 4).

    the Twelfth: 12 August, also known as the Glorious Twelfth, by law the
    start of the red grouse and ptarmigan shooting season.

278 *that very clever . . . little fleas*: the famous mathematician Augustus de
    Morgan's *A Budget of Paradoxes*, published posthumously by Longmans
    in 1872, included this adaptation of a verse by Jonathan Swift: 'Great fleas
    have little fleas upon their backs to bite 'em, | And little fleas have lesser
    fleas, and so ad infinitum. | And the great fleas themselves, in turn, have
    greater fleas to go on; | While these again have greater still, and greater
    still, and so on.'

    farriery: a farrier specializes in horses' hooves and shoes.

    Major Tifto had a little 'box' of his own: OED, box, n.2,14, 'a residence
    for temporary use while following a particular sport, as a hunting-box,
    shooting-box, fishing-box.'

    grass-plat: more commonly, 'grass plot'. *OED*: 'a piece of ground covered
    with turf, sometimes ornamented with flower beds.' See also *The Warden*,
    ch. 5: 'Who would not feel charity for a prebendary, when walking the
    quiet length of that long aisle at Winchester, looking at those decent
    houses, that trim glass-plat, and feeling, as one must, the solemn, orderly
    comfort of the spot!'

280 *strap a 'orse*: to groom a horse.

headstall: key part of the bridle holding the horse's head in place.

suffrage: John Stuart Mill's *The Subjection of Women*, which among much else advocated for women having the vote, was published in 1869 and was considered a radical document. It took until 1918 for the first large women's suffrage act to pass in Parliament.

a month at the treadmill and a month of starvation: Tifto talks about the good old days of harsh prison punishment, but actually, 'after the 1865 Prisons Act and under Assistant Director of Prisons Edmund du Cane, prisons were made even tougher. Hard plank beds replaced hammocks, food was deliberately boring and inmates had to work hard on . . . monotonous, even pointless tasks,' including the treadmill, 'a large wheel on which prisoners walked' (https://www.nationalarchives.gov.uk).

284 *As the place was entailed he could not sell it*: the elderly John Scarborough's hatred of the laws of entail propels the plot of Trollope's late novel *Mr. Scarborough's Family*, as Scarborough creates doubt about who his one rightful male heir is.

285 *white plastered heads*: footmen (as distinct from the aristocracy who in certain ages and circumstances might wear powdered and scented wigs) would often grow their own hair long and use flour or highly refined starch to whiten it. Each night, at the end of their duties, they would have to wash it out. Trollope may be saying that the whitened hair would give the effect of being plastered down across the footmen's heads. It is also possible that he meant 'powdered' rather than 'plastered' (he refers to 'powder-headed footmen' on p. 597).

292 *Lazarus . . . Dr. Gwynne*: fictional college and warden of Oxford. In *Barchester Towers*, Dr. Gwynne is described as 'a high churchman at all points; so high, indeed, that at one period of his career he had all but toppled over into the cesspool of Rome' (ch. 14).

They paid their own shares: the cost of the expedition is divided equally into two between Popplecourt and Silverbridge. Dobbes and Nidderdale each pay a third of Popplecourt's expenditure directly to Popplecourt but Silverbridge pays for himself, his brother, and Frank.

gillies: attendants who do the more mundane tasks of the hunt. Dobbes imagines using them as a kind of private army to thrash any intruders.

300 *playing lawn-tennis with Miss Boncassen*: unlike most other sports, the new game of lawn-tennis encouraged social intercourse between the sexes. The first patent was given to Major Walter Clopton Wingfield in 1874 and the first Championships took place at Wimbledon in 1877.

'When Youth and Pleasure. . . flying feet': Byron, *Childe Harold's Pilgrimage*, Canto III. Lady Mabel quotes the description of the Duchess of Richmond's famous ball in Brussels, in the course of which the Duke of Wellington received despatches concerning the French troop movements that led up to the Battle of Waterloo.

309 *parti-coloured stockings*: OED, particoloured, 'partly of one colour and partly of another or others; variegated.' There are citations with the spelling 'party-coloured', including Wordsworth's 'The Waggoner', and Trollope spelled it this way in his manuscript. *All the Year Round* changed it to 'parti-coloured', while Chapman & Hall followed the manuscript.

316 *an hotel at Ischl*: the spa Bad Ischl in Upper Austria was widely known as the site of the Habsburgs' summer residence.

321 *insurmountable . . . the rich man*: Gospel of St. Luke, 16. As the narrator goes on to say, this is 'an odd illustration for him to use', given that the rich man fares badly in the parable. The Duke is thinking about two people from entirely different walks of life and not about the larger implications of the story.

322 *'Men have died . . . for love'*: 'men have died from time to | time and worms have eaten them, but not for love' (*As You Like It*, Act Four, Scene One). The Duke believes he has 'remembered it all', but in fact has not quite done so, as he's left out a few words. It is worth noting too that Rosalind in Shakespeare's play gives in ultimately—something the Duke is determined to avoid.

328 *Richard will be himself again*: 'Hence, babbling dreams! you threaten here in vain! | Conscience, avaunt! Richard's himself again,' from Colley Cibber's famous 1699 adaptation of *Richard III*. The word 'again' is in Trollope's manuscript and mistakenly fell out of the printed versions. Even if she is joking, Mabel does not help her cause by comparing herself to Richard.

330 *Dobbesdom*: published in *All the Year Round* and beyond as 'Dobbydom', though Trollope wrote 'Dobbesdom' in the manuscript. 'Dobbesdom' must be what he intended; there is nobody named 'Dobby' in the novel.

331 *the Semiramises, . . . and the Charlotte Cordays*: Semiramis: heavily mythologized Assyrian leader, early 800s BC; Pocahontas: heavily mythologized Native American, born in the 1590s, died 1617; Ida Pfeiffer (1797–1858), Austrian explorer and author; Charlotte Corday (1768–1793), most famous for murdering Jean-Paul Marat in his bathtub during the French Revolution. Of the four, it is likely that Trollope, as a regular traveller himself, considered only Ida Pfeiffer unequivocally 'great'; in 'The Two Heroines of Plumplington' (published posthumously in 1882), one character says that 'She was a great traveller, and went about everywhere almost without anything. I don't know how she managed it, but I'm sure that I can't.' Mabel's scattershot collection of 'great women of the world' fits the moment; she has only a vague sense of how to proceed.

335 *macassar*: oil to groom men's hair. Mr. Pook is being humorous when he says that the horse looks good even without macassar.

337 *about seventy thousand pounds*: over eight million pounds in today's currency (Bank of England inflation calculator). Counting up what he had earned from his books as of 1876, Trollope gives the figure as also 'about seventy thousand pounds' (*An Autobiography*, ch. 20).

340 *the ring, . . . always suspects*: for the first use of 'ring', *OED*, 2.18c is most
relevant: 'to hold the ring'—'to continue victorious or hold one's own in
a series of fights.' For the second usage, Trollope may have 'the bookmaking
profession' in mind (2.18b).

344 *a sell*: *OED*, 2a: 'a contrivance, fiction, etc., by which a person is "sold":
a planned deception, hoax, take-in.' There is also a citation from 1857
(T. P. Thompson, *Audi Alteram Partem*) that attributes this usage to 'the
language of the turf'.

her own telegraph-wire: the telegraph network extended itself across the
UK during the 1870s, and Trollope's own interest in this new technology
is evidenced in his story 'The Telegraph Girl', *Good Words* (1877). To have
a telegraph wire in one's own house was, however, an unusual luxury, also
enjoyed by Paula Power, heroine of Hardy's *A Laodicean* (1881). [M&O'G]

346 *his lordship's simple bond*: printed as 'single bond' in *All the Year Round*
and thereafter, despite what Trollope wrote in the manuscript. Though
Shylock's 'single bond' from *The Merchant of Venice* (Act One, Scene
Three) fits the context, Comfort and Criball would not be so punctilious
in their literary allusions.

347 *Jockey Club rules*: according to its present-day website (https://www.the-
jockeyclub.co.uk), the Jockey Club was founded in 1750 and eventually
became 'the official governing body for horseracing in Britain'.

349 *Pitt was a great minister and Pope a great poet*: originally, 'Pitt was a minister, Pope a poet, and Disraeli a novelist.' Trollope added 'great' before
'minister' and 'poet' but nothing before 'novelist'. This would have looked
odd in proofs, and understandably the reference to Disraeli was dropped.
Trollope despised Disraeli as a man and as a writer—see *An Autobiography*,
ch. 13 for a brutal assessment of his fiction—and would not have been
willing to call him great.

350 *mooncalf tone*: *OED*, mooncalf (noun), 2c, 'a person who idles time away in
dreaming; someone absent-minded, distracted, or given to sentimental-
ity.' Silverbridge barely wants to admit that he has been hunting at all.

Nimrod: Mesopotamian ruler described in the King James Bible (Genesis
10:9) as 'a mighty hunter before the Lord'. Trollope in *The Prime Minister*
names one of the clubs the Nimrod.

352 *coverts*: areas and thickets where any game can hide. They might be natural
habitats or specially developed by gamekeepers.

359 *marker*: someone with various duties officiating a billiards match—most
particularly, keeping score.

360 *the Duke's daughter*: unaccountably, this has always been published as 'the
Duke's children', despite what Trollope wrote in the manuscript.

361 *the Skald*: Mary asks either about the particular old Norse poet that
Mr. Boncassen has just mentioned, or perhaps about skaldic poetry more
generally. Either way, she is glad to have a reason not to speak with
Popplecourt.

362 *Moore's elegies*: Popplecourt's mangled reference to Moore's *Irish Melodies*, written by Thomas Moore in the early nineteenth century. Corrected to Moore's *Melodies* for *All the Year Round* and thereafter, but the original error was almost surely intentional on Trollope's part. Popplecourt is no great reader and is making a clumsy effort to impress Mary.

375 *a Sir Guy who was a king's friend*: in ch. 22 of *Can You Forgive Her?* Glencora tells a garbled story about Sir Guy de Palisere, meeting the king, either Richard 1st or Edward III, 'I forget which,' and providing refreshment, 'as he came from the war, or from hunting, or something of that kind.'

376 *Arabian Nights*: the first English translation of these Arabic folktales appeared in the early eighteenth century. See also note to p. 193.

380 *Island of the Blest*: from *The American Encyclopaedic Dictionary*, Volume 6: 'Greek Mythol.: Imaginary islands, situated in the West, thought to be the abode of good men after death. The following passage from Cook's translation of Hesiod's *Works and Days* (l. 170) shows the ancient belief as to the nature of the enjoyment to be found there. "There in the *Island of the Blest* they find | Where Saturn reigns, an endless calm of mind; | And there the choicest fruits adorn the fields, | And thrice the fertile year a harvest yields".'

381 *Apollyon*: angel of death or the abyss; adapted from Hebrew 'Abaddon'. In John Bunyan's *Pilgrim's Progress* (see note to p. 223) Apollyon is described as a 'foul fiend', a formidable monster 'hideous to behold'.

392 *locus poenitentiae*: Latin phrase signifying ability to withdraw from an agreement.

396 *People's Banner*: one-time Liberal, now Conservative, scandal sheet, edited by the unscrupulous Quintus Slide until he is fired at the end of *Phineas Redux*. 'It became Mr. Slide's duty to speak of men as heaven-born patriots whom he had designated a month or two since as bloated aristocrats and leeches fattened on the blood of the people' (*Phineas Redux*, ch. 22). When a rival newspaper prints a double column showing the completely opposite opinions that the *People's Banner* has espoused, Slide 'did not pause to defend himself, but boldly attacked the meanness, the duplicity, the immorality, the grammar, the paper, the type, and the wife of the editor of the evening newspaper' (*Phineas Redux*, ch. 22).

399 *jolly as a sandboy*: a proverbial phrase, like 'happy as a clam'. The first citation is from 1821; and in 1841, Dickens named an inn The Jolly Sandboys in *The Old Curiosity Shop*. A sandboy would often bring sand to a publican and then spread it on the floor. He would be paid, in part or whole, by beer.

407 *President of the Council*: Lord President of the Council—a prestigious position but one without many duties.

409 *quints*: see ch. 55 of *The Eustace Diamonds*, 'Quints or Semitenths', where Palliser is humorously described as 'the financial Hercules of the day'. He is flummoxed about what to name 'the new Palliser penny', and gathers the

Prime Minister and others at his house to talk about it: 'By what denomination should the fifth part of a penny be hereafter known? . . . Should he
stick by the farthing; or should he call it a fifthing, a quint, or a semi-
tenth?' See also note to p. 437.

414 *King Cophetua*: from the sixteenth-century ballad 'The King and the
Beggar-Maid', referenced by Shakespeare in a number of plays. See
also *Framley Parsonage*, ch. 35, titled 'The Story of King Cophetua', and
Tennyson's 'The Beggar Maid' (1833). In the story, Cophetua not only
falls in love instantly with the beggar Penelophon, he decides instantly
that she will be his wife. Their marriage turns out to be a happy one.

he must give up his seat: perhaps Silverbridge feels he would have to resign
as a matter of principle, since he was elected as a Conservative, or perhaps
he is mistaken about the law. In any case, he would not have to give up his
seat if he switched parties.

415 *a gentleman who . . . would have to begin again*: in this reference to the myth
of Sisyphus, Mabel suggests that she too will have to 'begin again' in her
pursuit of Silverbridge, or indeed any suitable marriage—and that like
Sisyphus, who keeps pushing a boulder up a hill only to have it roll down
again, she will fail.

417 *White Elephant*: reference to any useless, unwanted article.

423 *Great Reform Bill . . . second Reform Bill*: the Reform Act of 1832 and
Reform Act of 1867 widened the franchise.

424 *paid very dear for his whistle*: proverbial phrase originating from Benjamin
Franklin's 'The Whistle, a true Story; written to his Nephew': 'I conceive
that great part of the miseries of mankind are brought upon them by the
false estimates they have made of the value of things, and by their giving
too much for their whistles.'

strange Conservatives: strangers; not from the local political constituency.

426 *You have read Carlyle's* French Revolution: Carlyle's book was published in
1837 and was still well known four decades later. Whether Frank has actually read it is open to question. As the narrator suggests, there is 'much that
was superficial only, much that was mere tinsel' about him (p. 21).

427 *I regard myself as a philanthropic patriot*: in *An Autobiography*, Trollope
talks about the 'conscientious philanthropic Conservative' (ch. 16) who
believes that inequality is of 'divine origin', and 'that the preservation of
the welfare of the world depends on the maintenance of those distances
between the prince and the peasant by which he finds himself to be surrounded;—and, perhaps, I may add, the duty is not unpleasant as he feels
himself to be one of the princes.' It is a view that Trollope as 'an advanced,
but still a conservative Liberal' has strong objections to.

Robespierre and his pals . . . prison: though both Frank and Silverbridge
decry the excesses of the French Revolution—as did Trollope—the latter
at this stage of the novel is far more willing to criticize the status quo that
existed before the revolution.

429 *a Presbyterian in Scotland was not a dissenter*: the Scottish national church was firmly Presbyterian.

430 *buff*: traditional Whig colour, along with blue. The buff and blue are mentioned in the first stanza of Robert Burns's famous 1792 poem, 'Here's a Health to Them That's Awa': 'Here's a health to them that's awa, | Here's a health to them that's awa; | And wha winna wish gude luck to our cause, | May never gude luck be their fa'! | It's gude to be merry and wise, | It's gude to be honest and true; | It's gude to support Caledonia's cause, | And bide by the buff and the blue.'

431 *But to go through it . . . indeed!*: in ch. 16 of *An Autobiography*, simply titled 'Beverley', Trollope devotes many pages to his woeful experiences running for Parliament in that Yorkshire town. See also *Ralph the Heir*, written less than a year after his 1868 election failure, for a fictionalized account.

433 *every Salem and Zion and Ebenezer*: usual names for Nonconformist chapels. Hostility between the establishment and the Dissenters was widespread: see Revd. John Clifford, *Baptist Handbook* (1877), speaking on 'Religious Life in the Rural Districts of England': 'It is intolerable that landowner and squire, justice of the peace and priest of the Church, should form a confederacy to close the chapel doors' (*Nonconformity in the 19th Century*, ed. D. M. Thompson, Routledge, 1972). Edward Miall, a leading Congregationalist, said in the House on 9 May 1871: 'Every town has its exclusive circles of social intercourse—the one appropriated to Churchmen, the other to Dissenters.' Mr. Williams, and Tregear's parents, regard his election as a victory for the Church over the Nonconformists (who in the West Country would very likely be Baptists or Wesleyans). The use of the word 'dissenter' rather than 'Nonconformist' was rather old-fashioned by 1876. [HL]

435 *a magistrate a thousand miles up the country in India*: with the 1858 Government of India Act, the British Raj was created, giving the Crown, rather than the East India Company, control over the Indian subcontinent. In this new system, the district magistrate would be in charge of administering and collecting revenue in a particular region.

437 *the beauty of tenths . . . the hideous deformity of dozens*: though the Royal Commission on Decimal Coinage had explored the issue in 1856–7, decimal coinage was not instituted in the UK until Decimal Day, on 15 February 1971. Prior to decimalization, the coinage was as follows: one pound could be broken down into twenty shillings, or you could have two ten-shilling notes or four crowns or eight half-crowns. Crowns largely disappeared except for souvenir minting, but half-crowns were still used often. There were 12 pennies in a shilling; each penny could be divided into two half-pennies or four farthings. The Duke's problems mainly related to making this part of the currency fit in with units of ten.

438 *they would not preserve foxes for him*: landowners had a difficult decision to make. They could preserve foxes for the local hunt or they could preserve game for shooting, but the two objectives did not always go well together.

As predators, foxes could decimate game and, at the same time, could cause great havoc to the local poultry.

441 *Caesar wouldn't keep a wife*: variation of the proverbial phrase 'Caesar's wife must be above suspicion.' *Plutarch's Lives* relates how Julius Caesar divorces his wife, Pompeia, after she is accused of adultery. Though he offers no evidence, Caesar proceeds with the divorce anyhow, saying he must have a wife who is so virtuous, no one would even suspect that she could stray. Trollope was proud of his own *Commentaries of Caesar* (1870), and in his autobiography said that Caesar was 'probably the greatest man who ever lived' (ch. 6). As is often the case, one can't know just how playful or serious Trollope intended to be when offering his opinion; he also says that his nonfiction book *The West Indies and the Spanish Main* is 'the best book that has come from my pen' (ch. 7), a view so perverse that no one has ever been able to explain it.

444 *draw*: to lure a fox out of the coverts.

448 *bounce*: OED, 4a: 'a loud or audacious boast.' See also *The Way We Live Now*, ch. 44: 'Melmotte's supporters began the battle with an attempt at what the Liberals called "bounce,"—to carry the borough with a rush by an overwhelming assertion of their candidate's virtues.'

453 *He and I once had an adventure there out hunting*: narrated at the end of *Phineas Redux*, ch. 16.

455 *crammer*: OED, 3, slang: 'a lie.' The earliest citation is from 1861, in the periodical publication of George Augustus Sala's *The Seven Sons of Mammon*: 'Every other word he says is a crammer.'

460 *top of his bent*: *Hamlet*, Act Three, Scene Two. 'They fool me to the top of my bent.' Hamlet indicates that he is not being fooled; and here, Mabel is yet to realize that Silverbridge will not be swayed by flattery.

465 *the Coldstreams*: the Coldstream Guards, regiment of the British Army, originating in the English Civil War.

469 *perfect love casteth out fear*: 'There is no fear in love; but perfect love casteth out fear, because fear hath torment. He that feareth is not made perfect in love' (1 John 4:18, King James Version).

479 *Then the Duchess interfered . . . or two*: see ch. 75, *Phineas Redux*, 'The Trumpeton Feud Is Settled'.

   uxorious: published erroneously in *All the Year Round* and thereafter as 'vigorous'. Mr. Spooner is certainly not a vigorous man.

480 *appanages*: also spelled 'apanages'. OED, 4, 'a specially appointed, and hence, a natural or necessary, adjunct, accompaniment, endowment, or attribute.' One citation is from Swinburne's 1875 *Essays and Studies*: 'This fretful and petulant appetite for applause, the proper apanage of small poets.'

481 *I never go out myself now*: as Violet Effingham, she hunted often. It is likely that she would continue to hunt if she wanted to; rather, the implication is that her husband is so full of hunting talk that she doesn't need to do it herself.

481 *He came into his property last year*: the elder Mr. Maule was particularly ungenerous when he was alive. See ch. 21, 'Mr. Maule, Senior', in *Phineas Redux*.

first whip: also called 'whipper-in'. Responsible for many duties in assisting the Master of Foxhounds. *Manual of British Rural Sports: Comprising Shooting, Hunting, Coursing, Fishing, Hawking, Racing, Boating, Pedestrianism, and the Various Rural Games and Amusements of Great Britain* (first published in 1856), by Stonehenge (John Henry Walsh), includes several pages about the first whipper-in's responsibilities, calling him 'truly a Jack-of-all trades'.

give him a line: referring to the fox's scent.

gorse: hiding place for fox; also called a gorse covert. In *Hunting Sketches*, Trollope also mentions the woods and the forest as hiding places, but calls the gorse 'the most delightful'.

482 *we found our foxes without drawing them . . . We chopped one*: the dogs have caught the fox before it had a chance to run.

483 *the delight of leaving a friend in a ditch*: published erroneously in *All the Year Round* and thereafter as *having a friend*, which has slightly salacious overtones.

stiff-built rail: something 'stiff-built' will remain sturdy, even if hit with horses' hooves. The rail could refer to any sort of barrier: a hedge or a fence or a wall or a barred gate, any obstacle that it would be advisable to clear comfortably in order to avoid a probable fall. In *Hunting Sketches* Trollope writes of a 'stiff-built wall six feet high' and how when he rode in Galway he 'found the six-foot walls all shorn of their glory.' It is possible, then, that Trollope meant to write 'wall' but mistakenly used 'rail' instead.

literary ignoramuses: published erroneously in *All the Year Round* and beyond as 'literary ignorances'. In the heated discussion that Trollope describes, it is easy to imagine this word—and harsher ones—bandied about.

U.R.U.: The Ufford and Rufford United Hunt Club; previously misprinted in *All the Year Round* and beyond as A.R.U. See, earlier in Trollope's career, *The American Senator* (ch. 1), and, later, *Ayala's Angel* (ch. 39).

484 *The Pope of Rome . . . self-preservation*: Trollope had to make his own choices about his manner of 'self-assertion' in *An Autobiography*, completed only three weeks before he began *The Duke's Children*. His statement here about the benefits of self-assertion suggests that he was aware of the risk he took in his autobiography by stating forthrightly that he was not a genius, that he was like a shoemaker showing up for work every day and not waiting for inspiration to strike.

the Shires: the Midlands in central England.

Land and Water; Bell's Life; Field; Bayley's: hunting magazines from the nineteenth century, though Trollope used a different spelling for *Baily's Magazine of Sports and Pastimes*.

486 *Michaelmas Daisies . . . unseasonable name*: published erroneously in *All the Year Round* and beyond as 'unreasonable'. Because Michaelmas, the Feast of St. Michael and All Angels, falls on 29 Sept., the name is 'unseasonable' for a midsummer flower.

488 *we'll see if we can't . . . out of them*: to push the horses more than usual so that each one is taken out four times a week.

489 *check*: when the hounds lose a line.

"*whoo-whoop*": the huntsman's call at the kill.

492 *crupper*: *OED*, n.1: 'a leathern strap buckled to the back of the saddle and passing under the horse's tail, to prevent the saddle from slipping forwards.'

496 *I shall always hate . . . her plan*: published erroneously in *All the Year Round* and thereafter with 'place' rather than 'plan'. Either reading from the manuscript is acceptable, but in context 'plan' is obviously correct. Even if Lady Cantrip devised the plan, it is one that the Duke encouraged—and one, too, that Lady Cantrip would have been glad to abort. Yet it suits Mary to displace all her anger onto Lady Cantrip and to spare her father.

Hyperion to a satyr . . . Look on that picture, and on this: *Hamlet*, Act One, Scene Two and Act Three, Scene Four. Hamlet compares his dead father to his uncle, now step-father. Mary's immediate impulse to focus on the 'picture' emphasizes a stark physical difference: Frank is extraordinarily handsome, while Popplecourt is not good looking at all.

501 '*I am just twenty-one*': in the previous chapter (p. 498), Nidderdale says that Gerald is under twenty-one.

'*Facilis descensus Averni . . . janua Ditis*': *Aeneid*, VI, line 126f. More commonly, *Averno*, though *Averni* has been printed in some editions of the *Aeneid*. John Dryden's translation is well known: 'The gates of hell are open night and day; | Smooth the descent, and easy is the way: | But to return, and view the cheerful skies, | In this the task and mighty labor lies.'

502 *footpad*: *OED*, n.1, 'a highwayman who robs on foot. Sometimes used to distinguish from a highwayman, who usually robs on horseback.'

503 *pips*: *OED*, n.3, 'each of the dots or symbols on a playing card, die, or domino.'

direction: address.

505 *Lord Buttercup*: changed in proofs from Lord Balamb (baa lamb), which had a more logical connection to his father's title, the Earl of Woolantallow.

Conservative young Lord as he was: though *The Fortnightly Review* (founded in 1865 by Trollope and others) was at first open to a wide variety of views, it soon became known as a staunchly Liberal magazine.

507 *craning*: *OED*, 4: '*Hunting*. To pull up at a hedge or other obstacle and look over before leaping; . . . [to] hesitate at or shrink back from a danger, difficulty, etc. (*colloquial*).

507 *cat-o'-nine-tails*: 'a whip with nine knotted lashes; till 1881 an authorized instrument of punishment in the British navy and army' (*OED*).

518 *the grouse were . . . February or March*: Lady Chiltern playfully suggests that if Parliament were to begin in April, then the start of the grouse-shooting season, which always begins on 12 August (see note to p. 273), would need to be pushed later. Silverbridge, however, claims that Parliament could finish its work by the end of July.

'I should so hate to fig myself out and look like a guy': dressed up in an eccentric manner. *OED*, fig, v4, 2: 'to fig out: to dress, "get up".' This meaning of guy (n.2, 2, 'a person of grotesque appearance, esp. with reference to dress; a "fright" ') comes from the Guy Fawkes effigy. See also *The Last Chronicle of Barset*, ch. 60: 'what are you doing there, dressed up in that way like a guy?'

Take the goods the gods provide you: well-known quotation from Plautus's comedic play *Rudens*: 'if you are wise, be wise; keep what goods the Gods provide you' (H. T. Riley translation).

521 *The same feeling reversed may keep you silent respecting Sir Timothy*: misprinted in *All the Year Round* and thereafter with 'policy' instead of 'feeling'. Though it is perhaps just possible to see how a compositor working quickly might have read the word as 'policy', he must have been especially inattentive here, repeating a word he had just typed.

whip: 'The use of the word "whip" within Parliament has its roots in the 18th century hunting terminology "whipper-in". It refers to a huntsman's assistant who drives straying hounds back to the main pack using a whip. . . . One of their responsibilities is making sure the maximum number of their party members vote, and vote the way their parties want' (https://www.parliament.uk).

525 *literary spinster*: unmarried woman 'with a pen for a spouse', as Louisa May Alcott wrote in *Little Women*, though the term can also refer to an unmarried woman who spends a lot of time reading, or to a spinster who is depicted in a work of literature. Mr. Boncassen is certainly joking; he does not envision Isabel remaining single. Mrs. Boncassen probably feels the same—though it is also possible that she has some genuine concern.

531 *Hebe*: Greek goddess of youth and cup bearer to the gods. In Book 9 of Ovid's *Metamorphoses*, at the request of her husband, Heracles, she restores the old man Iolaus to youth.

532 *He was inclined to think that he could not abdicate*: it would be possible for Silverbridge to renounce the title—the dukedom which he does not yet have—but not to pass it on to Gerald or anyone else.

since Macaulay's enthusiasm . . . of Clarissa: as recounted by William Thackeray in an 1860 letter, the great Whig historian and politician Thomas Babington Macaulay, while in India as part of the Supreme Council in the 1830s, claimed that 'the whole station was in a passion of excitement' about the novel after he urged everyone to read it. Trollope himself was not a great fan of *Clarissa*, writing in an 1868 review that even a new abridged version was too long.

533 *I've been horribly cheated*: in *The Way We Live Now*, the Longstaffe family falls victim to the con-man financier Augustus Melmotte.

534 *oaf*: published erroneously as 'owl' in *All the Year Round* and thereafter. Though 'owl' would work here too—*OED*, n.3, 'a person likened to an owl, esp. in being active at night, or in looking solemn or wise (frequently with implication of attendant dullness or underlying stupidity)'—it makes sense that Silverbridge at this moment thinks of Dolly as a more basic 'oaf', which is what Trollope wrote in the manuscript.

535 *Titania and Bottom*: the highly mismatched lovers from *A Midsummer Night's Dream*. Silverbridge would consider Popplecourt to be, like Bottom, an ass.

536 *hook it*: slang, to 'make off' (*OED*, 3) or run away.

538 *Ezekiel Sevenkings*: various readers have suggested Walt Whitman, who had become well known across the Atlantic by the 1870s, as a model. It is possible, though Whitman lived mostly in New York and New Jersey and was not from the 'far West'. Trollope's final words of *An Autobiography* have a Whitmanesque flavour: 'Now I stretch out my hand, and from the further shore I bid adieu to all who have cared to read any among the many words that I have written' (ch. 20).

539 *'You are not going to accept the Chilterns?'*: in other words, to resign from the House of Commons. Though technically an MP cannot resign, according to a 1680 resolution if he 'shall accept any Office, or Place of Profit, from the Crown', he can be 'expelled'. By getting appointed to the office of Crown Steward for the Chiltern Hundreds when he wishes to give up his seat, he is considered to be in such an 'office'. Silverbridge pretends that Lady Beeswax is referring to Lord and Lady Chiltern instead, leading her to consider him 'incoherent'.

543 *Anglican tendencies*: Mr. Boncassen does not mean 'Anglican' in relation to the Church of England. Though the *OED* says that it is now rare to use 'Anglican' to mean 'English', it does cite some nineteenth-century examples. See also *The Prime Minister*, when the narrator mentions 'the anti-Anglican tendencies of foreign railway officials' (ch. 67). In that case too, 'Anglican' means 'English'.

547 *sore-boned*: left out altogether in *All the Year Round* and published erroneously as 'sore-bored' in Chapman & Hall and thereafter. The (thin) skin and (sore) bones figuratively describe an overly sensitive politician much like the Duke of Omnium when he was Prime Minister.

551 *'all the blood of all the Howards'*: the best of the aristocracy; from *Pope, Essay on Man* IV: 'What could ennoble sots, or slaves, or cowards? | Alas! not all the blood of all the Howards.'

554 *Penates*: ancient Roman household gods.

coign: *OED*, n.1, 'in the Shakespearian phrase *coign of vantage*: a position (properly a projecting corner) affording facility for observation or action.

(The currency of the phrase is apparently due to Sir Walter Scott.)' Originally from *Macbeth*, Act 1, Scene 6, spoken by Banquo.

555 *Islington*: now a borough of London. It was once a settlement in its own right but had become a middle-class suburb by the time Trollope wrote; famously depicted a decade later in *The Diary of a Nobody*, by George and Weedon Grossmith, first serialized in *Punch*, 1888–9.

567 *but I have a doubt. I should have liked to be Duchess of Omnium*: published correctly in *All the Year Round* but erroneously in Chapman & Hall and thereafter as *'but I have a doubt I should have liked to be Duchess of Omnium.'* The omission of Trollope's full stop entirely changes the meaning; Mabel has no doubt at this point that she would have liked to be Duchess of Omnium.

568 *still I want some man's house, and his money, and his carriages*: published in *All the Year Round* and thereafter with 'name', rather than 'money', despite what Trollope wrote in the manuscript. Mabel is not much interested in another man's name; the money is a different matter.

569 *'There is a tide in the affairs of men'*: *Julius Caesar*, Act Four, Scene Three. Brutus: 'There is a tide in the affairs of men, | Which, taken at the flood, leads on to fortune; | Omitted, all the voyage of their life | Is bound in shallows and in miseries. | On such a full sea are we now afloat; | And we must take the current when it serves, | Or lose our ventures.'

572 *A man does not I suppose . . . of propriety*: published erroneously in *All the Year Round* and beyond as 'without any consideration or purpose', which suggests that love is always, to some extent, calculated.

573 *caviare to the general*: *Hamlet*, Act Two, Scene Two; something too good for most people to appreciate. '[F]or the play, I remember, pleased not the million, 'twas caviare to the general.'

577 *to a moral*: *OED*, moral, n.7, slang: 'a moral certainty; a person or thing certainly destined *for* or *to do* something. Now chiefly Australian.'

University boat-races: the traditional annual boat races on the River Thames between the Universities of Oxford and Cambridge, which continue to this day.

583 *upsetting to me*: one *OED* meaning, 'presumptuous', could apply to Tifto himself but hardly to the Duke's heir. Tifto's speech isn't exactly a model of standard English usage; he seems to mean that he was upset when Silverbridge snubbed him.

586 *Henry Walker*: Trollope may possibly have written 'Vesey' rather than 'Henry', but given Tifto's desire to transform himself into a solid citizen, the more common 'Henry' seems likely.

587 *Treasury bench*: front bench in the Commons, first row of seats to the Speaker's right where the Cabinet members sit.

589 *buckram*: *OED*, n.2a, 'a kind of coarse linen or cloth stiffened with gum or paste.' In *Henry IV*, Falstaff claims that he was robbed by men in buckram suits, with the number of men growing the longer he speaks. By saying

that a great leader 'should know how to carry his buckram without showing it', Trollope essentially means he should be able to make things up without being too obvious.

590 *trench on*: *OED*, 7b, 'to encroach or infringe (however slightly) *on* or *upon* a region which is the domain of another.'

591 *brewers were very anxious about publican licences*: the 1872 Licensing Act had been introduced by Gladstone's first Liberal government and reduced the number of licences. Accordingly, the brewing interest or 'beerocracy' supported the Conservatives, and Gladstone blamed the loss of the 1874 General Election on the opposition of this interest group. [M&O'G]

592 *once in four years when the President is elected*: Trollope ignores the considerable difference that congressional elections make, as every two years the entire House of Representatives and roughly one third of the Senate must run for office.

593 *gout in the stomach*: perhaps mentioned because of it being in a fairly unusual location. More typically, gout would occur in the 'great toe' as Mr. Spooner experiences it in ch. 62.

599 *the chapter of accidents*: *OED*, Phrases, P4: 'the unforeseen course of events, (the unrolling of) fate. Also *the chapter of possibilities*.' A play, *The Chapter of Accidents*, billed as a comedy in five acts, was written by Sophia Lee and performed at the Haymarket Theatre in London in 1780. The *OED* also has citations for 'a chapter of accidents', and this is how the phrase was published in *All the Year Round* and beyond. However, Trollope wrote 'the' and there is no good reason to change it.

601 *had him on the hip*: *OED*, Phrases, P1: 'at a disadvantage; in a position in which one is likely to be overthrown or overcome.' Among the *OED* citations are *The Merchant of Venice* ('Now infidell I haue you on the hip') and Trollope's *The Belton Estate* ('feeling that she had the culprit on the hip').

604 *retrick his beams*: *OED*, v.1., '*to retrick one's beams*: to recover mentally or physically from a setback; to rally one's strength or spirits; to refocus. Now rare.' Referring to the horizontal beams of a wooden ship of the period and the need to retrick the timbers when necessary in order to avoid being 'on your beam ends', which could lead to shipwreck. One *OED* citation is from *The Small House at Allington*: 'We have retricked our beams in our own way, and our lives have not been desolate' (ch. 33).

606 *leather or prunella*: *OED*, leather, n.1d, leather and prunella: 'an expression for something to which one is utterly indifferent.' See Pope, *Essay on Man* iv, 194, 'Worth makes the man, and want of it the fellow; | The rest, is all but leather or prunella.' The *OED* additionally cites Trollope's Thackeray biography; in it, he talks about how one can be 'enraptured by the wit of Sam Weller or the mock piety of Pecksniff', but still considers certain types of American humour as 'leather and prunello' (not 'prunella'). Trollope continues: 'It is a matter of taste and not of intellect, as one man likes caviare after his dinner, while another prefers apple-pie.'

610 *It is certainly better . . . a commoner*: especially because legislation is initiated in the House of Commons, though some Victorian Prime Ministers (Lord Russell, Lord Palmerston) led from the Lords.

611 *I would return to the Exchequer again*: a job that the Duke loved and was entirely suited for, unlike his more troubled reign as Prime Minister. He sacrifices an opportunity to become Chancellor of the Exchequer in *Can You Forgive Her?* so as to save his wife and his marriage, though later he finally attains the position. From ch. 29 of *Phineas Finn*: 'Plantagenet Palliser, himself the heir to a dukedom, was the young Chancellor of the Exchequer, of whom some statesmen thought much as the rising star of the age. If industry, rectitude of purpose, and a certain clearness of intellect may prevail, Planty Pall, as he is familiarly called, may become a great Minister.'

I wish the title . . . at once: see note to p. 39.

615 *put into Coventry*: more usually 'sent to Coventry'. Often said to have originated from the Civil War, when Royalist prisoners sent to the city of Coventry would be ignored by the local population.

618 *niddle-noddling*: *OED*, 'to nod unsteadily to and fro; to nod the head rapidly and continuously.' Among the *OED* citations are this one from Trollope, and a later one from Virginia Woolf in *The Waves*: 'the trembling figure of Christ's mother was born niddle-noddling along the streets.'

It is but ten days across the Atlantic: Trollope would know, as he crossed the Atlantic several times, visiting New York in 1859, 1862, 1868, and 1875.

620 *I felt sure that he would succeed:* either Mrs. Finn is forgetting about her early reaction to Frank (at the end of ch. 4, she thinks he is 'not. . . fit' for Mary, regardless of his finances), or, more likely, she is referring to an early change of opinion that is not depicted in the novel.

621 *my own way whatever it is*: Trollope's cut of the novel's final sentences does not indicate a change of heart in how the book should end. Rather, he was continuing his space-saving practice of eliminating many sentences at the ends of chapters. Other examples, late in the book, include the passage about Major Tifto becoming Henry Walker (p. 586), and Isabel telling Silverbridge she will teach him about American politics '[i]f you behave yourself well' (p. 592). For more on the novel's ending, see Introduction, pp. xxvii–xxviii.

INDEX OF NAMES AND PLACES

MICHAEL G. WILLIAMSON

I have lived with my characters, and thence has come whatever success I have attained.
(An Autobiography)

The Duke's Children follows the sequence begun in Anthony Trollope's Palliser series, although it can also be enjoyed and appreciated in its own right. He indulged his well-loved preference for reintroducing characters and place-names from his previous novels. The list below includes all the characters, together with some of the significant place-names appearing in the book along with references to novels in which they also appear (in italics). A key to the novels referred to can be found at the end of the Index. The page numbers indicate the pages in the present work in which the reference first appears.

AMAZON, Miss: A rowing lady. A guest at Mrs. Montacute Jones's garden party. p. 238

ARCHBISHOP: A colt (young male horse). p. 51

AULD REIKIE, Marquis of: Principal seat of Auld Reikie in Scotland. Uncle and guardian of Lady Glencora M'Cluskie (future Duchess of Omnium), and father of Lord Nidderdale. His wife, the Marchioness. Trollope uses the old Scottish soubriquet for Edinburgh as the title, which translates as 'Old Smoky', to indicate the importance of the family. *SH, CYFH, WWLN.* p. 465

BALDFACED STAG, The: An inn in the Brake country. The temporary lodging of Lord Silverbridge. p. 488

BEARGARDEN CLUB, The: A rather bohemian gentlemen's sporting club situated close to St James's St. and thought to be loosely based on the Savage Club. This is the club patronized by Felix Carbury in *The Way We Live Now* and described in more detail there. Specifically designed to be appealing to 'young, parsimonious, profligate' members. *WWLN.* p. 23

BEESWAX, Sir TIMOTHY: Conservative, member of Parliament (MP) and Leader of the House of Commons during Lord Drummond's period as Prime Minister. His wife, Lady BEESWAX and daughter. *PM.* p. 122

BEVER, Mrs. ARTHUR de: In whose memory the monument called 'The Temple of the Winds' was built by the river at Maidenhead. p. 245

BLOGOWNIE and TOODLEM MINES: The coal mines on Lord Popplecourt's property in Staffordshire, the royalties of which increase at a rate of £2,000 a year. p. 361

BOBTAILED FOX, The: An inn half a mile from Egham where the Runnymede hunt holds their meetings. p. 439

BONCASSEN, Mr. EZEKIEL and Mrs. BONCASSEN: An American scholar and his wife visiting England so that he can use the resources of the British Museum. Their daughter, ISABEL. They initially stay at the Langham Hotel but eventually rent a house in Brook St. p. 211

BRAKE HUNT, The: A relatively successful hunt situated in the Shires. The Master of the hunt is Lord Chiltern, who lives at Harrington Hall. From the place-names given it is probable that this hunt was loosely based on the Quorn or Cottesmore hunts. *PR.* p. 435

BUBBS, Mr. and his wife, Mrs. BUBBS: Mr. Bubbs is a potential elector at Polpenno. Mrs. Bubbs, of course, does not have a vote, but seems to be in charge of Mr. Bubbs's decisions. p. 430

BULLOCK, Mr. MARLEY: A ruined race-horse owner. p. 281

BURGH, Mr. HERBERT de: An unlucky hunting man. p. 499

BUTTERCUP, Lord: Son of the Earl of Woolantallow. A junior minister. p. 505

CAMBORNE, The Earl of: Liberal nobleman who originally held Polpenno as a pocket borough; in the novel, the Camborne Arms still bears his name. p. 423

CANTRIP, Countess of: Wife of the Earl. Lady Cantrip offers herself as a chaperone and companion to Lady Mary after the Duchess's death. *PF, PR, PM.* p. 13

CANTRIP, Earl of: Liberal politician of London and the estate of Custins in Dorset. Two married daughters. The younger is married to Lord Nidderdale. *PF, PR, PM.* p. 84

CAPULET, The Marchioness of: A lady in society. p. 244

CARBOTTLE, Mr.: The Liberal candidate at the election in Polpenno. p. 424

CARLTON TERRACE (In some editions and other Palliser novels also referred to as CARLTON HOUSE TERRACE or CARLTON HOUSE GARDENS): The London home of the Dukes of Omnium which backs on to The Mall. This house was based on Carlton House Terrace, which still stands today. The Savage Club (see BEARGARDEN CLUB) occupied 1, Carlton House Terrace from 1936 until 1940. *PR, PM.* p. 28

CARSTAIRS, Sir SIMON: Recently deceased Liberal member of Parliament for Polpenno. p. 424

CASSEWARY, Miss (Miss CASS): Distant cousin and companion to Lady Mabel Grex. p. 71

CASSEWARY, Rev. Mr.: Of the Parish of STOGPINGUM, Barsetshire, and brother of Miss Cass. p. 445

CHILTERN, OSWALD, Lord: Family name of Standish. Son and heir of the Earl of Brentford, who was a former Whig Cabinet minister and early sponsor of Phineas Finn. At the time of the novel the Earl is probably still travelling abroad with his daughter, Lady Laura Kennedy. Lord Chiltern is currently living at Harrington Hall and is the Master of the Brake hunt. *PF, ED, PR, PM.* p. 389

CHILTERN, Lady VIOLET: née EFFINGHAM. Wife of Lord Chiltern. *AS, PF, ED.* p. 356

CLANFIDDLE, Countess and her two daughters including Lady VIOLET: Members of society. p. 260

CLORAL, Mr.: A chemist at Silverbridge. p. 110

COALHEAVER: A colt (young male horse) owned by Lord Silverbridge. p. 257

COALITION: A filly (young female horse) held in joint partnership by Lord Silverbridge and Major Tifto. p. 50

COMFORT and CRIBALL, Messrs.: Of Crasham Court, Crutched Friars. Moneylenders. p. 346

COURCY, Lady ROSINA de: Unmarried daughter of Earl de Courcy of Courcy Castle in West Barsetshire (Whig/Liberal family). *BT, DT, SH, PM.* p. 356

CREAM CHEESE: A colt (young male horse) owned by Lord Silverbridge. p. 51

CRUMBLEWIT, Sir OLIVER: President of the Phrenological Society. p. 218

CRUMMIE-TODDIE: A grouse moor in the west of Perthshire. p. 292

CUSTINS: The Dorset country seat of the Earl and Countess of Cantrip. p. 273

DOBBES, Mr. REGINALD: A sportsman. p. 273

DROUGHT, Sir ORLANDO: Conservative MP. Serves as First Lord of the Admiralty during the Duke's coalition Government. *PR, PM, WWLN.* p. 122

DRUMMOND, Lord: Conservative and later Prime Minister. *PR, PM.* p. 158

DU BOUNG, Mr.: Brewer and local Liberal politician of Silverbridge. *PM.* p. 88

ERLE, BARRINGTON MP: A Liberal politician. Related to the Earl of Brentford and the Standish family. Strong supporter of former Whig/Liberal Prime Minister William Mildmay. *PF, PR, PM.* p. 396

FAWN, FREDERICK, Viscount: Of Fawn Court. His young wife, Lady FAWN. A relatively ineffectual Liberal politician. *PF, ED, PR, PM*. p. 330

FINN, Mrs. MARIE: Wife of Phineas Finn; formerly Madame Max Goesler. *PF, ED, PR, PM*. p. 10

FINN, Mr. PHINEAS MP: Liberal politician who has a London house in Park Lane and a country house in Surrey, both of which came to him following his marriage to Madame Max Goesler. *PF, PR, PM*. p. 10

FISHKNIFE: A colt (young male horse). Winner of the Derby. p. 135

FITZGERALD, Mr. BURGO: First romantic but impoverished love of Glencora, Duchess of Omnium when she was Lady Glencora M'Cluskie. *CYFH, SH*. p. 90

FLETCHER, Mr. ARTHUR MP: Former Conservative MP for Silverbridge; husband of Emily Lopez, née Wharton. *PM*. p. 59

FOTHERGILL, Mr.: Manager of the old Duke of Omnium's estates. A West Barsetshire magistrate. *DT, FP, SH, LCB, PR*. p. 479

FOWLER: Huntsman of the Brake hunt. p. 485

GATHERUM CASTLE: The principal seat of the Dukes of Omnium in Barsetshire. *DT, FP, CYFH, PF, ED, PR, PM*. p. 62

GEORGE, Lord MP: Conservative politician. p. 123

GEORGE and VULTURE, The: The Conservative hotel at Silverbridge. p. 108

GLASSLOUGH, Lord: Member of the Beargarden Club. p. 50

GLOMAX, Captain: Master of the Ufford and Rufford United hunt. *AA*. p. 483

GOTOBED, Mr. ELIAS: An American Senator and minister. His wife, Mrs. GOTOBED. *AS*. p. 538

GREEN, Captain: Major Tifto's companion. Described as his 'inferior' friend. p. 278

GRESHAM, Mr.: The most significant Liberal Prime Minister during the Palliser series. Possibly based, in some respects, on William Gladstone. *PF, ED, PR, PM*. p. 7

GREX, Earl of: Has a London house in Belgrave Square and the estate of Grex in Yorkshire. Holder of the Order of the Garter. p. 69

GREX, Lady MABEL: Only daughter of Earl Grex. Second cousin to Frank Tregear; also second cousin to Lord Silverbridge. p. 69

GREX, Lord PERCIVAL: Only son and heir of Earl Grex. p. 69

GREY, Mrs. ALICE: née VAVASOR. A cousin and friend of Glencora, Duchess of Omnium, and wife of John Grey. *CYFH, ED*. p. 10

GREY, Mr. JOHN: Of an estate near Ely. Previously Liberal MP for Silverbridge. *CYFH, PF, ED, PM*. p. 10

GRIFFIN, Mr. GREEN: A racing man. The owner of the winning horse at the Derby. p. 128

GWYNNE, Dr.: Master of Lazarus College, Oxford. *W, BT, LCB*. p. 292

HARNAGE, Mr.: Lord Gerald Palliser's tutor at Trinity College, Cambridge. p. 137

HARRINGTON HALL: The current home of Lord and Lady Chiltern and the headquarters of the Brake hunt. *PR*. p. 474

HINDES, Mr. JACK: A gambling acquaintance of Lord Gerald. p. 465

HORNS, The: Villa residence of the Palliser family in Richmond on the River Thames. A wedding present to Lady Glencora and her favourite home. *SH, CYFH, PF, PM*. p. 84

JAWSTOCK, Mr. JEREMIAH: Of Juniper Lodge, Staines. A leading member of the Runnymede hunt. p. 440

JONES, Mrs. MONTACUTE: Wife of a rich industrialist and a leading society hostess, with property in Grosvenor Place, London; Curry Hall, Gloucestershire; Roehampton, and Killancodlem in Perthshire. *IHP*. p. 155

JOSEPH: One of the Duke of Omnium's footmen. p. 514

KILLANCODLEM: Mrs. Montacute Jones's estate in Scotland. *IHP*. p. 284

LAZARUS COLLEGE: A fictitious Oxford College. *W, BT, LCB*. p. 292

LENNOX, Rev. SOMERSET: Lord Gerald Palliser's private tutor. An Oxford man. p. 188

LONGSTAFFE, Mr. ADOLPHUS (DOLLY): Son of Adolphus Longstaffe, Squire of Caversham. Member of the Beargarden Club. Sometimes referred to in other Palliser novels as Longstaff or Longestaffe. *WWLN*. p. 52

LUPTON, Mr. MP: A Conservative politician. *PM, WWLN*. p. 123

MACLEAN, Mr.: A tutor at Trinity College, Cambridge. p. 139

MATCHING PRIORY: The Yorkshire country home of the Palliser family. *CYFH, PF, ED, PR, PM*. p. 8

MAULE, Mr. GERARD: And his wife, Mrs. ADELAIDE MAULE, née Palliser. Both keen hunting participants. *PR*. p. 479

MELROSE: A horse (hunter) owned by Lord Silverbridge. p. 507

MIDLOTHIAN, Countess of: Related to both Glencora, Duchess of Omnium and Alice Grey, née Vavasor, and who interferes in respect to both their marriages. *CYFH*. p. 10

MILDMAY, Mr. WILLIAM MP: Former Prime Minister. 'The great Whig Minister of the day'. *PF*, *PR*, *PM*. p. 520

MONOGRAM, Sir DAMASK: An impoverished sporting baronet. *WWLN*, *PM*. p. 134

MONK, Mr. JOSHUA MP: A Radical/Liberal politician. Chancellor of the Exchequer in both the Omnium and Gresham ministries. *PF*, *PR*. p. 123

MONTAGUE, Countess: A lady in society. p. 244

MORETON, Mr.: Agent to the Duke of Omnium (sometimes referred to in other books as Mr. Morton). *PM*. p. 62

NEWCOMB, Mr.: The curate at Polpenno. p. 430

NIDDERDALE, Lord: Cousin to Glencora, Duchess of Omnium and heir to the Marquis of Auld Reikie. Married to the younger daughter of Lord and Lady Cantrip. *WWLN*. p. 10

OMNIUM, GEORGE PLANTAGENET: The former Duke of Omnium. Now deceased. Uncle of the present Duke. Lord Lieutenant of Barsetshire. *FP*, *DT*, *SH*, *CYFH*, *PF*, *ED*, *PR*, *PM*. p. 99

OMNIUM, GLENCORA, Duchess of: Now deceased. Formerly Lady Glencora M'Cluskie and a great heiress of her father, the Lord of the Isles. *SH*, *LCB*, *AS*, *CYFH*, *PF*, *ED*, *MM*, *PR*, *PM*. p. 7

OMNIUM, PLANTAGENET PALLISER, Duke of: Principal seat at Gatherum Castle, Barsetshire; also Matching Priory, Yorkshire; The Horns, Richmond; and Carlton Terrace in London. Former Liberal Prime Minister of a coalition Government between the Conservatives and Liberals. *SH*, *CYFH*, *PF*, *ED*, *PR*, *PM*. p. 7

PALISERE, Sir GUY de: Prominent distant ancestor of the Palliser family. p. 375

PALLISER, Lord GERALD: Younger son of the Duke of Omnium. p. 8

PALLISER, Mrs. JEFFREY: Wife to Mr. JEFFREY PALLISER, who is a cousin to Plantagenet Palliser and next heir to the dukedom should Plantagenet's line fail. Country house in Gloucestershire. Mrs. Palliser offers Lady Mary a temporary home after the death of the Duchess. p. 13

PALLISER, Lady MARY: The only daughter of the Duke and Duchess of Omnium. An elder sister, Lady Glencora, is mentioned in *The Prime Minister* but not in *The Duke's Children*. p. 7

PEOPLE'S BANNER: A popular newspaper widely read and often concerned with scandalous issues. Originally edited by Quintus Slide. *PF*, *PR*, *PM*. p. 396

PEPPERMINT: A jockey who rides Prime Minister at the Derby. p. 135

PERRY: A member of the Coldstream Guards and friend of Lord Gerald Palliser. p. 465

PINEBOTT, Mr.: Conservative attorney at Polpenno. p. 430

PLAYFAIR, Sir HENRY: A racing gentleman. p. 351

POLPENNO: A borough in Cornwall returning one member of Parliament. p. 422

POLWENNING: The estate of the Tregear family near to Polpenno in Cornwall. p. 23

POOK, Mr.: Horse trainer to Lord Silverbridge. p. 335

POPPLECOURT, Lord: Of the estate of Popplecourt in Suffolk and a further estate in Staffordshire with productive coal-mines. A racing peer and politician sitting in the House of Lords. p. 125

POTTLEPOT, Lord: A racing peer. p. 49

PRIME MINISTER: A colt held in joint partnership by Lord Silverbridge and Major Tifto. p. 50

PROBY: A Cambridge undergraduate. p. 191

QUOUSQUE: Defeated horse at the Derby. p. 133

RABBIT, DICK: First whip of the Brake hunt. p. 481

RAMSDEN, Lord: Conservative Shadow Chancellor. *PM*. p. 120

RATLER, Mr. MP: The Liberal Whip in the House of Commons (appears sometimes in the Palliser novels as RATTLER). *PF, PR, PM*. p. 426

ROBY, Mr. THOMAS MP: The Conservative Whip in the House of Commons. Later also Patronage Secretary and Secretary to the Admiralty (mistakenly also appears as Mr. ROPER in some editions). *PF, PR, PM*. p. 521

RUNKS: Son of Old RUNKS, Veterinary from Rufford. p. 491

RUNNYMEDE HUNT: A fictitious hunt which, as its name suggests, is based to the west of London with its headquarters near Egham in Surrey. Runnymede itself is the site of the signing of the Magna Carta by King John by the River Thames. Major Tifto is the current Master. p. 47

ST. BUNGAY, Duke of: Now an elderly but wise and significant supporter of the Liberal party. His wife, the Duchess of St. Bungay; two daughters, Ladies ADELAIDE and FLORA FITZHOWARD. His residences include St. James's Square, London and the country estate of Longroyston. *CYFH, PF, ED, PR, PM*. p. 166

SARCINET: A spotted chestnut mare (female horse) owned by Lord Silverbridge. p. 51

SCHOTZDAM, Madame: A singer. p. 257

SEVENKINGS, Mr. EZEKIEL: An American poet. p. 538

SILVERBRIDGE. The third most significant borough in Barsetshire. Originally a pocket borough in the gift of the Dukes of Omnium. Held as a Liberal member of Parliament by Plantagenet Palliser before he succeeded to the dukedom. Then by John Grey and Arthur Fletcher. *SH*, *CYFH*, *PM*. p. 39

SILVERBRIDGE, PLANTAGENET PALLISER, Earl of: Elder son of the Duke of Omnium. Referred to as 'Silver' by his brother. *CYFH*, *PF*, *PM*. p. 7

SIMCOX: Lord Gerald Palliser's tutor. p. 350

SLOBODY, Sir SIMON: A hunting gentleman. p. 507

SOLOMON: A bookmaker. p. 52

SPOONER, Mr. THOMAS PLATTER: Of Spoon Hall, and his wife, Mrs. SPOONER, née LEATHERSIDE. Both are keen hunters, but, particularly, Mrs. Spooner. *PR*. p. 479

SPROTTLE, Mr.: Secretary to Mr. Boncassen. p. 215

SPROUT, Mr.: Bootmaker and local Conservative politician of Silverbridge. *PM*. p. 104

SPRUGEON, Mr.: Ironmonger and local Conservative politician of Silverbridge. *PM*. p. 104

SQUERCUM, Mr.: Dolly Longstaffe's man of business who has chambers in Holborn. p. 364

STIRLING, Lord: A racing peer. p. 351

STOGPINGUM: Parish of Rev. Mr. Cassewary in Barsetshire. Previously joined with the Parish of Eiderdown to form the benefice of Stoke Pinguium and held, in absence, by Dr. Vesey Stanhope in *Barchester Towers*. *W*, *BT*. p. 445

STUBBS, JACK: An unfortunate hunting gentleman. p. 494

STUFFA, Mdlle.: The 'nightingale of the season'. Married to Mr. THOMAS JONES. p. 53

SUNFLOWER: A colt (young male horse). p. 52

TEMPEST, Rev. Dr. MORTIMER: Rector of Silverbridge and a Conservative. *LCB*. p. 110

TIFTO, MAJOR T: Of Tally-ho Lodge near Egham in Surrey. Master of the Runnymede hunt. p. 39

TOOBY, Mr. and Mrs.: A farmer in the Brake country and his wife. p. 493

TOPPS, Mr. MAHOGANY: Prominent member of the Runnymede hunt. p. 439

TREGEAR, Mr. FRANCIS (FRANK) OLIPHANT: The younger son of Squire Tregear and his second wife of the estate of Polwenning, near Polpenno, Cornwall. Second cousin of the Earl of Grex. p. 14

TREGEAR, Miss: Frank's older sister—perhaps half-sister? p. 425

TREGEAR, Squire: Of the estate of Polwenning and his second wife, Mrs. TREGEAR. Parents of Frank. Squire Tregear also has a son by his previous marriage; it is not specified whether his daughter is from his first marriage or his second. p. 26

TRINITY COLLEGE, CAMBRIDGE, The MASTER of: Trinity College is a real Cambridge College and the one that Lord Gerald Palliser attends as a student before he is expelled. p. 138

TRUMPETON WOOD: A wood on the estate of the Duke of Omnium in the Brake country in the Shires. The subject of much debate about lack of preservation for both hunting and shooting (in some some editions referred to as TRUMPINGTON WOOD). *PR*, *PM*. p. 475

TYBALT, Lord: A peer in society. p. 244

UFFORD AND RUFFORD UNITED HUNT: Captain Glomax is the retiring Master in *The Duke's Children* and Sir Harry Albury is the Master in *Ayala's Angel*. Referred to as the U.R.U. *AS*, *AA*. p. 483

VANSINOFF, General: A Dutch traveller. p. 218

VILLIERS, Mr. GILBERT: A racing gentleman. p. 336

WALKER, Mr. GEORGE: Liberal Attorney at Silverbridge. *LCB*. p. 110

WARBURTON, Mr.: The Duke of Omnium's private secretary. *PM*. p. 352

WEAZELING, Lord: Liberal Lord Chancellor. *PR*, *PM*. p. 120

WILLIAMS, Rev. Mr.: Rector of Polpenno. p. 425

WOOLANTALLOW, the Earl of: Father of Lord Buttercup. p. 505

KEY TO NOVELS CITED

AA	*Ayala's Angel*
AS	*The American Senator*
BT	*Barchester Towers*
CYFH	*Can You Forgive Her?*
DT	*Doctor Thorne*
ED	*The Eustace Diamonds*
FP	*Framley Parsonage*
IHP	*Is He Popenjoy?*
LCB	*The Last Chronicle of Barset*
MM	*Miss Mackenzie*

PF   Phineas Finn
PM   The Prime Minister
PR   Phineas Redux
SH   The Small House at Allington
W   The Warden
WWLN   The Way We Live Now

American Literature

British and Irish Literature

Children's Literature

Classics and Ancient Literature

Colonial Literature

Eastern Literature

European Literature

Gothic Literature

History

Medieval Literature

Oxford English Drama

Philosophy

Poetry

Politics

Religion

The Oxford Shakespeare

A complete list of Oxford World's Classics, including Authors in Context, Oxford English Drama, and the Oxford Shakespeare, is available in the UK from the Marketing Services Department, Oxford University Press, Great Clarendon Street, Oxford OX2 6DP, or visit the website at www.oup.com/uk/worldsclassics.

In the USA, visit www.oup.com/us/owc for a complete title list.

Oxford World's Classics are available from all good bookshops. In case of difficulty, customers in the UK should contact Oxford University Press Bookshop, 116 High Street, Oxford OX1 4BR.

	Late Victorian Gothic Tales
	Literature and Science in the Nineteenth Century
JANE AUSTEN	Emma
	Mansfield Park
	Persuasion
	Pride and Prejudice
	Selected Letters
	Sense and Sensibility
MRS BEETON	Book of Household Management
MARY ELIZABETH BRADDON	Lady Audley's Secret
ANNE BRONTË	The Tenant of Wildfell Hall
CHARLOTTE BRONTË	Jane Eyre
	Shirley
	Villette
EMILY BRONTË	Wuthering Heights
ROBERT BROWNING	The Major Works
JOHN CLARE	The Major Works
SAMUEL TAYLOR COLERIDGE	The Major Works
WILKIE COLLINS	The Moonstone
	No Name
	The Woman in White
CHARLES DARWIN	The Origin of Species
THOMAS DE QUINCEY	The Confessions of an English Opium-Eater
	On Murder
CHARLES DICKENS	The Adventures of Oliver Twist
	Barnaby Rudge
	Bleak House
	David Copperfield
	Great Expectations
	Nicholas Nickleby

A SELECTION OF   **OXFORD WORLD'S CLASSICS**

CHARLES DICKENS	**The Old Curiosity Shop**
	Our Mutual Friend
	The Pickwick Papers
GEORGE DU MAURIER	**Trilby**
MARIA EDGEWORTH	**Castle Rackrent**
GEORGE ELIOT	**Daniel Deronda**
	The Lifted Veil and Brother Jacob
	Middlemarch
	The Mill on the Floss
	Silas Marner
EDWARD FITZGERALD	**The Rubáiyát of Omar Khayyám**
ELIZABETH GASKELL	**Cranford**
	The Life of Charlotte Brontë
	Mary Barton
	North and South
	Wives and Daughters
GEORGE GISSING	**New Grub Street**
	The Nether World
	The Odd Women
EDMUND GOSSE	**Father and Son**
THOMAS HARDY	**Far from the Madding Crowd**
	Jude the Obscure
	The Mayor of Casterbridge
	The Return of the Native
	Tess of the d'Urbervilles
	The Woodlanders
JAMES HOGG	**The Private Memoirs and Confessions**
	of a Justified Sinner
JOHN KEATS	**The Major Works**
	Selected Letters
CHARLES MATURIN	**Melmoth the Wanderer**
HENRY MAYHEW	**London Labour and the London Poor**

A SELECTION OF   **OXFORD WORLD'S CLASSICS**

WILLIAM MORRIS	**News from Nowhere**
JOHN RUSKIN	**Praeterita**
	Selected Writings
WALTER SCOTT	**Ivanhoe**
	Rob Roy
	Waverley
MARY SHELLEY	**Frankenstein**
	The Last Man
ROBERT LOUIS STEVENSON	**Strange Case of Dr Jekyll and Mr Hyde and Other Tales**
	Treasure Island
BRAM STOKER	**Dracula**
W. M. THACKERAY	**Vanity Fair**
FRANCES TROLLOPE	**Domestic Manners of the Americans**
OSCAR WILDE	**The Importance of Being Earnest and Other Plays**
	The Major Works
	The Picture of Dorian Gray
ELLEN WOOD	**East Lynne**
DOROTHY WORDSWORTH	**The Grasmere and Alfoxden Journals**
WILLIAM WORDSWORTH	**The Major Works**
WORDSWORTH and COLERIDGE	**Lyrical Ballads**

TROLLOPE IN **OXFORD WORLD'S CLASSICS**

ANTHONY TROLLOPE   The American Senator
An Autobiography
Barchester Towers
Can You Forgive Her?
Cousin Henry
Doctor Thorne
The Duke's Children
The Eustace Diamonds
Framley Parsonage
He Knew He Was Right
Lady Anna
The Last Chronicle of Barset
Orley Farm
Phineas Finn
Phineas Redux
The Prime Minister
Rachel Ray
The Small House at Allington
The Warden
The Way We Live Now

A SELECTION OF   **OXFORD WORLD'S CLASSICS**

HANS CHRISTIAN ANDERSEN	**Fairy Tales**
J. M. BARRIE	**Peter Pan in Kensington Gardens and Peter and Wendy**
L. FRANK BAUM	**The Wonderful Wizard of Oz**
FRANCES HODGSON BURNETT	**The Secret Garden**
LEWIS CARROLL	**Alice's Adventures in Wonderland and Through the Looking-Glass**
CARLO COLLODI	**The Adventures of Pinocchio**
KENNETH GRAHAME	**The Wind in the Willows**
ANTHONY HOPE	**The Prisoner of Zenda**
THOMAS HUGHES	**Tom Brown's Schooldays**
CHARLES PERRAULT	**The Complete Fairy Tales**
ANNA SEWELL	**Black Beauty**
ROBERT LOUIS STEVENSON	**Kidnapped** **Treasure Island**

A SELECTION OF   **OXFORD WORLD'S CLASSICS**

ANTON CHEKHOV
About Love and Other Stories
Early Stories
Five Plays
The Princess and Other Stories
The Russian Master and Other Stories
The Steppe and Other Stories
Twelve Plays
Ward Number Six and Other Stories

FYODOR DOSTOEVSKY
Crime and Punishment
Devils
A Gentle Creature and Other Stories
The Idiot
The Karamazov Brothers
Memoirs from the House of the Dead
Notes from the Underground and
The Gambler

NIKOLAI GOGOL
Dead Souls
Plays and Petersburg Tales

MIKHAIL LERMONTOV
A Hero of Our Time

ALEXANDER PUSHKIN
Boris Godunov
Eugene Onegin
The Queen of Spades and Other Stories

LEO TOLSTOY
Anna Karenina
The Kreutzer Sonata and Other Stories
The Raid and Other Stories
Resurrection
War and Peace

IVAN TURGENEV
Fathers and Sons
First Love and Other Stories
A Month in the Country